SIRENS

A NOVEL BY

Eric Van Lustbader

SIRENS

THIS BOOK CONTAINS THE COMPLETE TEXT OF THE
ORIGINAL HARDCOVER EDITION.

Published by Fawcett Crest Books, CBS Educational and
Professional Publishing, a division of CBS Inc., by arrangement with M. Evans and Company, Inc.

ISBN: 0-449-24510-1

Thanks are due to the following authors, publishers, and
agents for permission to use the material included.

Epigraph: Excerpt from *Playback* by Raymond Chandler.
Copyright © 1958 by Raymond Chandler. Reprinted by per-
mission of Houghton Mifflin Company. *Page 9:* "The Light-
ning Play" by Kikaku. From *An Introduction to Haiku* edited
by Harold G. Henderson. Copyright © 1958 by Harold G.
Henderson. Reprinted by permission of Doubleday & Com-
pany, Inc. *Page 141:* "My Only Love" (Bryan Ferry). © 1980
E. G. Music Ltd. All rights reserved. Used by permission.
Page 170: "Fauvette" (Duncan Browne). © 1979 Logo Songs
Ltd. All rights for the U.S. and Canada administered by The
Hudson Bay Music Company. Used by permission. All rights
reserved. *Page 501–502:* "You Wear Those Eyes" (Ric Oca-
sek). © 1980 Ric Ocasek. All rights controlled by Lido Music,
Inc. Used by permission. *Page 543:* "Closets and Bullets"
(Martha Davis). © 1979 by Clean Sheets Music. Used by
permission. All rights reserved.

Printed in the United States of America

First Fawcett Crest Printing: June 1982

10 9 8 7 6 5 4 3 2 1

This is dedicated to the memory of my mother

For my father, that Nolan woman, Syd
and
the one and only V.

ACKNOWLEDGMENTS

Friends and family were extremely helpful during the writing of *Sirens*. Thanks are due to: Carol, M. J., Syd, Doris and Charlie, Marv; my father, who proofed, and, especially, to H. M., the wizard, without whom, etc.

"...There in a meadow they sit, and all round is a great heap of bones, mouldering bodies and withering skins. Go past that place and do not let the men hear..."

—Circe to Odysseus.
Homer, *The Odyssey*.

I looked around the empty room—which was no longer empty. There was a voice in it, and a tall, slim lovely woman.

—Raymond Chandler,
Playback.

THE LIGHTNING PLAY

Lightning-play—
that yesterday was in the east,
is in the west today

— **Kikaku**

1

Daina Whitney shifted down, edging into the neat hairpin turn on the western face of the hill, on her way up. As predicted the cool air had arrived just after dusk, scouring the canyons and hills of L.A., purging the indolent humid air eastward, sending the burnt-rubber smog from the valley back to where it had originated.

From the tops of Beverly Hills, the haloed lights seemed to kneel below the swaying crowns of the palms, sweeping away, exploding in the haze of distance.

Daina coaxed the silver Mercedes into the center of the snaking road, shifted briefly into third. She listened to the throaty roar of the car's exhaust and thought of the Ian Fleming line: "She drove like a man, with sensual delight...." Or something like that. The idea reminded her of Marion, her director on *Heather Duell*. They had been hard at work on the film for over six weeks, having just returned from location shooting in the sun-dappled hills north of Nice. Marion, who brought with him the reputation for manufacturing an authentic feel to everything he shot, nevertheless had insisted on filming all interiors in Hollywood.

"On the set I can control time, halt the light in the sky,

stop the wind from blowing, make it rain," he had told her on the day they had returned. "On location one is constantly at odds with the environment. I want to be able to control *everything*. That's why one comes to Hollywood, after all."

He walked around her, expostulating, venting steam like an engine on maximum. "But for that control one gives up a certain amount of volition. Being in Hollywood takes you right out of reality. The more you give to it, the more it sucks away at you—just like a superlative whore. And it feels so good you don't want it to stop."

Daina recalled the first time Monty, her agent, had mentioned this project. *Regina Red* had just been released to excellent reviews. It was a spectacular, controversial film, filled with directorial pyrotechnics. But, more important, it was her first starring role and, as Monty himself had pointed out, she was poised at a crucial nexus in her career.

"I think you're ready," he told her one day over lunch at Ma Maison, "to go beyond *Regina Red*." She had to lean forward to hear him over the chink of glasses and the gush of honeyed voices, rising and falling, as the upper crust of Beverly Hills strolled by them, alighting for a time at this table and that for a stinger or three. "I'm not knocking the film, mind you. Anything Jeffrey Lesser directs gets an enormous amount of attention. But I feel the time's right for you to go beyond that Zap! Pop! thing. You should see. I'm drowning in scripts for you."

"Well." She laughed. "That's a switch."

"Be careful, Daina. Now it's the easiest thing in the world to get you a film. But what we don't need is for you to become involved in a piece of shit. You want to see shit? Like I said, come to my office. There's a pile of it there. This town grinds screenwriters up into hamburgers. I haven't seen a reasonable idea floating around here for months."

Of course she heard the "but" hovering unspoken as he had meant her to, but she was not going to give him the satisfaction of seeing her ask for it. She felt like a dog on a leash, knew that part of this feeling stemmed from the boredom of inactivity while Mark was busily filming his political epic. And, perversely, this only seemed to infuriate her further.

"I don't," she said sharply, "want to wait a year for some

mythical project that you're dreaming might come along. I want to work. If I don't, I'll go crazy."

It was then that Monty smiled. He had, she thought, a completely irresistible smile. It was wide, taking in his whole face, but most especially, it was warm. When he smiled like that she found herself trusting him implicitly because he had a way of making you believe that the gesture was just for you, that he had never done it quite this way with anyone else.

"How would you like," he said happily, "to work right now?" And handed her over a blue-bindered script.

"You bastard," she said, laughing.

Monty gave her just overnight to read and she knew why. He wanted her excitement level to remain high.

Away from the office, at breakfast in Malibu, he said, "What do you think?"

She already knew from his face what he thought. Her eyes teased him. "I'm not sure. I haven't finished it yet."

"Goddamnit, Daina, I told you—!" He stopped, seeing her laughing silently at him. "Ah," he said. "Well perhaps if I can answer some of your questions I can help make up your mind."

She sipped placidly at her iced coffee, feeling a measure of satisfaction. "Who's directing it?"

"Marion Clarke."

She raised her eyebrows. "You mean the Englishman who directed that Stoppard on Broadway, oh, two years ago?"

Monty nodded. "The same. He won a Tony for that one."

Still she was puzzled. "What's he doing here? And in films?"

Monty's heavy shoulders lifted and fell. "It's what he wants to do, apparently. And this isn't his first film. He's done two others but they really don't count. They were done on a shoe-string. Twentieth is putting a lot of bucks behind this project."

"How'd they come to get Clarke?"

"Uhm..." His brown eyes slid away from hers, contemplated the bright brass of the early sunlight lacquering the Pacific. Several gulls spun desultorily near the water's surface, searching for breakfast. "The producer brought him in. Apparently he had seen the script fairly early, made some vital changes, got a guarantee from the producer and began a full-fledged rewrite the result of which"—he nodded his small bird's head; his hollow cheeks quivering as if they might shake loose the perpetual tan—"you have just read."

"This producer," Daina said guardedly. "Who is he?"

Monty rubbed at his thick nose, diddled his fork up and down in a brief tattoo on the wooden tabletop. "Now, Daina—"

"Monty . . ."

He knew that warning tone, said almost reluctantly, "Rubens."

"Oh, for Christ's sake!" He winced at her bark, his knuckles white where he grasped the edge of the table as if in preparation for a violent squall. "That sonovabitch's been trying to get me into bed ever since I got out here! Now you want me to work in one of his films? I don't believe you!"

She got up, thrust the chair from her with the backs of her legs, went out of the cool clutter of the restaurant onto the soft sand. She moved away from the edifice. Behind her, the morning traffic hissed by, heading for Sunset.

She bent down, took off her shoes, headed toward the lapping surf. At the verge of the sea, she felt the contradictory hardness come into the sand, its coolness. Then the water washed over her feet, tickling her ankles. She shivered, feeling an odd kind of terror grip her at the thought of working with Rubens. She had studiously avoided him for so long and now it had come to this. Her anger at Monty was misplaced, she knew, and, abruptly, she was ashamed of how she had yelled at him.

She felt rather than saw Monty coming up behind her. He had difficulty negotiating the beach, his breath coming in hard, quick pants. Belatedly, Daina thought of the pills he took for his heart.

"I think," he said softly, "that you're being a bit of a prima donna. This is the role of a lifetime. You—"

"I don't like it when you start planning things behind my back."

"Rubens and I are old friends. We go back, what?, ten years or more. If you'd look at the situation objectively, Daina, you'd see it's the perfect thing for you."

Now she was angry again. "What does Rubens know about my acting abilities? I know what he's hoping for."

"I think you're wrong about that," Monty said.

She dismissed his words with a wave of her hand. "One

buddy standing up for the other." She turned away from his steady gaze, her feelings in turmoil. Rubens, she thought acidly, the name that opens all doors in Hollywood. But what doors did it open inside herself?

To the west, out over the Pacific, the sky glowed, hanging suspended as if it were a stage backdrop, reminding her of that hard struggle up from no parts to bit parts to supporting roles.

Sunlight gilded the bridge of her nose, glinted off her eyes, turning their deep violet opaque. Her normally sensual lips were pressed tightly together.

When she spoke again, her voice was low and furred with menace. "I am not," she said, "a whore. If Marion Clarke wants me for *Heather Duell* he can damn well call you himself!"

"That," said Monty calmly, "is precisely what he's done."

Marion Clarke was not at all what she had expected. He was older, his seamed face dominated by a long patrician nose. His soft metallic-gray hair was combed forward over his wide forehead in the style of a Roman senator. She found herself wondering whether he was from the English upper class, Oxford and all that, with the kind of old-world bent John Fowles extolled as the highest virtue. And would Hollywood, she asked herself rhetorically, bring him down like a crass white hunter shooting a magnificent wild animal?

She stared into those piercing blue eyes, like shards of ice, and thought, No, not with this forbidding exterior. But then he spoke and all the ice turned to running water and rainbows.

The first time she met him—on the lot where all the interiors would be shot—he was carrying a copy of the script rolled into a tight cylinder. But when she introduced herself, he handed it to his assistant—a thin young man with no hair—then took her arm in a firm, controlling grip and began to stroll with her away from the clots of people. He guided her with his palm, rather than with words, and by this she thought she understood the nature of the control he wished to exert, as all directors did—over her.

"How well do you know the script?" His voice was light, neutral.

She laughed, a trifle uneasy. "I'm afraid I haven't had time to memorize the thing."

But he was already shaking away her words as if they were an annoying cloud of gnats invading an otherwise glorious summer's day. "No. That's not what I meant."

She waited for him to go on but he did not. Indeed, he seemed lost within his own thoughts. They were approaching a cobweb of streets—some television producer's idea of a New York neighborhood, though it bore no resemblance to any area of the city she had been to. Lights were up but not on. The asphalt had just been slicked with water so that it shone. The lights came on all at once and almost immediately a long black Lincoln slid by them, so slowly there was almost no hiss from the tires. Someone called for more water. The lights were cut. No one bothered them.

"Well?" he said sharply.

She wondered what he wanted. "Should we do a scene?"

"Do you recall," he said as if that was precisely what he had had in mind all along, "the scene directly after your husband is shot?"

"When I turn around and scream at El-Kalaam?"

"Yes. From there."

"I don't—"

But he had already begun it and she had no choice because he was working with her from within rather than from without as most film directors in her experience had done, manipulating.

It was like quicksand, drawing her in or, rather, downward until she lost herself and began to panic because she did not remember the lines or how she was supposed to react.

Then something he said seemed to trigger her and she knew what Heather Duell—what she—had to do. And, simultaneously, she understood what Marion was up to, that the lines themselves were meaningless, that it was Heather, the character, he was out for her to define, to see if she could, if she had it in her just the way Heather had to have it in her. To survive the body blow to her life. Just to go on. *To live.*

And without knowing just when—as it always was, she had found, with truly great performances—she crossed the barrier, becoming Heather Duell.

Daina came out of it dazzled and breathless, having been

given a glimpse of the montage of the film, the accretion of shots she might eventually view daily, metamorphosing into the whole cloth, filled with deep tonal feeling. She had been given a taste of the heart of the matter and now she was certain that she wanted this role more than she had ever wanted anything in her life.

Her chest was tight and there was a pounding in her temples, familiar but so much stronger than before that she was dizzied. It seemed to her like the vicious, awesome, stupendous thrust of life itself breaking time down into minute, rapid lifetimes, separate, apart, diverging, multitudinous, proliferating endlessly. And she realized just how long it had been since the ending of *Regina Red;* how she ached for the eye of the camera to mark her again, to surround her with its great technicolor rectangle. Wide-screened, she would be born again. It was time for another life; she could feel the ripples along her musculature, live wires tingling her brain and she knew that she would not sleep tonight, perhaps not again until she knew this part was hers.

Docilely, she let Marion lead her back past a pair of half-filled garbage cans, down an ersatz alley with its machine-made "dirt," its carefully torn and faded posters flapping off brick walls that were, after all, only plaster and plywood and, abruptly, they re-emerged into Hollywood.

"Now listen to me." He stopped, turned to face her. Light flooded his face, tingeing his pink drinker's cheeks. "You may think that *Heather Duell* is an action story. The people at Twentieth certainly think so." Each word seemed to escape his lips separately as if with a life of its own. "Rest assured that we shall not take that aspect for granted." He smiled a little through his thin wide lips as if it were a grudging outlet, a churning factory's chimney blowing off steam. He lifted a forefinger. "But do not be deceived. This is another kind of film entirely.

"Terrorism as a concept is as epidemic in this decade as communism was in the twenties. They are political ideals just the same. But this is not a film about the Jewish-Palestinian struggle. We are not about to make a film about *war*, d'you see?"

He raised the forefinger even farther so that its tip touched the silver side of his head. "It is something wider we are after; something everyone will understand. It is the terrorization of the mind that is the ultimate danger; the effect it has on one individual." He pursed his lips contemplatively. "After all, Heather Duell is not so much different than you or the millions of women who will see this film.

"Up to that moment which so drastically alters her life, what contact has she had with terrorism, violence, the torture of the soul? James has kept all of that from her.

"But now"—he jabbed his finger as if he were a schoolmaster on the trail of a particularly salient point—"now she is hit between the eyes and—this is what will fire the film—with this new confrontation with terrorism, how will she be changed? What will happen to her? You see?

"*Here* is the true power of *Heather Duell*—why I have come so far to direct it; why Rubens has put so much of his own money into it—not the guns, the masks, the stench of cordite and fear. These are marvelous appurtenances and used judiciously they will help make this into a blockbuster film.

"But that's not enough. Along the line one must make a conscious choice, d'you see? It's not enough to make films that merely entertain, Daina. We are the dream makers for the world and as such we have a terrible responsibility not to continually fill people's heads with sawdust. We must strive to be bringers of emotion, to offer the public something it would not otherwise discover. *This* is our uniqueness."

Marion was on the tips of his toes now, his cheeks reddened by a rush of blood. "This is a horror story of the mind; a clash of wills; the delicate tickings of fears that escalate with every passing moment; an unexploded bomb that threatens the fabric of civilization because it cuts to the core. And what of Heather Duell in all this, eh? This is what you must ask yourself, Daina. Will she live or will she die?"

Marion was like that, Daina thought now as she changed down to take a particularly sharp curve in the road. You had to begin to live the role for him and for yourself before he let the cameras roll and catch your expression for all time.

She thought of the last scene she had done with El-Kalaam. The clash of wills, as Marion had called it.

And those memories of anger and energy set images of Manhattan billowing through her mind: blue shadows in the street; muscular canyons of smoked glass and steel; the hot August wind laughing down Riverside Drive; the park filled with Puerto Ricans in sleeveless shirts cooking plantain and black beans over makeshift charcoal burners, the brown butt of a .22 sprouting from the back of a waistband. Street Spanish buzzed through her head as if from an old, out-of-sync film. Was it only five years ago?

She shifted down again. The narrow road was nearly vertical here, which was why she came this way, loving the colors and the textures streaking by her, the challenge to her reflexes and her coordination. The top was down. The Los Angeles night stole in, a luminescent, fleeting lover.

She spun into a sweeping S-turn and abruptly felt herself on the verge of some great adventure, as if she were Cortez experiencing an intimation of greatness on the plunging seas, bound for gold-encrusted Mexico.

Monty was so right. *Heather Duell* was her film now and it would either make her or break her. She felt a shiver trace ghostly fingers down her spine and she twisted in the leather bucket seat. So much depended on other people. Everything had to come together, all the divergent strands, for success to come. Was she riding a rocket or—

Her fingers twitched on the wheel, cream and pale blue stucco walls flew by, she pushed savagely at the gear lever, nearly put the clutch through the carpeting in her anger. What was she worrying about anyway? She was an actress. It was up to her to take those dead lines typed across the white page and give them life. She had to become Heather Duell, allowing the role to grow up around her without conscious thought until she entered into a new reality. A new life. Leaving her—the *her* that was Daina Whitney—apart and drifting, merely an interested observer of another personality.

And by what arcane process was she able to accomplish this feat? She did not understand it, only knew that it gave her immense power.

She stepped hard on the accelerator.

Her excitement was a fever pushing her onward. She breathed in the night scents of the foliage on the hillside. Mark should be back from location by now, she thought. Their times away from L.A. had overlapped, he leaving after she had. They had spoken to each other infrequently and written not at all and, increasingly, she had heard disquieting stories about the tangled progress of his film: a war movie—virulently antiwar: "Coppola failed to cut it," he'd often tell her—

that because of his constant script revisions he was far behind schedule. And the money—it had to come from somewhere.

She felt a warmth seep into her as she dismissed those thoughts. Now was day's ending and she drew her image of him around her like a quilt, feeling his strength enter her flesh, her bones, as she imagined him caressing her back, his hot open mouth over hers....

She turned into the driveway of her house and cut the engine. Lights were on inside, a cheery greeting, but the exterior lights were off. Typical of him, she thought. He's so involved in the political, the mechanical has no meaning.

She went happily up the steps, swinging her handbag as if it was a baton, humming. The deep green ivy, jauntily overgrown on each side of the doorway, was glossy in the last of the light reflected in the vast bowl of the sky. She put her key into the lock in the wide oak door and went through.

She stopped, frozen, just over the sill and watched in a kind of horrified fascination the two bodies coupling on the bare parquet floor.

Blood shot through her as rage pumped adrenalin and there was a rushing in her ears as she stared at the animal thrusting of Mark's black buttocks back and forth, back and forth like the pendulum of an infernal clock ticking off the instants of love left in the world.

Oddly, dazedly, she found herself thinking that it must be cold for the girl there on the floor. Then, dimly, she heard the panting and the soft liquid sucking and the knowledge of this reversal humiliated her, made her feel as lost as a little girl, recalling to her her first—and only—silent intrusion upon her parents' bedroom early one morning. She felt a kind of vertigo, a strange frightening pressure along her chest as if she had somehow wandered into a pocket of heavy gravity. She felt terribly chilled; numbed into immobility.

Then the girl moaned and the spell was broken. It was as if Daina had been touched by electricity, violent and elemental. She drew her arm back, flung her bag and leaped forward so that she was upon them at almost the same moment the thing caught Mark alongside his head.

"Hey!" His neck twisted as his head came up. He began to lift off the girl.

"No, no, no!" Her voice rose to a scream, her long pale

fingers writhing along his bunched biceps. "Don't leave me now! Not yet! Don't—Oh!" Her breath shot like an explosion.

Daina's clenched fist dove toward Mark's flushed face. It slammed into his ear. He panted. Then her shoulder crashed into his and he tumbled off the girl with a pop like a cork coming out of a bottle.

His arms came up. "Hey, hey. What the hell—!" His rampant hardness was already deflating.

"You stupid bastard!" was all she could cry. "You stupid bastard!" She thought she would choke on all the unsaid words.

Alone on the floor the girl bucked and rolled, her fingers clamped between her wet thighs, her red breasts shaking. A thin dribble of fluid still linked her with Mark.

"Christ, Daina!"

But, hitting him, she would not let him speak. He had already done far too much of that. She swung at him not as a woman might but as a man, the training she had undergone in preparation for the film coming to good use, added to what she had learned in New York where she had grown up, learning how to defend herself, how to throw a football thirty yards in a perfect spiral. Red, red rage altered nothing.

"Daina, Daina, for Christ's—oof!—for Christ's sake will you listen to me?"

But she would not, knew he was good at that, his logic, his reasoning the heart of his political stance. Her fist caught him flush on the mouth, her knuckles twisting at the last instant so that her gold and jade ring—the one she had bought herself as her going-away present when she had said good-bye to New York to come out here—scored lengthwise across his lower lip, tearing through the tender flesh. Blood spouted in red ribbons.

He leaped away, his eyes wide with fear of her. He knew, in this terrifying moment, that he could not control her. She saw it contorting his dark handsome face.

Daina's eyes burned and she reached for her heavy handbag again. "Get the hell out of here, you sonovabitch!" She could not use his first name now. "Get out now! And take this"—she swung a foot into the girl's thigh, bringing her out of her thrall—"with you."

Warily, never letting his gaze waver from her, Mark circled around until he could safely pull the girl onto her feet.

She was slim, frail almost, her perfect skin burned brown by the California sun. She had no tan line, indeed, even now, exhibited no sign of shame, and now that Daina got her first good look at her, she realized with a tiny thrill that she could be no older than fifteen. Her small breasts seemed to be all erect nipple and she had shaved her pubic mound.

Mark tried one last time, his clothes and the girl's clutched under one arm like moulting feathers, but she cut him off: "Don't. Just don't say a word. You were just a lodger here. Just a lodger and nothing more. I don't want to hear anything you have to tell me." Tears glistened in the corners of her eyes and she was having difficulty seeing. "There's no excuse—nothing...."

And he was out the door, stumbling into the night, pushing the naked and now shivering girl in front of him, around to the side of the house where he kept his car.

As if from somewhere deep beneath the sea, she thought, she heard the brief cough of a motor starting into life, the echoes raking the hills, fading far too slowly. Through the window she saw two ruby pinpoints like adder's eyes flickering in eerie afterlife, now visible, now extinguished by the sighing trees, the lemon bloom of the headlights already expunged by distance.

She stood quite still, listening to the sibilance of the wind in the trees, felt like some freak hauled out of her habitat, a mermaid stupid enough to have been caught in a fisherman's net, dragged from the depths of the cool dim sea into the bright breathless world above where all was new and strange and certainly quite frightening.

The coldness swept over her again and she put her arms around herself, kicked the door closed with a bang. Her flesh was raised in goosebumps. My house. My house. The phrase kept whirling around in her mind. This is my house, she thought. He was just a lodger here. A goddamned transient I invited in eighteen months ago. To share—my God. My God!

She whirled away from the window, went limply into the living room, paused at the bar. She stared at the array of liquor and, in reaching for the bottle of Bacardi, gave a galvanic start so that the clear liquor roiled inside like a stormy sea. She poured herself three fingers of the rum, swallowed it all in one great gulp as if it was medicine. Her eyes closed and she shuddered. She pushed the thick cut-crystal glass away from her, shook her head and ran into the hall.

Hurling herself into the bedroom, she flung open the closet, ripped down all his clothes, went to the bureau and dumped the rest of his things onto the center of the carpet. She threw what she could into his one battered suitcase that, so he had said, had felt the heat of La Paz and the glitter of Buenos Aires, the mysteries and miseries of Moulmein and Lom Sak, and she snapped it shut. With this weight in one hand and the remainder of his clothes under her arm, she loped clumsily through the house, banging her toe on a chair leg, cursing, through the front door.

Outside birds sang sweetly, flitting through the treetops. A dog barked angrily from the other side of the hill, perhaps at the sly encroachment of a coyote upon its territory. A radio blared rock music briefly before being shut down.

She went to the side of the hill where the long grass grew wild and the brambles were thick and clawing. She looked at the suitcase as she hefted it. It had been his constant companion as he had moved from Burma into Thailand and thence, so he maintained, across the border at great personal hazard into forbidden Cambodia. For this was the cause he claimed to espouse, bleeding for a maimed and dying people on the other side of the dawn because he felt at least partially responsible for their torment and destruction. But what he had been exposed to there in the crossing must have, like radiation, blinded him to other just as basic concepts closer to his own home. Like some spaceman returning home from a walk on the moon, she thought now, he had changed, his mind bent out of shape, his emotions a grotesque parody of what they had once been. The flames of some unknown pyre had seared him.

At last she lofted the heavy thing out into the night, watching it tumble as if in slow motion, end over end over the hillside filled with dark bracken, a jungle's dense underbrush. Twenty yards down, it hit the earth corner on. The lid flew open under the impact and clothes spewed forth in a silent explosion.

Then, quite deliberately, Daina let fly Mark's loose clothing, one piece at a time until there was only one item left. It was a silk shirt she had bought him for his last birthday—his favorite, he had once told her. Crumpling it into a ball, she hurled this too into the wake of the other debris. It caught for an instant partway down the hillside in a branch of the giant acacia, waving there like the last pennant on a battlefield already lost. Then the cool night wind, tugging at it, took it upward high in the air like a kite loosed from its governing string, away and away. But she had turned from it before it was out of sight.

She shivered inside the house, the front door closed, locked and chained for the first time in many months.

The cicadas. The ticking of the kitchen clock. She stared sightlessly, clutching at herself. Numbness was ebbing slowly. She reached for the phone and dialed Maggie's number, but on the fourth ring, when she got the service, realized that she must be in the studio with Chris and, tonight, she had no desire to get involved with that frantic scene.

Said "Goddamnit," went back down the hall to change. The thing to do, she decided, was to get out of here herself. The Warehouse was a place where she could cool off and relax.

She paused, seeing herself in the bathroom mirror, a ghost-flash across time and space. A tidal flow pulled her into the cool tiled room. All movement ceased for a moment. She might have been a statue adrift in the diffuse inarticulate light. With an abrupt jut of her slim tanned arm, she stabbed on the vanity lights, a rainbow framing her face in illumination. Without taking her eyes from the reflected image, she sat slowly down. Lifting her hands, she pulled back the forest of honey hair spilling across her shoulders. She observed her face as she would an image on the screen, noting the strong oval structure, the wide-apart eyes, long and slightly tilted at their corners, with the spray of gold amid the violet irises, the high cheekbones. She thought she looked more like her mother than her father.

She began to cry even though a moment before she was quite certain she would not. She put her head down, cradled on her folded arms, and sobbed. She rocked a little, finding some small comfort in the motion. When it was over she got up and, turning on the taps, washed her face.

But the water in the sink sounded like Mark's voice whispering, *Darling, darling!* And she shook, disgusted by her self-pity.

Grow up! she told herself savagely. What the hell do you

need him for? Her body had a ready answer for that. It was the one thing all evening that made her smile.

She undressed in quick bursts and stepped into the shower. Moments later, she was pulling on a blue silk shirt. She had thought first of jeans but, somehow, tonight pants seemed all wrong and she drew on a deep blue and pale yellow print wrap skirt. She looked at herself, at her hard high breasts— Kim Novak breasts, Rubens had once said to her, jokingly— her narrow, not thin, waist, her long dancer's legs.

In the night and the silver Merc, she throttled down, around the hairpin turn, then launched herself on a mattress of motion. The wind spun her hair and the lights of the valley, haloed in haze, seemed to wink at her through the onrushing foliage, black as the sky.

The car throbbed beneath her like a heart. She sped past a high rock-and-concrete retaining wall and for an instant it threw back to her the sharp scent of gasoline, masking the perfume of the honeysuckle. It made her think of the streets of New York, roaring and drunk with life, careening onward, unstoppable, majestic in their rawness.

These were odd, disquieting echoes from a time in her life when she had nothing of her own, no one to turn to. Alone, full of fear and suppressed anger, she had found the only way to survive was to turn to the streets; only the people there treated her as a whole person who thought and felt and lived as a separate, discrete entity.

Now she felt the old longing for Baba and tears rolled down her cheeks again. Don't, she thought, do this to yourself. You've been down that road before and you know where it leads. She shivered. I'm close to the edge. Marion's pushing me to new depths is scary enough without Mark blowing up our relationship in my face. God damn him! She felt cut off, displaced, the opulent houses rushing by her could be no more alien than if she had just arrived from another solar system.

She wiped at her eyes, tore at the gear shift, felt the Merc leap ahead, skidding around a sharp turn. A mist was rising, whipping by her like spirit sails, and she was abruptly terrified, feeling as if the world was filled with a nothingness as great as the one she felt inside herself.

With a savage groan, she leaned forward, shoved a cassette in the player and, turning the volume full up, heard the hard biting electric pulse of the Heartbeats: the sharp staccato punch of the drums against the weighty underpinning of the bass; guitars and keyboards leading to Chris' angry voice shot like bullets from the speakers; *All the times I've tried/ To make you, break you/Sting you, wring you/You know I'll find you wherever you go.* . . . She threw her head back, letting the wind tear her hair back from her face. *Bound and tied/ Rubber bubbles in my mouth/It's no time to run away—No way/Taken by forces/In the dead of night.* . . . Her lips peeled back from her teeth from the force of the wind and, for just this moment, she did not have to think, merely feel the visceral pull of the music as if it were a tide drawing her out to sea. *Taken by forces/Without a fight.*

L.A. was a blue-lemon hemisphere below her, pulsing beneath the heavy smog as if some deeply buried soul was striving to be free of the torturous grip of the city.

She rushed downward to meet it.

The Warehouse was a mass of blazing lights, reflecting and bobbing like a community of luminescent sea creatures on the skin of the water. At this hour Marina del Rey was not crowded; Admiralty Way desolate in a way no diurnal inhabitant would recognize. Large yachts were reduced to two-dimensional shadows, their whipcord antennae sending mysterious signals into the sky.

This was a restaurant she loved above all others in L.A. She knew everyone here and they all did their best to make her feel at home. It was sufficiently far from Rodeo Drive in Beverly Hills to remove her from the modish fame mainliners whom she detested.

It had been built to resemble the waterside establishment of its name and came complete with great seasoned oak barrels, enormous wooden crates stamped with the names of the world's most exotic ports of call: Shanghai, Marseilles, Piraeus, Odessa, Hong Kong, Macao and even San Francisco. Strung from the ceiling were bales caught in heavy hemp nets.

It was a large and rather rambling place, reminding her of a New England country inn—its sea side an enormous glass-enclosed sunken balcony with the most dazzling harbor view within a fifty-mile radius.

As usual it was packed, but Frank, the maître d', smiling

and chattering on aimlessly about her clothes, her face, whatta bella, whatta bella, led her to a waterside table while heads turned and, on a long, snaking line past the bar, others were told politely but firmly that there would be at least an hour's wait for a choice table.

She ordered a Bacardi on the rocks with a twist of lime and it was brought almost at once. For what seemed an endless time she sat sipping at her drink, staring at the reflections of the people at the bar, quietly drinking their dinners, blinking bleary-eyed at each other. And for the first time she thought she knew what it might be like for them.

She turned her head away, found that she was focused on her own reflection in the glass. She traced the line of her nose, imperfect and unstraight, feeling immensely pleased that she had never had it fixed. Only my mother had wanted that, she thought.

Not Jean-Carlos. She had felt not a little trepidation as she had walked up the steps to the second-floor school he maintained at 8666 West 3rd Street in Los Angeles.

"Greetings, Daina!" he had said, grinning broadly and pumping her hand in both of his. She could feel the thick, yellow calluses, hard as concrete. "Welcome to school." He put one hand on her shoulder. "We are all on a first name basis here. *Sin ceremonia.* My name is Jean-Carlos Ligero."

He could not, she thought, have been Mexican. He had short, curling red hair, a narrow forehead beneath which burned a pair of clear blue eyes. "Hah, *chica*," he said in his rumbling voice that seemed to emanate from his chest and not his larynx, "*this* gives you character," and ran the hard pad of his fingertip down the bridge of her nose.

He had a wide mouth over which arched a perfectly groomed, dark red, pencil-thin mustache. He had a hard, aggressive chin; overall, his head was rather squarish. Slim-hipped, he moved with the grace of a dancer but with absolutely no effeminacy.

"Are you from the islands?" She took a shot.

His skin crinkled as he smiled. Lines scored his face as if they were direct evidence of the ravages of time upon human flesh. His teeth stood out startlingly yellow against the sun-burnished skin. "*The* island, *cara.* Cuba!" The smile disappeared like clouds racing before a dying sun. "I escaped from Morro Castle twenty years ago; took three others with me and left Fidel behind...also my family: my brothers, my sister.

"Now..." He stood before her, his hands balled into fists on his hips. They stood in the center of the vast room. A pair of enormous skylights brought a diffuse, smoothly constant light to all parts of the room, even the corners. Along one wall was a polished wooden dancer's barre above which hung a long mirror and, beyond that, a webbed network to create shadows. The floor was wood, covered in part by plain gray mats. Otherwise, the room was bare.

"Is this it?" Daina said, looking around.

"What were you expecting?" He smiled archly. "Something a bit more exotic, perhaps. Stripped from the pages of a James Bond novel."

She smiled back at him, relaxing at last.

"Come," he said, gesturing. "Let's see your hands."

She put them up in front of her.

"First things first," he said seriously and produced a manicurist's scissors. "You can accomplish nothing with these." He went deftly to work on her nails, paring away all the excess until they were man-cut. He ran his fingertips over their semicircular edges one by one, nodding to himself, satisfied. Then he stepped away from her.

"You understand why you are here?"

"Yes. James, my husband in the film, has taught me to be an accomplished hunter."

"All right." His voice was clipped but still, as he had put it, *sin ceremonia*. "This specialized training is for a film, yes, but what I will teach you over the course of the next three weeks is no fake. This must be made crystal clear to you. It is no joke. You are to learn the real thing: the lore of guns—how to hold them, recognize them, load them, fire them. How to handle yourself with your hands, with a knife and so on." He shrugged. "Some directors, they don't care too much...so long as it looks good when they do the take they are satisfied, no? These people I do not handle. I send them elsewhere. I cannot afford to waste my time." He raised a long forefinger. "Marion and I have spent many pleasant evenings with—he knows rum...and the sugar cane. We drink, we chew, we talk. He knows what he wants, this man, so he comes to me. 'It will take longer,' I tell him, 'but when your people are through with me, they will know what they must know.'"

He clapped his hands together. "All right. We begin."

Daina looked again. "But there's nothing here except those mats."

"*Paciencia*," Jean-Carlos said. "All you will need is right here in this room." From out of nowhere, he produced a pistol, threw it at her. She caught it clumsily.

"No, no, no," he said easily. "Do it this way." And he showed her. "This is an automatic," he said. He turned the pistol over to show her the underside of the butt. "Here, a clip of bullets is placed." He turned the weapon back over. "You see, it has no cylinder." He raised his forefinger again. "Never trust your life to an automatic. They jam much too often for comfort. Use a revolver. Here"—from the same nowhere he produced another gun—"try this Police Special. It's a heavier pistol, I grant you, but it has its compensations. Heavier caliber bullet, greater stopping power, very accurate. As a huntress, all these factors are important to you.

"No, this way." His strong, capable fingers guided hers. "Use both hands, that's right. Does it seem heavy? Yes? All right." He took a pair of weighted strips, wrapped them around her wrists, securing them with the Velcro pads. "Now this is the way we'll practice for the first two weeks. After that, the weight of the pistol will feel like nothing at all. And like any fine marksman, you will forget about it entirely."

True to his word he worked her hard, driving her until she could recognize a dozen different handguns, a score of rifles from across the room, until she could shoot confidently and accurately, use a knife to skin an animal torso, crack through bone joints—all in the space of the three weeks before the cast's departure for Nice. "There will be more later," he told her. "But for now—you are ready."

"Daina—hello."

She looked up now over her shoulder, saw Rubens standing at her side. He was tall and broad-shouldered. He had flat black eyes in a bold, hawklike face made even more so by his deep tan. He was of that handsome Mediterranean type that could as easily have its origins in Greece as in Spain. He had a strong, determined mouth, longish hair as black as his eyes.

But all this physical detail was merely icing. Rubens had only to walk into a room for others to feel his formidable presence. He radiated power as if he were some newly designed mobile nuclear reactor. And, perhaps inevitably, because of this, rumors followed him around like chips from a comet's tail.

It was said, for instance, that he had never lost a boardroom fight—and there had been plenty of those; that he was not content at victory but was driven to grind his opponents into the ground.

It was said, too, that he had divorced his wife—a beautiful and talented woman—because she would not touch him in public.

In a sea full of sharks, Rubens was known as a shark eater, a reputation he continually sought to further. And for that he was greatly admired, sought after, cajoled and stroked by a populace used to twisting their backbones out of shape.

"Rubens." Daina, lifting her Bacardi and lime, thought, The absolute last person in the world I want to see tonight.

Because everyone else deferred to him, she had made up her mind not to the moment they first met: he had been represented as the cold heart of L.A., the high-gloss mainstream all the fame-junkies lusted after; a symbol rather than a man.

He put one hand on the back of the wicker and chrome chair opposite hers. "Do you mind?"

She was terrified and, finding herself shaking, clasped her hands in her lap below the tabletop. But she was dismayed to find another, stronger emotion inside her. The aloneness shook her and now, looking up at this man, she could not help thinking of the other, fleeing into the night with that little girl, her taut backside winking as she ran easily, laughing. Mark.

She was on the verge of tears again and only her training stopped her from looking like a complete fool in front of him. She did not want to be with Rubens but his company was preferable now to being alone with herself.

She cleared her throat. "By all means." Her voice did not sound like her own.

"Vodka and tonic, Frank," he said to the hovering maître d' as he sat down. "Stolichnaya."

"Stolichnaya. Yes, sir. Miss Whitney? Another Bacardi?"

"Sure." She lifted her empty glass. "Why not?"

He nodded, took it from her.

Rubens waited until the drinks came and they were alone again. The barflies were buzzing, their raucous, brittle laughter in sharp contrast with the carefully controlled movements of their hands and heads. In short, they were just like the drunks in any bar in any quarter of the world.

"It's nothing I've said?"

"What?"

"Your blue mood."

She sipped at her drink, wondered what his angle was. At another time, it might have been a challenge but now . . . "Just a bad day."

"Everything all right on the set?"

She was suspicious now. "You know everything that goes on on the set. You know it's not that. What are you getting at?"

He spread his hands. "Nothing. I walk in, see that look on your face . . ." He lifted his glass, took a drink. "I don't want to see my stars unhappy. I thought I could help."

"Help me right into bed." It was out before she knew it and she thought, Oh, Christ, now I've done it.

"I'll leave then." He took hold of his glass.

She watched his face, her mind whirling. Even if you are a bastard, she thought, you're all I have tonight. Lucky me. "No, don't go," she said halfheartedly. "I'm just in a shitty mood. It's nothing to do with you."

He stood up, gave her a rueful smile. "I'm afraid it *does* have to do with me. You have every right to say what you did." He spread his hands again, a characteristic gesture. "It's true. You know it. I know it. I've wanted to get you into bed ever since I was first introduced to you a year and a half ago. But you'd just met that crazy black director—what's his name? Mark something—"

"Nassiter," she said quickly.

He snapped his fingers. "Yah, right. Nassiter." He seemed to stir the name about with his tongue. He shrugged. "Well, who's faithful around here." He looked around them conspiratorially. "Everyone's screwing everyone else. And I thought—"

"I don't," she said tautly, "do that."

"No," he said. "You don't." She thought he looked a bit sad. "But unfortunately it took me eighteen months to discover that fact." He lifted his glass to her in a toast. "See you around."

And she thought that perhaps she had been all wrong

about him. That all along she had been seeing him in just
one way, judging him on the equivalent of a screen image;
that she had let others shape the way she reacted to him—
all those stories, rumors, excited whispers: lust of the fame
mainliners. No, no, no. Daina Whitney would have no part
of *that*.

She almost laughed at herself then for being such a se-
rious-minded bitch, always looking under the rug for hidden
motives.

But, simultaneously, she recognized a deeper, darker motive for her pushing him away. Rubens was, they said, heart-
less and as hard as diamond dust. But he was also power; he
was L.A. Is that why she felt drawn to him? What could he
be, ever, to her? He was dangerous and she knew it and she
began to sweat with the knowledge. Now she saw abruptly
how the events in her life had led her quite directly to this
moment. Yes. Trauma had fixed her even before she left the
house tonight. But she knew now with a growing certainty
that had it not been this way, it would have been another.

She felt deep inside her a stirring: his heat, her friction;
a combination that she had not allowed herself to acknowl-
edge. Until now.

Slowly she put her hand over his. "Stay," was all she said,
looking up into his face. She felt his fingers hard, calloused
beneath hers and unaccountably, she thought of Jean-Carlos.
Rubens, too, had that tough animal grace: great power held
tightly in check. Sparks flew off the surface of him.

For the first time, Rubens seemed unsure and she said,
"Oh, c'mon. You've been a bastard and I've been a bitch.
Doesn't mean we can't spend a couple of hours together. Could
be it was all a misunderstanding."

He sat down again, took a long pull at his drink. She took
her hand away, watched him staring at her.

"What are you looking at?"

"You know you are really the most extraordinarily beautiful woman I've ever—"

"Oh, Christ, Rubens!"

"No, no." He lifted a palm toward her. "I mean it. I've
never—this sounds so odd—I don't think I've ever really seen
you before. You were the new girl—"

"A trophy."

"Guilty." But there seemed little apology in his voice. "*Mea culpa.* You get so used to the assembly line. It's like any other place, except here we deal in human flesh." He waved away those words. "Anyway, it gets hypnotic after a while. The girls come and they go...speaking of Michelangelo." He laughed and she did too, intrigued by his reference to T.S. Eliot. "It's easy, so damnably easy that sometimes it makes you want to scream."

She made a wry face. "You mean it's not every man's fantasy of paradise?"

"I'll tell you something," he said seriously, leaning forward across the table. "Paradise is a place fit only for a dream. It cannot fit comfortably into the real world. And d'you know why? There's no danger in paradise. We—" he gestured with his free hand "—all of us—need danger in order to survive. To live and to do...the things we have to do to get one notch higher each year." He was carefully monitoring her expression. "D'you think you're any different than the rest of us, Daina?" He shook his head. "You're not, you know." He pushed his empty glass aside so that there was nothing between them on the tabletop.

"Take *Heather Duell* as an example. Are you going to be happy if the film doesn't turn out to be the blockbuster we all believe it is? Of course not. You won't be happy until you're number one. But without that drive, that confidence in your own ability to do it, you wouldn't survive out here...or anywhere.

"You have a certain quality that I can't place. It's almost as if you're a displaced person from another time, another place." He cocked his head to one side. "I don't know. You'll think it a line if I tell you there's something different about you."

"No," she said. "I wouldn't." Now she was really intrigued. He couldn't know, of course, she knew that. Yet he saw it in her. Would he guess? She thought there was a chance.

"It's almost—" And there was that distinctive gesture again, the edge of his hand brushing away at the air. "But no"—he shook his head—"it can't be."

"Can't be what?" Now it was she who was leaning across the table.

He smiled, almost shyly, and for just an instant she thought she had caught a glimpse of him as a little boy. She found herself smiling back at him.

"Oh, well, you'll probably be offended." He waited a moment as if deciding. "If I didn't know better, I'd swear you came in off the streets. But I've read your background: upper-middle-class family in a fashionable section of the Bronx. Then, not now," he amended. "What could the streets of New York mean to you? Movies, books...."

Baba, she thought, shutting her secret heart away, away. But she was surprised and pleased that he had guessed, though she would never tell him that.

"How was New York?" she said.

"Oh, you know. Just the same. The garbage is piling up, everyone hates the mayor and the Mets are still losing."

"But it's spring there," she said wistfully. "I'm afraid I'm forgetting what the different seasons are like. It's like being in a land without time."

"That's just why I like it here," Rubens said.

"Don't you miss the East Coast?"

He shrugged. "Oh, well. My company's got offices in New York so I go back there at least once a month. I like it but I don't really think I miss it." He took a sip of his drink. "I like staying at the Park Lane when I'm there. I really do enjoy that...view north out over Central Park up into Harlem. That's interesting, looking out over where the poor live."

"So business made you come out here."

He nodded. "Eventually. But it was reading Raymond Chandler that began it all. I fell in love with L.A. through him."

"You know, it's funny," Daina said, looking out at the water. "In all the other cities of the world I've been to—Rome, London, Paris, Geneva, Florence, all of them—mornings invariably hold the most magic; a kind of virginity that is almost transcendent when all the mechanization is stilled enough to allow the heart to soften." She shook her head. "But not here. In this city, it's the onrush of night. That's because L.A. has no virginity to lose each day. It was born a whore."

"Harsh words for a town you've chosen to live in," Rubens observed.

Daina dipped a fingertip into the last of her drink, swirled the half-melted ice cubes around and around. "Oh, there are other qualities to this place." She looked at him through her

lashes. "It's the most luxurious city on earth, filled with petulant sighs and platinum bracelets."

"If you love the nights so much, we should be doing something now."

"Like what?"

"Beryl Martin's throwing a party. You ever meet her?"

"I've only met the studio's publicity people."

"Well, Beryl's the best of the independents. She can be a
bit sharp, but when you get to know her you appreciate just
how brilliant she can be."

"I don't know."

"Well, we can leave whenever you want. And I promise
I'll take good care of you."

"I've got the Merc here."

"Give me the keys. I'll have Tony drop it off home for you.
I don't need him to drive the Lincoln now."

Rubens avoided Sunset, preferring the dark rushing
streets to the neon glitter and crawl of the Boulevard. Gradually, the sprawling mock-Spanish houses gave way to
chrome-and-glass-fronted banks, brightly lit used-car lots
with colored pennants fluttering.

Beside him on the Lincoln's plush crushed velvet seat,
Daina reached forward, flipped on the radio, spinning the
dial until she caught radio station KHJ. It was only moments
before the Heartbeats' current single, "Robbers," came on.

"You love that stuff, don't you?" Rubens said.

"You mean rock or the Heartbeats?"

"Both. I keep hearing that goddamned song wherever I
go."

"That's because it's number one all over."

"I don't understand it," he said, making a left. "Those
guys've been around for a hell of a long time, haven't they?"

"Seventeen years or thereabouts."

He braked into a right-hand turn, ignored the red light,
plunging onward like an undaunted explorer into a night
illuminated, it seemed, only by the twin swath of the big car's
wide headlights. "Christ, you'd think they'd have blown
themselves to bits by now or, at the very least, gone their
separate ways like the Beatles."

"They're one of the last remnants of the first British mu-

sical invasion," she said. "God knows how they've stayed together this long."

"Lots of bread there, no doubt. That's a good incentive."

She turned her head. "You wouldn't be interested in moving into that—"

"Good God, no." He laughed. "I'd sooner slit my wrists
than have to depend on a bunch of drugged-out musicians
who've never outgrown adolescence." He glanced in the rearview mirror. "Besides I don't like what they play. Never
have."

"Don't you like music at all?"

"When I have the time to listen, yes. Jazz, a bit of classical
if it's not too heavy."

"You want me to turn it off?" She reached for the dial.

"No. Leave it. You like it."

They were nearing the flats of Beverly Hills now, the
houses longer, lower, more ornate.

"How's your friend Maggie? Doesn't she live with one of
the band?"

"Yes. Chris Kerr, the lead singer. She's fine. She's been
with Chris while the band's in the studio working on their
new album. She's still looking for the role to break her."

Rubens grunted. "I'll bet she'd give the caps off her front
teeth to have your role in *Heather Duell*."

"Not if it meant I wouldn't have it. She's happy for me."
She saw his look. "Really. She's my closest friend out here.
We went through a lot of bad times together during the last
five years."

"All the more reason," he said, turning into a long sweeping driveway lit on either side by Japanese stone lanterns.
"Now's the time they separate the girls from the women."

Naturally she lost him in the first burst of glittery light,
wild noise, and swirl of perfumey scents. He stuck in the
corner of her eye as he was led away by an earnest-faced Bob
Lunt of William Morris. And soon they had their heads together like sophomores in a football huddle.

Rock music blared, Linda Ronstadt alternating with
Donna Summer, giving the party an odd schizophrenic atmosphere. Daina recognized people from all the major studios,

along with a sprinkling of independent producers and directors, all of whom outnumbered the actors.

"Ah. Daina Whitney."

Beryl Martin was a large woman with a face that most closely resembled a parrot's. Her beaklike nose would have been the dominant feature in a flat-planed, oval face the color of putty had it not been for the remarkable green eyes, set like emeralds within pouches of flesh.

"Hello, Beryl."

The older woman whirled her great bulk around in a remarkably lithe spin. "Well, how do you like me? In the flesh, I mean?" She laughed, not expecting a response. She took Daina's arm, led her to the crowded bar where she got drinks for them both.

"You must tell me," she said warmly, "how you manage to be such good friends with Chris Kerr. I mean he...well, all of those rock people, really, are such freakish figures. Or"—she cocked an eyebrow speculatively—"is that the secret?" She giggled. "They're so *outré*." She hugged Daina. "How delicious!"

"That's not it at all," Daina said, halfway between fascination and annoyance. "I don't understand why you find musicians so incomprehensible. I think most people in our community invite them to their parties because they feel both excited by and superior to them."

"Musicians..." Beryl rolled the word around in her mouth as if it were a morsel of food. "Uhm, no. *Musicians* are people who play in symphony orchestras or jazz combos. Rock and roll is played by, oh, what should I call them? Outlaws." She shrugged her meaty shoulders. "I don't know, they all seem so stupid."

"Well, Chris isn't," Daina said, a bit put out that she needed to defend him. "You don't understand him because he comes from a totally different background. He's an alien here. I imagine he still feels uncomfortable around you; he had nothing for so long."

"I'll tell you a secret about me," Beryl said lightly. "When I first came out here I had fifty cents in my pocketbook. I weighed one-fifteen and could've been a model." She turned her face into the light. "See, I've got the bone structure. But so could ten thousand other girls far more pretty than I. Some of them did, eventually.

"I, on the other hand, was obliged to get down on my knees and put my mouth in a number of increasingly influential laps in order to raise myself up, so to speak." She shrugged again. "Sometimes that worked and sometimes I got thrown out anyway. This is a very callous town." She laughed, spraying the air with a fine mist of liquor and saliva. Her skin was warm and dry; she smelled of Chanel No. 5.

"Then one day I got a thought. Right in the middle of the act. I got so excited I almost bit it off." She guffawed. "I was doing this publicist while he was on the phone with a client. I knew right away who she was and that his pitch was all wrong. He had no angle.

"At that moment, the bastard puts the heel of his hand against the back of my head, pushing me further down on him. That's when it dawned on me. What am I doing here sucking cock when I can be out getting this actress print space? So I, ha ha, dribbled a little on his pants, and, when he went to the men's room, I stole a look at his classified Rolodex to get the actress's address.

"The minute I left his office, I drove over to the *Times* and pitched Epstein my angle to the story. He bought it. Now all I had to do was convince the actress to take me on."

Beryl drained her glass, smacked her lips in pleasure. "Well, let me tell you, it was easier than I thought. She'd been stuck in neutral for so long, she'd forgotten what first gear was like. The *Times* piece sounded like overdrive to her. That was the beginning." She patted her stomach. "All those breakfasts, lunches, dinners and there went my model's figure. At first I was upset but then I thought, What did weighing a hundred and fifteen ever get me? A hit-and-run concession in L.A.? And after a while, I learned to love the weight. I turned it into part of my image. And anyway"—she winked—"now it's the men who have their mouths in *my* lap. Ah ha!"

"There was no other way for you?"

Beryl shook her head. "In the days I'm talking of, no. Now it's a bit different: women can *choose* that way to go."

Daina laughed. "Yes. There's more talk of liberation every day but very little else."

The heavyset woman gave her an appraising look. "I see there's quite a bit more to you than even Rubens told me." She nodded. "But now I can see why he's taken such a proprietary interest in your career. I must say I thought you were quite good in *Regina Red* but the press—or should I say the lack of it—has been scandalous. Paramount should've hired me. You're certainly not being used to the right advantage. Not at all. I think Monty missed the boat on that one. He should've gotten you some guarantees. Hell, if I'd've been aboard, *Regina Red* would be selling *you* instead of the other way around."

"He did what he could," Daina said. "After all, it was my first starring role."

"Hell, honey, that's no way to think. Jeffrey Lesser was goddamned lucky to get you for that role. Yes. All that flash would've been for nothing without good, solid acting and you provided that." Beryl put her arm around Daina's shoulders. "I also hear you stood up to him pretty well."

"Oh, you know Jeffrey. He enjoys intimidating people. He broke Marcia Boyd down within three days. He badgered her over one scene...did one hundred and fifty takes...for no reason, really. He's just foully neurotic. Marcia got more and more hysterical until she had to be replaced. He loved that one."

"And what happened when he tried it with you?" Beryl said in a softly conspiratorial tone. "You don't look like the hysterical type to me."

"I don't bruise that easily."

"Brava!" Beryl clapped her hands together around her glass. "What spirit!" Her voice got even lower now so that Daina was obliged to lean toward her in order to hear her over the brash noise of the party swirling around them. "But he tried, didn't he?"

Daina nodded. "Yes, he did. But I just stood there and gave him back everything he gave me."

Beryl looked astonished. "And he didn't have you thrown off the set?"

Daina laughed. "Oh, no. You see, I discovered early on that Jeffrey feels much safer if he can alienate the entire cast, because he believes it generates the kind of tension from which the best acting springs."

"Is it true?"

Daina shrugged. "Who knows? I do think that he does it because deep down *he* can function best with that tension. I saw what happened between him and Marcia and I learned how to handle him."

"You clever thing!" Beryl squeezed her arm affectionately.

"What are you two talking about?" Rubens said, coming up between them from out of the clouds of milling people.

"Oh, nothing you'd be interested in," Beryl said in an off-hand manner. "Just girl talk." She left them amid gales of laughter.

"What was that about?" he asked her. "I haven't seen Beryl laugh so much in a long time."

"Kindred spirits," Daina said. "I think we got along."

"That's great." He seemed inordinately pleased.

Daina, glancing into the midst of the party, took Rubens' arm, swung him around. "Christ," she breathed, "I think Ted Kessel's on his way over here."

"What's wrong with him?"

"That weasel! Life's not complete for him unless he's screwing someone. You know *Regina Red* was originally supposed to be a Warners film."

"Sure."

"Well, it was Kessel who balked at the last minute. And d'you know why? He complained that the lead should have more of a box-office name. He was nervous because I wasn't well known enough and, in his opinion, I'd be a liability."

"I wonder which cover-up he's using to explain your success away to his bosses?"

Kessel had seen them and was, indeed, on his way over. He had close-cropped white hair and the kind of glossily pink, clean-shaven jowls one could only get from hot towels and a straight razor. He wore tan slacks and a safari jacket with only the bottom button closed, revealing his hairless chest and rather distended beer belly.

"Daina, what are you doing with this pirate!" he said heartily. He slapped Rubens on the back while leaning forward. "Is this little tête-à-tête business or pleasure? Do you mind a ménage?" He laughed.

"A little of both, actually," Rubens said. "We're planning Daina's next film."

"Already? Why, you're not even halfway through with this one."

"Ted," Rubens said with his arm around the other man, "when you become this successful, you've got to plan ahead."

Kessel made no mention of *Regina Red* but looked, fish-eyed, from one to the other. "Twentieth's got an option, I suppose."

Rubens seemed to wait a very long time before looking at Daina and saying, "No, they don't."

"Really? Well, you got a studio in mind?" Daina could almost see him licking his chops. "You know my position at Warners, Rubens. You just say the word and I'll have a deal memo messengered over to you in the morning." Now that it had come this far, he was no longer speaking to the both of them.

Rubens looked dubious. "I don't know, Ted. I mean you don't even know anything about the project."

Kessel's fat fingers fluttered in the air. He was on the scent and nothing was going to shake him. "Doesn't matter. We'll leave that totally up to you, Rubens. Your name's like gold."

"And Daina. Her name's like gold now, too."

"Yes, yes. Of course it is," Kessel said quickly. "We've all been hearing the most remarkable things about *Heather Duell.*"

Rubens, knowing the man was anxious to hear more about the film, said, "There are an enormous number of guarantees we'd want."

"Hey, what'm I here for? They can all be worked out, believe me."

"Oh, I believe you, Ted," Rubens said, taking him around the shoulders again. "And I'm sure that Daina believes you, too. But you see..." He looked around. "Ted, I'm going to tell you something in the strictest of confidence...."

"Yes?" There was a sheen on his cheeks as he strained for the tidbit.

"Whichever studio it's going to be," Rubens said, "it'll never be Warners." His laugh exploded as Kessel angrily jerked himself away from the fraudulent embrace and, his face and neck flushed red, stalked out of the room.

"I see you're not headed back to my house," she said cynically. She could not help it still; it seemed her only defense now.

If it bothered him he was careful not to let it show. He answered her seriously. "No. I know you love the sea."

At that precise moment, as if he had magically managed it like the greatest of prestidigitators, they broke past the Pacific Palisades, winding down the quiet road into Malibu.

Daina touched a stud, rolled down her window all the way and switched off the radio. In the silence she could discern the draw and hiss of the surf as steady and comforting as a heartbeat. But as they drew closer, the sight of the sluggish Pacific made her ache for a glimpse of the harsh deep-blue Atlantic, pummeling sharp bleak rocks, covering them with frantic white spume, the water so cold it turned your skin pebbly, your lips blue.

The long Lincoln thrummed quietly along Old Malibu Road, past silent dark houses set one against the other so that she could only catch intermittent flashes of the sea.

"It's getting late," she said in reflex. "I'm on call."

"That's all right."

They slid to a smooth stop before a bare stretch of sand. Incredibly, there was no house there.

"Where are we?"

"Come on," he said, climbing out of the car.

She got out, took a deep breath. At least this is the same, she thought, inhaling the rich scents of the sea, salt and phosphorus and something more, the amalgam of living creatures floating, swimming, undulating in one long continuous chain.

She looked at Rubens over the shining car top. He had taken off his suit jacket and now, putting one foot behind the other, slipped off his shoes.

He reached out a hand and, coming around to his side, she took it, trembling, letting him lead her over the road, out onto the sand. They half ran, half stumbled, sinking in, passing a line of lights to their right as if it were the verge of civilization. Now they were in territory new and unexplored.

Down to the water's edge they went and he urged her forward still. She bent, slipped off her shoes and, not knowing why, she walked with him into the water.

At first their clothes billowed out with trapped air, making it easier to float, but all too soon the pockets belched up their contents and then their clothes clung to their skin, heavy as lead.

They launched themselves, swimming out from the shore, Rubens slightly in front leading the way, and it was not until they were almost upon it that Daina realized that their destination was a boat.

It was a thirty-three-foot sloop moored through a buoy and then an anchor. At its curving side, Rubens reached upward, his long muscular arms over his head. His fingers apparently caught in something for he hung suspended in midair for some seconds before splashing back down into the water with a rope ladder. It was slippery with seaweed.

"Coming up?"

With a start she turned her head upward. The boat loomed darkly above her left shoulder. A dripping hand was held out to her. Rubens had already climbed aboard. She lifted one leg in the water, almost but not quite reluctant to leave its low-gravity embrace.

On sudden impulse she dipped her head under the water and opened her eyes as if that might make hearing here easier. She listened for what seemed a long time, until her burning lungs made it imperative that she surface. But she had heard nothing save the tide in her ears, a kind of muted roaring, shapeless, almost soundless, as if it were the fierce, inchoate bellow of entropy lapping at the universe—a land beyond the grip of time, where all things lived and died simultaneously, were recognizable and anarchic in the same instant.

She breached the surface, shaking her head to free her eyes and nose of water, blowing her breath through her mouth. She felt vaguely defeated and sad. She took a deep breath of the night and reached for Rubens' proffered hand.

"Do you fish?" he asked her, handing her a fluffy deep blue towel. "I do a lot of deep-sea fishing with this boat. It's ideal for it."

"No," she said. "I don't like it much." She dipped her head so she could dry her hair.

"Don't," he said. He put a hand on the towel until she lowered it. His eyes seemed to shine in the dim moonlight, as sharp and glittery as stars. "Please." She paused, looking at him, the thick towel draped across her slim wrists as if in preparation for some ceremony. "I like the way your hair looks wet. Like a mermaid's." He seemed faintly embarrassed by what he had said. He turned partly away. "What do you think of her?" His arm spread wide.

Daina looked around the craft. It was a one-masted sailboat. The deck was flat, a midnight-blue ribbed composition material, perfectly flat aft. Forward, she could just make out the slight sleek rise of the white cabin.

"It's beautiful," she said. "But what happens when you hit a patch of calm weather?"

Rubens smiled. "Underneath the deck is an inboard diesel. The casing bulges out from the line of the keel. It gives her a deeper draft but she's infinitely more stable in rough weather. Naturally there's more deck space, too."

With this talk of the boat, his abrupt unease melted. He sat easily against the port sheer-strake, the towel around his neck, his back to the land and his legs stretched out in front of him.

"I never suspected you had a boat."

He laughed. "No. It's a well-kept secret. There are times I've just got to get away from everyone and everybody. Tennis is my social sport; get a lotta business done that way as well as relaxing." He laughed again, a bright, breezy sound. "You know guys. They pal around, sweat together, sunburn together, grunt a little together and right away they think they can trust each other. It's our form of Mah-Jongg."

She got off her backside as if stung. "You mean that's the kind of thing we women can manage—Mah-Jongg."

"Well I certainly don't know the first thing about it," he said jokingly. But seeing her expression, he quickly added, "Now look, that's not at all what I meant. I only—Jesus, Daina, what are we talking about. I know you're not another Bonnie Griffin." Bonnie Griffin was an executive vice-president at Paramount who, Rubens knew, Daina had dealt with during the filming of *Regina Red*.

"What the hell does that mean?"

Rubens was perhaps already beginning to suspect that he had inadvertently poured gasoline onto the fire, thinking it was water, but he seemed unprepared as yet to back down. "You know very well what I mean. We both know what she is. She breaks chops every chance she gets."

"And that's what you think I do." Her eyes burned savagely in the moonlight, ironically making her even more desirable.

"That's not what I said and you know it. I only meant, well, you know how girls are when they get together...."

"No. How are they?" But she knew very well indeed.

"For Christ's sake, I only meant that guys are the same way. You needn't bite my head off."

They stared at each other for a time. Around them the sea rocked in tiny splashes like a child playing contentedly. The fittings on board creaked rhythmically in a kind of soothing litany, conjuring images of the land of nod and sugarplums dancing, recalling to her images like bright flashes of lightning of her childhood summer days and nights on Cape Cod.

"She's a hell of an executive," Rubens said. "But she is murder to deal with."

"It's only because—" Daina began, then shut up. They rocked back and forth on the tide. "Yes she is."

He smiled at her and the tension broke, a tropical current slicing through a formidable ice floe. He seemed to sigh, though it might have been the wind, and came toward her, looming over her, a lithe nocturnal creature she had been lucky enough to stumble upon in the dead of night.

His magnetism reached out across the closing expanse to embrace her in a kind of self-generated heat. Her thighs seemed to glow and her heart plummeted just as if she were in a swiftly descending elevator. He had not yet touched her but the moonlight, the slow drip of the seawater onto the deck as it rolled in pearly drops off his skin, the way his half-open shirt clung to the muscles of his chest, all combined to make him seem almost priapic. She felt her nipples stiffen, begin to ache with her need and she saw this inevitable end to the long night almost as if it were predestined. Her tongue came out unconsciously, touched her upper lip, moistening it. Her mouth felt as dry as if she had just trekked across a desert.

She became acutely aware of him staring at her, his eyes flicking momentarily to her breasts where her wet and clinging blouse had opened enough to show her deep cleavage; then back to her shining face. Her lashes were thick with water and her hair darkened and curled damply across her forehead, stranded over her ears and shoulders like sea grape. She began to feel as if she were the mermaid he had conjured.

"Come here." It was a whisper she was not even certain he had uttered yet it seemed at once as soft and as harsh as

the night coming in off the sea, bringing with it tantalizing
hints of the far-off lands it had brushed in days gone by:
Tahiti, Fiji, even Japan, floating serenely on the other side
of the world.

She came against his chest feeling as superheated as an
engine, sighed as her nipples scraped erotically against him
just before his open mouth came down over hers. His tongue
touched hers while his hands reached down to cup her buttocks and she felt herself lifted up onto the tips of her toes,
back arched, at once floating and supported by the fulcrum
of his hands, his fingertips lightly caressing her between her
thighs so that she was pressed inward and upward. Her pubic
mound found him already erect beneath his lightweight pants
and she moved her hips in a circle as they kissed.

Her arms were around his neck, her fingers gently caressing the nape, feeling the toughness and the resiliency as
they moved slowly down the ridged contours of his back.
When she reached his waist she clawed his shirt free of the
waistband of his pants, ran her fingertips inside, upward;
even her short man-cut nails shivered him.

Rubens had already opened the buttons at the rear of her
skirt and now he unwound it from her as if it were a harem
girl's cape until it was a dark puddle at her feet, a perfect
crepe flower from which she seemed to emerge. He pulled her
hips back into steamy contact with his groin and she gasped,
feeling him like a glowing poker through the tantalizing second skin of her silk bikini panties.

He worked on her shirt while she stroked his chest and
sides, feeling his taut muscles jump. Then he had her shirt
open and his hands were inside, cupping her breasts. She
heard him moan as he saw how hard her nipples were and
his head lunged forward, his hot lips closing around the tip
of one breast.

She thought again, as pleasure began to assail her, of the
inevitability of this moment but this time the effect on her
was different.

"No," she said. "Stop it." She put her hands against the
sides of his head, pulled his sucking mouth from her flesh.

"What's the matter?" His voice was tight and clogged.

She crossed her arms over her breasts, turned away from
him, into the wind. She felt lost, out of control, as if that
inevitability was no longer something she wanted but merely

a circumstance of life she had stumbled upon in the darkness. Fear clutched at her with icy fingers, making her shiver. She felt his hand at the crook of her elbow, knuckles against the side of her sensitive breast, shook him off wordlessly.

"Have I done something?"

She found that she could not even answer him. She thought of Mark, cursed him because she still wanted him, fires inside her dying hard, anger not yet the palliative it should be, would be in the time to come.

"Daina—?"

"Be quiet," she whispered. "Please."

It might help to tell him, she suspected, but she could not. She tried twice but was as helpless as a mute. She would never, could never go back to Mark—her heart experienced this like an arrow through its center—yet the old feelings had not shriveled, dropped off.

She went to the rail, stared out to sea. The night was chill, undressed as she was, but the gently lapping water was warm. The Pacific, she thought idly, was aptly named. Like Los Angeles itself, it was laid back, sleepily content to move in the changeless pattern it had grown accustomed to through all the long accretion of years. Nothing would interfere just like nothing could alter the city. It existed, sapping vitality, turning it into sunshine and smog, palm trees and Mercs, the wafting odor of money that they all inhaled like burning lotus leaves and, like Ulysses' crew, refused to budge themselves. . . .

She turned away now, toward Rubens who waited as still as a statue, watching her. She knew now what she must do—abandon herself to selfishness; it was either that or fade away like a puff of smoke into the L.A. haze. He was her lifeline; only he could save her tonight, his strength, his power seeping into her.

She walked toward him, her breasts swelling, her arms at her side and when she was close enough to him so that their flesh grazed, she lifted her arms, drew his head down to hers, feeling as his lips closed over hers that fluttering of terror that came from the adamantine suspicion in her depths that his appalling energy might consume her like a moth crisped by the irresistible flame.

"My breasts," she whispered as his arms came around her.

His head bent as his hands slid around her bare sides and gently lifted her breasts upward toward his opened lips.

Daina threw her head back, her long exquisite neck arched, her eyelids fluttering uncontrollably as she felt the tender pulling, the origin of a fierce fireline reaching down through her abdomen and into her vagina. Involuntarily her thighs spread and her mound began a frantic up and down movement against him that made him gasp.

He moved back and forth until her breasts were dripping with a combination of saliva and sweat and her nipples seemed raw. The heat threatened to overwhelm her and it seemed impossible that she was breathing oxygen; the night air had turned to musk.

She moaned a little, fumbled with his belt. He stepped out of his pants and immediately she surrounded him with her fingers, gently stroking his length, cupping the balls beneath. He groaned, licking the cleavage between her breasts. His hands were busy between her thighs, caressing her around the edge of her panties.

And at last they were totally naked, flesh to flesh. She took him in her fingers and rubbed the tip around her lips until the exquisite friction was too much for her and she felt him swelling in her palm.

Then they pushed together, groaning with the velvet contact as he slid all the way up her. The contact seemed to go on for ever, filling her belly, her throat. She was on fire. Her thighs trembled and her breasts shook with the racing emotions. Her breath began to come from way down inside her so that her hard flat stomach fluttered continually against him.

"I can't—" he managed to get out. "I'm sorry—oh—" Simultaneously, his head came forward, his lips opening to catch a swinging breast, his hands went behind her, cupped her buttocks so that she felt as if she were being split in two by the incalculable heat.

She heard him groan one last time and she clutched him to her, his lunge drawing a gasp out of her. Her orgasm was upon her, rushing at her from out of nowhere. She bit into the muscles of his shoulder without knowing what she was doing, tasting the salt and the scent of him in arousal and, at that moment, her inner muscles clamped down on him. She only felt the beginnings of his explosion as she came in every part of her, crying out and trying to merge herself with his hard, jetting flesh.

Afterward they dove wordlessly over the side, rolling over and over each other and the swells of the waves, an endless threesome at home in another element, carefree and ecstatic, touching each other from time to time with fingertips or the flat ends of their toes faintly puckered. Occasionally their thighs would brush and Daina would feel a residual jolt, like stepping on a live wire, almost too intense to bear, as if her flesh had become so sensitized that all contact verged on the painful.

They regained the deck and Rubens led her wordlessly below, opening the portholes and switching on low lights. There was a head, a tiny galley with stainless-steel fittings, a dining area with a table and facing booths that ingeniously could be converted into a double bed.

Rubens moved expertly around the galley, preparing eggs and bacon, coffee. It was very quiet on the water and, straining, Daina now heard the soft, elongated sounds for which she had been searching earlier in the sea, for she could discern now the dialogue of the whales, deep and echoing as they reverberated through the endless corridors of the Pacific. They were not sounding, no rush of black flukes, no high jetting of expelled water, no humped glistening backs rising from the depths to breach the surface, to take the long breath before another dive. These were the mysterious, haunting sounds they made in stalking the deep.

She put her face to the porthole, feeling the soft night wind on her face as she drank in the sounds, her eyes filling with tears as she recalled the bright hot days deep in that last high summer she had spent with her father before he died.

Her eyes were closed but the tears seeped out and down her cheeks just the same as the sounds of the whales brought back the Cape Cod days and nights, images whirled in a child's kaleidoscope, not merely pieces of bright glass colored by time.

With her eyes tightly shut, she could not see how her hands were clenched into tight white fists, her nails dug painfully into the flesh of her palms but, later, she could find the remnants, the semicircular series of red weals, and wonder at this stigmata. Now, however, she wiped at her teary eyes with a brown arm, sniffed.

Across the small cabin Rubens, occupied with the sizzling bacon and the precise parting of the eggshells, did not see or hear a thing and by the time he turned to her, proudly holding out the two plates of steaming food, she had returned to the woman to whom he had, moments before, made love.

2

In the endless moment just before he was shot, James Duell called out her name.

"Heather!"

The peaceful morning at the villa in the south of France to which they had been invited for a week had been abruptly shattered by the roar of explosives, the harsh bark of machine-gun fire.

Some of the assembled guests had no idea of what the sounds heralded and they glanced at each other in mute bewilderment. But others—James and Heather included—like the silver-haired American secretary of state, Bayard Thomas, were familiar with these noises and scrambled for cover.

Outside the light was harsh and bright. The villa was coming under a brutal lightninglike frontal assault that was bringing the American and Israeli Secret Service agents running from their assigned positions around the grounds.

Mist was rising. The high iron gates lay twisted and broken where the grenade explosion had tossed them. Through the gap shot perhaps twenty figures in olive drab fatigues stripped of all markings and insignia. For the most part they carried lightweight MP40 machine pistols. Their faces were made grotesque and unreadable by smeared lampblack. They were led by a tall, broad-shouldered man with a full beard and light brown eyes. He stood calm and unshakable, waving them on all around him. They opened fire as they ran with seemingly no regard for their own personal safety.

"Make certain you kill them all!" the bearded man roared in oddly clipped English over the chatter of the gunfire.

Secret Service men fell, twisting, riddled with bullets. One used a dead compatriot as a shield, backing away until he was caught in a ferocious crossfire that downed him. Another retrieved a wounded terrorist's MP40 to spray death back at them before he was shot in the face and was pitched aside. Still another ran in a ragged zig-zag away from the attack, pulling a walkie-talkie from beneath his clumsily flapping suit jacket. He was shot just as he began to speak rapidly into it.

Those agents still alive fought back and, here and there, a terrorist slumped to the blood-soaked ground. But, inexorably, the wave of attackers advanced, killing as they came on.

Inside the villa, James Duell managed a quick peek through the near corner of a shattered front window. "Christ Jesus," he said. He ducked back as a stray volley of machine-gun fire ripped through the opening. People scattered, screaming as bullets stitched a line across the wood paneling on the opposite side of the room. He turned back to Heather.

"Who are they?" she said.

"PLO, undoubtedly. You know what they've come for. Where's Rachel?"

"She was in the kitchen the last time I—"

"Come on!" He leaped forward, heading out from their sanctuary near the end of one plush sofa. Susan Morgan, a petite brunette of approximately the same age as Heather, jumped out of his way as he raced across the living room toward the open alcove and the kitchen.

"James, wait—!" Heather cried.

The great iron-bound wooden door to the villa flew open. Thick white smoke wafted in, making Heather and Susan begin to cough and, with it, ten figures who spread out, advancing through the living room. In a moment, another staggered in, his arm around a wounded compatriot.

"Everyone stay very still!"

The bearded man stood just inside the front door. An MP40 machine pistol was grasped in one hand. Just behind him and to the right was a small, dark-complexioned man with a dour countenance and eyes like a rodent's. He carried the somewhat more bulky AKM automatic rifle. On the other side of the bearded man was a statuesque woman with shining black hair, high cheekbones and an Asian cast to her eyes. She was dressed identically to the men, carried an MP40 on her hip.

At the very instant of the door's banging inward, James Duell had paused, turning to look and now he was caught in the open, midway between Heather's position and the doorway to the kitchen.

"Fessi," the bearded man said, glancing around the room at the frozen, frightened faces of Bayard Thomas, his aide, Ken Rudd, Susan, Heather, Freddie Bock, their industrialist host, MacKinnon and Davidson, the two English MPs, Rene Louch, the French ambassador to the United States, and Michel Emouleur, his very young-looking attaché. "See where the girl is."

The man with the rodent's eyes began to move through the room, passing the white-faced maid and butler as if they did not exist. He was perhaps a yard in front of James when there was movement from the kitchen alcove.

Rachel was coming. She was a dark-haired girl of perhaps thirteen with a fiercely beautiful face that already appeared to be somewhat rugged. Her clear blue eyes were very large. They took in the entire scene at once.

Something had taken possession of the man with the rodent's eyes. The muscles in his arms jumped as he swung the muzzle of the AKM up to track the movement. His finger grew white against the trigger and a vein stood out high up on his forehead. James, half facing him, saw the look of unadulterated hatred suffuse his face like an excess of blood.

In that instant, James broke into a run, thrusting his body between Rachel's emerging form and the black mouth of the AKM. But the air was no longer clear. It buzzed with the flight of steel-jacketed bullets flashing from the mouth of the automatic rifle.

Heather, standing transfixed by the sofa's end, heard James call out her name, very loudly, very clearly, just before his body was pierced by the bullets, sent hurtling backward off his feet, into Rachel's midsection. She staggered backward, caught at him, his weight too much for her. He slid heavily down her body, lay crumpled in a pool of his own blood, his eyelids fluttering.

The bearded man's brown eyes watched Rachel carefully. "So," he said. "The daugher of the prime minister of Israel."

With that the spell that had kept Heather immobile abruptly broke and she rushed across the room. The tall woman beside the bearded man made a move to stop her but the man pushed his compatriot aside, grabbed hold of Heather's wrist with his free hand as she flashed past, whirling her around in a tight circle. She cried out, came face to face with him.

He stared into her eyes, studying whatever it was he found there. "Open the left-hand breast pocket of my blouse," he said calmly.

"Let me go!" Heather cried. "My husband's been shot!"

"Inside the pocket you'll find a cheroot. Put it between my lips."

She stared at him. "Are you out of your mind! My husband's hurt!"

"He may die," the bearded man said, "if I don't get my smoke soon."

"You bastard—!"

"Do as I say," the man told her, tightening his grip on her wrist so that she winced in pain. "This is a lesson you must learn; one of many."

Her eyes darted around. She stared at James and bit her lip. But, at last, she did and, slowly, brought her hand up to his chest, dipped her fingertips into his breast pocket. She brought out the cigar, a long thin black cheroot, placed it carefully between his lips.

"Now, light it," he said, never taking his eyes from hers. She struggled a little, her hair flying and he said, "Your husband is waiting for you, living out the last moments of his life perhaps."

Heather's hand went back inside his breast pocket. She flicked back the cover to the chrome lighter, held the flame just off the tip of the cheroot until he had it going to his satisfaction. He grinned at her and she saw the gleam of the gold jackets on three front teeth. "There," he said. "That's much better." He puffed while she returned the lighter to his pocket.

"Let me go," Heather said again. "You said you would—"

He glanced around the room, drinking in the pinched upturned faces one by one. His expression clearly showed his enormous pleasure.

"When I'm finished with what I have to say." This time he did not look at Heather. He was addressing the room. "Gentlemen," he said slowly, chewing on his cheroot, "ladies, you are all now hostages of the Palestine Liberation Organization. You are helpless. All resistance is futile. What security you once possessed is now entirely gone." There was a gasp from Susan Morgan. "We hold the villa; we hold you. Mr. Secretary of State, Mr. Ambassador, let me say now your worth to the outside world is far more than it is to us here."

As he spoke, his voice took on color and resonance, a richness that made what he said impossible to dismiss or take lightly. "We are involved in a war—and, make no mistake, we are *all* involved—a war of freedom and justice. The Palestinian people have been robbed of their homeland—their very birthright—by the Zionist interlopers.

"We are here to gain back the land that is rightfully ours. The PLO must be recognized by Israel and the United States as speaking for the Palestinian people; we are their will. Our land must be restored to us; thirteen of our brothers, tortured by the Zionists, must be released from their incarceration in Jerusalem. All this must happen or you will die. But"—he lifted a forefinger—"if you cooperate with us all will be well; no one will be harmed."

Once again he looked around the room. "I am El-Kalaam. It is a name you will come to be familiar with during this time. And, if you are fortunate—if your governments are wise—you will come to bless it for it will not be the name of your executioner."

With that, he let go Heather's wrist and she ran, full tilt, to where James lay half conscious on the floor at Rachel's feet.

"Idiot! You should have called me—even in the studio."
"Oh...well. I know how you are when you're with Chris."

Maggie McDonell's deep blue eyes stared with reproach from the fragile oval face: the porcelain skin with its fine dusting of freckles. Her hair, which she wore long, was the color of butterscotch and permed so that it looked electrified. She had the bones of a bird—a model's flawless figure with no sharp jut or heavy line to mar the smooth flow of her flesh. Clothes draped over her slender form with exquisite perfection.

Exhausted, Daina flopped down on the pale green Haitian cotton sofa, reached for the long vodka and tonic Maggie had mixed for her. She took an enormous draught as if it were water.

"But this was serious," Maggie said. "I mean throwing Mark out.... You should have called me."

"I was better off on my own anyway. I wound up at Beryl Martin's party."

"Now *that* should have bored the hell out of you."

"You're just jealous because you weren't invited," Daina said lightly.

"That's only," Maggie said, swinging away to pour herself a drink, "because I'm not the star you are."

Daina closed her mouth. She had been about to tell Maggie about her night with Rubens. Now she was not so sure she should. She recalled the offhand comment he had made. Separating the girls from the women. It made her think of the first time she and Maggie had met at a casting call for bit parts for *Coming Home*. Daina had just arrived in L.A. and had felt an almost compulsive need to form the kind of solid friendships she had enjoyed in New York. And she had come with the prejudice that she could not do this with anyone who was not also newly transplanted.

"I'm from St. Marys, Iowa, and I don't know much," Maggie had told her. They had hit it off immediately; Maggie wanted to know all about New York, a place she had always wanted to visit but never had. The comfort of their friendship had kept the long days and even longer nights of failure and inertia from collapsing their lives altogether. They had much to thank each other for yet, curiously, never had.

Daina remembered, too, the day Maggie had burst out of her shell one foggy morning as they met for breakfast at a McDonald's. Maggie was a rock freak. She had grown up in St. Marys with a transister radio glued to one ear, dreaming

of bright bursts of thunder, the shouting Greek chorus of the
frantic kids—which she felt, simultaneously, a part of and
disconnected from.

"Chris Kerr," she had said as if evoking a magic spirit.
"I saw him perform last night." And laughed like a little girl
until Daina joined her though she did not yet understand
what was so amusing. "The band, the Heartbeats, was at
Santa Monica Civic last night. My God, the swell of the noise
when he came out was deafening...like being engulfed by
a storm. And I thought, Here he is. All the music rushing
around inside my head with a life of its own—a life I gave
it because without it I'd've gone mad alone in St. Marys with
my hard-working, dull-as-coal family—and now here's the
man who made it; who made my heart throb so hard it hurt.
Ah, Christ, it was too much!"

Maggie's eyes, as bright as beacons, blinked several times
as if the images were running still behind them. "The first
rush of their music was so overwhelming that I thought, This
sex, what rock is all about, *that's* what our parents were so
frightened we'd pick up. But the music allowed us to vent the
unfocused anger we had when we were teenagers and didn't
even know was part of us. There's a kind of release...." Her
eyes shone as if she were about to cry.

"I'm glad you finally got to see him," Daina said.

"Oh, but that wasn't the end of it." Maggie's long thin
fingers with their hard unpainted nails touched the back of
Daina's hand where it lay on the cool tabletop. Their Egg
McMuffins lay cold and congealed between them like an offering. "There was a party after the concert. The record label
threw it and, y'know, we always have access to those things
because you know how the presence of actors is something
like a quotient of their success. They goggle at us as if we
weren't real or something. Obviously they haven't found out
yet how absolutely insufferable some of us can be."

Maggie took her hand away and, now that the first torrent
of words was spent, relaxed somewhat, sitting back in her
orange plastic seat, blowing through her rounded lips. "I
mean the concert was amazing enough. It just blew me away.
I mean, look at me! Small-town girl, brought up with miners
too tired to have anything on their minds, who went down
early from black lung disease..." She said this quite dispassionately without either rancor or bitterness. That was her

way. Inside, at the core of her, Daina knew, her heart had
been coated with a gray grime that no amount of happiness
could ever scrape entirely away. Her father, then her older
brother, had died in just that way while breaking their backs,
she said only half jokingly, for the company store. "...in the
midst of all this. Like a real-life trip to Oz only—and this is
so curious—at some time during the concert it all got turned
around so that this, this concert, became real life and those
years in St. Marys were reduced to a dream I once must have
had while ill.

"I remember the singles I bought in Des Moines when I
went to visit my aunt Sylvia. I had to smuggle them into the
house: 'I Want to Hold Your Hand,' 'Route 66,' 'The Hippy
Hippy Shake.' You wouldn't know how it is."

"I can imagine," Daina said.

"No you can't. You were born and brought up in New York.
What's America to you but New York and L.A.? Oh, sure,
once you might've seen Chicago or maybe even Atlanta. But
all the rest is just some weird kind of alien landscape that
exists only in stories or films or an atlas."

"But, Maggie," Daina began. "I've been to—"

"Doesn't matter. It's not the same as living there. Don't
you see?" Her voice was anguished now. "I was living in a
bloody black coffin of a world, flat and slow and changeless.
You can't possibly imagine what that music meant to me.

"And now that I'm here...D'you know some mornings I
wake up and it takes me ten minutes or more to realize that
I'm actually here, that it isn't a dream, that when I turn my
head, open my eyes, I won't see those school pennants hanging
forlornly on the wall over my head or my cheerleader sweater
draped over the back of the rickety wooden chair Gran gave
me." Her fingers, interlaced, twisted back and forth. "If I
hadn't left St. Mary's when I did, I know I'd never have gotten
up the guts to do it at all. So I ran—all the way out here."

"We're all running, Maggie," Daina said kindly. "All of us
who are doing what we're doing. We're all searching for a
golden harness to strap across our shoulders." She sighed
deeply. "Only trouble is, we seem to be running in place these
days."

Maggie had smiled. "At least it keeps us in shape."

Daina laughed, said, "Go on. What happened at the party?"

Maggie grinned. "We met, Chris and I." She lifted a slender arm, mimed the movement of a ballerina. "And I conquered."

"You're kidding!"

Maggie shook her head. "I was so bloody disdainful at first. Y'know, I'd heard about how sleazy these rock parties can become when they decide to get down; so—"

"Exciting," Daina whispered.

"Yes!" Now Maggie put on an upper-class English accent. "But one ultimately gets bored with slumming." She giggled, dropped the stylization. "So we left."

That was the beginning and, a week later, she had moved in with Chris, out here in Malibu with the gulls crying and the somnolent surf's constant slide and hiss, the women with bobbing breasts jogging down the beach in search of a pickup with fame and, deep in the night, the soft lowing sounds of the whales.

"Christ, but that bastard deserved to get thrown out on his ass," Maggie said now, taking a sip of her drink. "You're well rid of him, Daina. I guess I can tell you now I never fancied Mark much."

"You didn't?"

"I suspected him. His politics...I don't know. That kind of altruism is too pure to be real. And he was so good with his rhetoric...so goddamned slick. He can talk his way in anywhere."

Daina nodded. "Which is how, I suppose, he was able to shoot in Southeast Asia."

"It's almost done, isn't it? The film."

"I guess so. He had just come back from putting on the finishing touches. Shooting's over and he had time to—" She took a long convulsive pull on her drink.

"Here," Maggie said, "let me freshen that." She took the empty glass out of Daina's hand, went about pouring the liquids. "Sorry about the mess but when Chris's in the studio recording everything gets turned upside down."

"How's the new album coming?" Daina accepted the filled glass. It chilled her palm.

Maggie gave her a quick smile that faded out all too soon. "Hard to tell at this stage. Everything's so jumbled about still." She had always used a number of British idioms. Daina imagined it came from her love of English rock and roll. "There's always, you know, a great deal of tension when they get into the studio. The pressure to create is enormous and, well, some of them are still pretty irresponsible. Naturally, it's up to Chris to round them all up and get it going." She sat down in a deep chair, put her glass against her cheek, closed her eyes for a moment.

It was dark in here, even with the scattered lamps on. Outside Daina could hear the gentle hiss of the Pacific but in here was absolute stillness now that their voices had ceased. Sitting across from Daina with her eyes shut, Maggie seemed to have lost the vitality of life. Daina looked away, at the enormous Persian carpet covering the floor, a complex swirling pattern of deep greens and sapphires, earth browns and a black so dark it seemed infinite. The walls were enameled umber, broken here and there by a Calder, a Lichtenstein and, incongruously, a Utrillo, all originals. Along the opposite wall ranged a monstrous component stereo system including reel-to-reel and cassette tape decks and a pair of mammoth four-foot speakers, all of studio caliber.

Maggie's eyes abruptly opened and she leaned forward, putting her glass down on the curved ebony coffee table. Her hands passed over the wheat rolling papers, the plastic bag of grass. Her wet forefinger rubbed along the surface of a small square ground-glass sheet, picking up the traces of the white powder. She rubbed the coated end along the pink ridges of her gums. It was, to Daina, a curiously obscene gesture. "You really ought to loosen up a little and try some." But she was too self-absorbed to see Daina's negative reply.

Maggie ran her hand along the table edge. She had picked up that quintessentially L.A. habit of touching things with the palms of her hands in order not to mar the gleaming surface of her long, manicured nails. She sighed. "Remember the way it used to be when we were starting out? We were both so scared then; both so...equal."

"Maggie, you can't expect—"

"But we're not anymore, are we?" She gave Daina a sharp look. "You've changed, goddamnit! Why did that have to happen?"

"Oh, for God's sake!"

"But I don't *belong* in commercials," Maggie wailed. "It's demeaning. Christ, it's not *acting* at all! I just posture. It's garbage!" She picked up the large silver lighter between the heels of her hands, flicking the flame on and off. "I am sick to death of waiting for something real to come along. I'm going nuts!"

"I'm sure you've talked to Victor," Daina said calmly. "What's he say?"

"He tells me to be patient, that he's getting me what he can." She got up, searched about the room as if she had an excess of nervous energy that needed venting. "I've had it, Daina. I mean it. I need someone to *do* something for me." She returned with a small glassine bag, dumped white powder onto the ground-glass square.

Daina watched in silence as her friend snorted the coke.

Maggie turned to her, sniffing. "What do you think I should do? Fire Victor, maybe?"

"Victor's a good agent," Daina said. "That's not the answer. And neither is jamming that stuff up your nose."

"Makes me feel like I'm on the top of the world," Maggie whispered. "You know that. Please don't get on me about it again. I've got no other choice."

"You do," Daina persisted, "but you don't want to hear it. You've changed, Maggie. You used to believe in yourself; you used to think you were the best. Remember the night-long arguments we used to have about who was best, you or me?"

"Kid stuff," Maggie said. "The world turned out to be quite a different place, didn't it, Daina?" Her eyes had a hurt look as they gazed at Daina from under her lashes. "You won everything and here I am, stuck with a career that's going absolutely nowhere." She bent, took more coke. "So don't you say another word about this stuff, huh? When I'm high I can forget I'm nothing more than a glorified groupie, hanging on to Chris—"

"Maggie, you know it's not like that. Chris loves you—"

"Don't talk about what you don't know!" Maggie said sharply. "When it comes to me and Chris, you don't know a goddamn thing, got it?" She was shaking, spilled coke into her lap. "Oh, Christ! Now see what you've made me do!" She began to cry, trying to scoop the white powder back into the glassine envelope. Most of it fell onto the carpet at her feet. "Oh, hell!" With a convulsive gesture, she threw the envelope across the room.

"Honey, stay off it," Daina said gently. "Just for a few days."

"I only do it because it's what Chris wants," Maggie said

in a small voice. She wiped at her eyes with the back of one freckled hand.

"That's no reason to do anything."

"Oh, I don't want to lose him, Daina. I'll die if he walks out. Anyway, I've gotten to like it."

"Maggie, don't you—"

"God, I'm such a shit. You're the last person I should be blowing up at."

Daina touched the soft down along Maggie's arm. "How about some coffee for us?"

Maggie wiped away the last of the tears, smiled and nodded.

"I'll be right back."

"Oh, listen," Maggie called from the kitchen. "Use the bathroom in our bedroom. The john in the one in the hall's being fixed."

The bedroom, at the front of the house, was a large ol, spacious and airy. A pair of high windows overlooked the Pacific. The walls were painted a lustrous midnight blue. Covering them were silver-metal-framed posters advertising concerts from the Fillmore East and West theaters, the most famous of all rock venues in the sixties, now defunct. She saw the Heartbeats on a bill with B. B. King and Chuck Berry in blue and silver; Cream in pale yellow and umber; Jimi Hendrix in deep red and sand; the Jefferson Airplane in forest green and light brown, the colors and psychedelic lettering of Rick Griffin representing each musical headliner in an almost medieval manner, as brave and gallant knights with their colored pennants fluttering, about to enter the lists to do battle. And like the knights, she thought, they're all gone now in one way or another: dissolved, transmogrified or destroyed. Except for the Heartbeats who had persevered for seventeen years and were still on the top of the heap.

She skirted the king-size bed with its midnight-blue-and-pale-green-striped comforter turned back to reveal its cream nether side like the belly of some great sleepy lizard. On it she saw a portable cassette tape recorder, empty, its flip-up lid gaping. Alongside was a broken-spined copy of Tom Disch's *Getting Into Death*, Christopher Isherwood's *Berlin Stories*, an oversized volume of Kenneth Grahame's *The Wind in the Willows* with illustrations by Arthur Rackham and a dog-eared paperback edition of Colin Wilson's *The Outsider*.

Along the opposite wall was a table piled with the music trade weeklies, *Billboard, Record World,* and *Cash Box* along with *Variety* and papers from England, *New Musical Express, Melody Maker,* and *Music Week,* and a two-week-old issue of *Rolling Stone* with a cover story on Blondie. Then the dark doorway to the bathroom.

Hanging just to the left of the doorway was a gilt-framed 8-by-10 black-and-white publicity shot of the band. Judging by the gaudy clothes it obviously dated back to the sixties.

Daina stared at the photo, fascinated. She had never seen the Heartbeats in their early incarnation, having come upon them a bit later in the early part of the seventies. Here she saw five members not four. There was Chris, the guitarist-singer, tall and handsome; Ian, the bassist, dark-haired and black-eyed, thin and wiry as a girder; Rollie, the drummer, chunky as a teddy bear with that perpetual smile plastered across his amiable face; Nigel, the keyboardist—who wrote the lyrics to Chris' music—glowering into the camera in that peculiar manner that had become, over the years, the band's signature. But then he was the most image-conscious of the lot. She knew them all but one, the man in the middle. He wore his hair quite long, pulled back severely from his high-hill, deep-valley face as if he were wearing it in a ponytail. Overall, she would say his face had a rugged quality, stemming for the most part, perhaps, from his thin-lipped mouth and broken-bridged nose that seemed too long for his head.

But it was his eyes which intrigued her. They were inordinately expressive and at total odds with his other features so that the manner he exuded was one of disquieting mysteriousness. His gaze was a mixture, a kind of icy haughtiness, which, it seemed to her, was merely a facade hiding a rather fragile intellectualism. Some elusive emotion swam in the depths of his eyes as if trapped. She felt an overwhelming urge to reach out a hand to help him.

She shook her head, laughed to herself. Some imagination, she thought. Surely all of that could not be contained in a mere two-dimensional image.

When she returned to the kitchen, the coffee was perking, the rich aroma pervading the room.

"No instant around here," Maggie said brightly. Apparently her blue mood had faded. "Chris insists on fresh-perked all the time and I must say I can't blame him. I'm beginning to be able to tell the difference myself." She turned and poured. "Here you go."

Daina took the filled mug. "Hey, Maggie, I saw an old photo of the band in your bedroom. Who's the fifth guy?"

"Oh, Jon." Maggie sipped at the coffee, made a face and put in some milk. "Jesus, I've been trying to drink it like Chris does—black. But I can't."

"What about Jon?" Daina persisted. "What happened to him?"

Maggie sucked a drop of milk off her fingertip. "There's nothing much to tell, really. He used to be in the band, y'know, early on. Died just as they were making it big." She turned to the counter, spooned sugar into her coffee, tasted it again. "Uhmm, that's better. An accident. Someone—Rollie maybe—once mentioned that he was a bit unstable. The pressure got to him, I guess."

"Have you ever talked to Chris about him?"

"Oh, he never talks about Jon. Too many painful memories, I reckon. He and Nigel grew up with Jon in the north. Came down to London all in a group to make their fortune." She wriggled her nose. "But you know what it's like in their business. So many casualties."

The drumming sound of an engine interrupted them and they both looked up.

"Papa's home," Maggie said with a grin. She left her coffee standing on the counter, went into the living room with Daina in her wake. "He's got a new toy—a motorcycle," she said, reaching for the doorknob. "A bloody big Harley they custom made for him. The body's all clear so you can see the workings. He threatens to take me on it all the time but I'm petrified of the thing. I won't get on it even when the motor's off."

The throaty sound died and they heard the crickets and the surf beginning again their background wash, coloring the night in cool pastels.

Maggie threw open the door, said "Hey." Chris grabbed her up in his arms and kissed her. He was massive and Maggie was dwarfed beside him. He was over six feet, his skin bronzed by the sun—the reason, he said, he had decided to settle in L.A. rather than return to London. Of course there were the taxes, which made it more advantageous for the band to live abroad—Ian had a house in Majorca; Nigel a villa in the south of France. They were tax exiles all, like so many other prominent rock musicians.

He put Maggie down, came into the room. He saw Daina and his face split in a wide grin. "Hey, how you doin', Dain?" They kissed. His hair was a dark brown, falling in thick waves, his eyes a deep green that, at times, verged on black.

"You're back early," Maggie said as they went arm in arm back to the sofa. Chris sprawled across it.

"Well, I wouldn't've been but there was another bloody row. I nearly put Nigel's head through th' floor. Serve th' lazy sod right. Bloody hell!"

"I thought it had gotten straightened out this time," Maggie said, rolling a joint. She lit it, took a drag, passed it over to Chris.

He took a long drag with a hiss like a steambath. He seemed to hold the smoke in a long time. "You know those dumb bastards," he said on the exhale. "It goes in one ear an' out th' other 'cause there ain't nothin' in there but air." He took another drag and his mood seemed to change abruptly. He sat up, knocked off a bit of ash into the huge bronze ashtray on the ebony table. "But, hey, I'm glad you're here, Dain." He reached around to the pocket of his Western shirt, extracted a white plastic cassette. "Guess what I got here, girls?"

"Tracks?" Maggie said excitedly.

"Better'n that." He grinned. "Got here a mix of two of my songs for th' new LP. First time I've written stuff without Nigel."

Maggie turned to Daina. "Wait'll you hear these songs. They're nothing like what the band has done before. A whole new direction."

"Yeah," Chris said, getting up and heading across the room for the stereo. "A breath of much-needed fresh air." He crouched in front of the system, flicked switches. Lights came on, ruby and emerald pinpoints twinkling like far-off stars. He put the cassette in the tape deck.

"Okay. Ready?"

They both said they were.

He sat back on his haunches, said, "The first's a thing called 'Race.' The second's an instrumental." He punched a button and at once the room was filled with music. Great guitar's chording, a bass pulse steady as steel, the punch of the drums like the pebbled bottom of a stippled stream. Then they heard Chris' rich distinctive voice: *Remember the times/ In the back of a Ford/With the dashlights glowing/Did we know the score?/That one day we'd grow up/Ent'ring the finals—/Those days of palm trees and lotion seem far away now.*

The music soared on in a short bridge, a prelude to the second verse: *I've abandoned the rhymes/Off which we have lived/The limos, the parties/The big girls who give/All that they can/In the back of a van/Ah, those bright nights of delight and co-caine seem far away now.*

Coming out of the second verse the guitar, now double-tracked so that it sounded infinitely thicker, took the melody into an adrenalin-pumping chorus. There was a repeat and then the ride-out again chillingly guitar-dominated.

Silence for the space of several seconds and then the instrumental began. It was the musical antithesis of "Race," a slow haunting melody built on minor fifths, which continued to spiral upward in languorous abandon, reminding Daina of Samuel Barber's "Adagio for Strings."

The ending faded out so gradually that she only became aware that the song was over when she heard the tiny click of the machine shutting itself off at the end of the side.

Chris swiveled around. "Well?"

"I'm stunned," Daina said. "I don't know what to say."

"Did you like it?"

"I loved it."

"They're just great," Maggie said. "I mean, Nigel will probably mess his pants."

"He hasn't heard it yet," Chris said. "None of 'em have. Ian'n'Rollie've just heard what they set down. Nigel's heard nothin' and it's gonna stay that way till I've got the final mixes down." He jumped up. "Well, I'm goin' out for a spin."

"Chris, you just got home." Maggie's voice was plaintive.

"Dain," he said, "would you like to take a ride?"

"Sorry," she said, getting up, "but I've got a five o'clock makeup call." She said her good nights, acutely aware of Maggie's eyes on her, filled with anger and envy. She shivered as if it were a physical thing that had brushed her.

*   *   *

The long dark blue Mercedes limo sat across her driveway like a massed fortress, its shadow as she drove up seeming larger than the house behind it.

She came up quite close to it, shut off her engine and got out. The night was stirred by a wind that brushed her cheek, rippled her honey hair.

The sharp click-clack of her heels on the gravel drove away the sing-song wheezing of the crickets. As she approached, the rear door swung silently open. There was a light on inside, the kind of rich warm glow that only came from a beautifully shaded lamp. Cars did not have lights like that.

She bent her head, got in. "The Tonight Show" was on the small-screen color TV, Johnny Carson silently mouthing to Stockard Channing while bouncing his double-erasered pencil on his desk top.

"I missed you when you didn't come home," Rubens said.

"I'm home now."

"I meant *my* home."

She turned away from him, looked out at the darkness of the night. Trees obscured the steepness of the hill, the enormous sweep of lights beyond. The seat beneath her felt as hard as a church pew.

"It never should have happened."

"What never should have happened?"

"Last night," she told him, still looking away. "I was angry, upset . . . something had happened. And you were there."

"I've always been there."

She said nothing, wrapped herself in her arms. She felt cold.

"You're not going to tell me it was a one-night stand—"

"I'm not going to tell you anything."

"—because I know you're not like that." Her head swung around to look at him, the lamplight soft on the sharply defined curve of his cheekbone, his lips. "You don't give your body easily, without thought. No matter what you tell me, I know that." He leaned over, flicked off the TV. Johnny and Stockard died.

"And I also know that it wasn't just a fuck last night. I know that because I've done it so often over the last couple of years to too many girls to count. I know what that's like, all too well. We didn't fuck last night."

"No?" she said, her voice rising. "What *did* we do?"

"We made love. I know it and you know it."

"What if I do?"

He reached out, touched her. "I don't want to lose that."

She brushed away his fingers. "What do you think," she said coldly. "That you can buy me with a line like that?" She was close to sneering at him but the anxiety was rising in her far too rapidly for her to realize it.

"Okay. I said it the wrong way. Sue me."

"You're very cute, you know that." Her eyes were bright and fierce. Every moment she sat here with him, she felt that odd fluttering in her chest, almost as if she were about to have a heart attack. She put her hand on the door handle.

"Don't," he said, oddly echoing her line from the night before. He put his hand lightly over hers, took it away quickly. "There's no reason to be afraid of me."

"You've got to be kidding." But he had hit it and she knew it; the panic soared inside her.

"Here." He opened the bar, made her a Bacardi on the rocks. He did not forget the twist of lime.

The ice cubes clinked against the side of the glass as she took it from him, took a long pull. She leaned back, closed her eyes, sighed.

"You can leave now, if you want."

His voice came to her as a disembodied force past the darkness imposed by her closed eyelids. He might have been a doctor.

"I don't," she said slowly, "want you to own me."

"Daina, I'll tell you the truth. I don't think that's possible. I think that the fact that I *can't* is the real reason I—"

"If I fall in love with you, it might be possible."

"Isn't it a little early—"

But she had opened her eyes, was staring directly into his. "Is it?" she said.

Now it was his turn to twist away. "I don't know that," he said after a time. "All I know is that I came here to ask you to move in with me."

"Just like that? No strings attached."

"What strings? You think this is some kind of business deal?"

She ignored that, closed her eyes again. She could almost feel again the gentle rocking of the boat, the long, haunting melodies. "You remember when I told you something had happened last night? Well, I threw Mark out. I found him...well, never mind that. He's a bastard and he got what he deserved.

"But"—unconsciously, perhaps, she drew herself further into the corner of the seat—"it left me shaken. He had been living with me for almost two years. There had always been some kind of...stability. And I never realized how much I relied on that until he was gone.

"Last night I was alone, a stranger in a strange land; it was as if I were an out-of-focus snapshot. Then you happened by and—" Her head whipped around and she impaled him with a stare that made him shudder internally. "When we made love"—and here she pronounced each word as a separate entity—"I have never felt so out of control. I have never felt so acutely being a woman. Not in the generic sense but in the traditional sense. I had my place and you had yours and—"

"I never said anything; *did* anything to—"

"No, you didn't. It was a combination of me and...a part of you. The furnace of your power. *That's* what frightens me; it diminishes me in some way."

"No." He shook his head. "It's your fear that diminishes you, nothing else."

Her eyes stared back at him defiantly.

"Come home with me."

"Not tonight," she said, opening the door. The muscles of her thighs jumped and twitched as she watched the limo disappear down the hillside.

That night, wrapped in her bedcovers, she dreamt of a time long gone: the days of Woodstock. People for as far as she can see in all directions. Fringe swinging and beads clicking like the beat of some cosmic clock; hair streaming across staring eyes, down bare backs like the manes of sweating horses. The air is humid with dope. Here, beside her, a couple make love oblivious to the forest of humanity around them, there a man in a tangled ponytail lifts his pink, naked son over his head while a stringbean of a boy is lofted upon the surface of the throng, head lolling insensate—tripped too far on acid, fell down the well—and he is directed on the moving litter of palms toward the first-aid station, sent there with love.

Last of the announcements floats through the air as prel-

ude to the music running rampant like a long-caged bull
stampeding through the crowd like a living thing. What are
they saying over the loudspeaker? Over half a million souls
camped here, touching, yearning. And what a cheer that announcement brings! An entire generation displaying their
solidarity in the Age of Aquarius, brought together by the
war; there are no gods before them, merely the muse of
the music echoing loud, louder, loudest in order to drown out
the din of death in the rice paddies, snouted submachine guns
flickering and napalm falling, a hideous rain of gelatinous
fire. Hell no, we won't go!

And the music rages on, trumpeting their defiance, incandescent in its adamantine resolve, igniting a firestorm in
her mind or, perhaps more accurately, triggers the sunshine
she's dropped.

Now images leap and squeal like laser bursts as her body
tremors in the bass' vast booming like miniature earthquakes
enfolding her in a physical web.

During this long celebration she has cooked for the crowd,
sewn ripped denims for strangers who became family in the
close communal atmosphere, been thrown up on and, some
time yesterday—or was it the day before?—saved a frail
young girl from swallowing her own tongue during an epi-
leptic seizure as violent as the music. She has eaten little
and slept not at all and now, in the midst of the milling
throng, she sits back and is taken by forces she does not
comprehend, losing for a moment her humanity, slipping
atavistically into the millennia, becoming pure animal.

Abruptly there is a shattering as if she has caused all the
mirrors of time to come crashing down. She arises to see
herself one dot among the countless masses, part of a throbbing organic conglomerate and, twisting herself around, sees
only the sea of humanity, and feels herself lost as if there is
no longer any *her*, any Daina, left at all but only a great
seething *they*. She is a cog in a wheel, a cell in a body, a spoke
on a mandala that is turning at a rate of speed, she realizes
now, not of her own choosing. She feels immersed in a depthless sea, drowning on a tide she never even suspected existed.

She turns. The music rattling her bones as if they were
plastic. Faces, faces, a torrent of faces bobbing, rushing at
her like raindrops. Then Daina is gone and she realizes that
she too is but a raindrop.

Terrified, she leaves. She leaves. She leaves. It takes a long time. Like leaving Manhattan on and on and on. Faster and faster, gaining a kind of crazed momentum. Houses without end rush by her. People without end. Faces like windows, doorways, backstreets. Until, at last, trees, grass, the wind and, above her head, the vast blue-and-gray-streaked sky, echoing.

And, having left, she is spent.

Heather was on her knees, gently lifting James' head up from the spreading pool of his own blood, cradling it against her thighs. Her arms were streaked red.

"James," she whispered. "Oh, James, whatever possessed you to do such a foolish thing?"

His eyes opened, large and blue, and he tried to smile at her. His lips were moving but there was nothing coming out save an odd, chilling kind of chirping that had only a passing resemblance to human speech.

Rachel tried to claw her way to where they were but Malaguez took her by the back of her blouse, jerking her backward and away.

"I'm sorry," she said to Heather. "I'm sorry."

All around them, the terrorists were rounding up the rest of the people. The Americans and the Frenchmen were jammed uncomfortably together on the plush sofa; the two English MPs stood huddled on the far side of the marble fireplace as members of the cadre began to bind their wrists and ankles. One of the terrorists brought the maid and butler along, shoved them angrily down at the feet of the MPs. With a wave of his arm, El-Kalaam sent four of his men outside to scour the grounds and patrol.

"Heather." It was a croak.

"Oh, Jamie." The sound of her own voice or his set her off to crying again. "You were right. They want their land back." She took her face out of her hands, looked hopefully at him. "But they said if we cooperate with them, we'll be out of here soon enough."

"Don't do it, Heather." His eyelids were drooping.

"Of course I'm going to do it," she said hotly. "The sooner

this nightmare...is over, the sooner we'll be able to get a doctor in here to fix you up."

"Is that what they told you?" He shifted a little in her arms, his mouth twisting in pain. "Never mind about me. You just remember not to believe a word they say."

Off in one corner near the front door, a tall thin man with a bushy mustache looked up from his fallen compatriot. The palm of his hand was across the wounded terrorist's forehead. "El-Kalaam, he's delirious."

The bearded man, who had been conferring with Malaguez, a short, broad-shouldered man who was almost bald, looked up. "Will he begin making noises?"

"It has already begun," the man said. "He cannot help himself."

Without another word, El-Kalaam strode across the room and, making certain every hostage could see what he was doing, unsheathed a hunting knife. It had a twelve-inch blade that shot light-sparks from its gleaming surface. El-Kalaam bent and, without preamble, made a quick, violent motion with the edge of the blade against the wounded man's exposed throat. There came a soft, horrible gurgling and the body, gripped by the tall man, jumped as if speared. A froth of blood formed on the dead man's lips just as if he were a child blowing bubbles.

El-Kalaam wiped his blade on the dead man's trousers with two economical movements, sheathed the weapon at his left hip. He jerked his head. "You two, take him outside."

"My God!" Heather whispered hoarsely to her husband. "He just murdered one of his own men."

"I'm not surprised," James said thickly. "He's a professional, Heather. Beware of him. Words are only a political expedient for a man like him. He speaks merely to set the stage for his actions."

"All right," El-Kalaam said, looking across the room. "That's enough for them. Rita."

The statuesque woman took three strides, reached out, jerked Heather to her feet. "Come along now," she said harshly.

"What?" Heather was bewildered. "You can't just leave him like that."

"You had your time with him," Rita said. "What did you expect? That we would bandage him up for you and send the

two of you on your way?" She laughed, a musical sound at
odds with her tone of voice. "Oh, no."

"But that isn't fair!"

"Fair?" Rita scowled. "Fair? What is fair in life? It it fair
that we should be deprived of our homeland? Is it fair that
our women and children are starving to death? That our men
are tortured and butchered by the Zionist pigs?" She shook
her head violently. "No! Don't dare talk to me of fairness.
There is none in this world."

"I want someone to—aaah!"

Rita had grabbed her arm, forcing it around behind her
back.

"Enough of this! Come with me!"

El-Kalaam came toward them. "What is going on here?"
He looked from Heather to Rita. "I gave you a simple order.
I expect it to be carried out."

"It is being carried out," Rita insisted. "She just—"

"Give her to me—" he began.

"Bastard!" Heather screamed. "Bastard to do such a—"

El-Kalaam was like a snake lashing out at her, pulling
her off her feet. "Bitch!" he cried frenziedly. "What are you
trying to do?"

Heather pulled away from Rita, began to fight him off.

"Cut!" Marion yelled, leaping up off his chair. "Cut!" He
ran past the gaping crew. "Goddamnit, George, what the hell
d'you think you're about?" His hands spread as he attempted
to pry George Altavos, the actor who played El-Kalaam, away
from Daina. "George—!"

"What does this bitch mean by ad-libbing lines on me!"

They were struggling now, all three of them in the center
of the set while everyone stood as still as statues awaiting
the outcome. And as they fought, a whispering sprang up—
not from any one discernible source but from everywhere at
once.

"This is *my* scene!" George yelled, now grabbing at Marion
as much as he was at Daina. "It's how we damn well *rehearsed*
it! Now she's adding lines—"

"Will you, for the love of God, calm yourself!" Marion said.

It was Yasmin who broke the deadlock. She played Rita
and now she thrust herself between Daina and George with
such force that Marion was obliged to grasp George's arm in
order not to be spun away.

"Yasmin," he said, panting, and the dark-haired woman took Daina by the elbow, led her off the set until they could no longer hear George's rantings.

"That sonovabitch!" Daina cried, flinging herself away from Yasmin's grip. She rubbed her shoulder. "He really hit me! Christ, what's the matter with him?"

At that moment, Don Hoagland, the assistant director, hurried up. "I'm terribly sorry about this, Daina," he said. "What George did was inexcusable...inexcusable." He shook his head. "I want you to know that Marion is with him now—"

"Sure," Daina said, sardonically, "giving him exactly the same speech, no doubt."

Hoagland gave her a small smile. He was an Irishman with a clipped silver mustache and slicked-back hair who worked every project with Clark. It was easy to see why; he had a silver tongue. "Really, Daina," he said more quietly, "that's not true at all." He touched her hand, an endearing, avuncular gesture. "The fact is, Marion's beside himself. He thought the additions you made were perfect. I thought he was going to throttle George back there." He patted the back of her hand. "Don't you worry. We'll all take the rest of the day off and by tomorrow morning, it'll all be forgotten."

"George had better have his head on straight by then," Daina said.

Hoagland smiled at her. "Marion'll make certain of that." He turned away. "Don't worry about a thing."

"Are you okay?" Yasmin asked when they were alone.

Daina wiped at her face, looked at her as if for the first time. "Oh, yeah. Sure." She smiled then. "Thanks for pushing yourself in between us."

Yasmin waved at the air. "Forget it. I think it was my fault really that this whole thing erupted today and I'm very sorry about it."

"You mean this's going to happen again?" Daina said, wiping at her face.

"I don't know. Part of it depends on me, I think." She nodded her head. "Let's go outside, though. It's still a bit evil in here."

They went across the darkened part of the soundstage with its snaking cables and piled hardware. Bright sunlight hit them as they opened the heavy metal door, went down the concrete ramp to the back lot.

"My trailer or yours?"

Daina laughed. She pointed. "I'd like some of that rotten coffee." And they went over to the huge truck dispensing food and drink from its open sides.

They took their cups into the shade, stared out at the endless passing parade of actors and actresses in and out of costume.

"The truth is," Yasmin said after a while, "George and I have broken up. I moved out last night."

Everyone knew that George and Yasmin had been living together.

"What happened?"

Yasmin shrugged. "I'd had enough of him. His bitching and moaning about getting it up while he's working; his insecurities about getting older, losing his hair.... 'Where have all the leading roles gone to?'" She looked at Daina then away at the busy lot. At length her eyes dropped to her coffee. "Hell," she said and threw the cup away. "I don't know why I'm lying. It's a habit, I guess."

Daina looked at her. "You don't owe me any explanation, Yasmin."

The other woman smiled. "Perhaps not. But I think I owe it to myself." She put her nervous hands on the railing against which they leaned. "The truth is, we—that is George and I—had struck a bargain. At least I thought of it as such. He wanted to go to bed with me and I wanted this part in *Heather Duell*." She shrugged. "It's simple, no? Everyone does it at one time or another. We both won." She sighed. "I didn't want anyone to get hurt."

"Well, you didn't sign a contract," Daina said. "I mean, people are people, not things. They have feelings and they may say something at the time, really mean it. But feelings change. We're not made of stone."

"George certainly isn't," Yasmin said sadly. "He's in love with me." She turned to Daina. "I didn't know until just now how much I'd hurt him, Daina. I didn't mean to but it's happened anyway. As if neither of us have any control anymore. As if we're both sliding away."

"How do you feel about him?" Daina said, thinking of Rubens.

"That's the really awful part. I don't know. I mean just between us girls, I did what I had to do and I'm here now talking with you because of that. Our weapons arsenal is just different than theirs, that's all." She laughed shortly. "The only problem is, I'm not a conscienceless bitch. I still care about George."

"Then the only thing to do," Daina said, "is to tell him that."

"Oh, he won't listen to anything I have to say now."

"Then you'll always have it on your conscience. D'you want that?"

"Poor George," Yasmin said, squinting into the baking sunlight. There was movement ahead of them. They both stared at the enormous silver stretch limo coming toward them. All the windows were coated with that silvery substance that allowed you to look out but not in. All the grillwork was clear acrylic. Many of the crew had stopped what they were doing to turn their heads, wondering who was inside.

It came abreast of Daina and Yasmin and slowed to a halt. The rear window on their side slid soundlessly down and music erupted from the interior—shrieking guitars and flailing drums. Daina saw Chris' grinning face in the dim depths. He wore a pair of black-lensed, steel-rimmed sunglasses. As he slid across the seat, she could see that he wore a pair of tight jeans, washed so many times their color had faded almost to white, and a fire-red T-shirt with a black and silver guitar silk-screened obliquely across his chest. It was the same shape as his custom-made instrument.

"Hey hey hey," he said lightly. His fingertips curled around the rim of the window. "You busy, or what?"

Daina came over. "Are you crazy? How the hell did you get in here?"

He laughed. "All God's chillun is fans you know." He looked around them. "This a bad time or what? You shooting?"

"No. I'm off for the day courtesy of a temper tantrum."

"Well, goodo. Get in, then."

Daina turned her head. Yasmin had come up beside her. She introduced her to Chris. He nodded, said, "Hey," turned his attention back to Daina.

"Oh, hell, d'you mind?" Yasmin shook her head, smiled. Daina opened the heavy door, got in. "See you later," she said to Yasmin as Chris pushed a button and the window slid up, sealing them. She smelled his scent, clean and strong and masculine. She sat back in the plush seat that held her like a hand. A darkly iridescent barrier isolated them from the front of the limo where the driver sat.

She saw the set sliding by. It was like looking through a pair of the ultimate sunglasses, all colors subdued, green shadows everywhere over-hanging the sun and the stark linearity of the buildings, superseding reality.

She looked at Chris as they passed through the heavily guarded entrance and headed toward the freeway. His dark hair was uncombed, his nose as sharply defined as a razor's blade. It was difficult to tell just how old he was—late thirties?—his face streaked by the powderflash of accelerated time within which they all lived, these special people, patched with shadows of another world as if he were a survivor of some ongoing existential war that mere mortals could only guess at.

"Well." He grinned, snapping his fingers pop-pop-pop as if in time to music only he could hear, making the muscles of his biceps bulge beneath the thin T-shirt. The blast of high-energy rock had long since ceased and only the faint whisper of the limo's thrumming engine remained.

"You're up early," she said. Then, "Where's Maggie?" because, perhaps, she was slightly nonplussed by this immediate intimacy. He had never made this kind of gesture toward her before. She wondered just what kind of gesture it really was.

"Home," he said, his fingers popping. "Out." He shrugged. "Just you'n'me, fancy free." He looked for a time at the ribboning silent traffic through which they slid like a sleek shark through a school of timid fish. "Hey, you don't mind now," he said, turning back, "Maggie not bein' here do you? I mean..." He spread his hands, palms up.

Daina smiled. "No, it's all right. Anyway I needed to get away from there for a while."

"Hey, right. Goodo." He shook his head, his thick hair like the mane of some mythological creature. "So—" He slapped his thighs. "Glad you could come."

He seemed ill at ease and Daina thought, Christ, he's not going to leave Maggie. Not now. I don't need to hear that kind of confession.

Overpasses darkened the interior even further now and then, steel-reinforced concrete clouds lifting above a metal landscape.

Daina was on the verge of asking him if something was the matter when he blurted, "So what did'ja think of th' last album?"

Daina stared out the window for a moment. The traffic had slackened as they approached the Pacific. She wondered whether to tell him the truth. As with all artists it was often difficult to know what he really wanted to hear. Far too many were greedy to settle for the easy lies, the smooth alibis by which they survived in this dreamland. What kind of person was Chris really?

Abruptly she realized the fallacy in this line of thought. Who cares what he wants to hear, she said to herself. If he's upset by what I say, too bad. But I won't lie to him.

"To tell you the truth I was disappointed."

"Oh?" He regarded her impassively. "Tell."

For just an instant she wondered whether he was serious. "All right. I think you've done that stuff before. And better. Songs like 'Face on the Floor,' come on, it's retreading old ideas. 'Barroom Blitz' is far better and you wrote that, when? Two years ago?"

"Three."

There was silence for a time. They wound down the Pacific Palisades onto the Coast Highway.

"Chris, I'm not sorry I said any of that. You asked me and—"

"S'okay." He waved a hand at her. "Glad you said it really." His head turned toward her. "'Cause I've been thinkin' th' same thing an' it's been hammerin' away inside my skull." He snorted in derision. "Nah, th' fact is, th' new album's goin' all t' shit an' you wanna know why? It's th' same bloody thing all over again. I've told those sods over'n'over t' quit fuckin' around but it does no good. We've got a balls-up anyway. Got nuthin' on their minds...."

"What'd they say?"

He rubbed his palms down his thighs. "First they ignored me. Then when I didn't shut up we got into fights—you know over dumb things like if dollies can come t' th' session which everyone knows they can't. Hard'n'fast rule but—Christ, I put Rollie's head through his snare drum one night last week. Took two engineers t' separate us."

"What about Nigel? You two are such good friends—"

"Oh, yah Nigel," Chris laughed. "He's some bloody help he is. Got so much blow up his nose, he doesn't know whether he's inside'r'out an' every time I try t' tell him what's what that bloody bitch Tie sticks her nose in just like she's been doin' since th' beginning." He clasped his large, long-fingered hands in front of him. "It's no good for the bleedin' music anymore, Dain. I'm tellin you...."

"Chris, isn't this mess something your manager should be clearing up? After all, he—"

Chris' head went back and he laughed sardonically. "No, babe, no. Benno's th' bloody instigator he is. I went to see him weeks ago, when all this shit came flushin' out the loo—" He reached into his boot top, plucked out a joint. He lit up, inhaled, offered her the joint. She refused and he continued. "You've never met Benno have you? Well, he can charm th' poison out of a cobra if it suits him. I know that, see? Even so, I sat down with him, *mano a mano* like they say on the Boulevard, an' told him everything. Promised he'd take care of it. 'But you gotta be patient,' he said. 'You know how they all are, Chris. Volatile as hell. So it'll take time. But you know that.' So like a first-class berk I waited.

"Then Nigel comes in with th' most diabolical lyrics I've ever heard. I mean it sounded like he'd cribbed all th' ideas off our last album an' there I am holdin' my prick an' ten tunes for th' sessions that can't even get off th' ground. Bloody hell!"

They began to pull into a Jack in the Box along the right side of the highway and Chris leaned forward, pounding on the partition with his fists until it zipped down just enough for him to shout, "No, damnit, I said the Polynesian place!" The partition slid up and the limo swerved out into the sparse traffic, gaining speed again.

"That's when th' fights started," Chris continued as if there had been no interruption. "I mean they're all actin' like right bastards. So then one night Nigel comes to me an' tells me that Benno's pissed because we're way behind in th' studio an' if we don't get the bloody LP out on schedule we'll miss th' date for the kickoff of th' tour—you know how they like t'do it. Release a single just before the start of th' tour; then blast out with th' album part way through. Business hums, babe. So I said, 'You dimwit, if you'd done your bleedin' job we'd have th' songs t'get this thing done but instead everyone's coppin' an attitude an' it's a complete balls-up!'

"An' you know what that bleedin' sod has th' cheek to say t' me? 'Yer right, Chris. But you're th' one's coppin' an attitude. We've got this formula, man, an' it's bringing us a shitload of bread every time out.' He points a finger at me. 'Nobody in this band's gonna change that. We're gonna go on makin' th' music we've been makin' until th' kids tell us they don't wanna hear it no more an' that's th' end of it, clear?'"

They came up on a long, low, thatched structure on the sea side of the highway. The limo slowed and stopped, waiting for traffic to clear, then it arced gracefully, grandly into the rough gravel driveway. The chauffeur, an older man with a jowly, pockmarked face, opened the door for them. They got out, went up the wide dark-stained wooden steps, past the twin nine-foot carved Tiki gods guarding the entrance.

Inside it was as dark as midnight. A light-haired woman in a green and blue sarong met them, guiding them through the mock-thatch-walled main dining room out onto a glass-enclosed patio. A hammock was slung from the sloping ceiling. She sat them at a table overlooking the Pacific, rolling unendingly onto the brown beach. The spindrift, flung as if reluctantly into the air, caught the sun, sowing the sea with tiny rainbows, insubstantial bridges to nowhere.

Daina waited until the drinks—combinations of rum and rich fruit juices served in hollowed-out coconut shells—had been served. She removed the brown plastic Tiki-shaped swizzle stick, bent it against the edge of the table.

"Chris, I have to ask you something and it's not because I'm not interested, because I am, but—why haven't you talked this over with Maggie?"

"How d'you know I haven't?"

"You wouldn't," she said, "be talking to me then. This isn't the kind of thing you take a poll on."

He smiled thinly, sipped at his drink. "That's true enough." He put his hands flat on the table so that they covered the menus. "So look, Dain, don't get me wrong. I love Maggie, I really do. But sometimes, well, she just has trouble gettin' past th'—well, you know how she feels about th' music. Find-in' a worm in th' candy jar's just not on for her so she won't see it, know what I mean?"

Daina knew. "How d'you know I will?"

He took the swizzle stick from her, broke it in two, shrugged. "Got a feelin' is all. An' th' truth is..." He grinned like a kid.

"What's so funny?"

"Oh, well, when Maggie first introduced us, I remembered you right off."

"Remembered me from where? We'd never met before."

"No, but I knew I had seen you somewhere. Woodstock."

She laughed. "Oh, that's crazy. There were more than a half a million people there. How could you—"

"You were down in front, very near th' stage, an' it's so odd, y'know, 'cause I still remember thinkin', Now where th' hell did that bird get those black jeans. I'd been lookin' for a pair o' those since I'd come to America."

He rubbed at his nose. "We went on late th' third day...Sunday, I think it was. Yeah, yeah. There was some kinda hassle with th' Airplane's management, that's right."

"I don't get it. You remember me just from my jeans?"

He grinned. "Don't tell me you've forgotten? Christ, just as we broke into th' first number you stood up, stripped off your top an'—"

"That's enough! I remember!"

Chris laughed. "How could I forget that body?"

"I wish I could say I was there for all the peace and love."

He looked at her oddly. "What difference does it make why you were there?"

"It was a bad time for me. I was running away from everything I didn't want to face. All I could think of when the bands weren't playing was a piano piece my father used to listen to. I went to sleep hearing it when I was little. It always made me cry then. Afterward, it reminded me of him."

"Which one is it?"

"Maurice Ravel's 'Pavane Pour Une Infante Défunte.'"

Chris nodded. "Oh sure. I know th' piece. In Soho, I ran across an old geezer. Wasted on gin all th' time but he taught me how t'play th' piano a little. Used t'play th' 'Pavane' all night long, cryin' inta his glass. 'Quel triste,' he used t'say t' me. 'Quel triste.' Poor bloody bugger. He—"

"Hey, man, Chris Kerr! I don't believe it!"

They both looked up to see a beefy, slouching individual with a handlebar mustache yellowed around its lower edge by nicotine. His long greasy hair was tied back in a ponytail. He was wearing a pair of stained and faded jeans and a San Diego State sweatshirt with the sleeves cut off at the shoulders.

"Chris Kerr. Hey. Far fuckin' out!" His smile was full of brown teeth and red gums. He completely ignored Daina. "Mike Bates. Hey, you remember, man. We met backstage in New York. The Academy of Music—you know, now it's the Palladium. Back in, oh yeah, sixty-six. Winter, man. You guys were nothin' then. Playin' second bill to Chuck Berry."

"I don't think I remember."

"Oh, sure you do." The smile had turned into a grin. "Solid Jamaican ganja. Primo stuff." He made the motions of smoking grass.

"You know, we're right in the middle of lunch. We're discussing—"

"Hey, but meeting you like this," Bates interrupted. "Wow, it must be karma." He was twisting the wide leather watchband he had on. "Hey, yeah, it was wintertime all right. Snow on the streets, colder than a witch's tit, and you guys were nothin' over here. Now look at you." He put his hands on the back of a chair at a nearby table. "Me, I wasn't doing much of anything then, and now"—his meaty shoulders lifted, fell—"about the same." He began to pull the chair over. "Doin' a little dealin' here and there, nothin much but if you—"

"Don't do that," Chris said. "Like I told you, we're in the middle of discussing something important. If you don't mind—"

"Oh. But hey, it'll only take a couple minutes of your time, I promise." He began to sit down. The chair groaned beneath his bulk. "I got a scheme I've been hatchin' for a while now. It's all worked out—"

"Don't you listen?" Daina could feel the tension flooding through Chris.

"Wow, man, all it needs to get rollin' is a bit o' bread. You got bread to burn, Chris, I know that. Just a little financin'."

"That's it for you," Chris said. He took the man by the back of his sweatshirt, jerked him to his feet.

Daina pushed her chair back, ran to the doorway of the

terrace, calling for the manager. He appeared in a moment, a swarthy-skinned individual with a burly Mexican bouncer beside him. He snapped his fingers and the Mexican went down the steps on the balls of his feet.

The manager called out something to him in rapid street Spanish, and the Mexican reached out with both blunt-fingered hands. They gripped Mike Bates' shoulders in a steel-like embrace, jerking him backward so violently Daina could hear his teeth click.

But Chris merely leaped forward, his fingers grasping at Bates' chest. Daina moved toward them and, despite the manager's sharp warning, slipped between them, wound her arm around Chris'. She was very close to him, could feel his panting breath on her cheek, see his eyes, pupils dilated wildly.

"Chris," she said softly, putting more strength into her grip, "let him go now. Let the Mexican handle it. They have him now, Chris." It sounded like the crooning a mother uses to soothe her child. "They'll get him away as soon as you let go. Come on now."

He let go reluctantly and the Mexican hefted Bates off his feet, hustling him out of the terrace area.

"Bastard!" Bates called. "Don't you believe in sharing the wealth? What's a couple of thousand to you! You didn't act like that when we blew weed back in sixty-six, you cocksucker!" Then he was gone, hurtled by the Mexican through the darkness of the restaurant and out the front door.

"I am so sorry," the manager said, wringing his hands. He tried to smile, did not quite make it. "Stardom, eh?" he said by way of apology. "It is with you always, no? Such a burden." His tongue clucked against the roof of his mouth as if he were a saddened old woman. He reached up, slicked back his dark, oily hair. "Please try not to think too badly of us. Eat. Eat! Lunch is on the house." He turned, clicked his fingers as if they were castanets. The waiter appeared.

"Bloody parasites," Chris said as Daina led him back to the table. "They meet you once an' think you owe 'em for life. Christ, but they make my blood boil."

The food came: steaming platters of half-shelled shrimp, thick-cut spare ribs in a glaze as bright as red lacquer, sweet-and-sour fried wonton, roast duck, fried rice; and more drinks in their split-coconut-shell containers. An endless parade marching toward them until the table was overflowing and still the manager, standing in the shadows discreetly watching over them, clicked his fingers and the waiter arrived and departed again and again like the sorcerer's apprentice, staggering under his load.

"Christ," Chris said at length, throwing the last of the denuded ribs onto the mound he had built up. "I'm in a stinkin' hole, I am."

Daina put her coffee cup down. "You talk as if you've got no control over the situation. The solution's simple. If you don't like it in the band anymore, get out."

He looked at her. "That's th' first thing Maggie told me." He wiped his greasy lips on a crumpled paper napkin. The manager clicked his fingers and the waiter began to clear away the piles of plates.

When they were alone, Chris said, "I didn't think th' two o' you would have th' same opinion. I mean she's only a child, really." He gestured vaguely. "You're not as naive as all that, Dain. You know nuthin's as simple as that. Not in this life."

"What are you saying? That you *can't* just walk out? Any contract can be broken, you know that." He said nothing, looked out the window. The blue of the Pacific had vanished in the brilliant sun dazzle. "All I want to know, Chris, is what you want to do."

"Y'mean if I had my druthers?"

She nodded.

His gaze turned inward and this somehow made his face sad. Her heart broke to see him that way. Now he was another person, totally at odds with the brash, exuberant pop star who pranced across the high stage to the screams of fifty thousand adolescent throats.

"I dunno," he said after what seemed a long time. He was far away. "I don't wanna lose th' band. We're a team...they're all th' friends I've known for close t' fifteen years. Th' hangers-on come'n'go, bringin' their dope so they c'n be next t'you. They're part o' th' business, y'know, an' after a while y'get t' be able t'peel 'em off just like leeches. They think they're gettin' an inside look but they're not. None of us would let 'em in that far; we're too insular." He laughed shortly. "Sometimes I think it's what makes us so weird, like inbreedin'. But th' band, we love each other...they love me more than any mum or dad ever did. I want all of us t' stay together for all time. Y'know, us against th' world, like it's been since th' beginnin'.

"But"—he clenched his fist and she could see the cords of his neck standing out with the strain—"I know somethin's gone wrong. I don't know what it is but I c'n feel it." His eyes stared straight into hers and she felt an odd premonitory shiver race down her spine. "Like it's got a life of its own, it's already outta control, ready to eat us alive." He was shaking with a kind of inner tension Daina could readily understand. To her it was the emotional charge she built up inside herself just before she went in front of the cameras. It began in her legs, made the muscles jump and ping and when the spasms reached her knees, it was time to go.

Abruptly Chris hit the table with the flat of his hand so hard the coffee jumped from her cup. "Hey," he cried, "you know what we're gonna do? I got that bloody elephant Harley in th' boot o' th' limo." He grinned broadly, the carefree boy again. He reached over, grabbed her hand in his. "C'mon! We're gonna hit th' road!"

And out above the slow pearling spread of the sea they sped atop the blood-red motorcycle, its bulging clear central nacelle acting as a reflector, intensifying the color of the metal struts. The great engine throbbed and vibrated between her legs, her arms were around his waist and she felt the keyed-up hardness of his muscles, thinking only briefly of Maggie who refused to mount the machine.

Her breasts pressed against the forgiving wall of his hunched back, the warm wind tearing at her cheeks as if full of envy, rippling her long hair, turning into the fan of a seashell; the sun hot on her bare arms, spilled into her squinting eyes like poured gold.

Chris gunned the engine and the Harley leaped beneath them like a live steed, carrying them along, faster and faster until it seemed as if they were outstripping time itself with the coastline gone, merely a blur of brown-ochre-green-white-red that had nothing to do with them, reduced to light lances upon the moving filaments of her body, energy like fire burning through her veins. Exhilaration.

Ecstasy without end. . . .

3

For what seemed a long time, she sat behind the wheel of the Merc. Bel Air was still and silent around her. This far in, not even the interminable hiss of the traffic along Sunset Boulevard could be heard.

She was parked just out of sight of the beginning of Rubens' wide, sweeping, crushed-marble driveway, deciding whether or not to go in. High above, a plane droned furrily through the haze, heading toward Los Angeles International Airport.

She stared straight ahead at the high line of jacarandas that bordered this section of the property but what she really saw was in her mind: New York's heavily muscled skyline breathing in sunset and sunrise, filling her with the power of a goddess. That great kinetic city crashed in her mind like a shout of victory.

Her lips, half open, emitted a soft sound, as if it were the ghost of that shout, dimmed by time and distance. She lay back against the cool leather of the seat, her long fingers gently stroking the curve of the wheel.

The western evening was coming but all she heard were the echoes of that cry swirling like wine through her mind while her thoughts tried to recapture the essence of that sleazy, granite soul. Her pulse beat one-two, one-two, tiny tremors in the hollow of her throat, on the inside of her wrist, *Mark, Mark,* making her heart pound against the cage of her ribs. Tears glazed her eyes and she bit her lip, thinking, Oh, you bastard!

Abruptly she gunned the engine and, slamming the car into first, spun into Rubens' drive. The huge house with its orangey Spanish tiled roof and repeated white stucco arches seemed far away indeed, its brilliant color softened by the plashy pink glow of invisible Hollywood, which illuminated the sky like a benediction from a falsehearted priest.

Twelve massive poplars whipped by her, turning her world cool and dark, the flat face of the Mexican gardener's assistant zooming by as he took off home on his Honda.

Maria pulled the door open to the ringing of the chimes but the housekeeper was on her way home, too.

"*Buenas tardes,* Señorita Whitney," she said with the hint of a formal bow. "The señor is just finishing his tennis."

"Oh," Daina said. "Who's with him?"

Maria smiled. "No one, señorita. Today he plays the machine." She closed the door softly behind her as Daina went quietly down the hall, past the enormous El Greco on the left-hand wall, through the arch and into the living room.

Rubens, in white tennis shorts and shirt with a double stripe of dark blue down each side, was just coming in through the window doors at the rear of the room. A white towel was draped around his shoulders. He had a blue and white sweatband on his right wrist. Behind him, in a blaze of spotlights, she could see a third of the Olympic-size swimming pool and, just to its right, one corner of the composition-clay tennis court. He smiled at her.

"You came after all."

"Did you think I wouldn't?"

He waggled the flat of his hand. "Fifty-fifty. I had a bet with myself."

She came toward him. "Which fifty did you take?"

He grinned. "The winning one." He went over to the bar, made them both a drink.

"I think you cheated."

He stirred her Bacardi, dropped in a twist of lime. "I'm always honest with myself."

She took the cold glass from him. "And very sure."

"Training," he said, taking a long pull at his Stolichnaya. "Bullies used to kick sand in my face."

She laughed, certain he was joking but she sobered immediately, staring down into her rum. "I almost didn't come."

He said nothing, took a cigarette out of a slim gold case, lit it. The smoke hissed from between his lips, he flicked the ash into the earth surrounding a small potted cactus.

From the depths of her sadness came an intuition that he would say, What's the difference? You're here. That's all that matters. So she was surprised when he said, "What happened?" She saw the concern on his face, knew then that perhaps she had wanted him to say the other thing, to be callous because that would make it so much easier for her to get up and walk out on him; not to have to feel anymore.

"I don't think I want to talk about it."

"Oh, come on," he said, coming out from behind the bar. "Why else did you bring it up?" He took her arm, guided her down the three steps to the pit where the immense sapphire velvet couch curled in a U-shape beneath the high ceiling.

"Okay," he said when they were seated. "Spill it."

Her eyes flashed. "Now you're making some kind of joke of it."

"I am?" His eyes opened wide.

"That Raymond Chandler dialogue—"

"It's a holdover from my former life as Philip Marlowe. I'm not making fun of you."

She looked at him for a moment. "I threw Mark out. He—"

"You've already told me that."

"Will you stop it and listen to me—"

"You're much better off without him, I can tell you."

"Why, because he's black?"

"Not in this day and age."

"It still matters, don't bullshit me."

"Yes, it does. But I was going to say, it's because of his politics not his color." He sipped at his drink. "It took a lotta people a long time to allow Fonda her comeback."

"It didn't have anything to do with her politics."

He lifted an eyebrow. "No? Oh, excuse me. I didn't think you were that naive."

"Just what do you know?"

"What I've told you." He put his drink down on the white

slate coffee table in front of them. "Look, your rocket's at the launching pad. You don't want anything to disconnect the cable now." He eyed her. "Do you?"

"No." She looked away for a moment. "But this has as much to do with us as it does with Mark and me. The timing's all wrong, don't you see? I've just come out of a long, hard relationship. Then you come along and make me feel like a pendulum, swinging back and forth over a pit. I feel like I'm going to fall in at any minute."

He reached over, touched her. "Then don't think of that bastard anymore. He was always running around with—"

"Don't," she warned.

"What's the matter," he said, "are you too delicate to hear this? You know what he was sleeping with down at the set and on location. He couldn't get enough of those sleazy—"

"Stop it!" Now his face was very close to hers. She could see the gleam of sweat, the short stubble of beard. But most of all, she inhaled his animal scent.

Rubens' voice was low now but perfectly clear. "What you ever saw in Mark Nassiter I'll never know but I'm glad you threw him out." He put his free hand up, turned her head toward him. "It sickens me to see your face now, to know that you still feel something for him, a bastard who spent a week and a half pursuing that little fifteen-year-old bitch—"

"You knew!" With a violent jerk, she pulled free of him and stood up.

"Now wait a minute—"

Now she slapped him, hard and without warning, leaving a rough red welt on his cheek. "You bastard! Why didn't you tell me?"

"D'you really believe you would've listened to me?"

"You stepped on me just the way you've stepped on every other woman in your life. You used it." She glared at him. "I must be out of my mind. Really."

She turned on her heel, went up the steps to the living room proper but he caught up to her there.

"Now, look, that isn't the way it was at all."

She whirled, stared up at him. "No? Liar! You didn't know just what was happening when you ran into me at the Warehouse? Say that to my face and I'll spit in your eye!"

She thought she saw him tremble then and the blood drained from his face, not slowly but all at once. She felt the

coiled readiness of his body, knew instinctively that this was
how he reacted to a situation of this sort: with violence. Because of that she could not stop herself, wanting as she did
to push him further, to provoke in him a response strong
enough to prove to her once and for all that he truly cared
for her. "I mean it, Rubens. You leave the lying for business.
You're so used to twisting women around your finger, you've
forgotten they're human beings. Well, I'm a human being,
damn it, and I don't like being lied to. You understand you
can't treat me that way."

The air between them had turned to lead. It was as if an
entire world revolved on this one point, so delicate was the
moment.

"All right," he said, after an eternity. "That's the way it
was in the beginning. I got a call ten minutes after it happened—"

"Thanks," she said. "For nothing."

"Now just a minute! You said..." He grabbed her arm but
she gave him a look that caused him to turn her loose immediately. "Maybe we both have to listen sometimes, huh?
Maybe that's part of the problem."

"I'm not going to stand here and listen to your crap." She
turned away. "You've trained yourself so well you don't even
know when you're lying anymore. The truth has no more
meaning. It's only what's best for Rubens at the moment.
Christ, I don't know how I could've felt anything—"

"What can I do to convince you?"

She gave him a brittle smile. "Oh, you'll get no help from
me on that."

"And you'll just walk out."

"Why not? There's nothing for me here."

"If you leave now, you'll never know for sure."

"Believe me, Rubens, I know."

"I still want you to move in."

"Oh, please."

There was a peculiar, tense silence. It was as if the two
of them stood in a leafy glade divested of not only their clothes
but the carefully cultivated layers of civilization. An atavistic
tension laced the air. Only their eyes moved minutely. Their
nostrils dilated, scenting. In the next moment, they would
have bared their teeth, growling at each other.

"You don't really want to leave, Daina." His voice, if not exactly filled with menace, had taken on a steely edge.

She knew perfectly well what he meant. She had had enough of his intimidation. She was acutely aware of how much she wanted the role as Heather Duell but she was perfectly set in her mind about what to do. After all, how many millions were already invested in the film? Too many for him to allow her to walk off the film. It was just another tactic. Just as he had backed off from hitting her a moment before, he would back off from this.

And what if it's not a bluff? she asked herself. He has the power. He *could* do it. Then where would I be? If I were a man, it would never have come to this. Power. All I lack is the power.

She wavered then for just a moment but was fixed by a last thought: If I allow myself to be ground under his thumb this time, it'll happen again and again and I'll never get out. I'll never have the power.

"You won't take me off this film." It is the only way I have of defending myself, she thought.

Rubens' face was as expressionless as a mask. "You want this role too much, Daina. You *need* it."

"I'd rather go down the street to Ted Kessel. You've turned this into a prod to debase me."

"All right." His voice rang with a peculiar tone. "As of now, you're off the film."

For an instant, she thought her heart had stopped beating. Had she misheard him? Had she dreamt it? But no. She had miscalculated, pushed him too far.

She turned away from him, went across the long living room toward the hallway. She could see the old man El Greco had chosen to paint, his elongated face making him seem that much wiser. His calm eyes watched her as she approached.

Her heart was breaking and tears stood at the corners of her eyes, unmoving, as if by her own force of will she was preventing them from dropping over the edge, to roll down her cheeks and shame her. The old man of Spain—the kind of resolute Jew—saw her shame but she resolved that Rubens never would.

She thought then of her other shame, of a time she had locked away inside herself, and her grief became all but unbearable. She sought solace from the old man but, after all, he could not reach out and touch her, merely speak to her with those expressive eyes. And what he said to her was, I have survived. You will, too.

She was near the hallway when she heard Rubens speak. It was a sound that came to her from out of another world.

"Please come back here," he said softly. "I didn't mean any of that."

Still she stared into the old man's eyes.

"Can't you forgive me?"

She turned now. "Why must you be so hurtful?" She knew tears were glistening in the corners of her eyes. "Why should you even say that to me?"

"You won," he said. "Don't you see that?"

"Won what? This isn't a contest."

"Oh, yes," he said easily. "It's all a contest." His tone was admonishing now. "You know that."

"Then how could I win against you?"

"When my foot came down, you twisted it away. You said no, despite the fact you wanted that role more than anything else."

"Almost more than anything else."

For the first time in what seemed a century, he smiled. It was a nice smile, she saw, warm and gentle. "'Almost' is what separates you from—"

"The bimbos."

"—everyone else." He came up to where she stood. *"Everyone."* His arms came around her and she let them stay there. "You're not afraid of me," he whispered. "That's something I need in a woman." He kissed her neck. "More than you could know."

"So you terrorize me to—"

"No." He shook his head. "You terrorized *me.* The moment I knew you really meant to walk out, I also knew I could never allow that to happen. I'd do anything..."

"Give me anything I want?" Her voice was very soft.

"Yes." His voice was even softer as his arms tightened around her and he buried his face in the hollow of her shoulder.

Without conscious thought, her hand came up, her fingers digging into his thick hair as she pressed her body hard against his. Her nostrils were filled with a kind of musk so powerful it dizzied her and she found herself clinging to him as if for support.

But he was already sliding down her body as if his flesh had turned to rainwater. She stood as still as she could, her fingers still twined in his hair. But as she felt his hands at the opening of her silk wrap dress, pulling aside the flaps, she began to tremble.

She gasped when she felt the soft scrape of his fingers along the flesh of her thighs and then, incredibly, his lips were right against her mound.

His tongue snaked out, licking at her. The muscles of her thighs jumped and all strength seemed to seep from her legs. She bent all the way over him until her breasts flattened against the muscles of his back, moving herself up and down against the soft lance of his tongue.

Pools of pleasure made her feel heavy; her heart thundered in her chest; her lips were parted and her hips began to jerk. "Oh, God," she groaned as her orgasm opened up inside her, rubbing her breasts against his back, feeling her nipples against his flesh, dissolving in the torrents of pleasure.

Afterward, she lay atop him. She caressed him for a time, her fingertips moist with her own secretions until she saw his eyes glazing. He groaned deeply at the contact of their hot flesh and the feeling of him filling her was so wonderful that she shuddered.

Eventually, the whispering of the palm trees lulled them to sleep where they lay on the carpet beside the huge pink and gray marble fireplace with its high, empty mantel.

She awoke in the middle of the evening when, in the houses all around her, TV sets were still burning brightly, and stared into his sleeping face. She put a hand up, her fingers gently stroking the line of his jaw where she had earlier slapped him. His eyes opened.

"It shouldn't be like that," she whispered. "A contest. Not between two people." In her mind, she had added "who love each other," but she could not say it.

He looked into her eyes. "It's important to master that because this town is full of fools. They think money is the great intimidator. They don't realize the more you rely on money the weaker you become until your brain goes flabby with disuse and you make all the wrong decisions." She put her hand along his chest so that she could feel the breath going in and out of him as she watched his dark, shining eyes.

"Force of will," he said, "is an infinitely better weapon than money because it works all the time. All it needs is you. But no one can give you that advice, you've got to learn it the hard way like I did.

"On Avenue C in Manhattan there's no money anywhere. It takes time to get out of that hellhole and in the interim you've got to survive."

He moved minutely against her and she could feel the tension flooding into him, turning him hard as a rock. "Times I'd come home in the dark, nursing a bloody cheek, a fractured jaw...my nose was broken so many times, I stopped counting." He gave a mirthless laugh like the bark of a vengeful dog. "Oh, how the Ukrainians loved me! 'Hey, Jew,' they'd call to me. 'C'mere, Jewboy. We gotta present for you.' Fist in the stomach, knees in the groin, leather straps across the face. 'Here's your reward for killing Christ, you piece of shit!'

"They beat me with a kind of cold, methodical fury, as if they had picked up from their parents the knowledge of un-feeling bestiality those Europeans had suffered at the hands of the Germans. It was nightmarish, as if the Nazis had, even in defeat, managed to resurrect themselves through the children of their victims, cheating death to become immortal."

She lay there with her arms around him, feeling something writhe inside him. He was silent for so long, she thought the story finished.

"There was one," he said so abruptly he startled her, "who was always in the forefront, a large, tousle-haired kid with lambent blue eyes. He always wore his shirt open, even in the dead of winter, so you could see the silver crucifix around his neck. I used to think it was there to remind him of what he was.

"Anyway, it was his voice I heard first during those en-counters; his fist, his knee, his laugh...his spittle on my face.

"Oh, I put up a fight. But they were bigger than I was and there were always too many of them. My mother cried to see me bleeding but she said nothing to my father. The one time he noticed my broken nose, he took my hands in his, turned them into painful fists, said to me, 'Haven't you learned yet to defend yourself? You've got fists, use them!'

"For a time after that, I dared not go out of the house. I

was convinced they were waiting for me. I knew 'they' were
not important. It was the big boy with the blue eyes who
invaded my dreams just as he punished me for my imagined
sins.

"Then one day, I *did* go out. It was Saturday, during the
summer, and I thought perhaps they'd be at Brighton Beach.
I walked for blocks without seeing anyone I knew; it was as
if I were a stranger in my own neighborhood and, feeling this,
I allowed my resentment to surface. I looked down at my
hands, flexed them. My father had been at least partially
right. I had to use something...something I'd find inside
myself to defend myself. I knew it would never be my fists
but they weren't all I had.

"At that moment, I looked up and saw the white Caddy.
The white Caddy was a car that used to show up around the
neighborhood once or twice a week. I knew what it sold—
well, generally. Dope was only something I had heard talked
about. The white Caddy turned the corner into East First
Street. I stopped by the lightpost at the corner, watched it
down the block. It stopped about a third of the way down and
I saw a figure emerge from the shadows of a tenement doorway. It was the boy with the blue eyes. He gave the man in
the white Caddy some bills and got in return a couple of small
glassine envelopes.

"For the next week, I charted the white Caddy's movements down East First Street. Invariably, it stopped outside
the same tenement but I never saw the boy with the blue
eyes come out again. Several times, one of the other Uke kids
took delivery. But just as often, I saw them use any one of
the younger boys who hung around the stoops. They never
used the same one twice.

"The following Saturday it was raining. No beach that
day. I slipped out of the house, up Avenue C to East First
Street. On the way, I had to duck into old man Wcyczk's fruit
store to avoid the Ukes. They were heading downtown, on
their way to the Loew's Delancey movie theater. The boy with
the blue eyes was not with them and I knew why.

"I went down East First Street, parking myself high up
on the stoop just west of his. In ten minutes I was drenched
and in the next ten I began to shiver despite the heat but at
last I heard the hissing that was like no other and knew that
the white Caddy had turned the corner and was coming.

"It stopped just past where I was sitting. For a moment, nothing happened. Then the nearside window hissed down and I heard a voice. 'Hey, kid. Hey.' I looked up. A hand beckoned. 'C'mere a minute.' I got up and went to stand beside the open window. 'Here's a coupla bucks. Take this package up to 6F in that building.' A blunt finger pointed to the blue-eyed boy's apartment.

"Inside, on the stairs, I carefully unwrapped the package. There were three glassine envelopes. I repacked them, went up the stinking stairway to the top floor. I could hear a radio blaring, blotting out the sound of the rain on the roof. I put the package away and knocked on the door.

"He didn't recognize me right away. Why should he? I was the last person he expected to see. But I waited patiently until he did know. 'I see you haven't learned your lesson yet, Jewboy,' he said. 'I'll have to fix that.' He lunged at me but I danced away. 'You don't want to do that,' I said reasonably. 'I've got your dope.'

"Of course he was too stupid to recognize the truth when he heard it and it wasn't until I had spilled the contents of the first envelope into the sink and run the water over it that he believed me. 'Don't,' he said, 'do anything with the rest. I need it.'

"'But the Jewboy has it,' I said, taking out the second envelope. I had never seen someone beg before...I mean really get down on his knees and beg. I saw the tracks in his arm. He disgusted me. I poured the contents of the envelope down the drain. 'Now there's only one,' I said. He looked up at me and all the beautiful blue had disappeared; his eyes seemed as brown as mud.

"'Here,' I said, dangling the third envelope above his head, 'is the Jewboy's gift to you.' I let it drop into his trembling palm, watched the agony come into those half-dead eyes as I said, 'I don't know very much about this. What would happen to you, d'you think, if you shot the stuff I put in there?' Then I turned and walked out of there. But his face was fixed in my mind forever."

Gradually, in the ensuing silence, Daina felt all the tension flowing out of him as if they were floating above a subterranean river. She felt his breathing slow, knew he was close to sleep.

"Rubens..." she said softly. "What happened to the boy? Did you cut the heroin?"

For a long time he did not answer. He turned on his side, holding her as she held him. "It doesn't matter."

"How can you say that?"

He kissed her, so tenderly she felt herself close to tears. "That's not the point of the story," he whispered so softly it might have been the night wind. "Now go to sleep, my darling."

"Power," Marion said to her. "This is why one gravitates to Hollywood. There is more power concentrated here than in any other city in the world. Oh, except Washington." He gave a mordant laugh. "And don't they wish they had our money!"

They were walking along the periphery of the set, passing in and out of the frame of the three enormous Panavision cameras rearing like saurians out of a primeval swamp.

"Coming to Hollywood is the ultimate test of myself as a human being." Marion carried with him that rather formal English hauteur, a certain distancing from the mere common citizen of the world not fortunate enough to be a member of the Empire. It was nevertheless endearing because it was part of his peculiar provincialism, a throwback to the ideals of the nineteenth century. You never thought he had anything but your own best interests in mind. "I could have stayed in the theater for the rest of my life. After all, when I was a lad that was all I dreamt of—being part of the West End and, of course, Broadway. But one is changed by success, it's quite true. Well, take yourself. Since *Regina Red,* you have been 'turned on' so to speak. The public has been made aware of you in the most intimate terms, d'you see what I mean? Your life *must* be altered because of that.

"In my case, the successes I had in the theater made me long for other...grander...things. I made my decision to come to the heart of power, first, to see if I could survive and, second, to see whether I could conquer it." He took her hand. "But one learns quite quickly that merely to survive here is a victory and not an unimportant one. Many of the great ones have not and d'you know why?"

The place was beginning to fill up with the cast and crew

and he pulled her away, into a last pocket of shadowed gray calm. He looked her full in the face. "It's because, in the beginning one is so intent,"—his hands made small orbits between them, punctuating his words—"so totally wrapped up in the gathering of power. And one comes to believe that is the end of it, that one has accomplished *everything*." He was whispering now but his words carried more weight than if he were shouting. "It's not true, Daina. The really formidable task is learning to use one's power intelligently once one has it." He looked sad. "It's not power itself that corrupts but ignorance in the *application* of that power."

Behind them, the buzzing had reached its peak and movement was everywhere as people eddied about, taking their places. "My dear, I believe it's already far too late for our friend"—she knew he meant George—"but for you it certainly is not. Controlling him is unequivocally my job so I want you to know that if you ever find yourself in the crossfire again just stand aside and come to me. I don't want you involved in all this. You're far too brilliant an actress to allow our friend's, uhm, aberrations to disturb you."

"He wants this role and I believe he's right for it. But it's difficult for him. *Heather Duell* is obviously written for a woman—for you—and from time to time his resentment boils over." He laughed and now it was a rich, jolly sound. "He may be a swine for all seasons but the two of you have a chemistry on screen that's absolute magic. You see, clever chap that I am, I showed him the rushes of yesterday's scene. Now he may be many things but he's no fool, our friend. And he was man enough to admit that I know what I'm doing." Marion laughed again, turned as a figure approached. "George!" he cried. "Come reacquaint yourself with the leading lady!"

"Yes," El-Kalaam said into the telephone. "That's quite correct, Mr. President. I've just been on the line with the prime minister of Israel. He has spoken to his daughter and is quite convinced she is alive and well. For the moment." He glanced over to where Bayard Thomas stood. "Your secretary of state was quite a bonus." Thomas' normally ruddy face was as white as the hair on his head. His piercing blue eyes, too, seemed to have gone pale. His gaze dropped. He stared down at his wrists. He seemed to be shaking.

Across the room James sat half propped up against the bookcase. He appeared to be breathing easier but there was still a lot of blood. Both Heather and Rachel were watching him.

"What was that, Mr. President? I didn't quite catch what you said. This transatlantic line... No, that doesn't matter." He kept staring at Thomas, willing him to meet his gaze. The American secretary continued to stare at his shaking hands.

El-Kalaam grinned suddenly. "Your secretary just wet his pants, Mr. President." He clucked his tongue against the roof of his mouth. "A shameful act."

His face sobered. He checked his chronometer. "It is now twenty-four minutes past ten A.M. At six P.M. this evening I will expect a call from you informing me that our thirteen brothers have been released from their imprisonment in Jerusalem. By eight o'clock tomorrow morning, you will have met our other demands. You know what they are. There will be no further negotiation.

"If, at the end of that time, we have not heard over local public radio, thirteen hundred megahertz, of your total acquiescence, the daughter of the prime minister of Israel, your secretary of state and everyone else here will be summarily executed." He replaced the receiver with great care.

"This is outrageous," Rene Louch said. "I demand that I and my attaché be released immediately. France has no quarrel with the aims of the PLO. On the contrary—"

"Shut your mouth," Malaguez said coldly. El-Kalaam turned to Rudd. "You must take better care of him," he said with a note of amusement in his voice. "I think he's getting too old for his office."

"El-Kalaam!" Louch called. "Listen to me!"

"He has not yet learned," El-Kalaam said without inflection. He was staring at Susan now but it was obvious he was speaking to Fessi.

The rodent-eyed man seemed not to move at all but the thick butt of his heavy AKM smashed into Louch's midsection. The French ambassador went down as if he were poleaxed. His torso flew forward and his knees collapsed from under him. His arms went inward, his fingers scrabbling for his stomach. A peculiar high wheezing came from his open mouth and tears rolled down his cheeks. Then Fessi tapped him on the back of the neck with the edge of his hand and Louch passed out.

El-Kalaam wrinkled his nose and clucked his tongue as he had done when he was on the phone. He bent from the waist, lowered the muzzle of his MP40 until the metal bit into the other man's chin.

El-Kalaam lifted upward until Louch opened his eyes and was staring him in the face. The Frenchman's skin was sallow and sweat-sheened, his eyes red-rimmed.

"Don't ever," El-Kalaam said with great kindness in his voice, "speak to me unless you are told to do so first." He pursed his lips. "It must come as a great shock to you, I know. But there are no allies here. You are the enemy just like all of them"—his arm swung out and he indicated the other hostages—"are the enemy. You are one and the same." He jerked at the muzzle of his machine pistol as he stared down at the other man. The face bobbed. "Isn't that so?"

The French ambassador stared at him, mute and bleary-eyed. El-Kalaam fetched him a close-handed blow to the side of the head. He bent, pulled the other man's face off the floor. "Say it is so, *Mr. Ambassador*." He said the appellation with exaggerated diction. The scorn was manifest.

Louch's tongue came out, wiped at his dry lips. "It's..." His voice faded out and he cleared his throat, began again. "It is so. We...we are the enemy."

"Quite so." El-Kalaam stared at him for a moment. Then a look of distaste crossed his face and he turned to Emouleur. "Clean him up as best you can," he said. "What else can an *attaché* expect to do?"

"What?" the young Frenchman said. "With my hands tied behind my back?"

El-Kalaam took the muzzle of his machine pistol away from Louch's face and the man collapsed at his feet. "Use your tongue." He turned away.

On the other side of the room, James was continuing to lose blood. His left arm appeared to be paralyzed, lying dead and useless at his side. He was using his right hand to claw at the left sleeve of his shirt.

"Please," Heather said, standing beside Rita. "Let me help him. What harm can he do you now?"

El-Kalaam seemed to ignore her. "This is very interesting. Quite"—he cocked his head, watching James' struggle—"inspiring." He went and stood before James. "I want to see if he can do it by himself."

"And if he can't?" Rachel said. Malaguez was just behind her and to one side. "He saved my life. I would like to help him now. If you won't let Heather, then let me."

"Let you?" El-Kalaam did not take his eyes off James. "I wouldn't let you tie your shoelaces by yourself. You'll go nowhere near him."

James was concentrating on what he had to do. His handsome face, knotted and sweating in pain, worked as he struggled to get a piece of cloth between his teeth. He grunted and the cords of his neck stood out as he stretched it to its limit. Then he had it.

A moment later they all heard a sharp shredding sound. James dug two fingers into the rent, pulled sharply down. One long half of his sleeve came away in his hand. Moments later, he had his bandage.

Some odd look had come into El-Kalaam's eyes. "That's very good," he said, watching James adjust the bandage. "You did that like a professional . . . soldier."

James took his time replying. He wiped at his forehead with the back of his good hand, dried it on his trousers. It left a dark stain. He sat back against the bookshelf, took as deep a breath as he could. It came ragged, turned into a cough at the end. Immediately James wiped away the pink spittle from between his lips. But El-Kalaam reached out, turned his hand palm upward. "Bloody," he said and James snatched his hand away, cleaned it off. Heather stifled a cry, closed her eyes.

"I know a bit about soldiering," James said, not looking at her.

"Do you." El-Kalaam put the tip of his MP40 against James' chest, pushing away the shirt. He peered inside. His face was unreadable. "And how is that?"

"I was born and raised in the Falls in Belfast," James said. His head went back; his eyes closed.

"Don't, Jamie," Heather said. "Don't tax yourself."

Rita made a move to silence her but El-Kalaam waved her back. "Leave it alone," he said calmly. "It doesn't matter now what she says. He'll tell me. . . ." He crouched down in front of James. "Won't you?"

James' eyes came open. He stared straight at El-Kalaam.

"The Falls," El-Kalaam said softly. "You were raised in the Falls of Belfast."

"Yes, the Falls," James echoed eerily. "Where the bloody English come in with their Proddy informers to kill and torture the young boyos who fight for their freedom."

A wolfish grin had spread across El-Kalaam's face and he turned his head to glance at MacKinnon and Davidson. "Don't you two English gentlemen want to come closer? Don't you want to hear about the atrocities your government perpetrates on the Irish Catholics?"

MacKinnon and Davidson stared at El-Kalaam, white-faced and stoic. "We live with that knowledge every day of our lives," Davidson said. "It's a fact of life."

"You see how it is with them?" El-Kalaam told James. "You see how they rationalize away their sins?"

"We all have sins," James said softly. "I left the Falls because I knew I'd be more successful in business in the States." He turned his head in Heather's direction. "You know where most of the profits go, my love." Her eyes closed; tears appeared, sliding down her cheeks.

"To the Irish Republican Army, eh?" El-Kalaam nodded. He cocked his head again, staring into James' pain-filled face. "But I wonder. Is that really why you left Belfast?"

"I suppose I always suspected deep down I was a coward. My brother, my sister's fiancé, they fought the Proddies... and died for their ideals. They didn't have a shilling to give to the cause... they gave their lives. They made their choice. Now I've made mine."

"Choice?" El-Kalaam said. "What choice?"

James was quiet for a time, then he looked at El-Kalaam. "Between the defense of honor and submission to the lawless."

El-Kalaam stared at him. He got to his feet, backed away.

"He's right, you know," Ken Rudd said over the hysterical hushing of Thomas.

"What are you doing?" Thomas whispered harshly. "Are you out of your mind? You saw what he did to Rene Louch."

Rudd gave him an icy look.

El-Kalaam swung around to face the American aide. "Words," he said. "Only words."

"Words are what Americans have lived and died for over two hundred years," Rudd said. "Freedom and liberty justice—"

"I'll show you what words mean." El-Kalaam's voice dripped contempt. He made a curt gesture. "Rita."

The tall woman came around from behind Rachel. She took her machine pistol off her shoulder.

"What are you going to do?" Rachel said. Her eyes were very wide.

"Quiet!" Malaguez hissed, training his gun on her. "Just stay where you are and watch."

"I don't want to watch this!"

"Ah, see," Fessi said, grinning. "The Israeli has no stomach for this."

"Leave her out of this," Bock said. He had been silent up until now. "The women shouldn't be involved at all."

"You see," El-Kalaam said to Rudd, "all this talk is quite meaningless. Only action has impact."

While he had been speaking, Rita had singled out the butler. He was a thin, balding man with a pronounced stoop. His eyes were rolling and he had begun to tremble.

"What are you up to?" Rudd said.

"James knows what is about to happen, don't you, James?"

James' head lolled on his neck. His eyes stared at a fixed point on the opposite wall. He gave no sign he heard.

"What's happening? El-Kalaam—" Rudd's voice was interrupted by Thomas' hysterical bark: "Shut up, will you!" His eyes squeezed shut. "Shut up and they'll leave us alone!"

Rita had led the terrified butler into the center of the room. Now she backed away. There was a sharp click as she threw off the safety of her machine pistol.

"For the love of God!" Emouleur cried.

The maid burst into tears; Susan's indrawn breath was a gasp.

"This is no way to—" Davidson began.

The harsh shout of the machine pistol made everyone jump. Heather cried out. The butler spun around, one foot off the ground. He was hurtled against the far wall in a welter of blood. He bounced off. Rita squeezed the trigger again. The noise was deafening. The butler's arms opened wide, the hands grasping at air. His body danced; his eyes rolled up into his head. He was covered in blood. It smeared against the wallpaper as he slid down, his long legs folding under him, his head bent far forward onto his chest.

The maid, a young blonde with far too much makeup, was

whimpering. As if by silent assent, the rest of the hostages had limped and crawled away from her. She was cowering in front of the fireplace.

Rita whirled. Orange fire leaped from the muzzle of the MP40 again and the maid seemed to jump back. The marble mantel struck her across the shoulder blades, arching her forward. Her mouth tried to work but no sound came out. Her fingers contracted into claws as she went down on her knees. She swayed there for a moment before she collapsed onto her side.

"All right," El-Kalaam said through the cordite smoke. "Now you know we mean what we say. Words are as nothing before us; courage a useless commodity before the power we wield. It is ultimate and irrevocable."

His head swiveled around the room, his dark eyes drinking in the shock and stark fear on the pale faces. He smiled a little as he watched them all. There was silence now. He patted the barrel of his machine pistol, spat loudly onto a spot on the floor midway between the corpses.

It was not only that Rubens was becoming humanized to her but, perhaps more importantly, his terrorist beginnings on the Lower East Side touched a nerve deep at the core of her being. She knew what it was like to hate so much it became a taste in the mouth impossible to wash out. And, of course, she had known the punishment for such blinding hate.

It was not surprising then that she found herself back at Rubens' and not at her own house at day's end. She had a swim, after which Maria brought her out a tray on which was a large, perspiring glass of Bacardi, deliciously frigid, and a plate of chicken sandwiches because "the señor will be late tonight and he asked if you would wait dinner for him."

She had downed half the rum before she was sufficiently chilled to return inside. She sat in her still-damp bathing suit, sipping the remainder of her drink, feeling her thick hair heavy and curling on her shoulders. She stared at the outsized oil painting just to the left of the fireplace. Settled on craggy rocks was a grossly overweight mermaid, her face a full moon of pink fat out of which two jolly green eyes peered enigmatically. Her long hair sparkled with a network of sea jewels: a flotsam of tiny shells. The wet scales of her tail gleamed in the light. Her mouth was half open, as if she were singing a song. Below and behind her, the sea curled and rushed as if about to engulf her. It was a curious feature of the painting that the water and the mermaid's eyes were precisely the same color so that one had the vertiginous sensation of looking through her, down into the depths of the ocean. Daina closed her eyes.

Perhaps it was logical that when she fell asleep that night she dreamed of the dungeon. She had never spoken that word in all her life and, for years, when reading a historical text that contained the word, she would sit and stare at it for long, trancelike moments, as if she were afraid it might spring to life. For it was this word she had used in her own mind to describe the room three flights down, burrowed into the ground like a sickly mole waiting to die. Lightless and airless, it hung in her subconscious, drawing her back to that time in her life when she had no volition, no control...as if she had returned to the womb.

She awoke, as she always did from that recurring dream, drenched in sweat, the vile taste of rubber so strong she wanted to get up, go to the bathroom to cleanse her mouth. But that would take time for she still thought of herself as strapped to the bed.

"Daina," Rubens said. "Are you all right?"

For a moment she could not answer. She stared sightlessly at the ceiling. Then she felt him stir beside her, his skin sliding against hers and it was all right.

She rose and, silently, went into the bathroom. When she returned, he was sitting up in bed, watching her.

"What happened? You cried out."

"It was only a dream." She stood at the foot of the bed, naked still.

"You said that like a child." And then, very softly: "You're so beautiful."

She smiled at that. "How this town breeds beauty! Soon it will be so common that it will lose all meaning."

"I wasn't speaking about your face...or your body."

"What then?"

"Your imprint: voice, gestures, intonation...your presence." He held out his arms to her. "All of you."

She let her hair float out across her shoulders like a cloud as she knelt on the bed, coming toward him. "You're not the way," she said, "everyone says you are." She shivered a little when she felt his arms begin to enclose her.

"I'm very cold," he said but she did not know whether he really meant it. There was a depth of illusion about him she could not yet fathom.

"Were you cold with your wife?"

"*Especially* with my wife."

"You see," she said with a kind of mock triumph. "The stories they tell about you must be true."

"What stories?" She could feel the butterfly softness of his lashes as his lips touched her collarbone.

"I've heard it said you divorced your wife because she would not touch you in public."

"I've heard that one, too."

"Well," she said. "Is it true?"

"Does it matter?"

"I don't know." She pulled a little away from him so that she could better see his face. She reached up, brushed a lock of hair off his forehead. "Yes. It would say something about you."

"Oh, yes. It would say I'm quite an egomaniac. I'm quite sure that's the conclusion most people would draw."

"Then you didn't."

"I did, in fact. But that was only an outward manifestation. My wife was as cold as I am purported to be. I learned that from her."

"You're not so cold." She put the flat of her hand along his cheek.

"No. Not with you." He put his hand up, covering hers. "And that surprises me."

"It shouldn't." She stared into his eyes. "It's very logical, really. You've possessed me, penetrated me. But what is that? Only flesh and flesh; nothing at all, compared to—"

The front door chimes rang. Rubens kicked his legs like a college boy, got up. Daina rolled over in the bed, peered at the clock. It was just after midnight.

"Do you have to answer that?"

"Yes." He pulled on a midnight-blue silk satin robe that William Powell might have worn. There were white starbursts all over it. The chimes came again and he went down the hallway.

She turned over on her back, spread her hands out on the

cool sheets, closed her eyes. Voices. Sleep would not come. She sighed, called her service. Maggie had left a message to call.

"Hi. What's up?"

"Just a bit down is all." Her voice sounded muffled and tired. "Where are you?"

"Home," Daina said. "Ah, no. I'm at Rubens' really."

"What are you doing there?"

"Living."

"Ah ha ha." The laugh was harsh, a brittle sound. There was no animation to Maggie's voice at all. "I see. Well how is it?"

"Okay. Listen, Maggie, I'd rather talk about you."

"Boring. I'm just sitting here crying."

"I'll come on over. You shouldn't be alone."

"Stupid. No. I don't need anyone."

"Yes you do. That's the trouble. Chris'll be in the studio all night working...."

"Even if he's not he won't come home."

There was silence for a time while Daina wondered what to say. "He's having problems with the band is all." And knew it was the wrong thing as soon as she had said it.

"How d'you know?" A sharpness had crept into Maggie's voice.

"Oh—well—I ran into him yesterday. We talked for a bit. You know, just chitchat."

"No, I don't know. What the hell's going on, Daina?"

"I don't know what you mean."

"Are you with Chris now?"

"Maggie what's the matter with you? I told you—"

"I know what you told me!" she snapped and hung up.

"Damn!" Daina said and redialed the number. She tried three times but the line was busy.

She got up and began to dress, pulling on jeans and a velour top. She went down the hall and into the living room.

Rubens was there with a rather tall, athletic-looking man. He had a deep tan and sun-streaked hair brushed straight back from his face. He might have been a surfer straight off Laguna Beach. The only incongruities were his rather wet-looking brown eyes and the perfectly round horn-rimmed glasses he wore. He reminded her of someone from her childhood but she could not think who it was.

"Daina Whitney, meet Schuyler Foulton, my attorney," Rubens said.

Foulton shifted an oxblood hand-stitched attaché case from his right hand to his left, shook her extended hand.

"All right," Rubens said, snapping his fingers, "let's get on with this."

Foulton flipped open the case, produced a sheaf of papers, which he handed over. Rubens immediately began to study them.

Daina watched Foulton. There was a thin sheen of sweat on his face. It was a face, she thought, too pretty to be termed handsome. She thought the glasses made him seem younger than he was. She wondered again whom he resembled and then turned away, stifling a laugh. Foulton looked just like Clark Kent.

She turned back to him. "Would you care for a drink?"

"Schuyler's not staying that long," Rubens said brusquely, without looking up from his reading.

"No...thank you." Foulton's face was slowly turning red.

Rubens held out a hand, snapped his fingers. Foulton reached inside his jacket, produced a slim, elegant gold pen. Rubens took possession of it, drew circles around two paragraphs on the page he was reading. Only then did he look up. "What the hell is this?" He tossed the sheaf through the air and Foulton caught it clumsily.

Foulton glanced down at the page but only perfunctorily. He knew what was there. "That's the wording the board sent me from New York."

"The board? You mean Ashley had this drafted this way? I expressly told him I wouldn't go for anything less than a five-year deal with escalators and two one-year options."

"I, uh, I spoke to him this afternoon. He says they're worried about being locked in. The liquidity—"

"Screw the liquidity! It's to our advantage to be locked in with Colombine. Do I have to spell out everything to those cretins?"

"Ashley said—"

"I don't give a damn what Ashley said!" Rubens exploded. "Who do you work for, Schuyler?"

Foulton said nothing, stared at the carpet between his shoes.

"You know something, it's a damn good thing we're living

in the twentieth century. What they used to do to bearers of bad tidings...Cut off their heads."

Foulton cleared his throat, looked up. "I think it was cut out their tongues."

"Either way." Rubens went down into the pit, reached into the side of the coffee table. He depressed a recessed stud and a drawer slid soundlessly open. Inside was a white telephone. He put a thin plastic card in a slot, waited while the phone automatically dialed a number. "Come by yourself?" he said while waiting.

"I, uh..."

"Bill drove you."

"I don't think this is—"

"C'mon, Schuyler, Daina isn't about to say anything. Why don't you have him come in. You know he's welcome and he might be getting lonely out there." He turned away from them both and his voice changed as he spoke into the receiver. It was as soft as a lover's caress. "Hello, Marge. Yeah. How are you? And the boys? Good. Sorry to wake you. Yes, I know. Just poke him. He'll wake up." He turned, stared at Foulton the way a mongoose might regard a cobra. When he spoke again his voice had turned as cold and hard as flint. "Ashley, you bastard, what the hell do you think you're doing. Yes, I know what time it is. Schuyler's just handed me the Colombine contract. You know what it's good for, Ashley? Toilet paper." He listened for a moment and his voice lowered, crackling with menace. "Listen you little bastard, if you've screwed this deal I'll carve you into hamburger. D'you know what paragraphs seventeen and nineteen mean to us? No? Colombine has the option to out after three years and if they do we'll take a helluva bath. No you didn't, did you. This contract's *bupkis*. What the hell have you been using for brains lately. Don't start that. I know what Maureen's been doing to you ever since you hired her. How? Who d'you think's running this ball of wax? Yeah. Just so you shouldn't forget, being three thousand miles away." He waited a beat. "Ashley, you'd better get this deal together before Thursday because that's when Schuyler and I are gonna fly in with the new contracts. Right. Oh, and Ashley, as of now I'll handle Colombine personally. Right. You do that." He slammed down the phone. "Schmuck."

He turned to Foulton. "All right. You heard that. Get them

done by ten tomorrow." He smiled. "Didn't you ask Bill in?" He waved a hand. "Daina, go ask Schuyler's friend to come in for a nightcap, will you?"

"No," Foulton said before she could move. He turned to her. "I don't think he was serious about that."

"Hell, man, of course I was!" But his bonhomie was utterly false, so transparent in fact that Daina could feel the undercurrent of anger seething just below the surface. Only the thin veneer that growing up civilized had provided for him kept him under control. What had set him off so? she wondered.

"You've got to get over this phobia, Schuyler, really. Daina doesn't care that you're gay. She works with them all the time, isn't that right?"

She said nothing, not wanting to be a part of the cruel banter.

"It's not that," Foulton said. "You know—"

"Oh then it must be Bill. Well hell, Schuyler, Daina doesn't know Bill." He looked at her for a moment. "You know Bill Denckley, the dermatologist? Bill of Beverly Hills? Schuyler here lives with him. Bill's sitting out there in the car waiting for him." He smiled again, showing his teeth. "Hey, I've got an idea—why don't you strip for us? Show Daina the black-and-blue marks that Bill—"

"Rubens, please don't." Schuyler shifted his attaché case from one hand to the other, wiped his free palm down his pants.

"Oh, now, there's no reason to be shy, Schuyler, old boy. Just think of Daina as one of the guys, eh? That ought to put some spark in you—"

"Rubens, that's enough!" Daina said sharply. "Stop it."

He was about to say something more but what he saw in her face perhaps dissuaded him and he shook himself, as if to rid himself of the excess verbiage he had been about to spit out. Instead he said in another tone of voice, "How's *Over the Rainbow* coming?"

Schuyler cleared his throat, darting a thankful glance toward Daina before he answered. "I just completed the third month accounting, and I think we are going to have to monitor the spending a bit more closely."

"How far over budget are those bastards?"

"Three million . . . so far."

"How far are we in?"

"Six million, roughly."

"They're also behind schedule."

"It's that crazy set designer, Roland Hill. He just keeps building them bigger and brighter. They're waiting for a neon skyline of New York that's costing us a quarter of a million because Hill refuses to do miniatures."

Rubens turned to Daina. "These bastards get one hit under their belts and right away they're running away with things." He put his glass down. "Set up a meeting, Schuyler. For sometime, oh, next week."

"At the office?"

"No, here. I want those egomaniacs relaxed when they walk in here. They sure as hell ain't gonna be when they walk out. Now about the Colombine—"

"You'll have the contracts by ten," Schuyler said softly. "I'll send them over by messenger."

"Don't bother," Rubens said. "I'll come by the office first thing."

Foulton nodded. "Nice meeting you, Miss Whitney." He took her hand in a cool embrace. "I've enjoyed your films."

"Thank you," she said pointedly. "Come again soon."

They heard his heels on the hall tiles. The door closed quietly after him. A car's engine coughed to life, its sound soon diminishing into the high palms.

Rubens was staring at her. He turned and went across the room to the bar. For a time, the space between them was filled only with the tiny sounds of ice cubes against glass.

"Why did you treat him that way?" she said at last.

"I don't want to talk about it," he said angrily.

"All right. Fine." She went to the hall closet.

"Where are you going?"

"To see Maggie. She's—"

"Don't do that."

She turned around to face him fully. "She's my friend, Rubens."

He took a step toward her. "I'm more than your friend."

"I'm not going to stay with you tonight...not after the way you terrorized Schuyler."

"What's he to you?"

"It's what he's to *you*, Rubens. My God, he's your friend."

"I do it because he enjoys it."

She shook her head. "I was watching his face. You hurt him. Badly. And you did it because you enjoyed it."

He gave her a peculiar look. "I can see I've underestimated you again."

"Christ. And that bothers you."

"I'm not certain that it does." He took his drink, came around from behind the bar. He nodded. "All right. I'll tell you. Schuyler and I went to school together. I worked my way into that place—his father put him there." He waved a hand in the air as if to erase his words. "But that didn't mean a thing. We were roommates, became good friends...did all the things friends do together: went to football games, helped each other cram for exams, doubledated—"

"Ah."

"Yeah. It wasn't until much later that he told me he had come out." He gulped at his drink with enough appetite that she could see his agitation. "I didn't take it well then and I still don't now. I mean, I know what was going on with him and broads years back. We used to stay up all night talking about Kim Novak and Rita Hayworth, comparing them to our own girls. So I keep thinking it's just a temporary aberration." He turned away. "His fiancée still calls me from time to time, asks me if there's any hope. She still loves him."

"Rubens," she said softly, "you can't make him be what he's not."

"You know what it is," he said. "I don't think he knows himself what he is. I get so angry at him sometimes I could throttle him. I don't want to abuse him, not really. But every time Regine calls, crying"—his hand balled into a fist—"I think, why does it have to be like that? How can he choose that fag dermatologist over her?"

"You act as if it's your decision. It's not." She put her fingers along his arm, squeezed. "But then I don't love him like you do."

He snorted. "I don't love Schuyler." But there was no conviction in his voice and he did not break away from her touch.

"D'you think it's unmanly to love him?" It was a question to which she did not really expect an answer; she merely wanted to voice the question he should be asking himself. "What's more important than friendship?"

He seemed to relax a bit. "I really do owe the bastard an

apology. Sometimes I treat him as badly as I imagine Bill does."

"Do they do what you said they did?"

He smiled. "No. Of course not. It just drives Schuyler nuts. I think Bill really loves him." He twined his fingers in hers. "He's not a bad sort, really, for a dermatologist." He laughed, turned to her. "You know, you've got a very disquieting ability."

"What's that?"

"You're able to make me see things about myself." She became aware of the intensity with which he was staring into her eyes. Her knees grew weak from what she saw there. He seemed transfixed, mesmerized, as if by some mysterious process she had been transformed into a fabulous magical creature. He was breathing through his half-open mouth and when he reached his free hand upward to touch her cheek, his skin felt hot.

"Don't go, Daina." His voice was thick. "Not now. Not tonight." His touch was electric. A tingling began behind her eyes, melting all the memories inside her so that for that moment she came to him purified of the fire and ice of her past. "Please."

But she could not keep that unspoken promise to him, however much part of her wished selfishly to stay with him all night. From out of the darkness she heard, above the ticking of the bedside clock and Rubens' own regular breathing, Maggie's agonized voice.

She thought of all the gray days they had spent together sharing meals at Taco Belle or Hamburger Hamlet; how many nights they had cried in each other's arms out of frustration and anger at getting nowhere. No parts, no films, no life. How many invitations to bed, how many producers they had turned down, she could no longer remember. They had only each other in those bleak days. Her heart broke at the thought of what Maggie must be suffering now: to see her best friend so successful; to be so mired herself.

Daina sat up and, with a violent shake of her head, got out of bed. The parting of her warm flesh with Rubens' was a shock and she turned her mind away.

Silently, without waking him, she dressed in jeans and

cowlneck sweater. She found her car keys and was halfway across the threshold to the hallway when she heard him stir and say: "Where are you going?" His voice was furry with sleep.

"I've got to see Maggie."

"What the hell for? She hates your guts right now."

She turned around, saw his face almost all in shadow. Just a tiny crescent of light lay along one cheek like a scar. "You stopped me once from going. Don't do it again. Please."

"I'm only pointing out something to you that should be self-evident," he said, getting up on one elbow. "If you want to waste your time, that's up to you."

"She's my friend, Rubens." She took a step toward him. "You should understand that. Friends are important where you come from." She paused. "Isn't that right?"

He was silent for a moment. "She's only waiting for a chance to stab you in the back."

She leaned forward. "This is only a game to you, isn't it? You don't care one way or the other about Maggie. You just don't want me to leave you."

"No," he said bluntly, "I don't." He sat all the way up; she felt him staring at her. "Now we're both angry," he said, "over nothing."

Daina came over to the bed, bent over him, kissed his lips. She put her fingertips up until they touched the line of his jaw, removing for a moment the scar of light.

"I'm not leaving you; I'm going to see Maggie. There's a difference. You're wrong about her. Whatever she and I fight about will be nothing a day from now...but only if one of us makes the first move to heal the wound. She won't—not this time. She's too filled with frustration and despair." She took her face away from his but squeezed his hand with her own. "Don't be angry with me. My friends are important to me, too. And she needs me."

"I need you, too."

She smiled at him. "You're stronger than she is right now. Don't make it into a contest."

"No contest," he said from out of the darkness. "Do what you have to do."

Lights were blazing as Daina turned the silver Merc in at the side of Chris and Maggie's beach house. The hiss of the waves was swept away by the chunky pulse of the Heartbeats' music emanating from the interior.

Mounting the sandy stairs, Daina knocked on the door. The music was loud enough so that there was no immediate response, and she was forced to wait for the lull between songs. Then she hit the door hard with her balled fist.

"Come in, it's open.... Oh, it's you," Maggie said as she saw Daina. "Who was expecting you?"

"Why'd you hang up on me?" Daina said, walking over to where Maggie sat curled into a corner of the sofa. There was an almost-empty bottle of German white wine on the coffee table; the ashtray bristled with ground-out cigarette butts. A half-smoked roach lay in a wire holder.

"Where's Chris?" Maggie said sullenly. "You too chicken to bring him home yourself?"

"Maggie, I don't know where you got the idea—"

"I want to know!" She shouted down the music, no mean feat. "What've you two been doing behind my back?"

Daina crossed the room, stabbed a button on the stereo amplifier. Silence descended and, in its aftermath, the dull crash of the soft surf outside. She went and sat on the couch next to Maggie.

"I'm sorry I didn't get a chance before to tell you Chris and I had talked."

"He could've come to *me* for advice." Her eyes filled with tears. "Why'd he go to you?"

Daina reached out a hand and, as if the contact caused her to speak, Maggie said convulsively, "Oh, God, Daina, I can't stand it! You've got everything and I've got nothing...nothing. Now you've taken Chris, too."

"Chris loves only you, Maggie. We're just friends and sometimes friends can talk about things they can't talk to lovers about." She enfolded Maggie in her arms, feeling the bitter tears running hotly down her neck, the succession of sobs like miniature quakes.

"Shh," she whispered. "Shh," as she would do to a hurt child, as she wished her mother had done to her just once. She stroked Maggie's hair. "We still have each other; we'll always have each other."

"But you're going away." Maggie's voice had turned small and sad, all the hard-edged anger leached away by her tears. "You're going and I'll be left."

"Where am I going?" Daina said softly. "I'm still here." She was crying herself now because at last she saw what was happening to them and knew she had to stop it before their friendship was destroyed. She took Maggie's head in her hands so that they could look at each other. "No matter what happens, we'll always be friends. It will always be the same between us. I promise, Maggie."

Maggie looked into Daina's eyes and a forefinger came up, took one sliding tear off Daina's cheek. Then, sighing deeply, she put her head against Daina's breast and closed her eyes. Together, they rocked each other to sleep.

"Rita," El-Kalaam said, "untie the women."

Heather and Susan stood in front of the sofa as Rita, slinging her MP40 back over her shoulder, withdrew a serrated knife from her hip scabbard. She slit their bonds, stepped away from them.

El-Kalaam stood before them. "You will unshackle your feet when I am finished speaking. Is that understood?"

Heather stared at him, unblinking; Susan had her face partially averted. She wiped tears away from her eyes with the edge of one hand.

"What's the matter, Lady?" He took one quick step forward so that he was very close to Susan. "Do I smell bad?" She would not turn her face back. "Perhaps I do not have enough money for you to look into my eyes, uh?" He took one of her hands, glanced at the diamond rings there. "These are the eyes of a poor man, Lady. A dedicated man. A professional." He let go her hand. "That's something you would not understand, uh. Because dedicated men, we all smell bad." He gathered himself up. His face suffused with blood. Heather, watching him, made a move toward Susan but it was too late.

"You will answer me when I speak to you!" El-Kalaam bellowed, and struck Susan across the face. She reeled and, her ankles hobbled, toppled to the floor.

"Get up!" El-Kalaam said.

"Leave her alone!" Freddie Bock yelled. "Don't you strike her again!"

Fessi had been staring at the two women, licking his lips

as his eyes roved up and down the contours of their bodies. Now he scowled and, his movement a blur, smashed the heel of his fist into the side of Bock's thick neck. The industrialist cried out, staggered back.

"Swine!" Fessi hissed and spat onto Bock's shirtfront. But he looked from Bock back to Susan and a small smile played across his lips.

"Get up!" El-Kalaam said more harshly. He had paid no attention to this by-play. "Get up, get up!" He bent down, jerked the petite brunette up by her hair. She was sobbing.

"You women are all so useless. All you know how to do well is cry. You cannot do anything else satisfactorily."

"What about this woman here?" Heather said, indicating Rita. "She just killed—"

"Who gave you permission to speak?" El-Kalaam's eyes squinted, his head thrust out on its muscled neck.

"I just thought I'd—aghhhh!"

His huge hand gripped the sides of her jaw. He trembled with the pressure he was exerting on her. "No," he said. "You *can't* think. Remember that." He was trembling more now. "Cry, damn you!"

But Heather continued to stare into his eyes, unblinking. He took his hand away, leaving marks, white turning red. He slapped her hard: once, twice, three times in rapid succession. Tears started at the corners of her eyes as her head rocked.

"You see?" His voice turned soft. "You're like all the rest. Don't forget that, either."

He regarded them both. "The servants are gone." His tone had turned ironical. "They've served their purpose. They lost their lives so that you could be warned; so that you could all gain some small amount of wisdom." His head swiveled to take them all in. "Those that do"—he shrugged—"may survive." His voice grew loud and harsh. "Those who do not heed our warning will follow these two"—he kicked out, made contact with the butler's thigh—"into the lime pit out back."

He smiled and his entire countenance changed. His mouth was filled with gold caps. "But enough of such gloomy talk. Time is passing and there is a rumbling in my stomach. You two"—he pointed to Susan and Heather—"will do the cooking and the washing up for all of us." He grunted. "At least you can handle that. But"—his hand whipped out and he grasped

Susan's ringed hand around the wrist—"we can't have this, can we?" He took off her gold bracelets. "You can't do common housework with this much money on you." He twisted off her rings. Susan gave a little gasp as each item was removed from her.

El-Kalaam turned her hand palm up, gave her a broad smile. "Not used to being so naked, uh? Well, you'll have plenty of practice now."

"And what will you do with all that jewelry?" Ken Rudd said. "Distribute it among your cadre?"

"For Christ's sake," Thomas said, red-faced, "haven't you learned your lesson yet? Keep your big mouth shut and nothing will—"

Rudd clenched his jaw, turned on his boss. "If you don't stop that sniveling, I swear to God I'll fracture your jaw."

Thomas went pale, then flushed red. He looked around the room. All the hostages were staring at him. He squared his shoulders. "Don't you dare talk to me that way, Rudd. I was the one who took you in. Don't you feel any gratitude? I'll see you drummed out of the diplomatic service for such insubordination."

"We'll see who does what to whom," Rudd said calmly. "*If* we get out of here. You're a goddamned coward, Thomas. That's something the president's got to know."

Grinning, El-Kalaam approached them. "How the mighty American eagle's been laid low!" He laughed. "But the young man deserves an answer." He hefted the bounty he had pulled from Susan. "This is not for any one individual. It will go to aid the Palestinian people in their struggle against the Zionist terrorists."

"Ah, yes," Michel Emouleur said. "The talk of a true revolutionary."

El-Kalaam turned. "And that is what I am." He reached out, put his hand on the young attaché's shoulder. "I see that is something you understand, Frenchman, uh? I am not wrong."

"I understand the need of the Palestinian people to establish their homeland." Emouleur nodded. "The French hold no love for the Israelis."

"No," El-Kalaam said. "And why should you?" He put a forefinger against his lips, looking thoughtful. His finger tapped and his head cocked in that peculiar way of his.

All at once his knife was in his hand and he was cutting through the young man's ankle bonds. "I think you can do us more good this way than tied up." He kept his hand on Emouleur's shoulder. "You just talk to these people, my friend. Speak to them of the revolution and of freedom. The Jews," he said. "The Jews—"

"Yes, yes, yes, El-Kalaam," Rachel said. "We all see how it is. That's all you can do: feed on the hate that's inside everyone. Every Jew knows what it's like to have all hands turned against him. This is no different. Nothing ever changes."

"Paranoia was always a strong Jewish trait," El-Kalaam said. "I see you're no exception."

"I think you're confusing paranoia with persecution," Rachel said.

El-Kalaam waved a hand, dismissing her words. "Rita, take the women into the kitchen so they can fix us something to eat. Fessi, take the, uhm, the young American and the Englishmen. Let them take down the bathroom door and then we will set up the hot box, uh?"

As Heather and Susan went toward the kitchen, Rachel reached out a hand, put it on Heather's arm. "Courage," she said. Malaguez jerked her away.

"Just words," El-Kalaam said.

Rita prodded Heather in the small of the back with her machine pistol. "Move," she said. "Or he'll put you in the hot box. And you don't want that."

Daina was adrift on the night, as if she were floating over the rooftops of the city—the one long sprawling far-flung suburb. If I were in New York, she thought, I would scale the heights, ascend at the speed of sound to the top of the World Trade Center and there peer out over the twinkling lights as far away almost as stars, west across the Hudson to the New Jersey countryside, north past the highrises to the smoldering tenements of Harlem.

She could not go back to that empty house that did not even smell like her anymore. Rubens was in Palm Springs on business and, though he had told Maria to let Daina in, she had no desire to rumble around the house by herself.

Automatically she went west in the silver Merc, along the

brightlight Freeways—Foothill then Ventura—to Los Feliz,
Western, until she came onto Sunset four blocks east of the
Huntington Hartford Theatre. Without thinking, she made
a left onto La Cienega, found herself outside Las Palmas
Soundcorders where Chris and the band were recording the
new album.

She blinked several times as if waking from a dream and,
once realizing where she was, got out.

She could not, of course, gain entrance. The Heartbeats'
whereabouts were always kept secret although it did not seem
to matter. Leaks abounded and the need for security was
legitimate. The heavily muscled black man who barred the
door was only the first of several human barriers the band
put up. He would not let her through or even send a message
back to Chris. In fact he denied that the band was even there
at all.

His shaven skull shone blue in the buzzing fluorescent
lights of the entrance. He wore a flame-red shirt and a choc-
olate-brown suit. Around his bull neck hung a silver coke
spoon and a double-edged razor also in silver. He pushed his
wide pink palms at her, the paws of a beast, seemingly oblivious to her verbal protestations.

She was about to give it up when she caught a glimpse of
Nigel walking by behind his bulk.

"Hey, Nigel!" she shouted, jumping up so she could be seen.
"Nigel! It's me, Daina!"

The black man moved her out. "Hey now." His voice was
low but menacing. "Didn't you hear what I tol' you, mama?
Get yo'self out—"

"Hold on, Gerry." Nigel shouldered his way past the black
man. "Hey it *is* you!" He turned. "S'okay. She's okay."

The black man shrugged, stepped aside. He made no apology. Nigel took her by the hand, leading her down a short
flight of carpeted stairs. Immediately the lighting dimmed
and softened, the pastel walls curving away in the shadows.

He stopped by a soft-drink machine. "It's been a while,
Daina." He dug some change out of his jeans pocket, rolled
quarters into a slot. "Want a Coke?"

"No thanks."

"Come here t'see Chris?"

He half turned, peering at her over the rim of the waxed
paper cup. He sniffed, slurped greedily at the soda. She saw,

over his left shoulder, a half-shadowed figure. It had the body
of a bulldog with impossibly wide shoulders. It moved slightly
and the face came into a dim patch of lemon light. It was
properly craggy but curiously lacking in ferocity. The calm
gray eyes seemed to regard everything with the same studied
detachment. The first time he looked at her, Daina was quite
certain that those flat gray disks were lenses and that, had
she touched his stomach with the end of her finger, a color
Polaroid would have been delivered to her out of the un-
smiling slit of his mouth.

Nigel stirred, seeing the direction of her gaze. "S'only
Silka," he said softly. "Protects us from everyone." He danced
a little, as if throwing off excess energy, and the carved ivory-
and-black onyx fetish around his neck jigged against his collarbone with an audible jingle-jangle.

Daina shifted her gaze back to Nigel. "I hadn't seen everyone in a while—you know we're all so busy—"

He poked at her with a bony forefinger as if she were a
doll. "You becomin' a star, darlin', you are."

"—knew you were doing the album here so I—"

"Bugger that!" Nigel crunched down on the crushed ice,
grinding his teeth from side, up and down. "Uhm." He swallowed. "We're goin' on th' road in a week. That's where you
oughta see us, yeah!" He spread his legs like a legendary
gunfighter, hands at his narrow hips as if to draw a pair of
six-shooters. "On stage! Zow! Super tour. We haven't been on
th' road in, uhmm, almost year an' a half." He swayed back
and forth like a cobra being charmed by a melody only he
could hear. "It's like war—yeah, combat y'see. Y'get trained
for killin' for bein' there on th' front line hearin' all th'
pop-pop-pop of th' gunfire all round like it was th' air itself,
a new kinda, y'know, atmosphere. Then all at once smellin'
th' stench of burnin' flesh an' blood an' havin' th' *feel* of that
weapon always in your hands warm'n'close. Becomes a way
o' life." He crumpled the empty cup, threw it carelessly away.
Silka never took his eyes off them. "An' so then y'get sent
home—R&R some bleedin' shit like that y'know an' what
happens? Too bleedin' quiet for you t' sleep is what. Lie there
in th' crumpled bed wide awake just waitin' for th' sounds o'
the bullets screamin' past your head; solid thump o' th' mortar
fire; an' th' house it smells too clean, sweet—*gentle!* An' you
begin t'understand. It's your bleedin' hands innit. They're

empty—bloody empty an' without that weight in them they begin t'sweat an' y'can't make 'em stop, wipe 'em down your thighs, along your ribs, heat 'em, chill 'em, nuffin helps...."

At first she had found Nigel's preoccupation with war extremely discomforting even though Chris had given her ample warning before their first meeting. Nigel had, he had told her, one of the largest collections of World War II military paraphernalia in the world. His gun collection was monstrous. And since then he had begun to pick up here and there the deadly hardware of Vietnam because, he had said, they were far more sophisticated.

Nigel's deep-set eyes burned with an intense inner fire as he spoke to her. "Well that's what it's like when we're off th' road. Like bloody R&R. Mollycoddled at home. Don't know 'bout these other bastards but makin' records's boring as hell for me. Bleedin' four walls start t'close in on me y'know; sooner we get it over with, better I like it. Wanna go out there, y'know? Out in th' night where th' lights'n'th'mikes-'n'th'high stage standin' there all by itself with just us on top'n'those kids, fields of 'em, screamin' their guts out for us, waitin', stampedin', cryin' out, makin' that last rush at th' encore just to *touch*....

"In the middle of th' set I go out t' th' lip o' th' stage an' I c'n see th' first two rows. They're all standin' y'know—I mean *all* of 'em—wavin' their arms, carryin' roses. I kneel down an' they go crazy an' even 'cross' th' photographers' pit I c'n smell it—th' dope'n'th' beer'n-somethin' else I can't describe, somethin' that even after all these years still has that effect on me. It's th' smell of—youth: a *yearnin'* toward what we've become up there on that stage 'cause we've transcended our humanness y'know, we're no longer y'know Nigel'n'Chris 'n'Ian'n'Rollie *we're th' Heartbeats,* n' that reek of sex that comes across is so strong that I know, I know if I just touch m'self I'll come—all those massed exhalations like a wind blowin' at me from some dark doorway.

"I c'n look down an' see those faces shinin' in the light reflected off our follow spots. An' y'know what it's like?" His arms spread wide. "A great mirror reflectin' th' music back at us. Those faces shine like suns with an unearthly light. They're transfigured, yeah, in a state of grace an' then I feel like I c'n reach out an' when I touch 'em I c'n rearrange 'em into any shape I please just as if th' flesh'n'th' bones've been turned to putty.

"An' that's what's important. Not th' bleedin' bread—th' bread's only good for spendin' y'know. But *this*—bleedin' hell—this's what makes th' world go. An' my instrument's like that bloody M-16. When I take th' mobile keyboard during 'Rough Trade Nites' an' go roamin' I'm a grunt in the bleedin' jungle just lookin' for th' enemy so's I c'n blow his brains out."

Daina watched him as he spoke. He had the kind of face, she thought, that would seem odd in anyone who was not a performer. Like the excesses of a silent screen performance, Nigel's features, on close inspection, were overdone. There was too much of everything, as if two faces had mistakenly been crammed into one. His face was all angles, high-cheek-boned, limned in makeup more theatrical than cosmetic so that when he used eyeliner it did not make him seem effeminate so much as sinister. And it was precisely this image that early on in the Heartbeats' career he had latched on to and carefully nurtured.

Anyway, demonology was never far from his lyrics, skulking there, a permanent shadow as his songs stalked the seamy side of life. Blackhearted women, drug-induced euphoria, phantasmagorical street fights where the open switchblade shimmered the air, the ultimate punctuation, and the unfettered release of teenage aggression made up the gist of the tunes the Heartbeats were most famous for. And it was primarily this dark edge, perfectly honed, that had kept them current in an industry notorious for instant burnouts. No one—not even the most radical of the raw New Wavers coming out of England—thought to disparage the band as they regularly did the "Boring Old Farts"—the other supergroups—who had been around for years.

Nigel had always reminded Daina of a caged animal, restless at his core, impatient and dispirited by turns, as up and down as a yo-yo. He was certainly manic, she thought, in a way that was perfectly acceptable in a performer.

"Hey, catch this." He dug out a rolled-up polythene bag from inside the waistband of his jeans. "Mate o' mine just flew this in himself. Th' bastard's wall-eyed'n'crazy as a bedbug but I gotta admit he has th' best shit goin'." He dipped a thumb and forefinger in, rolled a flaky substance as dark

brown as chocolate. "Bet y'don't know, darlin'. This's pure
Cam-bleedin'-bodian buds. Tol' you this guy's looney. But I
should worry. He gets in, gets out. No one knows, right?
Here—try some. Blow your mind it will."

But instead of stuffing it into a pipe, he tried to stuff it
into her mouth. She turned her head away, put up her hands.
"Hey, no, Nigel. Not this time."

He shrugged, grinned, popped it into his mouth and began
to chew. "I wonder 'bout you sometimes." But he seemed to
be thinking about something else altogether.

"Don't you smoke it?"

He guffawed. "Jesus no, darlin'. This here shit's too good
for that. Y'eat it, man. Only way. Wait'n'see. S'no lie. Ah
hah!" He rolled some quarters into the slot, got another Coke,
ripped off the lid while he chewed on some more buds.
"Ummm, this's th' express. Get's me through this boring shit."
He swallowed, gulped at the soda, put the buds away. "Chris
is inside, diddlin' with th' computer. I always split for that.
Christ, he takes this recordin' shit too seriously, y'know. We
did okay in sixty-four when we had two soddin' tracks instead
o' the sixty-four we got now. Bloody hell! What we gonna do
with sixty-four bleedin' tracks, use the Berlin Philharmonic?
We're a bleedin' rock'n'roll band not some arty-farty bunch
o' nances. Hell, we been through all that shit, come an' gone
in sixty-eight—I mean who cared y'know? We went along
with *Sergeant Pepper* an' all—Chris an' Lennon bein' such
buddies in those days an' all. But screw that—was a long
bleedin' time ago y'know? It's not our kinda music, not
rock'n'roll. Our business's blowin' th' top o' your skull off. In
th' streets, man. Barricades bristlin' with hardware. We're
th' bleedin' gutter, mate, I c'n tell you, not th' *campus*. Eyes
all glazzy afta one of ours, y'know? Ears buzzin'. Rockin'n'-
reeling it is. That's it all right. What life's all about, innit,
th' gutter?"

The sound of the studio door being opened gave him pause.
A blast of recorded music blatted at their ears, abruptly wiped
to silence, and the garble of the tape being rewound. She
could hear Chris' voice: "There." And the music starting up
again at precisely the same spot as the door whooshed shut
with a kind of pneumatic finality.

"Hey, Tie," he said, smiling.

A woman stood regarding them, her back to the door. She

was of medium height, as slim-hipped almost as Nigel. She stood with one hip jutting out, a pose that in anyone else would have been characterized as sleazy. But in Tie one saw only the darkest of overtones, some deep and abiding chill.

She had a failed face, the countenance of a fallen angel: striking and triangular, the wide European mouth, the high cheekbones, the stiletto-thin nose.

Magnificent would have been the first word to come to mind had it not been for her eyes. Black as coal, they defeated the whole, placed wrong on that face or, perhaps, just a little bit too small.

She wore a strapless waist-cincher that thrust her breasts up and out lasciviously, and a black raw-silk skirt, slit to the thigh on both sides, revealing a deliberate glimpse of satin garter belt.

They all called her Tie but her real name was Thaïs. She came toward them, her odd, stony eyes on Daina. "I was wondering where you were so long, darling." She did not look at Nigel though her words were obviously for him.

"You remember Daina, don't you?" Nigel said. "Chris'n'Maggie's friend."

"How could I forget?" Her heavy lips curled upward in a smile that did not reach her eyes. "Why'd she come? You know we never allow—"

"Hey, c'mon. Hey." He put his arm through hers, close to her side so that the back of his hand pressed against the bulge of her breast. "Daina's a friend, Tie. Come all th' way down here, huh?" He winked at Daina. "Works her butt off all day, comes down here for a bit of a lark. Hey. Hey." He danced a little, linked with Tie.

"I'm going to the ladies' room," she said. Now her baleful gaze swept past Daina, focused on him. "Want to come along?" Her voice was deep and husky. It was obvious she had had theatrical training even if Daina had not known her European screen origins.

He grinned at her. "Sure. Yeh. Always ready." With an effort he broke away from her stare, turned to Daina. "You go on in, if y'want. Chris an' th' guys'd be glad t'see you. Ha! Rollie's got pic o' you on th' inside o' his kit. That right, Tie? Ha ha!" She pulled at him and, together, they disappeared around a slow turning in the tunnellike corridor.

Inside the door, the studio was all blond-wood planking

laid obliquely along the walls and lacquered so it shone, interspersed with pale blue soft trapezoidal acoustic panels.

She stood three steps down, at the verge of the control room with its outsized bank of dials, switches, faders—sixty-four of them, one for each track—and patch-in terminals, all computer-controlled.

Beyond the double glass panels, she could see the studio proper, filled with the band's massive amps with their glowing ruby lights, various instruments, yards of thick snaking cables, boom mikes. In one corner was a small acoustically enclosed booth with a window for vocal recording. Against the back wall a concert grand piano stood, a padded khaki drop cloth over its top and sides. A couple of young lanky recording assistants were on their knees working at a cable outlet, preparatory to recording the last of the album's instrumental overdubs.

Still in the shadows of the doorway, Daina paused and thought about Nigel. "He gives me the willies," she had said to Maggie after her first meeting with him.

"Don't be silly." Maggie had smiled reassuringly at her. "It's only a pose, darling. Quite a successful one, I'll admit, but only that. He dotes on it. All this demonology bullshit—I think he got into it originally because of Tie. The facade of sensationalism. I'm perfectly sure that's why she has all those affairs with other women. It makes good copy—"

"The busts would be more than enough," Daina had said archly.

"Oh not for him. Nigel needs this kind of thing twenty-four hours a day. And of course Tie feeds it into him just as fast as he can take it." She shrugged her shoulders. "But I mean how evil could he be? He and Chris've known each other all their lives."

"Hey, Daina, how are ya?" Rollie, coming in through the connecting door to the studio proper, grinned at her, came up the steps, gave her a hard but affectionate bear hug. He wore a pair of torn jeans and a blue and white Dodgers warm-up jacket. When he was in town, he was at all their home games, more often than not watching from the dugout.

Rollie went off to speak to Chris who was huddled together with Pat, the band's engineer, developing the computer program for a final mix. Then he went out into the studio, crossing the snaked landscape to his drum setup, began to go over it carefully, tapping experimentally on each drum and cymbal in turn with one drumstick tip, making adjustments where he thought it necessary.

The control room was bilevel, a lower section abutting the front of the control panel along which was a comfortable couch and a small table. Daina went down to it and sat. Dim lights shone over her head from recessed pits in the deep-brown acoustic ceiling. She heard the sharp hiss of the spinning tape, the brief flare of backward notes like a child's tumbled conversation with herself. It stopped and out of the absolute silence afforded by the room there came a blare of music so loud it made her jump. The massive speakers—the same ones, she saw, that Chris had at home—were mounted on either side of the room over her head. She heard Chris' voice saying quietly, "Okay."

Silence stole in again for a moment, then a chair creaked and Pat said, "I gotta go take me a piss an' stretch my legs. Be back in a bit." The door to the hall hissed shut behind him.

Daina turned around, got up on her knees. The top half of her head protruded above the machinery.

"Hey, is that you?"

"Maggie not here?"

He shook his head. "Got a call earlier, she said. Maybe to do with a part."

"That's great." For a moment she contemplated telling Chris what Maggie had accused them of, then thought better of it. Damn her, she thought, for thinking that. She's so insecure sometimes.

Chris nodded. "Maybe now she'll get off my back. Christ, she's drivin' me round th' bend, she is."

"She's just worried."

"Yah." He shook out a cigarette, lit it with a practiced snap of his lighter. "Ain't she always?" His face got fierce as he lurched toward her over the control panel. "You gotta believe in sumthin', Dain, t'get anywhere." He clenched his fist. "You gotta believe in yourself 'cause all round you are people just dyin' t' put th' knife in; who'll love t' tell you what a screw-up you are." He was very close to her and his eyes darted back and forth over her face as if searching for something. He laughed, abruptly changing the mood, sat back in his chair. "That's why we get along so well, you'n'me, huh?"

Daina nodded. "That's part of it."

"You don't see me as a freak; you ain't out t' grab ahold o' th' comet's tail." He laughed again. "Hell, no! You got a comet o' your own." He stubbed out the cigarette, half-smoked, produced a small metal cannister. "Wanna little blow?"

She shook her head. "I ran into Nigel outside. He tried to ply me with loco weed."

"Uh. He's in some bloody foul mood t'night. Must be a fuckin' full moon." He sniffed up a tiny spoonful of coke.

Daina, watching him, said, "Why don't you get into a really healthy habit like drinking."

"Ha." Chris pinched his nose, ran the white residue on his fingertips along his gums. "Uhm, that's purely a prole vice. They put m' dad away for it once. Bloody rummy before he ran away t'sea. It's what cured him, really."

"The sea?"

"Nah. Bein' away from me mum." He laughed without any humor. As if his words had a bitter taste. He eyed her. "Sure you don't want any o' this? Nah. You're a good girl, you are."

She laughed. "Got to think of my image."

"So do I," he said, taking another spoonful. "Here's to image!" He sniffed mightily and the powder was gone. He put the cannister away, wiped his nose. "Yeh, well, better you didn't take any o' Nigel's weed; you'd be right out of it by now."

"He still makes me nervous," she said, "after all this time."

"Who, Nigel? Hell, he's only a little boy tryin' t' make his mark on th' grown-up world."

"That's what I mean. How he loves his guns!"

"Oh, that. Well, y'gotta know him as long as I do, t'understan' that. See, t' him, everythin's fleetin', insubstantial. But a gun he can hold in his hand. It's got weight, it's got power. It's potent. He pulls th' trigger an' kills an animal. He can feel it, touch its coolin' fur. He knows what he's done."

She shuddered. "It's reprehensible."

"Why?" He aimed his forefinger, cocked his thumb, aimed and shot at an imaginary target. "Bang! Bang! He don't kill people."

"Sometimes he sounds as if he wishes he could."

"Oh, well, that's Nigel all over, innit? The sod was always th' most image-conscious of us lot. Sure." He nodded. "An' I oughtta know—we grew up on th' streets o' Manchester t'gether." He lit another cigarette, took one puff and ignored it. "That's what comes from not knowin' your dad, never havin' enough money t' pay th' rent, never knowin' what you'd come home t'find."

Chris took one last drag, dropped the cigarette away from his yellowed calloused fingertips. "I remember when we were sharin' a flat in th' old days when we was just able t' scrape up th' odd gig. Filthy bit of a thing one flight down in a basement smelled of old cardboard'n'piss so bad I useta put a clothespin on me nose before I could fall asleep.

"One night I calls me mum—didn't have no phone; froze our bollocks off at th' corner in winter—an' she tells me, 'Son your dad's back. Just nipped round t' see us. He wanster see you. Brought you a Christmas present he did.'

"I got white in th' face, came back t' th' flat, didn't even hear Nigel say, 'What's th' matter, mate?' an went off t' me mum's flat.

"Waited in th' street till th' bugger came down th' steps. Then I bust him in th' face, broke his nose so's th' blood's all ova the place. Teeth go flyin.' Kick him twice in th' balls hard as I can. Nigel had t' drag me off th' bleeder.

"So me ol' man's a mess on th' pavement y'see, all blood an' teeth an' all, moanin' away. Nigel's got holda me an' I'm shakin' like a leaf an' he throws me aside, that crazy bleeder, an' he whips out a gun—a German Luger—an' aims it at me ol' man's head. I made a grab for th' arm, made it just as he squeezes th' trigger. Boom!

"Like a bomb explodin', bits o' macadam blew into our faces an' I said t' Nigel, 'Are you bleedin' off your nut, mate? Y' coulda killed him.' And he said, 'So what? Look what he did t' you an' your mum.'

"But it was loyalty, y'know. Christ, he was crazy t' try but I understood what he was about." He looked at her. "Know what I mean?" He grunted. "Had reason enough, I reckon. His ol' man left his mum alone t' fend for herself. Worked all her life."

"What ever happened to your father?" she asked.

"Funny, that. Course, he packed it in; went away an' I never saw him again. But coupla weeks later, me mum said t' me, 'Heard there was a bit ova fracas in th' street while ago. You have a fight with your dad?' 'He told you,' I said.

But she shook her head. 'Never said a word, luv. Was Mrs. Faithfull downstairs who saw it.' An' I thought, How's that. The bleeder never said a word. That gave me a feelin' inside somehow, all warm like.

"An' me mum said, 'Son, it's about time I told you all about your dad.' He's a seaman, she told me. Had to ship out. What could she do? Stand in th' way of him earnin' his livelihood? Not bloody likely I c'n tell you. But every month, she said, just like clockwork comes a packet o' money from him. Course she left out th' rummy part—had t'find that out on me own.

"He's meant to've drowned off the Cape of Good Hope in seventy-seven. Mum showed me th' letter his captain sent. He went over th' side in a longboat in th' middle of a bleedin' storm to rescue two crewmen. Swept away in an instant, 'like the sea had spirited him away,' the captain wrote." He snorted. "A bleedin' hero, see what it got him." Chris' head went back and his eyes closed. He breathed evenly and deeply as if he were asleep but his finger flipped a toggle switch and music shot from the enormous speakers over their heads.

Daina slipped down onto the couch, losing sight of him. She put her arms over her head, closed her eyes, allowed the notes to beat against her eyelids like patterns of light.

As if from far away she heard the door open and someone walk in as the music faded out into a soft tape hiss.

"Ah, Chris, there you are."

It was not Pat, who had a pronounced Southern drawl. This voice had the clipped consonants, the utterly flat vowels she associated with the area around L.A.

"What, may I ask, is going on here, anyway?" the voice went on. "Every goddamned night it's another fight between you lazy bastards I gotta put right." Someone lit a cigarette. "Chris, at the risk of becoming redundant, let me go over this with you again. If this album's not completed and mastered inside a week, we're going out on tour with no new product. You know what that means? Not even a goddamn single to—"

"Oh, go screw yourself, Benno. In th' long run it's gonna make no difference at all."

"That's where you're wrong, buddy boy. Why don't you just stick to the music and let me handle the business end, all right?"

"That's th' problem, coach. It's all a bloody business now."

"Oh, you break my heart, you know that? Without the business this group'd be bankrupt. You spend the money before it even comes in. Christ only knows how much goes up your nose."

"Get out! I don't spend that much."

"I'm telling you right now, Chris, to get this album wrapped up."

"But it's all down t'me, don't you see that? No one else was prepared for this one—or haven't you noticed? I'm th' one expected t'get it all together but I mean Nigel came in here holdin' his dick an' Ian didn't even want t' listen t' th' new tunes I'd written."

"Now listen, Chris—"

"No, by Christ, you bleedin' listen, you sod! I'm fuckin' tired of carryin' this band around on my shoulders. I'm bloody sick of takin' everyone else's responsibilities on. I mean why should they bother? They know bloody well it'll get done without them."

"What are you saying?"

"Th' situation's all bollixed up an' I want out."

"I see."

"'I see'? What th' hell does that mean?"

"This's the first time I'm hearing it. What d'you want me t'say?"

"Oh come on. I'm hip t' your—"

"You can't leave, Chris. You have responsibilities—"

"Don't you go tellin' me my responsibilities, mate!"

"I was talking about all the kids—"

"You're a real hard case, ain't you, Benno? Oh yes you are. A real corker. You don't for a minute give a shit about th' kids, do ya? Naw. Naw. It's the bleedin' income."

"Chris, the Heartbeats haven't been successful for, uhm, seventeen years with no reason. Even you can see that."

"Yeh. Sure."

"It's the music. The kids dig the music. You start deviating from, well, what everyone's gotten used to and it's disaster time. For all of us. For Christ's sake I'm not thinking about myself. We're a goddamned *industry* now. Lotta people depend on what happens from album to album. Now I've heard some of your own tracks, this new stuff you're—"

"Now we've come to the heart of the bleedin' darkness haven't we, mate?"

"Pat played me the roughs—"

"*My* music—"

"I got a right to hear it, y'know. You forgotten who the hell I am?"

"I could never do that, Benno."

"All right then."

"The music's none o' your business—"

"But it *is* my business when I think it might affect—"

"Who died an' made you God?"

"You rotten bastards think you've got the monopoly on Goddom or what? Certain decisions've got t'be made. That's why I'm here."

"Yeh, an' the music's none o' your—"

"*Career* decisions, Chris—"

"Listen you bastard—"

"This one's already been made."

Silence enfolded the control room, thick and choking.

Daina's eyes flew open as the fire burned brighter in her chest. Anxiety rose inside her like a fettered bird.

"What th' hell're you on about?"

"Just what I've said. The band will not allow you out of your contract."

"The band?"

"There was a vote, you see."

"Without me? Who called it?"

"Nigel—and I. It needed getting done. There had to be a clarification of—"

"Get the hell outa here, man. You disgust me."

"That won't solve anything."

"Out, Benno. Now. In another minute you'll be crawlin'...."

"When you calm down you'll see—"

"You ain't gettin' any more music outa me."

"Chris—"

"Not one bleedin' note! Not until I'm free."

"There are legal measures but I don't want to go into them now. When you—"

"Know what, Benno? All of a sudden, I don't feel so good y'know? Might be serious. Somethin' like infectious hepatitis. That means six months at least I'm outa commission."

"I can get a doctor to—"

"This album. Th' new single—th' bleedin' *tour*, mate. Boom-boom."

Out of the silence Benno's voice was filled with an odd calmness. "I don't for a minute think you're serious about any of this, Chris. Once you get out on the road, San Francisco next week, you'll feel altogether different."

"You just ain't listenin'. I'm through with th' lot o' you."

"You're making a serious judgmental error, Chris."

"Jesus, you're beginnin' t' talk like that bleedin' battery o' lawyers o' yours. Split. Just split."

"I'll talk to you in a couple of days then."

Daina heard the door open, sigh shut, then Chris' exhaled voice, "Jesus bleedin' Christ!"

She sat up like a jack-in-the-box, her head spiraling higher.

"You still there?" He came around from behind the wall of the console. "Yeah." He grinned at her. "Th' only one. Sure emptied out in here all of a sudden." He rubbed at the tip of his nose. "That bastard manager!" Abruptly he gave a barking laugh, shrugged his shoulders. "Oh, what the hell. Nothin' I c'n do 'bout it t'night. What say we get outa here but quick."

He took her to The Dancers, a members-only club off Rodeo Drive, right around the corner from Georgio's. Inside, it was a palace of mirrored rooms. The main one was round, cinctured by a Lucite bar. It had a see-through floor below which grew a tropical torrent of foliage. Looking down caused almost instant disorientation. The walls were black enamel, covered by electronicized moss, skeins of patterned colored lights, moving in endless waves. Every hour, as if to mark time, the dancers in the center of the floor were drenched in sparkling silver "stardust" drifting down from some hidden source.

They pushed their way through the crowd and in the sweat and frenzy and constant cacophony of the music lost themselves in an orgy of movement.

They seemed oblivious in their intensity to the stares of the tanned and painted faces bobbing wide-eyed next to them like sampans drawn to the side of an imperial junk, begging, dark lips pressed to pink ears so shouts could be heard over the beat.

Soon after, the cameras arrived and, after certain clandestine phone calls from the management, a peculiar school of pilot fish arrived. They seemed to survive for just this purpose—to be near, to rub up against, to be at the same function as, to nick one more notch in the tired Fiorucci jumpsuit, but always to gaze lovingly at, to drink in the aura, the emanations, the electricity, like latter-day vampires feeding off sustenance without substance.

Chris whirled Daina around, his hands on her hips as they gyrated, sweat flipping off their faces like cascades from a waterfall while below them the furled fronds of the dwarf palms dipped and swayed as if they, too, found the rhythmic pulses irresistible.

And still they danced on, with Chris' T-shirt dark with sweat; with Daina's blouse clinging damply to her skin, unmindful of the flashbulbs popping all around them like shooting stars and the noise of the place like a constant roll of thunder so that, at some time unknown to either of them, the music ceased to be music anymore, became a kind of pulsonic grunting, a percussion they picked up through the soles of their shoes and was all they had to guide them on long after their ears gave out with a soundless shout and packed it in, exhausted with overload.

At some time they found themselves at one section of the bar. Chris bought them enormous gin-and-tonics, which they proceeded to pour over each other's head rather than drink. They laughed and snorted, drinking greedily of drinks they could not taste—all the harsh smoke had rendered their taste buds insensate. Chris threw his head back and she watched curiously his Adam's apple bounce up and down before he scooped the shaved ice out of the bottom of his glass, thrust it down the front of her blouse.

She jumped, screaming a scream no one could hear over the din and, whirling, Chris drew her out again onto the floor where there was no more room as the shoals closed in for a good look, fascinated, moving a bit, the music inescapable, hips twitching, breasts quivering, flanks out-thrust and tense.

And Daina was lost, captivated by everything that was happening to her, as if each sight, each sound, each smell was a bolt of a living energy lancing through her. A shell had burst open without her knowing, its fragile skin ripped open by forces now far too strong to contain. She was plugged in, connected, part of the delicate powerful circuit and she trembled at the energy she felt.

For a time she lost Chris to the back rooms which, she surmised, were filled with pinched faces, frosted hair, cocaine, and Quaaludes. But that did not stop her. She was surrounded by music so loud, percussive, prismatic, it was like an injection straight to the heart.

Her mind was a dance, unbounded by time or space so that she kept slipping away from here to a room without light three floors down, sunk into the ground like a cesspool, guarded by concrete dogs; to the rubble of an urban street filled with wire-mesh, chain-link fences guarding mounds of broken brick, bonfires in ashcans and breaking shadows along sooty, windowed walls.

And she thought, I am, I am, *I am!*

Chris returned, kissed her, hugged her, whirling her back out onto the disappearing floor and back here, below their blurred feet, the forest bowed deferentially to their passage. And the music buzzed around her brain, kept them alive and moving, a nonstop nightcoach journey, as if they were both attempting to flee Los Angeles without ever really leaving.

Just another illusion that, in the soft light of dawn, seemed never to have existed at all.

It was still on Old Malibu Road, so early that all they could hear was the sea hissing on their left. Daina braked before turning in and parking the car.

Chris was slumped against the right-hand door, asleep. She shook him gently and his eyes opened halfway. "Uh?"

"We're home."

"Home?"

She got out, pulled the door open for him. "Yes. Home to Maggie."

"Maggie. Oh yeah." He rubbed his fingers in his eyes. "Musta been dreamin'." She had to lean in to help him up and out. "Was in Sussex." He was talking half to himself. "Haven't been there in a while." He leaned heavily against her.

"Chris, I've got to go to work."

"Saw Jon wavin' t' me. From th' kitchen. Just liftin' his arm. Wavin', wavin' like he was beckonin' me. Odd."

She began to walk him slowly to the front door. "What's odd about that?"

His head swung around and he almost stumbled as they

hit the sand. His large eyes stared at her half crossed. "Jon's dead," he said thickly.

She nodded, leading him up the steps to the door. It needed a lot of patience. "Jon died a long time ago." She said it as a mother might to quiet an unhappy child.

Chris nodded, broke away from her on the terrace for a moment, clutching at the wooden railing. He weaved, almost tripping over one of the potted plants. All color drained from his face, his mouth dropped open. Daina was afraid of what he might do. Then he seemed to regain control of himself. He turned toward her so that his back was against the railing. "Long time ago." His voice was only a croak, an eerie echo of what she had said. "I was there."

It was enough, she thought. She went to where he stood and took him up, bringing him to the door. "I know," she said sympathetically.

"You don't know nuthin."

She managed to get her left hand on the doorknob, turned it. It wouldn't give and she thought it was locked until she realized that it was because she was using her left hand. She turned in the other direction and the door swung open.

She half dragged him into the foyer.

"Maggie?" she called.

All the lights were on and Daina squinted against the glare. Outside, in the dawn, occupied as she had been with getting Chris into the house, she had not noticed.

They stumbled into the living room and she stopped dead. Chris, whose head had been lolling against her shoulder, roused himself, his dark eyes flicking back and forth.

"Jesus!" Daina breathed.

"What th' hell happened here?"

The room was a mess. The long leather sofa was on its side, the cushions and back slit over and over in slashes long enough to have been made with a machete. The Oriental rug was chewed up as if by a rabid animal. The bookshelves had been cleared, pages wantonly ripped out of volumes, a snow-fall of literature covering everything. Daina saw a broken-spined copy of Joseph Conrad's *Lord Jim*, a book on the Tarot without a cover, on and on.

The enormous stereo system had been beaten in, the metal and glass fascias of the components dented and shattered, the great speakers skeletal husks within which only ripped wire hung forlornly. At least this was true of the one nearest them. The other had been spun around and now faced toward the dining room.

"Maggie!" Daina moved toward the dining room, seeing the smoked-glass tabletop shattered and spiderwebbed with cracks. She stepped over a litter of pages from a biography of Cervantes, overlaying bits of wood and twisted metal, and that is when she saw what was inside of the far speaker.

At one time it had been a thinking, feeling human being. She had to keep telling herself that in order to believe it, for what confronted her now was a mockery of anything even remotely human.

The face had been shattered as efficiently as the tabletop so near it. It was only half covered by the hair that fell down over it. Patches of bare, reddened scalp showed that great clumps had been viciously ripped out. One shoulder must have been broken when the body was stuffed into the empty innards of the speaker box and almost certainly both legs fractured. Pink and white bone protruded rudely from the flayed and ruined flesh. Blood was everywhere, drying where it was not pooled.

Daina screamed and immediately put her white knuckles in her mouth. She bit down but felt nothing. Her nails dug into her palm.

"Dain, what is it?" Chris came up beside her and she felt the warmth of his body quite distinctly, as if the space directly in front of her was as frigid as the depths of outer space. She felt her stomach lurch menacingly and she coughed and, tasting the acidic sourness, began to gag. Oh, my God, oh, my God. The phrase bounded over and over in her brain, which suddenly seemed monstrously empty of everything but that hideous sight. Terror was creeping in on silent cat's feet and she felt as if some part of her vital life force had been ripped from her.

Oh, my God, oh, my God! It rebounded like a handball from soft wall to soft wall. She could not stop it; could not even make any sense of it. It was as if she were abruptly thinking in some alien tongue.

Chris' hands gripped her shoulders painfully. "Agghh!" he screamed. "Maggie!"

Daina had known it, of course. That was why her mind had been jabbering on like a loon. But until he vocalized it,

she had not allowed the thought into her consciousness. Now
it would not get out. Like some horrific uninvited guest, some
monstrous plague carrier staggering in to infect everyone
around it, this thing, this bit of knowledge that she desperately did not want to assimilate, tore at her relentlessly with
talons of steel and a beak of iron, rending her flesh, exposing
her heart to the acid of the air.

She feel down on her knees before the grotesque boxed
thing and sobbed. She tried to turn her head away, to close
her eyes, and could do neither. She was pinned there, staring,
crying while Chris stood impotently over her, bellowing into
the new morning that had brought horror and rage and pain
to them both.

PART TWO

DEEPER THAN THE NIGHT

*There's a river flowing
  by a willow tree
    when you find you're there
    remember me....*

—Bryan Ferry,
  "My Only Love"

4

Baba. It was the only name he had. But of course if he had another he would not have told her.

Baba picked up on her the third night she came by. He was a mammoth man with a great woolly beard and a nose so wide it seemed to cover the whole center of his creased face. His skin was the color of mahogany except for a line of puckered flesh the color of café au lait just under his left eye. He knew a lot of French as did she but he had not learned it at the High School of Music and Art as she had. He said he had lived in Paris years ago but she was never that sure. More likely he had picked it up inside Attica or somewhere.

In this early autumn of 1968, it was already cooling off rapidly even here in the heart of Manhattan—one Friday it had been in the high 70's and three days later winter had begun its grip; somewhere over the weekend autumn had come and gone without being noticed. Baba wore a Navy peacoat with those large plastic buttons with an anchor carved in their center and a pair of white chino bellbottoms. But he was no sailor.

Everyone who hung out along the 42nd Street strip, extending from Broadway to Ninth Avenue, had a spot and

Baba's was just outside the Selwyn Theatre on the south side of the street. This, Daína soon found out, was by far the rougher side. It was on the calmer north side that once in a great while cops—always in pairs—could be seen, strolling, having a smoke. They would only venture onto the south side to stop a brawl inside one of the movie grind houses and then it was only in packs of a comforting size.

There was never any problem at the Nova Burlesque House, next door and one flight up from the Selwyn's tacky marquee. Its ancient blue-green neon sign buzzed constantly and its 8-by-10 black-and-white glossies of bimbos who never appeared on that tiny stage, who had never even been near New York, fluttered tiredly in the sooty breeze off the Hudson. But then the Nova had its own security force.

Baba, standing outside the Selwyn, pushed anything he could get his hands on—as it turned out, there was an appalling variety. Publicly he hawked loose joints, speed, acid cut with cheap speed. But privately, if he knew you, he was a source of just about anything. Daina had not even heard of a third of the shit he trafficked in.

It is difficult to say just what he saw in her right off. Certainly she was beautiful but he could get—and did get— all the women he needed. And then again, as she found out later, he had a distinct propensity for Asian women. So what was it that made him speak to her as she walked by him for a third time in her plain brown corduroy jacket, faded Levi's stuffed into black calf-high boots with tips so pointed she thought of them as lethal weapons.

"Whatchew think yo doin', mama?"

She stopped, looked into his ursine face. Her hands were dug deep into the pockets of her jacket; it was too early in the season to have thought about gloves. His liquid eyes regarded her curiously. Their pupils and irises were the same color, taking up almost all of the available space so that just a touch of the surrounding yellow could be seen.

"Not doing anything," she told him.

"Ain't yo got nowheres else t' go?"

"I like walking here."

Baba laughed deep in his throat, his eyes crinkling up, almost disappearing in the dark flesh of his face. "Shit!" His features hardened and he turned his head, hawked and spat.

"Yo cruisin' fo' a bruisin', mama, yo keep this up." She frowned. "Whatchew see in this per-fumed garden anyway?"

"Nobody but me," she said, "to answer to."

The tip of his thick tongue came out, shockingly pink against the almost-black lips. "Uhm. That right?" His eyes rolled, roved up and down her body with such intense carnality that she found herself blushing. "Prime cut o' white meat like yo be picked up by any one o' these sumbitches toolin' roun' here. They chew yo up, mama, spit yo out so yo doan know yo'self no mo'."

She glanced apprehensively around at the passing throngs of blacks and Puerto Ricans. Here and there whites hurried by. There was laughter, loud bantering. A couple of long lean blacks ran down the block toward Eighth Avenue, ignoring the red light on the corner. There was a squeal of brakes, shouts and cursing.

"You mean it's a tough world."

He shook his head. "Yo picked the place, mama. Some bad dudes hang 'round here. Mighty evil cats as I say. Yo gots t'be careful. Whatchew wanna be twitchin' that pretty white ass o' yours out here with us outlaws, huh? Yo do much better at home where yo' white boyfrien' will take care o' yo."

"I told you I liked it here."

His face darkened and he squinted one eye at her. "Shit, mama, yo ain't cruisin' any dark meat, uh?"

"Huh?"

"Niggas, mama. Do niggas turn yo on? 'Cause sho nuff yo gonna end up with a face fulla blood, some handsome dude with a pea-green suit come sweep yo off yo' feet, beat yo then spread them pretty legs o' yours, oooh. Yo go on home now."

"I'm not," she said stolidly, "cruising. I'm here because . . . I can't be where I should be anymore."

"I tell yo this, mama, yo sure as shit doan belong here."

She stared up into his face, dug her hands, now curled into fists, deeper into her pockets. She moved back and forth from one foot to the other. Her cheeks were rosy with the cold, and when she and Baba spoke their words were accompanied by tiny excited bursts of steam from their open mouths. "This what you do all day?" she said.

He snorted. "Fuck no. By day I got me a seat on the New York Stock Exchange. This's on'y a sideline y'see." He tapped the side of his head, the fingertip lost within the woolly hair.

"It's this rascal plate upside m'head, mama, did me in. Steel 'stead o' brains is all. They all dribbled out during the war. Te'bble shame."

Even she could tell an Amos'n'Andy sham and she giggled at his clowning. "I'll bet you weren't in the war. You're not nearly old enough."

"Oh, yo' wrong 'bout dat, right enough. Coulda gone to Nam 'cept I'se out here in the ozone doanchew know. Army doan want no outlaws. Couldn't find me anyways even if they'd a mind to try. Come down here, they'd be shown the combat zone for sure, huh!" He slapped his huge hand against his meaty thigh.

A pair of Puerto Rican youths stopped, looked at Baba. Their faces were as smooth as cream, their long black shining hair pulled back into ponytails. They were in uniform: ragged jeans, short baseball jackets. One had on a pair of Adidas—"For fast getaways," Baba said later—the other, scuffed black winkle-picker boots. "Hold a sec," Baba said and went over to deal.

The street around her blinked and semaphored, all its brash multicolored neon crawling its endless skein through the night, manhandling the darkness. A gritty wind whipped down the gutter, whirling litter like forlorn handkerchiefs mistakenly raised in salute. She sniffed the stench that was part of any west wind, the industrial wastes from the New Jersey landfills.

Baba took a handful of green for a couple of tightly twisted polythene bags filled with yellows and reds. A baby-blue Caddy tooled by as slowly as if it had engine trouble. It had a four-foot whipcord antenna, gaudy spiked custom wheel covers and more chrome than any three cars put together.

Daina screwed up her eyes, trying to peer into the interior but the dark green tint of the windows made it next to impossible. She saw only a dark moonlike face and, next to that, on the passenger's side, a Medusa's head of braided black hair.

Baba, finished with the Puerto Ricans, bent down as the window whipped silently down. He had to bend almost double to stick his head in. Baba spoke for some time but Daina could not hear what he said. From somewhere he produced a small flat brown-paper package. His hand went in with it, emerged with a roll of bills. Baba said a couple of more words and stood up. The Caddy began to pick up speed, the window whipping back into place like a zipper.

When Baba strolled back across the pavement to where she stood, she said, "So what are you going to do, stand here all night?"

"What yo up to, mama?" He stared hard at her. "Yo doan know me a'tall. I could be serious trouble."

She smiled. "I don't think so." She reached up, touched his face. "What would you do to me? Steal my money? You can have it." He was so startled that he could think of nothing to say. "And what's the worst? Rape me?"

"Huh! Like as not lotta dudes 'round here be off like a shot behind that one. Yo ain't gonna find no help. What the fuck's matter with yo, mama? Ain't yo got no sense a'tall? Shit! Din yo' mama learn yo nuthin?"

"I don't think you're anything like the others you've been telling me about."

"Sheeit, mama! I'se just like the rest. Just bigga than most, thas'all."

"Let's get something to eat, okay?"

"Hey. I could take yo by the hand right now, up there back o' the burlesque house, make yo sorry yo came down here." His thrust-out head was quite close to hers and his yellow eyes seemed to have taken on the feral glow of the nocturnal predator.

"C'mon," she said. "Let's grab a bite, huh?"

His hand grasped hers in a powerful grip and he began to pull her toward the shabby entrance to the Nova. She made no attempt to resist him.

"I'm gonna fuck yo silly, mama," he growled, angry now. "Yo gonna need a wheelchair to move around afta I'm through with yo."

"It won't be rape," she said, "if I want it."

That brought him up so short. He whirled to face her, glaring. "Whatchew up to now, mama?"

"Just letting you know you can't rape me."

"Well, I sure as hell mean to give it all I gots."

She turned her head up. "Okay."

He stared down at her serious face for what seemed a long time. Then he threw his head back and laughed longer and harder than he had in years.

* * *

Detective-Lieutenant Robert Walker Bonesteel stepped carefully around the debris. "Okay, split," he said to the pair of uniformed cops without looking at them.

They had been the first to arrive at the house, two seasoned street dogs whose seamed faces spoke volumes to the more than casual observer. Still, it was likely they had been expecting the run-of-the-mill celebrity overdose when they came into the living room because the balding one had said, "Christ Jesus!" when he got his first look at Maggie's corpse and the other one had turned right away, as white as a sheet.

However, a moment later it was back to business: their notebooks were out, their pencils poised as they began to ask questions in their odd, mechanical voices, as if all self was submerged beneath a metallicized exterior.

That was when the tall man had come in through the door. He had dirty-blond hair and very wide-apart blue-gray eyes. He was slim-hipped, elegantly dressed, and moved with some authority. He kept his hands in his pockets.

The balding cop grunted, flipped closed his notebook. "Pack it up," he said disgustedly. "The Homicide boys are here."

"And not a moment too soon," Lieutenant Bonesteel had said. He beckoned at the open door. A pair of men came in, followed by a thin, slovenly dressed individual with a crew cut and lines of dirt in the sharp creases at the back of his neck. He was munching on a tuna fish sandwich.

Bonesteel went across the litter without disturbing any of it. When he reached the speaker box, he stared straight down. He moved to the side, crouched down, cocked his head as he looked at the wooden sides, then at the carpet behind the bizarre coffin. He stood up. "Doc," he called.

The thin man came over, stood looking down into the seeping speaker box. He took a bite of his sandwich.

Bonesteel pointed to the wooden side. "Pics of that," he said. "Okay?"

The thin man nodded, motioned for his men and they got out the cameras and lights.

Bonesteel went over to where Daina was sitting, holding Chris by the hand. He made no sound when he walked and, as she watched him approach, she was somehow reminded of the burly Mexican at the Polynesian restaurant in Malibu.

"Miss Whitney?" He had a soft voice, raspy, the consonants rounded but there was no drawl. "Are you the one who called?" Up close she could see his beard stubble was as light as corn silk. "Ma'am?"

Baba and the cinnamon smell of New York were still strong inside her; the trauma had triggered the memory like a night barrage and she was still tottering between two worlds. Her eyes focused. "Yes?"

"You are the one who phoned the police." He said it slowly and carefully as if she might have a hearing impairment.

"Yes." She ran the fingers of her free hand through her thick hair, pulling it away from her face on that side. She saw that he was watching the point of her physical contact with Chris. "I'm all right. Really."

"Good friend of yours?" He spoke into her eyes.

She wondered whether he meant Maggie or Chris. "A good friend of us both."

"Walk."

Bonesteel turned his head toward a beefy, rumple-suited man who had just entered.

"All clear outside."

Bonesteel nodded, hooked his thumb. "You take the rock star." The man bent down, took Chris by the elbow, led him across the room, sat him down at the dining table, opened his notebook.

"Miss Whitney, I'll have to take your statement now."

There were constant flashes from the assistant medical examiner's men as they went on with their photographing and she turned away because the light hurt her eyes.

"Here," he said, producing a white Styrofoam cup filled with a dark liquid. "It's not quite coffee but it's hot."

She took it between her palms. By the time she was finished talking, the men had put away their cameras and were trying to maneuver Maggie's corpse out of the box. They seemed to work as gently as if she were still alive. At one point, the assistant M.E. called for a hacksaw. At last they had her out, carried her away sealed in a gray plastic body-bag. For the first time in what seemed like days, Daina was able to breathe without a pain in the center of her chest.

"I want to speak to Chris," she said after a time.

Bonesteel nodded. "Soon as Sergeant MacIlargey gets through with him." He took the empty cup from her fingers. "You want to call anyone, Miss Whitney?"

She thought of Rubens, wanted very much to call him. But she knew that when he left town, there was no number where she could reach him. She had no idea where he was in San Diego, only that he would be taking the 8:00 P.M. flight back today. She looked at Bonesteel. "You're very formal, Lieutenant."

"Stars get the star treatment, Miss Whitney. Captain's adamant about that." He turned as the thin man came up to him. "What you got, Andy?"

"Uhm, not much at this stage." The assistant M.E. sucked at his teeth. "All I can tell you so far is the victim died at approximately four-fifteen this A.M., give or take the usual amount."

"What'd you do, use your divining rod?"

The thin man barked appreciatively. "Some days I'd sell my soul for one." He sobered up quickly. "One odd thing, though."

"What's that?"

"She was a long time dying."

Bonesteel gave a quick glance at Daina, made a rapid hand motion, and the assistant M.E. nodded. "Got to roll," the thin man said. "I'll shoot the goods over to you pronto. Won't be till afternoon, though. I've got to get some rest." Despite what he had just said, he went out more briskly than when he had come in.

Bonesteel sat down next to Daina, leaned over so that his forearms rested on his thighs. He clasped his hands together. He had the extraordinary ability to remain motionless when he spoke.

"Miss Whitney, there's just one item I'd like to backtrack on before I let you go. You told me that you and Mr. Kerr were at The Dancers from approximately twelve-thirty to just after five o'clock this morning, is that right?"

"More or less," she said. "I said around midnight."

"All right, midnight. Give or take a few minutes." He smiled at her. "By the way, were you with Mr. Kerr all the time?"

"Most of the time, yes."

"That's not what I asked you." His voice had not changed but something in his eyes had.

"Of course we...there were times when we were apart."

Bonesteel looked at his clasped hands. He waggled his knuckles back and forth. "About how long would you say?"

She shrugged. "I don't know...I can't remember."

"Twenty minutes, maybe...a half hour?"

"It could have been that."

He looked at her directly. "Could it have been longer?"

"Look," she said angrily. "If you think Chris had anything to do with this...He loved Maggie. We both did."

"I don't think anything yet, Miss Whitney," he said matter-of-factly. "I'm just trying to get at the heart of the matter."

"The heart of the matter," Daina said, "is that Maggie's dead."

His eyes seemed to bore into her skull. "If you're that angry, you'll do everything you can to help me."

"Yes. I will."

He seemed to make up his mind about her. "All right."

"Chris, what the hell happened here?"

They both looked up. Bonesteel stood.

Silka's huge frame blocked out the light streaming in through the open doorway.

"Who're you?" Bonesteel said.

Silka looked right through him, began to cross the room. Bonesteel stepped in front of him, put a hand out. In his palm was his wallet open to his L.A.P.D. badge. "What d'you want here?"

"I work for Chris Kerr and Nigel Ash," he said. "I don't have nuthin' to say to you." He looked at Daina. "You all right, Miss Whitney?"

"Yes, Silka." She got up. "We both are. It's Maggie."

Silka looked around him. "Where is she?"

"Headed for the morgue," Bonesteel said bluntly.

"You ain't funny at all," Silka said.

"He's not joking." Daina put a hand on his arm. It felt like a steel girder. "Maggie was murdered early this morning."

Silka's eyes blinked as if he were taking a photograph of this scene just as the assistant M.E.'s men had. "Oh, Christ!" he said and broke away, heading toward Chris.

Bonesteel hooked a thumb. "Who's the tank? Bodyguard?"

Daina nodded.

Bonesteel shook his head. "Where was he tonight? He should've been here."

Daina touched his arm, as she had Silka's. "You said something before about me helping you. What do you know that you're not telling me?"

"I won't know much of anything until I get the Medical Examiner's written report and the developed photos."

"You looked at the side of the speaker box. What did you find there?"

"I looked in a lotta places, Miss Whitney." His voice was noncommittal.

"But that was the only one you asked for pictures of especially." She looked at him. "You wouldn't want to tell me what it's all about."

He lifted his arm as if he were a dancer. "See for yourself." He said it, she thought, as if he did not believe she had the fortitude to return to the spot where Maggie had died.

She went across the room, through the litter, knelt down at the side of the box. The assistant M.E.'s men had used the saw on the opposite side. Here the wood was unmarked but there was an unmistakable stain. The pattern seemed unrecognizable to her.

"It's a sword," Bonesteel said, standing over her. "A sword within a circle."

She looked from him back to the stained wood. Now she could make out the odd kind of cross surrounded by its crude circle.

"It's painted in blood. What's it mean?"

He reached down, pulled her to her feet. "Time you were leaving," he said not unkindly.

"I want to talk to Chris first." She went over to where the two of them were standing. MacIlargey walked away to confer with Bonesteel. "How is he?" she asked Silka.

"Not so good, Miss Whitney." He was holding Chris firmly around one bicep. "He's taking it very hard."

"Chris." She reached up, touched his face with her fingertips. "Oh, Chris."

He blinked several times, looked at her. "I'm okay, Dain. Okay."

But she saw that he wasn't and at that moment she found that she had made a decision. She rummaged in her purse, came up with the keys. "Here," she said, curling his fingers around them. "Silka will take you to my house. Use it for as long as you want."

"I was gonna take him back to Nigel's," Silka said.

"Take him home," Daina said. "To my place."

Silka looked uncertain. "Tie'll be awfully upset. She wanted—"

"Do as I say," Daina said softly. "He doesn't need Nigel and Tie now."

Silka's eyes flickered. He said nothing but she knew he would do as she asked. She fumbled in her purse. "I'll give you the number where he can reach me if he needs—"

"I already know it," Silka said without a trace of overtone.

"Oh." She stared at him. "All right." She leaned forward, kissed Chris on the cheek. "Take good care of him, Silka."

"I always do, Miss Whitney." They went out and, after a moment, she could hear the liquid roar of the limo as it left.

Now that he was gone, she felt a kind of numbness creeping through her. She flexed her hands. I need a drink, she thought. But she would not take one in front of the lieutenant. She had seen his type before, in New York.

Bonesteel turned away from his partner. "Where can I drop you?"

"What time is it?" she said.

He consulted his watch. "Just after eleven A.M."

She nodded. There was time for a drink and a little sleep before she went to pick Rubens up at the airport. "That's all right," she said. "I've got the Merc here. I think it'll help if I drive."

Bonesteel nodded, ushered her out the door. MacIlargey stayed behind. It was overcast outside, the light thin and diffused through a shell as white and fragile as porcelain.

She got in behind the wheel and Bonesteel closed the door of the car. "I'll call you in a day or so," he said.

"When you have something."

"Yes."

She looked up at him. "Lieutenant—"

"Walk."

"Ugh, no." She smiled. "I can't call you that. You look like a Bobby."

"No one calls me Bobby." He watched her, nodded. "Goodbye, Miss Whitney."

* * *

"Whatchew see in this per-fumed garden anyway?" Baba
had said to her that first night.

"Nobody but me," she had said, "to answer to." But even
then she suspected that he knew why she had left the house
on leafy Gils Place in the Kingsbridge area of the West Bronx.

She had been thirteen—a time when circumstances,
rather than ritual, had led to childhood's end—her father
already dead, a silent but unforgotten sentinel in his walnut
casket six feet under in a cemetery she had not been able to
return to since the day of the funeral.

She would not remember the exact date of his death but
the time of the year—the core of the August dog days when,
even on the Cape, at the verge of the unruly chill Atlantic,
the sun streamed down with blinding maliciousness—was
indelibly wrought upon her heart.

It had to have been August because she could vividly recall
how crowded the water was, knew that it was not until this
late in summer's stifling heat that the sea warmed up sufficiently for most people to enjoy it for long.

For herself, it had never made any difference, not caring
at all if her lips turned blue and the skin at the base of her
nails went eerily iridescent. Her mother—whom she had
always called Monika—would wave to her, shouting for her
to come out of the sea, to dry off and to warm up in the sun,
but she never would; not until Monika had come wading out
to get her, pulling her back to land. But by that time she was
already chilled to the bone. She would emerge from the water
dripping and shivering until Monika wrapped her in one of
the enormous bright red beach towels, rubbed her arms to
get the circulation going, and great buzzing blue-green horse-
flies bit painfully at the salt sheen of her ankles.

That had been the beginning of it, she believed, that deep
dark summer when her father died so suddenly, so shockingly
and—so uselessly. For a while she hated him irrationally for
doing that to her, just when they were getting to know.... And
for that time, she thought she understood Monika's carping,
her hate, freshly exhibited.

But then that feeling left her and she knew—understood—
that it was not his fault and that he had loved her. That much
of himself he had left with her. So she came to the full knowl-

edge of what her mother was, of how much she had envied her husband his career success and how she felt he had kept her from fulfilling her potential, as she was now fond of putting it.

But Daina soon learned that Monika's idea of fulfilling her potential was targeted in one area—the bedroom.

For Daina the beginning of 1965 was a time of her first period, a filling out of her figure so that no one—not even Monika—could take her for a child anymore.

It was a time of energy and anarchy. Rebellion laced the air like a spice and the groundswell was emerging, the earth juddering to the shocks of long hair, jeans, communes, fringed jackets, drugs and the flowering of the power of rock and roll.

The new generation had appropriated Churchill's vigorous V sign, giving it a whole new meaning. Easy riders roamed the highways while the children of the middle class, the post-World War II babies, began their long hard period of breaking away. And, though younger, Daina felt the same dissatisfaction with the molds that had been part and parcel of being young for so long. Daina was convinced that her father would have seen the inevitability of it all but, of course, she recognized the canonization, did not care because what was left was only, perhaps, what she could make of him.

In contrast, Monika's world was defined by rules. She still had much of the old world in her and, now that she was on her own, it was quite obvious—to Daina, at least—that day by day she was falling back on the notions that had been drummed into her as a little girl in Győr. She was from northwestern Hungary—the land of the Magyars—and the legends of these fierce, independent warriors were constantly on her lips.

"Your eyes," Daina's father had said to her once, "are your mother's. They've nothing to do with me. You see that color— the burning of the violet that floats there; the tilt to the corners: those are Magyar eyes, Daina." She was tucked neatly in bed and he sat on the soft quilts outside, the deep red cloth-covered book Monika had bought for her open on his lap. He began again to read the story to her, as he had so many times before—about the coming of age of two Magyar boys as they were caught up in the struggle between Magyar and Hun and how Attila's pursuit of the legendary White Stag led to the end of the war with the Magyars.

Daina's father looked up from the pages of the book, said

to her, "Remember, darling, if the bad times come, within you lives the White Stag, proud and mythical and unconquerable." But years later, during that last summer with him, when she had asked him if he had really meant what he had said, he merely laughed and ran his long fingers through her golden hair.

Now it was too late and she was obliged to make of it what she might. She went to the library, pored over books on the history of Hungary, Austria and, finally, Russia, but in none did she find any reference to the White Stag. At last, she became reconciled to the fact that the creature had been another of her father's conceits. When, as a child, she had asked him to tell her stories, they invariably came from his mind not out of a book. So, too, she came to think, the White Stag.

There was a period in her life when she dreamt often of that mythical creature moving across an unfamiliar countryside to the melody of Ravel's sad "Pavane," each note falling like a flower's petal, and she would awake with her eyes full of tears.

Monika understood none of this and once when Daina attempted to explain it, her face drained of color and she hit Daina across the mouth. "That's baby talk!" she cried. "All this mystery and legend. It would dominate you as it did your father. Well, I won't have it, do you hear? He's gone now. You'll forget all about this white horse—"

"A stag is a male deer, Mother. Not a—"

"Now you listen to me," Monika said, grabbing her arm tightly. "You'll do as I tell you and learn to like it."

Thus did she drive Daina far away, to a land at the edge of the world, where twilight reigned and the lawless stalked its streets as surely as if they were nightmares given life.

The traffic on the Pacific Coast Highway was bad but it was nothing compared to what was waiting for her on Ocean Avenue. She was obliged to wind up all the windows and put on the air—a last resort as far as she was concerned. But this time of the day it was either that or risk asphyxiation. This was no place for an asthmatic.

Fuming and stalled in the lineup, she stabbed on the cassette deck, set to playing what was already in there. She came in on the middle of "Narsty," a track from the last

Heartbeats album. There was Chris' voice as hot and demanding as it had ever been and of course her thoughts swung
to—bits of pink flesh and pools of red so dark they looked
black in the dim light: mutilation beyond comprehension.
Her finger reached out to end the music but she held it there
in midair not an inch from the controls and thought, No, no,
no. If I turn it off now, I'll never be able to hear their music
again without images of Maggie, torn like a discarded doll,
and I can't live with that. I can't....

Of course in those days drugs had come her way—they
were so much more prevalent than any adult would believe.
Apart from a bit of grass, she had stayed away from it all,
having seen what it had done to a classmate who had pro-
fessed no addiction. He had been found early one morning,
blue-skinned beneath the plastic bag that covered his head,
surrounded by the stench of glue, in the center of the deserted
orchestra of the Fillmore East, as cold and lifeless as a slab
of refrigerated meat. For three days, the pushers at school
were driven out but she knew that anger was misplaced.

It was a hot and dusty trail to the Marina and after a
while, Daina felt as if all flesh had been flayed from her.
Despite or even because of the air conditioner she began to
feel as if a shower was far more important than a drink. The
music banged against her skull, insistent and ragged, and
she stared out before her, the lowering sunlight bronzing the
tops and hoods of all the Mercs, Mazdas, Porsches, Audis,
Trans Ams, and Datsun Zs, and she felt a part of this long
gleaming, articulated serpentine monstrosity: all metal and
glass and nothing else.

Baba lived on Forty-first and Tenth Avenue; a fifth-floor
railroad flat in a rat-infested tenement the first floor of which
was given over to a Puerto Rican bodega, where the roaches
were so numerous and familiar they almost seemed like the
true tenants. "I use'ta fight 'em," Baba told her seriously.
"Now they'n'me've got a kinda understandin': I don't bother

them an' they doan bother me." But that is not where he took her, at least not at first.

They took the subway, emerging up the stairs in Harlem, walking up Lenox past 138th and the Zanzi Bar, dark and buzzing, squatting on the northeast corner of what could just as easily have been the nether bank of the river Lethe. At least she came to think of that stark, rollicking place as a landmark to the barrier between, well, here and *there,* their feet taking them across an entire continent so that they passed into another, nether world where all faces were brown and she felt as conspicuous as a snowflake on an obsidian beach.

Yellow eyes went as wide as saucers when she walked there because this was not her turf, was not even, strictly speaking, America, land of the free, home of the brave, but some bottled-up ghetto filled with the shiftless and the sly— pink Caddys parked next to old men rubbing gnarled gray hands across a trashcan fire. But not a word was spoken and all was crystal silence. Because of Baba.

Still she was uncomfortable for she saw in their eyes things that would haunt her for years. These people did not need to open their mouths—they screamed their hatred of her with their eyes. Her skin crawled and her stomach knotted and, for this moment, she was sorry for what she had asked for. She was an alien on a distant planet, a place where she might conceivably be tolerated while in the company of this dark moving mountain but where she could never belong. Then she glanced once into Baba's face, saw the unconcern, and her stomach settled down.

She had read many times about London after the Blitz but had never been able to fully visualize the enormous devastation. Until now. Walking through Harlem she thought she knew. Half-demolished buildings loomed on all sides, shattered brickwork and rubble scattered, bent wire and wood-frame fences needlessly guarding black holes in the ground, the burned stubble of a once-rotten tooth.

Dogs roamed in packs, huge and thick-furred with long muzzles, like wolves, and bright yellow eyes that iridesced in the slither of the mobile headlights of the passing traffic. They barked hungrily, nervously circling the cinder fires staining garbage cans black. She saw a cockroach as long as her finger scuttling in the gutter before a dog pounced on it.

Drums sounded from far away in the direction of the upper edge of night-black Central Park. Flames lit the street where the lights overhead buzzed and fizzled. She thought of Dante and shivered a little against Baba's side, as big and comforting as a wall.

He took her to a restaurant sandwiched between a six-floor tenement that looked as if it might burst into flames at any moment and an old-fashioned grocery with a faded sign provided by Coca-Cola. In long languorous strides a young couple danced in the cool light thrown on the pavement from the open door. A portable radio set on the lid of an aluminum garbage can spewed James Brown's "It's a Man's World."

Daina stopped as he was about to take her in. Across the avenue, the fat old woman—as dark as tar—left the recesses of her mojo store to smile and have a look. Daina was fascinated by the ghostdance. The couple seemed on that magic, flickering night not to be made of flesh and sinew and bone but of starlight and the wind. It was as if they had always been there on this street, part of the world, surely closer to the essence of life than any of Daina's days in Kingsbridge in pursuit of everything that now seemed false and meaningless. And she realized dimly that it was because there was no civilization here, at least not as she had been taught it. She found herself thinking that in this filth and poverty and ignorance was an essential purity that everything known to her would obscure and therefore destroy. It was perhaps idealistic and not a little sappy—which was why she would never tell anyone—but still she knew that at that moment she was right; that she had indeed been witness to some extraordinary act so that she felt transported back through time to the instant when civilization had been born. And she was at once exalted and sad for she understood that they possessed some basic quality that she did not and would never, perhaps, acquire and she resigned herself to the role of spectator at an arcane rite.

"All right," she said softly when it was over and Baba took her inside.

The restaurant was low-ceilinged, the walls and floor all of old Italian tile, in some places worn and shabby, even chipped, but, for the most part, lustrous still. There was no telling whether the proprietors had allowed the decor to stand for aesthetic or financial considerations.

They were shown to a corner table by a thin waiter with skin so light he might have been dusted with flour. Baba grinned at her and said: "Now yo done it, mama. Yo gone eat some real nigga food." He took the menu from her hands. "Yo let me do the orderin'."

He told the waiter what he wanted and when the first course came—flash-fried chitlins made so crispy they were a racket to eat—he said, "So whut about yo' boyfrien' back home in the Bronx?" The way he said it made it sound like the other side of the universe instead of just north of cross-town.

"Told you I didn't have anyone."

"Pretty girl like yo?" He shook his head, crunched into the chitlin before him. "Well, hell, yo got yo' fam'ly, mama."

"My dad's dead." She looked down at the red-and-white-checked tablecloth. "And as for my mama, she doesn't really give a shit what—"

"Hey now. Ain't no way for yo to talk, mama."

"Why not? You talk that way."

"T'se an outlaw, mama. On the edge o' town. Doan you go pickin' anything like that up from me. I gotta talk this way so's I c'n be unnerstood." He winked at her. "Anyways, I'se a nigga. Doan know any utha way to talk. Now yo sumthin else again, mama. Yo had schoolin'. Brought up proper. Yo got no reason usin' all them fucks'n'shits."

"I think they're just words like any other words. You've heard of Lenny Bruce—"

"Uhm." Baba shook his woolly head. "Mama, yo got a lot to learn. Don't make no difference whut you or I think, doan yo know that? All that matter's whut them out there"—he tossed his head—"thinks. An' they doan like none o' that shit, y'unnerstan'. Dig: they likes things calm'n'easy. Nice, unruffled feathers." He pointed with a greasy forefinger. "Eat yo' soul food, mama. Smack yo' lips. Enjoy 'em like yo was a nigga, yo'll make me happy."

They ate in silence for a while. The place was narrow and crowded. There was an almost communal atmosphere with a great deal of high-spirited talk and casual banter between tables. It was something she had never seen in any place downtown.

They were near the back where a double plate-glass window looked out across a weed-choked back lot filled with piles of black rubble. Blobs of lemon light from second- and third-story windows haloed shabby brick walls seemingly far away but in reality just a block distant. In the night the gaps created by the collapsed buildings caused the illusion.

Baba turned his head as the front door opened to admit a man with a long shining face as black as midnight. He made his slow circuitous way toward them through the restaurant. He wore a fawn-colored suit with lapels so wide they touched his shoulders, a dark brown shirt open at the neck to expose six or seven rows of thin-link gold chains. He had a long wooden kitchen match stuck in one corner of his mouth and when he came closer Daina could see that he was continually sucking his teeth with great energy. She also saw the rictus at the side of his mouth, where he left the match, a slight turn-up of his lips that never varied despite his expression.

"What say, m'man?" he said in a voice like a semi chewing up a gravel drive. He stuck out a pink palm and Baba slapped it.

"Hey."

The man eyed Daina. "Whatchew got here, nigga?" He hooked a chair leg with the tip of one Thom McAn ankle boot, pulled the chair out and sat down. "Seems t'me yo got yo' black self one fine slice o' prime meat there."

"Smiler, yo got sumthin important t'tell me? If not, yo'all c'n blow."

Smiler gave him a gold-toothed grin. "Say bro, yo gettin' a might touchy, seems t'this nigga."

"Whatchew got shakin', man?" He had stopped eating. Now he wiped his fingertips very carefully as he watched the other man. "Clean it out as I says."

Smiler chewed reflectively on his match, the red and white tip bobbing. "Whassamatta, nigga, yo forget white meat's meant t'be shared—'specially slab boss as this'n?" His hand heavy with callus came down over Daina's. She tried to pull it away but his thick fingers imprisoned her.

"Doan do none o' that, Smiler."

Smiler grinned. "Why not?"

Baba reached out with deceptive speed for such a large man and, without looking down, grabbed Smiler's forefinger from where it lay gripping the back of Daina's hand. In a blur he had snapped it up and back until there came a loud crack as the joint gave under the enormous pressure.

Smiler yelped, tried to jump up, but caught in Baba's grip he could only squirm like a fish. Tears stood out at the corners of his eyes and his face contorted. The pain could not erase his awful half smile. His chest heaved and a trickle of sweat inched down his left temple, forced to detour by a throbbing vein.

Still maintaining his grip, Baba leaned across the table and in a low voice said, "I tol' yo t'get on with it, man, but yo' too much a bad-ass nigga t'pay me any mind."

"Hey, bro..." Smiler's eyes rolled, the sweat was really sliding now, staining the collar of his shirt.

"On'y way I sees t'get through t'you is do sumpin yo c'n unnerstan', dig?"

Smiler gritted his teeth. "Hey, bro. Hey, hey, calm down now. Yo hurtin' this nigga—"

"I don't give no fuck 'bout yo' pain, nigga, that clear? Yo got nuthin upstairs, yo gots t'pay the price." He put his face close to Smiler's shining one, his elbow on the cloth of the tabletop, increasing the pressure. Smiler gasped so hard the match dropped out of his mouth.

"Christ, bro, yo killin me, I ain't lyin'."

"'Pologize t'the lady, man."

"Uh...uh—"

Baba leaned in, gritting his teeth, and all color seemed to fade from the other's face.

"So—sorry...."

"Sorry, *ma'am*. This here's a lady, mothafucka. Sumthin yo wouldn't be able t'rec'nize."

Smiler looked desperately at Daina. "Sorry, ma'am." And his eyes closed with an almost infinite weariness.

"Baba," Daina whispered. "Stop it now."

He took his hand away from the other's and relief flooded Smiler's face. He swept his injured hand off the table, held it protectively within the other palm.

"Jus' like crackin' a chicken wing fores yo take a bite, eh, Smiler?" Baba chuckled. "Kay. What's up?"

Smiler looked at him out of reddened eyes. He rocked a little bit in the throbbing aftermath of the pain. "Shit comin in at three A.M. Same place."

"Yo check it out?"

"At th' other end, yas. Fine shit."

Baba nodded. "Thas a cool two G's fo' yo'all, nigga. Buy yo'self some fancy threads with dat kinda bread." He laughed. "Keep yo' ol' lady in smiles, dat's fo' damn sho."

But Smiler wasn't laughing. He gripped his ruined finger with a peculiar kind of rigidity, seemingly terrified of moving it. He stared at it, his lips moving, but no sound came out. The sweat was drying up on his face.

"Doc fix yo up no time a'tall, yo see." Baba returned to his food. "An' nex' time yo'll know betta, right, nigga?"

Smiler looked at him. "Yas." He stood up, did not even glance in Daina's direction. It was as if he saw Baba all alone at the table. "Nex' time I knows betta."

He pushed past the chair, threaded his way out of the restaurant. When he got outside Daina thought she saw him cross the street.

"You didn't have to hurt him like that, did you?" she said.

Baba put down his fried chitlins, said, "Like I tol' yo, mama, yo gots a lot t'learn 'bout these folk. On'y thing niggas like Smiler knows is pain. Sad fact, fo sho, but it's true enough. They don't hear so good sometimes so yo gots t'get their attention. It ain't easy."

"That means you had to break his finger?"

"Uhm." Baba sat back, wiped his thick lips. "Let me tell yo a story, mama, illustrate m'point. Years ago ol' Smiler use'ta be a free-lancer. The Lord on'y knows how he made his bread 'cause he ain't got enough goin' upstairs t'make a bird fly but he managed somehow. Until the day he come up against a big shot outa Philly—a P.R. t'boot. Now this guy, he's a nasty sumbitch but he ain't stupid an' he sees how he can, y'know, fit ol' Smiler inta his business plans.

"So he makes Smiler an offer. Nice one, couldn't complain, 'less like I says, yo' pilot light's a bit dim. Smiler, he says 'Get fucked' t'this dude an' the man goes away. But he can't for long, cause he's gotta itch t'move north t'New York an' he sees how Smiler's his ticket in, grease t'meat. Now he's insistent an' ol' Smiler, he won't be budged, no how.

"Now this P.R. fella's gettin' bugged an' he sends a sol'jer over t'Smiler's t'bring him in fo' a talk. On'y problem is, Smiler's out on a buy that night an' the stupid spic blows away Smiler's ol' lady by mistake.

"Now it takes a while fo' things t'settle in with Smiler but once they do, he rolls. He goes out afta the dude. Not too bright. But like I says..." He shrugged.

"'Tell you what,' this dude says to Smiler. 'One broad's jus' like another. Yo take whichever one yo sees here you like, kay?'

"'Yo spic muthafucka,' Smiler says, 'I'm gonna pull yo' arms outa their sockets fo' yo.' But, of course, ol' Smiler, he can't move fo' the two spics holdin' him, an' this dude, he says, 'Yo know the problem with yo bastards is yo gots no sensa humor. None a'tall. So's I tells yo whut I'm gonna do. I'm gonna do yo a big favor an' fix that.' He gets up an' flicks out a gravity knife an' he goes t'work on the right side o' Smiler's face, cutting into the nerves. 'Now,' this fucker says, steppin back an' wipin' the blood off his blade on Smiler's sports jacket, 'yo'll smile alla time an' *nobody*—not even me— will be able t' accuse yo of havin' no sensa humor.' Huh!" Baba went back to his food.

Daina stared at him. "What's the point?"

"Of the story?" Baba wiped his greasy mouth. "The point is, mama, that Smiler's now workin' for that spic dude. Uh huh. Took one of his broads, too. Been with her now...uhm ...three, four years."

"I don't believe any of this."

"Hey, mama, it's all true. *Emmis,* like they say downtown. Dat's the way it all works here. That dude, he got ol' Smiler's attention. Eventually. Huh!" He laughed again, launched into the last of the white meat.

"Well, I think it's disgusting."

He gave her a quick look over the torn piece of crackling skin and he did not have to open his mouth, did not have to say to her, "Yo came out here on yo' own, mama. No one brought yo," because that look said it all and she, too, went back to the remnants of the meal.

Around them, the atmosphere became more raucous as they sank deeper into the night. Bottles of corn mash whiskey appeared from somewhere, one placed in the center of every table along with enough glasses. These looked to Daina like the glasses she had used at home while brushing her teeth.

Baba reached out, poured himself four fingers of the liquor neat. There seemed to be no ice or water with which to dilute it and when she asked him about this, he said, "Yo doan wanna do that, mama. Sacrilege."

She waited until he had downed his before saying, "Aren't you going to pour me some?"

He eyed her a moment before putting down his glass. "Yo got some streak inside yo, mama, yo know that?" But he poured her some just the same, watched her, smiling, as she choked it down. Her throat felt like it was on fire and she swore she could feel the path the liquor took all the way down to her intestines as clearly as if it were a fluorescent-lighted flight path. She brushed the water out of her eyes, shoved her glass across the table for a refill. Baba shook his head, laughed and poured for them both.

"I'll bet you've got some big family," Daina said after a while.

"Nah." He rolled the glass on edge between the two walls of his enormous hands. "Got no fam'ly, leastwise not now. My daddy, he come up here from Alabama. I hate them mutha-fuckas down there worse'n I do spics but I gotta say one thing fo' 'em—they tell yo they hate yo right off." He shrugged his huge shoulders. "Up here a lotta 'em pretend, y'dig? They's yo' friend but it don't mean shit 'cause behind yo' back, they's sayin' the same thing. Nigga." He looked at her. "Yo tell me, mama, what's worse."

"All of that...color thing," she said. "I don't know. I don't understand."

"Well that sho as fuck makes two o' us, mama." He sipped at the bourbon. "Had me a pair o' brothers, once upon a time. Tyler, he was the oldest. They got him one night outside o' Selma. Three big mothers with shotguns come along, drunk as skunks one Satidy night, sees Tyler and his girl neckin' an' they blows them t'kingdom come. Shit." He poured himself more liquor. Daina said nothing, just looked at him.

"Then there was Marvin," Baba continued. "He was the youngest. Nice nigga. Not like his old man or the rest of us. Graduated high school; wanted t'go t'college, too, but, well, we had no bread. So he up an' enlisted in the army 'cause that was the on'y way, those muthafuckas pay his way." He stared down into the depths of the brown liquor as he swirled it around the edge of the glass. "Stupid bastards shipped him off t'Nam. So after all, he was jus' one more ig'orant nigga who tried t'beat the system an' failed. Shit.

"I wrote t'that nigga every week. Said, 'Listen here Marvin, yo take care o' yo'self. This here's a white man's war, see.

Don't yo get yo'self hurt over that.' But Marvin, he writes back, 'Yo gots t'unnerstan', Baba. I'm an American; yo an American. Over here there ain't no niggas an' no white men. There's us an' the enemy. Doan make no difference t'them *what* color I am.' Poor muthafucka. Then he writes me his platoon was ambushed on a night patrol. He an' another bastard all that's left an' they hold their position. Next morning, grunts find 'em back't'back with a pile of Cong laid around them like a wreath. Marvin's a fuckin' hero, about t'get the Silver Star.

"So what happens. The next week, he's leadin' his own patrol, steps on a mine an' all that's left o' him is his head and part o' his chest an' he gets shipped back home in a pine box, covered in the American flag an' the Silver Star pinned t'one corner. What the fuck'm I supposed t'do with that, huh?" There were glittery points standing out in the corners of Baba's eyes. He pushed the glass away from him. "Shouldn't be drinkin' this stuff, see what comes of it. Shit!"

Daina reached out across the table, took his hands in hers, saw how the black swallowed up the white, felt his warmth, and she rubbed the skin of his wrists.

He cleared his throat, disentangled himself, took his hands off the table. "Enough o' this, mama. Ain't no good a'tall."

"Well, well, well, Baba. This is quite a surprise."

They both turned to look up at the man standing in the narrow aisle between the tables. Had they not been so engrossed in conversation, they would most certainly have spotted him the moment he came through the door. For one thing, he was dressed all in spotless gray, even down to his elegant suede shoes. He wore a wide silk cravat instead of a tie. But what he wore was hardly the man's most remarkable feature. He was tall and slender, with a kind of animal grace when he moved in even the tiniest way. His hands were long-palmed with stubby, powerful-looking fingers. The backs of the hands were heavily freckled, covered in golden hair. He had a narrow face with rather long, pinned-back ears and curling reddish hair cut short. His face, too, was freckled and his wide-set, heavy-lidded eyes were so pale a blue that, in bright light, they were colorless. His mandiblelike mouth and sharp, prominent chin gave him a ferocious countenance.

Baba smiled slowly, lifted an arm. "Daina, meet Aurelio Ocasio. Ally, sit down why doncha?"

"Don't mind if I do. Young lady—" He took Daina's hand in his and she felt the faint coolness of the fingers, smelled his cologne. Ocasio lifted her hand, thought better of kissing it, let it go. He sat down opposite Baba and next to Daina. As he did so, he signaled a couple of dark-haired Puerto Ricans who sat at a cramped table for two up against one wall near the front door.

"You robbing the cradle these days, Baba," he said with a harsh laugh. He poured himself some bourbon, made a face. "Christ, how can you drink this shit. Don't they have rum in this place?"

"Little too far west fo' that, Ally," Baba said pointedly.

"Ah hah. Well we're gettin around these days, more'n'more. Business is boomin'."

"So I see."

Ocasio gave a glance toward Daina and she saw how long his eyes were, like the narrow slits of a fox. "*Dígame, amigo,* you're not thinkin of branchin' out by any chance."

"You mean Daina?" Baba laughed, took a gulp of bourbon. "Don't get yo' bowels wet, Ally. She jus' a frien' o' the fam'ly."

"You ain't *got* no family, *amigo*."

"Ah ha, well I do now. Whatchew think o' that?"

Ocasio took a very deliberate sip of his drink, watched the liquid run down the side of the glass. "I think that's just fine, long as you keep it that way. Wouldn't want anyone steppin' on my toes...ah, specially you, *amigo*, you got such big feet, eh?" But he did not smile and nothing about him connoted humor in even the driest sense.

"Since when've I ever been innerested in that kinda action? Doan know nuthin 'bout it anyways."

"Time passes, *amigo*. We all get the itch, you know. Ambition is the downfall of us all."

Baba put his glass down onto the table directly in front of him. "Whatchew aimin' at, Ally?"

"Uhm, well. Smiler tells me you're about to raise your rates as of this shipment...."

"Tha's right. Inflation, m'man. Even outlaws gotta eat."

"Inflation, uh. You're sure that's it?"

Baba eyed him.

"Couldn't be you're anglin' for some kinda financin' so's you can expand, could it?"

Baba laughed. "Where yo' pickin' up this ratshit, Ally? My

oh my times they's changed. Yo once had the best sources on the street. Whassamatter, they give up on yo in these evil days, uhm?"

Ocasio shrugged, as a welterweight might throw off a deft combination before he began to counterpunch. "You know them sources as well as I do, *amigo. Los cochinillos!* They are without honor but they have their good days as well as bad."

"But rates is rates, m'man," Baba said, draining his glass, "an' I gots t'keep up with the times."

Ocasio placed his glass down beside Baba's. "Don't we all," he said as he got up. "Glad we had this little visit. *Adios.*" He signaled his men and one opened the front door for him. Neither of them had eaten or drunk anything since they came in; no one had disturbed their silent conversation.

Baba wiped at his mouth as the door closed, turned away to look at Daina. "An' he talks 'bout honor; calls his men pigs. He's the fuckin' pig, that spic."

"You don't like Puerto Ricans much, do you?"

"Huh, no, mama. I sure as hell don't. They givin this city a bad name. Stink up the place!" He smiled. "One thing though yo c'n say 'bout em: they's lower down than us niggas." Then he threw his head back and laughed loud enough to turn heads in that hubbub.

At the Warehouse she sat by the window staring out at the deepening night, the bobbing lights like blobs of cast-off paint scattered across a canvas, sipping a chill Bacardi and thinking, for once, of nothing at all. She listened to the muted buzz of conversation from the main dining room at her back, the soft clink of the ice against her teeth when she drank and watched a forty-foot schooner, strung with colored lights, heading out from its berth, the top edge of its long cabin and sleek hull glowing whitely, two slashes in the darkness, an equal sign equaling nothing.

"Mind if I sit down?"

She looked up, thought, Oh, Christ no.

George Altavos stood two paces from the table. Apparently he had come from the packed bar because he had a drink in one hand.

"Saw you come in a little while ago." His voice was only slightly slurred but he might have been drinking here for hours. "I thought at first I'd just pretend you weren't here." He brayed a laugh. "Pretty funny, that. You and me at the same watering hole, not talking to each other."

"Army Archerd would love to get hold of that item, I'll bet." She tried a smile, missed.

"Yah. And Rubens would run me right off the lot." He tried to hide the bitterness in those words.

She looked up at him. "Why don't you clarify that statement."

He opened up his mouth to say something, jerked his drink to his lips instead. When he took the glass away, he said, "I don't think you fucked your way into this picture, if that's what's on your mind."

"What's on my mind," Daina said clearly, "is how you treated me on the set the other day."

He set his empty glass down on her table. "We didn't get a helluva lotta work done today." He ran his fingertip around the rim of his glass until it gave off a little squeal. "It was very vibey. You know, weird. Everyone was freaked." His dark eyes locked on hers.

It was a form of apology, no matter how oblique. "Sit down," she said.

In or out of makeup, George was a remarkably handsome man. Not in the careful, unvarying modern Hollywood way; he had a rough-hewn quality that harked back to the old days of the thirties and forties when the stars seemed bigger and less even-featured. His oval, open face was dominated by dark hooded eyes that made him appear sleepy all the time. He left his toupee behind when he wasn't filming.

She let him order drinks for them both before she said, "I'm sorry to hear about you and Yasmin."

"Yah, well, it's not much of anything. Just a passing fancy."

The drinks came and he watched her carefully for some time. "I'm gay," he said.

Daina put down her Bacardi. "I didn't know."

"No one really does. Except Yasmin." He fiddled with the plastic stirrer, making it click against the side of the glass. "Yah. I saw her and thought, Hell, maybe she's the girl to change me." He shrugged. "She wasn't. I guess you can't change human nature." He put his finger around the stirrer, took a long swallow of his whiskey, looked down into it. "I

used to drink these with soda but I gave it up after a while."
His head came up abruptly. "You know why? It took me too
long to get drunk." He took another long sip. "It's quicker
now. Much quicker."

Daina shrugged. "If you're not happy..."

George waggled a finger at her. "No, no. You mistake
anger for unhappiness. I come from a large family. I've got
four brothers and three sisters. They're all married
now...happily, unhappily, what's the difference? The point
is that whatever they've done, in marriage and in divorce,
they've trod the safe and narrow. Every Christmas when I
go back, when we all get together in that big house in Animas,
New Mexico, I feel like I'm gonna die." He finished his drink,
waved at the waiter for a refill. "But you know what? I *want*
to go back home, I'm still looking to please my parents. They
don't know I'm gay; it would kill them. My father, so macho
still at seventy. I walk around Animas so full of guilt. Yet
I go back, again and again, as if I'm searching for something."

"Did you ever take Yasmin with you?"

He gave her a kind of grimace. "She was going to go this
year." He waved away his words as the waiter set down a full
glass, took his empty one. He started on it right away. "It
doesn't matter."

But Daina thought it did. "George, if it's right, it'll happen
with someone else."

His smile was bleak. "Ah, no. There was no one else but
her. I don't think there will be another woman." He shrugged.
"What the hell. I am what I am, right? And relationships are
so much easier when you're gay. Just sex with no strings. No
hysterical women calling you in the middle of the night, wondering just where the relationship is going. You're always
free to get on with your life; you don't have to explain all the
brief encounters to anyone."

"George, it sounds to me as if you're using homosexuality
as an easy way out."

"What's wrong with taking the easy way once in a while?
I've had it up to here with problems." He pointed a finger at
her. "You know how I got into acting? I thought if I could
learn to change my personality, I'd begin to...like girls. Oh,
yes! Stupid, isn't it?" His hand fluttered in the air again. "No,
no, I was just confusing ego and personality. All that dissolution of personality, the roles in front of the camera, all that

did was to *accelerate* the process...that long slide into nothingness."

He rattled the ice cubes against his glass as if he were a disgruntled simian shaking the bars of its cage. "I'll tell you what acting did for me. It made me want more. It got so that I wasn't content anymore in letting myself go in front of the cameras. I needed to do that in real life, too.

"So I began to cruise because I found out that, like acting, it's where the ball game begins and ends for me. Because I see them as precisely the same thing. It's like living on the high wire. You know that it's just a matter of time till you make a mistake and go off. Anyone would think that's a frightening thought. But no. It's the thought that drives you on, why you go out again and again to confront...that *thing*, whatever it is, full of an inexorable magnetism.

"And you think, Will it be tonight? as you pick up the blond muscle boy on the beach at Santa Monica, surfing his little heart out. Okay, so he ties you up, goes in for a little harmless beating before he gets down to fist fucking you. So far, so good.

"But suppose...just suppose that innocent blond exterior is hiding the soul of a psycho. He decides maybe he won't untie you after all. He goes through the house, taking your money, jewelry, starts to break up the place and then he comes back to begin work on you—"

"Stop it!" Daina cried, clapping her fists over her ears. "Stop it!" Heads turned in their direction and Frank, the maître d', came hurrying up to make sure she was all right.

George waved him away and when they were alone said, "I suspect that's what Yasmin despises in me. I'm such an unthinking bastard most of the time." He touched the back of her hand briefly. "Murders are committed every day. What happened to your friend isn't unique. It's a consequence of—"

"I don't care about other people," Daina said fiercely. "Just Maggie!"

"A consequence of modern living," he continued doggedly. "None of us knows right from wrong anymore. Death has lost all meaning."

"How can you say that!"

"Because, Daina, it's perfectly true. The dark side of our

nature has bared its fangs, has taken a bite and now struggles to gain the upper hand, to accelerate the decay."

He gave her a wide, wicked smile. "El-Kalaam would understand that, don't you think?"

"Why not?" she said. "El-Kalaam is a terrorist. You speak like a terrorist."

"But that is precisely the point!" George pressed his palms against the table. "El-Kalaam is more real than is George Altavos. I'll admit that I resented this project at first...almost didn't read for the part. But Marion, our bloody genius Marion came and got me out of bed and I read. He did not want anyone else. But I was not yet convinced. He saw right through to the heart of the matter while I was still floundering around with my ego...battling you."

He rubbed the edge of his cold glass across his lips until he was stained with its moisture. "El-Kalaam's mastered what I've sought to understand. And now we're one, Daina, the terrorist and me. One."

She left him drinking at the table. It was impossible for her to stay with him longer though there was still some time before she had to head for the airport. She recognized, even as she left, walking rather unsteadily to the Merc, that part of her was fascinated, wanted to stay. But on another deeper level, she had become terrified. George seemed so out of control that she had begun to shake as if she were ill.

For a long time she sat in the car, the windows all rolled down. Soon the cool night breeze had dried the sweat along her hairline but this gentle bathing could not cleanse her of the thoughts that came creeping in a furtive skirmish line, thoughts she would rather not face.

With a convulsive movement, she inserted the key, fired the ignition. The rich thrumming, the familiar scent of the exhaust thrown back at her, masking for an instant the smell of the sea, was comforting. She switched on the headlights, headed out, back along Admiralty Way. She snapped on the radio, turned up the volume, coming in on midsong: *I like fast company/I like the sound of danger in your voice/Now I like to wait until the fire is part of me/And you like to wait until you've got no choice....Here comes the night again/It turns me round to face you....* And she laughed loud and hard, pressed the accelerator down and down, flying away from and moving toward that same marker; the banner of an unknown champion.

Through the great sparkle-dazzle of the city he took her, up through the darkness of Central Park with its intermittent icings of Christmas lights like magical spiderwebs from *Fantasia* scalloping the cracked black branches of the trees. The bright clear horizon was all around a planetarium cyclorama of tall buildings, the silent sentinels at parade rest overlooking this sooty woods.

Baba, immense beside her in a dark blue velvet suit heisted no doubt off some Calvin Klein truck on its way down Seventh Avenue. Nevertheless it fit him perfectly because he had had the sense to take it in to Herchel, a *schneider* of the old school, who ran a beaten-down establishment on Ninth Avenue but turned out impeccable alterations.

As for Daina, she was wearing a shantung silk dress, a plum-colored wonder she had weaseled out of her mother with a maximum of effort. It showed a lot of leg and, because all that held it up were a pair of spaghetti straps, a great deal more cleavage than it otherwise might have. Daina thought it had been worth every moment of the effort.

At seventeen she was very much filled out and had not had any trouble ordering drinks in a bar since she was fifteen. She wore her long hair up away from her face and had long ago had her ears pierced at a jeweler's in the Village that abutted one of the numerous coffee houses she used to frequent.

She rolled down the window of the taxi, let the chill night air beat with velvet fists against her cheeks. She opened her mouth until her gums were numb.

On their way to a party. Uptown. And the park opened up its mailed fist for her, softened by the pink glow of Manhattan, lights from the spires gilding the foliage with make-believe frost.

They debarked at an enormous prewar building on 116th Street just on the borderline between east and west, at Fifth Avenue.

"Free territory," Baba said as she stared up at the stucco-and-concrete facade encrusted with gargoyles just as if it were an ancient French cathedral. Its architecture was assuredly

European in inspiration, characteristic of small pockets of upper Manhattan not yet leveled by the master urban plan proliferating the blight of high-rise city housing to take care of the burgeoning immigrant population or—as some would have it—members of the multiplying welfare roles. "Everyone's free to come and go here."

They stood on the pavement before the ornate entrance. A light sleet had begun to fall and the traffic began to whisper in the moisture. To their left, at the corner, a streetlight emblazoned the frozen snow in a cool halo about its summit.

"You make it sound like a war."

He nodded his shaggy head. "Sho' as hell is, mama. Spics wantin' t'move up now. They's gotta haul it over our asses. Ain't on'y whitey we gots t'watch, mama." He took her arm, began to lead her indoors.

"Baba," she said, "why d'you live where you do? I know you don't have to."

His yellow eyes looked at her. "I'se comfitable there is all. Ain't nobody hasslin' me. No petitions t' get me up an' out like that. Jus' me—an outlaw at the edge o' town."

The lobby was all marble and gilt got up around a series of mirrors, darkened here and there by the slow disintegration of their silver backing, making reflections oddly incomplete.

To the left a Christmas tree rainbowed the immediate vicinity, to the right a marble staircase led upward in shadows. Immediately ahead was a wooden-doored elevator. She looked through the diamond-shaped window as it descended to street level.

The party was on the seventh floor and they heard the burst of boisterous noise the moment they stepped off the elevator.

Their host met them at the door. He was an enormously tall black man who moved with the grace of a giant cat. His hair was but a glistening stubble, his nose as sharp as a beak, his wide-set eyes always on the move, darting here and there as if in search of total security. He grinned, pumped Baba's hand, leaned down, kissed Daina on the cheek. "Charming," he said. "Charming." Guiding them inside the hot, noisy place, his movements were deft, economical and, as he turned away, Daina saw the gold ring in his ear. His name was Stinson.

Swirl of movement; swirl of comment as they were borne into the smoky maelstrom's heart. Dark faces all around, painted and gay; red lips pouting in bows, doe eyes opened wide. A great burst of laughter, a single shot, as if from the entity itself.

Baba got them drinks, introduced her around. There were lawyers and dancers, loan sharks and actors and all seemed perfectly interchangeable, belonged here after all, bound to this time and place as if it were a mast. But in their eyes she could see the longing when they glanced at her. They tried to hide it but they rarely succeeded. It was her they envied—her innate *whiteness:* the color commodity, the one thing they could not have. Because it allowed her free access. It was the key to the city.

"Hey, Baba, hey. Whatchewsay!" A short man with a slight limp and light skin sidled up. His face was lopsided and the skin on the left side was glossy, pulled taut with the imperfection of plastic surgery. It was oddly hairless—the slight stubble on the right side of his jaw standing out as if it were a full-grown beard.

"Happenin' bro." He put his arm around Daina's shoulders. "This here's Trip, Daina."

"Hi."

"Hey hey hey. Bring on the nubiles, Baba, yo sly fox."

Daina laughed. "It's nice to meet you too."

Trip was delighted. "M'*man!*" he exclaimed. "She got a brain!"

"Outthink even you, you sawed-off sonovabitch," Baba said. He took a swig of his drink. "Listen, mama, I gots t'go do some bizness. Yo stay with ol' Trip. He'll take care o' yo till I come back, right bro?"

"Sho nuff."

"You know everyone here?" Daina asked.

He smiled, quite an unspectacular gesture given the nature of his face. "Oh yah. Ev'yone. Yo want some introductions? Don't blame yo none. That bastard Baba's ugly sumbitch ain't he?"

"Oh, I don't know. He's—" But she recognized being ribbed and broke off with a laugh. "He's like a teddy bear."

"Oh yah, mama. Some monster bear he is. Ah ha! Yo want a refill on that?"

"Okay. Sure."

He guided her over to the bar, began to fix her drink. "Yo ain't a little young fo' all this by any chance."

She looked at him. "Would it matter if I were?"

"Not a bit. There you are." He handed her the drink. "Just curious is all. Baba's always level-headed...."

"Meaning?" And when he would not answer, she provided her own. "What's he doing with someone so young."

"None my bizness, mama."

"No it's not." Music sprayed over them and they were bumped and pushed by dancing couples as they moved toward a sparsely populated wall. All the furniture was filled to overflowing. "But just the same I'll tell you. I don't mind provided..."

"Yas?"

"Provided you tell me what you do."

"Oh, mama. Yo doan want t'know that."

"But I do."

Trip's odd head bounced back and forth on his neck like a coilspring doll. "Oh, oh, oh, yah. Okay, mama. Yo jus' make sure yo doan tell Baba I tol yo." She nodded. "I break heads."

In all the commotion she was certain she had misheard. "What?"

"Mama, I break heads." He smiled sweetly. "Whassamatter, I ain't ashamed. It's an honorable profession. My father did jus' the same till it caught up with him one day and he was blown away." He drummed his fingers against the wall. They were long and thin and very powerful. They looked like surgeon's fingers. "My mama, if she'd known, it woulda killed her. But she's daid now so's it doan matter none. 'Cept t'me of course."

"But you're..."

"So small," he finished for her, shrugged. "They all say that at first. Size doan make no difference at all, mama." He winked at her. "Now tha's a secret if ever there was one. Mos' people, they goes fo' bulk, y'know. Gives them a sense o' security." He shook his head. "But bulk, that doan mean nuthin, mama. Yo gots t'know whut t'do with whut yo gots, y'dig. Yah. Yo gots t'learn yo' trade real well, jus' like anythin' else. Yo fuck aroun' yo goan get yo' ass handed t'yo, y'dig."

"But I don't understand why you'd choose—"

"Choose!" His eyes got hard and she could feel a sudden tenseness come into him. "Ain't got nuthin t'do with *choosin'*, mama. Tha's fo' white folks who gots the time t'go t'college. I didn't *choose* nuthin. I am where I am 'cause I gots t'be. Ain't no two ways 'bout it. Shit!

"Some muthafucka comes in, blows my father away, whut am I s'posed t'do? Sit there an' cry 'bout it? No way, mama! I went out carryin' my father's .357 Magnum in both hands an' while the bastard was gettin' into his Continental, I says, 'Scuse me, suh, but they's something on yo' windshield.' An' pulled the trigger on that mutha. Blast like t'throw me back ten feet, put a hole in the screen big enough t'drive a semi through. I took a peek in an' upchucked all over that muthafucka's velvet seats 'cause the bastard lost his head, jus' a dark stump in there, pumpin' blood like the Roosevelt Dam."

He stared at her. "*That* was my choice, mama, if y' c'n call it that."

"What happened after that?"

"Whut happened. Shit but yo iggorent, chile. They come afta me. The bastard had a lotta friends." He smiled now as if at a fond memory. "But I was learnin' fast. There were contracts out on most of 'em so I made my first money while—"

"You killed them all? You're not serious."

"Fuck I am, mama. But doan yo go askin' Baba. Sho enough he'd kick my tailfeather if he knew I shot off m'mouth t'yo like this."

"I told you I wouldn't say anything," she said. "I just want to know.... You're not pulling my leg or anything."

"Why I wanna do that, mama? Shit I doan joke 'bout these things, yo ask anyone here. Hey hey, yo ask Stinson, okay. Go on."

"Oh yes," Stinson said, his eyebrows raised. "Trip's most serious about those matters. I must say he's a most comforting man to have as a friend. Very loyal." He smiled, stroked her hair. "Are you having a good time?"

"I couldn't be having a better time," she said. "But I'm curious about one thing."

"What is that, little darlin'?"

"How do they survive?"

"Oh, well, lot's of times they don't or, even more likely, they run their course, if you know what I mean. But of course that's all that life is anyway, running one's course."

"But it's such a—clandestine way to live."

He smiled again. "Well that's part of its appeal, isn't it. Here they are wanted, admired, known—they even tread the path of gods in many ways. What more could there be for them? They possess here a kind of fulfillment that blots out the pain of their past, of the early breakup of their family units. That's a very strong pull, the family. It's what drives them on, really, because it's all they could ever count as their own when they were children."

"You talk as if you're above all this—not part of it...."

A peculiar look came into Stinson's eyes and he blinked several times. "Yes, well. I suppose that's my own way of...putting those memories aside. Not to forget, mind; never to forget, oh no. Only to get on with the present without allowing the past to entangle you so." He looked down at her as if from Olympian heights. "I am a dancer, Daina. I don't shoot anyone. Yet in your world I am as much a pariah as is Trip." He regarded her for a moment as if at last she had taken him out of himself.

"Odd that you are here," he said slowly, "at this very moment. That you aren't afraid—"

"There's Baba."

He gave her a peculiar look. "Yes. Quite right of course. But you're here all the same. You must have come *to* Baba rather than the other way around I imagine."

"Yes, that's so."

"Well then. You came. But not a runaway per se. At least not as we've come to know runaways. You didn't come to whore or to get a fix." He put a forefinger gently against his lips. "Then why *did* you come?"

"I'm...I don't think I'm quite sure."

"Well"—he stroked her hair again—"it doesn't really matter now. But it will," he mused. "It will...."

"So," Trip said, coming up, "what'd this sumbitch tell you? What a twisted muthafucka I am?"

"Nothing of the kind," Daina said. "In fact, just the opposite."

Trip looked from her to Stinson. "Well is that so? Mighty decent of yo, bro!"

"Decency," Stinson said, "had nothing whatsoever to do with it."

"What'd he say?" Trip giggled. "I mean what'd th' mutha

say? Baby, it's gettin' so's a hardworkin' street nigga cain't unnerstan' yo no mo'."

"Shit, Trip. Cut the act in front of this lady. Who you think you're foolin with that bit?"

"Whut yo mouthin', baby?"

"See, Daina, it's this way. Trip figures the less seriously you take him, the easier it's going to be to waste you one day. And you know something? He's absolutely right." He turned to Trip now. "But you know something else, baby, this is a party here. Ain't no bizness goin' down for you here. This here's neutral territory. It's off limits to the big bang and all that other rough stuff." He poked a forefinger into Trip's chest. "So ease up a mite. Relax and enjoy yourself."

"Hey, baby, yo go an' relax fo' jus' a moment an' tha's when they come an' scrape yo off the walls. Listen, m'man. I know whut it took fo' me t'get here, y'dig?"

"Hey, baby," Stinson said, in an excellent parody of Trip's voice, "yo ain't no fun a'tall." He grinned and left them.

"Where's Baba?" Daina asked, looking around. And saw the red hair, the pale eyes of Aurelio Ocasio. He had just come in the door. He wore a chestnut-colored suit with a red carnation in the buttonhole, a brown cashmere overcoat over his shoulders as if he were consciously mimicking Sol Hurok's entrepreneurial pose.

Trip saw where she was looking, pulled her away. "Yo doan wanna get involved with the likes o' him, mama. He's bad news."

"Baba's got some kind of deal with him."

"Yeah. Well I doan wanna know 'bout it an', anyways, ol' Baba knows whut he's doin. That man's gotta eye fo' the ladies. Long as they ain't spic or nigga, he'll gobble 'em up an' spit 'em out so fast they doan know which end's up. Yo stay away now like I tol' yo."

But it was too late. Ocasio had obviously spotted her in that room of dark faces and was already bearing down on them.

"Well," he said, grinning like a piranha, "if it ain't Baba's girl." Somehow he made the last word sound like *whore*. "What're you doin' this far uptown? Seein' how the other half lives? Slummin' your way into our hearts—or should I say beds?"

"I don't think," she told him, "you should say anything."

"Oh ho!" He laughed but it was anything but friendly.
"You hear that, Smiler?" He half turned so that she could see
the thin dark face. Smiler grinned, licked his lips as if he
were at a feast. "She got a lip on her. You know I like that.
I'm tired of all these empty-headed broads I usually tumble.
Now how 'bout you an me splittin' this place and—"

She heard the gentle click at her back, knew that Trip had
extracted his switchblade, but before he could use it, a great
black hand descended onto Ocasio's outstretched wrist. The
golden hairs disappeared beneath the dark mountain and
Ocasio swiveled his head. "Eh?"

"Whatchew on about, Ally?" Baba rumbled.

"Ah ha, nuthin, m'man. Just having a conversation with
the lovely lady is all." He looked down at the hand encom-
passing his wrist but Baba did not take it away, only tightened his grip.

"Yo know, Ally, I'se a tolerant nigga. Live an' let live is
how I likes t'live my life. But y'know ev'ry once in a while
some joker comes 'long makes me forget all that." He jerked
hard on Ocasio's wrist so that pain rippled across his lips like
an adder's shudder. But those pale, pale eyes were as opaque
as stones, showing nothing at all.

"I doan like liars, Ally, an' tha's whut yo are. A liar. I
heard ev'ry word yo said an' I didn't like even one of 'em. Yo
know whut I think? I think yo' gettin' outta hand. Yo need
a little sumthin t'think about these cold winter nights so I'm
gonna give yo one.

"Yo out o' my end as o' now. Yo had it. Yo go find yo' fine
self some other connection, baby, 'cause I had it with yo." He
looked past Ocasio. "An' yo, Smiler, whut yo doin' suckin' up
t'this spic? Doan yo have no self-respect?"

"I gots plenty o' that, bro. Fo' sho."

"Then yo tell this spic muthafucka good-bye, baby. Come
on, I want t'hear it. Yo gots a job with me, Smiler, if yo gots
the guts t'stand up an' be a man."

By now most of the dancing had ceased while people gathered in a loose semicircle to gawk at the spectacle.

Smiler looked around at all the guests, gave a quick glance
toward Ocasio who did not look up from his seemingly avid
contemplation of the back of Baba's pinioning hand. He glared
around him again, stared at Baba. "Okay, baby. Yo got it.
Yeah. I'se an independent now jus' like yo."

"Yo hear that, Ally?" Baba said softly. "Now get on outta here. Yo got no bizness talkin' to ladies, y'hear? Go find that blond slut yo been sleepin' with all these months. Yah, baby." He flung Ocasio's hand from him as if it were leprous.

In the hubbub that started up, Daina heard a sigh from behind her and Trip saying, "Baba, m'man, yo got some set o' balls."

"Hey," Baba said, moving them away from the epicenter of the commotion's aftermath, "balls ain't got nuthin t'do with it. Ain't no cocksucker gonna tell me whut's whut no more. I'se done with all that, put it behind me, y'dig? They's jus' some things I won't tolerate, tha's all. I c'n put up with a lot o' shit, specially when it comes t'bizness. But that mutha's gone come to a mighty bad end one o' these days." He looked down, saw the still-open switchblade in his friend's hand.

"Sheeit. Yo see whut I mean? I shoulda stayed outta it while yo carved him inta a sucklin' pig!" He grinned, put one arm around Daina, slapped Trip on the back. "God *damn!*" he cried. "Let's party!"

Daina was two car lengths away from the Pacific West Airways entrance when she saw Rubens striding through the magic-eye doors. He had an elephant-hide overnight case in one hand and a matching attaché case in the other. The familiarity of his face, his walk, made her smile.

"What the hell's happened to you?" he said, peering in through the open window on the passenger's side. There had been some rain and she had put the top up. She turned to look at him and he said, "Move over. I'll drive."

She did so without protest, waiting with her head against the door post while he threw his bags in the back seat, came around and got in behind the wheel. He leaned over, put his hand at the back of her neck, pulled her toward him. His lips brushed hers and she pulled her head away long enough to say, "You should've left me a number," before she buried her head in his shoulder. Her arms came up around him, holding him tight. He had sense enough not to say anything for a time. Horns blared behind them and the traffic hissed by. It had turned very cool.

At last she let him go. "Maggie was killed early this morning." Her voice did not sound like her own. "She was murdered."

"Murdered? How? By whom?"

She told him what she knew.

"A sword within a circle of blood," he said when she told him what Bonesteel had found on the speaker box side. "Are you sure?"

She nodded. "Why?"

"Well, last year there were a couple of particularly gruesome murders in San Francisco and, just after New Year's, two or three more in Orange County. All of them were identified with that sign, drawn in blood either on or near the victim's body."

Daina shuddered. "I knew that lieutenant knew more than he was telling."

"Daina, how did you hear about this?"

"I was with Chris last night. He was so stoned, I had to drive him home; he'd never've made it on his own. We came in and...found her stuffed into—"

"Oh, Christ." He let out a long sigh, put the Merc in gear and accelerated out of the airport.

"What the hell were you doing all night with Chris Kerr?" he said as he took them onto Sepulveda.

"I dropped by the recording studio and we went out dancing. What's wrong with that?"

"He's got some rep."

"As what?"

He gave her a quick glance. "Oh, come on, Daina. The man can't keep his hands off the girls."

"I'm not one of the girls."

He jammed down on the accelerator and the Merc leaped ahead, humming. "No, I will admit you're a bit over the hill for his specialized tastes."

"You're a real bastard, you know that?" she said hotly. "He needed some help; I gave it to him. He's a friend of mine."

"Some friend."

"You've no cause to be jealous. The two of you are quite similar in some respects."

"Jesus, I hope you're joking."

"I'm not."

He turned off onto Wilshire, slowing. "You really are the limit."

"Rubens"—she touched him—"we shouldn't be fighting. Not now. I saw something this morning no one should ever see."

He took them through Westwood Village, heading for Sunset. The kids were out and the line was long for *Regina Red* at the Plaza. "Look at that face," Rubens said, glancing at the poster of her outside the theater. He drove very hard along Sunset, downshifting through the turns instead of using the brake. It was not until he made the sharp right into Bel Air and slowed again that he said, "I took us that way to see how you were doing. I can wangle the true grosses out of Paramount but I like to see the lines for myself."

She put a hand on his arm. "So do I." She saw that Maria had put the lights on before she had left and the trees lining the long driveway blazed in the artificial glow. "I wish you had called."

"I did," he said. "You weren't home."

She looked away. "Sorry. That was stupid."

"It's okay," he said, pulling up. He shut off the engine. In the sudden stillness, she could hear the crickets singing in counterpoint to the soft pinging of the motor cooling. "But I did call Beryl. I wanted to get this thing rolling."

"What thing?"

He touched Daina's hair. "I hired her."

"For the film?"

"For you."

"What's Monty think of her?"

"Forget about Monty."

She took his hand away from her. "You *did* clear this with Monty, didn't you?"

"Monty's out of Beryl's league." He was watching her face intently. "Way out."

"Rubens, I want him to know. If he doesn't approve—"

"Listen to me. Monty's getting old. He's tired. His heart's not what it once was. I think—now, just listen to me—I think it's time you looked elsewhere for an agent."

She looked at him sardonically. "And I'll bet you have someone in mind."

He chose to take it head on. "One or two."

"I'm not getting rid of Monty, Rubens, so forget it."

"He'll pull you down, Daina. He's a weight you don't—"

She rounded on him. "Just discard him as if he were a useless rag doll."

"In a sense that's just what he's become. You're grown up. He's part of your past, now. He's obsolete; there'll be no place for him where you're going. There are others who can help you more."

"But there's no one else," Daina said, "who can help *him*. I want to do that and not you or anyone else can take it away from me."

"I want you to come to Maggie's funeral with me."

"Oh, Christ, Daina."

"Please, Rubens. It means a great deal to me."

He sighed, twined his fingers in hers. They were in bed, the windows full open, the night scents drifting in. He had fed her and bathed her, put her to bed. For a time she had drifted in that warm twilight between sleep and consciousness. The comfortable bed, the delicious coolness of the sheets warming to blood heat, the gentle patter of the shower as Rubens soaped himself, the knowledge that soon his body would be against hers all combined to make her drift off. But she did not want that now because the memories that had for so many years remained buried were surfacing like sulphurous bubbles breaking the skin of a dank and hidden swamp.

"Tell me," she said now, pressing his hand, "what happened in San Diego."

"It was a real sonovabitch." He stared up at the ceiling and something in his voice changed, making Daina feel as if she were in a plunging elevator. "I had to go to San Diego to find out that little bastard Ashley's been creating his own empire at my expense. This guy Meyer I went to see—he's got a permanent suite at the Del Coronado Hotel. He's got emphysema so he had to leave New York—he told me Ashley's been rounding up support among the board members. Meyer says he's going to try to oust me."

"But that's stupid," Daina said. "The company's yours, isn't it?"

"Well yes...and no. When we did the *Moby Dick* remake two years ago, things got a little hairy. The finances began to escalate all out of proportion." He shifted onto his side to be closer to her. "But the cast and crew were already on location. We had a couple of bad breaks: storms, a union strike. But it was an important film. I believed in it and we needed capital in a hurry. Now if we'd been cofinanced by a major studio—like we are on *Heather Duell*—there'd have been no problem. As it was we had to go elsewhere."

"But *Moby Dick*'s been very successful."

"Oh, yeah. I was right to make it. But that's all after the fact. At the time, we were in a hole and my friend Ashley tells me he can get the bread within two weeks. That was better than I could do and, rather than risk suspending the shooting, I told him to go ahead."

"How'd he do it?"

Rubens' eyes left the ceiling, paused on her face. "Well, let's just say that since then, every time I go to New York, I see more and more unfamiliar faces around the board table." He grunted. "Up to now I've been too busy with other things to stick my nose into it too deeply. I saw what a hole I had put the company into. It was my pride. But I realized with *Moby Dick* that the days of the true independent producer are gone. So I've been working out a long-range deal with Twentieth that would give me enough freedom."

He grunted. "Then I get this call from Meyer. He and a small number of powerful people are still on the board from the old days. But the others—it's like a tick infestation. Once they get under your skin . . . it's very difficult to get rid of them."

"But not impossible."

"Oh, no." Rubens laughed and she felt the reverberations through his body. "Nothing's impossible. You've just got to have nerves of steel."

Her head was against his chest. She listened to his heartbeat, like the tide, filling her ears.

"What are you going to do?"

"Part of it's already done; I went to see Meyer."

"What did Meyer say?" Her voice had dropped to a whisper; she was on the verge of sleep.

"Meyer." His laughter exploded again. "Meyer's a funny old guy. I'm glad he's my friend. He's no enemy to have."

"And what did he tell you?" she repeated.

"That I'm not, either."

* * *

The Nova Burlesque House had an unprepossessing, even a vaguely self-effacing, exterior. This had no doubt been carefully thought out for it was no tourist trap filled with females superannuated and fleshy or—as was the case with the live peep down the block and across the street—sad birdlike creatures complete with ellipsoid black-and-blue marks across haunch and ribcage, and dark, sunken junkie eyes.

Here specialty acts were clandestinely paraded for a select audience filled with every sort of fetishist imaginable and some—the staff always had a story or two—so shocking as to send chills down your spine. Or so they said. One never really knew or cared, for that matter. For the staff were a jolly lot who took their work with the equanimity of a well-disciplined high-wire artist.

No sad sacks performed here, for the audience, not to mention the staff who considered themselves strict professionals, would tolerate no such rip-off. For that kind of trash one only had to darken the doorstep of the numerous burlesque houses on Broadway. But not here.

Downstairs, on the street level, was a rather seedy porno store, dispensing with great élan an oddball assortment of perverse goodies that ran the range from under-the-table films in grainy black-and-white utilizing child performers—not the shaggy dwarves an unwary buyer would be stuck with elsewhere—to high-level black rubber bondage magazines that had about them the carnivorous air of the Inquisition. There was, of course, the straight nudie stuff but most of the store's customers gave that short shrift.

Though this store did a brisk business—businessmen from as far away as Dayton, Ohio, made a beeline here as soon as they hit town—its real profit came from the back where a lucrative numbers running operation oiled its cogs and wheels late into the long dusk. And, indeed, the Nova's much vaunted security force was comprised of members of this blue-collar cartel.

Daina recognized them the moment she laid eyes on them but that was hardly surprising since they were fond of displaying just enough of their pieces, lying snug and warm in chamois holsters in the sweaty pits under their arms. But despite this rather swaggering conceit, these men were among the nicest she had ever met. For one thing they were, to a man, filled with their proliferating families and never missed an opportunity to drop for her their plastic accordion cases with color snapshots unfolding like endless clowns emerging from a tiny auto. They deplored the fact that she was not at home with her mother. They mothered her but she knew it was Baba they loved.

He had a kind of off-the-street office here, unofficial and cramped, which he shared with the Nova's spectacled bookkeeper who, Daina discovered one winter afternoon filled with an atrocious pelting rain, lived on a quiet tree-lined street in Bensonhurst where his wife of thirty years was a member of Ladies' Aid and the local library association. It was understood that when the Nova's manager needed a place to sit, Baba would be displaced. He did not mind.

In fact Baba was the most easygoing person Daina had ever met. Nothing seemed to ruffle his vast exterior and this made her feel safe with him. He was a rock promontory upon which she could stand and watch that turbulent dangerous sea with impunity.

He did not seem to mind when she watched the shows from the wings, believing, perhaps, that corruption came only from within. For her part, Daina was fascinated by the phantasmagorical parade of eye-popping flesh. She never believed a body could move in so many curious ways. Yet, gradually, she came to understand that the art—for she felt certain it was an art—was a part of the mind as well as the body. The women she was introduced to here were part of no world she had ever been to nor had even heard of, equipped as they were with X-ray eyes able to unzip the soul of every man who passed through the theater's portals.

And it was here, at the Nova, that she began to see the curtain rising; to understand the focus of acting. You could do what you wanted; be whom you wanted; live out, for all intents and purposes, the darker side of what lay partly hidden inside you, without fear of retribution or embarrassment. It was only a role, after all, though the audience was always to believe otherwise. How wonderful to be able to live many different lives in almost simultaneous abandon! Rolling free to do . . . what?

Anything you wished.

On a chill winter's evening when the darkness had clamped down upon the shell of the city with such force that it seemed as if the dissipated glow of the streetlights were in a losing battle, when the west wind tore down 42nd Street with animal hunger, Baba took her in off the street, up the worn wooden rickety stairs to the lobby of the Nova.

Rooster was in his booth, dozing over a stained container of cold coffee in which could be seen floating some grotesque insect dragged down out of the air, no doubt, by the scent.

The somnolent Rooster, head propped up by the heel of one dark hand, was flanked in his tiny sanctum sanctorum by a pair of the saddest and dustiest plastic palm trees Daina had ever encountered. No one else was around. They could hear the percussion-heavy music that accompanied the show, muffled by the walls.

"Stick 'em up, yo muthafucka," Baba said in Rooster's ear and the other jumped up with admirable alacrity, his sleepy eyes wide, his hand scrabbling under the counter for the sawed-off shotgun that always lay there at the ready.

He saw Baba and his face relaxed. "Christ," he said breathlessly. "One o' these days yo gone get yo' haid blown off, jokin' like that!"

Baba laughed, clapped Rooster on his thin shoulder. "Yo should'na been asleep at the wheel. Ally come in here with his men an' wipe the floor with yo, yo not mo' careful."

Rooster snorted. "That cocksucker knows better'n that, bro. We fix his tailfeathers right fine," he said, picking up the shotgun and patting its barrel. "Why yo think we haven't widened the stairs, smartass." He hefted the weapon toward the dark and empty top of the staircase. "Boom! Blow the muthafuckas all the way back to Porto Rico, hah!"

Baba waved the barrel aside. "Watch where yo point that sumbitch. I made a promise t' my mama I wasn't gone die."

Rooster snickered, put the shotgun away. "Doan yo worry 'bout that none, bro!" He turned to Daina. "How yo doin', Miss?"

"Fine, Rooster."

"Now yo listen here real good. This ovastuffed ape doan treat yo fine, yo come here, right? Yo know where yo' friends are."

"Huh!" Baba grunted. "Doan listen t'a word he says, mama. He's jus' itchin' t'get inside yo' pants."

"Yo a cruel mutha, Baba," Rooster said with sad eyes, "yo knows that? Cruel."

"But I ain't lyin'." He laughed. "My office free?"

"Yas. Jus' Marty. It's gettin' near the end o' the month."

They went down the entrance past the lobby, filled with harsh blue light, to a sloping hallway at the side of the theater to a locked door of painted tin reinforced with steel. Baba slapped it with his palm until it opened a crack.

"Hey," he said into the dimness and the door opened just far enough to admit them.

Tony was the guardian of the gate at this hour, a bull-shouldered individual with a low forehead and curly brown hair. He had a neat mustache beginning to go white around the edges. He had small eyes of an indeterminate color, three kids, a chubby wife who seemed to be forever pregnant, bandy legs and a smell that seemed to stay with him whether or not he bathed. He punched Baba lightly on the shoulder, gave Daina a small squeeze while asking her, for the umpteenth time, if she would like to see the pictures of his family.

Baba dragged her away, knowing that she had endured Tony's familial sermon more times than she cared to remember.

She stopped on the way to the office in the rear to peek past the dusty curtains in the narrow wings and see what part of the savage parade was on view at the moment. Denise, a long willowy brunette in her late twenties, was in the midst of performing some fairly startling acrobatics with the lower half of her body. By now Daina knew most of the steady acts by heart, although from week to week some came while others departed.

Now Denise was inserting the egg and, requesting a volunteer to come and upturn his mouth beneath the V of her widespread legs, commenced to crack the egg with the muscles of her vagina. The music ceased, there was not a sound from the audience, not even a rustle until, with a sharp crack, the raw egg broke apart and the gooey inside dropped messily into the waiting mouth. Then Daina could hear the collective sigh coming from the semidarkness out front and the applause began to well up.

Baba had already gone back to the office but she stayed on, knowing that Denise had not yet begun to warm up.

She watched, fascinated, as Denise, naked, did a reverse strip, slowly, erotically picking out stockings and drawing them on, caressing her long legs as she did so. She turned, wrapped a garter belt around her waist, attached the tops of the stockings. She moved without once glancing at the audience and in such a way so as to make you believe that she was at home, alone, preparing to go out.

She turned away from the front of the stage, went across to the vanity that had been wheeled out for her and began to carefully make up her face using eyeliner, blush, lipstick, mascara. At length, she turned back and was even more beautiful than she had been before, the makeup—never too heavy—accentuating her eyes and mouth.

She picked up a brush and began to pull it through her long hair. With each stroke, her breasts bobbed, dipping and springing back.

She stood up, running her palms up over her hips, her torso, climbing to her breasts, cupping them, squeezing them, pinching the nipples until they erected. She licked her lips and one hand briefly brushed across her mound. Her thighs spread for a moment and her hips bobbed. Then she had lifted a bra from the top of her vanity, slipped it on. She bent forward a bit, rubbing the fabric across her stiff nipples before encasing them. She bent, stepping into stiletto-heeled pumps.

She drew up a long lavender dress, stepping into it, wriggling, lifting the zipper at the side. Save for the slit to one thigh, she was demurely dressed.

Jewelry came next: earrings, a pair of bracelets high up on one arm and a diamond necklace that hung down into the cleavage between her breasts.

She walked slowly to the front of the stage and stood there at the verge. From behind her she produced a pair of doeskin gloves, the same color as her dress. She had a ribbon in her hair that made her seem rather girllike.

With a kind of sensuous abandon, she drew on the long gloves, rubbing a fingertip between each finger as she did so. Then abruptly, shockingly, she reached out into the audience, pulled a man up on stage with her.

Without preamble, she unzipped his fly, drew him out into the spotlight. She bent slightly, pursed her lips, blew on him, then, enclosing him in the velvetlike fist, she began to gently rub back and forth, up and down and, miraculously, he began to harden until he was as stiff as an arrow. Now she worked in earnest, moaning as she pulled in long strokes until, feeling the warning tremble, she peeled back her dress so that the jerking tip grazed her pubic hair, inundating her mound with semen.

Backstage, Daina found Erica sitting on a stool, her bare legs crossed, smoking a small cigar with a white mouthpiece. She had a frayed robe around her shoulders but her hard apple breasts were bare. She enjoyed her nudity, Daina had observed.

"How does she do it?"

Erica looked up. She had cornflower-blue eyes and short blond hair. "Whom do you mean, *liebchen*, Denise? Ah." She puffed on her cigar, her wide sensual lips compressed with the effort. "It is very simple, really. She gives them precisely what they want. We know them." She shrugged. "It's human nature, don't you see? What could be more obvious?"

"But it never fails."

"Oh, well, Denise is quite good. It's like radar I think." Erica put her cigar into a green metal ashtray blackened in the center. "She knows which ones to pick. But of course they fight to be in the first row. She doesn't really go out there into the audience." She regarded Daina. "They come to her." She smiled a bit, a cold odd gesture that Daina found unfathomable. "That's an essential lesson in life, *liebchen*, eh?"

Daina went along the wall of the room, tracing her outstretched finger along the dusty surfaces of the mirrors.

"Are you happy here?" she asked after a time.

She heard the sharp indrawn hiss, knew that Erica had taken up her cigar once again.

"Happy," Erica repeated. But it was not an echo, rather a new meaning given to an established definition, as if she had somehow accomplished a sophisticated play on words. From her lips that word meant something else altogether. "Have you any idea, *liebchen*, what it is like to make a break with the past? Understand me, I do not mean simply *to leave* but also to disavow, to forget, to take a solemn oath not to remember." She let out all the blue acrid smoke. "Can you understand this?"

Daina stared at her, wide-eyed. "I'm not sure," she said. "I think so."

Erica, bestowing upon her that odd chilling smile again, said, "No, *liebchen*, you cannot. No one can unless...unless they accomplish it for themselves."

"Is that what you've done?"

"Oh yes." That smile would not dissipate and Daina found herself trembling. "Yes it is. You see I am quite special. Quite...unique. I have run away from it all—run to the other side of the world and now, yes, I am happy because I am what I want to be."

For what seemed the longest time there was silence. But Daina could no longer hold back the question, "And what is that?"

A burst of applause, sustained, came at them through the wings. Erica stood up, put a spiked collar around her throat. Her cornflower-blue eyes, wide and innocent, looked at Daina and her coral lips opened. "A cipher, *liebchen.* Just a cipher."

And whirled out of the room just as Denise, sweating and disheveled, came in.

"My God, what a crowd!" She put on her robe, sat down and shook out a cigarette. "Hi, honey. See the show?"

"Most of it," Daina said.

"You never get bored, do you?"

"Uh uh."

Denise smiled, wiped the sweat from her forehead. "That's good. It means you'll pick up the stuff. Not"—she lifted her hand—"that I'm advocating you going into this. In fact, now that Baba's not around, I ought to tell you to get the hell out."

"I don't see you leaving."

"No, well, that's a bit different."

"I don't see how."

"Well, darling, I love it. And anyway I'm in and out—make my own hours. That's good but I've got to because I've got to work around my classes at NYU. The Ph.D. program's a bitch—" She stared at Daina. "You don't understand do you? Nah, why would you?"

"But I think I do. I think it's the same reason why I'm here and...with Baba. It's because when I go back I feel...different."

For a moment Denise said nothing, then she held out a hand. "Come here, darling." She stroked Daina's back. "You're right you know that? Yes. But still—" Her eyes clouded. "But still"—she leaned forward, kissed Daina on her forehead—"you're up here dreaming dreams."

She smiled, patted Daina on her fanny. "Go on now," she said in a low voice.

"I'll be back tomorrow." She was reluctant to leave.

"Would you go on? I've got to study."

"Ah," said Marty, looking up at Daina through his bifocals. "I thought you might be in today. I brought you a jelly dough- nut." He lifted a small white package off the littered desk, shook it.

"Hey thanks, Marty. You remembered." She took the bag from him, extracted the doughnut.

"Whattayou mean, remember? Course I remembered. It's what I'm paid t'do." He tapped the side of his balding head. "Remember. My wife says, 'Marty, it's not just figures you remember.' There's a reservoir up here. I'm swimming in things I'd like to forget. Here"—he cleared the seat of a crum- bling easy chair of piles of papers, stacking them on top of the old safe—"sit down."

She did and as she began to eat, he said, "So how's school?"

"Okay I guess."

"You're doing well, aren't you?" Suspicion had crept into his voice. He waved his hand. "This isn't . . . you aren't fooling around are you? Education's an important commodity, you know. Even Baba will agree with that, won't you, Baba? You see? You don't want to end up like poor Denise."

"Poor Denise? What do you mean? She's going to graduate school at night."

Marty leaned over, wiped the rime of confectioners' sugar from the sides of her mouth.

"This is no place for a girl with so much brains." He pointed a stubby finger at her. "That goes for you, too."

"Aw, giver a break," Baba growled from the corner. "She knows whut she wants."

"Phooey!" Marty slapped at the air between them with the flat of his hand. "She's too young to know anything about what she wants."

"I don't think age has anything to do with it," Daina said.

"Not now you don't," Marty told her. "But later on you'll see."

"She won't see shit less I c'n get these figures t'match," Baba said gloomily, "so let's hold it down."

"Here," Marty said, leaning over, "let me see that."

"Get yo' hand outa here, Jack. Yo gots no business pokin' round here."

"What's the matter? You think I don't know what those figures represent? What's it to me?" He tugged the ruled yellow sheet out of Baba's hand. "C'mon. It'll just take me a minute and then you can go take Daina out for a good meal. This month you can afford it."

Marty had just begun to peer at the scrawled figures, mumbling, "Where'd you learn how to write anyway?" when the door to the office flew open. A man in a tan overcoat straight-armed a .38 Police Positive into the room, moving that black lethal mouth from one to the other. He wore a red, white, and blue ski mask so that only his eyes and his thick red lips were visible.

He moved two steps into the cramped room and they could see another man, similarly dressed, slightly taller, at his back. From the dimness beyond they could hear Tony's plaintive voice: "How was I t'know? They was in the audience; pulled out the masks before anyone knew what was—"

"Shut your face!" said the taller man. He gripped a .357 Magnum in both hands, his legs slightly spread.

No one in the room moved.

"Kay," said the man in the red, white, and blue ski mask. "Let's have the bread."

"What bread?" Marty said.

"Hey, asshole, don't kid around." He swept the barrel of the .38 in the direction of the old safe set against the back wall between where Marty and Daina sat. "Open it," he said. "Now."

"No one here has the combination," Marty protested. "And besides—"

Daina jumped at the roar of the explosion. Marty flew back against the wall, his arms outspread. His pencil clattered to the floor, rolling, and blood spurted from the hole in his chest. The concussion at such close range had thrown his bifocals off his face. "I can't see," he grunted. Blood drooled out of the corner of his mouth, his chest heaved twice as if laboring under enormous pressure and deflated like a punctured rubber raft.

"Marty," Daina said softly and then a bit louder: "Marty!"

The man moved the .38. "You," he said, "shut up!"

"What's goin' on in there?" Tony yelled.

"I'm warnin ya, Jocko—" said the taller man.

"Tony," Baba said. "It's all right. Don't do a thing."

"What am I gonna do, a Magnum starin' me in the face?"

"That's the spirit, Jocko."

"Kay now," said the man in the ski mask. "Let's have it."

"Let's jus' all calm down first," Baba said softly. He did not move a muscle and Daina thought, What does he mean, it's all right. It's not all right. Marty's been shot.

"Hey don't you go tellin' me what—"

"Jus' good bizness, baby." Baba spread his hands, palms outward. "Doan do yo no good blowin' brains out. This poor bastard's not gonna open any safe fo' yo now is he?"

"What'd you do?" asked the taller man. "Blow one of 'em away?"

"Had to. Now they know it's serious. There must be half a mil stashed around this joint somewhere."

"Yah, baby," Baba said, smiling cordially, "an' I'se the only dude what knows where, dig? Now let's all talk like gemmun. Doan want no mo' shootin' is all."

The man in the ski mask shook his head. "Talk won't do it, nigga. You just fork over the bread 'fore I start to think of what I c'n do with this little girl here."

"Sho," Baba said, the smile still stitched across his face. "Yo callin' the shots, m'man—"

"You bet nigga. Let's go."

"I gots t'get up first, okay?"

"Yeah, yeah," the man said irritably. "Just move it."

So Baba did. His hands flat on the desk top, he somehow levered his huge frame through the air, across the desk. At the last possible instant, his powerful legs unfolded, shot straight for the muzzle of the .38.

The soles of his boots struck the pistol from the man's grip and, instants afterward, the full force of his formidable bulk slammed into the intruder.

The man went down as if pole-axed. Baba, astride him, lifted his right arm. His fist descended in a blurred arc, smashing into the left side of the ski mask. There was a sharp crack and the man screamed.

Daina jumped as the .357 Magnum roared. She fell off the chair, holding her ears.

Baba was already moving out across the doorsill. Daina heard grunting, horrible animal sounds and abruptly the taller man hurtled backward into the office. Baba, his face set in a snarl of rage, flew in right behind him. He grabbed the man by the front of his overcoat, jabbed a short, vicious uppercut to the center of his chest. There seemed no sound in all the world save the awful cracking of bone. The man collapsed under the terrible blow, the muscle of his heart shredded by the debris of his shattered sternum imploded by Baba's fist.

Baba looked up at her. He was not even breathing hard. "Yo okay, mama?"

She nodded mutely, turned her head. "But what about Marty?"

Baba took her up in his massive arms, stepping over the bodies and the blood, pushing through the cluster of curious people crowding in backstage. He glared at Tony as he passed him, said in Daina's ear, "Yo forget 'bout him, mama."

Daina closed her eyes, willing herself to stop trembling, but all she could think of was that quiet tree-lined street in Bensonhurst where Marty had lived. And what, she asked herself, will his wife tell the other members of the Ladies' Aid?

It was impossible to see through the high iron gates into Forest Lawn. The phalanx of reporters and paparazzi surrounding the entrance served to mask, for a time at least, just what lay beyond the forbidding portals.

"Jesus," Rubens said, turning his head. "Beryl was right. You'll have a great opportunity to talk to them about the film."

"Don't play at being such a cold bastard," Daina said softly. Splinters of memory were still surfacing like the returning jetsam of some enormous wreck. "This is for Maggie."

"Funerals are never for the dead," he said in a tone that indicated he was speaking from experience. "They're only to soothe the fears of the living." And then as if it were an afterthought, "I have no interest in funerals."

"Why? Because you have no fear?"

"Yes."

She had said it as a joke but his answer had been perfectly serious. She watched him for a moment, pulling cigarette smoke deeply into his lungs. The hiss of its release seemed like a dragon's sigh. She sat back in the limo's seat as they approached the milling mob, took his strong hand in hers, squeezing the fingers very hard.

It was early in the morning and the sun had not yet begun

o burn its way through the thick haze, but flashbulbs pop-ing in tiers as they parted the throng brought out a pallid ncandescence that seemed spectral and eerie as if it had been designed by the special-effects director of a horror film.

There was heavy security but, despite that, the paparazzi had managed to infiltrate the place. They seemed to Daina almost inhuman in their fanatical desire to concoct bastard innuendos designed to promote an image of Hollywood prev-alent east of Palm Springs. They lay on their bellies behind ornate marble monuments or crouched behind trees like chil-dren at play, snapping roll after roll of high-speed film shot through monstrous telephoto lenses.

Stepping out of Rubens' limo, Daina felt a shock go through her. She was facing a woman who looked so much like Maggie that for an instant Daina felt totally dislocated. She was flanked by Bonesteel on one side and a rather small man in a dark-colored suit a size too large on the other.

Bonesteel introduced them as Joan and Dick Rather. Joan was Maggie's sister. Dick had a cast in one eye. He told them he was from Salt Lake City, where he and Joan now lived. He sold vacuum cleaners. Daina had not been aware that anyone could still make a living selling vacuum cleaners.

"It's very disconcerting." Rather rushed the way some peo-ple do when they are upset and they don't know what to do except talk, as if they are afraid that only silence will bring the grief. "I've often talked about coming out here to visit, living all my life so close and, you know, never having been but"—he was looking straight ahead, directly at Daina, away from his silent wife; it seemed a very deliberate gesture—"Joan has always found one excuse or another. Now this, and suddenly we're here...it doesn't seem real somehow." His eyes seemed to be pleading with her as if to say, Tell me this is just a bad joke.

"I'm sorry," Daina said and she thought she saw him wince.

"Sorry?" Joan said. "What do you know about being sorry?" They were the first words she had spoken since they had come together and Daina was struck by how dissimilar her voice was to Maggie's. It made her feel relieved.

"I was her best friend, Joan," Daina said.

"Mrs. Rather." Those cold blue eyes were unblinking. "What do you people"—she said this word in a way someone else might say "slime"—"know about friendship...or family, eh? I haven't seen Maggie since she left St. Marys. That's a long time ago." Her eyes seemed to burn with that cold quiet fire born to some Protestants, who never seem able to express their inner feelings. "Too long, for sisters. Much too long." She took one step forward and Daina saw her husband grip her elbow as if he suspected she might be ready to lunge. "I cannot imagine why she came out here or what she might have seen in this place. Perhaps, because she was not a particularly happy person, she fit in here in some way. None of you here is happy. I know that. All that makes you happy is eating each other up alive—"

"Joan—"

But she gave Dick Rather such a withering look that he immediately closed his mouth.

"I consented to allowing Maggie to be buried here because I was told that was what she wanted. She chose to be here for better or for..." She could not finish the sentence and for a moment Daina thought she saw the bright sparkle of a tear like a brief fireworks display in the corner of Joan's eye. In the next instant there seemed no trace of it. "I blame you all." Her voice was very low, as if the swirl of emotion had turned in upon itself like a tightly coiled fist. "You all knew her." She said "all" but it was quite obvious she meant Daina. "Saw how vulnerable she could be. Yet you let her"—she had to choke out the next word—"live with that demon. Nothing good can ever come from that kind of thing. Only evil." She pointed a finger. "You killed her!" she whispered. "You killed Maggie! And I...I can't even remember her voice now." At last her voice cracked and her body began to shake. Rather gripped her by the shoulders and her face turned away from them. But not before Daina saw that her eyes were still dry.

Daina reached out. "Joan—Mrs. Rather. I understand how you feel. There's no need for antagonism. I—we both loved Maggie."

"Don't you dare lecture me!" the other woman snapped, drawing away from Daina's touch. "You miserable creature. You and all the others like you. I don't need your sympathy. I'm quite certain it's as real as your conception of friendship."

"Let me tell you something," Daina said. "All my friends are important to me but none is as important as Maggie was. We grew up in this town together and over the last five years we spilled our guts to each other. There was nothing we didn't share." Joan Rather had gone white, recoiling backward so that her husband gasped, reaching out to grab her before she stumbled. But this reaction of what she took to be loathing only spurred Daina on.

"You think I don't care that she's dead?"

"I think, my dear, that you care about as much as you can. Which is to say very little indeed."

"And where were you when she cried all night long? It wasn't you who held her in her arms. It was me."

Two points of color appeared on Joan Rather's makeupless cheeks like opening parasols.

"You have no right to talk to her like that," Rather said. "Not after she—"

"Shut up!" Joan Rather barked and her husband's jaw snapped shut with an audible click. She addressed Daina: "You don't fool me with this talk of sentimentality. Should I break down and weep on your shoulder, calling you a saint? No, no." The tendons stood out along the sides of her neck. "If you're all that my sister could call a friend then I feel very sorry for her."

"Joan, please—" Daina felt it important now that she be able to get through to this woman. Easy enough to say that her love for Maggie would endure no matter what. But this was Maggie's only sister—her family. To be cut off so abruptly, so absolutely from this woman filled Daina with a kind of creeping dread she could neither tolerate nor define. "I don't want to argue with you. We both loved Maggie. Surely that should be enough to bind us—"

"Bind us?" There was an odd high, almost hysterical quality to Joan Rather's voice now. "We have nothing in common. Nothing at all." She jerked her head toward her husband. "Come on." She would not address him by name. "There are other places for us to stand."

Daina watched them go with a sinking heart and she thought, I'm sorry, Maggie.

She turned her head, saw Chris and the other members of the band several paces away. Chris looked drawn and haggard. Tie was standing between him and Nigel but she had her long fingers through Chris'. While Daina watched, she turned, said something in his ear.

"I want to go over and see how Chris is," Daina said.

Rubens looked at her. "Go on," he said. His voice had gone metallic.

"Won't you come with me?" she said, touching his arm.

"You go on," he repeated with as little emotion.

"Don't do this, Rubens," she whispered. "Not here, not now. Please."

"I came here with you," he said not unkindly. "Now you're on your own. I don't want to have anything to do with them."

He had ended on an odd inflection and she said to him, "Go on, darling. Why don't you finish it?"

"I'm not jealous, if that's what you think."

"That's *precisely* what I think," she said, giving him a sad smile before she turned away, walking carefully across the newly mown grass. The smell reminded her of old rambling houses on the Cape, the chop-chop-chop of the mower at dawn rousing her from sleep, hot August days deep in the heart of summer, the rank windblown smell of the quahogs piled in the shallows, and Daddy's face close beside her, his warm smell, lit by sunlight and salt, permeating her being. She closed her eyes, bit her lip, felt her pulse beating strongly against her eyelids. A voice was crying inside her, plaintive and forlorn and, abruptly, she tasted rubber in her mouth, so powerful that she almost gagged.

"Well," Tie said, in her oddly accented English, "I see the prima donna isn't holding up so well this morning."

Daina opened her eyes. Tie was the only one at the funeral who was not wearing dark clothes. On the contrary, she had chosen, as if with exacting care, a peach-colored raw-silk suit with a skirt slit up one hip, seamed stockings and very high-heeled red shoes. She wore a ruby choker and matching stud earrings. She looked as if she had dressed for an advertising photo session.

Daina ignored Tie, said, "Chris, how are you?"

"He's just fine," Tie cut in before Chris could open his mouth, "now that he's staying with us."

"I thought he should be alone," Daina said, wondering why she felt the need to defend her actions. "He certainly needed the rest."

"Oh, yes," Tie said. "The rest. In *your* house. How very altruistic of you." She smirked and, beside her, Nigel mirrored her expression. She pushed out her chin. "What's the matter? The producer's not enough for you?"

"What are you talking about?"

"I'm talking about you and Chris," Tie said savagely. "We all know what was going on ... how it made Maggie so unhappy."

"You're out of your mind!" But Daina found herself recalling the last phone conversation she had had with Maggie. Where had Maggie gotten such an idea?

"Maggie was an outsider," Tie hissed. "And so are you. She tried to worm her way in where she didn't belong." Her hand came out, palm up as if the nothingness held there were some kind of offering. "And there she lies." Tie seemed almost to be laughing now. "She died for her sins."

"Sins? What sins?" Daina sought Chris' eyes. "What's she talking about?"

"Magic," Tie said. "Black magic. She sought to break our inner circle."

Behind the band, a scuffle had broken out. Over Tie's shoulder, Daina could see Silka manhandling a paparazzi. The man struck out feebly, and Silka, picking up the man in one arm, snatched his camera away with the other, hurled it against the bole of a tree. It shattered, the ruined film popping out like a child's Slinky toy. Nigel turned to look but Tie did not. Chris seemed to be assiduously studying the tips of his boots.

When Silka returned from handing over the man to the security guards, he looked Daina right in the eyes as if to say, I told you about Tie.

"Is it over?" Tie asked and, when Nigel nodded, she said, "Chris likes you and so does Nigel. Don't make the same mistake your friend did. Nothing that's between us need concern you. Leave it alone."

"Leave it alone?" Daina said incredulously. "She was my friend. How can I leave it alone?"

Tie opened her mouth but before she could say anything, Bonesteel had taken Daina's arm and was saying, "It's time. I'll take you back."

An unnatural silence hung over them all as if they were locked in some kind of primordial struggle. Sides were forming, a flow of black and white, and it seemed to Daina that these people were involved in a monstrous game, that this kind of baiting was all they had left in life to keep them alive. Joan's words flowed through her mind: *All that makes you happy is eating each other up alive.* No, Daina thought, it's not true. We're not like that. *I'm* not like that. Once, I could've been like my mother, like that. But I learned.

She looked over Tie's shoulder again, saw Silka watching her. He put his forefinger up to his lips, pressed it there until she had allowed Bonesteel to turn her around, lead her back toward Rubens.

"I want to talk to you," she said softly.

"Not here," he said. "Not now." The echo of her own words sent a chill down her spine. "I have nothing to tell you yet."

"Yes you do—" But he had already left her beside Rubens, taken his place near the Rathers. She supposed he had called them.

The minister began. It seemed a long ceremony, bloodless and soulless. The minister had not known Maggie yet he spoke about her as if she had joined his church as a child. Perhaps Joan had been led to him earlier, given him the essential facts of Maggie's life.

Midway through, Daina realized that Rubens was right. Funerals weren't for the dead but the living, for there was no trace of the woman who had been Maggie here. Just a round of oval faces, masked in varying degrees of sorrow.

At last, two burly men lowered the coffin into the ground on its stout ropes. For Daina, her eyes filled with tears and her heart breaking, more than one person was being buried here.

Joan detached herself from her husband, walked stiff-legged to the edge of the grave. The minister intoned, "Ashes to ashes. Dust to dust..." while she bent down, gathered a fistful of loose earth. She seemed utterly, terrifyingly alone. For a moment, she stood there rigid and unmoving. Tie turned her head, said something to Nigel. With a convulsive gesture Joan stuck out her arm, flung the soil downward like dark rain onto the coffin's gleaming lid.

5

"I don't know what it is that makes them keep at it," Marion said one morning on the set.

"Keep at what?" Daina asked.

He folded the copy of the *Manchester Guardian* airmailed to him every day. Marion was a man who hated being cut off from news of home. "Yank papers," he was heard muttering from time to time. "Don't know how to report the news of the world." But in fact it was news of Britain he hungered for.

He looked at her over his bone-china cup filled three-quarters of the way to the brim with freshly brewed tea, a combination of English Breakfast and Darjeeling Marion had flown over from a shop he frequented in Belgravia. "The English and the Irish," he said quite carefully. "The C. of E. and the Catholics." He took a sip. "It sticks in my craw." He pointed a finger at the folded paper. "Take this for example. There was an enormous raid put on in Belfast about three weeks ago. It says here the thing was organized by Sean Toomey, that patriarchal head of the Irish Protestants in the north." He looked disgusted. "As usual, the English did all the dirty work, going into Andytown, pulling out the suspected IRA boys." He shook his head. "It was a real blood-bath."

"But it's been going on for so long."

"Just so!" He set down his prized cup with a bang. "And where does it get us, I ask you! Blood and more blood. Families decimated. Sorrow and despair." He pushed his cup away. "Now you see the real reason I'm making this film; show people the utter stupidity of it all." He gave the *Guardian* a backhand swipe so that its pages flew across the floor like birds with broken wings. "Ach! I don't know why I bother reading the bloody stuff anyway!"

But the next morning he was back at tea, studying the paper as if nothing at all had happened.

El-Kalaam was crouched on the floor next to James with Malaguez beside him. They had a map of the villa and its immediate environs spread out between them. They were going over it, piece by piece.

"They're certain to have men here soon," El-Kalaam said. "We must be certain there's no chink in our armor. It wouldn't do to be surprised at this late stage, uh?" His forefinger traced a rough rectangle on the map. "Moustaffa's here now. Go and see that all is well." Malaguez nodded and wordlessly obeyed. On his way out, he passed Rudd and the Englishmen on their way back down the hall. They were carrying the bathroom door. Fessi prodded them and they set it against one wall. He allowed them to rest then.

El-Kalaam glanced over at James. "You don't look at all well, my friend. Rita!" he called. "Some water out here. Keep the man's wife in there with you."

In a moment, Susan appeared. She carried a glass of water. Her makeup was gone and her carefully coiffed hair was falling around her ears. El-Kalaam ordered her to kneel before him; she complied.

"You see how easy it is," he told James. "They were born to take orders." He jerked his head at her and Susan let James sip at the rim of the glass.

In the kitchen, Rita was supervising the women's cooking. She had not touched a pot or pan herself.

"How is it," Heather said as she stirred the soup, "that he allows you in the cadre? It's obvious he hates women."

"He does not hate women," Rita said with a note of defensiveness in her voice. "He has no respect for them. Men and women are only different because they serve different functions in life."

"I don't see any difference—"

"It's foolish to even talk to you. Keep quiet and stir your soup."

Heather turned her head away. "It's just that I don't understand. Part of the revolutionary role is to make yourself understood."

Rita looked at the back of Heather's head for a moment. "When my man was killed by Israelis in a raid, I found I could no longer function as I—as a woman functions. Perhaps part of me was killed along with him." Heather turned around to face her. "I could only think of one thing. I took my brother's machine pistol and went across the border into Israel."

"By yourself?" Heather said. "Alone?"

"I don't remember it all. Only sometime later hands pulling me away from bodies—there were three of them, they told me later—I swear I had never seen before."

Her head swung around. "It was El-Kalaam who pulled me away. The killing frenzy was still on me and he took me out into the desert so that I could empty my machine pistol. When it was all over, he asked me to join him.

"I am not like the others," she said softly. She took a bit of food from the counter, ate it. "I am half dead." She pointed. "You're burning the soup." Her voice was a whiplash.

"You're wrong about women," James said from his sitting position against the bookcase.

"I'm not wrong about anything I say." El-Kalaam lit a cheroot.

"You are about this," James persisted. "You don't know Heather."

El-Kalaam grunted. He took the cheroot out of his mouth. "I don't have to. She's the same as this dark-haired one." He glanced up at Susan. "Get out of here now. Can't you see we've finished with you?" Susan went back inside the kitchen. "All Western women are the same. One need have no fear of them. They know nothing. They don't think; they just talk." He made a flapping gesture with the fingers and thumb of his hand.

"How would you like to make a wager on that?" James' blue eyes were bright.

"I don't make wagers," El-Kalaam said. "Not even with my equals." He puffed on his cheroot, glanced over at James. After a time he said, "What is it your wife is supposed to know how to do?"

"Shoot a gun."

El-Kalaam's face broke into a grin and he threw his head back. He laughed. "Oh, you are the lucky one. Lucky I don't take that wager."

"You're a coward then."

The smile left El-Kalaam's face and he scowled menacingly. His body tensed. His hands balled up into fists. Then the emotion was gone. The grin was back. "You seek to insult me, but it won't work. I won't be baited."

Rita appeared. "The food's ready."

El-Kalaam looked up. "Have the brunette feed Fessi and the others. The wife"—he looked pointedly at James—"will serve me and then you."

"What about Malaguez?"

"He'll eat as soon as he returns. I don't want anyone else out of the villa at the moment." Heather came out of the kitchen carrying a platter of steamed vegetables. El-Kalaam beckoned her over to where he sat. "Kneel down," he said.

After a moment's hesitation she did. Very slowly he began to pick at the food. He used only his right hand. "Keep your eyes down while I'm eating," he told her.

Susan came out of the kitchen, followed by Rita. They went across the room to where Fessi and the other members of the cadre sat. The front door opened and Malaguez came in. El-Kalaam looked up. The other man gave a curt nod and El-Kalaam went back to his meal.

"What about my husband?" Heather said.

"What about him?"

"He needs to eat."

Delicately, El-Kalaam took a slice of vegetable between his thumb and forefinger. Very deliberately he placed it between James' lips. James tried to chew. The food dropped onto his lap.

"You see?" El-Kalaam shrugged. "It does no good. No good at all."

"He needs something liquid. I made some soup."

El-Kalaam ignored her, turned to James. "I beg your pardon," he said ironically. "You were right, after all. She *is* good for something." When James did not answer, he turned back to Heather. "Your husband tells me you can shoot a gun."

"Yes," she said. "I can."

El-Kalaam snorted. "And what do you shoot? A paper target? Ducks on a pond? Or perhaps you're a rabbit killer? Oh yes, I see it in your eyes," he said triumphantly. "You can handle a gun all right." He pushed the platter away, disgustedly. "Go feed Rita. When you're finished you may give your husband the soup you made." He rose. "If he can keep it down."

He strode across the room to the telephone, dialed a number. "The prime minister," he said into the receiver. "It is now close to three A.M., Pirate. What have you to show for your time?" He listened for a moment. His face darkened. "What do I care for your problems. If it's a difficult or an easy task makes no difference to me. Our Palestinian brothers must be freed by six tonight.

"And if not...? You recall your old friend Bock, don't you, Pirate? Of course you do. Why else would you have sent your daughter here? You and Bock go back a long, long time. To the old days in Europe. We know all about that. You would not trust her with anyone else, isn't that so?" His voice was thick with rage. "Well, I trust you've got a photograph of your old friend Bock, Pirate. Watch for him. If our brothers are not free by six you're going to need that photo to recognize him."

He slammed down the phone, turned to Malaguez. "He thinks we'll get nothing out of him but he's wrong." He pounded one fist into his palm. "Those accursed Israelis are inhuman." He took a deep breath. "Well. They need a lesson. Malaguez, bring Bock along. Fessi, you know what to get." He stopped, brought Heather up beside him. "Come."

"Where are we going?"

El-Kalaam said nothing. He took her along down the hallway, past the bathroom with its open doorway, to a room at the far end of the villa. Once it had been Bock's suite but now the cadre had turned it into something else.

The windows had been boarded up, the huge bed overturned against it. No light came in through the window.

There was one lamp on in the room. The shade had been removed and the light was a harsh glare. Heather squinted. El-Kalaam moved her out of the way as Bock was brought in.

Malaguez took him into the center of the room. He stood with his calves against a slat-backed wooden chair. They all waited silently until Fessi came in. He closed the door behind him. He was carrying what appeared to be a length of garden hose coiled over one shoulder. There was a brass nozzle at one end, a screw-on socket of the same metal on the other.

"I understand," El-Kalaam said to Bock, "that you are quite a fine public speaker. That is unusual in an industrialist. Capitalists are often too busy giving orders or stuffing their faces with expensive food, uh?" He cocked his head to one side. "But then a man who makes his living exploiting the poor should know how to speak to them, at least."

"I was poor once," Bock said. "I know what it means."

"Ah hah! Yes indeed." He spread his arms wide, grinned. "All this is for the poor. Oh, I can believe that." His voice changed and his eyes narrowed to slits. "Well, I tell you, Bock, you will have to do some speaking now. You will convince your old friend, the prime minister, of his folly. He tells me he's experiencing delays, that there are many political factions in Jerusalem who must be appeased."

"He's quite correct."

"Do you take me for a fool? Do you think I don't know who runs Jerusalem? If the Pirate orders our brothers released, they will be released. It is folly, this stubbornness. He values your life; he values his daughter's life, doesn't he?"

"He values the welfare of his country more," Bock said.

"Spoken like a true Zionist!" El-Kalaam cried. "But this is the real world, my dear deluded Bock, not, Allah be praised, some Jewish pipe-dream you people insist on living. Decisions of life and death will be made here during the next eighteen hours. Part of the responsibility for what does or does not happen falls on your shoulders."

"We Jews have had six thousand years of life-and-death decisions," Bock said. "I know what I am doing. There's nothing more for us to talk about. You'll simply have to get along without me."

"Smart Jew," El-Kalaam sneered. "Very smart." He poked Bock in the chest with a forefinger. "Very stupid is all you are. You'll see. And remember this conversation. You'll beg

me to send you off to do my bidding." His face was very close
to Bock's. "Yes, you will."

He turned to Fessi. "Go attach it."

Fessi disappeared into the bathroom. Small sounds emanated from the open doorway. Then Fessi reappeared, nodded
curtly.

"Malaguez," El-Kalaam commanded.

The broad-shouldered man untied the flex from around
Bock's ankles.

"Sit him down."

Malaguez slammed the butt of his MP40 onto Bock's shoulder. The industrialist moaned, sank down onto the chair.

"That's better."

Malaguez tied his wrists behind the chair's slatted back.
"Ready."

Fessi took the nozzle end of the hose from behind his back.
He brought it close to Bock's face.

"You're so filled up with Zionist ideals," El-Kalaam said
coldly. "Now you will feel how it is to be filled up with something else." Bock's eyes swiveled from him to the nozzle Fessi
held.

"Have you ever seen a drowned man, Bock? I believe you
have. During your days in Europe, uh? The bloated bodies
like carrion. The stink. You looked at the face of your best
friend and couldn't recognize it." He looked down into Bock's
sweating face. "Yes. You've seen them drowned and gone.
And you've thought, Better them than me, uh, Bock?

"Well, now you'll feel what it's like to drown. And, in the
end, you'll do what I wish."

Bock gritted his teeth. Sweat dripped off his round chin.
"Never."

El-Kalaam reached out and pinched Bock's nostrils closed.
He shook his head but El-Kalaam held on. After a time he
opened his mouth to breathe and Fessi shoved the brass nozzle
into it.

"Never say never, Bock," El-Kalaam said, still holding his
nose shut.

Bock's eyes got big. As Fessi fed more of the hose in, he
began to gag. He sat up straight. His eyes began to water.
He made horrible mewling sounds around the obstruction in
his mouth.

"It's tough, isn't it, Bock?" El-Kalaam said. "Being so helpless." Bock's eyes were rolling wildly and he began to shake, first his legs, then his thighs and, lastly, his torso. Heather could see the muscles of his throat convulsing. "What a poor creature you are, Bock. But it's only typical of your race."

"What are you going to do with him?" Heather asked. "You're choking him."

Without looking at her, El-Kalaam said, "Fill him up with water, Fessi. But not too quickly. We want the effect to last. It's more...persuasive...that way."

"Torture."

El-Kalaam shrugged. "It is only a word. Women are good with words. Men deal in action. Results are what count. One must always sacrifice something to get what one wants. In this case—"

"Then you've sacrificed your humanity," she said.

He turned so swiftly it was a blur. His hand came up and he slapped her across the face. "Who are you to tell me of humanity?" he thundered. "Shooter of guns. Hunter of small animals. You kill without purpose, for sport. I kill for my people, my country, so that we may return to our home. There is justice in what I do but you—" he spat at her feet. "There is no excuse for what you do." He jerked his head. "Malaguez. Take her out. Let her wait with the brunette."

In the awful silence of the living room, they could not block out the intermittent cries that drifted toward them from the far end of the hall where the terrorists were working on Bock.

At last, Malaguez returned down the hallway. There had been no sounds for several minutes and Heather, her arms around Susan, bit her lip in anticipation of the outcome.

Malaguez stopped, beckoned to Heather and Susan. "You will both come with me now."

He was waiting for her when they broke for lunch. She walked back, exhausted, to her trailer and, opening the door, found him rummaging around in the half refrigerator in the far corner next to the dresser.

"Looking for clues?" she said as he stood up.

Bonesteel turned to face her, a small bottle of Perrier in his hand. He smiled. "Just looking for the lime."

"You're too late," she said, closing the door behind her. "I'm all out."

He unscrewed the top, took a swig.

"Wouldn't you rather have a glass?" she said acidly. She was annoyed that he had not seen fit to talk to her before this.

He waved the bottle at her. "It's okay. I'm used to eating on the run." He wore a lightweight pale mauve suit that did not come off any rack. Daina wondered how he managed to pay for it on his salary.

"You certainly are well dressed for a cop." She sat down in a plush chair, took her shoes off.

He grinned. "That's what comes from being a kept man." It had perhaps been meant as a joke but something in the back of his blue-gray eyes refused to laugh, remaining sullen and withdrawn. He leaned back, his buttocks against the top of the refrigerator. "You said you wanted to talk to me. What about?"

"You said you'd want my help."

"Oh, yeah, well, I don't think—"

"You've changed your mind."

He put the bottle down, went across to the small window, peeked out at the bustling lot by hooking his finger, pulling back an edge of the curtains. "I don't want you involved."

"Why not?"

He turned to look at her. "Miss Whitney, coming from such a smart lady, that's an awfully dumb question."

"I want to help."

"I appreciate that." His eyes said something else. "But there's nothing for you to do."

She took another tack. "You weren't very honest with me the other day."

"Oh?" He did not seem surprised. "What about?"

"That bloody emblem you found on the side of the . . . speaker box." She swallowed, willing herself to forget the horror that had lain inside.

"It's police business, Miss Whitney."

"*My* business, too."

She leaned forward and he sighed, massaging his closed eyelids for a moment. When he spoke next, his voice had taken on the droning inflection of a lecturer who was either incompetent or very bored with his material. "A little over two years ago, on November thirteenth, the body of a twenty-three-year-old college student was found within the north-west borders of Golden Gate Park in San Francisco. She had been brutally beaten and disfigured before she died. Beside her body was a rock on which had been drawn what was later identified as a sword within a circle. It was also later confirmed that this *emblem*"—he deliberately used the word she had used—"was drawn in the victim's blood. No suspect was apprehended."

He went back to the refrigerator, took another long swig at the Perrier. "Three months later, again on the thirteenth, the mutilated body of a twenty-five-year-old woman was discovered beneath one of the piers along the Embarcadero. Again, the peculiar emblem was found, this time crudely drawn on the inside of her thigh.

· "By the time the third victim was found—a twenty-seven-year-old model—the San Francisco police had brought in several psychiatrists who specialized in criminal psychopathology." Bonesteel grunted. "Bookworms. All they could come up with was that the killer would probably strike again in three months' time on the thirteenth. They said he must be driven."

Bonesteel's mouth twisted in the parody of a smile. "The bastard fooled 'em all. He struck in May, again a three-month interval, but this time on the eleventh." He dropped the empty bottle into the wastebasket by the side of the refrigerator. "It drove the San Francisco cops mad. Especially since the model's corpse was found by an army colonel's wife inside the Presidio.

"Then some bright light at the *Chronicle* came up with an angle. Using the emblem as a hook, he began to refer to the killer as Modred, the black knight from King Arthur's court. It was just the thing the public responds to. It stuck."

Daina got up.

"What do you want?" Bonesteel said.

"Just a club soda."

"I'll get it." He knelt in front of the refrigerator.

"I'd like it very cold," Daina said. "The ice is right there."

He scooped up a handful, poured in the club soda, handed her the glass.

"How do you know all this?" She wanted to see if he would tell her everything.

"Modred's fourth victim was discovered in La Habra."

"Orange County. That's quite a way from here. Isn't it a little out of your jurisdiction?"

Bonesteel shook his head. "I'm like those shrinks in one way. This kind of thing's my meat. Only I'm out stepping in the shit every day while they're leaning back in their leather-covered Barcaloungers, filling their pipes." He crossed his arms over his chest. "That La Habra thing was early last year. The sixth was early this year in Anaheim. Your friend, Miss McDonell, was the seventh." He stood up. "Now you see why there's really nothing you can do to help."

"Are you any closer to finding...him?"

"Modred?" He gave her a thin smile. "I wish I knew. The more data we accrue, the better chance we have of course. But"—he shrugged—"no one knows what he's up to, not the shrinks, not the county boys, not me. Only Modred knows. The shrinks tell us he's trying to communicate, in his own twisted way. We just haven't figured out what language he's using. It's tough."

Daina threw her head back. "And meanwhile women like Maggie die one after another." Her eyes blazed. "Why the hell don't you *do* something!"

There was nothing to say and Bonesteel, watching her, allowed her bitter words to fall, one by one, into silence until the tiny sounds from outside—a muffled laugh, hands clapping, the clash of metal against metal, a car's engine starting up—stole in on them.

"I'm sorry," Daina said, putting her drink down. "I'm tired and angry and I don't know what to do about it."

"It's not," he said, "just a job to me."

Something harsh and guttural in his voice made her look up quickly, just in time to see the feral yellow flare far back in the blue-gray of his eyes. To Daina it seemed like it might be a banner she had become familiar with. She looked at him again, as if she were seeing him for the first time.

"Will you find Modred?" she said.

"Yes, Miss Whitney, I'll find him." Abruptly, he seemed tired. He could not be more than thirty-eight or nine, she thought, but now he looked more like fifty. "I find them all. That's what I do."

His words were conveying more to her. She did not know what it was but it made her shiver. "Won't you call me Daina, Bobby?"

He had told her that no one called him that. Perhaps it was the name that held him in check. "All right," he said softly. "Daina."

She held out her hand. "You'll let me know?"

Bonesteel reached behind her, toasting them both with her glass. *"La Morte de Modred."* The ice danced in the glass as he drank.

They had come and taken Marty's body away—as well as the two others—and Baba would not let her find out where he was to be buried or which home in Bensonhurst the funeral was to be at. "What yo think, mama," he said, "we c'n jus' show up in there? Huh! Yo do what I tell yo, forget 'bout it, hear?"

She tried to do as he asked but it was impossible. She saw again and again in her mind's eye Marty's face, shocked and outraged, as he was slammed back against the office wall, the splash of blood as bright as a tropical bird's plumage, a soft grunting such as a mating animal might make.

She could not forget the tiny kindnesses he had lavished on her—"I can't help it," he would say to her, not at all apologetically. "I've got three sons. I always wanted a daughter." Her desire to say good-bye to him one last time was strong indeed and Baba's words brought home to her the completeness of their isolation from the mainstream of society. Being an outlaw had its bad aspects as well as its good ones.

To take her mind off it, she asked Baba how he had been able to do what he had done to the two men but he had just laughed deep in his chest and told her a story about a fight he had once had with a trio of anxious white Marines. "Yo learn t'be arrogant, mama," he said, "an' sho as shit yo gon get whupped. Them Marines found that out from me the hard way."

Thus the days and nights of utter peace had been pierced and this time of unadulterated fantasy, when she had been able to lock away the bleakness of the quotidian world within whose flesh she had encysted herself, was coming to an end. The wolf had been at the door and for a while she had barred him most successfully. But as the green leaves of summer eventually darken to russet and gold, foretelling the onset of winter, she could once again hear the howling, the insistent scratchings of his heavy forepaws and, at last, the splintering of the wood.

But today it was only a pounding on the door to Baba's office. Sergeant Martinez came in. He was a man who looked as wide as he was tall. However, no one could possibly mistake his bulk for fat. He had no neck and this made him appear as if he were continually strangling inside his policeman's uniform. His face was made up of a series of broad planes that held no shadows. The bridge of his wide nose and his round cheeks were heavily dusted with freckles and his eyes were a pale blue as if the blazing sun of his native Puerto Rico had bleached most of the color from them.

He slammed the door behind him, took several paces into the room toward Baba. "I ought to run your black ass into the station right now."

Baba looked up from his work, staring coolly at the cop. "Hey," he said softly, "what yo' doin' here? Ain't yo' time o' the month."

"Never mind the lip, *chico*. All that's gonna change as of today." He shifted his hips so that his revolver's large leather holster jutted out rudely. "This goddamn shoot-out's making a helluva stink at the precinct."

"Calm down," Baba said. He put his hands flat on the desk. To his left, the back wall was still dark with Marty's dried blood, ignored as if it were a mural by a painter who has dropped from favor.

"Calm down, hell!" Martinez stuck his chin out belligerently. Baba had once told Daina he thought the cop had picked up the habit from watching old gangster films. He thought it made him look tough. "The captain's talkin' 'bout gettin' involved himself." He bent forward at the hips so that his head and bull shoulders were over the desk top. "You know what that means? *Madre de Dios!*"

"Oh, yeh," Baba said. "It'll be the end o' yo' little racket here."

Blood came to Martinez's face, making his freckles fade. "My little racket," he said carefully, "is all that's keepin' your black ass in business."

"I know," Baba said in precisely the same tone of voice he had used with the two gunmen before he had destroyed them. "That's sumthin yo never tire of remindin' me of."

"'Cause you *need* the remindin', n—"

He stopped short but Baba supplied the word he had been about to say: "Nigga."

"You got this white *guapa*," he said thickly, pointing in Daina's direction, "you think you're somethin special." It was the first time he had acknowledged her existence. He shook his head from side to side. "But you ain't nuthin but a piece o' shit I gotta scrape off the heel of my shoe from time t'time. That's all you gotta remember." He stood straight up now. "Oh, yeh, an' one other thing you gotta remember: you pay me *twice* a month now." He stuck out his hand, a pig's hoof. "T'day you pay, *hijo malo*. Judgment Day."

For a long moment, Baba said nothing, declining even to move. Daina could see Martinez's increased breathing through his uniform jacket. A thick trickle of sweat crawled down the line of his sideburn, crossing his freckled face.

"Yo know the trouble with yo, Martinez," Baba said after a time. "Yo been so long thinkin' o' yo'self as a white man, yo beginnin' t'pick up white traits."

"You see these eyes, *hijo malo?*" He pointed. "They're blue, hey? Blue. You see this hair? No kinks. *I* ain't no nigga."

"No," Baba said quietly, "yo worse than a nigga. Ain't that what whitey tells yo down the station house?" He saw the other man stiffen. "Oh, yeh, they's some pressure now t'put a cupla yo spics on right now but yo knows where it's really at, doncha, baby. Sho nuf."

The cop's eyes got small and hard. "You better watch your mouth, nigga."

Baba ignored him. "Yo picked up whitey's greed, Martinez, an' it's gon get yo inta a heap o' shit yo not careful with yo'self. Ev'ybody on the force's got sumthin goin', so why not yo, yah? But there's a difference, baby. Whitey's got the muscle t' back up his vices. Yo ain't. Yo jus' a filthy spic, low man on the totem pole."

"*El dinero*," Martinez said hotly. His thick hand hovered in the air, opening and closing as if with a will of its own. His hair beneath his cap was wet and glistening with sweat. "*Ahora!*"

Slowly Baba stood up, shook his head. "Yo come back at the end o' the month like always, yo gets yo' bread. Ain't worth my while t'pay yo mo'."

"We'll see how you feel about that after I run you in."

"Yah, yah, yah. I see." Baba nodded. "Oh, this gone look real fine. Porto Rican cop on the take." He licked his lips as if in anticipation of breaking the story. "Gone read real well. Captain's jus' waitin' for sumthin like this t'bounce yo' ass out the door."

Martinez's hands balled up into fists. His face went dark with blood and he shook a little.

"No, baby," Baba said sadly. "We in this t'gether...yo from one end an' me from the other. Yo doan want no change, now do yo?"

Martinez seemed on the point of saying something but at the last second he bit his lip and, crashing his great fist down on the desk top, stalked out of the office.

Baba sighed deeply, sat back in his chair, his hands behind his head. He swiveled around to look at Daina, shrugged his immense shoulders. "Ain't his fault, I s'ppose. Whitey treats him like a used scumbag. Doan ever let yo'self be treated like that, mama." He turned, looked out the wire-laced window at the grimy spangled facades of the buildings across Forty-second Street. "Shit, they's taken away the on'y thing he had left: his pride."

Just before noon the light crane toppled and almost killed three of the production crew. The cast had the rest of the day off.

Daina and Yasmin left a furious Marion on the set. It had taken him five hours to get the lighting correct. "Get away from here, all of you!" he had cried, not unkindly. He was about to lay into the engineers and he felt that no one else should be privy to such flogging. The cast and the crew worked hard for him and he was, in turn, intensely loyal to them.

It was a smoggy day, the atmosphere thick and wet, when one wonders what airborne filth was settling on one's skin, and Daina found herself wanting to be near the sea; the city, even with all its flamboyant spread-outness, was making her claustrophobic.

But the sky above the beach at Malibu was perfectly clear, which was, Daina thought, typical L.A. weather. When it was lousy here, the sun was shining in Beverly Hills and vice versa. She parked the Merc by the side of the road at the vacant lot and the two of them stripped to their underwear, swam out to Rubens' boat.

"I envy you," Yasmin said as she toweled off her hair. The deck pitched slightly beneath their bare feet. "I really do." She threw out her olive-skinned arms. "I mean to have all this—and Rubens, too. I hope you enjoy it while you have it." Her enormous dark eyes were shadowed. Daina was aware of the hard thrust of her large breasts beneath her flesh-colored half-bra. The sight reminded her of the campus at Carnegie-Mellon but the sudden heat at the tops of her thighs made her think of Lucy: that halo of red hair, those perfect breasts and the two of them alone in one room. Stop it! she ordered herself, turning away. Her cheeks burned with a kind of shame she was at a loss to explain or even comprehend.

"Take it from me," Yasmin was saying. "I ought to know. All fame is fleeting." She gave a laugh that was more musical than it had been perhaps intended to be.

Daina said nothing, her mind far away, busied herself with drying off. The breeze was stiff out here. Watching the sunlight spinning off the tops of the waves like skeins of gold thread, she wished she could ride those waves out into the deeps. She felt a warm palm on her shoulder and it made her jump. An electric thrill went down her spine and died away.

"Daina, are you all right?"

She scented Yasmin's faint spice close behind her and for just a minute her eyes closed, her nostrils dilating. When she turned around, her face was entirely composed. She smiled. "Sure," she lied. "I was just thinking, if I looked out that way I could see Chris and Maggie's house."

Yasmin's hand remained where it was, building up heat between them. "You mustn't think of that," she said. "It's not good to store up such sad thoughts." She put out her other hand, turned Daina all the way around to face her, putting Daina's back to that part of the shore where the house lay. At that moment, Daina thought Yasmin's face was exquisitely soft, alive, full of a compassion no man could possibly duplicate. "Now is the time for you to be strong. There is no solace in weakness. *We* continue. *We* live. That's all that matters."

With that, a peculiar weakness came into Daina's knees. She had felt this sensation once before, in college on a steamy night in late May in the midst of final-exam week. She had been seeing Lucy's brother, Jason, a golden-haired boy full of muscle and stamina. They had tried to stay away from each other during that hectic week but even final-exam anxiety could not stem their lust.

On a night when Lucy had made plans to study at a friend's, Jason had come over. Never had his lovemaking seemed so exciting, never had she found herself so lost within her own passion. And then, as he rode deeply inside her, she heard the door to the bedroom open, thought she could discern the soft pad of bare feet amid the gruntings. She felt the weight of someone else in the bed with them.

Afterward, she told herself over and over that she had only been dimly aware of these things, that most of her being had been involved in the highly sybaritic pursuits. She felt soft hands caressing her back in just the way that moved her most, spiraling downward to her buttocks. They were cupped, spread slowly apart, long fingers in the wet crease, moving up and down, up and down in concert with Jason's increasingly lustful thrustings.

She moaned, beside herself with pleasure, and it was then she had felt the breasts against her spine, the hard nipples brushing her skin and the thick bush of hair insinuating itself between her spread lobes.

She pulled her lips from Jason's, turned her head, saw Lucy's face shining, alight with lust, so close to hers that the other girl bent her head only a fraction, covering Daina's lips with her own. The feel of Lucy's slithery tongue, her hot panting breath inside her own mouth, was somehow the limit of intimacy. It caused Daina to shudder. And with that bodily reaction, self-consciousness came. My God, she thought wildly, what am I doing?

With a soft cry, she tore herself away from Lucy's clinging mouth, her stinging nipples. She wrapped her fingers around the base of Jason's rampant penis, pulling him out of her. He groaned deep down in his throat and she felt him begin to jerk in her hands.

"No!" she cried. "No, no, no!" And leaped off the twisted sheets, running from the room, her palms hot and sticky from the initial jets of his orgasm.

Remembering it again, Daina was overcome with shame. Not so much that it had happened but at the thought that she had known who it was who had crept into her bed that night—that she had known and had wanted it all along.

Angrily, she broke away from Yasmin's grip.

"That's it!" Yasmin shouted, misinterpreting the movement. "Anger is far better than tears."

"I'm through crying," Daina said. Her voice sounded oddly harsh to her own ears. "For anyone."

Yasmin came and stood beside her. Together they looked out at the bosom of the Pacific. "What is there left to cry about anyway?" Yasmin said softly. "For either of us." She tugged at the ends of the towel Daina had given her, which rode around her neck. "It's all in the past...all that rotten bullshit. And the past is forgotten." She sighed. "Only at the Wall is it remembered."

Daina turned her head, gave the other woman a quizzical look.

"Oh, you know," Yasmin said, "the Wailing Wall. Don't look so surprised. I'm half Israeli...Sephardic, which is why my skin is so dark; my mother is a Frenchwoman, fair-skinned and fair-haired. In Jerusalem, at the Wall, the long torturous history of the Jews is remembered...and revered." She put her elbows on the polished wooden railing. In that position, her breasts hung lushly, her buttocks taut, straining the sheer silk of her panties. Daina thought she felt a bit dizzy.

"I learned very early on," Yasmin was saying, "to know what I want and to take it...by hook or by crook. We Israelis are very tough."

"Then why should you feel any remorse for George?" Daina said sharply. "You got what you wanted." She knew that the anger she felt was with herself.

If Yasmin was offended, she chose not to voice it. "I'm only human after all." She smiled. "My father is a very humane man. He told me he got that way by having been forced to kill the enemy during the war."

"Would he do it again, d'you think?" Daina said. "Kill, I mean."

"Yes," Yasmin said immediately. "Because it would mean the defense of our homeland. But more, in that moment of confrontation, there is no question of humanity, only survival."

Daina thought of Jean-Carlos and of what he had said

when she had asked him how he had broken out of Morro Castle. "I had to strangle a guard," he said without a trace of pride. "The time came when I was presented with the opportunity. It was only a split second, mind you. There was no time for philosophy or rationalization. And this is what I found out in that moment: the organism has the will to survive. It is deeper than anything. I do not speak now of duty or of heroism. These are different matters, entirely.

"What I am describing is the moment just before death. *Your* death. The organism has the will and the will allows the resources to be tapped.

"I was being beaten and had I allowed it to continue I would surely have died that day. Not to accept that opportunity would have been sheer madness. There was no question of humanity. Absolutely none. I ceded control of my body to the animal. I let him take care of me and he did. You, Daina, must learn the same thing. You must learn not to fear that part of you."

"I don't know whether I can," she had said, thinking of her time of impotence years before.

"We shall see," Jean-Carlos had said, putting his scarred forefinger against the side of his nose. "We shall see."

"Yasmin—"

The other woman turned her head so that her long blue-black hair, sailed out by the wind, brushed Daina's cheek. "Yes?"

Daina had been on the verge of asking the question—the same one she was certain now that she had wanted to ask Lucy. She could not then; she could not now. The same fear still transfixed her. She could not accept that part of herself; there was too much letting go involved. What would I become, she thought, what would happen to me if I should say to Yasmin, Will you go to bed with me?

She wiped her forehead with the corner of her towel and said instead, "How about some lunch? There're cold cuts in the galley."

But belowdecks, it was even more difficult because the quarters were so cramped. Daina became acutely aware of the sweep of Yasmin's dusky shoulders, her lithe torso, the contours of her slightly rounded belly and the heat that seemed to emanate from between her thighs. The dark hump of her pubic mound was all too apparent as she walked or sat or stood.

"I'll tell you something that's odd," Daina said, to get her mind off sex. "Do you remember that day Chris picked me up at the set?"

Yasmin, spreading mustard across a thick slab of wheat bread, nodded. She added lettuce, sliced tomato, made the sandwich whole.

"Well, at lunch we ran into someone who Chris had known years ago. I'd have thought it would've been a happy reunion but it wasn't."

Yasmin leaned over, opened the refrigerator, took out a can of Lite beer for each of them. She took a bite of her sandwich. "So?"

"So when it happened, I was confused by it. The guy was abusive but even before that I got the feeling Chris didn't want anything to do with him."

Yasmin opened her beer. "Maybe he never liked the guy."

"No, that wasn't it at all. I think I'm coming to understand it now. It's as if those people from your past remind you of what you once were and, in some way, that diminishes what you have become. People are like anchors: you can move to them in times of trouble but then again they can drag you down."

"Oh, your tastes change, you begin to move in different circles."

"That's only part of it." Daina had begun to see just how different Yasmin and Maggie were. In memories of Maggie, what she thought of now were the whinings, the weaknesses, the insecurities. She felt again Maggie's unbounded unhappiness like a chill breath from beyond the grave.

Yasmin had stopped eating and was watching Daina carefully. "I know," she said. Without moving her gaze, she dipped her long fingers into a jar of green olives. Her nails clicked as she drew out the cylinder of pimento from the hollow center. She ate that in tiny, nibbling bites as if it were the greatest delicacy.

"It's what happens when you become a star, isn't it? You feel it, too. It's happening to both of us."

Yasmin took the olive between her fingertips, extended it across the short expanse of the table. "Here," she said quietly. "Open up." While Daina chewed on it, she resumed eating her sandwich. "Not to both of us, darling. To you. You're the one Beryl's working on. You're the one this film's about. Don't think the studio doesn't feel it, too. They may be fools sometimes but they're not complete idiots.

"I think George was the first of us to understand it, really. Even before Marion or Rubens. *Heather Duell*'s become a locomotive. It's generating so much power, so much word of mouth already, that the momentum's out of all control. Tnat's why Beryl's having such a ball with it. It was her idea to do that twelve-page color insert in this week's *Variety*. No words...just photos: you, me, George, Marion even. But you were on the front and the back. The project's a publicist's dream."

Daina, though she had worked beside this woman for months, began at last to view her as a person and not just a personality. "What resentment you must feel."

"Oh no." Yasmin shook her head, her hair obscuring one eye. "I'm too much the pragmatist for that. I know that built like this"—her hands came up under her heavy breasts, thrusting them out and up so that Daina felt a spasm in the pit of her stomach. She turned her head away—"I'll never get the leading roles. The last actress who could was Loren and times were different then." She shrugged, dropped her hands, picked up the remains of her sandwich. "Perhaps I'll go into the hospital when we wrap," Yasmin said around a bite of food, "and have my breasts reduced." She swallowed, frowned. "What do you think about that?" She waited until Daina's head came back around and their eyes locked. "Maybe just a little bit to reduce my cup size from D to C."

Daina's mouth was dry. "I don't think you should change anything. Your body's your own. Why should you give it over to them?"

"Why do you want to be a star?" Yasmin said seriously.

Daina's eyes dropped and, after a time, she said, "All right then. I think it would help."

"Of course it would!"

Daina's voice was thick with anger. "It disgusts me, making yourself over in man's image!"

"Not man," Yasmin said. "Hollywood. There's a hell of a difference."

"It's obscene, any way you look at it!"

Yasmin put her hand over Daina's. Leaning slightly across

the table, her eyes so clear, so sincere, she was a female as
Daina was a female; their sex a sacred bond between them,
not at all sexual now but rather sociological, perhaps even
anthropological. "What will you do for stardom, Daina? How
fiercely does that flame burn inside you?" Her fingers tightened, draining the blood from Daina's flesh. Her voice was
now a whisper. "How much do you want it?"

Daina stared into those eyes. They seemed like mirrors,
reflecting two tiny replicas of herself and, as she watched,
she thought she could see the images moving as if of their
own volition. "I want it." Who said that, she or the replicated
figures?

Yasmin sat perfectly still. "What if you had to sleep with
Rubens in order to do it?"

"I love Rubens."

"What if that were part of it? That you were required to
act as if you loved him in order to—"

"Stop it!" Daina tried to pull her hands away. "You're
frightening me." But how hard had she tried to free herself?
Part of her was fascinated. She heard Baba's words echoing,
Doan ever let yo'self be treated like that, mama. Oh, yeah.
Baba knew where it was, all right.

"I don't believe you're frightened at all," Yasmin said with
some conviction. "I think you want to convince yourself that
you're not like that." Again she squeezed but no pain ran
through Daina's fingers, only a kind of electric current so
different from that she felt with Rubens, it seemed momentarily alien. "I think you know just what I mean."

"Yes," Daina whispered. "All right, yes. I'd sleep with him.
But pretend to love...I don't know."

"Yes, you do." Her gaze was steady. "We're two peas in a
pod, Daina. You know that, too."

Daina tossed her head. "No, I don't."

Yasmin shook her. "Look at you." Her voice was chiding.
"You're so terrified, you're trembling. What've you got to be
afraid of?"

Daina felt the anguished pull of her stomach as it tightened. "I don't know," she said, "what I'm frightened of."

"Oh, yes, you do." Yasmin was very close now, her musk
strong. "You finally know what it is you want." She took
Daina's hand in her own so that the palm lay open, waiting.
Daina felt the strength of the other woman as she gripped

her fingers from beneath. "All you have to do now is reach out and grab it." She snapped Daina's fingers into a closed fist.

"Rubens wants me to fire Monty."

"And so you should," Yasmin said. "It's the smart move to make; the *only* move."

"There's something else at work here—"

"Do it, Daina."

"There's loyalty—"

"Loyalty never helped anyone's career. It won't do a thing for yours."

Daina said nothing but silently she cried: You see how it is, Monty. You're only a corpse to them. But you're more than that to me. She turned away, hiding her face from Yasmin's sight, and thought: What am I to do?

Malaguez brought Heather and Susan into the hot box. Susan gasped aloud when she saw what they had done to Bock. She twisted from Malaguez's grip, threw herself across the room. On her knees she held Bock's head, cradling him against her breast.

"Malaguez," El-Kalaam said. "I want you to supervise the others outside. You know what to do. Send Rita back." Malaguez nodded, left. A moment later, Rita appeared, her MP40 slung obliquely across her back. Her large dark eyes flickered from Bock to Susan and back again.

"Will he do what we want?"

"Soon," El-Kalaam assured her. He turned his attention back to Bock. "Get away from him," he told Susan and when she did not comply, he made a motion to Fessi. The rodent-eyed man stepped forward, pulled her roughly by her hair, jerked her head back. Fessi grabbed her with his other hand, pulled her, gasping, to her feet. He took her a little bit away from the center of the room. One hand roamed her body as she twisted.

El-Kalaam came forward, bent over Bock. He took the industrialist's chin in his hand, lifted up his head. Bleary, bloodshot eyes stared dazedly into his.

"Are you awake, Zionist?" He slapped Bock firmly on each cheek until the color rose in the other man's face. "Yes, I see you're quite awake now." He glanced upward for a moment, at Susan. "Your lady friend is here. I thought it only right for the two of you to be together at a time like this."

"A time like what?" Susan said. Her eyes rolled wildly. "What more are you going to do to him?" She began to cry.

El-Kalaam pinched Bock so that the industrialist's eyes focused. "It's too late for you now, Bock. Your stubbornness has taken us all beyond the pale. You're responsible for events now. We are blameless."

"There is too much blood on your hands already," Bock murmured. "Too much blood."

"Enough talk now. Just watch."

Slowly Bock turned his head. His eyes widened. "Susan," he breathed. "What is she doing here?" He seemed greatly agitated.

"She's going to help us put on a little show."

"No." Bock's head went from side to side. "Not Susan, no."

"Oh, but Bock," El-Kalaam said, "that's no way to act. This show's being produced just for you."

"No," Bock said, his head wagging. "No, no, no." His voice began to rise in pitch.

Fessi's fingers left red welts where they poked and prodded Susan's flesh. Then he put his hands on her shoulders, forcing her down. He took out his pistol, aimed it at her. Bock began blubbering.

"For the love of God," Heather said.

"Shut up," El-Kalaam warned her.

Fessi stared down at the top of Susan's head.

"You see what is about to happen, Bock," El-Kalaam said. "See what your stubbornness has brought upon your woman." Somewhere in the villa the telephone rang. El-Kalaam made a motion to Rita who went across the room to where the phone sat next to the upturned bed. Susan was whimpering. Fessi gripped her until she cried out. In the background: Rita's hushed voice speaking into the phone. "It will be as it was before with you. She will be overcome and she will faint. And when she awakes, it will begin all over again." Fessi closed his thumb and forefinger around Susan's neck.

"El-Kalaam." It was Rita's voice. It froze them all. "The prime minister is on the line." Still El-Kalaam did not move or turn his head from the grotesque scene before him. "It's six o'clock," she said softly but clearly. "The deadline for our brothers' release has come and gone."

"What does the Pirate want?" His face had gone hard.

"He wants an extension on the deadline," Rita said. "There are problems. He wants to talk to you. He assures us that—"

"Tell him," El-Kalaam said with deliberate calmness, "to get out his old photograph."

"Don't you want to..." She held out the receiver.

"Tell him and hang up."

Rita did as he ordered.

Bock, who had been staring at Susan and El-Kalaam all this time, moaned and was sick again.

A look of disgust and loathing passed across El-Kalaam's face as he watched Bock writhing on the floor in front of him. "He's no good to us anymore," he said. "No good at all. Except perhaps as a lesson the Pirate must learn."

He reached to the heavy .45 caliber army automatic holstered at his right hip. He drew it out, transferred it to his left hand. He took Heather, brought her forward until she was standing directly in front of Bock's crouching form. "Rita," he barked, "put your pistol to this woman's head."

Rita came across the room, placed the muzzle of her automatic against Heather's right temple. Heather's lips parted and she began to tremble.

"Now, rabbit killer," El-Kalaam said, "we shall see what you are truly made of." Carefully he placed his own .45 in the palm of her hand. He curled her fingers around the grip one by one. "Your husband wanted to make me a wager. He said you could shoot a gun. You're a huntress, aren't you? All right. All you have to do is pull the trigger." He came closer. "Look, look. You don't even have to aim."

Heather stared down at the enormous gun in her hand.

"Put your finger on the trigger," El-Kalaam said almost gently. "Your husband said you knew how to shoot. Will you make him out a liar?"

"James does not lie," she said. Her forefinger curled around the trigger of the automatic.

El-Kalaam reached out, put one hand along the barrel of the pistol. He brought it up, aiming it at a spot just between Bock's eyes. Heather looked down the barrel at Bock's shining upturned face. His eyes goggled at her and there came a strange rattling from his throat.

"Pull the trigger, Heather," El-Kalaam said. It was the

first time he had called her by name and she jumped. "Just think of him as a frightened rabbit held in your sights. You've killed many rabbits."

Slowly Heather's eyes squeezed shut. Tears clung to the corners, sparkling in the harsh, defining light. They ran down her cheeks, dropping, left-right, onto the floor at her feet.

"How many rabbits have you killed, Heather?" El-Kalaam's voice was changing again, softening even more. He was a wise old uncle whose advice was taken unquestioned.

"Many." Her voice was just a whisper. Her eyes were still tightly closed. Her head trembled a little.

"Many." El-Kalaam nodded. "And in all those times, when you had the heads of those rabbits in your sights, did you ever think twice about taking their lives?" She did not reply. His hand reached out. "Well, here we have just another rabbit. Imagine those round unthinking eyes, that pale fur. Tastes so good in someone's pot, uh?"

Her eyes flew open and she stared at Bock. She began to shake and her head whipped back and forth. "I can't. I can't."

"You can and you will," El-Kalaam said. "Or else"—there came a sharp click as Rita pulled back the hammer on her pistol. Heather gave a start—"Rita will be obliged to kill you."

Heather wrapped the fingers of her left hand around her right wrist, her right arm held perfectly straight.

"Look at this," Rita said. "She just might do it."

Heather saw again the target in her sights. Bock's eyes stared up at her. Her finger tightened on the trigger but, just as she squeezed it home, she swung her arms away. The boom of the automatic was deafening. Plaster rang down on them from the ceiling.

"All right," El-Kalaam said.

Heather began to shake.

He took the .45 from her hand, brought it to bear on Bock's head. He pulled the trigger. The bullet went into the industrialist's left eye. He threw up his hands in reflex. Blood spurted, drenching Heather and El-Kalaam. Bock stared up at Heather with his one good eye. He lurched to one side and collapsed.

"That," El-Kalaam said to Heather, "is the difference between you and me. I know when to kill; you don't."

* * *

Now all natural light had left the sky, replaced by the distant pinkish neon of Chandler's L.A. night. Somewhere far, far away palms and jacarandas whooshed in the glow and coyotes growled in the sumptuous hills. But not here.

From close by the sound of simulated gunfire pop-popped like a string of firecrackers. Floods burned on the target range where the extras were earning their pay pushing back, in one isolated pocket, the gathering darkness.

With a weird kind of detachment Daina saw herself sitting in the semishadows, a principal actor in a play at the coming of dusk. The soft ending of the day cloaked her as if with sable.

She thought of the day's shooting and trembled a little. All around her was the black skeleton of the complex lighting structures and as they caught her eye they seemed to her to be the physical embodiment of the film. Its skeleton was up and each day they added on more meat: flesh, sinew, muscle, skin until now it was constructing itself, like some fearsome mythical beast they had, with their exceptional powers, conjured into the real life. They had seen the rushes—Marion, beside himself with glee, had insisted on it—and been stunned. Even the crew. *Especially* the crew: that jaded lot who had seen it all. Until now. *Heather Duell* was indeed being born and its power was awesome, undeniable.

At her feet were piled the trades: weekly *Variety, Hollywood Reporter* and *Daily Variety*. All contained articles on the film and on her. There was a piece in today's *New York Times* that was more laudatory than she could have imagined. Ostensibly it was about *Heather Duell* but it really revolved around her. "On the wings of her latest starring role in *Heather Duell*, Daina Whitney appears destined to be the most talked-about leading lady in Hollywood. According to noted publicist Beryl Martin and several highly placed executives at Twentieth Century-Fox..."

It was very quiet now. Even the extras, having learned how to simulate killing, had departed.

Absolute darkness descended as abruptly as it does in the desert, a flare of blackness. She turned her head as if she heard a sound.

At last she got up, leaving the papers where they lay. She was overcome by that intense satisfaction that only the artist—the painter, the writer, the actress—can feel: the living and dying within a lifetime, again and again with each new project.

Her arms reached out and up for the sky. This is why I became an actress, she thought. To know this feeling. But she understood that it was more than that. It was control. This was the legacy she carried with her from the Nova Burlesque House. She found herself wondering for the ten-thousandth time which was more important to Denise: her sensual life on the Nova's tawdry stage or the exacting work she put into her Ph.D.

Daina went quickly down the metal steps to her trailer, her heels ringing like hammer against anvil, across the light-smeared tarmac toward reality—or away from it. She was not really certain now.

There was a fire burning in the huge fireplace. That in itself was odd. On the wood-and-brass table behind the sofa, eight reels of 35mm film were neatly stacked in two piles within their gray metal octagonal cases.

"Maria!" Daina called. There was no answer. It was Maria's night to stay late. Daina set her suitcases down in the hall, away from the El Greco. She had stopped at her house on the way back from the studio to pick up all the clothes she thought she wanted. She had already decided to buy the rest.

She crossed the expanse of the living room. The bright colors of the fire clashed with the cool blues and greens of the steatopygous mermaid on the wall, giving her skin an unnatural glow that seemed to make her squirm uncomfortably atop her rock. Daina went over to the table. There were no markings on the metal cans of film. She lifted up the one on top, saw the title, *Over the Rainbow,* stenciled in black and, just under it, handwritten in flowing script: *Director: Michael Crawford. Writer: Benjamin Podell.* Before she replaced the top can, she turned it over. It and the top can in the second pile had been placed upside down. She left the cans the way she had found them.

"I'm afraid I'm off to New York this Friday. But on the plus side, Beryl just called and—"

She turned in time to see Rubens coming down the hall

from their bedroom. Odd, how she thought of it that way now.
Silently, she gestured toward the bags.

Rubens stopped strapping on his watch, looked where she
was pointing. "So it's really happened." He seemed quite surprised.

"I decided the morning Maggie was killed."

He looked at her quizzically. "I don't understand."

"Death makes you see life differently. Maggie was there,
then she was gone. Everything's finite, full of sharp edges
that'll slit you open if you stumble too far." She licked her
lips, her mouth dry. "You're what I want."

He came slowly across the room toward her. She watched
his movement, all motion from the waist down, like a dancer.
"And what about Chris?" he said.

"What about Chris?"

He was close to her now. She felt his heat. "What I mean
is," he said patiently, "do you want him, too?"

"Chris is my friend. You're my lover. I don't understand
you."

"I'm not certain a man and a woman can be just friends,
Daina. Especially when the man is Chris Kerr."

"First Maggie, now you."

"What was that?" he said sharply.

"Maggie accused me of the same thing." She stared at him.
"You remember, the night you begged me to stay here with
you."

"Not beg, surely."

"Don't go, Daina." She mimicked his voice perfectly, putting just the right amount of emotion into it. It was so accurate, she even surprised herself. "Not now. Not tonight.
Please."

For a moment his face went red all the way down through
his neck and she saw something hard and bright come into
his eyes. Then it was gone and he was laughing. Still she
would not let him touch her. "I want this settled right now,"
she said. "Whatever Chris' sex life is like is his business. It
has nothing to do with me."

"You mean he's not like everyone else?"

"*I'm* not like anyone else," she said softly, fiercely.

"I know that," he whispered. His lips were in her hair. She
felt his open mouth brush the shell of her ear and her eyes
closed.

"Forget it," she said, putting her arms around his wide shoulders, reveling in the hardness of his muscles. "Whatever you're hearing are lies."

"I'm sorry," he said. "But it's been coming from more than one source."

She pulled her head back in order to see his face. "Oh, who?"

He gave her some names and she began to laugh, nodding to herself as she did so.

"What's so funny?" he said, irked.

"Oh, it's just that all those people have one thing in common."

"What's that?"

"They are all," she said, "friends of Tie's."

"I don't understand."

She hugged him tighter to her. "I think Tie's more afraid of me than she was of Maggie." She was going to tell him about what Tie had told her at Maggie's funeral but it didn't seem very funny. "I suspect she's after Chris."

"Doesn't she live with the other one...Nigel Ash?"

"Yes, but that's never stopped her before. I think Chris is the only one in the band she hasn't slept with. So you see"—she kissed him—"this campaign's being put on for your benefit."

"Oh, we'll see about that."

She felt the anger leaping through him. "No, Rubens. Leave it alone."

"No one makes a fool of me."

"No one's made a fool of you." She took his chin in her hand, stared up into his eyes. They're so beautiful, she thought. "Besides, I want you to let me handle this."

"I don't—" He stopped, perhaps seeing something in her eyes; something he had not seen there before. He nodded.

"Now that that's settled, tell me what Beryl had to say."

He gave her a rueful smile. "That's what got me going, really. She said that this thing between you and Chris—whether it was real or not—was helping to get you a lot of space in magazines like *Rolling Stone* and *People*. Apparently there were a number of photographers at The Dancers the night you and Chris were there. She's got plenty of shots for the pieces."

"I'll have to thank Tie then, won't I?" She smiled.

"Ah yes. I imagine you will at that." He took her hand in his. "Come on. Let's get your suitcases inside."

After they returned to the living room, she asked him about the fire. "It's a bit warm for it, isn't it?"

"I didn't get it going for the heat," he said. The doorbell chimed and he glanced down at his watch. He did not move. "Business," he said. "Mike Crawford and Ben Podell." She recalled the canisters of film sitting on the table near the fireplace. "You remember them."

"I don't know them very well."

"Oh, you will by the time they leave," he said on his way to the door.

Crawford was a lanky, ruddy-complexioned Australian. He and the beefy, sandy-haired Podell had been the guiding lights of a TV sitcom that had shot to the top of the ratings list midway through its first season. They had stayed with it through its second year, renegotiating their contracts skyward and then had left to go into films. *Over the Rainbow* was their first venture. They were both in their late twenties and, from what Daina had seen of them, were arrogant and quite overconfident, no doubt from the instant stardom television affords the lucky. Still, Rubens had felt that their talents were original and forceful enough to take a chance on them.

He was sunny and full of good cheer as he walked them back down the long hallway into the living room. "You know Daina," he said, waving.

"Sure," Crawford said. Podell nodded. He seemed immediately ill at ease, his stubby fingers lacing and interlacing. Crawford sat down on the couch, opposite the fireplace, crossed his legs at the knee. He was dressed in an olive linen suit under which he wore a yellow-and-gray-striped shirt open to his chest. A gold medallion nestled in the sparse red hair there.

Podell, on the other hand, was dressed in faded jeans, scuffed Nike sneakers. He wore no socks. His yellow T-shirt had "Coors Beer" written across the chest in blue. The light-colored shirt made him seem even heavier than he was.

"How about a drink?" Rubens asked from behind the bar.

"Hey, great!" Podell said enthusiastically. "Gimme a beer." When he spoke, his face turned into a rubber mask. "Mike?"

Crawford bounced his leg up and down on his bony knee. "Oh, Scotch will be fine for me. Neat, please."

When they all had drinks, Rubens came around from behind the bar.

Podell, guzzling his beer out of the bottle, said, "Now what's all this shit about? We should be filming, not sitting around here like we were members of a goddamned club. We got work to do!"

Crawford sipped at his Scotch, scowled. "No, Benny," he said, not looking at Podell at all, "one must show a little tolerance. After all, one imagines that Mr. Rubens has a very good reason for calling this meeting."

"There're never any good reasons for calling a meeting," Podell said. He finished his beer and belched loudly. "Got another?"

Rubens waved toward the bar. "Help yourself."

"But you know," Crawford said slowly, as if giving this thought a great deal of consideration, "Benny *does* have a point. There is a *mountain* of work left to do on the film."

It was, Daina decided, a traveling minstrel show. And they were both quite good at it. They made their points without you ever realizing how hard they were working at it.

Rubens stood up as if on cue. "Yes, well about that." He managed to look at them both. "I'm afraid the work's going to have to be cut back."

For an instant it seemed as if his words hung in the air like icicles with a vivid life all their own. Then, out of the stunned silence, Crawford laughed. It was one of the oddest sounds Daina had ever heard, high and sharp as a pick.

Crawford slapped his thigh as he rocked. "Good Lord, Benny, don't you know when you're being put on?" Podell, however, looked as if he were about to hit someone over the head with his beer bottle.

"No joke, Michael," Rubens said. "Schuyler's given me the six-month breakdown. Everything's gone out of control."

"What the hell does that faggot know, anyway," Podell said. "We're making a goddamned masterpiece. Everything has to be right."

"No," Rubens said. "Everything has to be within budget."

Crawford cleared his throat loudly in order to forestall Podell. "I think what you're asking us to do is very difficult," he said calmly. "This film began with a certain vision. Benny and I signed on with you because we felt confident that you could provide us with the, uh, *follow-through* to implement that vision."

"You're almost four million over budget, Mike."

Podell threw up his hands in disgust. "Oh, Christ, it's only money!"

"I think," Crawford said, standing—he had apparently had enough of Rubens' towering over him, "that Benny has quite caught the flavor of the moment. We did not get into films in order to be dictated to."

"I think you're missing the point, Michael," Rubens said. "If you guys had maintained some kind of control instead of letting the set designer order a quarter-of-a-million-dollar neon skyline—"

"Have you seen that take?" Podell shrieked. "It's goddamn brilliant, man!"

"If you had acted responsibly," Rubens continued as if he had not been interrupted, "no one would *have* to dictate to you."

"Have you viewed the scene in question?" Crawford seemed to be having a bit more difficulty holding himself in check now.

Rubens nodded. "It's not worth the half-million bucks you spent that day."

"Christ, what *is* it worth?" Podell wanted to know.

"It never should have been shot."

"I think Mr. Rubens is exaggerating in order to make a point, Benny." Crawford went up the steps to the main level of the living room. "And now that he's properly chastised us, I'm quite sure we're free to go."

"Mike," Rubens said carefully. "I don't think you understand. We're not leaving here until the whole film has been rebudgeted. The entire team has to be streamlined."

"You're out of your mind!" Podell screamed. "Who d'you think we are—!"

"Just a moment," Crawford said, putting his hand on his partner's arm. "Let me get this clear. Are you giving us an ultimatum?"

"Just telling you what has to be done, boys," Rubens said, noncommittally. "It's nothing more than *any* movie man worth his salt would do."

"Christ, listen to this drivel, man!" Podell said. "I don't have to take this!"

Rubens said nothing and, after a time, Crawford said, "I rather do think Benny's right, Rubens." He gave them a thin smile. "If we walk off the picture, you're ten million in the hole." He cocked his head to one side. "I rather think that's a bit steep for you." He waved a red hand. "Besides, we'll just go down the road to Warners. They were champing at the bit to get us."

"Yes," Rubens said, nodding his head. "They were." Daina wondered what inflection he had given those words to make them so chilling.

Crawford seemed to shrug it off. "It all boils down to money anyway."

"Perhaps," Rubens acknowledged. "But you won't work at Warners. Or at Twentieth, Columbia, Paramount, Filmways, UA, you name it."

Podell turned to Crawford, ran his fingers through his long unkempt hair. "What's this bastard talking about?"

Crawford did not move. He stood his ground, staring into Rubens' eyes. "Think nothing of it—"

"Nothing?" Podell yelled.

"Benny, he's bluffing."

Rubens jerked his thumb over his shoulder. "Walk, buddy."

Crawford clucked his tongue. "Now, now, Rubens. You're good. *Quite* good, actually. ABC tried to do the same thing to us after our first season, when we demanded more money. After all, it was our right. They were making a mint off us. I think you'll agree we were entitled to commensurate compensation." He cocked his head again. "No? Well, no matter. In the end, they caved in. Of course they did. They had no choice. They had everything to lose." He smiled that rabbity smile again. "Just as you do. Ten million dollars of everything."

"This is the last time I will say it." Rubens spoke as if Crawford had not uttered a word. "Will you sit down with me and rebudget *Over the Rainbow?*"

"Rubens, you're making a very large mistake." Crawford's tone had gone cold. His mouth was grim and Daina thought he shook a little. "We're going to leave. But when you want to speak to us again—and you and I both know you will—we'll have to negotiate a whole new deal. More money; more points. I don't know how much. You'll have to speak to our attorney about that. You're going to pay for treating us this way."

He stopped speaking as he saw Rubens walking toward the table near the fireplace. He watched while Rubens picked up the top can from the nearest pile. "Know what this is?" Rubens said.

Podell snorted. "Can o' shit, man. Film, film, film. We see 'em every day."

Rubens flipped the can over to its front side.

"Hey," Podell said. "That's our fucking film you've got there! Gimme that, you bastard!"

But Crawford held him back. "What are you going to do with that, Rubens?" He could not keep the contempt out of his voice.

Rubens took the top off, freed the reel. It was filled to the rim with film. He shrugged. "What else *can* I do? It's going in the fire."

Crawford's tone was derisive. "Oh, come on, Rubens. You don't really expect us to believe you'd destroy the film. That's nothing but exposed negative—"

But Podell, in an agony of suspense, had already made the leap forward. His blunt fingers scrabbled at the outer edge of the reel. He spun off the film, looked at it. A harsh cry shot out of him like a bullet from a pistol. "Jesus, Joseph and Mary! These're the real goods!"

Crawford rushed to his side, lunging at the reel. "Let me see that!" The half smile left his face and his skin seemed to turn gray beneath the reddish hue. He looked up, as if into space. "My God, it's the baby!"

Rubens took the film out of his hand.

"No don't!" Crawford cried.

But it was too late. The reel, spinning from Rubens' toss, landed squarely atop the well-stacked logs. Fire licked at it.

"Mother of God!" Crawford put his hands over his face but Podell, enraged, dropped to his knees in front of the fireplace. The flames licked orange off his sweating face as he reached out with trembling fingers for the burning film. He screamed once, wincing as the flames caught his fingertips, went on, cried out again before Daina dragged him away. The heat was enormous, and harsh, choking smoke billowed up blackly into the recesses of the chimney. He was sobbing.

"Rubens," Crawford cried in anguish, "do something, for the love of—"

Rubens took two steps to the fireplace, reaching in very quickly and retrieving the reel. He looked at it almost unconcernedly but only Daina noticed that. "I don't know if it can be salvaged, Michael, really I don't."

"There must be a way."

"It'll take a lot of hard work, a lot of paring down, a lot of firings. That set designer will have to go."

Crawford lifted his head, aware at last of what Rubens was talking about. "Bastard," he said, quietly. The incident had drained him of anything more. "Bastard."

"It's only your egos that get in the way," Rubens said gently. "You're a pair of very talented boys, really."

Afterward, late in the night, after they had left, when she and Rubens lay side by side in bed and she felt delicious sleep seeping through her body, she turned on her side, said to him, "Would you've let the negatives burn, Rubens?"

"Of course," he said. "I'm as good as my word." Then he began to laugh. It began as a stream does with perhaps just a trickle, building as it flows into a thin line then widening until, rushing, it pours into the sea. "But, you see, it wouldn't've mattered. Only the first two hundred feet was their film. The rest was precisely what Crawford said it was: exposed negative. Junk."

She felt his breathing slow. It seemed to encompass her universe.

El-Kalaam called for Davidson and MacKinnon to be brought in. They stood stock still when they saw the scene confronting them: Bock curled on the floor, Susan on her knees, her head bowed. He was covered with blood and there was blood all around him.

"This is reprehensible," MacKinnon said, shaking his silver-haired head. "Utterly unconscionable."

"A political expediency," El-Kalaam said, slowly lighting a cheroot. "The two of you understand what that is very well."

"I understand that you're no better than a common thug," Davidson said. "I had thought my sympathies lay with the Palestinian people in this matter." He shivered. "Now I'm not so certain. You may have convinced Emouleur. But he is young and naive."

"We are at war," El-Kalaam said angrily. "We are forced into this. Our very lives are at stake."

"This cannot be the way—"

"To kill innocent people—" MacKinnon began.

"In war no one is innocent...everyone is expendable." El-Kalaam made a gesture at Bock's body. "Take him out. Put him near the front door. Malaguez will direct you. He will be thrown to the Israelis now. He will be of some help to us, despite himself."

Malaguez, who had accompanied them into the hot box, raised his machine pistol, and they bent, slinging Bock between them, maneuvered him out through the doorway.

Heather, released from El-Kalaam's grip, went to see how Susan was. She bent, put her hands gently on either side of Susan's head. She lifted up the brunette's face, gave a quick gasp. There was no recognition in those eyes. They were blank, uncomprehending.

"Susan," she whispered. And then more urgently: "Susan!" Susan was silent, her eyes vacant, unfocused.

"My God!" Heather cried. "Look what you've done to her. You've broken her!"

Fessi reached out languidly, encircled her wrist. "She's no concern of yours," he said.

Heather looked up. "You're a beast. A monster. Get your hands off me!" Rage drove color to her cheeks and neck.

Fessi giggled, put one palm over her breast, squeezed. "You'll be better than she was anyway."

"Leave her alone, Fessi," El-Kalaam said. He reached out, pulled Heather from the smaller man's grip. He grunted, turning her away from Susan. "Leave her alone. She is nothing."

"Yes," Heather said, staring into his face. "I see now. She's served her purpose. That's it, isn't it? She's just so much dead meat to you."

"She was dead meat the moment she stepped into this room," El-Kalaam said. He took the cheroot from between his lips, put his face close to hers. "But dead meat can still serve a purpose, uh? It can be eaten."

"She's a human being." Heather was weeping. "She deserves to be—"

"Go tend your husband," he said softly. "He must be starved by now."

He let go her wrist, made a motion toward Rita. Heather turned and, with Rita just behind her, went out of the room.

"I have to go to the bathroom," she said when they were in the hallway. Rita nodded.

There was no door, no privacy. Heather turned, surprised when Rita followed her in. "Couldn't you wait outside?"

Rita looked at her. "No, I couldn't," she said coldly. She made a motion with her chin. "You'd better get on with it. You have two minutes before I take you out of here."

For a moment, Heather stood there undecided. Then she went over to the toilet. Rita did not take her eyes off her and, slowly, Heather's face flushed pink.

When Heather returned to the living room, she saw Rachel huddled over Bock's crumpled form. Her shoulders were heaving. Heather went to her, put her arms around the child's shoulders.

"He was like an uncle to me," Rachel said. She tried to wipe away her tears. "He was so good to me."

She turned to look at Heather. "What did they do to him in there?"

"You've got to forget him, Rachel. He's gone."

"Tell me!" Rachel's voice was fierce. "I've got to know!"

"No," Heather said, "you don't." She took Rachel up, walked her away from Bock's body.

"Remember him in life," Heather said. "Not in death."

Rachel put her head on Heather's shoulder. "I won't cry now," she whispered. "Not in front of them."

Malaguez appeared, came over to where they stood. He took Rachel by the arm. "El-Kalaam wants you," he said. "He is calling your father." He pushed Rachel before him. They disappeared down the hall.

Heather went to where James sat. He had not moved. The blood had ceased to flow from his wounds but his face was very white and Heather saw that he had difficulty in breathing.

"Oh, Jamie," she said, kneeling beside him, "if only there was something I could do. I feel so helpless."

He opened his eyes, smiled at her. "There *is* something you can do."

"What is it?" Her face was lined with worry and anxiety. "Anything."

"Promise me you won't give in...even after I die."

Her fingers stroked his cheek. "What do you mean?" She gave a laugh that ended in a stifled sob. "You're not going to die."

"There's no time for this foolishness." He watched her eyes. "Promise me, Heather. You must."

She began to cry.

His hand came up, gripped her arm. "Promise me, damnit!"

Her eyes flew open; tears dropped into his lap. "I promise."

A long hissing sigh escaped from his half-open lips. He relaxed back against the bookcase. His eyes closed for a moment. "Good," he whispered. "Very good." His fingers dug into her flesh. "Now you must listen to me—"

"Let me get you some food. I made you soup. You need to—"

"Never mind that now!" His eyes blazed and his voice, though low, was fierce enough to check her. She looked around. Behind them, MacKinnon and Davidson were standing behind the sofa. Their wrists had been retied. They sat down on the sofa. Rene Louch sat by the fireplace staring stonily at his attaché who was animatedly talking to Rudd. He was attempting to talk to the secretary of state, too, but Thomas sat slumped in a chair with his forehead against his knees.

"You've got to understand some things, Heather," James said. "You can't ignore these bastards and you can't believe a word they say. If El-Kalaam tells you it's day outside, know that it's night. If he tells you everything will be all right, prepare yourself for a bullet through the head. He'll tell you *anything* if it suits his purpose. Men like him know only one thing: to kill or be killed." Across the room, Emouleur got up, went over to speak to the English MPs. James looked at her. "You'll have to kill him in order to save yourself."

"But, Jamie—"

"There is no other alternative, Heather!" His face was very close to hers. She could see tears glistening in the corners of his eyes. "Don't you understand? El-Kalaam is wrong. You must have courage. You must do what you know deep down you have to do."

"Jamie, I won't know how to—"

"His dominance lies in his absolute control over his environment. Once that's disrupted his power diminishes."

El-Kalaam and Fessi came into the living room. Fessi went to the front door, opened it a crack. He whistled low in his throat. In a moment one of the cadre appeared from outside. Fessi spoke to him in low tones before returning to El-Kalaam. "All is ready," he said. "He knows just where to place it."

El-Kalaam nodded, threw the last of his cheroot into the cold fireplace. Two of the cadre bent and picked up Bock's body. Fessi opened the door just enough to let them through.

"Hassam will show you the way," he told them.

Malaguez brought Rachel back into the room. She was white-faced, her mouth pinched. She would not look at El-Kalaam.

"Put her over there," he said to Malaguez, pointing to where Heather knelt. "I'm sick of her. Let the women take care of themselves."

Malaguez gave her a push and Rachel stumbled toward Heather. She tried to right herself, failed. Her arms stretched out as she fell. The side of her head hit the floor.

"Oh!" she gasped.

"Rachel!" Heather cried. And heard a brief strangled sound from close behind her. She turned to see James panting. His face had gone gray, his lips blue. His mouth was open and she could hear a rattle emanating from his throat.

"Oh, Jamie!" she said. She put her arms around him, rocked him. "Jamie, hold on!" She turned her head toward El-Kalaam. "Do something!" she screamed. "Can't you see he's dying!"

El-Kalaam stayed where he was. He watched silently as Heather shivered and James jerked, sighed and was still.

"My sympathies," he said at last into the quiet. "He was a soldier, a professional. We understood each other."

Heather, holding on to James still, watched him. Then she closed her eyes, cradled James' head against her breast, kissed his cheeks, his eyelids, his lips.

6

"I need your help."

"Well, that's quite a switch," Daina said.

Bonesteel watched the hummingbird hovering over one of the blue trumpet-shaped bells of the jacaranda that rose along the one area of blank brick wall. There seemed something different about him today. Daina had noticed it the moment he had appeared on the set just as they were wrapping for the day. She had been surprised to see him but immediately she had felt a tension like lightning radiating from him and had been intrigued.

He sat quite still, as he almost always did when he spoke, that peculiar lack of motion lending unusual weight to his words. "The situation," he said now, "has changed quite significantly since we last spoke."

She could tell by the way he said the word "significantly" that he had wanted to use another but had somehow felt constrained. Watching him carefully, she saw the added lines at the corners of his tight-lipped mouth, between his slate-gray eyes. She thought he very much wanted to tap his fingertips on the table.

His sharply angled face and right arm were in the last of

the dappled sunlight filtering through the spreading branches
of the acacia that sprouted from the center of the courtyard.
When he had picked her up in his dark green Ford LTD, he
had suggested this restaurant on Lindbrook in Westwood. It
was pleasant, spacious and, at this time of the evening, filled
with dancing light as the breeze fluttered the acacia. Above
them, the sky had cleared, filled now with a mauve and gold
light. One could almost imagine it belonged to another city.

Daina, imagining Bonesteel's words were filled with fore-
boding, finished her wine. Immediately he ordered them more
as if he needed her mandate in order to indulge himself.

"What's happened?" Daina said at last.

He seemed as tightly wound as a spring and, seeing him
this way, she found herself on the verge of being frightened.
She put her hand out, touched his wrist just above the place
he wore his gold Rolex watch. His head swung around, his
eyes contemplating her as if it were the first time he was
seeing her. "What is it, Bobby?" she said. "Can it be so terrible?"

"Yes," he said, almost as a somnambulist might speak,
toneless and sad. "It's quite terrible." He waited for the filled
glasses to be placed before them. Then he leaned forward,
said, "Everything's changed. We know now that Modred was
not responsible for Maggie's murder."

Daina felt a small chill race through her as if he had
thrown icewater in her face. "Does that mean you know who
killed her?"

For what seemed a long time he said nothing, staring at
the speckled drops of sunlight where they fell along his arm.
They moved minutely, faded as the sun sank lower in the
west. Then they were gone. Daina could imagine the swollen
disc settling its bulk into the calm Pacific.

At last Bonesteel looked at her again. She wondered what
he was thinking; those slate-gray eyes revealed nothing. "An
event occurred last night that made us re-evaluate our thinking. We found a young woman's body over in Highland Park."

"Was Modred's mark on her?"

"Yes."

"It's very close to when Maggie was ... died."

"Too close." He took a drink. "The shrinks tell us that
Modred could not have been responsible for both murders.

Given his makeup, it would be impossible. Not enough time has gone by."

"I thought you didn't put much stock in what they said."

He shrugged. "I don't—when they don't have much to go on and they're talking just to hear the sound of their own voices. It's different now. They've got a helluva lot of information."

Daina waited for him to continue and when he did not, said, "Are you going to tell me the rest of it?"

His eyes stared at her very directly. "You sure you want to hear it? You may not like it."

"I don't have to like it. I want to know."

"Yeah," he said. "I know you do." She thought she heard a trace of grudging respect in his tone. "What they told me led me to compare the emblems. The one we found near Maggie didn't match up with the one on the woman we found in Highland Park." He fingered the stem of his glass. "The only emblem that's different is the one on the side of the speaker box."

She felt him watching her carefully as if by what he saw there he would decide whether or not to go on. "The explanation's simple," he said. "In retrospect. Someone quite clever killed Maggie for his own reason and made it look like Modred's work." He pushed the glass away from him by its base. "And the really nasty thing is, if the real Modred hadn't gone to work again at just this time, we'd never have picked it up."

Daina felt her heart beating very fast. She knew instinctively that he was on the verge of telling her something that she very much wanted to know. She leaned forward and, instead of asking the obvious question, said, "You told me you wanted my help."

"Daina"—now his hand was over hers—"my captain would boot my behind out the door if he ever heard me talking to a civilian like this but...I believe your help is essential now if I'm ever going to catch Maggie's murderer." Something in what he said nagged at the corner of her mind. She let it go, concentrating on what he was about to say next.

An odd kind of calmness washed over him and at last he seemed to relax. "There is very little doubt," he said, "that whoever killed your friend is part of the band."

At first she was certain she had misheard him. "Band?" she said. "What band?"

"The Heartbeats."

The wildness of her pulse had invaded her head and she felt dizzy with the release of adrenalin. She felt she could no longer sit here quietly and absorb this information. "Let's get out of here," she said thickly, standing up.

Without a word, Bonesteel dug into his pocket, threw some bills onto the table. He did not wait for a receipt.

The Pacific was dark, the long gunmetal swells humpbacked, as deformed as they were sluggish. Where were the race of the waves in toward the rocky shore, the high white spuming, the echoing boom and thunder? Three thousand miles away, Daina thought, in the bosom of the Atlantic. She wished now that she could go with Rubens to New York. But it was a business trip and she understood why he could not take her. Still, they were not filming over the coming weekend; there were other places to go.

When Bonesteel spoke again, it was not about Maggie's murder. Daina tried to return to the subject several times, but he would not be budged.

"I was born in San Francisco," Bonesteel said as he took them along the Pacific Palisades. "Because of that I never forget the sea." They went down to the beach at Santa Monica, to a spot past the roller skaters and sidewalk surfers on their tiny iridescent boards.

"I think I became the family's instant black sheep when I moved down here. They're exceptionally narrow minded when it comes to things like that. They thought my move was quite traitorous."

"Why *did* you move?"

"I came after a woman." They went across the darkening sand toward the wandering high tide mark that was, at this time of day, as black as a tar pit. "I met her at a party in the Presidio and fell in love instantly." He put his hands in his pockets and she was reminded of the pose he had struck the first time she had met him. "Of course, she wasn't interested. She was from here and when she flew back, I followed her."

"What happened?"

"I pursued her until she finally broke down and married me." Far out on the horizon a dark shape loomed. Daina, squinting into the dimness, could not tell whether it was an oil tanker or a whale breaching the surface of the sea. "Now," Bonesteel said, "I can't wait until we're divorced. She owns Numans of Beverly Hills," he added as if by that fact Daina would come to understand his need to be rid of her.

He laughed harshly. "Now you know I wasn't kidding about being kept."

She was seeing a new aspect of him she would have dismissed as impossible several days ago. He seemed vulnerable now, a little boy, as if his fierce desire for separation from his wife was only a cover-up for his abiding love for her. She saw no weakness in this, rather an endearing quality that served to bring him closer to her. She did not want to push him, knowing that there was a lot for her to learn about what had happened to Maggie. But one of the Heartbeats? Surely he was mistaken in that.

"It doesn't matter," she said and instantly knew she had made a mistake.

His head whipped around. "Matter?" he said. "Of course it matters. It's why we're getting divorced." The sea, spinning its wheels, somnolent, trickled up to their shoe tips, faded back with hardly a gurgle to mark its passing. He looked out to where a plane skidded across the horizon. A blue light on its wing tip glowed on and off as if signaling them. "I thought, once, that I had a good reason for marrying her. Perhaps she reminded me of someone or something I could never quite have. "But"—he paused and turned back to her—"there was another reason. I don't know why but I get the feeling that if I show it to you, you'll understand."

The outskirts of what passed for the city slipped past them in a braid of pastel ribbons. The whispered call of the palms was interrupted only intermittently by the hysterical blatting of car radios, music exploding like flares, rhythm-heavy and full of anger.

The ornate facades of the banks and the procession of used-car lots, colored pennants bleached in the harsh buzzing arc lights, were their only companions. The streets were oddly deserted and when he turned onto Sunset, the strip seemed still and forlorn, lying straight as an arrow between enormous billboards advertising Robert Redford's new film and Donna Summer's latest album. It was a film set awaiting actors for the next day's shoot. L.A. never seemed more two-dimensional.

They whipped into the hills, hurtling onward until the light smear of Hollywood was a low phosphorescent surf, silent and immobile behind them, an ancient snapshot of some faraway reality.

He turned right onto Benedict Canyon Drive and even those lights vanished into the dark trees, leaving them with the soft fog-shrouded sky. They were alone in the night.

Well into the canyon he slowed, turning in beside a large, rambling redwood house. It was set into the rising slope of the western wall and, in rather spectacular fashion, was surrounded by lush foliage as dense and dark as a forest. It was a place, Daina thought, that Rubens would despise.

"Karin's house," Bonesteel said. "Home." He cut the engine and abruptly the chittering of the countryside stole in on them. "How I hate this place."

"I think it's quite beautiful," she said, looking at the profusion of camellia and lilac, mountain laurel and columbine that cloaked both sides of the stairway.

"The house is nothing," he said. "It means nothing, stands for nothing."

"Someone obviously went to a lot of trouble to landscape the grounds."

"Karin must've hired a fine hand," he said as if he truly had no idea of what went on here. "Come on." He opened the door and got out.

Daina came around the front end of the car. The air was thick with the perfumes of the flowers. She heard some animal moving in the underbrush at her approach.

Bonesteel took her inside. The hallway was dominated by a black hardwood sidetable, quite obviously an English antique. It was highly polished. On it was a spotless white linen doily on which sat a plum-colored fluted-glass vase filled with long sprays of Hawaiian red hibiscus. Above this rather perfect decorator's display hung an oval wall mirror. On the floor was a narrow Indian runner in dark reds and golds.

The hallway gave way to the living room, which rose up breathtakingly two stories to a cathedral ceiling cunningly spotlit from below to add even greater height. Windows on each side, rising nearly to the vaulted ceiling, made it appear as if they were living within the heart of the canyon's thick foliage.

The rear third of the room was overhung by a balcony on

which, Bonesteel told her, was the master bedroom. To the left was the kitchen and dining room.

Daina walked around the living room. The walls were a light blue, the deep pile rug under the main furniture grouping the palest lavender. The long modular couch and the matching chairs were eggshell. Tall plants were scattered about the room and, past a screen of ferns and the like, a Steinway baby grand sat in the right-hand corner beneath the balcony in back. The music stand along its top was up and Daina saw there sheet music: a Vivaldi viola concerto, transcribed for keyboard.

She turned to him. "Who plays?"

"She does." Bonesteel pointed.

To her right, atop the piano, Daina saw a color photograph in a rather ornate Mexican silver frame. A face gazed out at her: a girl already growing into a woman. She had dark, direct eyes, the hint of a smile about her generous mouth. It was, she saw, Bonesteel's mouth. Her hair, too, was dark, pulled back severely from her face by a pair of diamond barrettes. She had high cheekbones, which, when she lost the remainder of her baby fat, would certainly be devastating, and an odd, slightly crooked nose that saved her face from cold perfection, left an enduring impression that was more endearing.

"I used to play a long time ago," Bonesteel said, coming up beside her. But he was looking at the photo in Daina's hand. "I played well as a child but I stopped too soon. I was at a rebellious age. Now I'm sorry I did because it's far too late. I can still sight read but my fingers are too set in their ways." He stroked the piano's sleek flank.

"We bought this for Sarah and I started her early." He shrugged. "I don't know. I guess I wanted her to have the chance I threw away so unknowingly."

"Does Sarah live here now?"

"Oh no." He smiled, gently replaced the photograph on the piano. "She's in Paris. At a music conservatory, studying. She's quite something. At seventeen, she plays, well...." He left her, went across the room, inserted a cassette into a deck. "She sends us these recordings of her performances from time to time." He punched a button and the music began almost immediately. It was Mozart, showering over them like a cascade of silver dust.

She watched him while she listened to the superb playing—Sarah not only had technique, she played with passion. The soft half smile coloring his lips was the ghost of his daughter's expression in the photo. Daina was reminded of Henry and Jane Fonda, separated by sex and a generation, yet, at some moments and at certain angles, their faces one and the same.

And yet there was pain in that smile, a certain admission. After a time, its painful intensity was too much for her and she turned away from him before the music had concluded.

His words came back to her: *How I hate this place.* Of course he would. There was nothing of himself here, save the photograph of Sarah and perhaps the piano on which it stood. It was a cold, almost bleak house, as if a team of surgeons had marched in one day to decorate. If the interior accurately reflected his wife's personality Daina wondered what he had ever seen in her. Something unattainable, he had said. Isn't that what all men fell in love with in their women, the mystery of flesh and mind?

The silence washed over her. "She plays beautifully, Bobby." She saw that he was crying and his sorrow tugged at her. She went to him, put her hand on his arm. She could feel the welter of muscle there. "I'm sorry," she whispered. "I'm sorry." Knowing they were words without meaning, merely sounds to soothe a beaten heart.

"Stupid," he said, pulling away from her. "Just pure stupidity. I should never've put it on." He meant the music.

"I'm glad you did," she said. "Playing like that is meant to be heard."

"Karin doesn't understand it," he said so softly she had to lean closer to him in order to hear. "She thinks Sarah ought to be off skiing or iceskating. Something that'll toughen her up."

"Any discipline toughens you mentally," Daina said.

He looked at her, his slate-gray eyes blinking, and again she had the sensation that he was seeing her for the first time. "You know," he said, "you're not at all how I thought you'd be."

"I'm not rotten."

She smiled and he laughed. "Yeah, right. Not rotten at all." He turned away as if remembering something important.

"I still have to show you the reason—the *other* reason—I married Karin."

He crossed the living room to where a desk sat, prim and proper and glossy, in one corner, shadowed by a tall dieffenbachia. From the lowest left-hand drawer he produced a thick sheaf of white paper. Long before he put it in her hands, she knew what it was.

While she read he went quietly into the kitchen, made perfect linguine carbonara and arrugula salad with slices of Bermuda onion and ripe love tomatoes. He called her to the table as he opened a bottle of white wine but he served only her. They drank wine together.

"The manuscript is very good, Bobby," she said. "It has an anger and energy. It's"—and she was quite struck by this— "very much the way Sarah plays. It has passion."

"And Karin was my ticket," he said. "I loved her *and* she had money. How perfect, I thought. I'll have all the time I need to write. But writing's not going to a nine-to-five job every day." He poured them both more wine. "Anyone who's not a writer just doesn't understand and Karin, who understands nothing but her own business, certainly didn't. She wanted to know why I couldn't synchronize my work time with hers. And weekends! They had to be free for her social engagements."

Daina pushed her plate away. "In other words you were in a gilded cage. But to become a cop. How did that happen?"

He shrugged. "My family tradition is in the military. It seemed a natural choice." Something in his eyes seemed to go. "And I found I enjoyed the work."

"Investigating murders?"

"Bringing people to justice." The flat of his hand hit the table with a startling smack. "The law must be obeyed. Those who transgress must be punished. People walk around this city—any city—committing crimes as if they have impunity before the law. They have no regard—no respect—for human life. They're callous and their indifference to their own acts of violence is the worst kind of evil."

Daina was taken by surprise. From his usual sleepy tone, Bonesteel's voice had changed timbre, raised in volume as if he were preaching a fiery sermon from the pulpit.

There was a silence for a time. Bonesteel looked away from her as if abruptly abashed at his outburst. At length he cleared his throat. "We found a lotta dope at Chris' house: coke, Quaaludes, skag." He saw the look in her eyes. "Me, I don't give a damn. You expect that from these musicians. Some of 'em"—he shrugged—"live on the stuff." He finished off his wine. "You'd be surprised how much abuse the human body can take before it gives out."

"That's not like Maggie," Daina said. "Sure, she blew some coke once in a while." A white lie could not hurt her now. "But heroin..." Daina shook her head. "I would've known about that."

He looked thoughtful, tapping his unused fork on the side of his empty glass, setting up an overlapping ringing sound. "You're saying she wasn't familiar with heroin."

"Yes." She watched the peculiar look in his eyes. "What are you thinking about?"

"The M.E.'s report." His eyes focused on her. "Maggie died hard. For one thing she had been shot full of horse."

"'Had been'?" She echoed his words. "You mean you don't believe she shot up herself?"

"No, I don't."

"That's a relief. But you said you found heroin in the house."

He nodded. "I had it run through the lab. Choice quality stuff."

His words were again setting off intimations inside her. "What did the report show?"

Bonesteel sighed. "The junk shot into Maggie McDonnell was cut with strychnine."

"A hot shot." It was out before she could think.

"Well, well, well." He cocked his head. "What kind of nasty literature have *you* been reading?"

She felt slightly relieved that he had made the wrong guess.

He went on. "Normally, you'd be right. But what she was given was something a bit more diabolical than a pure hot shot. You see, there wasn't enough strychnine to jolt her immediately. It took some time...and it couldn't've been pleasant." He put his hand over hers. "I'm sorry." It didn't mean any more to her than when she had said it to him.

"Christ Almighty," she breathed. "I don't understand any of this."

He held on to her. "Someone shot her up. Then she was sexually assaulted, beaten unmercifully."

"Sexually assaulted?" She felt as if her blood had turned to ice. She shivered. "What happened?"

"Well, I don't think it's necessary to—"

"But I do!" she said fiercely. Her eyes burned into his. "I have to know it all now."

He watched her for a moment, then nodded resignedly. "To put it as succinctly as possible, the M.E. found traces of blood and semen in her vagina and in her rectum."

"Oh, my God." She had begun to tremble.

He held on to her tightly as if willing his strength to flow into her. He said nothing. The ornate antique French clock on the rosewood sideboard chimed in its gold-and-glass case. When it had stopped, he said softly, "There's more."

Her eyes were glassy. "More? *More?*" Her voice was thick. "What more could there possibly be?"

"Statistically speaking, over ninety percent of solved murder cases turn out to be committed by someone with very close ties to the deceased: family member, close friend or neighbor. Someone with a strong personal motive."

"But I just can't think why anyone would want to kill her."

Bonesteel closed his eyes for a moment. His grip upon her increased and when his eyes snapped open, she was certain all color had drained from his face. "I told you there was more," he said in a whisper. "Did you know your friend was two and a half months pregnant?"

For a long time after that she stared at him without really seeing him. She was seeing a broken bundle of flesh and bones and ripped skin beneath which had lain...At last her lips moved and he had to struggle to catch what she said: "My God, Maggie, what did you get yourself into?"

"You're certain you want to go through with this?"

His eyes were deep in shadow and she found herself thinking that without their guidance it was impossible to tell what he was feeling. Then she remembered how good he was at keeping his emotions hidden. Yet he had cried to hear Sarah playing Mozart on a cassette made nine thousand miles away.

She stared at Bonesteel in the half light. When he had first told her what he wanted her to do, she had been unsure.

But then she had been in shock from what he had told her about Maggie. Now she was certain.

"I want to find out who killed Maggie as much as you do." Her voice sounded hard even to her own ears. She kept thinking of the baby, so frail and...innocent. She knew Maggie, too. She never would've had an abortion. It was partly upbringing, partly how Maggie felt about life on her own. She could never knowingly take another life. No, the baby would've lived had Maggie not been...Hot tears flooded her eyes and she turned away from him, clamping her lids down with grim determination. Hadn't she said she was all cried out? But the unborn baby hung in her mind as if slung in a shining web. My God, how she wanted to see justice done. She thought now she understood a little of how Bonesteel felt. How had he put it? *An indifference to their own acts of violence.* The gross disregard of human life sickened her and she knew now that she would never be truly content until this matter was settled. She understood, too, why he had insisted on giving her his personal history. He was no longer just another cop.

"You know what you have to do." He was not asking her a question.

"I understand it all."

"Thank Christ you're an actress."

She knew that he wanted to laugh and she smiled so he would understand that it was all right.

After a time, he said, "I want to be certain you understand the danger invol—"

"Bobby," she said quietly, "we've gone through all this. I couldn't live with myself knowing there was something I could actively do and not do it. I want to."

"Chris is your friend." It was a gentle reminder.

"Chris will be all right."

"I think you really believe that."

"I do." She felt him close to her. It was so quiet in the house, she was certain she could discern their breathing. "Chris could never've killed Maggie. He loved her."

"Love has different definitions...different limits... depending on the person." Again she had the feeling there was more to that statement than she understood.

"I think he would've welcomed the baby."

"But you don't know."

"No one *knows* but Chris and Maggie." She waited a moment. "Do *you* think Chris murdered her?"

For a long time he said nothing. At last he put his arm on her shoulder. "There's really nothing to say until all the evidence is in, is there?"

Daina turned her head this way and that but his eyes remained in the shadows, impenetrable.

The Heartbeats were back together again. This is what Bonesteel had told her first. Of course she hadn't believed him. She'd been at Las Palmas when Chris and Benno had had their fight. The rift had seemed irreparable then. She had phoned Vanetta at the Heartbeats' office from Bonesteel's house and the secretary had confirmed that they had been in the studio day and night finishing up a new single and the rest of the album. "But they're not at Las Palmas now," she had said in her peculiar accent that was part black and part Cockney. "I just tried there. I think they've all gone back to Nigel's."

Daina took the Mulholland exit off the San Diego Freeway. Bonesteel had driven her back to the studio lot in Burbank. He wanted her to use her own car.

Nigel and Tie lived in Mandeville Canyon. It was on the other side of Bel Air—the west side—from Benedict Canyon, and was therefore more secluded and, some would say, more exclusive.

Mandeville Canyon was heavily wooded, filled with widely spaced houses rather more East Coast in design than the surrounding areas of L.A. Here lived equestrians with their horses and their jodhpurs and their short red jackets, riding alongside the omnipresent white picket fences. Daina thought it must have amused Nigel no end to move in here among people whose idea of rock music was bland and nonthreatening Linda Ronstadt or James Taylor.

He was considered a kind of fascinating pariah in their midst, which was just fine with him. He and Tie valued their privacy when they were home.

From the front the house did not look any different from its distant neighbors. Daina turned in at the wide crushed-marble driveway and had time to study the place on the way in. It was a white, two-story Colonial with columns that—

knowing Hollywood—had been shamelessly copied from
Tara. The trim was dark green, the steps brick. But the facade, Daina knew, had nothing whatsoever to do with what
was inside. Nigel had had the interior stripped and entirely
rebuilt. It was a funny place. Literally. For instance, she
remembered well the library downstairs that was done precisely like an old gentlemen's club in London at the turn of
the century: all wingback leather chairs, antique marble fire-
places and brass ashtray stands. The room was ringed with
balustraded wooden bookcases that contained, rather than
their namesakes, neat stacks of audio and video cassettes.
And, if one looked closely, one could see no fire in the fireplace
but an enormous television monitor hooked up to a video
recorder.

There were other marvels in the house, such as a bathroom
as large as a normal living room, which contained, among
other hardware, a refrigerator, a video monitor and a double
bed. There was also a small, soundproof studio in the back
of the house and an enormous pool complete with waterfall
leading to a totally isolated man-made pond.

Silka met her as she drove up to the front door and got
out. She could hear the barking of the Dobermans, silenced
by a command from the bodyguard.

"Miss Whitney," he said, coming as close to smiling as he
could. "What a marvelous surprise!" He came down the brick
steps. "No one informed me of your coming."

"I'm afraid no one knew," Daina said ruefully. "I hope I'm
not interrupting them. I know the tour starts this Saturday."

"Yes." Silka nodded his big head. "San Francisco, then
Phoenix on Monday, Denver on Tuesday, Dallas Wednesday
through Sunday and so it goes for six weeks. They're very
excited to be on their way." She knew he meant Nigel in
particular.

"Everything's all right between them?" He knew what she
meant.

"It's all been worked out. Benno's a genius at that sort of
thing. He's been around them a long time. Since their first
U.S. tour which was...oh, let's see, 1965? Yeah, it was sixty-
five 'cause he brought me aboard that year."

"How'd you know him?"

"Benno? Oh, well, we met at the American Society of Recording Manufacturers benefit dinner in sixty-four. We were

both hustling to make ends meet at the time. I had heard about the Heartbeats, even saw them a couple times when I was in Britain. But after that disastrous first U.S. tour, no promoter wanted anything to do with them. Their English manager just didn't understand America or the concept of selling a product. They were big in Britain so therefore, he figured, they should go down a storm in America.

"Anyway, I told Benno about the band at that dinner. I thought it was, you know, just small talk. I mean no one remembers what's said to them after affairs or parties. But Benno did remember and flew over there to see them. He convinced them to sign with him and, well, the rest's what you see." His thick arms swept up to encompass the house and grounds.

"You knew Jon, then," Daina said.

"Sure." But something had shut down behind his eyes. "We all knew Jon; we all loved him." He looked at her. "Have you heard the new single yet?"

"No, I'd love to."

"I'll take you inside then. They're going over it now."

Just before they stepped inside, Daina reached out to stop him. "Silka," she said. "How is Chris? Really."

He towered over her like a mountain, his head so high above her it seemed in the clouds. "He's okay," Silka said from deep inside his chest. "Really." He reached around, pulled the door shut behind them. It was dark and quite still in the hallway. "This tour'll do him good. You'll see." He seemed to be saying something more to her.

"I'm not here to stop him from going, if that's what you mean."

"It wasn't." But he seemed relieved. He turned away and they began to walk down the hall. "I've never seen her like this," he said. "She's really quite terrified of you."

Daina knew he meant Tie. "I can't see why." But of course she did. She merely wanted to see if he would tell her.

"She knows how Chris feels about you. She can't fathom the relationship. It worries her, I think, because she's usually very adept at that." He looked at her out of the corner of his eye. "She hasn't been able to pin you down in any way, and what she can't control frightens her."

"Well, that makes us even," Daina said. "I don't understand her, either." She thought, We're like two cats with our backs up. Perhaps it's only the territorial imperative.

"No," Silka said, stopping just before a heavily paneled oak door. "I think that's what terrifies her the most. You've got her dead to rights."

His hand shot out and the door rolled back. Sound blasted her with an almost physical force, the music drenching her with its energy. Her ears began to ache and her teeth were set on edge.

She felt Silka's fingertips on the small of her back, urging her forward, and she went in. The door slid shut behind her.

They were arrayed around the room in a rough semicircle before the two giant speakers, identical twins to the ones that had been in Chris and Maggie's house. The band was rapt, like idolators before carved figures of their god.

Remember the times/In the back of a Ford, Chris' voice rocketed full out, *With the dashlights glowing/Did we know the score?*

Tie saw Daina first and she got up. No one else moved or looked her way.

That one day we'd be all grown up/Finding the stars...

"Who let you in?" Tie drawled. The pupils of her eyes were enormously expanded so that they combined with the ebon irises in a seamless whole, gleaming and depthless and entirely alien.

"Do you mean I'm not welcome here anymore?"

In the night it's so right, Chris sang. *We'll be together again...*

"If it was up to me I'd have Silka throw you the hell out of here." Daina could smell the grass on her breath, a sweet musty scent she found repellent.

"But we both know it's *not* up to you." Daina put her hand out in order to move past Tie.

Angel and devil, Chris sang on, *meeting halfway between/In a land no one can call his own...*

The moment their flesh met, she saw something in Tie's face. Perhaps a muscle twitched or her pupils contracted for an instant. Then she was past and Chris had seen her. She opened her mouth, felt slim cool fingers enwrap her wrist, spinning her back.

"Where d'you think you're going?" Tie glared at her. She seemed to have trouble breathing. "It all comes down to Chris and Nigel." Her voice had become menacing. "That's it and that's all. It always has been."

"Even when Jon was alive?" Daina said.

Tie frowned as if she were truly concerned. "What do you know of Jon? Did Maggie tell you anything?"

"Whatever was told to me was done so in confidence."

Tie's looped fingers seemed to move minutely up and down her captured wrist. "You should be careful about believing all the stories you hear."

"Hey, Dain!" Chris was smiling as he came up. He stepped between them and Daina jerked her wrist away from Tie's grasp. "Hey, how are you!"

Abandon the rhymes/Off which we have lived, his recorded voice sang lustily. *The limos, the parties/The big girls who give/All they can/It's nothing.*

She tried to drag him away from Tie. "Chris," she said, "what the hell happened?"

"Hey," he grinned, "whattya mean?" She stared into his eyes, willing him to answer her. "Time's just not right, Dain. I can't leave now. Too many people dependin' on what we do, too much bread involved; too many years Nigel'n'me been mates." He stopped for a minute and she saw his face lose all energy. "You're not pissed at me or anythin', Dain. Hey, c'mon!"

She put a palm up to his warm cheek. "No, Chris. I guess I just wanted to understand, that's all."

He put his hand over hers, seeming as relieved as Silka had been earlier. "I'm glad," he said. "Tie—well, you know Tie—she thought you'd try to stop me goin' out on th' road with th' band."

She searched his face. "Why would I do that?"

"Dunno." She sensed he was nervous with the subject. "Guess I thought it too when I saw you here."

She smiled at him. "I came for a completely different reason." She turned her voice shy. "When Vanetta told me about the tour beginning this weekend in San Francisco, I had the notion that since we weren't filming then and I had some time off..."

"No!" Chris said, delighted. "You really want to come? I was thinkin' how you hadn't seen us on stage in so long." He swung her around. "An' it'll be good for you. Get you out o' this pit for a coupla days, nothin' t' do but relax!"

Bonesteel would not believe it; Chris was selling her the idea. "By going with them," Bonesteel had said, "you'll be able to find out a helluva lot more than I can right now." She wanted to throw her head back and laugh, thought, What the hell! and did.

Daina and Baba alone in his apartment, off the greasy streets filled with hunch-shouldered pimps and thirteen-year-old runaways giving ten minutes for ten dollars to yearning businessmen and scared adolescents in dingy hallways to feed their habit. It was mean out there as well as cold.

Out the window: a conglomerate of brilliant neon and iridescent red, the hallmarks of midtown Manhattan. In the winter, especially, it did not seem so tawdry. There was, at that point in time, a comforting immutability about the community.

The view was one of the wonderful things about the place. There were sparkles that could have been icicles, lines of white paint she pretended were hoarfrost. Coming here, Daina's mother would surely have been appalled, refusing no doubt even to climb the rickety wood and flaking iron staircase along which sat spectral cats, scrawny and immobile, eyes like emeralds, large and luminous in the inconstant light. They waited there in the warmth for the night to bring the rodent activity.

They were the guardians of Baba's building and Daina, at least, was careful to feed them at every chance she got. Naturally, Baba would warn her against such coddling. "They's gots t'be hungry, mama, t'go afta them monsters. They goan get spoiled on yo' feedin' and people herebouts never forgive yo."

Outside, the gutters of the streets were moldy with what once had been snow but had now been ground into submission, metamorphosing into gritty gray tubular humps, iced up and hard as granite.

They sat together on the worn carpet with the old beaten-down couch looming over them darkly, warmly. A couple of lamps were on, their colored shades softening the light. They ate pizza brought up from a wonderful place Daina had discovered on Tenth Avenue. Between them was a six-pack of Bud.

"Baba," she said after a time, "how come you've never taken me to bed? Don't you find me sexy?"

He looked at her with his big dark eyes. "I sho as hell do, mama. But y' know me. I ain't happy with jus' one. I gots t'have 'em all." He wiped his lips. "Sho as I thought 'bout yo an' me it'd be like all the rest." He looked away. "We gots sumthin else alt'gether 'tween us."

"But you already know I'm not like the rest; not like any of 'em who come trooping in here at any hour...." She trailed off, watching him stare at her. The light fell softly on his face, blending in the seams, the hard lines of wear, the blows of a world she still could not fully understand. "...Did you ever think about what *I* might want."

He grunted. "Like Marty said, mama, yo too young t'know 'bout that."

"You know that's not true."

"When it comes t'you I confess I doan know what t'think. Why yo still here, mama? In outlawland?"

"Because," she said, "I'm an outlaw, just like the rest of you."

But Baba shook his head. "Yo sho gots some crazy ideas. Cain't yo see this's all in yo' haid? Ain't nuthin goin' on here could interest yo."

"You're here. You interest me."

"Huh! Yo jus' likes t'go uptown." He laughed and his eyes slid away from hers. "Maybe yo best go, mama."

She shook her head slowly. "You're not getting away that easily." She got up, sat down next to him. "What's gotten into you anyway? I thought we had this all talked out ages ago."

He crossed his arms over his massive chest. "Truth is, yo makes me feel guilty, mama, and that ain't sumthin I've felt in a long time. Yo bein' here, seein' the things..." He shook his head. "It ain't right. Yo doan belong here. Yo belong back in Kingsbridge, that's where. Too much jack-shit here fo' the likes o' yo. Makes me feel evil."

She dug her fingers under his arm, hooked her arm with his. "But you're not that. You know it."

"No," he said bleakly, "I'se a goddamn prince I is."

She turned partially around, took his bearded face between her hands and, before he had time to protest, kissed him hard on the mouth. It seemed to last a long, long time and, when she parted her lips, slipped her wet tongue between them to explore his mouth, he allowed it.

She felt then his arms slide around her back, enfold her in an embrace that was so tender she began to weep.

"There," she whispered, pulling her face slightly away from his, "that's what all the fuss's been about isn't it?"

"Yo cryin'," he said with a strange kind of wonderment in his voice.

"Oh, Baba, I love you." She stroked the side of his face. "Don't worry about anything. Please. Let's just enjoy each other and not be concerned—"

He kissed her with a kind of gentleness she knew all the time was inside him and she began to work on his clothes, wanting nothing more than to press herself against his nakedness.

His body was peculiarly hairless and she found that she could not stop her hands from restlessly traversing the planes and valleys of his dusky flesh. Too, she could not stop the trembling in her frame. Now she felt the physical urgencies of her body like quicklightning, traveling her limbs and torso like a hobo hugging the rails. Yet all the while her mind kept screaming in a frenzy, the organism attempting to protect itself. Pleasure shot through her like intermittent thunder, deafening her, but still her fingers trembled as if she were an old woman.

Perhaps Baba saw this or, just as likely, sensed in her the dueling forces tearing her apart. In any case, he carefully carried her to the bed and slowly undressed her, his lips never far from her flesh, working on the parts of her newly uncovered. He felt her shudder when his lips closed over her nipples and, tonguing them, he found them erect and quivering, found further that when he moved his mouth to the undersides of her breasts and gently twisted her nipples with his fingers, she arched her buttocks off the sheets and cried out.

When she was naked, he slid down until he was kneeling on the floor at the foot of the bed. He lifted her legs until they draped over his shoulders and plunged his head forward between her thighs.

She was already so wet he was astounded and he groaned as he peeled back the petals of her lips, exposing her sensitive core.

"What are you...doing?" she had time to breathe before

his mouth descended again and his tongue slashed upward
from stern to stem. Her pleasure was so intense, so utterly
unexpected, that her legs jerked outward and up and, moaning, she began a circular grinding of her hips up against the
maddening incursion into her secret heart.

The pleasure was now a constant; everything flew from
her mind like pigeons scattered before a high wind. Her center had dissolved into liquid and nothing seemed to work.
She wanted nothing but for the feeling to go on and on. The
cords on the inside of her thighs stood out with the mounting
feeling and muscles began to twitch in involuntary concert
to the pounding of her heart. She thought of being high, of
being part of the music and now she knew the end of that
feeling, for she *was* the music—her own music that only she
could hear, feel, taste, and smell.

She knew she was going to come by the taste in her mouth
and the flesh she felt engulfing her jerking hips, radiating
outward like shocks from an epicenter, and when she felt his
fingertips on her aching nipples just as she, as she...

She cried out and almost doubled up, unaware of the movement of her driving hips but only of the fiery path his tongue
and lips took over and over as if burning a path in her
scorched flesh.

Drenched in sweat, her legs bent at the knees and curled
up, she whispered, "Baba come here," and felt his muscular
superheated body over her, felt even then in the glow of the
aftermath, a twinge of fear at his enormous size.

Then she was being flipped in the air so that she was atop
him, astride him as if he were a stallion she were about to
ride.

She leaned over and down, kissing his chest, his nipples,
her hands coming around to caress his torso while he lifted
her effortlessly up and at last she felt him hard at her dripping
entrance. She gasped, certain he was far too large for her to
accommodate but he sank up her with such ease that she
merely closed her eyes and sighed from deep inside her.

They spent over an hour languidly rubbing at each other,
gasping and groaning, pausing just before the frenzy overtook
them as if, having taken so long to get here, they could not
now get enough of each other, the agony of prolongation much
preferable to completion.

But there came a time when the excitement was too strong

to control any longer and, by mutual consent, they allowed
it to burn out of control.

Daina slipped her hands down Baba's sweating back to his
clenching buttocks, felt them hard as rocks, felt him swelled
inside her and this, along with the friction, was enough to
tip her over.

Still she was not fully content. She wanted to explore every
part of his body with her lips and she did. She could not get
enough of him and refused to take her mouth away from him
as he came in a series of hot tangy blasts that caused her hips
to grind down onto the bedding until she, too, came.

Afterward, she would not let him go, tonguing him until
Baba gently drew her away, whispering, "Enough. Enough
fo' now." Then she lay within his arms, feeling his heart,
inhaling his musk and hers, the pleasant odors of the aftermath of sex. "Anyways," he said softly, "yo gots t'go soon. I
gots me a buy t'pick up."

She opened her mouth, closed it almost immediately. She
wanted to spend the night with him just as they were but she
knew from past experience that he never allowed her to stay
on nights he had a buy. "Too dang'rous," he would say and
when once she had asked why, he had merely looked at her.

"That bastard Smiler come up here yesterday while you
was up in Kingsbridge," Baba said, stroking her shoulder.
"I tol' him never t'do that. Work's work and my private life's
got nuthin t'do with it. But he says he's never seen the place
and it was on'y this once so whut the fuck."

She had thought many times about asking him to give it
up but she knew better than to actually say anything. This
was how he made his living. He had chosen it and it was his.
Perhaps it was the only thing in the world that was. She
could no more think of depriving him of it than she could of
walking out on him.

"Yo tell me sumthin, mama...."

She snuggled closer to his warmth. "What?" she whispered
sleepily.

"It really don't make no diff'rence t'yo do it?"

"What does?"

"That I'se a nigga."

She put a hand on his chest, spread her fingers into the
shape of a starfish. Beneath she could feel the pulse of him,
the steady tide of his breathing. He seemed immense and

invulnerable. "In here," she whispered, "you're what I want. A man." She kissed the hairless skin over his heart.

He said nothing, staring up at the distorted patchwork of pale light coming in through the slats of the blinds. It pulsed across the ceiling with the passage of every car or truck.

Small sounds drifted up to them from the street below: a car's strident horn, the soft whoosh of the traffic along the avenue, a dog barking, some laughter, then words in Spanish. A cat screeched.

Daina looked clandestinely over at his dark profile, saw the glint of a tear at the corner of one eye. She pressed her lips to his neck and never told him what she had seen.

She awoke in the dead of night in the midst of a kind of vertigo. Immediately she reached out in bed for Rubens but she was alone. Why wasn't he home? Had Maria told her that he'd be late tonight? She couldn't remember.

The taste of rubber was in her mouth. She tried to swallow it away, thought, It's going to come back. All of it.

She began to sweat and abruptly she felt as if she were falling through the bed, the floor, through the very earth itself. Down to the core.

She stared at the ceiling. It seemed a million miles away. And whirling, whirling so fast it made her head ache. She squeezed her eyes shut but that only made the vertigo worse. Her eyes flew open. What had awakened her? She could feel the beating of her heart, a violent hammer in the steelmill of her chest, heard the rustle of her unquiet breathing. The sound, eerie and oddly magnified in the stillness, caused her to breathe even faster until she was panting.

She wondered if the noise of her own breathing could have awakened her. But deep down in her being she knew that something outside herself had caused her to come awake.

Fright ballooned from her belly up into her throat, lodged there like a stone. She fought it and at that moment heard the sound again. She stiffened, her ears straining in order to identify it. It came again and she tried to still her breathing. A thin, itching line of sweat crawled down her temple. The sound came from inside the house.

The sounds moved closer, seeming clandestine and tiny

and at last she understood that someone was in the house
with her.

She clutched at the sheets but she could not move. The
taste of the rubber was heavy in her mouth. She wanted to
gag. And now she thought she heard a low growling in a
foreign language. Spanish. It was Spanish. Her mind whirled,
still half clogged from her dream of Baba and New York. Part
of her was still three thousand miles away.

She was a girl again, helpless and afraid, suspended, paralyzed, in a world full of dark shadows and evil intentions.
Someone was drawing closer to her with each breath she took.
She felt herself stretched out on the bed, as spreadeagled as
a starfish. She tried to move her head, even her eyes so that
she could see who or what would come through the open
doorway to the bedroom.

A sharp click almost caused her to stop breathing. Trembling, bathed in sweat, she thought of a switchblade yawning
wide, as light silvered down its long lethal blade. And now
fear banged like a brass gong inside her, clanging its hysterical alarm in sonorous vibrations like ripples in a pool,
spreading outward.

Death hung on the air, as palpable as a beaded curtain
fluttering just above her head, descending with sadistic slow-
ness, intent on suffocating her. Her chest heaved and she
fought for breath. A shadow fell across the bed, across her
body, black and enormous and ominous, and she cried out,
though no sound came from her lips. Her mind was a cyclone
of images: death and destruction; messages carved into the
flesh of her body; vile sexual violations; great thorned sticks
bludgeoning her until bones splintered through rent flesh.
Blood fountained obscenely, nerves screamed with pain and
she was utterly helpless. She gasped.

And, arching up, screamed.

"What the hell—"

Crying out, not seeming to be able to catch her breath, she
began to choke.

She felt powerful arms pinioning her, the high heat of
another body pressed against hers. A masculine scent, somehow familiar. Her eyes flew open and she flinched away from
the contact. Still he held on. But this only increased her
terror. She found her face buried in the hollow of his shoulder.
She whipped her head back, her lips drew away from her

teeth as she reverted, whirled away down the long centuries. Her jaws snapped, opening again and she was not fully aware that she growled deep in her throat. She was mad to tear herself free of the grip of death but his strength was overpowering.

She lunged her head forward, her mouth opening, the teeth beginning to clamp down and bite when she heard him say: "Daina? Daina, it's all right."

She bit anyway, her mind still roiling, believing even now that she had been awake all the time. Heard the rip of fabric, tasted salty wetness, heard his surprised pain-filled cry. But it was nothing compared to the pain that filled her now.

"Daina...Daina...Daina..."

She recognized the tenderness in the touch; knew it was not death come for her. Only her mind at work like a steel trap, springing this awful, grisly surprise, an apparition at midnight.

"Rubens," she whispered hoarsely. "Rubens help me." And fell forward into his lap, shuddering and sobbing with anguish and the release from terror.

The nightglow of L.A. came into focus. From somewhere she heard Baba's voice saying, *Mama, yo either in o' yo out an' tha's the end o' it.* Now, with her involvement in Bonesteel's murder investigation, she knew she was in at last. She felt a great desire to tell Rubens everything but she knew that would spoil it in some way she could not understand. She could not tell him—or anyone—about Baba and this was the same thing, an extension of that feeling.

"I may have someone for you to meet," he said.

"Who?"

"Dory Spengler. He's a good friend of Beryl's." He turned over on his back. "He's an agent."

"Rubens, for the last time, I'm not going to fire Monty."

"Did I say something about that? I want you to meet Dory. There's a good reason."

"I'll bet."

"Will you do it?"

"All right."

"Maybe I should postpone my trip to New York," he said. "This thing with Ashley's too important."

"It can wait a week."

"I want you to go, Rubens." She put a hand along his naked flank. "I'm all right." She smiled into the darkness. "Anyway, Chris has invited me to San Francisco for the weekend to see the band perform."

"Good. You'll be out of here for a couple of days."

She leaned over his face. "That's just what Chris said. I don't believe you."

"Beryl's very high on the connection between you two. I've told you that. When I tell her, she'll be ecstatic. The trip'll be worth its weight in publicity for you, and you can meet Dory when you get back."

"Always thinking, aren't you?"

"Go to sleep," he whispered. His breathing slowed as he drifted off.

But sleep would not come for her. Dawn was just around the corner; yesterday was only a sour taste in her mouth. She turned away from the window and the gently moving curtain. She knelt on the bed, pulling the covers down until she had exposed Rubens' naked body. She stared at him for a long time. She felt an overpowering need to touch him, feel him next to her, crush his body to hers, to feel his weight straining her rib cage, his muscled arms encircling her. She reached out for him.

At last she sat up and with a long drawn-out sigh, swung her legs over the side of the bed, leaving Baba. She gathered up her clothes and her shoulder bag, padded silently the length of the apartment to the dark bathroom. The plumbing clanked constantly and the door, warped wood covered with who knew how many coats of cheap white paint, would not close fully.

Inside, with her hand halfway to the light switch, she paused, changed her mind. She set her clothes down on the rim of the bathtub, knelt atop the closed toilet seat, lifted the translucent glass window and let in all the combined light of Manhattan. The sky was white, the illumination diffuse as if they were living inside one of those shell-like Easter eggs.

She watched the city winking and trembling in the chill.

Behind her, she could hear, now and again, Baba moving quietly around the apartment, getting ready to go out.

Her head whipped around at the sharp sound. Someone was at the door. She heard Baba's voice then the sharp metallic scrape of the police lock being lifted out of the way. Friends were often dropping by without notice. Baba had no phone here, preferring to make all his calls from a variety of booths around the area. "Bizness," he always said, "belongs on the street." Still this was one night she would have wished for no interruptions, even so close to its end. She still felt the tingles inside her like grass rushes and her flesh was sore in many places, her lips bruised, slightly swollen: delicious.

She turned from the eastern scene at the window, went silently to the slightly open door to take a peek.

She heard the two loud reports just as she got there and she jumped, her heart hammering so hard she thought it must burst. She heard boots like a staccato rhythm on the bare floor, then nothing as a figure moved onto the thin carpet between the couch and the chairs. She heard a voice, low and menacing, say, "Stay where you are. You've done your night's work." Then there was silence for what seemed an eternity.

She stood quite still, her fingers whitely gripping the edge of the door. Terror clutched at her heart and she felt as if her blood had turned to icicles, paining her with every breath she took. Her mind was numb. She tried to think coherently, could not, just felt her lips moving, This can't be happening.

Abruptly she heard a gasp, so sharp and clear it might have been the report of another pistol. She tried to peer into the gloom, to see who the intruder was. She strained forward, thought she heard one whispered word: *"Cállate!"* Then nothing.

She rushed headlong out of the bathroom, across the long room. Pale light splashed in an oblique oblong across the floor from the partially opened front door. She ran to it, pushed it shut with all her might, slammed the police lock into place.

She turned, almost stumbled over him. He was lying, sprawled on the floor, his head and shoulders half propped against the wreckage of the overturned coffee table. Blood, dark and glistening like a shower of diamonds, covered his chest, drooled out of his open mouth. All the lamps had been extinguished.

She knelt beside him, saw the blood pumping out of him,

exquisite and deadly, life and life only, real and tangible to her for the first time.

"Baba!" she cried. "Oh, God, Baba!" Her hands went to his heaving chest as if, with her fingers alone, she could heal him with faith.

It was some time before she realized that he was trying to speak to her; there was so much blood coming out of his mouth he was choking on it.

She lifted his head away from the hard unforgiving edges of the table, cradling the great weight against her naked breasts. Blood spilled across her stomach, a dark warm river, pooling in the V between her thighs. The sharp stench of the cordite mingled with another smell, sweet and thick and clinging, that she could not identify. Baba felt cool against her and she wrapped him in her arms. Flecks of flesh stuck between her fingers like a shattered sweet.

Baba coughed, said something. She put her head down. "What?" she said bewilderedly. "What?" But she was thinking, Should I stay or leave him to call an ambulance. She missed what he said. "Baba, I can't hear you."

"Ally. Ally that PR cocksucker." His voice was thick, liquid, dull. She wiped the lacing of blood from his lips. "I work on the set-up for five years an' now he wants it all." His eyes closed for a moment and she was terrified he had slipped away.

"Baba?" she whispered fearfully.

His eyes flew open and she saw the spark within them. "Shit, mama. Yo know whut that spic muthafucka said t'me when he shot...says 'Know what's wrong with this city? Too damn many niggas.'"

"Shut up. Shut up. Who cares about all that now?"

He began to shiver. Sweat rolled off him like rain. Again she wiped tenderly at his face and she saw him staring up at her.

Her eyes filled with tears. "Oh, Baba," she whispered. "Don't die. Don't die." She pressed her palms more firmly against his chest. Through the film of blood she could feel his shattered ribs, the tired fluttering of his heart laboring on. His eyes never left hers. His lips opened with an effort, his teeth pink with the unending flow of blood.

"Mama..."

She clutched him. "Baba, I won't let you die. I won't!" But

she could feel the warmth flowing out of him, the life like a stream draining into the sea, dissipating all its power in that vast deep. She wanted to open her veins to him, do anything to give him life again but she was no goddess and he no mythical hero.

"Baba, I love you." But she could do nothing, now or before, when she had stood silent and unmoving in the safe shadows down the room while she watched the steel-jacketed pellets destroying him. She replayed that one instant over and over in her mind. Why didn't I move? Why did I just stand there? Now I'm helpless. Utterly helpless.

And at some point her eyes began again to focus on the outside world. She found that what she held was now merely a cooling and pooling form. There was no life anywhere to be seen or heard.

Outside, beyond the striped protection of the shades, the ululating sound of a siren wailed at her on its way to some emergency. There was none here now. She heard conversation from the street like the chittering of monkeys in the treetops, identifiable but indecipherable. Street Spanish. Then the sounds moved away down the block.

His eyes were glazed but she would not leave him. Her muscles were cramped and her flesh was raised in goose-bumps but the pain only made her less aware of what she must certainly sometime face.

I should have, I should have...oh, I should have...

She fled with her clothes close around her, with hate an impenetrable bead hidden in a locket strung about her neck. For a long time she thought that she would never smile again but, of course, that was just a young girl's foolish notion.

PART THREE

FOREST OF LIGHT

Hast Du was,
  Bist Du was—
If you have something,
  then you are somebody—

Viennese saying

7

L'Auberge Eclaire was situated along the sweeping roller-coaster of San Francisco's California Street. The limos swung into the tree-lined driveway, purred to a halt before the French-inspired frontage of dark red brick and scalloped beige masonry.

But in fact the hotel presented two distinct facades to the welcomed guest. For, soaring above the ivied six-story old-world section, gleamed the bronzed-aluminum and smoked-glass tower curving upward thirty-three stories to dominate this section of the city's skyline. The Auberge had become, in the three years since its opening, the most talked-about structure in San Francisco, overshadowing both the atriumed Hyatt Regency Hotel in Embarcadero Center and the Trans-america pyramid.

Silka left the car and the door locked behind him. For a time he could be seen with Benno Cutler conferring with the management of the hotel. Liveried bellhops opened the trunks of the limos, hustling the band's and Daina's luggage inside.

Silka banged on the door and the driver unlocked it. He

stuck his head inside, looked at Chris. "Extra security's been laid on."

"They th' same people we had before?"

Silka nodded. "Near as possible. They had to haul one guy in from vacation. He was fishing in Tahoe." He laughed. "Bastard's really anxious to bust heads."

"Use him," Chris said. "I don't want you tied up with that crap all th' time." He sounded like he was in the middle of a council of war.

"It's all set," Silka said. "Anyway, I've got to fix Miss Whitney up with her badges soon as we get upstairs, otherwise she'll be stopped at every checkpoint." He took a look outside. "Okay. Any time you're ready."

The enormous lobby was cool and dim with cream plaster Doric columns rising to a buff-and-gilt arched ceiling laced with cupids and seraphim.

To the left the lobby swung in a dogleg off which could be seen discreet hand-lettered signs for the bar, a nouvelle cuisine restaurant that did not open until six in the evening and, adjacent, a cabaret announcing the appearance of Shirley Bassey.

Nearer to hand pale green and gilt sofas and matching club chairs were scattered about, interspersed with tall ferns, their wide fronds creating subtle shadows as well as natural screens. The floor was mottled marble, covered in its center by an enormous Oriental rug.

The Heartbeats had booked the entire fifth floor of the old-world section of the hotel which was, in effect, the fifth and sixth floors because all the rooms there were duplexes. Tourists, of course, were relegated to the modernistic splendor of the steel-and-glass tower with its Nautilus-laden gym and Olympic-size indoor swimming pool high above the city.

The duplexes here had their own saunas and whirlpool baths, Daina saw. All that was missing was the Swedish masseuse and she could be ordered at the touch of a button. No wonder the Auberge was booked eighteen months in advance.

Chris and Daina were in the corner suite at the far end of a hallway filled with pearly black-and-white prints of San Francisco and men in dark suits and faces to match.

It was a rather spectacular apartment by any standards. Certainly Daina had not seen a hotel room to match it.

Around to the left was a full kitchen of copper and chrome and, beside it, a dining room with an oak table large enough to accommodate twelve people comfortably.

Facing them as they came through the enormous double doors was the living area, which might have been somewhat smaller than a football field but not by much. The entire far wall was made up of a series of windows through which the city, white as alabaster, shone in the bright sunlight.

To the far right, a spiral staircase, laden with tiny lights, led up to a pair of bedrooms, each with its own plant-laced bathroom, connected by the sauna and the whirlpool bath.

While downstairs roadies came and went with equipment and changes in schedules, harried press people fretted over tightly packed interview schedules that Chris and Nigel might or might not confirm, according to whim, and arranged for passes for the elite of the press corps with Benno, Silka hustled Daina upstairs and out of the maelstrom.

There seemed enough marble up there to build a fair-sized palazzo. She chose the bedroom with the deep green motif—the other was midnight blue. The curtains—both sets—had been pulled back. Sunlight flooded the room. Behind her she could hear Silka directing the bellboy with her luggage. Yes, she heard him say, it's really her.

She went to the window. The air seemed like crystal, the clarity perhaps magnified after L.A.'s almost constant smog. With her eyes she traced the lines of the buildings as they dipped precipitously down to the deep blue of the bay. Gulls wheeled low along the wharves and, out of the corner of her eye, she saw the bright red and gold flash of a cablecar as it disappeared over the crest of Russian Hill, plunging down to sea level. Far off, on a distant corner, she thought she could make out the brilliant costume of a street musician. The sight made her long to walk those streets herself.

She turned around, saw Silka staring at her. He was standing on the far side of the room where the sunlight lapped only at the tips of his shiny black shoes. The rest of him was in shadow. Daina recalled a football player she had once met, marveling at the size of him even without all his protective padding. It was as if he had been bred to lower his shoulder and knock the wind out of people. Now Silka struck her in just the same way.

"I want to get out of here," she said, "for a little while."

He nodded. "Chris has arranged a car for you. It's down-stairs whenever you want it." He crossed the room in two distance-dissolving strides. "But first we have to prepare you for tonight."

While he set up the Polaroid camera and the other para-phernalia that would process the color photo of her face onto a laminated card marked with infrared dye, which she must wear at all times while she was with the band, she said: "How did Tie meet the band?"

Silka grunted. "Picked them up one summer in Cap d'Antibes. Walked up to Jon wearing nothing but a monokini and lay down beside him. That was the kind of thing he couldn't resist."

"But then after Jon died—"

"Hold still, please." The flash went off and the mechanism whined out the developing photo. Silka put the camera aside. "Oh, yeah, she moved in with Nigel after Jon died but it wasn't what she wanted." He looked up at her as he worked. "From the moment she spotted them what she wanted was to make it with Jon and Chris at the same time." He shook his head. "But they drew the line at that. They were far too close to share a woman...brothers under the skin and all that...."

"And Nigel? What of him? They all came down to London together. Wasn't it all one big family?"

"Well, yes and no. 'Course they were all close but Nigel resented the special musical relationship Chris had with Jon. Together, they made magic music. How can you explain it? You can't. But Nigel had to try. He'd come to me and say, 'They're plotting behind me back, Silka, I know it. They want me out o' th' group.' At first I tried to tell him it wasn't true but he only wanted to listen to himself or someone who would echo what was in his mind."

Silka shook his head again. "He was a wild boy in those days, was old Nigel. Two, three times a week I had to come get him out of some bird's house when he'd been caught by the husband or the boyfriend with his pants down." He laughed amazedly. "The bastard just didn't care. He was in-satiable when it came to women. I mean, oh, they all were in their own ways but with Nigel it was different somehow, deeper and"—he shrugged his massive shoulders—"maybe pathological is the right word, I dunno. Anyway, he kept me plenty busy." His eyes clouded. "Then Jon died." He sighed, handed her the laminated tag. "There you go." The photo of her wasn't half bad. She pinned it on.

"And then the band changed," Daina said. "From what I've been told it had to, didn't it? Jon was behind all those outrageous publicity stunts that got the band so much press in the beginning."

Silka began to clean up. "Everyone knew what we wanted everyone to know. Half the time Jon was too ripped to think of anything. Tie whispered them into his ear. I don't—no one really knows how many were his and how many were Tie's. I don't think even she could tell you for certain because over time the process became blurred. It's always like that with the genesis of ideas, don't you think? I mean even when, one morning, you wake up and think, What a great idea! it's really a synthesis of what you've heard, seen, felt, acknowledged and, finally, act upon."

Daina found herself wondering what a man who spoke this way, felt like this, thought these thoughts, could be doing as bodyguard for the world's greatest rock band.

"That's what makes us different from anything else on this planet, isn't it, Silka? We have the power to act on all that."

She went out while the band had their interview with *Rolling Stone,* the limo taking her wherever she directed.

They went left onto Hyde, crossing Russian Hill, down into the part of the city she had seen from her window. A cablecar rumbled by. She could hear the muffled clanging of its warning bell as if from a great distance but by the time she thought to press the button to roll down the window, it had disappeared off the lofty heights, on its way to Ghirardelli Square where, she knew, it would empty of its passengers only to turn around at the terminal to begin its grinding journey up the steep slope to Union Square.

Vallejo and Green flashed by and she was on the crest of the hill. The street performer she had glimpsed before was gone but the streets, filled with people, were as friendly as she remembered. "Turn here," she said as they came to Union Street and the limo took her west.

Within three blocks the street was lined on both sides by

the tiny, eccentric clothing boutiques, art galleries, and restaurants she so loved.

She told the driver to stop outside Elaine Chen's where,
inside, they made the most inordinate fuss over her, serving
her steaming herbal tea while they paraded dresses, skirts,
blouses and sweaters before her.

Customers were no longer interested in the shop's wares,
clustering around her, asking questions about Chris, the film,
thrusting slips of paper at her to autograph. They had the
heat of the sun, gobbling oxygen, straining for a touch just
as if she were some slick-skinned alien. It made her feel ten
feet tall, as if she possessed enough power to light the world.

It was only when Elaine Chen herself appeared from the
bowels of the shop to shoo them all outside and lock the door
behind them that there was any kind of a chance to shop. But
then Elaine knew how to flatter her important clientele.

Back on the street, with her packages—she had bought
a pair of silk dresses, a satin blouse, and a remarkable grape-
colored jacket of silk and linen—she ran right into a slim,
rather effeminate-looking man in dark glasses, visored cap
and pale gray uniform.

"May I take those?"

Now Daina saw it was a woman, her voice high and musical. She smiled charmingly.

"Please." She held out one arm for the packages, gestured
behind her at the silver Lincoln stretch limo purring at the
curb. It was not the one that had brought Daina here.

"Where's my limo?" Daina said.

"Please," the liveried woman said. She began to usher
Daina toward the silver car. "Your face is too well known for
you to be on the streets this long."

And she was right, Daina saw. Passers-by and window-
shoppers were becoming no longer that. She was eclipsing
even the sights of San Francisco, she realized with a little
thrill. The woman beckoned. It was dangerous to be out on
the streets alone this way.

Daina nodded. "All right." And, handing her packages
over, stepped through the opened rear door into the dark, cool
interior of the car.

She might have been in a living room. There were no
conventional seats here but three butter-soft leather and rosewood swivel chairs. Between them was a bar, TV, a massag-

ing footbath in one corner, a bookshelf filled with hardbound editions of *Peter Pan, The Brothers Karamazov, Lolita, Candy, The Story of O, A Clockwork Orange,* and the complete works of Garcia Lorca. An odd assortment, Daina thought. But not half as odd as the man who sat in the chair nearest the footbath.

He had a long narrow skull, bald on top but with thick silver hair on each side combed straight back and not, as some vain men did in ludicrous fashion, to the side, trying to hide their baldness.

His wide, wrinkled forehead and bronzed, leathery skin reminded her of a beautiful black-and-white photograph of Picasso she had once seen. But there the resemblance ended for he had no deep lines whatsoever in his face though he was, she estimated, in his late sixties. Rather, the pleasant planes of his face were covered by a skin of unbroken tiny wrinkles as if one were viewing him through a fisherman's net. Too, his eyes were fierce bituminous chips with the power of a far younger man.

"Welcome, Miss Whitney," he said. "Do sit down." He had a voice like Alexander Scourby's, deep and rich and trained to be heard by many.

He wore a pair of charcoal slacks with deep pleats, a white short-sleeved linen shirt that had obviously been made for him and black huaraches beneath which she could see his bare skin. One leg was crossed over the other at the knee. His hands were in his lap. They were, she saw, large hands with great gnarled knuckles and bent fingers as if he were suffering from arthritis.

"I am Meyer," he said. "Karl Meyer. You know me." It was not a question.

She nodded. "Rubens has spoken of you. I thought you were in San Diego."

He regarded her curiously, only his large odd eyes moving. The air conditioning hissed inconspicuously. The mirrored windows echoed the scene. The outside world did not exist.

"You are frightened of me." He nodded his enormous head. "That is good. It shows you have good judgment." He smiled suddenly and she saw the welter of gold. It seemed to flash like the rising sun off the surface of the sea, spangling him.

"So this is Daina Whitney."

It was such an unexpected statement that she laughed.

"Pardon me," he said. "Have I said something amusing?"

"Well, yes," Daina said. "Everyone knows my face."

"Ah," Meyer said as if in complete understanding. "Of course." He leaned forward and one of his gnarled hands reached out. "But how many have touched you?" The point of his finger came down, tapping her on the back of the hand. "You are an icon now...or soon will be. Tell me, how does it feel?"

Daina said nothing. Her eyes had been drawn, as he had moved toward her, to the inside of his forearm. The blue numbers were thick with age but unmistakable.

Meyer, noticing where she was looking, said, "They felt we should not have names. Names were for human beings. All they gave us were numbers."

"I'm sorry," she whispered.

"Don't be." He kept his hands where they were, clasped. "It wasn't your world. Your world has other horrors to contend with." His eyes opened wide and she thought she could see another world there. He held up his hands. "When I was young, I used to paint. I dreamt of being another Cézanne or Matisse. I was very good," he whispered. "Very skilled. I had the fire." His eyes burned. "But I stayed too long in Europe. Too long. I could not believe what was happening there. When the Nazis took me and found out what I did, they did this"—he lifted those hands, spreading the crooked fingers to their limits like trees upon a moor—"to me. For fun. Broke my fingers, one at a time."

He stared at her hard for a long minute. Then he shrugged. "Well. At least I am alive, yes?" He patted her knee in a kindly fashion. "You never answered my question."

Daina fought to remember. "To love what you're doing; to create and to be recognized for it. What more could I want?"

He nodded sagely. "What more indeed?" He smiled. "Life is sweet for you, Daina, is it not?"

"But not without dangers."

"Oh no!" He laughed, slapping his knee. "What would life be like without danger. My God, what a colossal bore that'd be! I'd sooner slit my wrists." He grimaced and, reaching down, began to fumble with the leather straps of his huaraches.

"Here, let me." Daina bent forward and, carefully displacing his thick fingers with her own, undid the straps.

Meyer put his bare feet into the bath, pressed a chrome stud. The water began to vibrate and a small smile escaped his lips. "Ah, that's better." He leaned over, opened the bar. "Drink?"

"A Tom Collins."

"Coming up." His hands were very deft with the glasses, ice, soda and liquor and she began to wonder about the story he had told her or, more specifically, just how impaired those seemingly ruined hands were. She was also certain he would not have allowed her to see this chink in his defenses had he not decided he could trust her implicitly.

When he had made the drinks for them both and they had sampled the results, he said, "Age, my dear Daina, is a very serious matter. Of course, in a world of optimums, one ought not to take any notice of it. But this is a far from optimum world. I'm sure you will agree. When I was young, I was a very patient man. Painting in oils taught me that. Masterpieces cannot be rushed."

He sighed, put down his drink. "But age dissolves all patience, I'm afraid. One son lost in Korea, a second in Vietnam." His eyes turned away from her, inward. "There are no masterpieces anymore. There cannot be. Time is running out." His eyes returned to her. "When one is old, one turns more and more to fantasy." That sly, gold-tipped smile was back again.

"Now I only wish to create my own world—you've met Margo; there are many others. Yet only she travels with me. She understands the road, this car, me. We're all one.

"Now my mind is free to conjure up daydreams from which I fashion my own reality. I imagine it is something akin to what God must feel. If there ever was a God, which I most seriously doubt." He blinked like an owl. "God would never have taken both sons away from me. There's no pattern in that and the inexplicable, about which theologians are known to babble, is nonsense. No. The world is a vile place and when it comes to those one loves, there must be safeguards...don't you think?" He might have said it as an afterthought but now he seemed genuinely interested in what she might say.

"I don't know what safeguards there might be," she said, thinking of Baba and of Maggie.

Meyer lifted a finger. "Oh, but there are. There are." He

sipped at his Tom Collins meditatively. "Tell me," he said at last, "about Rubens. I want to know what you feel for him."

"I love him," she said.

"I wonder," he mused, "whether that's enough these days. It never has been. I loved my two sons but my love did not save them."

"I don't understand."

Meyer peered at her. "You must save Rubens."

She was alarmed. "From whom?"

"From himself." He patted her knee. "Let me explain. After my youngest son was shipped home with the medal he had earned posthumously pinned to the casket, I lost all feeling. I imagine it was finally too much for me to bear. My circuits had burned out.

"So I threw myself into business. Money seemed a poor second to my sons but that was all I was capable of. Meeting Rubens, getting to know him, teaching him, made those old circuits burn with life once more. But only for a time. Still, that is something one never forgets.

"Now, it is becoming increasingly clear to me that he has learned too well, becoming perhaps too much like me. I don't want that. No one should have to live his life as I do."

"Are you so unhappy, then?"

He sat back, sighed, taking his feet out of the bath and drying them on a towel. "I'm not unhappy at all. That is the point. I'm incapable of that now."

"I don't believe you," she said. "But if I did, wouldn't that be a blessing?"

"Oh!" he cried. "And all the other emotions that are no longer mine." His eyes searched hers. "Do you want him this way? Would you still love him?"

"I'd love him no matter what."

"I hope," Meyer said carefully, "you have the strength to stand by that always."

"I'll make you a deal," Meyer said, just before the limo let her off back at the hotel. "Take care of Rubens and I'll help you find out who killed your friend."

Daina took a deep breath, exhaled. "There's no need to make a deal."

"I want him safe, Daina," Meyer said seriously. "I don't

think there's anyone else he trusts enough or who's got enough guts."

"I don't make deals, Meyer."

"You'd be a fool not to take this one."

She burst out laughing but when she had sobered he was still regarding her with the same cool look. "You're serious."

He did not have to answer and, she realized with some surprise, she had not expected him to. She put her hand on the door handle. "Nothing will happen to him, Meyer." Then, impulsively, she leaned over, kissed the old man on his leather cheek. His skin was warm and dry. He smelled faintly from a rich, masculine scent. She looked at him one last time. "I'll tell Margo to come back here and buckle your huaraches."

His laughter remained with her long after his leviathan silver Lincoln had disappeared into the traffic on California Street.

When she returned to the suite, the *Stone* people were still there. Chris saw her, waved, "Hey, Daina, you're just in time. I wantcha in a coupla these shots, huh?" He put his arm around her as she came into the circle of people. The *Stone* people fell all over themselves to talk to her, find out what she was doing here, how the film was going. That was the magic word and she talked on while, out of the corner of her eye, she saw Chris climb over Rollie's outstretched legs to get to a tall black man who sat slouched in a chair in one corner, eyeing a silent TV screen.

He had a wide, glistening afro, a long face dominated by high cheekbones and rather almond-shaped eyes. His mouth was an artist's slash in the chocolate putty of his face. He wore dark green leather pants that tied up the crotch and a cream-colored Regency-style silk shirt with wide sleeves. Lines of beaded jade hung in concentric circles around his neck and close up to his throat hung a carved stone Buddha on a thin platinum choker. He wore a line of three diamond studs in the lobe of his right ear.

"Hey, Nile, hey," Chris said, slapping him on the knee. "Hey c'mon we need you for some shots."

Daina needed no introduction to know that this was Nile Valentine. He was an American-born guitarist who had emigrated to England in the mid-sixties. His first single, "White

Sun," had become virtually an overnight hit and with it Nile
had become somewhat of a sensation. His flamboyant guitar
style—a unique fusion of blues and psychedelia—had rev-
olutionized rock. When his second single, "Locked Beneath
the Earth," was released eight months later, it streaked to
the number one position worldwide and Nile's reputation was
secured.

While Chris guided Nile across the room, the *Stone* photographer began to group the band members. Of course Thaïs
was next to Nigel. She wore a fawn-colored suede skirt that
buttoned up the front. Most of those buttons were open so
that as she sat down, Daina could see all the way up her legs.
On the inside of her right thigh Daina saw what could only
be a tattoo. It appeared to be a double cross but she shifted
so suddenly that Daina could not be certain.

Chris finally got Nile onto the sofa with the attendant
splash of a great animal and he squeezed in between the
guitarist and Daina, put his arms around them both. On
the other side Rollie was, as usual, clowning and for perhaps the next ten minutes the photographer's motor-driven
camera ran off a continuous series of shots.

At one point, Thaïs leaned over Nile toward Daina, whispered, "Tell me, Daina, what's he like in bed?"

Daina glanced at Chris who seemed oblivious to anything
but the eye of the lens.

Now she had no thought about telling the truth. What
good would it do her in any case? Thaïs was determined to
believe what she wanted to believe. It amused Daina to give
it to her now.

"I've had better." Daina laughed. "But he certainly is
kinky."

"Has he ever brought one of his young girls in with you?"
Thaïs' ebon eyes seemed as lidless as a reptile's.

For a moment Daina was caught off balance and she could
almost hear the other woman's silent laughter ringing in her
mind. What young girls? she thought. Is Thaïs telling the
truth and, if so, what else don't I know about Chris? "He
asked me once if it would be all right," she said, her voice
betraying none of her unsureness—it was only another role
after all, "but I said no. 'I mean what if we're caught?' I told
him." Now they both laughed.

"You ought to see him sometimes when he goes on one of

his binges," Thaïs said softly. "Nigel has to go after him 'cause he's the only one Chris'll trust to drag him out."

Binges. Binges? Daina thought. What's she talking about? "I've been around a couple of times when he's just come back and Maggie—"

"Oh, Maggie knew nothing about them," Thaïs said. "She couldn't possibly have and stayed with him so long. Not knowing her—"

"All right," the photographer said, "now just a bit of a change, if you don't mind...."

Daina came and sat next to Thaïs. This was too good to let get away.

"But you never know," Daina said, "about people. I mean I was Maggie's best friend but I'm not sure now whether I really knew her."

"What d'you mean?"

"Well there was a lot going on that I didn't know about," she improvised.

"Oh yeah, yeah." Thaïs nodded. "Well it was Chris of course who got her started on the junk...but then everyone's into it sooner or later so I mean if it hadn't been him, it'd been someone else."

Daina felt abruptly dizzy, as if the world had canted off to one side, leaving her gasping for breath. She fought to regain her equilibrium, knowing she was good enough not to allow even a chip of what she was feeling to be exposed. Junk. The word had only one meaning on the streets and in the slang of this world. Christ, she thought. Could Tie be telling the truth? She turned away from the thought. What would that make Chris?

Abruptly she thought of Bonesteel and the world began to right itself. At least she had a way to check the veracity of what Tie was telling her. Bobby had the results of Maggie's autopsy. Surely that would show any—

"But of course you knew that," Tie went on, her eyes searching Daina's.

"I knew what she chose to tell me," Daina said enigmatically. Let her chew that one over, she thought.

Pop! Pop! Pop! Pop!

And the string was pulled, the session over. The group began to break up. Thaïs smiled down at Daina as she stood up. She smoothed down her suede skirt until only one thigh was visible. "You mean you never did any... investigating on your own? You were so incurious—"

Daina was on her feet, shoulder to shoulder with Thaïs. "If I did do any," she said softly, "that would've been between me and Maggie."

"How you must hate him for what he did to your friend."

Daina saw how she had been delicately led to this place: not softly but with tangential sledgehammers. She was furious with Tie, but she was determined that the other woman should not see this. Force of will was a habit with her now and she summoned this formidable talent as she said, "I love Chris. He's like family. And nothing you can say to me will ever change our relationship." A hard edge had crept into her voice, unbidden. It was the tone she used when in character in *Heather Duell*. She heard it only after the fact, as she observed the effect her words had on Tie, as if someone previously unseen had come up and grasped her by the shirtfront. And for once she seemed unsure about what to do next.

Daina smiled slowly, patted Thaïs on the arm. "It's all right," she said. "It's all over with and forgotten." She turned away. Nile had drifted back to his half-reclining position in front of the flickering TV. Slouched there with heavy eyelids and his thick, hungry lips, he gave a gaunt, unsettling impression as if he were filled with some kind of otherworldliness, haunted by an alien apparition, and from him came a phantasmic heat as if he were running an enormous fever that could not be controlled. He was still now, save for his long sinewy fingers that twitched and moved as if over an invisible fretboard.

"Composing," Chris said, as the room began to empty out. "He gets like that sometimes. Like a meditation."

Daina snorted. "Meditation? He's as high as the Mad Hatter."

"Well, yah, but so what?" Chris grinned. "We all are, so who gives a damn, huh?"

"Hey, Chris," Nigel said from the doorway, "limo's pickin' us up in fifteen minutes."

"Sound check," Chris said to her. "Gotta split. But wait dinner for me." He paused and a curious, little-boy look came into his eyes. "'Less you've got other plans...."

Daina laughed. "Go on," she said. "I came here to be with you." Which was not at all true, at least at the start. She had

come away from L.A. into this freneticism hoping that it
would help her. Now she felt that decision to be wholly for-
tuitous but for an entirely different reason. She had, she was
coming to suspect, breached a hidden doorway, finding inside
a circuitous Chinese puzzle stretching away from her like
ripples in a pond. From just one point, shock waves had begun
to radiate outward, revealing real worlds and false, hitherto
unknown.

She went up the spiral staircase, leaving Nile to his au-
tistic orchestrating. An idea was beginning to evolve in her
mind. Silka had said he thought Nigel might be pathological
but what of Thaïs? Was there any other explanation for her
behavior? How she had hated Maggie. And now me.

She looked at her watch. It was still early enough to get
Bonesteel at the precinct.

But he wasn't there. "Just a moment, Miss Whitney," an
aggressive female voice said in her ear, "I'll try him in the
car." It took a while but she got through.

"Well," Bobby said, "I didn't expect to hear from you so
soon. Anything wrong?"

"No. I just...Bobby I'd like some information."

"If I can, I'll give it to you. Shoot."

"What did Maggie's autopsy reveal about her?"

"I told you—"

"Something you *didn't* tell me."

"What's happened?" The quick change in his tone of voice
shocked her.

"Bobby..." The words were being squeezed out of her as
if of their own volition. "...I've got to know. About Maggie."

"What about her?"

She had had enough of that, exploded. "Goddamnit Bobby,
stop the bull! You know what I'm talking about don't you?"

"I can't believe you didn't know."

"It's true then. She had a habit."

"If it's any consolation, the M.E. tells me it hadn't been
going on for long."

"Well it's *no* goddamned consolation!"

"Daina, be reasonable. Look who she lived with."

"Jesus. Jesus." She tried to sort out her thoughts. "Why
didn't you tell me before?"

"I'm sorry," he said. "Really I am. But what good would
it've done?"

"You bastard!" she cried and slammed down the phone.

The music came again from downstairs in the suite but this time it contained the sheer cold brilliance of massed synthesizers. "Like working with synthesizers," Chris had said to her once. "You've got to be super careful not to reveal more than you want."

She bent over, her head in her hands, pulling at her hair. "Goddamnit!" She pounded her balled fists onto her thighs, the pain making her eyes water. But still she felt utterly impotent.

The Nova Burlesque House was the first place she thought of going. After all, there were many there who loved Baba and who, heavy bulges under their armpits, would give him his measure of revenge once she told them what she had been witness to.

She hurried down the bleak street, buttoning her pea coat as she went, oblivious to the flotsam of humanity who huddled, breathing shallowly, lost within themselves, or sleeping, shoeless, in papered doorways all around her.

Midway down the block she began to notice the burgeoning crowds, the refulgence of the roof lights of the police cars. She slowed her pace, her pulse beating strongly. She seemed to have difficulty breathing. She came to the further shores of the throng, saw the lines of stretchers and, hidden on the east side of the phalanx of police cars, the ambulances from Roosevelt Hospital.

Christ, she thought. No. And began to worm her way through the crowd. There was a live-wire tension as there always was when the cops came around here in force. But today, there seemed to be something more.

"What a blowout!" she heard someone say.

"Never saw so much goddamned blood!" From the other side.

She pushed and squirmed until she was near enough the front to see. The doorway to the Nova was blackened on the outside.

It reminded her of the way a suspected Viet Cong village looked after an American battalion had raided it. It made the six o'clock news on all three networks one evening. There was no smell of smoke but as she sniffed the air, she scented the same harsh smell she had noticed in Baba's apartment after he had been shot.

The line of stretchers kept coming and of course the cops were crawling all over the place. They were having a field day, gesturing to each other with as much relish as newscasters just after a major disaster.

Then she saw Rooster. He was on a stretcher, his face turned toward her. His eyes were closed. Blood had seeped through the cloth they had put over him. His normally glossy purple skin had taken on an odd waxy patina. She wondered about Tony and whether all those children and grandchildren would ever see him again.

Rooster was coming just abreast of her and, involuntarily his name was torn from her mouth. One of the policemen turned around and she saw Sergeant Martinez's porcine face. His eyes widened as he recognized her.

"Hey!" he called. "I wanna talk to you!"

She whirled away. She knew what he wanted to talk to her about. It had nothing to do with murder. She was the only witness left to his graft-taking.

"Hey! C'mere! Come back. *Putita!* I'll get you!"

His voice seemed to follow her through the crowd as if it had radar and could pick her out, surround her, draw her back.

Gasping, she shoved people this way and that as she drove a zig-zag path through the throng. People were milling all about and this was in her favor. But still she felt Martinez close behind her, heard the pounding of his huge, thick-soled shoes against the unyielding pavement.

At points, the crowd was so thick she had difficulty maneuvering. She began to pant, felt the sweat prickling her underarms, rolling down the indentation of her spine into the crack of her working buttocks.

Someone—Martinez or perhaps an annoyed passerby—grabbed at her sleeve and she lurched sideways, going over on her ankle and nearly losing her balance. She staggered for several steps. Her left ankle began to ache as she sprinted off, turning the corner onto Eighth Avenue.

Immediately, she ducked into a narrow alley, stood with her back against the wall, perfectly still except for her heaving breasts. Sweat poured off her in torrents and she felt as hot as if she had a fever.

She waited five minutes, then walked out as calmly as she could and into a Blarney Stone down the block near Forty-first Street where it was dark and beery-smelling and she could order a corned beef sandwich for ninety-five cents. She sat at a sticky table near the bar and watched the Knicks lose a close one.

The music was gone from below, which was perfectly all right with her. Its Dantean minor harmonics had only added to her depression.

She felt as helpless now as she had then. And just as terrified as if Martinez were breathing down her neck. And perhaps he still was, from his niche in her past, she told herself.

She got up. The only way out of it was through power. Real power. The kind that Rubens and Meyer wielded. Yes, they might have given up a lot but look at the return! And I, Daina thought, know what I'm getting myself into. Yes, there's pitfalls but if I'm constantly on guard for them, how can they hurt me?

And *Heather Duell* could do it, she knew that. *Could.* If everything went right.

In the bathroom, she turned on the tub, sprinkled in a packet of violet-scented bath beads, waited until the fragrance began to suffuse the small room.

She stripped off her clothes and sank gratefully into the hot water. She put her head back against the tiles. She gasped.

Nile filled the doorway, his half-open eyes regarding her with the utter tranquillity of a grazing bovine.

"What the hell d'you think you're doing?" she snapped.

"Everyone's gone," Nile said sadly. "And I'm through with the music."

"Do you realize," Daina said, "that I'm naked?"

He shrugged. "Don't make no difference t' me."

"How about me? Do I get a vote?"

"Door was open." He walked over to the toilet, sat on the lowered lid. "Chris introduce us?"

"Yes."

"Uhm. Uhm. Knew you looked familiar." His enormous head nodded. "Movie star, ain'tcha."

"That's one way of putting it."

He sniffed. "You sho smell nice."

"Thank you." She stared at him, saw that he was perfectly serious and burst out laughing. He was far too sweet to turn away. He seemed to her to have the air of a lost boy searching for his mother, an odd kind of Peter Pan who did not even understand the nature of his search—or of his longing.

"Are you coming to the show tonight?" she said.

"Yah. To the party too, afterward." He rubbed at his nubbly cheek. "C'n you keep a secret?"

"Sure."

He grinned, his long white teeth shining like a sun in that face. "Gonna jam there, oh yah. Chris'n'me we got it goin'. Gonna plug in an' blow eardrums. Hah hah! Yah!" He put a forefinger across his lips, lowered his voice to a hoarse whisper. "S'big secret. No one knows 'cept Chris'n'me. Now you. Ah! Don't you go tellin' anyone now. We wanna su'prise 'em all. Uhm. Y'need su'prises, y'know, t' keep from fallin' asleep. Otherwise life gets very, *very* boring, fall asleep alla time."

"The way you play, I'm surprised you find anything boring."

He gave her a sad smile so filled with emotion that she started. "Oh no. Y'got it the wrong way round actually. On'y thing *isn't* boring's m'playin'." His strong fingers arched, strumming the air. She saw the pale yellow buildup of the callous pads at their tips—the result of long years of working those steel strings.

"You play so wonderfully, Nile. It's so different from anyone else. You're a genius you know."

"Yah. M'friends said that 'bout me in the beginnin', too. M'friends." He shook his head. "Now they say, 'Hey Nile, watchew doin' with all that flamboyance on stage, man? The psychedelics, the lightshows; playin' your axe with your teeth. All that bullshit. You're the best, man, you gotta act like it. Jus' go out there an' play....'"

He drifted off into silence, his head in his hands, and his attitude was not lost on her.

"It ain't me," he said at last, "jus' standin' there." He shook his head. "It jus' ain't me."

"Then why d'you do it?" Splashing a bit as she sat up.

Nile lifted his head like an animal questing. He shrugged. "You gotta move with the times. I gotta rep I gotta live up to. I spent so many years, bitter years when no one here wanted t' listen t' the music I was playin'; spent so much time tryin' just t' *build* that rep—gave up *everything* in order t' get it an' now"—he laughed a chill bitter laugh—"now I find that the rep's far more important than the music I'm makin'." He turned to her. "See, the music's taken f'r granted now...and it's the rep that's gotta be maintained. I used my music t' build the rep but now it's as if they're two separate entities each in their own universe."

He shook his head. "Course I wouldn't've made it without some friends. Chris'n'Nigel'n, in those days, Jon...."

"You knew Jon."

"Oh, yah. Well, not for long though. There were a shitload of problems by then. Psychedelics were fadin', y'see. The Beatles had already done their nut with *Sergeant Pepper,* overnight changin' the face of music. An' it was Jon's contention that the band had t' produce its own masterwork in order t' keep up with the Beatles an' the Stones. The *Waxworks* album was the answer according to Jon, but then it was the gospel according to Saint Jon, y'know. It was all his or as mostly as counts.

"Naturally Nigel was against it from the first. He didn't want t' get away from the band's blues roots. It had made them an' he was terrified to monkey with the sound. Jon overruled him of course. But that was all ancient history when I arrived in England an' by the time I really got t' know them, things had changed drastically. Chris was none too happy with *Waxworks* after all. I guess he'd come around t' Nigel's way of thinkin'. Anyway he'd always be goin' off with Nigel here an' there—nobody but them knew where actually—leavin' Jon on his own. Ian'n' Rollie never cared, see, 'cause they always had their own birds, their own lives outside the band. But not these three. Band's their life, y'know?

"So Jon, he began t' freak. He wasn't the most stable of people t' begin with. Woulda been a field day for any shrink. Manic, paranoid, you name it Jon would act it. Reality never meant too much t' him."

Daina knew the progression of albums. "It was all downhill from there for Jon, wasn't it?"

"Uhm hum. Next album was *Blue Shadows* an' it was dominated really by Chris'n'Nigel. 'Course I did a little here an' there t' fill in when Jon didn't show or when he passed

out with his face in the loo. Christ, Tie had her hands full
those sessions."

"So they were true, all those rumors about you playing on
those sessions."

"Yah. My company wouldn't give permission an' anyway
I did it as a mate, y'know. Jon was in trouble, I gave the band
a helpin' hand. Any mate would've. But no one wanted it
publicized. Uhmm." He looked around. "You got anything t'
drop?"

"No."

He nodded. "Yah. Well." He got up. "I'll just amble out.
Let you finish what you started. Any Cokes?"

"Sure. Downstairs in the refrigerator."

"Right." With a quick grin he disappeared out the door.

By the time she emerged, wrapping a thick bathrobe
around her, the music had come on again, filling the downstairs with sad soulful sound.

Inside the limo it was another world entirely. She felt like
a fish in a tank. It was difficult to see out. The heavily tinted
glass let in only the brightest of light. A black, faintly haloed
world rushed silently by just as if they were all Nile, staring
intently at his silent TV screen. Except, Daina felt, they were
the ones on the TV.

The car was full of the sweet smoke of grass. Fireflies of
burning ash as they orchestrated their pulls on the weed,
sighed on and off like automatic doors.

Nigel leaned forward, opened the tiny refrigerator built
into the back of the front seat. He extracted a bottle of Kirin
beer and, opening it, tipped his head back. He sucked three-
quarters of the contents down his throat in one swallow.

Beside him Thaïs smoked a joint she had ostentatiously
dipped in a black paste she had concocted from THC. One
slim leg was crossed over the other, her right ankle hooked
behind her left, the pearl lamé of her dress falling away from
the firm flesh revealed by a high slit. She wore three gold
bracelets on her left wrist, each in the form of a serpent with
its tail in its mouth. The ancient Egyptian talisman that she
never took off was around her throat.

Chris, who sat next to Daina, had his head flung back

against the plush seat as if he were dozing. Nile had gone in the second limo with Ian and Rollie.

Thaïs handed her joint to Daina who passed it back to Nigel. He sucked on it. Thaïs stared at Daina.

Silka, in front with the driver, seemed to watch them and the road ahead at the same time. One long arm lay along the seat back like a cord of wood.

"Hey." It was Nigel's voice. It was soft but the atmosphere in the car had been so still, so thick with their studied nothingness—the void that, perforce, comes just prior to a gig—that Daina started.

"Hey, Chris."

"What is it?" Chris did not move a muscle, did not open his eyes.

"I don't know whether th' guys are ready t'do 'Saurian' t'night."

"'Course they are. They did it f'r th' record, they c'n do it t'night."

"I don't know—"

"Quit worryin'."

"Y'know I don't like last-minute changes. Too many things c'n go wrong. I don't wanna be up there playin' an' find m'pants down round m'ankles."

Thaïs giggled and Nigel glared at her.

"Things'll only go wrong if you think they will, mate." Chris brushed at the tip of his nose with the palm of one hand as if he had been bothered by a fly. "Anyway it wouldn't be th' first fuckin' time it's happened t' us. Remember that time in Hamburg with th' coppers all over th' hall? Or in Sydney when—"

"Christ, this is no time t' be strollin down memory lane!"

"What better time," Chris said placidly.

"I tol' th' guys we were takin' it out."

Chris' eyes snapped open. He was a blur as he reached across Daina, grabbed at Nigel's shirtfront. "You bleedin' berk!"

"Get th' hell off me mate!" Nigel shouted. He hacked at Chris' powerful wrists, twisted his body from side to side.

"Hey," Daina said. "Chris. Cut it out."

On the far side of the limo Thaïs sat motionless, her eyes dark and unreadable as she stared straight ahead. She held the roach away from her. Smoke drifted languidly upward from out of her partly opened lips as if she were a billboard.

"Tie," Daina called, still struggling between them, "aren't you going to do something to stop them?"

"Why should I?" she whispered. "The adrenalin's good for them both."

Silka grunted from in front and half turned. Somehow he managed to get both his thick arms through the gap in the mirrored partition. With seeming ease, he pulled them apart and held them there until their panting had subsided.

The two of them glared silently at each other. Daina could smell the sweat, the animosity that had sprung up between them, as clearly as if it were a freshly killed animal.

After a time Thaïs said softly, "There's only an hour before you go on stage." It seemed directed at both of them or, more accurately, at the space of contention between them.

Nigel twisted his head as if he had a crick in his neck, pulled his T-shirt down over his stomach.

"Close," Silka said, his voice like gravel crunching under a tire's tread.

Outside the night had abruptly come alive. Masses of kids filled the avenue before the hall like lemmings striving to be the first to reach the sea. Daina felt rather than heard a deep rumbling even through the limo's excellent soundproofing. Some sounds were not made to be kept at bay.

The flow of the kids receded and bulged as the look-outs on the periphery spotted the enormous Continental. A roaring like surf and the driver spun the wheel to the left. As they turned, the masses seemed to fly apart as kids began to run in the limo's direction. Hair flew in the night and shoulder bags swung dangerously in short choppy arcs. One blond girl went over on her high heels as she ran. For a moment she seemed to regain her balance as someone on her right brushed her back. But she was hit again before she had a chance to right herself and she fell. The crowd poured in on them, looking neither to the right nor the left, just coming straight on like a bolt of lightning. As if they possessed radar, they had locked on to the image of the Continental and, until it managed to outrun them, they could not be impeded.

Someone—in the semidarkness, the mass had begun to blur in its vast freneticism—stumbled over the girl on the ground. She tried to get up but they kept on coming over her, oblivious. She was stepped on; someone tried to leap her but, missing, pitched onto the asphalt of the avenue. Daina saw the girl's face lifted, her mouth opened wide in a scream no one heard.

Daina reached for the door, felt Chris' hand over her wrist. "What th' hell're you doin'?"

"There's a girl out there," Daina said breathlessly. "She's hurt. We've got to help her. Tell the driver to stop the car."

"Are you crazy? We stay still for a minute, they'll destroy us. We'll suffocate in that mass."

"But she's being trampled!"

"Won't do her any good if we're trampled too, will it?" Chris said. "First cop I see, I'll tell him, okay?" He turned around. "See, she's up again. There." He pointed.

The limo turned a corner. Now a cordon of police stood before them. Arc lights spun dizzying patterns off the crowns of their helmets. Nightsticks were out. She saw two police vans parked part way onto the sidewalk like metal guardians. Chris opened the window on his side, spoke to two officers. Then the hall's towering black silhouette loomed up.

The leading edge of the crowd crashed around the corner, a tidal wave with a mind of its own. An immense corrugated-steel door opened vertically in the concrete wall of the hall and they were inside, moving up a gentle incline. The limo came to a halt and a moment later its twin rolled in beside it. The heavy door slid down with a clang. They stepped out into the hollow emptiness.

"Everyone got their tags?" Silka asked. He checked them, one by one, and, nodding to himself, led them in a group away from the limos.

Concrete, painted a dull gray-green, rose above them for what appeared to be at least five stories, the space seemingly huge enough to house several commercial aircraft with room to spare. Buzzing fluorescent lights hung in orderly rows high above their heads, giving them all a pallid, sickly look.

There were uniformed guards all over. The two beside the wide elevator doors scrutinized their badges, carefully checking the color photos against the real faces. The elevator was as enormous as a studio apartment. It rose so slowly there was absolutely no sensation of rising.

At the backstage level, twelve stories up, they were greeted by four more uniformed guards who again checked them one by one. But once they were through the militarylike phalanx, Daina could see that a kind of controlled chaos reigned here. She saw the publicity people from the band's label herding a covey of reporters and photographers into one corner. Among them she could see the *Stone* people who had been at the hotel earlier. In addition, she recognized several people from *Time* and *Newsweek* who she had met before. She noticed that their tags were of a different color from hers and the band's. This was because they were only allowed backstage but had no access to the dressing rooms where an odd kind of pecking-order privacy reigned.

Flashbulbs popped as Silka led them across the open concrete expanse. Far from them and off to the right where the reporters huddled, Daina could see the thick deep red velvet curtains beyond which, she knew, must loom the high stage.

Silka took them off to the left, passing through a doorless aperture guarded by yet another pair of uniformed guards who checked the color of their tags. This led them into a long narrow hallway of concrete blocks coated with a battleship-gray enamel.

The band had two rooms on opposite sides of the hall in which to dress. Silka took them into the one on the left. Benno was already there. Inside were benches along two walls and, to the left, a tiled, doorless bathroom with a line of stall showers and a number of urinals separate from the enclosed toilets.

A long refectory table had been erected in the center of the room. It was laden with platters of fresh fruit and vegetables, along with iced buckets of champagne. In one corner was an old red and white Coca-Cola bin full of cans of soda surrounded by mounds of cracked ice. Bottles of Kirin sat at room temperature.

Ian and Rollie, having checked out their room across the hall, now came into this one. Each had a girl in tow. Rollie's was blond and buxom; Ian's was a redhead with the long legs of a showgirl. She wore tight black jeans and a white T-shirt emblazoned with a red, white, and blue bull's-eye and the word "JAG" across the chest.

Ian headed straight for the bathroom with her and a moment later they heard the hiss of the shower followed by a sharp scream. A great peal of laughter and then Ian reemerged with the redhead in tow. She was sopping wet, her hair curling around her cheeks, her mascara running in dirty lines, her breasts with their stiff nipples sharply outlined against the clinging cotton. He grappled with her for a moment, pawing at her before letting her loose, turning to Nile. "Hey, mate, how 'bout it? Want this dolly?" He grinned. "Got real talented lips." But Nile just played on with his own talented fingers, not even bothering to shake his head.

"No?" Ian straightened up. "Well, it's you an' me then, eh, laddie?" he said to Rollie. "Well okay, straight swap, eh. What say?" He took hold of the redhead and, spinning her willing form, danced her across the room toward Rollie who, with a great ruffle and flourish, flung the buxom blonde to Ian.

For just an instant, their paths crossed and, like starlets in a Busby Berkley musical, they whirled past each other with perfect choreographic grace.

Rollie put his arm around the redhead, looked her up and down. "Straight swap, you say, mate? No way. Look at the knockers on that blonde! This one—"

"Ah!" Ian interrupted. "I anticipated that degenerate fetish of yours, old boy. Redheads are relatively rare compared to blondes. I thought that kinda offset any—uh—so-called deficiencies."

Rollie laughed, ran his palm across the redhead's still-wet T-shirt. "Come on, luv," he said, leading her toward the door. "Let's get you something dry to wear."

Ian and the blonde followed them out as they all trouped across the hall to the other dressing room.

Chris and Nigel began to change out of their street clothes. Their stage outfits were carefully hung within plastic wrappers along the wall.

"Hey, Nile," Nigel said softly. "You up?"

"My eyes open, man."

"What you thinkin' about."

"'Bout my music, man. Tha's all. Just my music. Humm." His fingers arched, turning blurry, silvery as they performed in the air passages only he could decipher.

"Whassamatter, doncha want no pussy? Somethin' wrong with you, mate."

"Goin' into th' studio nex' week," Nile said placidly. "While yo'll be on the road bitin' tail, I'm gonna make me the best bloody album you ever heard. Humm. Hummm. Oh yeah. It's all inside me now"—fingers flexing still—"like a stream. My body's a melody goes on an' on an' on. Road with no end—only a sunset...night...another sunrise."

Nigel turned to Chris. "This bastard's babblin' again, man. Christ, he's in th' ozone."

"Know jus' what I'm sayin', m'man," Nile said. "You don't understand. Inside I c'n do whatever I please. Ain't got no friend sayin', 'Nile do this' or 'Nile you better do that.' No I only got me t' listen to."

"Huh!" Nigel grunted. "Sure. In th' studio you're just another cable th' engineer plugs into th' board. On th' road, you got th' halls filled with 'em, standin' and screamin' an' throwin' things an' when you stand up there in the spotlight, when you tell 'em t'do somethin'—they bloody well do it, mate. Tell 'em t' march inta the bloody sea an' they'll go. They'll go!"

"Uhm humm. You got your ideas, baby an' I got mine." Nile looked up and smiled dreamily. "But you oughtta be wearin' jackboots, baby. Yeah!"

Nigel went rigid. "What're you sayin', you bloody wog?"

Nile turned to Daina, "Used t' be different in th' old days. Th' sixties. Why I went t' London really." His eyes held a soft sadness. "Now it's all th' same, y'see, no matter where y'go. No place is far away no more."

"Listen, you bastard—!" Nigel lunged, grabbed the black man's shirtfront and, as if that physical assault was a signal, Nile moved his body to one side while bringing his forearms up under Nigel's grip. He broke the hold effortlessly, took one step forward and kicked. Nigel went down in a heap.

Nile stared down at him. "Nex' time," he said in that same sleepy voice, "you keep your opinions to yourself, y'hear?"

Nigel scrambled up, fists clenched but Chris moved between them. "That's enough," he said. "Quit needlin' him, mate. It's almost time t' go on. C'mon."

Nigel glared from behind Chris' grasp. "I want him outa here."

"He's my mate, too. Hey!" He shook Nigel. "Hey, man, I'm talkin' t' you! Straighten out!"

Nile looked on impassively. "Din mean a thing," he said. "Not a bloody thing."

Chris let Nigel go and they both went back to dressing. Chris pulled on a pair of mother-of-pearl-colored satin pants, took a scarlet satin shirt off its hanger. Nigel was already

lacing up the fly-front of his black skin-tight pants. He had
on a black T-shirt over which he would wear a black jacket.

The door to the hall opened and Rollie and Ian came in
with their girls. Rollie had on a white T-shirt with the band's
logo emblazoned across the chest and white jeans; Ian was
in a dark suit with a white silk shirt.

There were voices outside the closed door and the sound
of shoe soles against the concrete floor. Eerie echoes from
another world. Here it was very still. No one looked at anyone
else. Daina fancied she could hear the sound of their breathing like distant treetops laboring in a high wind. Despite the
air conditioning, tension had turned the atmosphere warm
and sticky, affecting them all save Thaïs. She finished one
roach, lit another joint from its last ember. There was a distinct rhythm to her inhalations and exhalations as if with
each toke she were reciting a mantra.

The only sound was the sharp cracking of the ice in the
open cooler as it slowly melted under the weight of the cans.
Then Rollie groaned, "Aw, shit!" and ran for the bathroom.
The redhead went after him. No one said a word as they
listened self-consciously to Rollie's animal noises as he vomited. The room was sweet from Thaïs' exhalations. Her leg
swung back and forth like a metronome.

"Always happens th' first night," Chris said to no one in
particular. He wrapped a silk scarf around his right wrist.
"You'd think that after all these years, he'd get used t' it."

They waited patiently for him to be finished like a commando cadre waiting for a brave but wounded compatriot to
make his recovery.

Nile, standing now, near Daina, apart from the rest of
them, began to snap his fingers in complex rhythm, his hair
shining with sweat, his great head swaying to the internal
beat on his long swanlike neck.

In the hideously compressed time before the beginning
they stood and watched shadows on the wall or nothing at
all and it was only the inanimate things that moved: the ice
dissolving, an olive slipping off a chilled stalk of celery, a
hanger slowly swinging.

They heard the toilet flush and then the sound of running
water, a female voice muffled, softly soothing, mother to a
child.

The door to the hall swung open and Silka stuck his head

and massive shoulders into the room. "Time," he said softly like the chiming of a clock. No one moved. His eyes lit on each of them in turn, then he looked in the direction of the bathroom until Rollie emerged, the redhead toweling his hair. Then Silka moved back, holding the door open for all of them.

Chris took Daina's hand as they went out across the long concrete apron—now deserted—toward the slowly billowing curtains. Sound from outside was completely dampened. They walked side by side with Nigel and Thaïs.

"How'd you like t' be on stage with us?" Chris asked her.

"I'd love it."

"Good. I'll fix it."

Silka had stopped them just before the curtains' barrier. Only the guards were with them now, arrayed at every possible position. Chris spoke to Silka for several minutes. The bodyguard's eyes slid away from Chris' for a moment, gazing at Daina as if she were a priceless Ming vase and the ambiguity of that stare—the intimacy combined with its absolute objectivity—disconcerted her.

Silka beckoned to her. He took her and Nile through a gap in the curtains. Haze in the air for a moment as heavy as smog.

The lights were still up in the hall. People choked the aisles coming and going. Music from the band's last album blared. The air was hazed with smoke. Several large balloons printed with the band's logo floated, bouncing from person to person, accompanied by great swells of noise from the crowd. One glanced off the head of a policeman and a great cheering went up.

Banners fluttered. At the far end of the tiered hall an enormous Union Jack hung suspended from the ceiling, its colors dimmed by distance and haze, giving it a peculiar dreamlike quality.

The high stage onto which they were led was studded with the outsized silhouettes of the band's amps, rising like black titan's teeth from the ebon gum of the stage. Center, on a raised plinth, was Rollie's enormous drum kit. Colored lights, now quiescent, rimmed this ministage. Below, on the stage proper, arterial cables streaked across the expanse, set in place by dull silver tape so that none of the band members would trip during the performance.

To stage right was the semicircular bank of Nigel's keyboards, which included a concert grand piano, a Farfisa electric piano, an organ and several synthesizers made to order. To the left were the skeletal steel stands upon which rested Chris' and Ian's numerous guitars.

Overhead a multitude of colored lights hung in a metal grillwork arc, a workman's rainbow, ugly in disuse.

Slowly the lights began to dim in the vast hall and the noise level jumped to almost unbearable heights. Speech was next to impossible in this din and Silka put his strong hands on Daina's shoulders, guiding her to stage left, near one of the tall banks of amps rising high overhead. He disappeared. She turned around but could not see where Nile had got to. She wondered where Thaïs would stand, guessed it must be on the other side of the stage, near Nigel.

Sunset had turned into night. Only a battery of glowing ruby pinpoints—the amps' pilot lights—stood out sharp and clear like stars. But she could hear the great restlessness of the packed house, an endless rustling as if a horde of serpents were writhing just out of reach.

Sound came up from the crowd and she looked up. A screen had slid down from the ceiling and a concealed projector at the other end of the hall came on. Swelling applause. By twisting her head she could barely make out the film of the band being shown. She turned away. Just beyond the lip of the stage she could make out the corps of photographers granted passes down in what might otherwise be the orchestra pit. They roamed back and forth like hungry felines, awaiting the appearance of the band with as much anxiety as the rest of the audience.

Daina could almost taste the excitement now. She felt as high as a kite. Her skin was in goosebumps and her muscles jumped in sympathetic longing for release. How long can they draw this out? she wondered.

At that moment she could feel movement near her like a brush of dry grass. The roadies had all gone from their last-minute checks of the stage equipment, were crouched in their assigned positions. The sound mixer was set, earphones covering his head. He spoke into a tiny square mike at the end of a thin stalk that clamped over his head. His hands raced over the lighted console in front of him.

The silhouetted bodies, moving like wraiths in front of the red pinpoints, set the crowd off even before the end of the

short film. The screen lifted. Noise swelled like a blister about
to burst, becoming at length so vibratory that it seemed as
if the entire hall shook on its foundations. Daina's heart thudded within her chest and there was a lump in her throat.
Energy, she thought. The energy's here. Her fingertips tingled as if in contact with an electric current.

There came a battery of blinding flashes from the kids
holding cameras so that the stage and parts of the halls exploded in weird illumination and the band, making their way
across the stage, were shot on and off with brilliant light,
their shadows ballooning starkly, enormously, then falling
abruptly away into pitch blackness in rapid-fire bursts.

Chris chorded the first notes and she thought, But it's also
power, pure power. And Nigel may be right after all. The
crowd howled its approval. Colored spots blazed down upon
Rollie and Ian; white follow-spots on Chris and Nigel.

Chris lifted his arms, his guitar aloft like the great sword
of an ancient warrior. His scarlet shirt bloomed into fire by
the spot.

Then the opening bars of "Devil's Disciple" drowned out
the insensate roar of the crowd. It was street-scratchy and
stark, as tactile as it was aural. Chris, chording maniacally,
raised one arm exultantly. The plastic pick flew from his
fingers and there was a mad scramble for it among the den-
izens of the first few rows.

Now the swell of the crowd and the music of the band
joined, fused, becoming more than the sum of the separate
parts and, like a volcano erupting, hovered on the verge of
pain. But it was a pain that reached down and massaged the
heart; a pain one could draw energy from or, perhaps more
likely, that released the energy encamped within each lis-
tener. Daina felt her eyes begin to tear, her back teeth vibrate
with the sheer force of it, feeling as she felt before the cameras, when she was Heather and the power was a tangible
ball of light she could encompass with the swift pass of her
hand before her eyes, darting like a dragonfly, picking it out
of the shimmering air, gulping it down whole so that her
insides glowed and steamed.

The song crashed to its conclusion and Nigel leaped from
behind his keyboards, grabbed his stand-up mike, yelled into
it, "Hello, San Francisco! We're back!" And the upturned faces

of the idolators seemed to burst apart in the thunder of approval.

They were all someone else now—completely outside themselves—grafted-on entities coming out of the casket where they had been kept all these long months off the road. Or, perhaps more accurately, they were extensions, there all along, carried around as excess baggage or the misshapen flesh of a hunchback. For surely these personas were perverse as well as merely distorted. Bereft of any human emotion, they strode the stage like giants come for a brief earthly stay. They might have been the shades of Norse gods, fierce, sexual, and virulent. There they were, transmogrified by the sweat and the love and the painful rhythm of their creation. But, Daina recognized, there was much more.

This magical transformation could not have taken place without the force of energy emanating in waves from out of that vast black pit in front of them, filled as it was with the tide of humanity. Young humanity—drugged and yearning for something they could not even understand.

And these two forces built upon one another, creating some third entity—some mythical creature of their own unique imagining—that took them all, spiraling upward higher and higher, whirling them around like leaves in a storm.

Chris, stretched to larger-than-life proportions by the hot spots, ran through a complex solo, his knees bent, back arched, sweat flying off him like bullets from a machine pistol. To his right, Ian pushed him along, providing a sinuous bass underpinning while Chris' plangent notes were bolstered by Rollie's percussive backbeat. Four measures on the ghostly swirl of bitter strings filled the air, shimmering, as Nigel worked the small synthesizer keyboard.

They were well into it now and the music picked up like a whirlwind, double-timed, superheated and tremendously sexual: an opened blast furnace. It was, Daina thought, like watching a prowling leopard in its cage at the zoo, mesmerized by the motion, too late realizing that it has abruptly padded out the open door in the side, leaving beast and watcher alone together with no barrier whatsoever.

What would happen then, when the bars came down and all the laws slid away into oblivion and chaos encroached upon the orderly procession of life. It might, she thought now, be the only moment of true creation, that change, the admixture of excitement and terror.

The thought swept her away on the spread wings of the music, breathless and vulnerable, her eyes shining, reflecting the perfect amalgam of intellect and sexuality that was this music's message.

The band careened into "Starlets in My Pocket" without a break and the lasers erupted like cannons, a trio of piercingly brilliant colored beams, so intense they became solid. They battled each other like duelists hovering in midair over the front of the orchestra. Applause swept the hall like heat lightning through a wheatfield.

All at once the percussion dropped out and it was Chris' guitar and Nigel's shivering synthetic strings intertwining, caressing each other like shy lovers and, incredibly, in the midst of the laser show, a hologram appeared: A young girl, long blond hair streaming down her back, turning and turning, as solid as flesh, eyes closed as if in ecstasy. Then, on the third pass, her eyes opened, staring out at the audience as she revolved slowly above their heads.

The kids were on their feet, screaming. Then Chris was alone in a solo. The hot white spot metamorphosed into green, then blue and, finally, into loving lavender as the notes he played turned legato.

Slowly he knelt on the stage, creating the languorous melody, its harmonics, all alone, head thrown back, his handsome face transfigured by the music and, suddenly, shockingly, Daina heard him beginning the first bars of Ravel's "Pavane Pour Une Infante Défunte." She stared, unable to take a breath, listening with her eyes as well as with her ears as he wrung those notes so familiar to her with love and so much haunting pain out of that unlikely instrument that she began to weep.

She looked out across the black stage, past the silent still figures of the band members to where Chris played on, splay-kneed, closed-eyed, feeling at this moment closer to him than she ever had before. All the secret misery of that shared moment of Maggie's death, expressed in the aching strains of that mournful, majestic melody. It was like a bridge of light, she thought, linking him to her just as surely as if he still held her hand. She felt him with each note, distance eradicated, a two-dimensional chalk equation on a black-board, never really existing.

There was no one in this vast dark place, this slowly rising and falling sea. Just Daina and Chris like two small craft come upon each other through a fog. Thus they clung to each other through the hot medium of the music, each coruscating note a caress more tender than any fingertip's touch. Daina shuddered and closed her eyes, her mind filled with color and light.

The "Pavane" concluded on one note that Chris held for an almost unbearably long time—the electronics of his instrument allowing him to subtly change the timbre, the high singing vibrato until, at last, he modulated the note into the opening of "Saurian."

Once again he was all alone and Daina's heart skipped a beat as she remembered Nigel's threat. As if she were watching an actor on stage who had missed a crucial line, she felt acutely Chris' nakedness out there.

He continued to play, turning the opening measures into an impromptu solo intro as the crowd gasped and applauded. The hologram was gone and so were the lasers. This song was too new for them to have worked out a suitable visual. But Chris, standing and playing, now turned from the audience to face the band and, as he did so, Daina saw the savage whiteness of his face.

His fingers, curved like the talons of some predator, were a blur as they worked the steel strings and "Saurian"'s melody poured out into the hall again. He stalked Rollie and, staring up at him, screamed out: "Play, you bastard! Beat those bloody skins or so help me I'll come up there an' wreck your face right now!" He made a violent, running movement up onto the plinth and with a convulsive start, Rollie began to lay down the percussive pattern. Chris' eyes burned like coals as he stared Rollie down and, jumping from the plinth, made his way over to Ian.

He seemed to Daina like that leopard, a wild animal on the loose, dangerous and deadly and totally unstoppable. "All right, now it's your turn!" He spit at Ian and the bassist, terrified, began to play.

Chris worked with him and with Rollie, creating an arrangement of the moment, a trio of illimitable power, and then finding them a home, a groove that surely neither Rollie nor Ian could have suspected was there. It was all improv now, rooted in the sheer force of Chris' will. Both Rollie and Ian stared at him while they continued to play, mesmerized, stooges to this awesome Svengali act.

Now the heat was there, shimmering and alive, rolling like a ten-ton truck out across the stage and into the audience. Chris whirled from them and sprinted across the stage to where Nigel stood behind the protection of his bank of keyboards. He seemed in that instant about to move but then Chris was upon him and he froze like a deer in a spotlight.

Chris, chording wildly, bounced up and down in front of him. His mouth worked like a ventriloquist's dummy and she knew he was shouting but the immeasurable din tore the words away before she could hear them.

For a moment, she thought she saw Thaïs' familiar silhouette lit by a green flood, the nose sharply defined, one eye glowing ferally, but it was gone so abruptly that she thought it might never have been.

Nigel began to play. He too stared at Chris even when Chris moved back to center stage and with all the musical elements now in place began to sing: "Deep in the night/Lit by rain and faces/I'll say good-bye to my love, to my love/Left in the hollowed palm hills/The fierce scandals/Burning at both ends..."

The crowd was on its feet, howling like dogs, stamping and clapping in time to the music. Daina looked out beyond the verge of the stage, saw sparklers fizzing in the darkness.

"Like a shot from a pearl-handled pistol, I'm gone," Chris sang. "Into the red dawn/The red red dawn/Like a saurian from the edge of time/A saurian stalking/I'll find what's mine/And I'll be waiting."

Now Daina could see, as the house lights came up fully, the kids in the first few rows. Their faces were turned upward into the hazed auroras of the colored spots, transformed as if by alchemy. Spectres of the rainbow, they lifted their arms wide, embracing the fount of physicality spreading outward from the great stacked amps.

"Like a saurian from the edge of time/A saurian stalking/I'll find what's mine/And I'll be waiting." The music behind him turned savage, cruel and sharp as flint until there was no more civilization, just the elemental fury that lived and danced inside all of them. Like a master snake charmer, the music had bewitched them, calling out all the hidden magic, terrible and awesome in its inarticulate rawness.

Thus they shed their skins: the silks and satins of convention and, like a New Guinea tribe who had never before laid eyes on a white man, who knew nothing of the atom age, they were joined together in a frenzy of motion and sweat, sensuality and sound that brought them to fever pitch, hurling them over the abyss.

Now the first bars of "Dancers in the Sky" bit into them and the lasers opened their needle snouts once more, pouring their living light into the far reaches of the rafters and, upon this ethereal highway of illumination, a pair of lovers appeared in hologram, beginning to move and, through the magic of technology, dancing to the beat of the music, disappearing at length with the last organ glissando from Nigel.

The audience screamed, stomped, and the hall shook as if lashed by an earthquake. Chris lifted his guitar over his head, waved it back and forth as if it were a banner. Nigel emerged from his portable synthesizer keyboard to stand beside Chris, launching them into "City Lights" with all the lights up.

Far too soon, the song ended and they left the stage. Now the hall lights dimmed. Applause built in strengthening waves. Kids rushed from their seats, loping down already clotted aisles, oblivious to the protestations of the guards and police.

Daina looked around her. In clusters, tiny lights wavered as the kids lit matches, held them aloft, multiplying until the place took on the incongruous appearance of a cathedral.

The band reappeared amid a hysterical welcome to play the first encore. The neon lights along the rim of the plinth glittered on and began their serpentine roll like an old-time movie marquee. The lasers returned, searching the upper reaches of the hall with lemon light. The place was emptying in back as the kids pushed and shoved their way forward toward the stage. More security guards emerged to help stem the tide but in this moment of conflagration, the task appeared all but hopeless.

The first wave crashed into the screen dividing the first rows of the orchestra seats from the photographers' pit. The photojournalists, cameras held high out of the way, scattered before the onslaught.

Far from calming them, Nigel roamed the verge of the
stage, playing with one hand while exhorting the crowd onward toward their goal. "C'mon c'mon!" he screamed in the
musical wind. "C'mon!" Beckoning them on in a crouch,
laughing and sighing in the heat and sweat. His eyes were
wide, feverish, as they raked the faces of the devoted, the
acolytes of his music.

The kids filled the photographers' pit now, trampling on
the guards and each other to get closer. They reached up,
looked up, screamed up. A boy lofted his girl on his shoulders.
She raised her arms, fingers hungrily clawing the nighttime
air. All the barriers were down but now it seemed reversed
to Daina. Now it was they who were on stage who were the
watchers in the darkness and this insensate crowd the un-
shackled beast. A girl with corn-row hair leaped for the stage,
levered herself up on one knee. Someone from behind gave
her an enormous shove and she fell face forward at Nigel's
feet. He stepped back. She came on. He shoved his keyboard
into her chest and she staggered backward, arms outflung as
if shot, flying backward off the lip of the stage and into the
howling crowd. One of the bodyguards rushed out from the
wings, dragged Nigel back from the verge where upraised
hands strove to claw him downward into their dark embrace.
Angrily, he flung the man from him and continued his prowl.

Someone threw a spray of white roses onto the stage and,
grinning, Nigel lashed out at them, kicking them high into
the colored air.

Daina watched the faces, sweat-streaked and inhuman,
the bodies bouncing to the insistent beat, eyes rolling wildly
like cattle trapped in a burning barn, lips pulled back from
teeth in ecstasy as they screamed, the band, the audience
feeding wildly off each other, pushing each other onward.

Chris and Nigel were at center stage. Chris chorded furiously; Nigel's fingers danced over the stubby keyboard; and
the music crashed over them all in a tidal wave of sound and
fury of war.

There was an intense flash on the left side of the stage so
near to Daina that all vision in her left eye was lost. It was
followed by an earnumbing roar, a shock wave like a physical
blow.

Daina staggered back. She gasped into fumes that sucked
all the oxygen from the air. Choking, tears running from her

eyes. Blind and deaf. A searing heat and, instinctively, she recoiled. It was all that was left her. Her lungs were on fire and she felt the laboring of her heart. All breath left her. She staggered and fell, saw in a vision from her mind or the real world a black mountain pitching forward on top of her. Thoughts fuzzy as shock set in. Mountain? The amps! They grew larger as they tumbled toward her, growing larger until they were all she could see. She tried to scream but could not.

Then she was in someone's arms. The world rushed by her but it was not she who was running. She seemed to be in midair. She turned her head, saw Silka's calm face so close to hers it was slightly out of focus. She blinked and her eyes teared again. She opened her mouth, coughed, lay her head weakly against his chest.

Around her, as if from out of a dream, she heard screams and clatters. Roadies ran past her. Policemen struggled past the intricate equipment. There came to her a great rushing din, pressing in upon the hoarse sound of the white noise in her inner ear.

Beneath all this, as Silka rushed her from the stage, she could plainly hear the shouts and the sound of someone crying.

"An M-80. Holy Jesus."

She lay on a bench with her head and shoulders cradled in Chris' lap.

"They must be bloody crazy out there. A M-80 thrown right up onto th' stage. Anyone see who did it?"

It was an obvious question but, of course, a futile one. In all that humanity?

"Sick bloody bastards," Chris said. "What's happenin' t' them anyway?" He was barechested, drenched in sweat. A thick towel was around his neck.

There were others in the room, moving around. She could make them out now, one by one: Rollie, Ian, Nigel...there was the buxom blonde and—

"How you feelin'?"

Nile's glistening chocolate face hovered above hers. His eyes were wide, startled, the ebon pupils enormously expanded.

"She's okay," Chris said. "Just give her some room." He lifted one arm. "Hey, Benno! Where's that doctor?"

"He's with the girl. The ambulance is here. As soon as he puts her in, he'll be up here."

"What happened?" Daina asked.

Chris looked down. "Someone threw an M-80 onto your side of th' stage."

"An M-80?"

"Eighth of a stick o' dynamite. Great for th' Fourth o' July but in a hall—Christ!"

"Someone was hurt?"

"You, my lady, were bleedin' hurt," he said. "I'd like t' get my hands on that bastard—"

"I'm okay. You said something about a girl...."

"Yeah. In th' audience. Poor bitch got th' brunt of it. Th' wall o' amps protected you from the worst of it."

"Will she be okay?"

"Dunno, luv." He looked up. "Ah, here comes th' doc."

"Hearing'll be a bit erratic on your left side for from thirty-six to forty-eight hours," the doctor told her when he had completed his examination. "You didn't black out. There's no sign of a concussion." He smiled. "You were very lucky, Miss Whitney." He took out his prescription pad.

"I don't want anything," she said.

"What?" He laughed, then blushed. "Oh, no. I was just ...uhm...about to ask you if you'd give me your autograph."

She laughed, held her head.

"Headache?"

She nodded.

"Perfectly normal." He shook out two tablets from a plastic bottle. "Tylenol 500. Take a couple every four hours."

She took the pen from him, wrote across the pad.

"Thanks."

"Doctor, how's the girl?"

"Ah, well, it's a bit too early to say yet. There are a number of tests...."

"Was she conscious?"

"No."

"Christ!" Chris said.

"How old was she?" Daina asked.

"Her I.D. said seventeen," the doctor said, getting up.

"I remember when I was that young," Nigel joked. But no one laughed.

"Don't forget the Tylenol, Miss Whitney. Take them right

away." He nodded to those around him, threaded his way out of the crowded room.

"I will," Daina said, staring at the white tablets in her open palm. Chris gave her a glass of champagne and she downed them with it. "Lucky Silka was there," she said, handing him back the glass.

"Luck had nothin' t' do with it," Chris said. "You were his assignment during th' concert. Think I'd leave you unprotected?"

"Chris…" It was Benno's voice.

For a long time Chris kept his eyes on Daina.

"Chrysler's outside with his team of marketing VPs. We gotta take those pictures now."

"Jesus, Benno, don't you have any feeling for what's going on here? That girl—"

"It's either that or we'll have them hovering around us all night. I'll leave it up to you and Nigel, huh?"

Chris gave a deep sigh, closed his eyes.

"Let's go, man," Nigel said.

"I gotta go for a minute," he told her. "Silka'll stay here with you—"

"They want her in the shots, Chris." Benno's voice was gentle.

"I don't give a damn what they want!" He rounded on the manager. "You know what you c'n tell those leeches, you bloodless bastard! They just want their snouts next to ours. Tell 'em no!"

"Chris—"

"Anyway, it's up t' th' lady…."

Daina smiled. "The show must go on, right?" She saw the look on Chris' face. "It's all right." She put a hand alongside his cheek. "I'm all right."

"Ready to roll," Silka said. "Almost." He turned to them from his position beside the limo driver. "Ready?"

It might have been D-Day morning, filled with the stink of tension and the gleam of oiled steel.

Chris sat very close to Daina, holding her hand. They had both showered and while Chris had changed, she had spent some time reapplying makeup.

In front of them, the enormous doors began to rise and

Silka made a visual sweep of all the electronically locked doors of the car. "Here we go," he said, turning away from them. The limo began to roll.

Down the ramp and out the door into the seething night. They could make out the wooden barricades and the police patrolling their small strip of space before the lapping sea of kids began, rocking and rolling, pushing and shoving, overlapping the pavement like an abnormally high tide.

Past the gray sawhorses, they were immediately engulfed in the writhing mass of bodies. Girls leaped on the long hood of the limo while the policemen tried vainly to pry them off. Balled fists pounded frighteningly against all the glass interfaces and heads were jammed up against the sides. A girl with heavily mascaraed eyes and feathered beads in her braided hair, opened her mouth, lasciviously licked at the glass with her tongue as if it were her lover's body; kept it up until unseen hands dragged her away but the window remained streaked with her saliva.

Noises assailed them through the Continental's soundproofing like the howling of a distant wind. A girl crawled up on the hood, digging a space for herself and, spreading her legs, ground the crotch of her skin-tight jeans against the windshield. Her lacquer-tipped fingers scrabbled at the flyfront as she attempted to push them off her hips.

Nigel leaned forward away from Thaïs, gripped the edge of the frame of the glass partition. "C'mon baby," he chanted. "Ooh, ooh take it off!"

"She's gonna do it," the driver said.

"Give 'er some bleedin' encouragement, man," Nigel said.

They all stared. The jeans were moving slowly down her hips. Down and down amid all that whirling confused melee. The car jounced on its heavy springs, swayed drunkenly back and forth as the hail of fists continued to beat on its top and sides in ancient rhythm.

"Jesus...!" the driver said.

"Well looka that." Nigel grinned like a cat. "No knickers."

The jeans had been pushed down so far they could see the beginning fringe of the girl's pubic hair as she continued to grind herself against the glass. Her fingers went into the tight V and she began to stroke herself.

"Hey hey." Nigel pushed at Silka's shoulder. "Get 'er in here mate! Ha ha!"

Thaïs said nothing, looked away at another part of the ocean.

The driver pounded on his horn.

"Hey, what you doin'?" Nigel was bouncing up and down on the seat. "Don't disturb her now. She's gettin' off."

"Ain't nuthin gonna bother her," the driver grunted as he continued to punch at the wheel.

But the force of numbers continued to climb as if on a graph vectoring the energy still to be spent this night. Embedded in the womb of some expensive creature, safe within the steel frame yet unsafe because no one knew to what extent this energy could rise.

Glass rattled in its frame; they saw rather than heard the screams of the crowd, giving them an eerie quality, a nightmare given life.

The girl on the windscreen had somehow disappeared, replaced by four others. The time for individuals had gone. Now the community held sway and Daina thought of Woodstock, of some other time when there was no thought of war among the generation.

Legs and arms pumping, eyes staring, the swirl of clothes, the heavy press of a blanket of bodies, entombing them in a collective embrace. And all they could do was sit and watch it happen before their eyes like the onset of a fatal accident: they were filled by a lurid fascination *not* to do anything but soak it all in.

"Y'know what?" Nigel had turned around, was staring at them. "Y'know what?" He raised his arms, extended them until his splayed fingers, his palms damp with sweat, pressed against the taut, vibrating fabric of the limo's ceiling. "It's all our own creation." His eyes went wide. "Yeah! Yeah, yeah, yeah!"

He began to jump up and down in that confined space. Up and down. Up and down and then, jutting out one finger, depressed a stud. The window on that side slithered down and he lunged forward at all that mob with a great fearsome expression on his face. He screamed like a banshee and they recoiled, scattered and began to run.

Moments later the police sirens began their electronic scream.

*　　*　　*

The entire rear of LoveIsALiquid had been cordoned off with plum velvet ropes on brass stanchions. It was upstairs on the restaurant's balcony whose front overlooked the lower level with its immense blond-wood bar and whose glass-walled rear gave out on a view of the city from twenty-five stories up. There was Coit Tower, the Transamerica pyramid and, far to the left, the floodlit Golden Gate, as pinkly orange as a sunrise.

Tube lighting in blue and green neon ran around the edges of the walls at bottom and top. High ferns swished and swayed with people's passing like old-time film cowboys. The sharp scent of juniper was in the air.

"These things always start small," Chris said in her ear as flashbulbs popped. Everyone stared at their passing, even the normally nonchalant, who thought themselves above it all. "With th' best of intentions of course." He moved her through the packed room. "Exclusivity is still chic an' we don't like t' be bothered." He laughed easily. "That's *our* excuse."

"Chris Kerr! Hey, outa my way!"

They heard him over the pulse of the music, the chatter of voices filling the vicinity. Daina, turning her head slightly, saw a dark blur emerging from out of the dense throng at the back of the restaurant.

"Hey, Chris!"

The crowd parted like sheep prodded with a stick and Daina could see the wide flat face, the long shaggy hair gleaming dully. Flash of white skin and black beard as he moved toward them.

"Hello, Chris!" He smiled. His arms were outstretched, broad shoulders brushing aside the last of the people like flies off a horse's coat. He had a chest like an ironworker.

"You know this guy?" Silka said in Chris' ear. Chris shook his head negatively and Silka said something to him.

Chris took one step back, taking Daina with him, and the enormous bulk of Silka was between them and the young man.

He crashed into Silka's body with shuddering force, his arms flailing. Silka, seeming not to move at all, brought his right forearm up, deflecting the other's fist to the side. Now they could see there was a gun in it.

"Let me at him," the bearded man said. He seemed quite calm. "I'm going to kill him." And tried to raise his arm.

Now Silka moved so that he faced the attack with just his right side and, with great fluidity, extended his hands. They were like sword edges as they drove between the other man's fists so that they exploded outward, expending the force of their momentum in this harmless way. He took the gun off the floor.

"Come on," Silka said softly. "Let's go, punk. You've no business here."

"What d'you know about it," the bearded man said. "You're just a hired hand." His lips curled in an odd smile. "A mercenary, that's all. Just following orders." The smile broadened as he lunged forward, trying again to get past Silka at Chris and Daina.

He came in swinging from the hip with both fists, holding his elbows in and his knuckles high, as men who are the best and most canny street fighters will do.

He expected Silka to come to the traditional defensive stance but the big man did no such thing. Instead of moving into the boxer's crouch, he straightened his left leg as he slid it backward along the limited space on the crowded floor.

Daina could see the bunching of Silka's muscles as they flexed in tension, as he brought the power flooding through them. Almost imperceptibly, his right shoe left the floor, slamming with appalling force into the juncture of the bearded man's leading ankle and instep.

The man cried out in pain and shock and, in trying to right himself, managed only to twist himself off balance. Silka's right hand rose only to the level of his chest; the hand, fingers as stiff as boards, slashed edge on into the bearded man's sternum so that all the breath whooshed out of him like a collapsed balloon.

Silka scooped up his limp form and disappeared into the buzzing throng. The entire maneuver had taken no more than a couple of seconds.

Immediately, Chris turned away. He clutched at her; his skin felt cold and clammy. "Christ," he hissed. "It's the Lennon thing all over again!" He was shivering and Daina put her arm around his shoulders. "What do they want from us?" he said to no one. "Why do they want t' blow us away?"

She led him up the spiral staircase, rimmed in pale pink

as if it were a strand of angel's hair. Music vibrated the steps of their ascent, buzzing through their legs. "Too many people now," he whispered. "We always end up invitin' th' world."

They sat in a corner near the windows, with Nile and Tie and Nigel, on a lipstick-red leather banquette, sipping Dom Perignon '73.

Clots of photographers roamed the place like greedy remoras sliding along a sleek shark's side, catching sniffs of Bianca Jagger and David Bowie, Norman Mailer, on the West Coast doing research for his next book, Bill Graham, once rock's greatest promoter. But always they came back to Daina until Chris laughed, said like a bee in her ear, "Tie's gonna hate you. She and Bianca, y'know—*very* heavy. But you...Ah!"

On the other side of her, Nile stared at a plate filled with undulating pasta rimmed with steamed oysters still in their shells as if it were some alien artifact.

"Nile," Daina said. "You okay?"

"Uhmm." He leaned his head back against the cool leather, closed his enormous eyes. She saw for the first time how long his lashes were. "Feel," he said, "nuthin inside. Too many nights runnin' all in'n'outta one another like a stream down t' th' sea, uhm hum."

"Why d'you do it to yourself?"

"Whut?"

"All the nose candy; all the...horse...."

"Oh, little girl. If you only knew." His eyes came open, stared into hers. "Best that you don't, though. It ain't gotcha yet. Don't let it. Hummm. Why's cause it's the only thing keeps me runnin' at all anymore. You got t'stoke those fires with whatever it takes t' make things run. Drugs in my veins like blood." He shrugged, smiled. "So what, right? Who gives a fuck anymore. Ah, whoever did?"

His hands came out and two long delicate surgeon's fingers turned the mounded plate in front of him around and around as if it were a sculpture he could not decide to place. "Ah ha. S'only dangerous when it's outta control an' the night screams in an' tears you apart. Till then it's a blanket that gets you through. Through an' through...."

"It's out of control, Nile," she said softly. "It always is, don't you know that?"

His lips pared back and his large white teeth clacked together warningly. "Don't go judgin' me. The way I live my life...I chose. Chose it all. My music...my life. All one. All there ever was for me."

"But now that you have everything you want—"

"Ah! S'all shit. Don't *you* know that? Ha. Right. Life's bein' unhappy. What makes my music...what it is." He looked away, out past the squeezed figures as overpainted as Kabuki actors, to the starless sky over the city. "Like that sky...what's there...unseen. Never t'know certain things. Never. Why the music's there in the first place...s'only reason for existing...."

She wanted to reply but Chris was pulling at her hand, dragging her away, saying, "There's Fonda. Now's the time t'introduce me."

Daina drank a great deal and ate almost nothing. She talked a lot and, it seemed, the more she talked the thirstier she got. There was always someone at her side to refill her glass with champagne—nothing but the Dom Perignon.

Thaïs came toward her through the pall, parting the curtain of noise, music, unmindful of the web of drifting conversations and monologues posing as conversations.

"Darling," Thaïs said in her awesome, husky voice, "are you having a good time?" as if she were this party's hostess. She hooked her slim cool arm around Daina's, led her toward the windows. "Jon used to hate parties like these," she said. "Took me hours of wheedling and cajoling to get him to show up. I had to shave him, dress him, brush his hair, make him up." Her eyes were opaque in the neon were-light, double-lidded. Windows that did not blink. "And do you know what, after all that?" Daina felt hypnotized by that unwavering gaze. "He would step into that crowded room and be turned on. His body felt nothing, numbed, but his mind flashed on it all. I'd look in his eyes and see the explosion there, the dark burning, a strange fire that would not go out until so many hours later that even the inveterate partygoers like Chris and Ian would be long gone and only the two of us were left conscious."

Thaïs had closed in and her long fingers, wrapped around Daina's wrist, gave her power a physical presence. For an instant, Daina felt a slight shiver of fear crawling down her spine. Then it was gone.

"But you knew all that already didn't you?"

Daina shook her head. "I didn't."

Thaïs' face was close to hers. She could smell her breath, sweet and slightly musky, her perfume, mixed with her sweat, tangy and harsh but not unpleasant. In fact, just the opposite—like an animal's. Daina closed her eyes, gave a shuddering exhalation.

"Don't lie, darling," Thaïs whispered. "I know that you know."

Daina's eyes flew open, encountered Thaïs' piercing gaze so close she started. "Know what?"

"About Jon. Don't be coy, darling." She wagged one upraised finger. "It's no sin to know. Only a mistake. Someone made a mistake, that's all."

"What are you talking abou—"

"If you were part of the inner circle, it would be different." Thaïs went on as if Daina had not said a word. "But you're an outsider. With no power here. And you'll have no power, do you understand?"

"I don't understand a thi—"

"It all began with Maggie, you see." A smile was frozen across her lips and her fingers were now painful as they gripped Daina's wrist more tightly. "She tried to gain the power; she tried to break in... to do more than was... expected of her. She had ideas, wouldn't listen to the warnings." The voice had thickened subtly in the last few moments until it was filled with venom. "But she was an outsider just as you are an outsider. She broke the laws and was destroyed."

"My God!" Daina twisted away from her grip. "What are you saying?" Her eyes were wide and fear flooded her veins like ice water. She found she was trembling.

"You don't want to know anything about it. It's none of your concern."

"It *is* my concern!" she cried. "She was my best friend!" Oblivious to the turned faces, the running feet, the renewed jostling all around them. Flashbulbs went off amid the rising bubble of voices.

Thaïs' cheeks went hot pink as the blood rushed into them. A small secret smile broke out over her wide lips, the neon light turning her teeth to dazzle. Abruptly she turned and slid away into the crowd.

For a moment, Daina stood rooted to the spot. Then, almost convulsively, she sprang after Thaïs, pushing her way through the milling throng, past Mailer and Jerry Brown and

Tom Hayden. But the bulking crowd moved in and stymied her. Her mind whirled and the room tilted as she hit the wall of solid flesh. She staggered but no one took any notice.

Sound blatted at her, losing all form and shape, hurting her eardrums. Her rapid heartbeat matched the insistent pulse of the bass. She struggled across the packed room toward the ladies' room. It seemed miles away, much too far for her to make but, abruptly, she was there, her trembling fingers turning the brass knob, the door swinging open. She pushed it shut behind her, went into one of the cubicles, collapsed onto the toilet. Her head came forward onto her hands and she felt the slippery film of sweat there.

Perhaps she passed out then or, more likely, hung onto the precipice, midway between, in twilight cerebration. She never knew how much time had passed when, at length, she opened her eyes and lifted her head. It seemed to weigh as much as a body. She blinked several times, staring uncomprehendingly at her fingers, stiff and white from hanging onto the cubicle door handle. She concentrated on taking deep breaths until she began to feel better.

She relieved herself, then went out of the cubicle. At the sink she splashed cold water over her face, feeling at length her energy returning. She cupped her hands and gingerly sipped at the water. Her throat burned but she resisted the impulse to gulp.

Sound and smell assaulted her like a fist in the stomach as she went out the door. She could see people moving beyond the long bank of windows, on a terrace, like cardboard silhouettes at a shooting gallery. She thought she might go there, to get out of the blast of the heat and noise, but Chris caught up with her when she was only halfway there.

"Hey, where you been? I've looked for you everywhere."

She had to start twice and then could only manage to get out: "Ladies' room." Her lips felt numb.

"Heard you had a bit of a row with Tie. Buzz on from somewhere."

"What...what she said to me..." She felt like a baby, unsure of the forming of her words.

He grinned at her. "Told you she was jealous. Doesn't like that kind of competition. She's queen of th' night...or likes t' think so."

"That wasn't it....She—"

"Hey c'mon," he said. "I was lookin' f'r you 'cause Nile an'
I're ready t' pull our stunt. Gonna play here, th' two of us.
Even Nigel doesn't know. *Especially* Nigel. It's gonna do him
in." They wended their way through the throng back toward
their table.

"Hey, Nile." Chris leaned across the table, brushing aside
empty bottles of Perrier and Tsingtao vodka, plates of crum-
bly Italian bread, saucers of golden butter. "You all set?
Gonna make th' announcement—then we wail."

Nile nodded, smiled beatifically even when Chris turned
away, whispered in her ear, "Kay, here goes."

She was still watching Nile as he reached out a hand to
her. She took it in hers, feeling its coolness like a breeze. He
stared into her eyes, opened his lips to speak. He gave a quiet
cough, fell forward, his chocolate face consumed, with a soft,
almost obscene sound, by the plate of pasta in front of him.
Tomato sauce splattered onto the white tablecloth, across
Daina's shoulder, staining her cheek.

Nile lay there, perfectly still. "Oh, my God! Chris! Chris!"
She pulled at him and he spun around.

"Christ!"

The party whirled on around them, oblivious, stoned, propelled by its own massive momentum, careening inexorably
out of anyone's control, filled with electric thrills and clandestine groping.

A tall blonde who had been sitting next to Nile, trying
vainly to keep his attention, giggled, ran her silver finger-
nails through his glistening hair.

"Hey, man," Chris said. "Hey, Nile. Hey!" He lunged across
Daina, sprawling over the table. Music blared and laughter
rang through the haze of smoke. Someone crushed a cigarette
out in the soft butter. The blonde leaned over, kissed Nile's
ear, gurgled delightedly.

Daina groped at him, putting the flat of her hand against
the clammy flesh of his chest through the gap in his open
shirt.

"Hey, man!" Chris knelt atop the table, dragging tablecloth and dishes askew. "Hey get offo' him!" he screamed at
the blonde, pushing her head away. He dug his fingers into
Nile's thick afro, pulled his head up.

Daina gasped; the blonde giggled hysterically, one hand
over her mouth. Nile's skin was as pale as café au lait. Chris

jerked his hand away involuntarily at the shock and Nile's
great head fell back like dead weight, hitting the back of the
lipstick-red banquette. The blonde turned away, vomiting all
over herself.

Nile's open eyes, already glazing, were raised, unseeing,
to heaven.

8

The sky, far out along the clean, unbroken horizon, was the color of the sea. It reminded her of the melancholy of late summer when the blueberries were so enormous she thought they might burst if she touched them with the tip of her finger, when she could smell their perfume a hundred yards away from the verge of the patch.

It was a time when the moon hung swollen in the sky, as dusky as a lantern in an ancient, faded picture book and she knew it was time for her boyfriend of two months to be leaving with promises of love and daily letter-writing that would never be fulfilled. Because summer was often like that: one great sea cruise that bore no direct link with the rest of one's life.

It was time to return to the still-steaming city, to the open fire hydrants, the sticky Indian summer of September and the coming of school, old friends in reunion once more, comparing notes, and the long slow slide into gray winter.

Beside her, Chris was crying.

Far off, the gulls lifted off from a spit of land, circling the dark gray water. As the first wan rays of the morning sun caressed the tops of the orange steel pillars of the Golden

Gate, they commenced their hungry cries. Daina put her arm
around his shoulders, hugged him to her.

She closed her eyes against the glare of the Sausalito
dawn, unaware of the dampness of the ground against her
buttocks, her own past welling up once again, drowning her
in bitter tears.

"Jesus Christ," Chris whispered, over the sound of the sea,
the aching cries of the wheeling gulls. His cheek was on the
crook of her arm, against her flesh where she had pushed up
the material of her zippered sweatshirt with "Heather Duell"
silk-screened across the back. Tears rolled from his eyes,
soaking into her. She felt each drop, separate and distinct,
like missiles from a slingshot. "Such a goddamn genius.
There'll never be anyone like him again."

Behind them, on the edge of the road, she could feel the
looming presence of the limo. The driver slumped inside, wire
sunglasses on, arms crossed over his fluttering chest, asleep
and snoring sonorously.

Beyond the deserted road, the town rose upward, splayed
across the hill, one-story shops and one-story houses amid
trees and lush foliage, a kind of hip suburban expanse. Here,
it was true country, even though it was just over the bridge.
Not like New York, she thought, where it took you a half
hour just to get to Queens.

"They're all goin', Daina." His voice was leaden and furry
from too much dope and heartsickness. "Too soon there'll be
no one worth his salt t' run in th' fast lane. No one but th'
young punks who think they know it all but don't really know
what it's about. Th' musicians—th' pure musicians're dyin'
out—dyin' o' some disease that has no cure."

"It's just the pace, Chris."

He shook his head emphatically. "No, you're wrong. It's
th' nothingness in between does th' killin'. That void's so
large that when th' music's over we dare not—any of us—
stick 'round too long 'cause it'll just eat us up alive. Swallow
us whole." He shuddered beside her and she pressed her lips
into his shoulder to calm him.

"What is it?" she asked. "That void."

He turned his head to look at her, his eyes bleak and teary.
"It's us, Dain. Us. I reckon we gotta pay for...what we do.
We can't...we can't live with ourselves. That's it, y'know.
That's th' secret. All of it. So we kick in th' afterburners, light

outta there so fuckin' fast we don't see th' dark. But it's creepin' in all th' time, all round th' edges. All round."

"Like I said: the pace."

"I dunno. Nigel'n'me'n'Jon, too . . . we all come from a place an' time where there was nothin' a'tall t'look forward to 'cept music. None o' us coulda worked at th' local greengrocer's an' we never woulda made it through university. An' what else c'n a poor boy do in England? Rock'n' roll's the driving force behind our lives. It sustained us when we were listenin' t'it; kept us from starving when we were makin' it.

"Without it, we're nothin' at all an' bein' where we are now . . . none of us can bear t'go back. Same with Nile. On'y thing he ever loved in life was his music . . . an' that's what killed him."

"Not the horse."

"It's all th' same, don't you see that? One goes with th' other, that's what I've just been tellin' you. You been listenin'? Outside o' th' music, we just can't . . . Christ almighty! . . . we can't stand up t' any of it." He closed his eyes slowly, almost reluctantly, as if he were giving up a precious object. A wind had sprung up from the west and he huddled closer to her. She stroked his hair, brushing the thick locks away from his face as the breeze took them.

"When I was much younger," Daina said, "my grandmother was still alive; my mother's mother, the only grandparent I ever knew. She was already very old—into her late seventies—and my mother was finally convinced by the doctors to put her into a home. She told me once much later that she had hated to do it but I never believed her really. My mother never had much of a conscience.

"But each day after that she would jump whenever the phone would ring late at night or very early in the morning, thinking that it was the home calling.

"And of course one morning it was. She seemed to listen for the longest time and then she put the receiver down without a word. 'Grandmother's died,' she said. 'She died at breakfast. Pop!'—she snapped her fingers—'Just like that. Fell over into her Cream of Wheat and never knew what had happened to her.'"

She stroked the backs of her fingers against his cheek. "Well that's what happened to Nile, Chris. Keeled over of old age at thirty-three. That's what I mean by the pace."

"But, Christ, he made such music!" Daina shook her head. "He was a wonder, ol' Nile. I once saw him break a string in th' middle of a solo. He never stopped playin'. Just took th' new string they handed him, wound it on, tuned up an' never missed a beat, not a note outta place. If you wasn't watchin', you'da never known at all...."

"Have you heard a word I said?"

He picked his head up off her arm. "I heard every goddamned word. Whatta you want me t' say? I know the implications but it's my life."

"Nile said exactly the same thing to me last night."

"Yeah, I'll just bet he did." He turned his head away, stared into the rising sun. Only the gulls crying now at the spilling of the new light like blood from a rent carcass.

"Did you ever feel," he said, after a time, "that if you stopped what you were doing—I mean cold quit—it would be all over, that something terrible would overtake—you'd dissolve into a kind of nothingness." He took her hand. "I mean I couldn't ever go back to what I once was...." A shudder seemed to pass through him.

The pale pink of the dawn's light brushed the spiral tops of the somnolent waves. Below, in the shallow troughs, the sea was still dark as gunmetal.

Daina thought of Rubens, of terrorists. "Dissolution's my business," she whispered. "It's what I do; what makes me happy. Like music for you, it keeps me going, my ground, the one long thread that gives my life continuity."

Just the soft cry of the seagulls, tugging the strings of sorrow.

"It's what happens *between* th' music that scares me, Dain," he said. "On th' plane, in th' airports, th' limos, th' restaurants. All I see in front o' my eyes are those tiny *bloody* seconds o' nothingness an' I'm lost in th' void. I don't know where I am or where I'm goin' anymore, just think on where I've come from: the miserable stinkin' basement flat in Soho." He looked away from her, would not meet her eyes. "What if I leave th' band an' it's all gone? I'll be nothin' again. Nothin'."

The gulls had found something out there, a school of fish perhaps swimming close to the surface, because they were very excited now, hanging close to the wavetops in tight, spiraling circles. She could see their bills snapping open and

closed, the snaking jerk of their necks as they pulled fish out
of the water.

"I don't think," she said carefully, "that that's enough of
a reason to screw up your life now." The gulls were a fluttering blanket, lifting and lowering in unconscious imitation
of the sea. Beyond, a white-sailed ketch tacked before the
wind. "I see—I can *feel* how miserable you are. Tie sees it.
Why d'you think she's tried to get friendly with me during
this weekend?"

"Forget Tie," he said. "She's just playing another one of
her mind games."

"She's as jealous of me as she was of Maggie. She doesn't
like our relationship. She doesn't trust it."

"Sure. She doesn't trust what she doesn't understand. Who
does?"

"What's that supposed to mean?"

He looked at her. "You just leave Tie t' me."

"You think you're so smart," she said angrily, "but I don't
think you know who's controlling who."

He glared at her. "When it comes t' bloody women, I know
what's what."

"Do you?"

He was filled with a little-boy bravado that only served
to provoke her into needling him. Why couldn't he see what
was so obviously hanging right in front of his face?

"Christ, but you make me feel a fool, sometimes," he said.
"Your force of will intimidates me, hypnotizes me." He rubbed
his palms up and down his thighs. "When I think o' the women
I've been with...an' others who I haven't even cared about.
There's an endless line right round th' world, just for me."

"Chris—"

"We fought 'bout you, Maggie an' me. We...I expect it
was 'cause we saw you differently." His eyes seemed to drop
away from her, to leak down into the past. "She saw what
was happenin' even if you didn't. No, don't interrupt. I don't
have enough courage in me t' start all over again." He gave
a deep, shuddering sigh. "I knew you had no idea, left it that
way 'cause I began t' realize that it was partially what drew
me on.

"I wanted t' be around you more an' more. It was a first,
really, an' it got me bloody pissed off. I mean that you
shouldn't react like all th' rest." He waved an extended arm,

painting the horizon in his telling. "All of 'em. Women. They lust after power—as big a hard-on as they c'n get. Then they compare it with all th' others: mine's bigger'n yours. Ha!

"But with you, for th' first time I felt...I just wanted t' be with you. It scares me....It still does in a way 'cause I don't understand that. I mean I don't feel like we've gotta be in bed all th' time or anything. Just...y'know...*be*." His eyes seemed to focus on the space between them. "We could even do it now...y'know...down there near the water where no one's—"

"Chris, no...." She put a hand on his arm. "I—"

"You think that what happened t' Nile's gonna happen t' me don't you? Sure. I c'n see it in your eyes. But you're wrong. It's all th' end, all th' goin'—like Joplin'n'Jon'n'Hendrix'n'Jim Morrison. But there're th' others, like Muddy Waters'n'Chuck Berry'n'them who just go on'n'on an' never heard of retirement or death; who aren't burnt out at thirty-three. Well, I'm one o' them. I ain't gonna die....I know what's happenin'—I'm no monster—"

"No." She leaned forward, kissed his cheek, held his head, stroking him with her long fingers, deliberately prolonging the gesture. "No," she breathed. "You're no monster. I know it, Chris." And she could not go on, could not somehow say to him: I'm afraid for you, afraid that Thaïs—what? She knew that in this he was not strong. He might have resisted her advances in the past because of Jon and in the present—or, more accurately, the immediate past—because of Maggie. But now...now there was no one to stand between them, not even Nigel with whom, it seemed, Thaïs was growing bored.

She saw him watching the line of her hair as it fanned out like a sail in the wind, lightening as the sunlight began to pour into the sky.

"I'm a survivor," he said. "I've been through it all...all th' bloody wars in th' streets back home. Got my head knocked plenty an' came back t' beat th' day. You understand what I'm sayin'?"

Beyond them, the white-sailed ketch raced for the far horizon where the sea skin still seemed dark and scaled with the remnants of the night, thin and straight as a newly forged sword blade. It seemed to her a solid and solitary creature skimming the edge of the world.

"About bed," she began. "We're friends, Chris—"

"Friends can go t' bed t'gether."

"Not where I come from." She took his chin, turned his face toward her. "Look at me. We've got something else...something different. And you're...looking to define it in some way so you can understand it." She looked into his face. "That's not the way. You know it; you feel it. You don't need me to tell you."

"No," he said. "It just would be less...frightening that way." He smiled at her, one of those patented Chris Kerr smiles that melted hearts and dampened crotches around the world. "An' I thought learnin' was all over." But he sobered immediately. "What is it?"

"Something else I found out. There's been no time to bring it up before now and...well, to tell you the truth, I'm not sure how I feel about it. One minute I could throttle you and the next..."

"You ever gonna get around t' tellin me?"

"Maggie was on it, Chris...horse. How'd it happen?"

"Whoever it was came in an' killed her, is that right?"

"Stop the bullshit. I know."

"Know what?"

"Don't you lie to me!"

She saw the tremor at the side of his mouth. He hardly seemed to be breathing.

"So you blame me, right? Well, it's convenient. I'm here and she's—"

"Don't," she warned, "you go on!"

"What th' hell makes you so righteous all of a sudden? You such a princess? You never did anything you were sorry for later?"

"You didn't answer my question," she said, unperturbed.

"No, I fuckin' well didn't!"

"All right. Forget it." She turned away.

The wind whistled through the low shrubbery, across the wide concrete wall, down toward the lapping water. To the west, the sky was clear, as pristine as an untouched canvas.

"You don't want t'know," he said after a time, so low that she asked him to repeat it.

"Not if it's another lie. I mean what's the purpose of our being together if we lie to each other." She gave him a swift look. "Was the 'Pavane' a lie, too?"

She knew she had hurt him and she was glad.

"No lie, Dain."

"Then don't lie to me now."

He nodded. "All right." He picked up the hard, dry shell of a reed, tapped it on the ground between his legs as he spoke. "One o' th' things about her was always that kinda innocence she had . . . not th' dumb blankness of th' groupies . . . nothin' like that. But . . . I'd been through it all an' she hadn't. I thought I could protect her from all that shit, y'know?" His eyes were pleading now. "She . . . I didn't let her know anything about what I took, much as I could. I didn't want her t' know, t' be *tempted*." He laughed, an abrupt, harsh sound and, in its own way, infinitely sad. "So one day I come home an' I find th' works right out there on th' kitchen counter. . . . One of her friends . . . I didn't even know 'er, turned Maggie on." He threw the reed away from him but the wind coming off the water merely blew it back into his face. He peeled it off his cheek, threw it behind them. "An' there it was, so *bloody* ironic. Some little whore . . ." He sighed. "You know how low she could get. Nothin' was happenin' with her career an' I had no time. . . ." He put his fists, white as snow, up against his face, pushing his features out of line. "But, oh, she was weak, Dain . . . she was so weak. She couldn't stand on her own . . . she needed me an' you an' a lotta others I reckon neither of us know. She couldn't . . . she never would've made it. She couldn't stand alone. . . ."

"Why didn't you stop her, Chris?" She said it so softly yet the accusation had a stinging blow.

"I thought about it of course. But then, look what I do. How could I? I'd've felt like such a pissant, tellin' her t' pack it in while I was still doin'—"

"So you just let her go on. You selfish bastard."

"What d'you think I coulda done?" he said miserably. "I beat her that once. Yeh, that's right. I was so bloody angry, I saw red. Just did it before I knew . . . Christ! It was me I was pissed at as well as her. But I knew she'd do it no matter what I said . . . *especially* if I told her not to 'cause then she'd have one thing t' hang over my head, t' gloat about when th' goin' got rough an' she hated herself just f'r wakin' up in the mornin'.'"

"How is it I knew nothing about this?"

"Because she loved you too much. She knew if you found

out, you'd think of a way t' stop her an'... Dain, she didn't *want* t' be stopped."

"How can you say that?"

"Because," he said with his face close to hers, "I know."

The flight back to L.A. was filled with dry, stale air and the microscopic grit under the eyelids one acquires only on planes.

First class was still a far cry from the Heartbeats' own Learjet Longhorn 50 that had brought her to San Francisco. While she watched Los Angeles International Airport tremble through the vapors beyond the burnished silver wing, the colors of the palm trees dulled and oily, she thought of the widebody Longhorn with the band's star-guitar logo emblazoned across its gleaming sides and in the middle of its vertical tail fin.

Of course it was monstrously expensive to maintain but that was more than made up for by dissipating the fatigue and boredom of the long mainly one-nighter tours. With the Longhorn, the band would set up shop in New York, for instance, while they played dates in the northeast, in Atlanta for the south and the southeast, and San Francisco for the west because they all insisted, Chris included, on getting out of L.A. while they were on the road.

Daina sat back and closed her eyes. She thought about the long, grueling session they had had with the police. She found it odd that the incident at LoveIsALiquid had been pushed to the background by Nile's death. It isn't really news unless someone is hurt or killed; then the vultures flock around— as they had at Maggie's funeral. She shuddered, the image of that smiling man bright in her mind. Silka had turned him over to the police and that had been the end of it.

And Chris? Though he had been momentarily shaken, he had wiped the incident from his mind. "It goes with the territory," he had told her that morning out at Sausalito.

She opened her eyes, looked out the window. She did not like to see L.A. like this, so close to the ground as if skimming the rooftops; its flat houses, row upon row, reminded her of a giant Levittown spreading itself like a disease, wiping out the green of the trees, the brown of dirt roads. Too, she did not like takeoffs and landings.... She felt her ears clogging

and, abruptly, the plane throttled back, a high metallic
screaming began and then, bump-bump, they were down and
rolling.

She felt a presence hovering over her and, grateful, turned
toward it. A pert young flight attendant with shining brown
hair and glossy pink lips smiled at her. "If you'll just keep
your seat, Miss Whitney, we will be taxiing over to the aux-
iliary air terminal where your people have set up the press
conference. Your luggage will be taken directly to your car."
She smiled again. "Thank you for flying with us."

Daina was the only one to debark when the plane stopped.
It would, she knew, return to the main arrivals building.

Beryl, resplendent in the kind of pale green chiffon number
only she could wear successfully, grabbed Daina by the hand.
"We're so glad you agreed to do the press thing," she said
effusively. "Frankly, I didn't know what to expect when I
called you." She pulled Daina along with her down a concrete
corridor filled with airline personnel and uniformed policemen. "The first reports were quite sketchy, as you can imagine." She peered into Daina's face. "It must've been awful."

Yes, Daina thought. It was awful, all right. But in more
ways than you'll ever know.

"This may seem a trifle ghoulish," Beryl was saying to her
now, "but when you think of it, tragedy occurs every day all
around us. And if you really think about it, we're all guilty
in one way or another of capitalizing on it. Why not? It's a
natural human desire. We're not any of us angels, after all."
The end of the tunnel was in sight and, beyond, was a blaze
of lights, a welter of human voices all seeming to talk at once.
"Ah, here we are." And Beryl escorted Daina into the press
room where, immediately, bristling cameras snick-snick-
snicked through their rolls of film, catching her in split-sec-
ond poses, the network TV cameras rolling, while concerned-
looking newscasters gave hurried sotto voce commentaries.

"I thought about writing you a prepared text," Beryl whispered. "But Rubens said no, you'd know what to say."

In point of fact, Daina had not the slightest idea of what
to say and, as she went up the makeshift wooden steps to the
podium, her mind was a blank.

But immediately the media crowd settled down, she knew
it would be all right. She saw Lorna Dieter from KNXT and
in the commentator's eye was something Daina had not seen

before. And, as her gaze moved from one reporter to another, she saw it there again and again, replicated, mirrored, building until she felt an odd sensation skewer her. A melody began to play in her mind. A heat built inside her. The melody had lyrics. And she felt the power surge through her as she heard her mind singing to her: *All the eyes you've hypnotized/ Are dancing to/Your American heartbeat.* She knew what to say and why she had to say it. She thought of Baba lying in his own blood while the indifferent cats stood guard in the hallway outside; she thought of Meyer with his face pressed to the death-camp barbed wire, dreaming of the day he would be free; and she thought of the dungeon, sunk deeper down into the foul-smelling earth than she ever wanted to go. She began to speak.

"When I was young," she said, "I learned the value of human life. I can't claim to know Nile Valentine well or for a long period of time. In fact, he was introduced to me over the weekend by Chris Kerr. But as one comes to know another person on an all-night flight from one destination to another, Nile Valentine perhaps told me things he would have exposed to no one else.

"You all knew him as a musician with a fierce talent and an insatiable appetite for living and in the end it was that same appetite that destroyed him.

"But I got to know another part of him that I think he tried to hide from all of you. It was a very human side and that is the part I'll miss most."

"Miss Whitney," someone called, "isn't it true that Nile Valentine died of a self-inflicted drug overdose?"

"I think," Daina said carefully, "you'll have the answer to that when the San Francisco Medical Examiner makes his report public."

"But isn't it true," the same voice persisted, "that the various members of the Heartbeats have been constantly involved in drug busts of a very serious nature?"

"We all read the same papers," Daina said easily. She smiled. "Except those of us who are addicted to TV." There was a general round of laughter.

"What about you? What kind of drugs do *you* take?"

Daina leaned toward them, the smile widening. "Penicillin when my doctor orders it; otherwise vitamins and iron." Laughter again.

"Miss Whitney, since there is a studio blackout on the subject, perhaps you'd care to comment yourself on the progress of *Heather Duell*?" This was a different voice.

"The film is an actress' dream," she said. "Working with Marion Clarke is like being in heaven." More laughter. "But seriously, the reason there's been very little given to you on the day-to-day progress is that it's all going so spectacularly, no one wants to jinx it." She waited a beat. "You all know how those studio executives come to rely on their Ouija boards"—laughter—"or voodoo dolls." She smiled as they continued laughing.

In the time she had been away, a new billboard had gone up opposite the one advertising Redford's new film. Beryl took the drive along Sunset as slowly as she could to give Daina as much time with it as possible.

It was not a typical billboard. There was, for instance, no copy. The thing consisted of two gigantic heads. On the left was a beautiful woman with long honey-colored hair and wide-apart violet eyes. Her pink lips were half open as if she were about to whisper an endearment to her lover. There was about her expression a kind of innocence that was almost radiant.

The sweep of her neck merged with that of the face on the right. This woman was tight-lipped and grim-visaged. Her gaze seemed to pierce the Hollywood haze as if she could see farther and with more clarity than anyone else. She had about her a strong-willed, determined air that was unmistakable.

Both these women were Daina. Or, more accurately, Heather Duell.

"My God!" Daina said. "Whose idea was that?"

Beryl frowned as she honked at a young blonde in ciré shorts who was roller-skating across Sunset. "What's the matter? Don't you like it?"

"I love it!" Daina craned her neck out the car's window. "But I didn't think anyone at the studio would have that much imagination."

"They didn't. Rubens got Sam Emshweiler to do it. He's an independent hotshot...designs million-dollar ad campaigns for print media." She stepped on the gas, going through a light on the edge of red. "He's the genius who got

Rubens' rear end out of trouble by launching *Moby Dick* so spectacularly."

"I remember it well. It was incredible."

Beryl nodded. "But unconventional. Rubens had to tear into Beillmann before he'd authorize the studio to put up their share. They get very nervous when everything's not S.O.P."

"What'd he do?"

Beryl could not help but grin, she glanced at Daina. "He told Beillmann he'd thought he'd misplaced the first two reels of the film. Of course Beillmann didn't believe him, so he called Marion, and Marion, who has really had it with Beillmann anyway, told him it was perfectly true.

"Beillmann went as white as a sheet because under Rubens' contract with the studio, *they're* liable for the replacement footage." Daina wondered whether it had been Schuyler or Rubens who had been responsible for that clause. "In any case, it got straightened out that afternoon. We didn't want to tell you because it would've spoiled the surprise."

Beryl turned off Sunset into Bel Air, slowing as she did. "Rubens was right. You did a hell of a job back there." There was so much respect in her voice that Daina turned to look at the other woman. Beryl would never win any beauty contest but she had other qualities that were much more valuable than a perfect face. At least to me, Daina thought.

She laughed. "Didn't you have faith in me, Beryl?"

"Faith," the other woman said, "has absolutely no place in this town."

Daina found it remarkable how adroitly Beryl had avoided the trap. Had she answered yes, she would have branded herself a liar; a no would have been offensive.

"But I know Rubens," she was telling Diana now, "and I trust his judgment."

"Hasn't he ever been wrong?"

"Only in the matter of his wife," Beryl said sharply as she turned into the long driveway.

Maria opened the door at their approach and Daina gave her the keys to the car trunk. "You'd better wash all the clothes, Maria, or send them to the cleaners."

"Rubens talked to you about Dory Spengler," Beryl said as they went down the hall toward the living room. Daina nodded and Beryl sighed. "You know, it'd be a whole lot easier on all of us if you'd just let Monty go. Then we could—"

"I've been through all this with Rubens." Daina's voice had a knife-edge to it. "I've no intention of rehashing it another time with you."

Beryl recoiled a bit. "I only meant you've put us in a rather awkward position, bringing Dory in while you're still paying Monty."

"As I understand it, that's one of the things you get paid to handle," Daina said. She waited to see if the other woman would come back at her. Since she did not, Daina went on, "That's the only way I'll work it."

"I could send him away now if you don't—"

Daina waved her hand. "Why? Just give me a couple of minutes to put on a suit, then take him out to the pool. I'm dying for a swim and we can talk out there. Oh, and Beryl, when Maria comes back inside, ask her to make us lunch. Something cold and light, okay?"

Dory Spengler was younger than she had expected. He had a deep tan that would, six or seven years from now, score heavy lines across his face. There were already tiny sprays of crow's feet at the outer corners of his bright brown eyes. He had a practiced way of looking at you, cool and level, that almost made you forget the work he had put into it. He had the reputation around town of a super deal-maker; as long as you were hot, he was your friend, but once you came down off the top, it was said, his memory was short indeed.

He was dressed in a light-colored linen suit and a white shirt open at the collar. He wore one narrow gold chain close around the base of his throat, half-hidden in hair.

"Daina Whitney," Beryl said, "this is Dory Spengler."

His mouth cracked open in a smile. "A pleasure, Miss Whitney." He held his hands behind his back. "I'm a big fan of yours. I can't imagine why we haven't met before. Unfortunately I was out of town for Beryl's party."

Daina said nothing, thinking of Monty.

Beryl's eyes darted from one face to the other. She cleared her throat, uncomfortable in the silence. "I'm sorry, Dory—"

Spengler waved her to silence. He was staring at Daina openly. "I understand this situation is somewhat, uhm, unique. It may take some time for Miss Whitney to accept me, certainly to get to know me." His hand lifted, fell, returned behind his back. "That's perfectly all right." He moved toward poolside. "We can talk while you swim. Is that all right?"

Daina gave him an appraising look before bounding two steps across the brickwork. She hit the water in a flat dive. Spengler waited until she had completed six laps before he said something.

Daina lifted her head, shaking it from side to side to free her eyes from the water. "What did you say?"

Spengler crouched down beside her. "I said, I've just come back from the South Pacific. I had a meeting with Brando."

Daina put her elbows on the pool's edge. "Brando?" She lifted her hair off her face. Drops of water rolled off her golden shoulders. "I thought he didn't have an agent."

"He doesn't. Not officially, anyway. There's no real need, you see. I only go out there when there's something specific to discuss."

Beryl could contain herself no longer. "Dory showed Brando a rough cut of what we have so far of *Heather Duell*."

"What? Even *I* haven't seen that."

"I know." Beryl smiled. "And if the studio found out about it they'd flay us all alive. They haven't seen it either."

"I also took him a print of *Regina Red*," Spengler said.

Daina felt her heart in her throat. "Why? No, wait." Using her arms she launched herself out of the pool to sit beside Spengler. "Okay, now I want to know it all. What did he think of it?"

"Hated it. But...he thought you were great." He put his forearms on his knees to help balance himself. "By the way, I've got to tell you I think *Heather Duell*'s sensational, judging by what we saw."

"Is that what Brando said?"

"Well, he's a bit more...eccentric. He liked it."

"That's great but what was it for?"

Beryl pulled a chair over, lowered her bulk into its embrace. "Dory's putting together a project for Rubens. Something, if it happens, that can't fail to be quite special. Right, Dory?"

"Yes." His eyes lit up. "We've got a script from Robert Towne that Coppola's wild over. So wild, in fact, that he's agreed to direct it and coproduce it with Rubens. But there *was* a problem."

"You know how Francis is. Everything's got to be letter perfect before he'll go ahead. He insisted on two elements. Brando for the male lead."

"Brando and I go way back," Dory said, "so I took him the script. He liked it, liked it a lot... wanted some changes"—he shrugged philosophically—"but that's the way he always is. It'll be his first real starring *role* since *The Godfather*. He's on screen nine-tenths of the film."

Out of the corner of her eye Daina saw Maria come out of the house with an enormous tray filled with sandwiches and pina coladas. She squinted into the sun. "You said there were two things Coppola wanted. The first was Brando—"

"And the second," Beryl said, "is you."

"You! Emouleur!" Fessi said. "Stop your talking and come get this man out of here. He's beginning to stink up the place."

Heather was still holding on to James. Emouleur went across the room, tapped her on the shoulder. "I'm sorry, Madam. I have my orders."

Heather did not move.

"Madam," Emouleur said a bit more forcefully, "your husband is dead. There is no point in this. You must let go of him now." His fingers moved along her shoulder.

"Get him the hell out of here!" Fessi shouted. Emouleur began to pry at her arm.

"Get away from me," Heather said.

"Madam, please—"

"I said get away!" She hugged James to her.

"Now!" Fessi cried. He advanced toward the young Frenchman.

Emouleur's face registered fright. He wrenched Heather away from James. She came onto her feet seemingly quite willingly. "All right now—"

She whirled, struck the attaché solidly across the face. He put a hand up, reeled away.

"That's enough!" Fessi screamed. "I thought you were man enough to handle this. Now I'll have to." A small smile played at the corners of his thick-lipped mouth. "I've been waiting for this." He addressed Heather. "Just waiting for you to do something like—"

Heather struck out blindly, smashing her fist into the side of Fessi's neck. He staggered, surprised, went to his knees. He blinked, swallowed. His head weaved from side to side. He wiped at his eyes.

"He's not dead meat," Heather said, staring down at him, "to be eaten by the likes of you."

Without looking up, Fessi grabbed at his machine pistol. A great rumbling came from him and Heather saw the muzzle of the weapon pointed at her. She did not move.

In one stride, El-Kalaam was between them. He struck out with his boot tip. The AKM went off, spraying bullets harmlessly against the far wall. Plaster chips whined away and dust hung in the air.

"You will not do to this one what you did to the other," El-Kalaam said coldly. "Put that thought away. You cannot have her. We have business to attend to. That is all you have to think about." Their eyes locked. He kicked at Fessi's flank. "Now get up and make sure Haddam has done his job. Tell me when the Israelis have picked up Bock's corpse."

Fessi rose. He did not look at El-Kalaam but at Heather. "You should kill her now," he said. "We'd all be better off." He went to the front door, closed it behind him.

El-Kalaam came over to where Heather stood, looked into her eyes. "Perhaps Fessi is right about you. You're an amateur but a dangerous amateur for all that. Perhaps I *should* kill you now."

"Go ahead," Heather told him. "Go ahead and shoot me. It will show everyone once and for all just what you are." She spat at his feet.

"It was her man Fessi shot," Rita said. "What else would you expect her to do?"

El-Kalaam took his hand away from the butt of his .45 automatic. "I know what you are," he said. "But you know nothing about me."

"I know enough. We both come from the same background in expertise. We're both hunters, right? You've gone your way and I've gone mine. But you're still curious about the element that binds us together."

"There's nothing that binds us together," El-Kalaam said with some heat.

Heather gave him a small smile. "You were right about my husband. You were both professionals. Two sides of the same coin. Darkness and light; about as different as two men could possibly be. But he knew you, El-Kalaam. He knew what you are. He knew you had to be stopped."

"Well, he won't have the chance now, will he? He threw that chance away when he put himself in front of Fessi's machine pistol. Whatever slim chance there was is over. He's gone and you're here."

"Yes," Heather said. "I'm here."

"Now I don't want you to worry, Daina," the doctor said. She was a big woman built along the lines of Birgit Nilsson and probably with as good a voice. "You've just been doing too much, too fast." She eyed Daina over the rims of her half-moon glasses. She wore an enormous white smock over an angora sweater and a tweed skirt. A displaced New Yorker, still rebelling against her environment despite having been out here for more than six years. She must sweat bullets going from her air-conditioned office to her air-conditioned Merc, Daina thought. She was in no mood for lectures and there was no doubt Marjorie was about to deliver one.

"You know," the doctor said slowly, "the best thing for you would be a couple of weeks in the Caribbean. Right now." She played with her gold Mark Cross pen, twirling it between her fingers like a majorette with her baton. "I've seen it happen before."

Daina groaned. "I know all of that."

"So what's the problem?"

"I can handle it."

Marjorie nodded, ran a hand through her carefully dyed chestnut-colored hair. "*Everyone* thinks they handle it. No problem. Meanwhile, someone is sneaking up behind them with a ball-peen hammer and while they're looking the other way, Bam!"

"The problem is," Daina said, leaning forward in the chair, "I've got the film to finish and then another project. The timing's all wrong."

Marjorie smiled disarmingly. "Is that what you'll say when you keel over and I've got to check you into Cedars of Lebanon, 'The timing's all wrong'?"

"I probably wouldn't say anything at all."

Marjorie tapped the point of the pen against the blotter sitting square in the center of her green baize-topped desk. "Look, all this clever banter is very cute but the bottom line is—"

"Oh, Christ!"

"The bottom line is"—she leaned forward as she emphasized each word—"that you've been neglecting your body. You know the human body is a wonderful mechanism, almost infinitely adaptable—it can take a helluva lot of punishment. But not without certain consequences. Some are long-range and some—depending on the severity of the abuse—become chronic." The pen stopped its tap-tapping and Marjorie took off her glasses, set them carefully down beside the gold pen on the blotter. Behind her a digital clock, just below a small, signed Dali, spun off the seconds, the minutes. "Do you understand the implications of what I'm saying?" Abruptly her voice softened. "Just take it easy, that's all. Try to get more rest. Your mineral levels are way off and you're on the threshold of anemia."

"I take plenty of iron," Daina said, thinking of the press conference.

"Supplements are all well and good," Marjorie said. "But that's all they are. Supplements. What you need are a couple of weeks in the sun and surf and about six months of at least eight hours of sleep a night."

Daina stood up. "As soon as the film wraps—"

"I wouldn't wait that long," Marjorie said. "Really I wouldn't." She began to scribble on a prescription pad.

"What's that?"

"Just some chloral hydrate. It's a mild sedative for—"

"I know what it's for and I don't want it!" Daina said hotly.

"You need something to get you through—"

"I'll get me through the next six weeks, doctor! Thanks very much."

Outside in the waiting room, Monty stood forlornly amid the florid forest of Beverly Hills minks draped around slender tanned shoulders.

"Daina!" he called anxiously. "Are you all right? I've been trying to get in touch with you ever since I heard about that press conference." Tension had creased his worn face and beneath his tan he looked pale. "Why wasn't I told about it?

I know how the press twists things around and you were upset, that man dropping dead practically in your lap." He began to follow her out the door. "But you should've told me where you were going, you know. I would've advised against it. I never liked those music people—"

"Monty—"

"All right! All right! I know you hate it when I bring that up. So okay. I'm only looking out for you." He raised his hands. "I forget sometimes. Anyway"—he shrugged—"I haven't seen you for so long, I've almost forgotten what it is you like and don't like." He turned to her suddenly. "I don't like what's going on down at the set. First Beillmann is too busy taking meetings to return my calls. Now, this morning when I tried to get on the set to see you, I was told my name was off the list. Daina, what's going on?"

She took his arm in hers, led him out the door. She looked into his red-rimmed eyes. "I'm sorry I haven't called you, Monty, I—"

"Ah, forget about that!" His hand lifted briefly, fell. "Who cares about that between friends. Tell me, what did the doctor say?"

They stopped on the sidewalk. Across baking Beverly Drive harsh sunlight underlit the glass front of The Breadwinner where, inside, sleek lovelies in minks lined up with their trays to receive heaping portions of tofu and mung bean salad, talking among themselves about their morning prowling Neiman-Marcus.

Daina smiled into his lined face. "I'm fine, Monty, really. Marion's working us all like demons that's all."

"And Beryl? Is she working you hard, too?"

"Hard enough."

There was a silence between them for a moment. "Someone should've told me about that."

"I told Rubens he should've—"

"The hell with Rubens. *You* should've told me."

She turned her face away but he moved so that he was still facing her. He lifted up her chin. "What's happened to you, Daina?" She said nothing.

She looked up, saw an odd kind of defiance in his eyes and a look she could not quite decipher. Yet it filled her heart with ice; her mind with self-loathing. Why?

"I want to hear it from your own lips," Monty said. His

face seemed so red it might be glowing with energy and she thought, Rubens is wrong; they're all wrong. He's not old; he's not tired. He's just the way he was when he picked me up off the unforgiving sidewalk of this town five years ago.

"I want to hear *you* say what everyone else has been whispering in my ear for a week."

"What's that?" But already her stomach was quailing and her voice was weak.

"That I'm out and Dory Spengler's in."

And now she knew the look he gave her for what it was. She saw betrayal in his eyes. Her own betrayal of him. Oh, God, she thought. No. This is what I've fought against.

"Monty, it isn't what you think at all."

"Then he *is* in!" A weird note of triumph sounded, distancing him from her, though that was not what she wished.

She took a step toward him, reached out a hand to take his arm. "I wouldn't let anyone come between—"

But Monty's face had already turned mottled as it drained of blood. He tried to scream at her and clutch at his chest at the same time. "Daina, you—! You—!"

But she never found out what he was about to say.

In the ambulance, heading up Little Santa Monica toward Beverly Boulevard and the Cedars-Sinai Medical Center, Marjorie touched the gray skin of Monty's chest where she had stripped the shirt open. She listened again with her stethoscope. She lifted her head, made a curt gesture to the paramedic riding with them. He lifted the plastic oxygen mask off Monty's immobile face.

"His heart's stopped," she said to Daina. Her stethoscope clicked as she put it away. "There's nothing more we can do for him."

9

For a while she did absolutely nothing. Lost all sensory touch
with the world. It might have been for a short number of days
or then again the most inordinate length of time. She never
really knew, was only aware that she did not go to school but
rather to the Dale movie theater, sitting through the same
film day after day. The repetition she found entirely comforting because it seemed to her the only thing she could
count on now.

After Baba's death she had returned to the Nova, to find
the men with the guns—Rooster and big Tony with his accordion roll of family snapshots, though their names were
quickly fading from her mind as if they were imaginary play-
mates she had once conjured up but now no longer needed—
so that they could act out the vengeance she wished to wreak
upon Aurelio Ocasio herself.

Yet now, though she might not even be aware of it, she
hated those guns as much as she did Ocasio for not having
the decency to keep themselves alive when she—and Baba—
needed them the most. If they had loved him and, by extension, her, they would be here now instead of in the morgue.

I'm the only one who loved you, Baba, she thought. And

all at once she could not see the actors on the screen. Tears coursed down her cheeks and she sobbed uncontrollably.

In the end, the coming of the new feature caused her to move on. She could not bear the thought of another sequence being superimposed on the semblance of order she had, in her desperation and her anger, set up in this tiny dark universe.

Outside, on the blustery street, she stood immobile and undecided until a chocolate-skinned woman passed her by and Daina, suddenly and irrationally, felt like smashing her pocketbook into the black face. It was then that she knew where it was she must go.

Directly across the street from the restaurant in Harlem Baba had taken her to that first night, on the same block, bleak and barren, where they had witnessed the ghostdance, was a mojo store presided over by a woman black as tar with wide hips and an enormous bosom, stuffed, glistening cheeks and eyes that seemed to spark when they caught the light.

Now it was her anger, denied an outlet in the adult world, turned backward down the path where a child's hate must take it.

When Daina arrived outside the shop it was still closed and she was forced to wait on the sidewalk, staring into the dusty, curtained window of the place, festooned with feathered fetishes and peculiarly molded, fiercely visaged voodoo dolls. All were tagged "Made in Haiti"—proclaiming their authenticity.

She jumped slightly as a shadow came to life against the black-on-black-patterned fabric of the window case. A pair of yellow-green eyes came toward her and, as sunlight struck them, she could make out their slitted, feline irises. The cat ran the side of its head against the pane of glass. Its body followed its flicking tail and then it was gone into the shop's dusty recesses. Hello kitty, she mouthed.

"Are you waitin for me, chile?"

Daina started. She whirled, saw the fat woman who owned the mojo shop. Her dark skin glinted with diamondlike beads of sweat. Her voice was musical, possessing the warm lilt Daina could now associate with the Island blacks. Foreign yet familiar.

The fat woman jangled, all the wide and narrow bracelets on her ample arm clacking together like a gaggle of geese as she probed in her handbag. She withdrew keys on a silver ring, inserted two, one after the other, into the locks on the front door of the shop. "Gowan in, chile," she said. "Street like this's no place for you."

Daina walked cautiously into the shop, her nose immediately wrinkling at the whirlwind of mingled scents assailing her. Something brushed against her pants leg and she looked down. The cat was entwining itself between her feet.

"You used to come up here with the big man, ain't that right, chile?"

"Baba." Daina almost choked on the name.

"Ah, Baba," the fat woman said. "I never knew his name." She put her bag down on the counter top, took off her voluminous coat. "Don't see him round here no more." She turned her head to look back at Daina as she hung up her coat. "You come here for a bit of love potion, chile? You an' him had a fight or—"

"He's dead."

"Dead?" The fat woman's eyes got big around. "Lord, chile, I'm most teb'ily sorry 'bout that." She bent a little, peering into Daina's face as she went behind the counter. "Well you just tell Lise-Marie what it is she can help you with."

"I want," Daina said, "something powerful. Very powerful. A...spell or something."

Lise-Marie nodded. She put her hands together on the counter top. "We got pow'ful spells for sure, chile. All kinds."

Daina looked at her. "I want one that will kill."

For a moment there was nothing in the mojo shop but silence. The black cat sat between Daina and Lise-Marie, licking industriously at one raised forepaw.

"Lord, chile, you're too young t'be havin' black thoughts like that." Lise-Marie came around from behind the counter. She reached out, took Daina's hands in her own. She turned them palms up. Her pink fingertips traced the lines there as if she were a blind woman reading a braille text.

As if they had found what they were looking for, Lise-Marie's fingers stopped their search and her eyes flicked upward to Daina's face. The whites showed all around and there was a thin film of sweat on her black skin. "You got a very pow'ful aura 'bout you, chile. There's great mojo power within you." She stepped back a pace as if she were afraid.

"Will you give me what I want?" And when she got no

answer Daina turned away. "I don't believe you about the power. I've got no power. I've got nothing now." Tears were forcing their way out despite her attempt to will them back. Angrily, she wiped at her eyes. "All right for you," she said. "You've got the power to help me destroy the man who murdered Baba." The name caught in her throat and now all the will-power in the world was of no use. "Oh, Baba!" she cried, her shoulders shaking. Tears scalded her cheeks but now she welcomed them.

She felt Lise-Marie's arms around her, the welcoming warmth, the sweet spice of the woman; heard the lilting voice crooning gently, "Tha's all right, chile. You go ahead an' cry. Cry for your man."

After a while, she left Daina and when she returned she was carrying a quart cardboard box from a Chinese takeout restaurant.

"Here," she said, delivering the parcel into Daina's hands. "It's all inside. Most everything you need. No"—she put her hand over Daina's—"don't open it now. Wait till you get home. Now, chile, this's what you've got to do...."

Rubens returned from New York with an exquisite emerald ring he had bought for her at Harry Winston.

He gave it to her as soon as he was inside the limo she had taken out to the airport to meet him. "I was concerned about you until I saw that press conference," he said. "Christ, you knocked 'em dead. We felt the shock waves all the way back in New York. You're getting more column inches than the president these days."

She held onto him wordlessly, wondering whether she ought to tell him about her meeting with Meyer. She thought it might be just the wrong thing to do. She was certain he'd resent anyone's interference including the old man's.

The ring—a square-cut emerald nestled in a sweeping setting of platinum—radiated a cool power and, when he plucked it from her fingertips to slip it on her, she found she was crying. Oh, God, she thought, how I've missed him. But instead of telling him, she reached her palm up, bringing his head down until his lips opened against hers. She felt as if she never wanted to let him go.

"You heard about Monty," she said after a time.

"Jesus, yes. I told him just last week he was working too hard."

"That's not all you told him, apparently."

"What I told him," Rubens said, "was for his own good."

"You hurt him badly. He thought of you as his friend."

"This had nothing at all to do with friendship. It was business. He had no business giving you a goddamn sob story. Who the hell did he think he was? He was a big boy. He should've known how to take care of himself—" He broke off, turned abruptly away from her.

"Rubens—"

"No. Damn it, no!" He waved off her hand. His voice was thick and she thought she saw his shoulders shake as if he were crying. "Bastard had no right to die." His voice was so soft she had to strain to make out what he said. "Christ," he whispered bleakly, "it had *everything* to do with friendship. Everything." He turned around and she saw his eyes were red; he had eradicated all other traces of his tears. "Well, why don't you say it and get it over with?"

"Say what?"

"'I told you so.' I shouldn't've let him think I betrayed him."

"You did what you thought was best."

He looked at her levelly. "D'you really think that?"

"Yes. And, in a way you were right; he *couldn't* handle it anymore. But there were other ways of dealing with it. We made a mess of that, you and I." She looked away for a moment. "The funeral's the day after tomorrow. I already took care of the flowers for us both." He said nothing and by some unspoken mutual consent, they left it at that.

"How was New York?" Daina said. "I miss it."

Rubens sighed. "Couldn't tell you. I was too busy tunneling through the corporate records. Schuyler confirmed everything Meyer told me." He put a hand on her thigh, searched her eyes. "Are you all right?"

She gave him a small smile, felt warmth seep back into her. "I'm fine. What did you find out?"

"Enough to hang that bastard Ashley," he said with some venom. "He had nothing when he came to me. I set him up. I let him go and he proved himself. So, like a fool, I threw away the leash." His eyes were bright as he leaned forward to light a cigarette. He took one puff, crushed it out. "You know, you're right about these things. They've got no taste." He snapped closed the top of the metal ashtray sunk into the inside of the plush door.

He leaned back and sighed. "Meyer once told me, long ago, that in business you've got to keep *everyone* on a leash. 'No matter what you may think at the moment,' he said, 'today's best boy will turn around tomorrow and bite your head off if you give him half a chance. It's human nature. You can't fight it, only protect against it.'" Rubens smiled at the memory. "At the time I thought Meyer was the most cynical bastard I'd ever met. I also thought I could go him one better. That's what I tried to do with Ashley—give him his head and let him run.

"And wasn't Meyer right? What does Ashley do but start to systematically screw me behind my back. Now I know better. Meyer isn't cynical...just realistic."

"Did you confront Ashley?"

"Oh, no. Not yet. No, I've set a little scheme going in the heart of the corporation that he's going to run for with open arms. Me, I'd stay away. But not Ashley. He's far too greedy, which means he's ripe for a scam. He wants to be conned. They all do, the suckers. It's their innate greed that pulls them under.

"I've got enough paper here"—he tapped his elephant-hide attaché case—"to finish him right now. But that's so cold and bloodless, terminating him that way. I'm no organization man.

"I'm sending Schuyler back to New York next week. Tomorrow or by Wednesday at the latest, Ashley will discover a way to funnel profits out of the corporation by assigning stock transfers to a subsidiary corporation. It will all appear to be neat, quick, and foolproof. And it is. Except that the second corporation doesn't exist, at least not in reality. It's a figment of my convoluted mind, prepared on paper by Schuyler to look as if it's been in existence since 1975."

"What makes you think he'll go for it?" Daina said.

"Because I've begun to put pressure on the board of directors—as has Meyer, without Ashley knowing it—to decline the offer of merger Ashley's cooked up with his friends. He says no, but once that merger takes place, I'll be out—and so will Meyer and all our group.

"Ashley thought he had enough support as the board now

stands. I've changed that. But with this stock scheme, he'll be able to build up enough percentage on his own to sway some votes his way—enough to decide the issue." He smiled. "At least that's how it'll look to him."

"You want to catch him in the act?"

Rubens closed his eyes. "Something like that." He laced his fingers with hers, squeezed.

When they got home they sat by the pool. He asked her about the weekend. She told him how much she liked the billboards, then said, "I'm not sure what happened. I could've sworn Chris was ready to leave the band...I know he wants to. And then someone dissuaded him. He says it was Nigel."

"But you don't believe him."

"No," she said slowly, as if his comment had cemented a thought she'd had. "No, I don't, Rubens. I think it's Tie."

"But she's living with Nigel."

Daina ran her fingers through her slick hair. "Nigel's creative powers are on the wane. It's really Chris, now, who's carrying the Heartbeats. Without him the band would likely be finished." She came closer to him. "Silka told me that Tie's wanted Chris from the very beginning but Jon and Chris were far too close to go along with it. I don't think the case is the same with Chris and Nigel, despite what the both of them say."

"Maybe Chris isn't interested in her."

She looked at him. "You don't know Tie. Anyway, I've a sneaking suspicion he's wanted her from the first but, because of Jon, he's left her alone. I think that's how she's gotten him to stay. I don't know what she'd do without that organization around her."

"I thought she was hard as nails."

"Well, she seems to be—on the outside. But she's weak inside. She was afraid that Maggie would convince Chris to leave the band and now she's terrified of my relationship with Chris. She can't believe we're not sleeping together."

"Hardly anyone does."

She put her arms around him. "Except you, of course." Leaning forward in her chair, she touched him. She put her head down, took a gentle bite at his flesh. "I missed you," she whispered. "I missed you. I missed you."

He laughed. "In the midst of all that excitement?"

"In the midst of everything."

"That's dangerous."

"I like danger."

"Speaking of which," he said as his hands slid down her, "I don't like the idea of you passing out on the set like that."

She shook her head. "It was nothing. Anyway, I saw the doctor."

"And?"

"I'm A-OK."

"Christ, I hope so," he said, "because I've got a couple of more surprises for you."

"Well, are you going to tell me or let me suffer like this?"

"Beryl's really done it this time. *Time* magazine."

She snorted. "You're dreaming. The both of you are hallucinating. Beryl couldn't've possibly gotten me in *Time*. I'm not that big yet."

"No?" Rubens drawled. "Apparently the *Time* people don't agree. When the issue timed to the first release of *Heather Duell* in New York at Christmastime hits the stands and people see your face on the cover..."

She turned to him, her eyes open wide. "You know, you *are* nuts. I mean certifiably. There's no way—"

"Wanna bet?"

That stopped her. Rubens never said "Wanna bet?" unless he was already certain of the outcome.

She sat very still, her palms pressed against her knees. Her heart beat in her chest like a blacksmith's hammer on his anvil.

"Christ! Who are you anyway?"

He shrugged.

"Come here." And when he did, she took his head in her hands, ran her fingertips through his hair.

"What are you looking for?"

"Horns," she said.

"Horns?"

"As in the devil."

"Ah, *those* kind of horns. Sorry. I had them clipped over a thousand years ago." He grinned, took her hands in his. They were cold and he stroked them to warm them. "Come on, Daina. It's you. You, you, you."

She came forward, her face against his chest. She could smell him, that combination of traceries: sweat and soap and Ralph Lauren cologne, which was peculiar to him. She pressed her ear to his chest just above his left nipple, closed her eyes, listening to the trip-hammer beat of his heart as if to reassure herself.

One arm slid around her back, caressing her spine. With her still against him, he leaned over, reached his other arm out toward a glass-topped bamboo table. From its drawer he produced a Swiss army knife, deep red with the cross logo in gold. He opened up one of the straight blades with a crescent of fingernail.

"Perhaps you'd like to cut me," he said.

"What?"

"To see if I bleed." He laughed, shoved the knife at her fingertips hilt first. "Go on."

She recoiled as if the thing was hot. "You're crazy. No." But he pursued her, placing the knife in her palm.

"Just a little cut," he said softly. "It won't even hurt. A quick flick of—"

"No!"

"All right." He took the knife from her loose hand. "I'll do it myself." And before she could stop him, made a slashing horizontal cut across the pad of his left forefinger. Immediately, dark red blood welled up along the length of the cut, beading on his skin like soft sculpture. "You see?" he said placidly, extending the finger into a shaft of sunlight so that the blood shone like a dusky ruby. Quickly then he reversed his finger, placed it on her forehead, drew a line down to the bridge of her nose. "Just so you know it's real."

She studied him through the sunlight. He seemed now no longer the deeply tanned, tennis-playing producer she had always assumed him to be. Although there was nothing outwardly different about his appearance, still the notion persisted that he had somehow metamorphosed before her eyes.

How had it been done? she asked herself. By what magic? And then she understood. She had always been—and this was, perhaps, the real reason for her holding him at arm's length for so long—somewhat in awe of the sheer quantity of power he wielded. The power had not gone; she had merely become used to it. And not only *his* power. What he had said before was true: *you, you, you.* She recognized that it was *her* power—the combination of the artistic and the business—that was currently shaping their days and nights.

"Yes," she whispered, taking his bleeding finger, putting the rosy pad against her lips, smearing them. "Me, me, me."

Rubens watched this with a kind of fierce, possessive pride. He seemed for that instant to be like Marion, who has worked so hard to set the scene and now has the pleasure of witnessing his star actor incandesce, surpass all expectation, enter the realm of legend.

Then, all this, neatly compacted within his intent gaze, dropped away like a ridge of purple heather sweeping precipitously down to the stormy sea and his eyes were once again as placid as a still pond.

They took to the water. "We've decided, Marion and I and Simeoni from Twentieth, to take the film to New York for just one week," he said. "We've booked the Ziegfeld for the first week in December. Strictly reserved-seat engagement backed by a ten-day media saturation campaign—no TV until the day after the opening. We've selected the five most important critics here and we'll fly them in on a junket for the first-night screening and a party afterwards...that's Beryl's baby."

He reached out for the green rubber raft, pulled it over so they could get on. "We'll all go in for the premiere, get as much publicity as we can, then do the L.A. premiere a week later so we can have a shot at the Oscar nominations as well as the New York Film Critics' Awards and the Golden Globes. You and me and Marion; Beryl, of course, and some of Twentieth's grand fromages. There'll be plenty of interviews and coverage."

She let her head fall back, exposing her neck, her long hair drifting like sea grape in the water, as his lips licked at the tip of her nose, her closed eyelids, her half-open mouth. She raised her arms over her head, grasped his shoulders, pushing herself down his flesh until she was half off the raft. Cool water engulfed her thighs. They stared into each other's eyes, squinting through the sunlight. They were content just to hold on to each other.

A long time later, they became aware of the doorbell ringing insistently.

Reluctantly he rolled off the raft, splashing into the water. He swam across the width of the pool. She watched him in languid fascination as he went through the garden and into the house.

She turned over on her back, staring into the sky. The water lapped lazily all around her. She let one hand disappear beneath the surface, bathed in coolness. She thought about nothing, drifting off to the edge of sleep.

"Daina!" It was Rubens calling her. "Come on inside and get dressed. Dory's here and I want you to hear what he has to say."

She went into the water.

"It's Beillmann," Spengler said without preamble when Daina came into the living room. He was standing with the fat mermaid over his left shoulder. She seemed to be laughing at him.

"Calm down, Dory," Rubens said, taking the other man's elbow and leading him toward the bar. "Let's have a drink first. Settle your nerves."

"What about Beillmann?" Daina said, following them across the room.

"I'll tell you what—" Spengler broke away from Rubens' grip. His eyes were hard and fierce. He looked at Daina once before staring directly into Rubens' face. "You said everything was go at Twentieth. Smooth as silk; no snags—"

"There *are* no snags," Rubens assured him.

"Oh, yeah?" Spengler snarled. "Yesterday Beillmann might have been tame but today is another day."

Rubens calmly unscrewed the cap from a bottle of Stolichnaya without going behind the bar. He dug out some ice, filled a low, wide-mouthed glass, poured the vodka over. He swirled the liquor around several times to cool it, took a long languid sip. "Something happened at the studio, I take it."

"You take it correctly," Spengler said. "We got ourselves a very big problem."

"You know, Dory," Rubens said without raising his voice, "I really do believe you could use that drink. Martini, dry, right?" He handed Spengler the glass. "Come on, now," he coaxed. "I want you relaxed when you tell me what the problem is."

Spengler took a sip of his martini, said, "That *ganef* Reynolds—George Altavos' agent—was in to see Beillmann this morning. He said George was threatening to pull out of the project unless the billing was changed."

"To what?" Rubens put his glass down very carefully.

"He wants his name above Daina's. Not side by side, mind you. *Above.*"

"And what did Beillmann say?"

"What d'you think he said? He caved in."

"What?" Daina said incredulously. "He said *okay?*"

Spengler nodded. "That's our boy." He turned to Rubens. "What d'you think of that bastard?"

Rubens came out from behind the bar. He had a peculiar look in his eyes. When he spoke, his voice was soft as silk. "What I want to know very much, Dory, is why you didn't do something. Hmm? You were there. Are you on our team or not? Why didn't you handle Beillmann?"

Spengler's martini was caught halfway to his lips. Now he lowered the glass.

"You know, Dory, when I recommended you to Daina, I thought I was doing her a favor. I thought you were bright, well-connected, and talented. Now I'm not so sure."

"I just thought you'd want to deal with this yourself," Spengler said.

"One of the reasons you were hired," Daina said, "was to make certain this kind of thing doesn't happen. Do you think I want George's name above mine?"

"That's not what we've been working toward, Dory," Rubens said. "You haven't been here very long but even a moron could pick that up."

"I don't appreciate being called a moron," Spengler said through clenched teeth.

"And I don't care much for people who can't handle themselves in a crisis. Now I'm going to clean up this mess."

Spengler was silent. The two men glared at each other for a long moment.

"There's another way," Daina said, looking from one to the other. "I think this is something I ought to take care of. It isn't a producer's decision. George isn't going to walk off this project; he needs it too much. Beillmann was bluffed. Come on, Rubens, we're going to see Buzz."

Buzz Beillmann had an office on the same side of the building as the president of Twentieth Century-Fox Films. It was, as befitting his position as executive vice-president, motion-picture development, a corner office and as large as a five-star hotel's suite of rooms.

His great rosewood and stainless-steel desk was situated on the far side of the vast room from the door so that, upon entering, one was obliged to trudge across the bleak expanse of dove-gray carpet as if making a pilgrimage to the Holy Land. Which, of course, it was to many people.

In line with this delicious illusion, Buzz Beillmann generally received his guests as if they were supplicants to the throne of Heaven. First there was a wait in the general reception area, after which, upon reaching the third floor, one was obliged to sit for perhaps another half hour—Mr. Beillmann was always "running late," according to his semiapologetic personal secretary—in the reception area outside his office. If one were truly one of the chosen, Sandra Oberst, a hard-nosed, sweetly smiling woman in her mid-thirties, would bring you a cup of coffee and tell you absolutely nothing. She was Beillmann's assistant and as such ran excellent flak for her boss. Every vice-president needed someone to weed out the wheat from the chaff, after all. The people downstairs were certainly no good at it.

Daina, upon walking into Beillmann's reception area, was determined to do away with the dragon guarding the giant's cave. The secretary seemed surprised that she asked for Miss Oberst but nevertheless summoned the tall woman with commendable alacrity.

Sandra Oberst bounded out of her office, both hands gripping china cups—no Styrofoam in Buzz Beillmann's domain!—filled with steaming black coffee. She must have been notified of their coming while they were on their way up to the third floor.

"Miss Whitney. Mr. Rubens. How nice to see you both." She had a peculiarly formal way of addressing everyone. With her, first names did not exist and Daina wondered what she called her lovers.

They both took the coffee Sandra Oberst offered. She stood, slightly spread-legged, before the corridor leading to Beillmann's office, as if concerned they might make a run for the door.

"This is an unexpected surprise." She cocked her head, clucked her tongue. "You know how Mr. Beillmann is about appointments, Mr. Rubens. This is a particularly heavy day."

She shrugged without a sign of apology, adjusted the enormous tinted glasses on the bridge of her nose. Behind them, her light eyes regarded them both placidly. "The whole week has been like this. May I help you with something?"

Daina looked bored and Rubens was looking somewhere else. "We were going to tell Buzz in person but...well, I know how close the two of you are. Telling you is almost the same as telling him, right, Rubens?"

"Oh, yeah." He had found a fascinating pattern of shadows on the carpet.

Sandra Oberst spent a beat being confused. "You mean you don't want— Well, I'm sure I can help you with anything you want." She put her perfectly manicured fingers up to touch the bun on the back of her head that looked as hard as a baseball. She was dressed in a man-tailored, navy-blue suit. The severe lines of her skirt only made her femininity that much more apparent. Her white satin shirt was fastened up to her neck where a large silver pin was stuck as if to make certain none of the buttons would come undone.

"We've got very little time, really," Daina said. "We've got an appointment with Todd Burke at Columbia in"—she consulted her watch—"just about twenty minutes." The other woman seemed to blink at the mention of the name but she said nothing. "Somehow he's gotten wind of the Brando project and he's invited us for a talk. Originally I told Rubens to turn him down—I mean I know we had a moral obligation to Buzz." She paused, watching the reaction Sandra had to her use of the past tense. The other woman crossed her arms over her breasts.

"But naturally," Daina continued with some equanimity, "when Dory told us about Beillmann changing my billing, I began to feel differently about it." The edge of her hand cut through the air between them. "But this is such unimportant stuff"—her voice was loaded with sarcasm now—"you just be a good girl and deliver the message to Buzz. Meanwhile, we'll be down the road talking to Burke. He's cleared his entire afternoon for us." She stopped, staring directly into Sandra Oberst's eyes.

The other woman had gone white beneath her tan and her makeup. "What is this, some sort of gag?" she said hopefully.

"No gag," Daina said. "I'm just fed up with the treatment this studio isn't giving me."

Sandra lifted her hands, palms up. "I don't know what you think I can do."

"Oh, nothing," Daina said, glancing at her watch. "You're just a messenger, that's all."

"Mr. Rubens, we've always had a good working relationship."

He shrugged, looked at her without expression as if to say, You know these strong-willed stars.

Sandra Oberst's glasses had begun to slip a bit and Daina saw that she was sweating despite the air conditioning. She looked, glassy-eyed, from one to the other. "I just...I don't know what to say." There was a tiny quaver beating that had not been there before.

"Of course you don't." Daina turned her head. "You see, Rubens. I told you. There was no point in coming here after all."

"Oh, Sandra's right. Twentieth and I have always had a good working relationship." He smiled at her. "Isn't that right?"

"Yes, Mr. Rubens," Sandra said, looking as if she had just glimpsed a ray of sunlight after a hideously destructive storm.

"But that, as you can see," Daina interjected, "is a thing of the past. We should've gone right to Burke's and forgotten to be polite to these people. They have no manners."

"Reluctantly," Rubens said, giving Sandra Oberst a rueful look, "I'm forced to agree with you. Give Buzz our regards." They both began to walk away.

"Just a moment!"

They turned back to see the other woman on the phone she had wrested from the secretary's grasp. She seemed to have it pressed to her ear with some rigidity. She took it away; it hung at her side like a useless appendage. "Mr. Beillmann would like a word with you."

"Oh, no," Rubens said. "We wouldn't want to disturb Buzz. He's probably in the middle of an important meeting—"

"Please," Sandra Oberst said. "He'd really like to have a word with you."

"A word?" Rubens opened his eyes wide, rolling the phrase around on his tongue. "Well, I suppose, under the circumstances—"

Daina shook her head. "I'm sorry, Miss Oberst, you've

made us late for our appointment. Please tell Buzz we'll call him later."

The other woman stepped out from beside the secretary's desk. "My God, you can't go now. He'll kill me."

"Perhaps you should've thought of that before," Rubens said. "Now it's too late."

Sandra smiled widely, desperately. She linked her arms with theirs. "You know," she said, "this misunderstanding is all my fault—really it is. We've had such a bad week, I'm just not concentrating today. I should've brought you in to see Mr. Beillmann right away. I really can't understand why I didn't." Daina knew it was because Buzz had given her instructions not to. "It's one of those days." She squeezed Daina's arm, one woman to another. "You know what those are like, Miss Whitney."

"Jesus, Daina," Rubens said. "Give the girl a break."

Buzz Beillmann was a beetle-browed individual in his mid-fifties. His short hair was iron gray, his thick skin the color of mahogany. He was a good golfer and an even better motion-picture man when he wasn't caught in a cross-fire. He was superb with ideas and figures but people tended to throw him. He hadn't had much practice being one.

His heavyset figure was waiting for them behind his desk. The long picture window behind his back faced west—he had been specific about that—so that his afternoon appointments (he saw only Twentieth people in the morning) would have the full benefit of the sun streaming into their eyes.

"Daina. Rubens," he said heartily. "What kept you so long? The minute I heard you were outside, I told Sandra to send you right in." His eyes squinted as they approached and a look of pain filled his face as if he were grappling with a particularly thorny problem. "I tell you, I don't know what I'm going to do with her." He shook his head. "She really should know better."

He came around from behind his desk, said to Rubens, "What do you think of her?"

"Seems okay to me," he said, looking at Daina.

But Beillmann seemed worried still. "I don't know. She's not the woman she once was. Tell me, Rubens—"

But Rubens had walked away, stood looking out at the

vista of streeted palms and gleaming Mercedes busily tail-
gating each other. He lifted a hand. "Talk to Daina, Buzz.
Ask her opinion. She knows women far better than I do."

"What d'you think, Daina?" Beillmann said as he went
across the room to the bar. "Drink, anyone?"

"I think," Daina said, "you'd better tell George that his
name is back below mine." Beillmann paused with a decanter
of Scotch in the air. "And, from now on, let Miss Oberst take
care of Dick Reynolds, so we don't have any more misunder-
standings."

Beillmann put the decanter down, turned. "Now, Daina,
let's not be unreasonable, shall we? I mean I know how you
people get overnight but there's a limit to how far any of us
will go." He advanced toward her. "I mean"—his hands were
outspread—"money's money and business is business. Isn't
that right, Rubens?" Rubens said nothing, did not even turn
his head to look at the other man. Beillmann, trying to ignore
this, continued. "I mean egos are fine to have. Actors can't
survive without them." He pointed a blunt thumb into his
chest. "Christ, I know that. You think I'm insensitive? I'm
doing this for the sake of the film. We're all one big family.
Someone comes in with a legitimate complaint—"

"It's not legitimate," Daina said.

"I have to act on what I think is best for all of us. I'm in
the middle of a juggling act, Daina. But, hell, I'm not com-
plaining. It's what I get paid to do. I'm just trying to explain
my position. I gotta think of everyone, not just one person.

"There's *always* a problem with you people. But we're prepared to handle every contingency. You're going to New York
and everything will be fine. Believe me." He spread his hands
and his voice took on a conciliatory note. "I know how it is
before a wrap and I sympathize. You're nervous and that's
perfectly understandable. But I've been through this a
hundred times or more. I know what I'm talking about."

"What happened to the original billing? I've got contract
guarantees."

Beillmann's smile widened just a touch as if he felt the
concrete beginning to buckle where he had struck. "I think
you'd better go back and read the fine print. The size of the
type is guaranteed, but placement is at the studio's discretion.
We rethought the idea, is all, and I'm totally convinced it
was the right decision. It makes sense to—"

"Don't give me that," Daina snapped. "Reynolds came in here and stepped on your big toe and you said, Ouch. *That's* what happened."

Beillmann's jaw jutted out and his face got red. He picked at a scab high up on his forehead until it began to bleed. "What's she talking about, Rubens?"

Rubens turned from his contemplation of the street. "I don't speak for her, Buzz. What she says stands."

Beillmann turned back to Daina. "You think I'm a push-over or something? Is that what you're getting at?"

"What I'm getting at," Daina said, "is that I've been meaning to tell you the color on the interior of my trailer's all wrong. I hate it. Paint it peach...a very pale peach. And when that's done, I'll come back."

Beillmann clutched at the side of his desk. "Hey, what?" He seemed bewildered. "What d'you mean, come back?"

"I'm afraid I can't concentrate properly when I've got to come back to such disgusting surroundings."

"Huh, what paint?" He eyed her suspiciously, then shrugged resignedly as if he had given up a great concession. "All right. Okay. You got it." He smiled. "What's a coat of paint to us? I mean, we're all friends, right?" He glanced from her to where Rubens stood watching him.

Rubens nodded. "Right, Buzz. You're on the track now."

Beillmann seemed to gain confidence. He went behind his desk, reached for the phone. "All I gotta do is—"

"And the lighting's all wrong," Daina said.

Beillmann froze, the receiver halfway to his ear. "Lighting," he croaked. "What lighting? Where lighting?"

"In my trailer," Daina said calmly. She took a step toward him. "I think track lighting would be much better."

Beillmann put down the phone, stared at her. "What, may I ask, do you need track lighting in your trailer for?" He just barely managed to keep the note of hysteria out of his voice.

"For the makeup people, of course. I want makeup done in my trailer from now on."

"Now wait a minute. D'you know what a storm that's gonna cause with the other—"

"And all the people—those studio nitwits you've been sending around to watch—off the set."

"You're crazy!" Beillmann stayed behind his desk as if clinging to the last shred of his authority. He worried the scab on his forehead. "This is insane, Rubens!" he cried. "You've got to stop this right now!"

"This has nothing to do with Rubens," Daina said fiercely. "This's just between you and me."

Still, Beillmann did not believe her. "Rubens," he said, "what the hell is going on here?"

"She's the star." Rubens shrugged. "I've got nothing to do with it."

"But she's your property!" Beillmann wailed.

"No," Rubens said. "She's *your* star, goddamnit, and it's about time you took responsibility for it. She's about to make you a hundred million dollars or more."

"Pie in the sky."

Rubens came away from the window. "If you can't even see that, I feel for you. A year from now, you'll be taking all the credit here for this project." He walked right past where Daina and Beillmann stood. "Come on, Daina. You were right all along. We've got nothing more to discuss here."

"Rubens, wait! Where are you going?" The door closed behind him. "Goddamnit!" Beillmann's hands balled into impotent fists. He glared at Daina. "Just who the hell d'you think you are to come in here and—"

"I know who I am, Buzz," Daina said icily. "It's you who don't have an idea of your position on this. What are you going to do when I walk out?"

"You're just a dumb girl." Beillmann seemed to be trembling, his heavy jowls wobbling. "I don't negotiate with girls."

"I'll tell you something, Buzz," she said, leaning slightly forward. "I don't like you professionally, and I like you even less personally. I'm a woman and you'd better get it through that dinosaur brain of yours that we're the only ones here." Her violet eyes bored into him. "It's just you and me and either we get this settled right now or it's all over and you won't ever have to negotiate with me again."

For an instant she thought he was going to blow up. Then he seemed to get hold of himself. "Okay. Okay," he said. "You've got the lighting and the closed set." He ran his fingers through his hair as he sat down with an audible sigh. "Jesus!" he breathed. He seemed to think it was over.

"Good," Daina said sweetly. "Now why don't you get on the phone with Reynolds and tell him you've changed your mind." She went over to the bar and opened it. "Otherwise the Brando project goes to Columbia." She poured them both Scotches on the rocks, turned to face him. He was staring at her with a kind of stony shock. "I'm sure the chairman of the board would be fascinated by how you let it slip through your fingers." She put his drink onto the desk. He was watching her with a look of terrified rapture on his face.

"Jesus Christ!" He swiveled away from her and, for a long time, his back was to her. When at length he turned around, he was smiling. He reached for the wide, sweating glass. Ice clattered as his shaking hand brought the Scotch up to his lips.

"Of course," he said, in a totally relaxed tone of voice, "Reynolds has no position." He picked up the phone. "No position at all." He waved a forefinger. "I warned those guys in publicity it'd be risky hanging this project on Altavos' name." He spoke into the receiver. "Dottie, get me Dick Reynolds right away. Try his house if he's not at the office. No, no, I don't want to talk to her now. And hold all my calls." He cradled the receiver, staring at the clear buttons on the base of the phone. He took another sip of his Scotch. One of them lit up and, when it began to blink and he heard the buzz of the intercom, he raised his head and looked Daina straight in the eye. "But then Reynolds knew that all the time, didn't he?"

Night. All the lights in the villa had been extinguished at sunset. What illumination there was came from the terrorists' flashlights.

Heather was sleeping on the bare floor. Rachel was beside her, curled up, her head in the crook of Heather's arm. A shadow detached itself from the far wall, came across the room without sound, high-stepping over the supine forms. When it reached the spot where Heather lay, it stood stiff-legged over her, one foot on each side of her body. The form reached out a flashlight, bent, jerked Heather up into a sitting position. At the same time, the flashlight beam came on, shining directly into her blinking eyes.

Heather cried out, squinted. She put her hand up to shield her eyes. It was slapped away. Her head lolled.

"Is it dawn already?" she asked thickly. "It seems as if I've been asleep for only a few minutes."

"Thirty." It was Rita's voice.

"What do you want?" Heather's head was turned away from the harsh illumination.

"You will not be allowed to sleep for more than thirty minutes at a time."

"But why?"

"Go back to sleep," Rita said. She switched off the flashlight. "You're wasting time."

Heather went back to sleep but as the night wore on and Rita returned every half hour she gradually became more and more agitated. She would be just drifting off to sleep when she was jerked up, the bright light splashing her face. And, finally, no sleep at all would come.

"Why are they doing this?" Rachel whispered to her during one of the dark intervals.

"I don't know."

"Every time I close my eyes, I think of her coming back, jerking me awake." Rachel moved closer to Heather. "It's far worse than no sleep."

"Yes." Heather turned her head, looking at Rachel. "Yes, you're right. The anticipation makes it impossible to go back to sleep."

"Heather?"

"Yes."

"I'm frightened."

Heather put her arms around the girl. "I know you are, Rachel. That's all right. It's healthy to have a little fear."

"I think I have much more than a little."

"Rachel, listen to me. Before he died, James told me I would have to fight these people. They have to control their environment completely, he said. That's their real power. Once that starts to break down, they become vulnerable."

"I don't understand." Her voice was small.

"It means we can't allow them to get the better of us. They're trying right now, you see. You helped me to understand this. What they're doing: the lack of privacy, the short sleep cycles. It's all part of a program to break us. We can't allow that."

For a moment, there was silence between them.

Rachel lifted her head up. "You loved James very much, didn't you?"

Heather closed her eyes but the tears squeezed through anyway. "Yes, Rachel. I did."

"Freddie Bock was like an uncle to me. Better than an uncle. I've got one back in Tel Aviv I hate." Her eyes roved Heather's face. Her small hand took Heather's, guided it to her own cheek. It was wet with tears. "What should we do?"

"Get some sleep."

A fierce light in both their eyes.

"What are you two whispering about?" It was El-Kalaam's voice.

"Girl talk," Heather said.

She was slapped across the face.

"Stupid bitch!" It was Fessi. He had hit her. Heather could just make him out beyond the brilliant ring of light, standing in front of El-Kalaam.

"What were you talking about?" El-Kalaam said again.

"I was comforting her. The girl was frightened."

"She has every reason to be frightened," El-Kalaam said. "Your situation is dire. We have heard no word yet tonight. Eight o'clock tomorrow morning is the deadline."

"El-Kalaam," Heather said, "you cannot mean to harm her. She's only a child. Surely even you—"

"This is war. Don't ever forget that. In war children are the same as adults. There can be no distinction between the two." His voice rose in fervor. "Our war is holy; our cause just. Allah tells us there are no innocents."

"Allah be damned!" Heather said hotly. "This girl has done nothing to you."

"Blasphemer!" Fessi cried. He raised his hand again. But El-Kalaam stayed him.

"I care nothing for her or for you as people," El-Kalaam said. "You are infidels. But whatever you can get for me, I will willingly take. She is a symbol, as you are in your own way. This is to be your role here."

"You'll never get what you want," Rachel said. Heather could see the girl's hand trembling against her own arm.

"Your father will not allow you to die. He will give us what we want, what is ours."

"He won't sell out his country," Rachel cried. "He won't!"

El-Kalaam thrust his face close to hers. The beam of the flashlight shone weirdly off his features. The pockmarks at the edge of his cheekbones were thrust into dominant shadow and biting light. Gold spangled his mouth every time he spoke. "You'd better pray to your God he will. Otherwise..." The muzzle of his machine pistol shot out of the darkness into the cone of light.

He shrugged as Rachel shrank back against Heather's side. "It makes no difference to me. In the end it will be the same. If you die, the world-wide outcry will bring your father's government down for sacrificing a little girl." He grinned wolfishly. "The only difference will be you, Rachel. Will you see tomorrow's afternoon or not?"

Rachel turned her head away.

"What a brave soldier you are," Heather said derisively. "*Soldier*. Terrorizing children."

"Listen, I don't give a damn what you think of me, d'you understand? You don't exist except to serve our ends in any way we choose."

Heather met his gaze. "You'll never get me to do something for you."

"Oh, yes, that's what your friend Bock said. You remember that. You remember what we did to him."

"I remember."

"And what happened to Susan."

"I'm not afraid of that."

"Perhaps not." He was studying her closely. "But I know there *is* something you're afraid of."

"What?"

He smiled benignly. "We found it in Bock and we found it in Susan." He shook his head. "No, I will not allow Fessi near you. You are his weakness and I believe you could defeat him in the end. Please be assured I will not give you the means to escape."

His hand whipped out. It took Rachel by the throat. He jerked her away from Heather's grasp. Rachel tried to cry out but only a weak gurgling sound emerged from her half-open lips. Heather lunged at him. Fessi held her back but still she fought.

"Yes, indeed," El-Kalaam said thoughtfully. He shook Rachel back and forth with so much force her teeth chattered. "I believe we have found your weak spot."

* * *

Bonesteel had, of course, begun calling her as soon as she returned from San Francisco. Daina knew what he wanted, believed, too, that she had a great deal to tell him. But he had so angered her that a solid wall of spite had built itself inside her and she would not answer his calls. She wanted, she realized sometime later, to force him to come out to the house.

This he did not do. But one morning on her way into the valley, she was stopped on Sunset. She pulled over, watching in her rearview mirror as the police car drew up behind her. She had not been speeding nor had she run a red light. There had been no reason to stop her.

No one got out of the police car. All she could see were two pairs of sunglasses behind the sunlight-streaked windshield. The car started up slowly and she watched it as it stopped beside her.

"Miss Whitney?" one of the young uniforms said, though he knew very well who she was.

"Yes?"

"I wonder if you'd mind accompanying us down to the precinct house."

"I'm afraid that would be impossible right now."

"Ma'am," the young uniform said sadly, "I'd take it as a personal favor if you would. My boss will chew my tail if I don't bring you along."

"What's this all about?"

"Official business."

"What, precisely, does that mean?"

"I'm afraid you'll have to ask Lieutenant Bonesteel that, Miss Whitney." He looked downcast. "I'm real sorry about this."

"Don't be," she said. "You're very polite. Was that the lieutenant's idea?"

"No, Ma'am." He smiled a dazzling L.A. smile. "It was mine."

She laughed. "All right." She put the Merc in gear. "What are you, a sergeant?"

"Patrolman, Ma'am."

She waved. "Lead on, Patrolman."

"Miss Whitney?"

"Yes."

He handed over his parking ticket book. "I wonder if I could trouble you for your autograph?"

* * *

Bonesteel's precinct house was in the heart of downtown
L.A. It was an ugly blocklike affair in an ugly blocklike part
of town. It looked like a bunker waiting for a war to begin
itself around it.

Bonesteel's cubicle was on the sixth floor. The oversize
elevator was filled with the astringent odors of stale sweat
and fresh fear. The patrolman took her up himself, depositing
her on Bonesteel's frosted-glass doorstep.

"Here she is, Lieutenant."

Bonesteel looked up from his papers. He was sitting behind
a desk littered with folders and flimsy colored sheets.

"Okay, Andrews."

"Lieutenant"—the patrolman hooked a thumb—"she's a
very nice lady."

"Cut the editorial comments, Andrews, and split."

For a time after the patrolman left they regarded each
other. Harsh fluorescent light spilled down from the recessed
panels in the acoustically tiled ceiling. In one corner, where
a metal vent was placed, the tiles were blackened as if by
fire.

There was one gray metal and green vinyl chair in front
of the desk and Bonesteel waved her to that now. "Want a
coffee?"

"I want to get out of here," Daina said tightly.

"As soon as we have a little talk. We have a bargain,
remember?"

"Our bargain did not include you acting like a bastard."

He seemed to think about that for a minute. He got up,
came around his desk and closed the door behind her. He did
not go back to his chair but hoisted himself onto one littered
corner of his desk. He stretched out one hand. "You see all
this? It's my monthly reports. I *hate* doing monthly reports.
I'm already two months behind, heading for three, and the
captain is riding my ass." He put his hands together, interlacing the fingers. "We've all got problems."

"If that's a joke," Daina said coldly, "it's not funny."

"I don't make jokes."

"I wonder," she said, coming toward him. "Do you really
have a heart underneath your Calvin Klein suits?"

His slate-gray eyes flickered for just an instant. "I like to dress."

"What'll happen when you divorce your wife?" she snapped. "Will she give you a settlement large enough to keep up your wardrobe?"

He stood up and his jaw clenched. "That's not funny."

"I wasn't joking." She confronted him defiantly, willing him to slap her. That was just what she needed. Then she could walk out of here and never see him again. Then she thought of Maggie. Could she trust Meyer to help her? I don't care anymore, she screamed to herself. But she knew it for a lie.

Bonesteel smiled. "Ah, I know how I made you feel over the phone. I'm sorry about that."

"Are you."

"Really I am. It was business. I had to see if you really knew."

"You mean you couldn't tell from before?"

"You're an actress, remember? You and Chris Kerr are like two peas in a pod. What if you were covering up about the drug angle because you were into it yourself?"

She held out her arms. "You want to check me for tracks?"

He watched her silently for a moment, not making a move. "I know where you've been." He said it so quietly she had to strain to hear.

"You do."

"Yes. I had to dig real deep for it."

"You don't know the whole story."

He shrugged. "Doesn't make any difference. They can do funny things to you in places like that. Some people come out with a craving, know what I mean?"

"Like morphine or horse."

"Like that, yeah."

"I'm clean, Copper."

He laughed. "Christ, I'm sorry I gave you such a rough time." He went around behind his desk, closed all the folders. "Andrews is right about you," he said without looking up.

"Thanks."

"You know, this is a lousy place for an interrogation. You filming today?"

"Just in the afternoon. They're doing some stunt footage this morning."

"Hell, I knew that, too." He went to the door, took her arm. "Come on, let's go home for a while."

"Pathological?"

"Yes."

"Are you quite certain that's what he said?"

"Of course I'm certain."

"What would a dumb bodyguard know about pathological?"

But Bonesteel was, essentially, talking to himself now and when Daina said, "I don't think he's dumb at all," she was not at all sure he had heard her.

He got out of the low-slung chair, went across the living room to the piano. He sat down, stared straight ahead at the Vivaldi concerto transcription open on the stand. He began to play. He did not nearly have the technique of his daughter or the talent. But he got through it without hesitations or false notes.

Daina had told him about the party, about Nile's death—he had wondered if there could have been any connection to Maggie's murder—the police questioning, her statement, the coroner's inquest the next day. He listened to it all with an odd acute intensity, his eyes burning bright as if he were feasting off her words.

She had repeated Thaïs' words at the party: "'She was an outsider just as you're an outsider. She broke the laws and was destroyed,'" but he had seemed to gloss over whatever import they might have to ask her to repeat what Silka had said about Nigel. "He was very wild in those days," Daina said. "But then they all were: Chris and Nigel and especially Jon."

"Wild, yes, he had said. But what if one of them were pathological. We already know how drugs turned Jon psychotic, magnifying his neuroses all out of proportion."

Now Bonesteel was through playing. He sat with his fingertips still on the keys he had depressed to sound the final chord of the concerto. He was staring at the photo of his daughter.

"Is that her favorite piece?" Daina asked.

"What? Oh, no." He smiled vaguely. "It's mine. Mozart is Sarah's God."

"Bobby," she said, leaning her elbows on the edge of the piano, "will you tell me why you so discount what Tie had to say about Maggie's death?"

"You mean I should believe Tie put a spell on her?" He snorted.

"That's not what I meant."

"I don't believe in magic. I leave that to Stephen King fans."

"What if Tie killed Maggie?"

He looked at her. "She's not capable of it."

"Her mind's evil enough."

"I was speaking," he said, "about her body. Physically, she's not strong enough to accomplish what was done to Maggie. That takes a man's bulk." He ran his hands along the keys as if brushing imaginary dust from their surface. "Besides, I discount almost anything she tells you."

"Why would you do that?"

"Because," he said slowly, "Tie's in love with you."

Daina laughed. "Oh, come on. She hates my guts." But there was a quick contraction in her stomach.

"Think about it," Bonesteel said, watching her face. "What do you imagine would terrify a woman like that most of all?"

But Daina already knew. "To have her emotions running out of control."

"I've seen it in her eyes, Daina," he said. "When I mention your name something inside her freezes."

"Because of her hatred. She's jealous of my relationship with Chris."

Bonesteel shook his head. "Hatred makes women like that melt. It's what they live on. D'you think she's ever loved anyone in her life? I don't. Not a man, anyway. Her men have all been weak—powerful, monied, but weak. She's provided the strength. But she can't do it on her own, otherwise she wouldn't feed off of man after man. But a woman is another thing altogether for Tie. Because I think that in them she sees reflected her own mystery."

And Daina caught an image in her mind: she and her father, a still, hot summer's day out in the middle of Long Pond on the Cape. In a rowboat, the flat wet deck stinking of salt and heating fish guts, rods gleaming in the air like fine strands of a great spider's web, delicate antennae searching.

"Look at the water, honey," her father had said to her in a hushed voice. "Look there—through the sun dazzle, at the dark drop of the hook."

They were both still as statues, sweating. The close afternoon waited on them with bated breath. Close to the lake's green surface a cloud of gnats parted, making way for a water spider skimming deftly by.

"Wait now," he whispered, his voice full of suppressed excitement. "Wait and watch that line."

The sun hammered down out of a cloudless sky onto her bare shoulders, all red and hurting by day's end. A goose called plaintively, taking off from the shallows of the far bank.

"Now," her father whispered hoarsely. "Now!"

And she saw it. The dark line had gone almost vertical with the pull, whirling so that the sunlight flashed off it as if it were a sword's edge, burning like a torch in the scant instant before the fish bit.

The ineffable mystery of her father's absolute mastery over that moment came back to her with such power that for an instant she was dizzied. And with a start she realized that for all her life she had been searching for the recreation of that moment when the entire world had been his and he held dominion not only over her but, it seemed, over all creatures. The ghost of an idea danced around the periphery of her consciousness. There was a way to save Chris from Tie—only one way—but Daina wondered whether she was up to the sacrifice. Yet the idea of flexing her developing power dazzled her, egged her onward.

"I think your going with the band just might've paid off," Bonesteel said, cutting into her train of thought. "Right now, I've got a fistful of hot air. Everyone's alibi is holding up, so far. Except for the time Chris was out of your sight at The Dancers, the other members of the band and the entourage have accounted for their whereabouts." He pointed. "But this broad who was Maggie's connection might lead somewhere." He eyed her. "You sure he didn't know who she was?"

"That's what he said."

"D'you believe him?"

"Why would he lie?"

He grunted. "Why does anyone lie? 'Cause he's got something to hide. If the lady brought him his dope, he wouldn't want her blown, now would he? Uh uh. I think our little boy's holding out on you."

"You're not going to bring him in and question him," she said with some alarm.

"I'm not that stupid," he said getting up. "You can do that for me."

"Oh, no." She put her hands up. "Chris's my friend. I don't want to keep lying to him."

"You know," Bonesteel said meditatively, "if I talk to him about it, I might make a slip and mention where I found out about this broad in the first place."

"I don't think he'd believe you."

"I don't think so either. But it might put a couple of doubts in his mind that weren't there before."

"I'll go to him first—"

"And tell him what?" She could see he wasn't gloating or even enjoying this. He reached out, touched her. "Look, Daina, I don't want to do anything of the sort. I don't want to put pressure on you. But I *do* want to catch whoever killed Maggie. And I'll damn well do whatever I have to to get the job done." His face was becoming flushed. "I don't have to tell you that this was not just another street murder where some young punk mishandles a gun or a stabbing after a barroom brawl. No, this is some demented mind's idea of fun and I don't relish the thought of people like that driving around town free and maybe thinking of doing it again." He shook his head. "Someone's gotta stop them."

"How is it that you're the one?"

"I've got the guts. It's as simple as that."

"You know, I really think you mean that."

"Why shouldn't I? You think this is some kind of macho pose?" He snorted. "When your piece comes out and you put your finger on the trigger, you better make damn sure it ain't no pose or you're liable to find your brains splattered all over your shoetops. You can't afford to hesitate. You gotta *know* deep inside what you're expected to do. And you do it."

"Have you killed a man?" she said softly.

"Yeah, once. Black man came over a wall in the dead of night. I was in uniform then. We'd responded to a squeal. Man had a piece the size of a shotgun. .357 Magnum. You can stop an elephant with that, just about. Blew my partner's head off while he was standing right beside me with his piece still in its holster. I never knew there was so much blood in a human being. The kid was nineteen and just married. I'd been an usher at his wedding and that gutless wonder of a lieutenant we had said to me, 'All right, Bonesteel, everyone around here thinks you're a hero. Now I want you to do something really difficult. Go tell the widow.'"

He walked away from her to the window where swirls of fog hid the tops of the trees and obscured the sky.

"What was it like?" Daina said, turning around to face him. "I want to know what it feels like to kill someone."

"It doesn't feel like anything at all," Bonesteel said, his eyes far away. "Because you make it that way. The hate and the...terror of being killed yourself damps down on it. I wasn't sorry I shot that bastard. I felt more when I had to tell Gloria that her husband of two weeks wouldn't be coming home again. But there's no desire, no real feeling at all. Just an empty black pit you have to get across before you can go on living again."

She came after him. "Jean-Carlos says you can't let yourself think when you pull the trigger."

He turned away from the fog. "Who's Jean-Carlos?"

"He's trained all of us in weapons. He's a Cuban refugee who broke out of Morro Castle."

Bonesteel sat on the edge of the off-white sofa, his hands in his lap. He seemed very tired. "You know, as long as I've lived in L.A. I still get surprised at how voraciously it turns the real into fantasy." He shook his head. "Training you in weapons."

"That's right. Pistols and knives—"

"Listen to yourself, for God's sake!" he exploded, jumping up. "Next you'll be telling me you really know what you're doing."

"We use real pistols."

"Oh, sure you do. Of course." He reached down between his legs, pulled out a drawer of the ebony end table. With a quick, practiced flip of his wrist he withdrew his .38 caliber service revolver from its stiff leather holster. He flung it at her without warning.

She cried out but Jean-Carlos' training surfaced and she handled the catch without a trace of clumsiness. She kept her finger off the trigger. "Are you out of your mind?" she said hotly. "This thing's loaded!"

"The safety catch's on." He said it deadpan and she knew that she had surprised him. He had expected her to drop it or shy away from it.

"We've worked on this kind of gun," she said. "I know how to use it."

"Okay." He got up, took her hand, leading her through the house and out the back door. It was warm and sticky. There was no breeze. Bonesteel pointed. "See that birch?" Daina swallowed, nodded. "It's only, oh, I'd say twenty yards away. See if you can hit the fork there at eye height." He reached out, flipped the safety off. "Go on," he urged. "Let's see you shoot."

Daina faced the birch head-on and, as Jean-Carlos had taught her, spread her legs slightly. She locked her knees and, holding the .38 with both hands, extended her arms in front of her. "For a target as large as a man," he had drilled into her, "you don't have to use the sight...just the barrel."

She squeezed the trigger and the gun exploded. It jerked upward in her hands but she stood her ground.

Bonesteel squinted ahead. "Nothing," he said. "There's no mark on the tree. Go on, go on. Try again."

Daina lowered the gun and, using the barrel to sight down, prepared herself for the recoil. She sighted again, carefully.

"Come on!" Bonesteel barked. "If someone is coming at you, you don't have time!"

She fired, heard almost immediately the whine of the ricochet. They went to the birch together and he put his thumb against the white flesh of the tree where her bullet had flayed off the bark. It was an inch and a half below and to the right of the fork.

"Not bad," he said, taking the .38 from her and walking back to the spot she had shot from. When she was at his side, he whirled, fired off the remaining four rounds without even seeming to aim. Daina did not have to go back to the birch to see the damage his shots had made right at the base of the fork.

"What a show-off you are."

"Naw," he said, flicking open the empty chamber and reloading the revolver. "Just showing you the difference." He clicked the cylinder back, put the safety on. "But I gotta admit you take it more seriously than I thought. Just don't get confused between reality and fantasy. What you were trained for was a part in a film. I was trained for the streets."

"And you've got the eye of a cop," she said, "to be able to see right down into someone like Tie."

But Bonesteel shook his head as he led her back toward his car. "That's not training; I was born with it. That's a writer's eye."

On a night when Rubens had left word he would be home late, Daina ignored everything and everyone and went right to bed as soon as she came home from the day's shoot.

She awoke in the night to an electric blue-white flash of lightning. It dazzled her and she squinted into a darkened corner of the bedroom. Thunder rolled from left to right like words on a page, singing. It seemed to echo on and on and, at its conclusion, she heard the doorbell ringing.

Pulling on a robe, she went down the hall in the unnatural silence. Thunder came again as she entered the living room. She had been dreaming of Rubens, of his flesh close to hers, his half-open lips breathing tidally against the pulse of her neck, her fingers searching for his hardness and stroking, stroking until she had put the tip of him between her moist thighs and they had both cried out at the same time.

She shivered a little with the strong sexual memory as strong as musk. She felt the lubrication forming, her nipples standing painfully erect, the material of her robe brushing their sensitive tips with every step she took. She shook her head to clear it, ran her fingers through her thick hair to bring it back off her face. She reached for the door and opened it.

A jagged fork of lightning split the sky and she shaded her eyes. From out of the darkness she heard her name being called softly.

"Yasmin?" she said. "What are you doing—"

Lightning flashed again and she saw the other woman. She wore a dark trenchcoat, which she clutched close around her throat. There seemed something wrong with her face.

"Yasmin?" Daina reached out, grazing her fingertips along her friend's left cheek. She heard a whimper of pain. "My God, what's happened to you?" She reached out without waiting for a reply, pulled the other woman inside, closing the door behind her. She heard the rain begin, pattering on the roof, against the windowpanes to the west.

With her arm around her, Daina took Yasmin down the hall and, in the living room, turned on a couchside lamp. She put her hand under Yasmin's chin, turned her face this way and that. Along the point of her left cheek, the flesh was red and swollen. Tomorrow, if she did not get an ice pack on it immediately, it would be as black as cinder.

"Come on," she said, leading Yasmin to the bar. She sat her down, fixed her a stiff Scotch on the rocks. Yasmin let it sit in front of her. She was trembling. Tears were rolling down her face.

Daina reached into the ice bucket, wrapped a handful of cubes in a thick towel. She came back to Yasmin's side, applied it carefully to the long bruise. Yasmin winced at the pressure but said nothing.

Daina made her take a couple of sips of the Scotch before she said, "Now, tell me what happened."

"I'm sorry I've bothered you," Yasmin said in a whisper. "This has nothing to do with you."

"Don't be idiotic, Yasmin. What else are friends for? Here—have another sip."

Yasmin coughed as she downed more of the Scotch and, eyes watering, waved the rest of the drink away. "I went back to George's house tonight to get the rest of my stuff. You know I still had some clothes and . . . personal items." She was crying again, turning her head away so that Daina had to follow her to keep the ice pack on the swollen flesh. "He was very drunk—very angry. I'd—I'd never seen him like that. I really . . . I thought he might've lost his mind. He screamed at me, ranted and hissed. 'I don't want you to leave, Yasmin,' he bellowed over and over again. 'I won't let you leave.' But I knew he couldn't mean it.

"I—I didn't tell you the whole truth before about why I left him. I wanted to stay, part of me really did but I was too strong for him. George is very old fashioned and he was . . . seemed to be overwhelmed by my sexuality. My aggressiveness in bed . . . frightened him."

"He hit you tonight."

"He took me . . . by force." Yasmin shivered and Daina put her arm around the other woman again, hugging her close, transmitting her warmth. "He raped me." Yasmin shook her head. "They say you can't be raped unless part of you wants to but it's just not true. I'm strong, Daina. You know I am." She sounded like a little girl now and Daina's heart broke. She kissed Yasmin's wet forehead. "But George was stronger. He possessed a kind of...I don't know, a demonic force. It was more than human. The more I...struggled, the more powerful he became. I knew...part of me thought, Well, if I lie still and stay perfectly unresponsive that might turn him off and he'll stop. But that meant"—she shivered again— "giving up on everything: myself, my womanhood, my humanity. I couldn't...I just couldn't bring myself to do that. So I fought harder and harder. It was awful, not like sex at all but like war...like death. I thought I was dying and, for just a moment, I *wanted* to die." She was sobbing in earnest now, her cheek against Daina's breasts as she rocked back and forth, back and forth. "That's what he did to me—me, who loves life more than anything! He made me want to die. Christ, Daina. Jesus Christ!"

After a time, Daina took her up, led her slowly across the expanse of the living room, down the hall. She sat Yasmin on the rumpled bed, went into the bathroom, ran the water in the tub. She poured in a soft violet scent.

When she returned to the bedroom, Yasmin was sitting where she had left her, her hands falling loosely in her lap. Daina knelt beside her, said, "Yasmin, I want to put you in the bath. Is that all right? Come on now." She reached up, began to unbutton the other woman's trenchcoat. "Come on." Yasmin turned her head sharply. Her eyes seemed wild. "Yasmin, it's only me. Come on now." She managed to get the first button open. "That's it."

One by one they were undone until Daina was able to strip away the garment very slowly and Yasmin was unfurled. Daina inhaled sharply, totally unprepared for the effect the other woman's body would have on her now. Perhaps it was the lingering effects of her erotic dream or the almost overwhelming feeling of tenderness and protectiveness she felt for her friend now. Whatever the case, she found herself tremendously, ashamedly aroused.

With quickened pulse she led Yasmin into the bathroom, set her in the tub. Yasmin lay back, her eyes closed, breathing deeply, the swelling tops of her breasts just visible above the slight suds of the violet bath beads.

Daina knelt by the side of the tub, replaced the ice pack against Yasmin's cheek.

"Daina...."

"Yes, darling."

"Would you use the soap on me?"

Daina's heart hammered in her throat and she felt a knot in her stomach. Oh God, she thought. But the fact that Yasmin needed her, that there was nothing sexual in the request....

She took up the bar of soap, began to run her palms over Yasmin's sleek limbs. She soaped shoulders, arms, legs, feet, sides, stomach. She pressed her thighs close together as if that might stop the feelings running through her. She felt her breasts swelling, the sweat breaking out along her hairline.

What is happening to me? she thought while her hands seemed to move of their own accord and between her legs she became wetter and wetter. She realized that she enjoyed being on her knees, that submissive pose, the rubbing of flesh to command, the intense feeling that Yasmin had come to her, that only she could comfort—

She froze. Yasmin's fingers had softly, gently covered hers, bringing them upward, over the other woman's fluttering belly, higher past her ribs, to the heated undersides of her heavy breasts.

For the first time Daina felt Yasmin's nipples. They were hard and soft at the same time, slightly rubbery and long, reminding her of a man's erect penis. Involuntarily, she stroked at the breasts, up from their wide base, out to the ends of the cones where she pulled at the nipples with harder and harder tugs, using only thumb and forefingers, milking them.

There was a fierce emotion rumbling through her chest and she struggled to keep the hated taste of rubber out of her mouth, the black images like sails fluttering around the periphery of her consciousness.

She knew now what was happening, knew that she wanted Yasmin with a force that was undeniable, that Yasmin had in fact come here with that in mind. And this knowledge that she was being seduced somehow heightened her pleasure, adding to the forbiddenness of what she was about to do.

She opened her eyes to see Yasmin staring at her from out

of her huge slightly almond eyes, their brown as soft as doe-skin. "Help me, Yasmin," she whispered. Her mind was whirling.

"Yes." Yasmin's wide sensual mouth curved in a tender smile. "My sweet Daina. I know what you want." She leaned forward, her lips opening like a flower against Daina's neck. "Let your robe slide off... like that. Like that. Ahhh!"

"They're beautiful, Daina." Yasmin sighed. "Have I ever told you how beautiful your breasts are?"

"No." Her voice, sharp and strangled, seemed to come from some other throat.

"Uhm, well, I should have." She twisted around so that she was on her side. "Your whole body"—her voice was like a bolt of silk, caressing—"beautiful."

With eyes stoned with lust, she watched Yasmin's hands slide up her rib cage toward the lower slopes of her breasts. Light filtered into the room in cool, pale bars, illuminating the lower half of the king-size bed with its coral satin comforter, the precise shade of intimate flesh. They lay side by side, naked.

Daina gasped as she felt Yasmin's warm hands lifting her breasts up and away, cradling them. Then the fingertips began to move, around and around the sensitive flesh, circling closer and closer to Daina's areolas. Sparks of pleasure rippled through her chest, pooled between her thighs. Her legs began to tremble and rise up but Yasmin calmly flattened them back onto the sheet. She had trouble breathing.

At last the fingertips reached the areolas, caressing them with a feathery touch. Daina groaned. Her nipples were so stiff they seemed painful. She felt Yasmin's lips against the shell of her ear. "Does it feel good?"

She nodded drunkenly.

"Then tell me, darling. Tell me."

Yasmin's head dipped into shadow, her opened lips swooping down to envelope Daina's nipples. Daina cried out and her thighs opened involuntarily. She arched her pelvis upward. "Oh, God."

"Tell me. Tell me." Those lips pulling, sucking, twisting the nipples.

"It feels—ohhh!—like heaven."

"Yes...yes!" It was an animal's cry.

Daina moved her hands down, frantically trying to rub herself, but Yasmin's fingers encircled her wrists. "No, darling. Let me do that." And she lifted up and Daina saw the hanging weight of her dusky breasts above her, lifted them into her hands. The feel of them, hot and hanging full, was like no other she could imagine. Her thumbs probed at the hard nipples until Yasmin groaned and moved downward.

Immediately, Daina's mons was enveloped in wet heat. She felt Yasmin's palms against her buttocks, the fingertips in the crack, one long nail probing....

At that instant, Yasmin's tongue stabbed out, directly into Daina's core. Daina arched up. It sounded as if there were an engine in the room, working at peak capacity. Her fingers locked in Yasmin's hair, pulling the face hard into her as she bucked up uncontrollably, crying out until she was hoarse.

After a time, her eyes opened and she pulled Yasmin's lush body over hers.

"Tell me," she whispered hoarsely, "what to do," not realizing that she had already begun, that the well, now opened, had made her so insatiable that two hours later, Yasmin was begging her to stop.

The silence of the night was broken by the jangle of the telephone. El-Kalaam, eating from a shallow bowl with the fingers of his right hand, let it ring for a long time. At length, he rose and walked to the phone. He picked up the receiver.

"Yes." His voice was calm, assured. His eyes were heavy-lidded, illuminated by the strips of light burning outside, seeping in through the gaps in the closed curtains across the front windows.

"So you received my little present." His thick lips curled into the semblance of a smile. "No, Pirate. His death is on *your* head. You did not meet our deadline. You earned the consequences of your actions." His voice went hard. "Don't tell me that and expect me to believe it! The truth? You wouldn't know the truth if it were staring you in the face....You had better do what you know you can do, Pirate. Killing is nothing to me; death is as the wind. But...then...I have no country. You stole mine and this is what I will get back! Give it to me, Pirate! You and the American president.

You can and you will. You have but six hours left. Use them wisely. After that, you will truly be helpless." He hung up the phone. "Emouleur."

The young French attaché came across the room, picking his way over sprawled bodies. El-Kalaam put his arm around him.

"Have you done what I have asked?"

Emouleur nodded. "Yes. I have spoken to the others about the justness of the Palestinian cause. About the thievery of the Israelis."

"And what have they replied?"

"It is hard to judge."

El-Kalaam put his face close to the other's. "Don't put me off, Frenchman."

"They—they cannot condone what you're doing to them."

"To them?" El-Kalaam cried. "What I'm doing to them? What about what's been done to us? To the Palestinians? Are they so blind or so stupid that they cannot see we've been driven to exercise extreme measures by the Zionists?" His voice was filled with fear and hatred. "There'll be no friends for us in the West. It has been corrupted by the Zionists. It has been turned away from the truth."

"I understand your plight," Emouleur said. "All of France understands."

"Well, we shall see. I want signed statements from you and the ambassador; the English MPs, embracing our point of view. Don't concern yourself with the wording. I'll give that to you now."

"I don't—"

"I want them right away." El-Kalaam grabbed Emouleur in a grip that made the young man cry out. "You are in charge of this." He shook the Frenchman. "This is your chance to prove your worth to the Palestinian people. You'll get no other." His eyes were fierce. "Don't fail me."

"This is not something they will agree to easily, if at all."

"Don't speak to me of difficulties," El-Kalaam hissed. "Revolutions aren't won with ease. There is personal sacrifice, pain, and self-denial. We don't read books here. We do! Are you a true revolutionary or not?" He watched Emouleur's face until the other man nodded.

"I will not fail you," the Frenchman said.

On the other side of the room, Heather and Rachel lay together.

"What did El-Kalaam mean when he said he'd found your weak spot?" Rachel said.

"He meant he thought he could break me through you."

"Through me? How?"

"If he hurt you in some way," Heather said.

"Is that true?"

Heather looked away, across the room to where Emouleur was getting himself up off the floor.

"You don't want to tell me," Rachel said. "But you must. A lie won't help me now...it won't help either of us. What will happen to us if we can't trust each other? They've taken away all the rest. We'll have nothing."

Heather gave her a small smile and a squeeze. She sighed. "I'll tell you something I never thought I would. When James saved your life and lost his own, I didn't understand it. I was angry. What have we to do with her? I thought. I only care about James; having him with me, alive.

"And when he said there's a choice to be made in every life, I didn't know what he was talking about. Now I think I do." She brushed her hair back from her eyes with her bound wrists.

"Yes," she said softly, "I believe he *can* break me through you."

"Don't let him," Rachel said in a rush. "No matter what happens, he mustn't break you or me. Didn't you tell me we had to hold out; we had to fight?"

"Yes, but—"

"No buts," Rachel said fiercely. "I mean it. My father won't accede to the demands of any terrorist group. Do you believe that he would or could destroy the entire State of Israel merely to save his daughter's life?" She shook her head.

"Then what will happen?"

Rachel looked at her. "We may die if El-Kalaam is able to carry out his threat."

"I think he will." Heather looked up at the blackness of the ceiling. "Oh, God," she whispered, "for the first time I'm contemplating my own death." She looked at Rachel. "We've got to get out of here. But I don't see how we can on our own."

"Maybe we won't have to," Rachel said. "My father will help us."

"But how? You said he'd do nothing—"

"To jeopardize the State. I said nothing about him not trying to get us out." She nodded her head. "He *will* try."

"D'you know when?"

"It must be just before the deadline. It can be at no other time. Perhaps there'll be a diversion. We must be ready."

"But how?"

Rachel put her head back, closed her eyes. "That I don't know."

Lise-Marie had provided everything within that small white cardboard box except for one important element.

"All this kind of magic—the mojo—is sexual," she had said, leaning over the counter while Manus watched unperturbed through yellow eyes. "You got t'get one square inch of silk stocking. Not nylon, mind, but silk."

"That's easy," Daina had said with murder in her heart. "There's a shop near where I live that sells them."

"No, no, chile." Lise-Marie waved away her words. "*New* stocking ain't no good a'tall. They got t'be *lived* in. *Used*, y'understan'? They got t'have the female oils inside 'em—oils that ain't your own."

Daina thought of Denise and Erica, but she had no more idea of where they lived than she did their real last names. For all she knew, they had used different first names while at the Nova. She was at last coming to realize the full nature of the duality of the life she had been leading.

So she was reluctantly obliged to go home. Her mother was the only person she knew who wore silk stockings; certainly no one she knew at school ever had.

She arrived in the early afternoon, hoping that would be the best time, that Monika would be out of the house, shopping. With no little trepidation she put the key into the lock and pushed open the front door, wanting only to creep up the carpeted stairs to her mother's room, steal into her bureau and carefully remove—

"So you've come back."

Daina jumped. With a mother's unerring intuition, Monika was sitting in the living room as if awaiting her daughter's arrival.

"Do you know how many sleepless nights you've cost me?"

Daina did not believe that she had cost her mother even an hour's insomnia. "I've been very worried about you, Daina." But, oddly, Monika seemed calmer than Daina had ever seen her.

"Where have you been?" Monika got up, came toward Daina. She was a large woman, taller than the Gabors, her figure just as lush. She had done something to her hair. It was long and lacquered, a kind of burnished silver that imperiously framed her beautiful, high-cheekboned face. "Not that I would expect you to tell me. Really I wouldn't. After all, we're all entitled to our secrets." Daina stood stock-still, listening. She had been expecting, at the moment Monika had first spoke, the start of another acrimonious screaming scene that had become the norm with them since her father had died. "I'm just concerned about you." Her eyes slid up and down her daughter's frame. "And I can see you've lost weight." She seemed to hesitate for just an instant. "Will you be staying long?"

"No."

"Well, you're welcome to stay." Monika's voice was soft. "No questions asked." She spread her arms. "I'd be lying if I said I didn't want you back home."

"I don't want to come back here. There's nothing for me."

Monika looked as if she were about to cry. She put one ringed hand up to her temple as if with each word Daina had thrust a knife deeper inside her. Her lips flickered in a smile that did not reach her eyes. "That's all right, baby. I think I can understand how you feel. You go on—" Then she was sobbing uncontrollably, her shoulders shaking.

"Mother..." Daina did not know what she felt. A heavy swirl of emotions engulfed her heart.

"Oh, damn," Monika berated herself. "I promised myself I wouldn't break in front of you." She looked up. Tears had run her mascara down her cheeks, giving her an uncharacteristic frail and vulnerable look. "It's all right if you have to go but...would you do me one favor? I'd feel easier in my own mind if you'd consent to have a checkup. Just so I know you're all right."

Daina acquiesced. A doctor's checkup seemed a small price to pay for keeping Monika quiet and smoothing over what Daina had come to think of as their last few days together.

It was in the middle of winter and Monika said that Dr.

Melville, the old family doctor, was away on vacation. "Anyway," she said breezily, "I've found someone who's much better."

I'll bet, Daina thought. In bed. Nevertheless, she went to the address in White Plains. Dr. Geist was a red-faced individual with an immaculately trimmed white mustache whose wirelike ends poked their way across his cheeks. He wore thick bifocals behind which lurked watery blue eyes. He had a habit of blowing air through his pursed lips when he was deep in thought or explaining a particular procedure to a patient. Consequently, his cheeks always seemed as round and puffy—they were, of course, already as red—as St. Nick's.

He gave Daina a thorough physical exam then asked if she would mind undergoing several more specific diagnostic tests. She said no, and he put her through them then sent her out into the waiting room, clad in that odd kind of uncomfortable smock one always gets in doctors' offices, which ties in the back and seems more trouble than it's worth.

After forty-five minutes, during which Daina, growing ever more impatient, skimmed through six-month-old issues of *Better Homes & Gardens* and *Time* without reading a word, she was summoned back into Dr. Geist's sanctum sanctorum. He was smiling genially and he stood up when she came in.

"I wonder, Miss Whitney, whether you'd accompany me over to the medical institute just across the Parkway?"

"Why?" Daina said. "Is something wrong?"

"Well," Dr. Geist said, coming around from behind his massive oak desk, "I use those people every so often when I need to run additional tests. I assure you it won't take long."

"But what's wrong with me? I feel fine."

Smiling still, the doctor put his arm around her, leading her toward the door. "Please come with me, Miss Whitney. You have no cause for worry. You're in good hands." Like all doctors, he wasn't going to tell her a thing, Daina decided, until he was ready.

White Cedars Medical Institute consisted of a rambling white five-story building that, with its row of bright stone pilasters and gables along the top floor, was trying hard not to look like a hospital. It was situated beyond an impossibly flat expanse of snow-dappled lawn, dotted here and there by large gnarled elm trees.

It all seemed perfectly fine until the doctor led her through a wire-and-glass-windowed door at the end of a long straight corridor and she heard the loud click of the lock behind her.

"What is this?" she said, turning around.

"Merely a security precaution," Dr. Geist said. "There are great quantities of contraindicated drugs here." He smiled again. "We wouldn't want them passing into the wrong hands, now would we?"

Daina was becoming annoyed at the way he spoke to her as if she were a child not yet old enough to make up her own mind about such matters, but she said nothing, allowing him to propel her forward. "Come along now," he said. "This will just take a moment. Everything's been prepared."

But now that she looked around her, she had the queasy feeling that something was amiss. This was, quite obviously, a part of the hospital that most patients did not see, no matter what the doctor had said. She saw, as they passed them by, that all the doors to the rooms were locked from the outside.

Abruptly she tried to pull away from him. "Where the hell are you taking me?"

The doctor made no sound, but with a silent signal of his free hand summoned a burly female attendant who took hold of Daina from the opposite side. Daina twisted from side to side. "Come on, dear," the female attendant said. "It's all for the best. You'll see. Trust doctor." Daina stared up into her beetling face, noting the dark line of hair on the big woman's upper lip.

Now, as they moved deeper into the hospital, Daina could make out muffled thumpings, rhythmic and somehow terrifying, from behind some of the locked doors, as if giant hearts were caged within.

At length, they stopped before a door identical to all the others. The attendant took out a key from her uniform pocket, inserted it in the lock. Beyond was a small cubicle with a bed and a dresser and one tiny window, screened by wire mesh, so high up all she could see was the dull gray of the winter sky.

"What are you going to do with me?" There was as much anger in her voice as fear.

Dr. Geist regarded her earnestly from behind his thick bifocals. He appeared distinguished and altogether assured.

"Miss Whitney," he said in his most stentorian voice, "you are seriously ill."

She felt her stomach contract but still she said, "What do you mean? I haven't even had a cold in three years."

The doctor's thin lips curled upward in what he thought of as a godlike smile. "We are not speaking of your body now, Miss Whitney, but of your mind. The mind is a strange, complex system and, most often, subjective knowledge gives off false signs. Only through truly *objective* observation can the proper diagnoses be made." Dr. Geist grabbed the base of one forefinger with the fingers of his other hand, twisting until the knuckle cracked. "You are unbalanced. To put it as bluntly as possible, you have developed a psychosis." He loomed over her, abruptly as big as a bear though she had not, before, thought of him as a large man. "This constant running away from home is an attempt on your part to deny reality."

Daina thought Dr. Geist must be out of his mind and she told him so as she tried to dodge past him to the door.

He blocked her easily and now his thick-fingered hands clamped down so painfully on her biceps that she whimpered involuntarily. "I'm terribly sorry"—now his voice sounded genuinely apologetic—"but we can hardly expect you to agree with such a diagnosis, can we? After all, you lack the proper, ah, impartiality to make the correct determination." He shook her a little as if that would get her back on the right track. "You have a deep-seated illness, Miss Whitney. You must learn to trust us. We know what's best for you." The thought seemed so amusing, it made him chuckle, a sound as thick as molasses; a sound that would haunt her long beyond her stay there.

He hugged her to him but the gesture contained no warmth, no intimacy at all, and Daina found herself wondering not for the first time what kind of special training doctors underwent in order to so cut themselves off from the rest of humanity. Were they, she wondered, so utterly, bone-chillingly cold-blooded in their private lives? Did they mount their wives with the same callous scorn? Did they pat their sons and daughters with such practiced indifference? Would any personal tragedy cause them to shed tears of grief? Daina suspected not. But she felt no pity for Dr. Geist or his family. When you lie down with swine, you're sure to get fouled. No, she felt only a burning anger like a cold flame at the center of her heart and, along with that, a wall of spite stronger than the hardest diamond. I won't give in, she vowed. No matter what, I won't give in to him.

"Now don't you worry at all," the doctor was saying in his lightest tone. "You're a very lucky girl to be in good hands. We know the quickest methods of recovery. We'll have you feeling ship-shape in no time at all, eh?"

"I feel ship-shape now," she said but all she got in return was Dr. Geist's raised forefinger waggling in her face.

"Very soon," he said, "you'll come to understand."

Daina steeled herself. "I want," she said, "to know what you're going to do with me."

"Have you ever heard of insulin shock therapy?" Dr. Geist said. His face seemed to gleam in the harsh overhead lighting. "No, I see by your face you haven't. No matter. It's better this way. You see, the process is quite simple. Massive doses of insulin are injected into the patient, producing a kind of shock coma. Now that's nothing to be frightened of. All it means is that we are, for the moment, defeating your conscious mind. So, while it, er, sleeps, we can bring your *unconscious* to the surface for there is where your problem lies." It's where *your* problems lie, Daina thought. "You, er, *tell* us what your problems are and in between treatments, group therapy resolves those problems.

"Tomorrow I shall take you down to the treatment room myself to get you, ah, acclimatized to the surroundings. Some, uh, peripheral factors may be a bit frightening initially."

"Does my mother know anything about this?"

"Miss Whitney," the doctor said slowly as if he were explaining something quite simple to a slow child, "it was your mother who came to me for advice regarding your, ah, condition."

"Condition?" Daina cried. "I don't have a condition."

"Of course." Dr. Geist smiled, sure of himself.

"You're as crazy as a loon." And when that didn't work: "I want to see her."

The smile stayed just where it was, fully as broad as he had been taught to carry it. "I'm sorry, Miss Whitney, but institution regulations forbid all visitors for a period of eighteen days. Phone calls, too, I'm afraid." He rubbed the palms of his hands together, all brisk business. "Now that we've gotten the, er, orientation out of the way, we'll let the hospital staff take over and we'll see you in the morning."

He was as good as his word. They woke her up at four A.M. and got her dressed in a fresh hospital gown. Dr. Geist was waiting rather impatiently for her as if she were late for their first date. But he smiled just the same when she appeared in the hallway just outside her door. She was accompanied by the same burly female attendant who had brought her in the day before. There were no windows in the hallway and the burnt lighting was kept at the same level twenty-four hours a day. It had a disconcerting effect.

Dr. Geist's face was freshly scrubbed, as red as if he had been out in his sleigh all night delivering packages down squeaky-clean chimneys. He smelled strongly of a cheap men's cologne she found anonymous in its abject familiarity. Again, his fingers gripped her like bands of steel.

"That will be all, Miss MacMichaels," he said curtly as Daina allowed him to lead her away. At the first branching, he took her right, then left down another corridor identical to the first. It was eerily quiet in the hospital at that hour and even the soft screek-screek of their rubber-soled shoes against the light-green linoleum was audible.

Halfway down the corridor, Dr. Geist stopped. He dug in the pocket of his tweed pants for a key and inserted it into the door before which they stood. Inside was a flight of metal steps painted dark green, leading downward. It was dank and cold and forbidding. The walls and ceiling were of unpainted concrete, unrelieved and grindingly monotonous.

By the time they had reached the second landing, Daina began to hear faint noises. They would shiver the air for long bursts during which she would turn her head to the side in an attempt to make sense of the sounds.

Dr. Geist took her down to the third level and, as they came off the staircase, the sounds returned, abruptly, shockingly in focus: people were screaming. The sounds were muffled but perfectly distinct for all that.

Daina shivered and tried to draw back but the doctor merely tightened his grip on her arm, half dragging her along by his side.

"Why are they doing that?" Daina said very softly.

"Try to ignore it," Dr. Geist said airily. "It is just a by-product of the treatment."

"You mean the insulin shock therapy?" And when he didn't reply, her stomach fluttering in fear, she said, "I don't want to scream like that."

"That, my dear Miss Whitney, is how you will speak to us," the doctor said dispassionately and she hated him all the more. "You will scream out to us all of your psychosis and once it is out in the, ah, light of day, we shall dissipate it like so much snow on a city street." She did not think much of his imagery.

He took her into a cell-like room, windowless and dim and, abruptly, she realized why the "treatment rooms" were so far beneath the normal levels of the rest of the hospital. It was the same reason that the therapy was administered at odd times: so that the screaming would not disturb the other patients.

Daina looked around the cell. There was only a zinc-topped table to which leather straps perhaps three inches in width were attached.

"These are nothing to be afraid of," the doctor said, flipping the straps up and down between his thumbs and fingers. "You must be strapped in for your own protection."

"My own protection?" she said weakly. She felt as if all the blood were draining out of her through the soles of her feet.

"Yes." The doctor turned around. "The insulin shock sets up a series of rather violent, ah, convulsions throughout the body. You might inadvertently hurt yourself if you were not restrained—"

Daina turned away and was sick in one corner of the tiny room. She remained half bent over with the paroxysms that by now were dry and accompanied by, in Daina's mind at least, the most disgusting gagging sounds, which only served to prolong her nausea.

"It is merely a sign of your body throwing off the ills that have haunted it from inside," the doctor said, not missing a beat. He ignored her actions. "Actually, it is a good sign, for in forcing your conscious mind to let go its control, we will possess the key to your cure. And day by day we shall bring it about."

Wiping her lips and breathing through her mouth because of the stink she had made, Daina looked at him. The tiny overhead incandescent bulbs made spot glares on his bifocals,

turning the lenses opaque so that he no longer looked like
St. Nick but Dr. Cyclops instead. "How..." She faltered. "How
long does the treatment take?"

"Two and a half months."

Oh, my God! she thought. I'll never make it through. And
then as he led her away from there back upstairs to her room,
Baba, where are you now? Take me away from here!

They began the next morning at four. Dr. Geist was waiting for her as before except this time he seemed calmer. Together, they trod the same path down and down and down
into the bowels of the hospital to where no one would hear
her screams, and at each landing Daina felt a little bit of her
life-force drain from her.

The night before her fitful sleep had been punctuated by
fierce dreams of what she would do when this moment came:
how she would fight back, fly her fists in the face of the burly
female attendant, take a great bite out of Dr. Geist's solid
thigh. But now that the moment had come she felt so ener-
vated that she docilely allowed them to strap her face down
on the table.

Gently, ever so gently, Dr. Geist lifted the hem of her
gown. Underneath, she wore nothing. He peered down at her
as if she were his own daughter. Bright light, reflected,
splashed off his lenses, zooming across the rough concrete
walls like a swinging car's headlights. Daina looked at the
stone floor and that is when the word dungeon exploded in
her mind like a bombshell.

Lightheaded and dizzy, she turned her head to see Dr.
Geist's right hand. It was filled with a syringe, its great
needle longer than any Daina had ever seen before.

"Will it hurt?" she said in the tone of a frightened child.
But all the while, tears of rage stood out in the corners of her
eyes and she clenched her hands into white fists. If only, she
thought, I wasn't strapped down. How she wanted to murder
Dr. Geist with all his platitudes about the goodness of medical
science and the mind-numbing expanse of his frozen smile.

"It won't hurt a bit," she heard him say as if from a thousand miles away but she didn't believe him for a minute. Not
with the buckets of blood he had undoubtedly spilled in the
cause of advancing the field. And not one tear dropping from
his unclouded eye.

She felt a cool breeze drifting across her naked buttocks

and with it came the most intense spasm of hatred she had
ever experienced. She thrashed upon the cold zinc-topped table as if she were a fish out of water. Dimly she was aware
of the doctor calling to Miss MacMichaels for assistance, but
that didn't stop her. Nothing could stop her now. No one. The
hate rocketed through her like a geyser and she imagined
her unpinioned hands wrapped around Dr. Geist's chunky
throat. She felt something pierce her flesh, sinking down and
down into her as she had come down and down into this
dungeon, and she cried out not in pain or in shock but from
the humiliation.

Her rage continued unabated, but now the face she held
so close to her own was growing dim so that she had to squint
in order to make it out. Then Dr. Geist was gone, the face
metamorphosing into that of her mother. Still her hands were
wrapped around the elegant neck, squeezing, squeezing. She
seemed to be panting, the breath coming out of her like gushes
of water spilled upon the stone floor until she was slipping
and sliding, her lips open in a soundless scream.

For some time she had her eyes closed with the force of
her hatred. Mother, she thought, how could you do this to
me? Jealous. You were always jealous of me. It was all right
when I was just a kid who you could diaper, feed and bathe.
But as soon as I grew up, I was your competition. You wanted
me to stay a child.

She opened her eyes because she wanted to see her
mother's face now, grotesquely distorted as she neared death
by suffocation. But it was not her mother's face she saw before
her but another's, shadowy and somehow terrifying. Daina
screamed and screamed until she had no breath left inside
her. Then for a time she floated in nothingness, insensate.

When she awoke, they fed her a thick lemony syrup that
tasted as if it were made of pure sugar. Still, all that sweetness could not take the strong taste of rubber out of her
mouth. The next day, lying in her room and staring at the
ceiling, she would remember the T-bar of black rubber she
had seen lying on the floor as they took her out of the "dungeon," her teethmarks scalloping its sides so deeply she
thought she must have bitten right through it during her
first treatment.

Upstairs, in her room, when she had recovered, they
brought her in breakfast. She had never been so ravenous in

her life but when she saw the size of the plates and their number she thought, No human being can eat this much food at one time. She ate it all.

And so it went, day after day: the treatment followed by the jolt of glucose and the prodigious meals. Dr. Geist came to see her every day. He talked to her endlessly. She did not listen to what he said. Her mind felt swollen like a balloon, filled with an odd mixture of thoughts and ideas as if she were some creature adapting to a wholly new atmosphere on some distant alien world. At those times, Dr. Geist seemed as unreal as a ride to the far side of the sun. She began to think of him as some form of grotesque day lily who bloomed anew with each light cycle only to wither and die with the coming of darkness. And she treated him with the same indifference she would a plant or, perhaps, a television that has been left on at low volume for companionship and nothing more.

At night, she would lie awake with the hatred of Monika and Aurelio Ocasio raging like a forest fire in her breast and it was that bleak and desolate hatred she clutched close to her when the terror of being incarcerated at White Cedars or the daily trip to the dungeon threatened to overwhelm her. Dr. Geist could have the part reserved for Monika—he had it anyway; it was a major topic of his daily talks with her. But her fear of his learning of her secret life with Baba and her secret hate of Aurelio Ocasio seemed unfounded as the days progressed and he made no mention of either of them. This was hers and hers alone: the love for Baba, the hate for his killer. She had been right. No one—nothing—could sever her from them. And, later, when she could bear to think about this time, she would be certain that her secrets were all that stood between her and madness—a real, pure form that she felt sure Dr. Geist would never recognize let alone know how to treat.

After a while, they started her on group therapy as part of her daily routine. The other members were all patients undergoing the same treatment.

At one of these, one of the patients, a heavyset man who had been there far longer than she, gave her one bit of hurried advice. "Eat everything they give you," he whispered.

She did not understand what he meant until one evening perhaps three weeks into her stay. Already she noticed the weight piling up on her. When the attendant brought in her dinner tray, she found that she had no appetite. She had visions of herself horribly fat, waddling into a room where everyone stopped what they were doing to stare at her. When the attendant insisted that she eat, she refused.

He departed only to return moments later with another attendant and a doctor she had not seen before. This one was long and lean with sandy hair and a bristling beard. His upper lip was curiously hairless.

The attendants had wheeled in a stainless-steel cart covered with medical paraphernalia. At the doctor's instruction, they strapped her into the bed. From the cart, they uncoiled a long evil-looking rubber hose.

Terrified, she began to scream as they tried to insert the hose into one nostril. She whipped her head back and forth until one of the attendants gripped her jaw so powerfully it brought tears to her eyes. She felt as if her jaw were dislocated. Immediately the other attendant inserted the hose. She coughed and gagged as the horrid thing went down her throat. The attendant who held her leaned close to her. She could see a pimple on his cheek, red and inflamed. "If you don't lie still," he hissed, "you'll never be able to stand it." He smiled, not unkindly. "We're going to do it anyway, so it's your choice." She lay back, trembling with tension and fear, her sweat rolling down her brow, tasting salty as it trickled through her lips, and they fed her through the hose. After that, she never refused to eat anything they gave her.

She did refuse to see Monika, though. Eighteen days after she had begun the insulin shock therapy, Dr. Geist came to her to tell her that her mother would be allowed to see her. "But only if you wish it," he said. She didn't and so she remained alone.

Not every day but often, she would have the visions of strangulation that had come to her during the early moments of her first treatment. Always they would be the same, beginning with Dr. Geist as her adversary—"That is quite natural," he said to her, nodding, when she had told him of it— then Monika, metamorphosing into that shadowy face that seemed so familiar yet so devastatingly terrifying. "You feel the moorings of your conscious mind coming loose," the doctor told her. "And underneath, before it succumbs totally and you pass out, you get glimpses of what lies in those depths."

On a morning after she dreamt of Dr. Geist dancing a jig by the light of an awful, swollen moon, the ends of his luminous white coat flapping about his thighs, she came face to face with the identity of her last—and "primary," according to the doctor—antagonist. It was her father. Her dead father for whom she felt only love. And here she was strangling him and screaming over and over, "Don't leave me, please don't leave me," and then: "I hate you for leaving me!"

Two and a half months after the beginning of her incarceration at White Cedars, Dr. Geist came into her room with a pile of clothes.

"It's time for you to leave, Daina. You're cured."

Cured of what? she thought. She put the flat of her hand on the pile. "These are not mine."

"They are now. We've bought them for you," Dr. Geist said gently. "You wouldn't fit into your old ones."

And indeed when she finished dressing and looked at herself in the mirror, she did not recognize either the face or the body reflected there. While she was unconscious it seemed as if some fat woman had come in to live. She was sickened by the sight.

On the doorstep of White Cedars, Dr. Geist stopped her. His hand was light on her arm. "Don't you want to know why your mother isn't here to pick you up?"

"No," Daina said, "I don't. We don't care much about each other."

"She cared enough to have you brought here," the doctor pointed out.

Daina almost laughed in his face. "She wanted me made over. In her own image."

"That's a sin," Dr. Geist said with a faraway look in his eyes, "many parents are guilty of."

She glared at him. Behind her she could hear the traffic hiss; a dog barking, children laughing. Those sounds were calling to her now. "They don't all go to such lengths."

"She only wanted what was best for you." His voice seemed abruptly heavy on the cold air. She had gone in in the dead of winter. Now it was nearly spring and the trees were beginning to bud, the first birds to make their summer nests.

"Wanted?"

"Daina, your mother's been in the hospital. She's been ill for about six weeks."

Daina looked away from him, away from White Cedars toward the red-tile face of the mall on the far side of the Parkway. For a moment, she watched the line of suburban mothers pulling into the lot with their Chevy, Buick or Olds station wagons, their hair still in curlers under multicolored scarves. She wondered what their lives were like. Were they as simple as she believed them to be? Were they happy when their husbands came home? When their children laughed? Were they frustrated when the garbage disposal broke down; unhappy when the PTA passed them by for vice-president? Or was there more...somewhere, hiding out, unseen and unearthed?

"Will she die?"

"Yes," Dr. Geist said softly. "Very soon now."

Beryl gave her the advance copy of *Playboy* on the set at the end of the day just as soon as they had wrapped and Daina brought it straight home to show Rubens.

Right in the center of the "Coming Attractions" section on films was the following paragraph: "**AND THE WINNER IS....** Although some of you might think it's a bit early to get into the Academy Award prediction game, I've heard some pretty remarkable things about **Daina Whitney**'s title role in the forthcoming *Heather Duell.* It's no secret that most of us have been waiting for another female part to compete with the likes of those played by Sally Field in *Norma Rae* and Jane Fonda in *Klute* and *Coming Home.* From all reports— and I'm inclined to believe these informed sources—the Heather Duell role could well put Whitney in contention for the Best Actress award. Flick is about the trial by fire of the wife of a wealthy industrialist caught in a house held by terrorists. Whitney, as you're no doubt aware, came to international prominence via Jeffrey Lesser's firework film of the future, *Regina Red.* If you haven't seen her in that, you don't know what you're missing."

She read this piece out loud to Rubens with no little relish. "Look," she said, turning the magazine back against her body. "They've even got a still from the film. How'd you manage that?"

"Beryl called Buzz Biellmann," he said and laughed. "I told you she was a genius." He came toward her. "Hey, the phone hasn't stopped ringing all day at the office and I know it's not gonna stop here. How'd you like to go out to the boat for a while?"

The sky was plum and indigo by the time they climbed on deck. Lights along the sweeping curve of Malibu shone in a glittering chorus line within the somnolent shallows. Daina thought of Yasmin and their afternoon here and shivered a little. The inside of her mouth seemed heavy and swollen with the other woman's musky taste. The thought that had been swimming the dark waters of her mind ever since she had allowed Yasmin to seduce her began to surface. If only she could connect it up. She thought of Chris, poor unhappy Chris. He had called her from, where was it? Denver? Dallas? She could not recall now. It doesn't really matter, she thought. The kids are the same wherever they go—the halls, the lights, the massive equipment. And the applause, the ringing applause building and building as the fans streamed down the already choked aisles with their hands upraised, forefingers pointing into the blackness of the night: Number One, Number One, Number One.

My God, but Chris had sounded terrible when he had called. As if he had been strung out. He didn't appreciate those grueling nights as Nigel did. He fed off his work in the studio not off his fans. There was some odd, twisted...all right, yes, vampiric relationship between those musicians and their fans. She had read an interview once, she couldn't remember where but some smart guy, some rock musician said, Okay, let's call a spade a spade. The relationship's vampiric. At the time, she had thought that so much copy. Those guys were famous for putting on interviewers who took the whole thing so seriously. Daina had read the cover story in *Rolling Stone* that had come from the interview of the band in San Francisco. They had run, as a heavily bordered inset, the photo taken with her and Nile and the group and the accompanying paragraphs were mainly about her. Deadlines had caused the obit on Nile to appear in the following issue.

Anyway, Chris had come off as very restrained while Nigel talked and talked. How could he stand it? The entire responsibility for the band's creative output was squarely on Chris' shoulders though, publicly at least, he and Nigel still collaborated on every song. Daina suspected that even for Chris there was a breaking point. Friendship could only take you so far. Well, they'd be back in L.A. in a couple of weeks. She resolved to talk to Chris again then, face to face.

She felt arms slip around her, Rubens' heat behind her. His budding hardness insinuated itself between the lobes of her buttocks. His hands came up to cup her breasts. She felt a warmth seep through her body that was only partially sexual, for it encompassed a great deal more.

"What are you thinking?"

"About how happy I am."

It wasn't a lie, she told herself but then again it wasn't the exact truth either. She had been thinking of Meyer, of what he had said to her—the pact they had made. She wanted now very much to protect Rubens, though she could not imagine from what. The old man worries a lot, she thought. I could see it in his eyes. Well, who could blame him? He's been through so much. And survived. That's the important part. Isn't that what Marion had told her so long ago about Hollywood? That the really important thing was to survive here. Because so many people came out here and didn't.

That's all it is, Daina thought now, as she watched the faraway lights of Santa Monica, haloed through the haze, as if they bobbed on the brink of heaven, he's getting old and he worries. Rubens is fine. I know it. I can feel it. There's no problem.

"You remember what I said back at the house about Beryl?" he whispered in her ear, holding her tight.

"That she's a genius?" She loved the feel of his hands on her breasts. It made her want to close her eyes and drift off, safe and secure.

"You're a genius, too," he said. "I've got to give Dory some credit." He laughed. "He's a good judge of character."

"*My* character."

"Yours, yes." He turned her around in his arms so that they faced each other. His cheeks were lit eerily by the red and green of the boat's running lights, one side darker than the other. It made him seem like two different people. "Daina, I've never loved anyone the way I love you."

Her eyes seemed to expand in the semidarkness and she made a tiny sound in the back of her throat halfway between a groan and a sigh. Her fingers caressed his neck, the tops of his ears, firmly pulling his head down to hers.

Their lips met with such exquisite suddenness that she

felt a galvanic shock race through her body almost as if she had stepped on a live wire.

"How you worked Buzz over," he said thickly, pulling his lips away from hers. "I'd never seen him react like that, especially with a woman. He's got no respect for anyone."

"You know," she said softly, watching her own reflection bobbing in his eyes, "I really enjoyed it. He was acting like such a pig. We spend all our lives in the power of men like that."

"You're not making something political of it, are you?"

"Political? No. There's nothing political about what happened between Buzz and me. It was sexual."

"Like this," he said, circling the center of his palm around her nipple.

"Like this," she said, kissing his neck with her open lips and darting tongue.

"Like this," he said, picking up the hem of her dress to slide his fingers along the long sleek length of her thigh.

"Like this," she said, cupping her hand over his balls and pressing gently against the intense heat until she felt the answering tremors racing through his thighs.

"Let's go below," he said thickly, "and put on our suits."

"What for?" she said, laughing. "Who's around to see us?"

He slapped her backside playfully. "Just do as you're told for once, okay?"

She kissed the tip of her forefinger, pressed it against his lips set in a mock-severe expression. They went down the companionway. Her suit, a plum-colored maillot, lay waiting for her, folded on one of the berths. By its side was a thick towel. She picked up the suit and something long and glittery fell out, slinking to the deck.

"My God!" she breathed, going down on her knees. She scooped it up, held it in front of her. It ran across the ends of her fingers like a river of light. It was a diamond bracelet. She turned her head up. "My God, Rubens."

He knelt down beside her. It was a time when, normally, he would have made jokes. That kind of deep sentiment was difficult for him to express or even face. But this time, he was serious. Gently, he lifted the bracelet off her hands. "I found it in Harry Winston's," he said. "It was one of those things. I saw it and knew it was for you." He looked into her violet eyes. "Which wrist?"

"The left one," she said and closed her eyes, kissing him. She trembled a little when she felt the weight of the bracelet encircling her. The click of the clasp as he pushed it home seemed as loud to her as a crack of thunder on an otherwise still night. Her arms came around him and she licked his face.

"Let's go into the water," she whispered. But her thighs had turned to liquid and he had to scoop her up, as easily as she had scooped the necklace off the deck, carrying her top-side.

On deck, he stripped off his clothes and then setting her atop the sheer-strake, began to undress her slowly and care-fully, taking his time, folding each garment as he stripped it off her flesh. She shone dark and full in the inconstant illumination of the boat's running lights and those burning feebly along the shoreline. There was a mist rising from the sea so that it appeared to Daina as if it were some primeval medium into which she dropped.

Together, they bobbed in the soft wavelets, washed and chilled, their skin raised in goosebumps. But soon, they ac-climated and they felt cold only on their faces, which were out of the water.

They treaded water lightly, looking only at each other. From out of the corner of her eye, Daina could see, now and again, the bright dazzle as a turn of her wrist shot reflected sparks against the dark skin of the sea, the white side of the boat. They played with each other for the longest time, touch-ing and stroking and kissing, and when he entered her he did so almost effortlessly so that only his heat told her it was at last him and not another tendril of the Pacific lapping at her core.

The coolness on the outside, the growing heat on the inside was a delicious contrast of sensations—as if she was being exhilarated and comforted at the same time.

He crushed her breasts to his lips with a fierce intensity so that his sucking pulled at nerve strings all the way down to her toes and she gripped his buttocks, pushing him up inside her until there was nowhere left to go.

She wanted desperately for this to last, for it never to end but the sensations were overrunning her and she was losing all control to the point where she held on to him as if he were the boat itself, biting his shoulder and feeling—ohhh!—that it was not enough to cry out incoherently as she approached an orgasm that went beyond all others, that there were words she wanted to tell him, about Meyer, about Aurelio Ocasio and, yes, this too, about Baba. She wished now in her ecstasy to deliver up to him those dark corners of herself she held most sacred, those secrets that she had buried in the center of her heart for all these years and would consider telling no human being but that she now wanted to share with him. Him!

But she did no such thing, merely cried out loud and long, delivering herself up totally to the pleasure sweeping through her. His lips brushed her arms, along her collarbones, that soft indentation at the base of her throat and, at last, his cheek lay along her throat as she transmitted the beat of her pulse to him in an endless message.

"That was so nice," he whispered and had to stop to get the water out of his mouth. "With you wearing nothing but diamonds like you were a part of the sky banded with stars."

The poetry of his words startled her—if only Biellmann or Michael Crawford could see him now; would they even recognize him as the same man? She thought not—and she stroked the back of his head wishing she had nails to scratch him lightly. But they were so short and so perfectly rounded they were no good for that at all. Just pulling triggers and gripping the rough hilt of a knife. She thought of the *Playboy* piece and Heather Duell's trial by fire. *My* trial by fire. Yes, mine. And perhaps, too, an Academy Award.

Reluctantly, they came out of the water, shivering, racing for their towels, and dried each other off. They drew on jeans and cotton T-shirts they always kept stowed in the boat and, on a whim, Rubens pulled up anchor. He fired the engines and, with his arm around her waist, took them out to sea far enough for the fog to devour them completely.

After a time, he shut the engine off and they drifted in silence. There was no wind, no stars, only the sea to let them know they were still within the real world.

Rubens went below while she dropped the anchor and by the time she had followed him down, he had turned the table into a double bed. Lilac-pattern sheets faced her. She undressed and climbed in beside him.

"Got a film loaded," he said in a soft, furred voice, his arm beneath her neck.

"Sleepy." She snuggled her cheek against his warmth.

"One of your favorites." He reached up with his free hand, flicked a remote and the TV screen bloomed to electronic life. "Don't you want to know which one?"

"Uhmm." She kissed his chest, her eyes closed. "Which?"

"Notorious."

She came awake, watching the film on and off. She dozed for moments, woke, dozed again but was so familiar with the dialogue that it did not matter. She dreamed the parts she missed.

Just after midnight—she knew by the soft chiming of the brass ship's clock—Cary Grant began to carry the poisoned Ingrid Bergman down the long sweeping staircase in tight, breathless close-up under the baleful but impotent gaze of Claude Rains and Leopoldine Konstantin, the actress who played Rains' mother so superbly in the film.

The phone buzzed. Rubens turned down the sound, answered on the second ring. While the silent images flickered from Grant to Bergman to Rains and the furious Konstantin, Rubens spoke into the mouthpiece. These people are icons, Daina thought, their images as immortally graven as those on Mount Rushmore.

"Yes," Rubens said. "I see."

The phone, she thought, still half asleep, part of the fantasy unraveling on the nineteen-inch screen. I thought Rubens came on the boat to get away from the phone. Hadn't he said that to her earlier? Isn't that why they had come out to the boat in the first place? She couldn't be sure. Of course he had had her present waiting for her here. Her present. Her fingers slid over the cool, faceted surface. There was nothing in all the world that felt the same as diamonds.

"No, no," she heard Rubens say. "You did the right thing calling me. Daina and I were still up. But, Christ, it's the middle of the night for you. Get some sleep now, Schuyler. I appreciate you letting me know." He hung up.

The film was over. The screen was blank. Rubens reached over, turned off the video cassette player. He turned off all the lights. They rocked in darkness.

"I didn't even know the boat had a phone," Daina said.

"It's just for emergencies, really."

She lifted herself on her elbow. "Is Schuyler all right?"

"Oh, yeah. Don't worry about him." It was difficult to see

him. The roll and pitch of the boat at anchor caused patches of pale light coming through the porthole to play across his cheek. They did not quite reach the darkness of his eyes. "You know Schuyler. He gets easily shaken sometimes."

"Rubens," she said slowly, an uneasy premonition snaking through her, "what's Schuyler got to be shaken about?" She put a hand on his chest.

"Police called him in to identify a body," Rubens said without a trace of emotion in his voice. He was back to the way the outside world saw him.

"Who was it?"

"Found him in the trunk of his own Caddy," he continued, ignoring her question. "Some kid spotted the car out in the sticks... across the river in New Jersey, down a landfill where they dump all that shit so they can build more of those cheap tract houses that go for eighty, ninety thousand now."

"Rubens, who did they find?"

"Kid woulda thought nothing about it, apparently, but his dog wouldn't get away from it, kept barking and scratching at the back end." He seemed to be relishing the telling and she knew now that he would not tell her who died until he was ready. "Kid came after his dog and that's when he saw the trunk wasn't fully closed. You know kids're as curious as women and he couldn't help himself. He looked in and up-chucked all over his Adidas."

Daina shivered despite her anger. "Rubens, for Christ's sake, who was in there?" She pressed the heel of her hand down hard against his rib cage as if this show of physical force might move him to tell her when words would not.

"Ashley," Rubens said slowly. "It was Ashley curled up in there with a bullet hole in the back of his head and almost no blood at all. It was very professional, the cops told Schuyler. Pinky-ring style."

She knew what he meant. In the darkness, she opened her mouth to say something, closed it immediately. Abruptly, Meyer's seamed face floated before her and she heard his words again as if he were there with her in the cabin of the rocking boat: *You must save Rubens from himself. He has learned too well.* She saw his grave eyes but remembered the gold-tipped smile. It was the smile of a man who gets what he wants and now as Daina stared down at the half-hidden countenance of Rubens, she saw that same smile though it was only gold-tipped in her mind.

"Didn't you tell me that Ashley had made a lot of new friends?" she said slowly, pushing the tip of her nose to one side in the universal, silent sign for the mob.

"Yes."

She kept her eyes on his face. "But they didn't kill him, did they?" They watched each other. Daina was remembering something else from her meeting with Meyer. *I'd love him no matter what,* she had said. And Meyer, watching her as Rubens watched her now, had said, *I hope you have the strength to stand by that always.* With her eyes she willed him not to lie, knowing that if he did, she might never trust him again.

"No," he said, after a time. "They didn't kill him."

"He found what you meant him to find."

"He was a greedy little bastard," Rubens said coldly.

"He was also a friend of yours... a long-time friend."

"Friends have a peculiar way of disappearing when you've got a lot of money. You'll see what I mean soon enough."

"Does Schuyler know what you've done?"

"He helped me set up the scam."

"But you sent *him* to New York."

Rubens pursed his lips. "The cops think Ashley was beat by the mob. So does Schuyler. Everyone does." His eyes were very intense. "So do you."

"Don't you feel anything... anything at all for Ashley?"

"I feel that he got what he deserved. I gave him a chance to call it quits and get out clean without making a fuss but he just wouldn't listen. He was too greedy and he thought he could beat me."

"No one can beat you, Rubens, is that it?"

"No one can beat me," he whispered. His arms reached up for her, pulling her down against him, skin against skin. "And now no one can beat you, either." She felt a heat rising inside her she could not resist.

PART FOUR

ICON

*'In that direction,' the
Cat said, waving its right
paw round, 'lives a Hatter:
and in that direction,' waving
the other paw, 'lives a March
Hare. Visit either you like:
they're both mad.'*

—Lewis Carroll, *Alice's
Adventures in Wonderland*

10

Daina did not, in fact, go back to the film until work had been completed on her trailer. This did not make her happy and, of course, Marion pulled his hair at the three-day delay it cost them. The whole job might have been accomplished in one, had not the electricians somehow gotten the wrong instructions and installed neon tube lighting in alternating strips of flushed pink and canary yellow. Consequently, the whole thing had to be ripped out of the trailer's ceiling so that they could start over from scratch.

Daina spent most of the time shopping. The first day it was a disaster. She was so mobbed in Maxfield Bleu on Santa Monica and Doheny that she was forced to flee to the relative safety of her Merc. After that, she took Rubens' advice. He hired a bodyguard for her—a dour man with Slavic cheekbones, short salt-and-pepper hair, thin lips, and absolutely no sense of humor. But he was exceptionally broad-shouldered and quick-reflexed, qualities that stood him in good stead when he had to rid Giorgio's of a young, well-dressed man hanging surreptitiously about.

She had gone into a dressing room to try on a pale green

dress with a flower print along its hem, when the door was snapped open.

"Oh, I'm terribly sorry," the man said. "I thought my lady friend was in here."

Daina heard the click-click-click of the 35mm camera going off just before he shut the door and, leaning out after him, called, "Alex!" She pointed to the man hurrying through the store and, pulling on her clothes, ran after him.

By the time she got to him, Alex had the man by the back of the neck.

"You can't do this to me! I demand an explanation! My civil rights are being infringed!"

Daina reached beneath his sports jacket and wrenched the Nikon out of his grasp. "What do you call this?" she said angrily. "An infringement of *my* civil rights! Can't I try on a dress in peace?" She unhinged the back of the camera.

"Hey!" the man cried, sticking his hand out, but Alex slapped it away, saying, "Now behave yourself," deep in his throat.

Daina exposed the roll of film, handed both it and the camera back to the man. "Next time," she said, "Alex will step on the Nikon."

"Christ," the man said, retreating, "I'm only trying to do a job."

From Giorgio's—where she ended up buying the pale green dress and several others—she had Alex take her to Theodore's on Rodeo, Alan Austin's on Brighton Way and, for the eight pairs of shoes she had been dying to buy, the Right Bank on Camden Drive.

After lunch, she hit Numan's of Beverly Hills, where she bought a wide leather belt of the deepest plum and kept a sharp eye out for Bonesteel's wife. It was only when she left that she remembered the other woman must still be away in Europe.

In Neiman-Marcus, she ran into George who was buying a present for his parents' anniversary. He was more febrile than he had been the night she had come across him at the Warehouse but, even more, he seemed to have changed in some basic way so that she felt as if she were seeing him for the first time.

"Well, well, well. Miss Whitney...and entourage. Can the paparazzi be far behind?" He primped at his hair while looking in a mirror set on one of the counters. "How wonderful it must be to be a star." But his voice told her he did not think it was wonderful at all; there was both envy and an odd kind of contempt.

He bowed. "I understand it is you whom we have to thank for this brief respite in our daily toil."

"Cut the crap, George," she said. "When are you going to grow up?"

"I think," he said meditatively, "I have done so during the filming of this project." He seemed quite serious now. "Or perhaps it's that I've finally come to my senses."

"What senses?" she grated. "When you beat Yasmin I wiped you off my list." She put her face close to his and there was so much anger in her that Alex began to move toward them, fearing perhaps that she would need protection either from George or from herself. "What you did was reprehensible. You're just a baby looking for a mommy to take care of it. You want someone to take you by the hand and feed you and pick out your clothes and take you away on trips and tuck you in at night and tell you everything's all right. Why d'you think you go home all the time. Isn't that what you said? Wander around, looking for something. Well, that's what you're looking for, George." Her eyes flashed and Alex was very close to them now, keeping the crush of people away.

"Well, I've got a flash for you. Everything *isn't* all right and, if you'd ever get your fish-faced mouth out of the Chivas Regal, you might realize you're the only one who can help yourself." They were almost nose to nose now and Daina tried to catch a whiff of Scotch on his breath; there was none. "Christ, you're a weak man, George. Otherwise you never would've hit Yasmin."

"She provoked me, goddamnit! She never should've—"

"To *hit* her? She provoked you to hit her?" she said incredulously. "Jesus, George, you'll have to do a lot better than that."

"I don't have to explain anything to you!" he exploded. "Not after what you did to me. I should have my name above yours. You know I should!" His voice had turned petulant.

"This film's about Heather," she said. "All you're doing is pulling a power play. You gambled and lost. Why don't you take it like a man?"

"It's my right," he said defiantly. "I'm a star of this movie, too."

But Daina shook her head. "You've got to earn the right, George. You're too goddamned wrapped up in who you are: your blond knights on their chargers and your delusions of terrorism. I'd watch that if I were you."

"Careful," he warned, his face darkening. "I know just what I'm doing. You don't know how dangerous I can be. I've been gathering new friends, giving money to—" He stopped abruptly as if he had realized he had said too much.

"Giving money to whom?"

"No one," he said, dismissing her words. "Forget it."

"Oh, yeah, sure." She gave it just the right amount of derision. "Another one of your daydreams." She had found the key to him now.

He laughed, certain he was back in control. He would tell her now, she knew, at what he thought was his leisure. "Shows how much you really don't know, Daina. Oh, yeah. I gota lotta surprises up my sleeve yet." His eyes narrowed and all hint of mirth left his face. "I know you think I'm just another dumb actor, hung up on his own face and method, and that was true, once. But not now." She knew he was in deadly earnest. Whether it was the truth or not, *he* believed what he was telling her.

"Film's *your* world. You're hermetically sealed and you'll never come out now until the time someone younger, prettier, more talented, hits the lights with enough impact to fling you aside. Then you'll wake up and see the real world all around you. But by that time, it'll be too late. It'll all have passed you by and you'll be nothing but a relic, a bag of bones thrown up on some foreign shore. But me"—he tapped his chest with the tip of his forefinger—"I already know there's more to it than you and Marion and *Heather Duell*.

"But it's the right track, you see. It merely takes the wrong point of view. Actually, El-Kalaam is the hero of this film. Or, more accurately, he *should* be. He's not. But"—he shrugged—"who cares? It's only a motion picture." He lifted his finger into the air. "But in real life...that's where it counts. That's where *I'm* working."

He seemed to be swinging back and forth between dangerous moods and she felt chilled to her bones. "What d'you mean, George?"

He smiled at her as if he had led her all this time to a trap and now was preparing to spring it. "I've begun to give money to the PLO."

"Are you out of your mind?"

"On the contrary." His smile broadened. "I've come to my senses, as I said. This is the perspective the film has given me. I was right when I told you that El-Kalaam and I are one." His hand balled into a raised fist. "I feel it now. I've got some purpose, somewhere to go."

"George, I think you're confusing fantasy and reality. Your role has nothing to do with real life."

"Oh, no. That's where you're wrong...just as Marion was wrong when he said he told me to funnel all of this zealousness into the film. The film was only important in opening my eyes to the truth. Acting's for pimps and whores." He gave her a lopsided grin and she saw that he had neglected to remove the gold caps that were part of his El-Kalaam makeup. She felt that chill come again. "To you the struggle for freedom is merely an abstract concept you read about in a book. You stir your coffee, pick up the paper, get into the fashion section. What's it to you, all the blood and guns?"

"The same as it is for you, George."

"Oh, no. You're wrong about that. Just the way you're wrong about all of this." He spread his arms out wide so that shoppers backed away, hurrying by, heads turned over their shoulders. "I know that the blood and the guns're for real. *They're* reality; not all of this shit."

Daina stared at him, felt a small shiver go through her. She became aware of Alex's hand on her arm.

"I think we'd better get you out of here, Madam," he said in her ear.

But it was not George who frightened her. It was Rubens. Or rather her love for him. How could she love a man who had given orders to kill another human being in cold blood? Rubens would reason that it was Ashley himself who had necessitated the action. And Meyer? What would he say?

Staring out the limo's dark-tinted windows at rushing L.A., Daina was certain she knew. Once, long ago, he would have concurred with Rubens' decision, had, perhaps, even given the same reasoning for an action of his own. But now, she knew, he would have found another way to handle the situation.

Perhaps, she thought, Meyer even knew about Ashley's impending murder. That could be why he chose that moment to speak to her. Her heart grew cold at the thought of it. Had he given her a chance to dissuade Rubens? Had she been so wrapped up in herself that she had missed the clues? Desperately she thought back but could come to no conclusive answer. She just didn't know and that, perhaps, was even worse.

Only you can save him. Isn't that what Meyer had told her? *Only you.* She could not let it happen again.

Rubens had done what he had done yet she loved him still. Was that wrong? Was it evil? She knew she had to melt his heart and, in the process, make certain hers was not turned to black glass.

Instead of going home she had the limo take her out to Chris' house. The band had returned from the wars, as Chris called it: six long grueling weeks on the road. The tour had been enormously successful: standing-room-only crowds wherever they performed, riots, tons of press coverage and, in New York where they were scheduled to play a week at Madison Square Garden, demand had forced them to add on three extra nights.

Daina had used the limo's phone to call the Heartbeats' office. Vanetta, their black English coordinator, had told her Chris was home.

"You mean the house in Malibu?" Daina had asked, feeling relieved that he was out of Nigel and Tie's place.

"Well," Vanetta said, "a house in Malibu, anyway. He had me arrange something with a realtor here. It's about a mile and a half past the old place." She gave Daina the address. "We had enough time to get everything set while the band was gone. Got its own studio in back and all."

It was a mulberry and gray beach house that seemed neither larger nor smaller than the one he had shared with Maggie. It had a wooden deck that ran out onto the beach. It was painted gray and smelled from Bain de Soleil and, somewhat more faintly, from new paint and tar.

She waited a long time after pressing the bell before the door opened and, at one point, she was about to turn away, having decided that Vanetta had made a mistake or, in the interim, he had left. But then she saw his Rolls on the far side of the house and she leaned on the bell again. Far down the beach Linda Ronstadt warbled languidly over the hoarse suck and hiss of the surf.

The door opened and she saw him framed in the dark doorway, still and lean. He wore a T-shirt with the sleeves cut off and a pair of black jeans. His hair was longer and more tangled than when she had last seen him in San Francisco and there were dark circles under his eyes, the badge of war. Music rolled out from inside, unfamiliar and intriguing.

He exploded when he saw her. "Dain!" He reached out, caught her up in his arms and they hugged each other.

She kissed him on the cheek, ruffled his hair. "I see you made it through in one piece."

"Oh, Christ, just about... an' no thanks t' Nigel. Th' bleedin' sod wanted t' go straight on t' Europe without a break. I finally talked him outta that one." He grinned. "But, hey, come on in. I'm glad you're here. Somethin' I wanna play for you."

They went through the spacious living room. The walls were painted a pale blue and the floor was covered with a deep-pile wall-to-wall carpet in dove gray. The furniture was upholstered in comfortable nubbly cotton over lacquered rattan. It was cool and relaxed and there was even a tall potted palm in one corner.

Daina caught a hint of a perfume that seemed vaguely familiar but which she could not place. It was not in the hall into which he led her. Color prints of the band performing dotted the walls. They passed by three bedrooms, one of which—the largest one—had obviously been slept in. It had a low-lying custom-made platform bed that could not be less than king-size. She glimpsed a black lacquer dresser and the half-open door to a bathroom before they were past.

They went down a short flight of polished wooden steps to the back of the house into the studio. It consisted of a tiny control booth separated from the studio itself by a double-paneled glass window and a soundproof door.

Chris was like a kid in a candy store to which he had been given the key. He sat down in the high-backed black leather chair before the console and stabbed at some square buttons. Pink and green lights lit up behind their frosted faces and the great tape machine behind him began its rewind whir. Jumbled noises, highly speeded up, then silence. Just a soft, almost inaudible hiss, coming through the mammoth speakers mounted high up on the wall.

Out of the silence, Chris whispered, "Listen to this." He stabbed at a button.

There came a blast of massed guitars, a phalanx of sound, blurred at first by the assault of its initial volume. But gradually the bare bones of melody emerged through the chord changes and the dominance of a lead guitar line, as slender and delicate as a filament.

Chris hummed along, singing out snatches of words here and there and, at one point, an exuberant burst of chorus that repeated what she took to be the song's title line: "The word for world is rock'n'roll."

Initially she was shocked. The music was definable as the Heartbeats' but only in the most tangential sense. The band's music had always had about it—at least after Jon died and with him his musical collaborations with Chris—a raw, streetfighter's edge to it, even on ballads that were as close as the band would ever come to being refined. But they were never that. Nigel, Daina suspected, would never have stood for it.

This music was different. The harmonics were the Heartbeats'—which meant to Daina, Chris'—but there was a sophistication that the band itself would never have been able to tolerate.

The music was over and the silence had returned. Chris sat with his head in his hands, almost trancelike, the overhead pinspots picking up red highlights in his hair. She could see nothing of his face.

"It's beautiful, Chris," she said.

"Yeah, but will it sell?"

Daina looked hard at him. She felt a difference; she still saw the resistance inside him but, mixed with that now, she recognized his burning desire to create. She was still not certain of all the factors holding him back but, abruptly, she recognized this moment as a crucial one in both their lives. I am, after all, his friend, she thought. I've got to tell him what I think.

"I don't," she said quietly, "think you're asking yourself the right question."

"Sure I am." He picked his head up, the peculiar overhead lighting pulling shadows along his already gaunt face as if great lines had been gouged into his flesh. It was a macabre sight but it somehow made him seem all the more vulnerable. "D'you think I want t' leave a money-making operation like this just t' fall on my face. Oh, th' critics'll be waitin' t' make mincemeat o' me, call it another ego trip. But it ain't that at all."

She came over to him, touched his shoulder. "I know it's not, Chris. This is the music you've got to make now."

"You know," he said with tears in his eyes, "what I'm most afraid of? I don't wanna be like Chuck Berry, cartin' my guitar round in ten years, playin' all th' old Heartbeats' hits." He closed his eyes, winced. "I'll tell you a secret even Nigel doesn't know. I can't stand t' even *listen* t' those numbers anymore, let alone play 'em. Christ, I've broken all those LPs over my knee an' thrown 'em away." He spread his hands, gave a small, sickly giggle. "I ain't got a single Heartbeats record in th' place." His arms came around her, his head buried in her stomach. "I can't play that stuff anymore, Dain."

"Then you don't have to," she said, smoothing down his hair. She leaned over, kissed the top of his head. "Leave the band, Chris. It'll be easier than you think. You've been giving everything and taking nothing. I know that's killing you." She waited in the silence for him to say something. "Chris?"

He drew away from her and she saw his eyes, large and haunted. "I can't leave," he cried in anguish. "They're my family. I just can't abandon them."

Daina knew that she was close but if she did not find out what was behind that look in his eyes, she could not help him fully. "Chris, you've got to tell me what's making this decision so difficult. I know you want to be free. What's stopping you?"

"No!" It was almost a shout. He lurched up, ran out of the room. Daina went after him, up the stairs and into the hall. She was passing the bedroom when something caught her eye. She stopped and went inside.

The room was something of a mess: clothes and newspapers scattered all around. A small Sony TV was on, the sound cut off. A cassette recorder was on the bed, loaded and ready to play.

She reached down, picked up the object that, glittering in the light, had caught her eye. It was a four-tiered necklace with the head of an Egyptian god in its center. Tie's choker. So that's it, Daina thought. Now that Chris is the creative force behind the band, Tie's finally moved in. What will Nigel say? she asked herself. Nothing, she suspected. He knew there was nothing he could do to keep her and he would not make a move that might threaten the band.

Christ, Daina thought, it's Tie who's keeping him in the band, nothing else. But she knew that Tie could be formidable indeed. Abruptly, her conversation with Bonesteel returned to her. *She's in love with you.* No, Daina thought, shocked, it's impossible.

But she knew that for a lie and now the thought that had been circling through the darkness of her unconscious began to surface so that sweat broke out in a thin line across her forehead and upper lip and she had to sit down on the edge of the bed. My God, she thought. My God! It can be done.

She looked down at the choker lying across her palm and closed her fingers over the god's head, making a fist. She squeezed for a moment, then threw the thing back onto the bed.

Without turning back, she left the room, looking for Chris. No wonder he could not tell her. He knew what her reaction would be if she knew he and Tie were together. Well, he'd never know she had found out.

Daina went through the living room and out onto the deck. She found Chris leaning on the cedar railing, staring out to sea. She smelled the cloying sweetness of the grass, saw as she approached that he was smoking a joint. He stood in a way that reminded her oddly of an invalid. In front of them the sea marked time as regularly as a drumbeat. The breakers dominated all sound, echoing and, in those echos, increasing in volume, scope and depth.

She came softly up behind him, her mind clear. She put an arm around him, stroked the side of his neck and said to him, "Come on. Let's go get blasted."

The beginning was easier than Daina had imagined it could be. She called Tie and asked her over for drinks. It was a time of the day when dusk was settling, straddling L.A. like a black lover, turning the brown smog plum in a brief, beautiful curtain call. In the valley, eyes were watering from

the pollution but here in Bel Air the rent was better than
Visine.

Tie arrived in Nigel's custom Silver Cloud Rolls rather
than her own Spider; it was like her to make a statement like
that. She wore a faille wraparound skirt in a black shadowstripe and a cream crepe de chine blouse. Her hair,
shorter than Daina remembered it, had darkened to auburn
while, oddly enough, her skin had taken on an almost opalescent whiteness.

Daina met Tie at the door, clad in skin-tight dark blue
pants and a pleated-front linen shirt, unbuttoned just enough
to reveal that she was not wearing a bra.

"Come in," Daina said, smiling. Tie tore her eyes away
from the unbound breasts. Her heavy-lipped mouth was
glossed the same shade of rich red as her long nails. Daina
saw the tip of her tongue like a pink adder's head, darting
between those scarlet lips.

Daina, on the other hand, wore only eye makeup and this
contrast, she knew, was just subtle enough to be dramatic.
She turned to lead the way down the hall and could almost
feel the heat of Tie's eyes burning her back.

"I must say I was rather surprised when you called me."
Tie's voice drifted down to her from behind. "We had some
fiery encounters in San Francisco."

"Perhaps that's only because we're both Chris' friends,"
Daina said as they emerged into the living room. Only the
etched-glass lamp in the conversation pit by the velvet sofa
was lit and this produced both a warmth and an intimacy
that was otherwise impossible in the enormous room. Daina
crossed to the bar. "Drink?"

"Do you have Tsingtao?"

Daina looked around. "I think we have a bottle around
here somewhere." She found it behind the Courvoisier. "Ah,
here it is." She broke the seal, poured the vodka over ice,
added a twist of lemon. "You know, we seem to be quite
different when we're both with him." She handed Tie the
frosted glass. "Have you noticed?"

Tie's black eyes regarded her coolly over the rim of the
glass. She waited while Daina fixed herself a Stolichnaya on
the rocks and they toasted silently, lifting their glasses as if
to friends departed but not forgotten.

"You seem to have become quite friendly with that cop," Tie said without ever having answered Daina's question.

"What cop?" She came around from behind the bar.

"The lieutenant investigating Maggie's death," Tie said, following Daina over to the couch. "What's his name? Bonesteel." She sat down with one leg bent under her so that the expanse of one pale thigh was revealed as the slit of the wrap skirt spread.

"No more than anyone else," Daina said levelly. She sipped at her drink. "Anyway, it seems I'm Chris' only real alibi."

Tie snorted. "He doesn't really think Chris killed her?"

"I don't know *what* he thinks." Daina put her glass down. "He's exceptionally uncommunicative."

"I know how to remedy that...and so should you." She looked at Daina over the rim of the glass: that same cool stare. "Why don't you find out what's on his mind. He can't be very complicated. It ought to be as easy as putting on your garter belt."

"What's your interest in this?"

Tie grunted, placed her glass next to Daina's. "Well *that* should be obvious. I don't want anything to jeopardize the workings of the band. And that includes the possible delusions of a cop." She took a tortoise-shell case out of her lizardskin pocketbook, snapped it open. "You know reputation's everything with these guys. He's made no arrests, he's bound to be feeling the pressure. He makes an arrest and the heat's off." She shrugged. "Just like that." She edged her ruby nails into the tortoise-shell case, extracted a tiny silver spoon, the business end of which she dipped into the layer of white powder. She did up each nostril, inhaling quickly and deeply each time.

"He's not going to do that," Daina said.

"What makes you say that?"

"He's not stupid."

"All cops are stupid," Tie said, replacing the spoon and snapping closed the case. "In one way or another." Belatedly, she said, "Want some?" And, quite deliberately, dropped the tortoise-shell case back into her purse.

Daina felt an urge to comment on Tie's generosity but restrained herself, saying only she would prefer to stick to liquor.

"Chinese and Russian," Tie said, reaching for her glass.

She meant the two vodkas. "The yin and the yang. Very interesting."

"Have you ever tried the Russian?"

"Not Stolichnaya."

Daina took her drink up. "You should. It's quite good." She extended the half-filled glass. "Here."

Tie turned her head a little. "I don't think so." But Daina had put one hand behind her head and was pressing the edge of the glass between her lips. She heard it rattle against her front teeth, tipped it up.

Then Tie's hands had come up and, in a blur, had thrust the glass away from her with such violence that Daina was inundated with the liquor. Tie threw the remainder of her own drink into Daina's face. "I told you I didn't want any!"

Daina closed the distance between them, felt the press of the other woman's ample breasts against her own, the heat of her body, the combination of perfume and mild sweat, mingling, creating a new musk.

Tie's breath was hot against her cheek as they struggled along the length of the sofa. "Bitch!" she cried. "You bitch!" Then she cried out in pain as Daina seized her arm, jerking it back against the top of the sofa. "Oh, oh, oh! That hurts! Shit!" She looked up to see Daina's teeth bared and she shuddered through her entire body, her eyes fluttering closed. "Let me up." But she said it so weakly it was almost a part of the silence that had grown up around them.

"Lie down," Daina commanded and Tie's eyes flew open. She was trembling. Daina had not relinquished her hold and she moved half over Tie so that they were both half reclining. The struggle had opened the remaining buttons on Daina's blouse and the swell of her breasts was exposed all the way down to her nipples. Tie's dark eyes were drawn as if by magnets. The tip of her tongue came out, unconsciously sweeping this way and that over her parted lips.

Daina straddled Tie, keeping her imprisoned between her powerful thighs.

"What are you doing?" Tie said hoarsely but her body told Daina she knew.

Daina's hands came up, pulled her blouse out from her pants, shrugging it off. She cupped her breasts. "Smell me," she whispered huskily. "Can you smell me?"

Tie tried to turn her head away but Daina saw her nostrils dilate at the heady scent. "Take them away," she groaned.

"Oh, no, no, no." Daina leaned forward, tracing the outline of Tie's mouth with one long nipple, rubbing it back and forth between her closed lips. "Don't you want to open your mouth, Tie?" The odd black eyes were clouded, the faille wraparound skirt rucked up around her thighs. A great heat emanated from between them. "Don't you want to... suck them?"

Tie moved her head away, fear and something more in her eyes. "What are you doing?" Her voice quivered and finally broke. "You must be mad."

"Yes, that's right"—her hands abandoned her own breasts, greedily dug beneath Tie's open blouse—"mad. I'm mad. But then"—she bent her head, licked at the cleavage between Tie's breasts, and grinned—"so are you." She began to grind her hips into Tie's. "Uhmm. I feel it. Oh I feel it. I knew you wanted it... secretly wanted it."

Quickly then she stripped off Tie's blouse and, making sure she had leverage, went to work on her skirt.

She went back to caressing Tie's breasts, feeling the responsiveness in the body beneath her coming reluctantly at first, then spasmodically. Tie began to pant, arching her hips up but when Daina began to pull her jeans off, she moaned, "No, no, no. Don't. Oh, don't. Oh!" Because Daina had touched her mount, found it already wet.

But Tie was still crying softly, "No, no," and Daina began to croon to her, as her lips and tongue worked their way down to the moist flesh, dipping into her navel, swirling the tip around, moving slowly downward to the first fringe of pubic hair.

And then, as Daina's lips were about to encompass Tie's sex, she pulled desperately away.

"Not yet," she cried. "Oh, I've got to have it," pursuing Daina's mount with her own. She worked for leverage and Daina gave it grudgingly to her. She hooked her left leg beneath Daina, spreading them and Daina's own in the process. They were now joined like a pair of scissor blades.

Immediately, Tie scooped Daina's upper torso to her, their breasts rubbing together as she ground herself into Daina. Faster and faster Tie drove the pace, her eyes closed, until Daina could feel the sexual tension running through her, singing like a live wire, her muscles bunching as she rode toward the peak.

And then her hands pressed down sharply against Daina's shoulders, pushing her down until her head was on a level with Daina's writhing hips. "Oh!" she moaned. "Make me come, darling." Her fingers twined in Daina's hair, the sharp nails scoring the scalp. "Ahgg! I'm almost there. Oh, darling!" She gasped as Daina lowered her mouth into that hot wetness. "Oh, yes, yes, yes!"

Daina knew that Tie was lost in her ecstasy, that all she could think of was completion, heard her say, "Why don't you leave him alone!" The cry of a little girl. Someone Tie had once been but so long ago, so deeply buried that she was never seen save for these brief moments. "Oh it's heaven! Darling heaven!" But the pressure had suddenly left the core of her and her eyes opened. "Darling, what are you doing? I'm ready to come. Suck me!"

"In a minute," Daina said, crawling up over Tie's shaking body. The other woman winced with the sliding contact. Tie moaned and her hips arched spastically up. "Wouldn't you like to have this all the time?"

"Oh, darling"—Tie's fingers gripped her powerfully— "don't talk now. Finish me!"

"I'll finish you," Daina said, using her thumbs and fore-fingers. "But first you must do something."

"Oh, ohh!" Tie's fingers came down over Daina's caressing their backs as they worked. "I'm just there," she groaned. "Almost, almost, ohhh!" Daina took her hands away. "Oh, don't stop now!" She grabbed at Daina's hands, tried to pull them back to her heated flesh.

"Thaïs listen to me."

"What...what is it?" Her hips continued to pump but Daina arched her body, keeping herself close enough so their skin brushed. "Darling..."

"You can have this anytime, Tie," Daina whispered in her ear, kissed the shell. "Anytime. Would you like that?"

"Yes...oh! Yes."

"Well then—go back to Nigel...or anyone else you please. But not Chris...."

"Nnnn. I want to come." Her hands moved to the juncture of her thighs but Daina, atop her, slapped them away.

Tie's eyes flew open. "Do that," she grunted. "Slap me there...."

"Like this?" She drew one hand back, slashed it up between Tie's wet thighs.

Tie's body jumped as if electrified. "Yes...oh yes! More!"

"Only when you agree."

"Yes, yes, yes!"

"Yes what?"

"Yes, I'll go back to Nigel." She giggled. "Chris's a lousy lover anyway. I just wanted to make it com...complete." Her hand scrabbled in the pocket of her balled-up skirt, came away with a capsule. "Little Locker Room." She took the capsule of amyl nitrite, held it under her nose, sucking up the gas. "I'd rather have you, Daina. Rather have you doing this to me...and me...doing this to you. Your fifty-foot face...your hungry lips...your icon eyes on me." Daina's head lowered and her fingers slid beneath Tie, lifting the other woman's hips off the sofa, plunging headlong into her core. "Oh God, oh God, oh God...yes!"

Tie began to tremble and jerk uncontrollably in an orgasm so powerful that at its end, she passed out. Which was just as well, for Daina, sickened, stumbled up and ran, making the bathroom just in time. She knelt in front of the cool porcelain bowl and was violently ill.

Oh God, she thought. Oh God, oh God, in unconscious reflection of Tie's own words uttered moments before. But the meanings were quite different.

As Daina stood shakily up, put her head in the sink and turned on the cold water, she felt an odd sense of disorientation. As if the fabric of her life was being twisted all out of shape, as if she no longer had control of her hands and feet and mouth or, rather, that these essential elements of her physical self were in the possession of some unknown being.

But it's you! her mind screamed at her. You! You! You!

Tie did not stir even when Daina returned to stand over her. Now it has begun, I must see it through, Daina thought. But this is the easy part. I won't even have to act.

Tie's eyes opened and her lips murmured something soft and indistinguishable. Her arms were over her head, her back slightly arched. It was a provocative, vulnerable pose and Daina reflected she had never seen Tie look so soft.

Languidly, Tie reached out with both hands, stroked along Daina's thigh. "Let me touch you there," she said in a whisper. And when Daina stepped back a pace, "Oh, please."

She pressed her cheek against Daina's stomach and one hand snaked through Daina's legs. "I've never knelt before someone." Her voice was clogged with emotion. "You didn't come. Let me...Let me—"

Daina thrust her head away roughly. "Get out of here!" Her voice was harsh and grating. Tie jerked as if the words had been a whiplash.

Daina bent, picked up Tie's clothes. These she thrust rudely into the other woman's lap, pulled her to her feet. Without saying another word, she dragged Tie down the silent hall to the front door.

"Put on your clothes and leave!" Daina commanded and left her standing there, shivering and wide-eyed.

In the blackness there was a stirring. The sounds of movement, furtive and stealthy. Abruptly, the sounds of choking, flailing, crash of a splintered object, a hoarse shout.

The flashlights burned. El-Kalaam's voice was heard over the tumult. Silhouettes: shapes and shadows dancing along the walls, grotesque, sharply defined. El-Kalaam fired three shots in rapid succession over everyone's heads. Order was returned. The lights came on.

Heather and Rachel were near the bookcase, where they had been sleeping. Thomas and Rudd were on the sofa, the English MPs close beside them on the floor. Rene Louch, tousle-haired and bleary-eyed, was sitting up against a floor-length mirror. Only Emouleur was still lying down. He was sprawled on his stomach with his head and shoulders in the deep shadows of the fireplace.

El-Kalaam looked darkly around the room. "Get him up!"

Rita picked her way forward, kicked at the young Frenchman's side with the tip of her boot. He did not stir. Immediately she bent down, put her fingers along the side of his throat. She looked up.

"Dead," she said. "Strangled."

"You've been given your answer, El-Kalaam," Rudd said. "No one's going to sign anything."

"I take it then you killed him." El-Kalaam's voice was cold, emotionless.

"I didn't say that. I wish it had occurred to me."

"Very good," El-Kalaam said. "But it won't work." He gave a curt jerk of his head and Malaguez took Rudd up by his shirtfront. "Take him to the hot box."

"Non!" Louch cried out. He struggled to his feet, leaning heavily on the mirror behind him. He swayed a little. "You have the wrong man. He did not kill Michel; I did."

"You did?" El-Kalaam said. "How interesting. And for what possible reason?"

"He was young, impressionable." The French ambassador tried to get his hair out of his eyes. "He did not see what you were doing to him; I did. He did not understand how you were turning him; I did. He would never have been the same. Never thought the same way or acted the same way."

"That was the point."

"Yes, I know. And that is why he had to be stopped. He had to be saved from himself or, rather, what you had turned him into." There was anguish on Louch's face. "I tried my best to talk to him but it did no good. And I—" He seemed to choke on his words. "The choice I had to make...was not an easy one. I could not allow our government to be dragged into this incident this way."

"I see," El-Kalaam said calmly. "Well, it does not matter." He turned away. "Lights off. Everyone stands for the remainder of the night." Blackness.

Harsh lights of morning. Colors came up slowly; in the wallpaper, the cream and gilt walls; brightness reflected off the wall mirror.

"Only two hours remain," Malaguez said to El-Kalaam.

"We all know what has to be done...one way or another." Fessi came up, joined them.

"I do not think the Israelis will give in," Malaguez said.

Fessi's face registered contempt. "The Americans and the English will persuade the Zionists to bend from their unyielding course. Between them they have enough power. It's been eroded but still...what would Israel do without the support of the Americans?"

"*If* the westerners understand our intent well enough," Malaguez replied. "We seem to bewilder them."

El-Kalaam grunted. "The westerners understand philosophy as well as they do Allah, which is to say not at all. What they *do* understand is bullets and gelignite and death. One must take extreme measures to get them into action. All subtlety passes through their minds like a shadow without substance. In time they will do what we demand."

"Time," Fessi said. "It weighs about my neck like a stone." He slapped his left hand against the side of his AKM. "I long for battle. Part of me wants the deadline to come and pass without the radio telling us of victory. I long to wreak death and destruction."

"That's because you're mad," Malaguez said. "Your mother must've dropped you on your head when you were—"

Fessi leaped for him; El-Kalaam stepped calmly in between. "That's enough!" he cried. "From both of you." He looked away from them to where Heather and Rachel stood against the bookcase. "Malaguez, take the girl. Fessi, go make certain the radio is tuned to the right frequency." Rita took Heather by the elbow. "Then join us in the hot box. Now we'll see what these two are made of."

They went down the hall single file. Nothing had changed inside the room at the far end of the hall. The windows were still covered, the bed overturned. The floor was slick with pink fluid. The rubber hose snaked across the floor toward the spot where Bock had fallen.

"What have you done with Susan?" Heather said.

"She was of no more use to us." El-Kalaam gestured to Malaguez. "Put her there."

Malaguez shoved Rachel down onto the stained seat of the chair where Bock had sat. Rachel's face was shiny with sweat. As she sat, she looked at Heather in silent communication.

"What we want from you is simple," El-Kalaam said in his most reasonable voice. "A statement from you." He looked at Rachel. "Just imagine how the world would react to a signed statement from you endorsing our aims."

"No one would believe it."

"Of course we could write it ourselves, sign it ourselves but that's merely a stop-gap. We need the authenticity of your own hand."

"Either way," Rachel reiterated, "no one would believe it."

He scowled blackly at her, then dismissed her words with a wave of his hand. "Of course they would. People are gullible. They believe what they want to believe or...what they are *led* to believe. There is a great deal of positive sentiment for our cause around the world. People are merely frightened of expressing it openly...the Zionist thugs are everywhere."

"All we want is to live in peace," Rachel said.

El-Kalaam spat and his face worked in a grimace. "Peace. Oh, yes, of course. *Your* peace. You wish to live in a world without Arabs."

"On the contrary, it is *you* who wish *us* destroyed."

"Twister of truth!" he cried. And then in a much softer voice: "It is just this kind of insane thinking we wish to free you from." He smiled crookedly. "We have the time—and the methods." He reached for her.

"Leave her alone," Heather said. "She's just a baby."

El-Kalaam turned. "A baby, you say? And do you think if I put a loaded gun into this *baby's* hand she would not blow my brains out in the first instant? Oh, yes, she would." He came across to where Heather stood. Rita was just behind and to the right of her.

"You still have not grasped what this is all about, have you? No, I see not." He pointed back to Rachel. "This baby is the key...the key to everything...to all our dreams. I do not care about the others in there...they're of no use to me. But this one...she is everything to me.

"Your husband grasped this from the first. It's why he did what he did. I admired him for that. He was an amateur trying, for one brief moment, to become a professional. He succeeded. But you," he said contemptuously, "you're nothing but a rabbit shooter. You have the rabbit-shooter's mentality. You have no real conception of life and death; when to initiate the one or the other. Your husband at least knew that. He was a revolutionary at heart. You're nothing but a housewife who's been trained to pull a trigger on a target range. You've got no brains, no courage."

He gripped her jaw, shook her head back and forth beneath the scrutiny of his gaze. "You just remember to keep your mouth shut from now on. Watch what happens. If you speak, Rita will open the side of your head with the butt of her machine pistol. Is that clear?"

Heather nodded mutely.

El-Kalaam made a curt gesture. "We begin."

"I've found out something you ought to know."

He did not use her name or his own; he was far too security conscious. Nevertheless she recognized his voice immediately. She thought of his warm spangled smile, his ruined artist's hands. She sucked in her breath. "What is it?"

"Not over the phone," Meyer said. "We should meet."

She thought of the film's hectic schedule; they were so close to a wrap now. Her heart sank. "I can't come down to San Diego."

"You won't have to," he said easily. "I'm in L.A."

"Where?"

"Oh, around." He laughed and she recalled the rich scent of his cologne, the dry leathery skin of his cheek. "Can you get away for an hour?"

Daina looked at her watch. "At dusk," she said. "We've got to catch all the light. How's six-thirty?"

"Fine." He paused. "Meet me in front of your friend Maggie's grave."

"You know where—"

"I know where it is."

"In that case," Daina said, "don't forget to bring flowers."

She had a studio limo drive her out to the cemetery that evening. She was doing this more and more now, leaving the silver Merc at home. It was, she had begun by telling herself, merely a factor of how tired she was. She had always loved driving but now it had become a chore to get herself to and from the set. And when she had brought up the point to Beillmann he had, without another word, picked up the phone and ordered her a limo.

Now as she lay back in the seat, turning into the light of the portable mirror so Anna could carefully remove her makeup, she saw that this service was nothing more than what was due her. She sighed a little, the feel of the cool cold cream soothing against her skin. For a time, she put Meyer out of her mind, along with the intense anticipation she felt at the meeting. What did he have for her?

She thought of New York and wintertime. It was hard to imagine them both now or, more accurately, *feel* them both.

Christmas in New York had somehow faded to the aspect of
a scene she once did in a film a long time ago on a set out in
the valley—dim and not quite real. She longed to go back
East, to renew her love affair with the city that never slept.
Champagne and caviar swam somnolently through her veins
and, above her head, the tall dusty palms slid by in the
stealthy arrival of evening. Here there was nothing but palms
and Mercs and time flowing by without tone or variation from
the changing of the weather or even the seasons.

"All done, Miss Whitney."

"Have Alex drop you off first, Anna," Daina said without
opening her eyes. She did not want to be disturbed until they
reached their destination.

Dimly she was aware of the limo's slowing, then stopping.
She thought she heard Anna say good night and she murmured a brief reply. *I've found out something you ought to
know.* Now Meyer's voice reverberated over and over inside
her brain. It was a tantalizing thread she followed here and
there without ever getting closer to its meaning.

She must have slept the last part of the journey for when
she opened her eyes again, the limo sat parked at the curb
closest to the cemetery entrance. The engine was off. She
looked straight ahead, saw the back of Alex's head. There
seemed nothing odd about it. Then the head turned and she
saw Margo's handsome face. A few wisps of black hair floated
down over her small ears. She smiled. "Come, my dear. Meyer
is waiting for you."

She disappeared from Daina's view only to open the back
door a moment later. She was bent slightly forward from the
waist. She was slim and very lovely, Daina thought. She held
out a bouquet of irises. "Meyer thought you might need
these." Daina laughed. It was she, after all, who had forgotten
the flowers.

There was no one around but Meyer. He stood before Maggie's grave, slightly stoop-shouldered. He was dressed in fashionable dark gray linen slacks and a cream-colored short-
sleeved cotton shirt. He looked unrumpled and fit. His wise
Picasso's head seemed even larger out of doors. He leaned
slightly on an ebony cane with a seemingly sharp silver tip
and a great knobby malachite handle "that was given to me,"
he told her later, "at the end of the war by an English colonel."

For a long time after she came up to stand beside him he

said nothing. She watched him clandestinely, searching perhaps for some sign of his age. But, except for the huaraches he wore, she could find none. There was no tremor to his hand, no nodding of his head. She watched a thin blue vein pulsing in the side of his head only partially covered by his fringe of hair. Above them the sky was opalescent with reflected light—mostly the neon from Hollywood and the Strip—but the smog softened it enough to create the illusion of pristine beauty. In this light, Meyer seemed immortal, untouchable either by mortal hands or by time itself. He had survived the death camps, the deaths of two sons and at least one wife. And here he stood, indomitable.

"I hear things about you," Meyer said and his voice sent shivers down her spine. "Exciting things." He turned his face to her and the light struck his eyes, enlarging them. "We haven't seen your like in a long, long time." Meyer had a way of using the word "we" as if it stood for the opinion of the entire world. "An incandescence on the screen." He took one hand off the cane, squeezed her arm with remarkable strength. "There is nothing you can't accomplish now, it seems."

"Sometimes I feel as if I'm ten feet tall," she said, almost dreamily.

"Tell me," Meyer said, "is it you who've changed or is it those around you?"

"I don't know what you mean."

"Well, for instance, that limo you arrived in." His hand left her for a moment to gesture vaguely out toward the cemetery's entrance. "Six months ago you didn't have it...couldn't get it, am I right?" He nodded. "So. Do you have it now because you're different or because those around you perceive you differently?"

Daina looked at him. "Does it matter?"

Meyer smiled at her. "Only to you, Daina."

She looked down at the irises Margo had put into her arms. She bent down, placed the bouquet on the grave. She stood up, feeling slightly lightheaded.

"How does it feel," Meyer asked her, "to put flowers onto an empty grave?"

He reached out and grabbed her before she could fall. She staggered against him but he was solid for all the pain in his bad feet and he held her until she had recovered.

"What do you mean?" she said. "I was here at the funeral when Maggie was buried. I saw—"

"What you saw," Meyer said patiently, "was an empty coffin being lowered into the ground. Your friend Maggie was not inside."

She did not think to question what he said. "Then where is she?"

"In Ireland." Meyer's arm was hard around her. "Buried back home."

"But Maggie was born in St. Marys, Iowa," Daina said.

"Not born, raised. She and her sister were spirited out of Northern Ireland just after they were born. They came here, were placed in a suitable family situation and—"

"But why?"

"Their real family name is Toomey," Meyer said. He waited a moment. "Does that sound familiar?"

"Wait a minute." Daina thought back to a conversation she had had with Marion. He had seemed upset, she had asked him why. *That disaster in Northern Ireland.* Wasn't that what he had said?

"Isn't Sean Toomey the patriarch of the Protestants in Belfast?"

Meyer nodded. "The same. Maggie was his granddaughter."

"My God!" Daina cried. "What are you saying?"

"I'm not drawing any conclusions," Meyer said evenly. "I let others do that now. I'm only telling you what I've found out. Wasn't that part of our bargain?"

"But Marion told me that Sean Toomey ordered the combined British and Protestant raid on that Catholic section of Belfast, what's it called?"

"Andytown."

"Yes. Andytown. And that was..."

"Two weeks, give or take a couple of days, before your friend was murdered."

She turned away. "I've got to go to the police."

But Meyer had her arm and he would not let her go. He turned her back toward him. "And tell them what?"

"Just what you've told me." She eyed his blank face. "Or don't you have the guts to stand by it."

"Calm down," he said. "This has nothing to do with me...or with you, for that matter." He drew her closer to him, using his cane to emphasize his points. "All right, let's say we both go to the Los Angeles police with what I've just told you. D'you seriously believe that Sean Toomey had his granddaughters sent over here without the knowledge of the United States government? And do you further think they'd allow this to get out into the press?" He waved the cane back and forth. "No, no, no. There are far too many IRA sympathizers in this country to allow that." He shook his head sadly. "They'd never get that grave opened. Never." He put his hands on her shoulders. "Daina, this information's for you and you alone. I told you I'd help you find out who killed your friend, nothing more."

"But you haven't even done that."

Meyer pressed a slip of paper into her hand, closed her fingers over it. "When you get a chance," he said, "see this man."

This time it was he who leaned over and kissed her cheek.

She could not help it; she went to Bonesteel.

Of course, he was skeptical. "You've got to tell me where this information came from."

"Bobby, I can't." She spread her hands. "Please don't ask me."

"Now listen—!"

"No, you listen. Either you believe it or you don't and that's the end of it."

"All right," he said. "I think it's a crock."

"Fine," she said, getting up. "Good-bye."

"Wait," he said. "Wait a minute." He drummed his fork up and down on the tablecloth. They were in the kitchen of Rubens' house. She had refused to come down to the precinct house again and could not think of a public place around the city where she would not be mobbed; she did not want Alex with her.

He gestured with the fork. "Oh, sit back down." His voice was gruff. "You're getting me nervous standing there."

It was Maria's day off but, looking through the window, Daina could see the Mexican gardener's helper hard at work on the roses.

"I don't think I like you much," she said, sitting down opposite him.

"But you haven't thrown me out yet."

"You know why. Without you, I'll never find out who killed Maggie."

He leaned across the table toward her. "And that's very important to you, isn't it?"

"Yes."

"Why?"

"She was my friend."

"A friend who was already on drugs, who lied to you constantly, it seems, who envied your success, who believed you were having an affair with her boyfriend—"

Daina slapped him hard across the face. "Christ, you're all alike, prying into everything!"

"That's what I do," he said without moving. His face was red where she had struck him but there was no obvious emotion in his voice. "I'm a garbage man. I sort through everyone's dirty underwear, sniffing at the excrement because, nine out of ten times, that's where I'm gonna find the twisted bastards who kill other human beings. Do you see the logic in that?"

She turned her head away. "It's disgusting."

"I suppose it's much more disgusting than grinding other people down under your high heel."

Her eyes blazed as she turned to look at him. "I don't do that."

"No," he said. "You only think you don't."

"Get out of here!" Her chair went over on its back as she left it. "I don't want any part of you!"

He came after her. "And what d'you think you're going to do about Maggie?"

"I'll handle it myself." She backed up against the wall. "Get away from me!"

She moved to slap him again but he caught her wrist in a grip she could not break.

"Don't be an idiot," he said, struggling with her. He was very close to her and they were both panting with the exertion. "We both need each other." His lips were close to hers and their eyes locked. Immediately his mouth came down over hers and she could feel his heat growing.

"What are you doing?" she said.

"What does it look like?"

Her breasts were exposed. She took his hands in hers, drew them up and away for a moment. She looked into his eyes and, surprised, saw herself there. She saw that she wanted him to make love to her not only because she liked him—that would not be enough. She needed his warmth now because he was not, like Rubens, a part of her world. His entering her would prove to her that she was more than an image. She moved to kiss him back but his face was as pale as if he were in shock. She could hear the sound of his harsh breathing. But the look on his face sent a cold knot of fear streaking through her stomach.

"What's the matter, Bobby?"

"I don't...I really don't know. I"—he looked down at his hands, took them away from her flesh—"find myself thinking about you all the time, fantasizing. Even, you know, in the precinct house, I get ribbed all the time...some guys are jealous because they know I'm with you."

She moved closer to him so that her bare breasts pressed into his shirtfront.

"I've thought about this so many times. What it would be like to..." He put his hands on her shoulders. "But now that the moment's here, it's like I'm paralyzed. All I can think of is that fifty-foot billboard of you, how you were in *Regina Red*. Then I see this and...and it's all disconnected. I can't seem to separate one from the other."

"But I'm only flesh and blood, Bobby."

"No," he said, pushing her a little away from him. "No, you're not. You're more now. You're an image, a fantasy to millions of people, a wet dream to I don't know how many guys. You're more than just flesh and blood now."

Her arms were around him, entwined. "That's nonsense and you know it." But the knot in her stomach was growing until it filled her chest cavity and she thought she might explode. What's happening to me? she thought.

"Don't you see?" Bonesteel said in an anguished voice. "I *want* to make love to you but I can't. We're from different worlds. I don't belong in your bed."

At that moment, Daina wanted to scream to him that she was just a girl from the streets, frightened and alone but, even then, something hard and immutable inside her would not allow it and she wound up biting the inside of her cheek to keep her silence. She cried out and Bonesteel, thinking it was out of anger, backed away.

"I'm sorry," he said softly. "I'm really sorry, Daina." Then he turned, went down the hall past the wise face of El Greco's Jew.

When she heard the door slam behind him, Daina sank to her knees and, covering her face in her hands, began to weep as she had not done since the long days and nights at White Cedars. She tasted the rubber in her mouth and almost retched. She held onto herself, rocking back and forth, crying, crying until, at last, she fell asleep on the carpet almost directly beneath the figure of the mermaid who looked down upon her with sorrowful eyes.

Somewhere, in the back of her mind, she knew how disconnected she was becoming. That was why, after all, she had tried to seduce Bonesteel and why she had broken down so completely when he refused her. Now she knew she was apart, different from all others but—and this she did not comprehend—only part of her rejoiced at this ascension.

She had seen Bobby as her last lifeline to the real world of workaday people, going about their quotidian routines as she had once done but did no more. She had entered another realm, and quite willingly so, with both eyes open and arms spread wide, but the crossover had been so seductively swift, so slickly oiled with pleasure that she had not been aware of the daily changes, that she was drifting farther and farther out to sea until this moment when she had looked up to find the shoreline gone.

Bonesteel had been quite right. He was not from her world, and her reaching out to him in the most primitive way had been an attempt to show him—and herself—that she was still human. Meyer's words came back to her, hauntingly. *Tell me,* he had said, *is it you who's changed or is it those around you?*

What frightened her most was that she did not know the answer. How does an icon react? She suspected that many before her had asked themselves the same question and that those who could not answer it had not long survived here.

When Rubens came home he found her sprawled on the sofa, a half-full highball glass in her hand and a bottle of Stolichnaya sitting in dried rings on the coffee table within easy reach.

"Goddamnit, Daina, what's going on between you and that cop?"

She looked at him with uncomprehending eyes and he leaned over, slapped the glass from her weak grip. It went rolling on its side across the cushion, dropping to the carpet with a dull thud, spreading a dark stain from its contents.

Rubens bent over her. "That gardener's assistant told me—" But she was already sobbing uncontrollably, clinging to him with such passion that his anger melted. "Daina." He whispered her name over and over again while he rocked her back and forth. "What's wrong?"

But there was nothing she could tell him.

El-Kalaam began by withdrawing his knife. Heather made a move toward him but Rita pulled her sharply back. She waved the MP40 under Heather's nose. She put her forefinger across her sensual lips, looked into Heather's eyes. She shook her head from side to side.

El-Kalaam had given his machine pistol to Malaguez who was standing off to one side. On the opposite side of the chair, Fessi was licking his lips. He fondled the trigger of his AKM. His lips were partly open and he seemed to be breathing in heavy gasps.

El-Kalaam advanced on Rachel. He brought the shining point of the knife to bear on Rachel's blouse. As it passed through the harsh beam of light it became a dazzling slab.

The sound of cloth shredding was very loud in the protracted silence. Rachel's flesh began to appear as El-Kalaam slowly peeled off her blouse in wide strips. Her skin shone dusky in the light. Her shoulder blades appeared and then her chest. She wore a thin camisole with a delicate line of lace across the top. A small pink rose in the center between her breasts.

"There," he breathed. The knife point hovered in the air. "How is that now?" His eyes locked with hers. Then his gaze moved down to her shoulders. The tip of the blade shot forward through light and shadow and light again. It broke one strap of Rachel's camisole. Rachel gave a little gasp. Involuntarily, her hands moved to cover herself but Malaguez held them in her lap. Her shoulders shook. She stared straight ahead.

"Look at that," El-Kalaam said. "What beautiful breasts. Don't you think so, Malaguez?"

"A little small for my taste."

"Oh, well, give them time, Raoul. You must give them time. The child is still forming. She's not yet a woman." A tear was forming at the lower lid of Rachel's right eye. It welled up, overran the lid, tumbled down her cheek, dropped onto the back of El-Kalaam's hand. He smiled.

"They're the breasts of a child," Malaguez said. "Give them to Fessi."

"The trouble with you is, you have no feel for the future, Malaguez." El-Kalaam contemplated Rachel. "They're the breasts of a child now, yes. But soon...ah, they'll bud into a woman's magnificent breasts." The smile left his face suddenly. "Unless, of course, something were to happen to them."

"Like what?" Malaguez said.

El-Kalaam shrugged. "Oh, I don't know. But you know what life is like. An accident, perhaps." There was a flicker in Rachel's eye. "Or...you know...someone vicious could come along...a woman-hater, say. Someone with no appreciation for the female human form. A homosexual—"

Fessi giggled. His eyes were wide and glittery.

"Or a psychopath, maybe. The world's full of crazy men, you know. And let's just say, for the sake of this example, that this psychopath caught the girl one night."

He stood very close to Rachel. Her breasts heaved up and down with her breathing. "He has a knife." The blade of his knife slid forward, passing through a patch of brilliant light. Its reflection skimmed along Rachel's cheek. Her lips began to quiver.

"This one is real crazy," El-Kalaam said. "He takes our pretty young girl by the back of her hair"—he grabbed Rachel, jerked her head back. His thick lips were pulled back

in a snarl—"and pulls." He peered down at her face. Light
played over the planes and valleys, turning her face patchy.

"Now he puts the edge of his knife under one breast."
Rachel flinched as the steel slid against her flesh. Breath
whistled through her teeth.

"And he says to her, 'It's time I made you look like a man.'"
The blade was moving horizontally below Rachel's breast.
Her eyes closed and she began to tremble.

"First one and then the other."

Rachel began to sob. Tears flooded through her closed lids.
Her head whipped back and forth against the high-backed
chair. "No," she said.

"What's that?" El-Kalaam said. "What's that?"

"No!" she cried, her voice rising in pitch. "No, no, no!"

"No, what?"

Rachel's eyes snapped open. Tears dropped onto her dusky
flesh, rolling down the contours of her chest.

"No, please."

"Ah," El-Kalaam said. He kept the knife just where it was.
"Now we're getting somewhere."

That morning, Daina had asked Rubens if he would leave
work early so that he could pick her up after the filming.
"I need a night out," she had told him, "and I want you there
beside me."

The big midnight-blue Lincoln was waiting for her as she
emerged from her trailer. Rubens' driver stood, holding the
open door until she had stepped inside. She caught a glimpse
of Alex, sitting on the passenger side in front, before Rubens
pressed a stud, sending the mirrored, impact-resistant plastic
panel up, cutting them off from the hired help.

"How are you?" he said, kissing her. He kept hold of her
hand.

"Crazy," she said with a slip of a smile. "We're almost
through. Just another scene or two that Marion's not happy
with and we'll wrap."

"Good," Rubens said just as if he did not get daily reports
from Marion himself. They both knew the reality of it but
they preferred this illusion.

"How is George holding up?"

"He'll make it through, I think, but he's got everyone worried about this PLO thing he's involving himself in. Even his agent's talked to him about it but it's done no good." She squeezed his hand. "Make me a drink, will you."

Daina insisted they go to Moonbeams, a chic two-story restaurant in Malibu that, especially in summer, provided a pleasingly spectacular alternative to the chic establishments along North Camden and North Canon drives in Beverly Hills.

Daina seemed distracted, as if her mind was far away. She felt the palpable waves of energy that emanated from her, rippling outward in ever-widening circles until they encompassed the entire restaurant. She was dazzled by the strength of her power, felt attracted and repelled by it at once. Everyone, from the maître d' to the chef, made an appearance at the table to ask if the food and drinks were as they should be. Consequently, she and Rubens spoke only a few words to each other through the dinner.

Afterward, they went across the flagstone path to the parking lot. Stray wisps of sand slid like ghostly serpents along the black asphalt, evaporating like smoke.

They confronted a sea of cars, lit by a pair of blue-white floods high up on aluminum stanchions. Great pallid moths fluttered in the intense illumination and one lone damselfly, its long, slender body an iridescent blue-green, hovered nearby, gorging itself on the host of smaller insects attracted by the beams.

Chrome glittered and all the colors of the cars, so carefully picked, so expensively custom-painted, were reduced by the harsh light to neutral tones without much differentiation. It seemed to Daina a vision terrifying in its utter banality, a hideous robotic landscape devoid of all aesthetics or life and she felt, abruptly, as if she were on some alien world, that the Earth she knew was merely a memory, spinning blindly one hundred million miles away.

She gripped Rubens' arm, said, "Let's get out of here." She thought she could hear laughing voices floating on the still, humid air, heavy and muffled like the sound of the surf, heels click-clacking across the flagstone path they had come down; far away, the hiss of cars passing on the coast highway.

They were almost at the limo when Daina saw two figures emerge from the red Porsche parked three rows away. She knew the car even before she recognized the people.

"Hello, Daina," Tie said. Behind her loomed the broad-shouldered figure of Silka.

"She was in no condition to drive," he said in his deep voice. And now Daina saw that Silka gripped her but could not stop her unsteady weaving.

She looked into Tie's eyes, saw the dilated pupils, said to Silka, "What's she on?"

He shrugged. "Whatever she could get her hands on: coke, a Lude or two...maybe a Dalmane."

"Daina," Tie said. "Daina." She reached out.

"What the hell's going on here?" Rubens said, eyeing Silka.

"Just a bit of a quarrel," Silka said. "It's really nothing at all."

"It's all right, Rubens," Daina said. She took Tie's arm, began to steer her away from the men. "I'll take care of it."

She put one arm around Tie's slim waist, the other held her hand. "Come on," she whispered. "Come on."

"Take me home," Tie said. "I want to go to bed."

They were alone within the sea of cars. "Silka will take you home soon enough," Daina said.

"But I don't want to go home with him. I want to wrap my legs around you."

"That's enough, Tie."

"I want to taste you."

"I said that's enough!" Daina hissed. She turned Tie around to face her, gripping her shoulders fiercely. "I told you what you have to do. Go back to Nigel and stay away from Chris."

Tie's features were twisted and now there was no trace of beauty or even sensuality in that odd face. "I don't want Chris," she whimpered. "I want you."

Daina kissed Tie softly and then with a great deal of hardness. She felt Tie's body stiffen then melt, could hear the little gasp of pleasure the other woman gave under the pressure of her lips and tongue.

"Now, go on," Daina said coldly. "Go back to your car. Show Silka you can do it on your own. He thinks you can't do it."

Tie looked at Daina for a moment. "I had to come back, Daina. When you threw me out—"

"That was only a reminder."

Tie gave her a soft smile. "I know." There was such love in her eyes that Daina almost winced. Then she was gone, walking along a row of cars, one hand sliding against the fenders for support but being very careful not to stumble or fall because she remembered what Daina had said about Silka.

When Tie was back inside her Porsche, Daina returned to where the men stood. They seemed not to have moved at all, not even to have spoken to one another.

"Everything's fine now," Daina said to both of them. But she was looking at Silka. She wondered how much he knew of what was going on. Certainly he wasn't stupid and he seemed to know Tie quite well. She suspected he knew all of it. "You can take her home whenever you want."

"You mean Nigel's," he said, watching her face carefully.

"Yes," she said, "that's precisely what I mean. Isn't that where she belongs?"

Silka gave her a little smile. "I imagine it is. Nigel misses her."

"He won't have to worry anymore."

Silka took out the keys to the Porsche, stood jangling them between his fingers. "Actually, I'm surprised this hasn't happened before. That time six months ago, I think it was, when Nigel was away, they were alone together." Daina knew he meant Tie and Chris.

"And nothing happened?"

He shrugged. "I don't know everything, Miss Whitney."

She smiled at him. "You know what, Silka? I think that whatever you don't know about the band you can easily find out."

Silka flipped the keys into the air, caught them again. "In that case," he said blandly, "you'll believe me when I tell you nothing happened." He smiled at her. "Thanks for taking care of her. She can get impossible at times like this."

In the limo, going home, she had to tell Rubens what the conversation was all about. It was a good story, one she could almost believe herself.

Rachel looked at Heather through her tears. There was such sorrow there, such remorse that Heather was forced to look away.

El-Kalaam stood up. His knife blade was wet with Rachel's sweat and tears. For a moment he watched her eyes. "Five minutes," he said. "I want what I said to sink all the way in."

Heather's legs were trembling and Rita had to use both hands to support her.

"Bathroom," she said thickly. "I've got to use the bathroom."

El-Kalaam turned around. The light of triumph was in his face. "I knew you had no guts. Where is your courage now? It seems I know you better than your own husband did." He laughed, jerked his head toward the door. "Take her, Rita. I don't want her stinking up the room."

Rita nodded, manhandled Heather toward the door. Partway there Heather stumbled. She went down on her hands and knees.

"Look at this," Rita said. "She can't even walk by herself." She bent down, scooped her hands under Heather's armpits. As she did so Heather caught Rachel's eye. She gave the girl a hard look. Then Rita had pulled her to her feet and she was hustled out of the room.

They went down the hall. As they came to the open doorway to the bathroom, they passed one of the cadre hurrying toward the hot box. He carried his MP40 at the ready and he seemed slightly out of breath.

"Come on," Rita grated. "Stop gaping." She pushed Heather into the bathroom. "You have two minutes."

Heather went to the toilet, lifted her skirt, sat down. She could hear a commotion coming from the direction of the hot box: voices raised, weapons being clicked over to readiness. The noises grew louder. She heard the sound of running boot soles coming toward her.

"Rita!" It was El-Kalaam's voice. "Come quickly!" His face

appeared at the doorway. He seemed enormous, framed in the bathroom entrance. He did not glance at Heather.

"What is it?"

"There's a fire some idiot started in the trash out back." He went off down the hallway. "Come on!"

"But—" Rita turned her head toward Heather.

"That's all right," Fessi said so close to her she was startled. "I'll look after her." He was grinning.

"I'll bet," Rita said acidly. "I know just how you'll—"

"Rita!" El-Kalaam's voice came again.

"Do whatever you want," she said as she pushed out the doorway past him. "Just keep her safe. We may need her." She ran down the hall after El-Kalaam.

Fessi came into the bathroom. The grin was stitched to his face. His eyes were locked on the juncture of Heather's legs beneath the skirt.

"What's going on out there?" Heather asked.

"La, la, la." Fessi's voice was thick. "What have we here?" He moved the muzzle of his AKM forward until it slid beneath the hem of Heather's skirt. Fessi's eyes were alight. His tongue came out, licked at his lips.

Heather said nothing. The muzzle of the AKM disappeared, probing higher. "Who's with Rachel?"

Fessi's eyes blazed momentarily. "I ask the questions here. I get the answers."

Heather watched him closely. Fessi's eyes widened and he took a step closer. His tongue came out and he licked his lips again.

"You liked what he did to Rachel," she said softly. Fessi came closer. "You'd like to do the same thing to me, wouldn't you?"

Fessi was very close now. Heather stood up. Fessi swung the AKM aside, put it down. He unholstered his .45 automatic, flicked off the safety. He reached out for her with his left hand. It went beneath her skirt. The .45 came up, the muzzle against the side of her head.

"Don't get any ideas," he whispered. His mouth slid along the edge of her cheek to her lips.

Heather averted her face. His hand moved on her and she bit her lip, refusing to cry out. Slowly, she put her arms up, her hands moving along his shoulders. His mouth crushed against hers. Her lips opened under his. They kissed for a long time. The sounds of running boots, hoarse shouts, came from the hallway.

Then, slowly, Heather moved her hands down his body. Fessi gasped. His eyelids fluttered and the gun wavered in the air.

Heather curled her right hand into a fist, lashed out at Fessi's crotch. The small man let out a howl, doubled over. The .45 fired, bucked in his hand. His face was white. His knees buckled.

Heather snatched the .45 out of his hand but he managed to slap it away. It skidded across the tile to the other side of the bathroom.

He was unbending now, reaching for her. He was cursing her low on his breath. Heather reached over him, took hold of the AKM. She raised the machine pistol, slammed the butt end down onto the base of his neck. Fessi let out a sigh, collapsed.

Carefully she stepped over him. She went to the open doorway to the hall. The sounds were louder now, shouts and calls. Then she heard the pop-pop-pop of gunfire from outside the villa.

She stuck her head out into the hallway. It was chaos in the living room, terrorists running toward the front door. She could see none of the other hostages. She could hear El-Kalaam's familiar voice raised as he gave orders.

She went back down the hall toward the hot box. She crouched along the wall, her finger on the trigger of the AKM. She kept her eyes on the half-open door to the far room. It loomed closer and closer. A fierce beam of light from inside the room stretched across the floor of the hall, obliquely up the opposite wall.

Just outside the doorway she paused, listening. But the sounds from the rest of the villa made it impossible to hear anything from inside.

For an instant, she closed her eyes. She took a deep breath. When her eyes opened again, they were fixed on the bar of illumination on the wall. Her lips moved as she silently counted to herself. On "three" she leaped forward. She banged open the door with her left shoulder. She was crouching, the butt of the machine pistol hard against her hipbone. She swung the barrel around in a brief arc. She saw Rachel bound to the chair. She saw shadows, no other person.

"Rachel!"

Gunfire from out of the shadows and she jumped, tumbled, rolled to one side. Bullets sprayed in her wake, tearing up the wooden floor. Plaster chips whizzed by her shoulder. The AKM came up and she fired into the darkness: one burst, two, three.

There came a harsh cry and she saw the top of a head. A body staggered out from the shadows. It pitched forward into the harsh glare from the one unshaded lamp. Blood glistened, running. The body fell heavily at her feet. It was Malaguez.

Down the hall came Fessi, staggering, the .45 clutched in his hand.

Heather stood over Malaguez, looking down.

Fessi came on, one hand between his legs. He lurched against the wall, back out into the middle of the hall.

Heather turned to Rachel. "Are you all right?"

Rachel nodded her tear-streaked face and Heather went to her.

Fessi, gritting his teeth and sweating, appeared in the doorway to the room. His gun came up, aiming at Heather's back.

"Look out!" Rachel cried.

The .45 went off. Heather was already turning. The bullet crashed into the wall close to her left shoulder, spun her around. She fell to her knees. Fessi, grinning, lowered the pistol to shoot again.

Heather pulled the trigger on the AKM. It bucked in her hand, spewing bullets. Fessi's body was slammed backward so hard he bounced off the wall. Blood splattered them all. He fell, outstretched.

Heather tried to shoot again but the AKM had jammed. She threw it from her disgustedly, picked up Fessi's .45. She turned back to Rachel, began to untie her.

"The attack's begun," the girl said. She stood up, took Heather's hand. "I told you my father would not leave us."

Heather looked around the blood-streaked room. "Come on. Let's go."

They went out of the hot box and into the hallway. They were immediately confronted by one of the cadre. He lifted his machine pistol. Heather shot him through the chest. He reeled backward, his arms outflung. He crashed to the floor, his head lolling.

Heather pulled Rachel down the hall. Past the bathroom there was a closed door on the opposite side of the hall. Heather opened the door. It was a bedroom. There was no one inside. She pushed Rachel into the room, followed her. She shut the door and locked it.

Across the room, the window had been blocked off as it had in the hot box by the bed being turned on its side.

"Think you can help me get this away from the window?"

Rachel nodded. Together they began to work the huge four-poster out from the wall. They sweated as they worked, straining at the weight. Beyond the locked door, they could hear the sounds of gunfire coming stronger, more distinct.

Abruptly, the sounds of raised voices very close. The bed gave a bit. Pounding on the door. The bed gave more.

"Come on!" Heather cried. "Come on! Push!"

Rachel put her shoulder to the other side of the bed.

Gunshots from beyond the door; bullets whining into the room. They ducked, continued to heave. The bed slid away from the window. It left a rather narrow gap.

Heather stopped pushing. "All right," she said. "Go on. There's enough room for you."

"But not for you," Rachel said. She continued to push. Now it was she who said: "Come on!"

Shots came again and they both ducked behind the edge of the bed. Heather reached out, pulled Rachel toward her. "Go on now!" she shouted. "There's no time!"

"No," Rachel said. "I won't leave you." Her face was determined. "Now, come on, we've only got a little more to go." She put her shoulder back to the bed. Her brow wrinkled with the effort.

Heather stared at her for a moment. Shots came again and she pushed, too. The bed squeaked along the floor. The lock on the door shattered with the next barrage of machine-pistol fire.

"Now, Rachel!" Heather screamed.

The door burst open.

Rachel scrambled behind the bed. She raised the wide window, leaped up onto the windowsill. "Heather!" she cried, reaching out.

"Go on!" Heather said. There was some desperation in her voice. She turned toward the doorway. "I'm coming."

Rachel jumped out just as Heather sighted down the barrel of the .45. A figure leaped through the open doorway. She heard gunfire. Fabric churned close beside her. The thunk-thunk-thunk of bullets hitting close. She squeezed the trigger, firing at the oncoming figure.

There was a scream but the figure came on. It was Rita. She cried out again. Heather could see her lips drawn back from the whiteness of her teeth. There was a blurred splash of crimson. One side of her head.

Heather turned, squeezed herself behind the bed. She scrambled for the windowsill, almost dropped the .45. Then there were hands—Rachel's hands—helping her up.

Just as she made the ledge, she saw the muzzle of an MP40 come around the edge of the bed.

"Come on!" Rachel begged. "Oh, please!"

Rita's bloody face loomed. Her hair was splashed with red. The muzzle of the machine pistol aimed at Heather's head.

Heather fired again and Rita's head jerked away. The barrel of the MP40 lifted into the air, spraying the ceiling with bullets.

Heather turned away. She jumped. Now she and Rachel were crouched by the side of the house. Gunfire came from all around them. Here and there, they caught a glimpse of a running figure.

Heather pulled at Rachel. They got as far as the first set of hedges when a wave of gunfire forced them down onto their stomachs. They lay still for a time, panting.

There was blood on the ground and more than one dead body. Now they could see the assault force, a combination of Israeli commandos and American Marines. The first wave had made the villa and were already inside; the gunfire attested to that.

Perhaps a half dozen commandos were crouching on their side of the front doorway. A tall square-shouldered Israeli with the hooked nose of an eagle's beak was commanding them. At his command, they raced inside. Rachel was absorbed by the course of the assault. Something caught at Heather's attention.

There was movement at the same window out of which she and Rachel had made their escape. Two men were wrestling in the open space, just inside the ledge. Heather turned to look.

It was El-Kalaam and one of the Israeli soldiers. As she watched, El-Kalaam's hand broke away from the hold the other had on it. The edge of the terrorist's hand came down on the side of the Israeli's neck. The man grimaced in pain but continued to fight. He thrust a knee up into El-Kalaam's midsection. The bearded man drove his forefinger downward in a vicious arc. The commando howled and bucked upward as El-Kalaam's finger punctured his eye socket.

El-Kalaam battered him again, threw him aside. He made a grab for the barrel of a machine pistol but now gunfire peppered the top of the window frame.

El-Kalaam ducked, gave one more heave at the MP40. It would not give and he leaped out of the window. Gunfire followed him.

He was about to bound off into the underbrush when Heather stepped out from behind the hedge where she and Rachel had lain. She stood spread-legged, holding the gun in both hands. She was stiff-armed.

"Stand where you are!" she called.

El-Kalaam whirled around. He saw who it was, began to laugh. "So," he said, "it's you. I thought you dead in all this fighting. I sent Rita after you."

"I killed Rita."

The smile on his face slackened.

"Malaguez and Fessi, too."

"Impossible." El-Kalaam frowned. "Not you. Not the rabbit killer. You don't know when to shoot." He shook his head.

"You don't frighten me. I'm leaving now. It's time to fight another day."

"If you move, I'll kill you."

His arms spread. "What? You'd shoot a defenseless man?"

"You're not defenseless, El-Kalaam. You're dangerous. Too dangerous to be allowed to go on living. You once told me I killed senselessly and you did not." She shook her head. "But you were wrong. It's *you* who kill senselessly. There can be no excuse—"

"Freedom!" he cried.

"Freedom's just a word you use to justify what you do. It has no other meaning for you. It, too, has its role to play for you. Nothing more. But that won't save you now. Nothing will save you. You twist the fabric of life around until it's so warped no one can recognize it." She was walking toward him as she spoke. "You've taken civilization by the throat and you're biting its head off."

A smile broke out again across his face. "Words," he said. "They're only words. They mean nothing to me." He lifted his hand. "Good-bye," he called and began to move.

Heather squeezed the trigger of the .45. It roared in her grip; the muzzle came up in recoil. Through the haze, she saw El-Kalaam reel back against the side of the house. He stumbled, took a step, fell to one knee. He clutched at his chest. Blood was coming through his clenched fingers. His eyes were wide and staring. A look of disbelief suffused his face. He watched as Heather advanced toward him.

"I don't—" he began. "I don't . . ." Blood poured out of his nose and mouth and he choked. He coughed, slid down the side of the villa. His head came back. His sightless eyes stared up at the bright blue sky.

Heather stood over him, the muzzle of the pistol aimed at his head. Rachel came out of her hiding place, raced across the grass to where Heather stood. She came against Heather's side, put her face into her stomach. She gripped her with both arms, her hands clasped together.

The hawk-nosed Israeli commander poked his head through the large window. For what seemed a long time, he stared at the scene in mute wonder. Then his head whipped away and they could hear him calling rapid-fire orders to his men.

In a moment, a dozen commandos came around the side of the villa. The commander came through the open window, jumped to the ground.

"Are you all right?" He looked at both of them. "It's over now." The men came up, surrounding El-Kalaam.

The fixed look in Heather's eyes faded and she glanced from El-Kalaam's fallen body to the hawk-nosed commander. One of the commandos kicked El-Kalaam's corpse, cursed.

Heather dropped the gun onto the lawn. She bent, lifted Rachel up into her arms. She turned from all the commotion, taking the girl quickly away through the hedges.

11

And fade to black.

But the applause was already welling up, rising to a torrent as the red-lettered crawl began to seep down on the screen. Then they began to stand. It began somewhere in the middle of the enormous, packed house, spreading itself until everyone was up and applauding wildly. Here and there were bright piercing whistles. The house was rocking.

It was, as Rubens had predicted, the week before Christmas. Marion had brought the film in on time and *Heather Duell* would open here at the Ziegfeld on 54th Street just west of Sixth Avenue in New York, for a week-long reserved-seat engagement.

This was the VIP screening for the New York and national press. Rubens had Twentieth fly in a select corps of Hollywood's most influential critics and columnists for the screening and the subsequent party. But, cannily, he had held on to one hundred tickets himself. The studio brass had screamed for them for their executives, who never showed up anyway, preferring to give the tickets to their secretaries. He had had Beryl come into town two weeks early to set up a local pro-

motion on the top three AM radio stations in a ticket give-
away.

Now he was reaping the rewards. An industry audience
was notoriously unresponsive but Rubens had gambled on
the instincts of the public. It had been an appallingly risky
throw of the dice because everyone knew what he was up to.
He and Marion and Beryl had had a summit on just this
subject almost one month ago to the day. When he had pro-
posed the plan, Marion had at first balked. But then again
he was the closest one to the project and, as Rubens had
persuasively pointed out, the one least likely to view the
situation objectively.

At last Marion had unhappily relented. "I'm putting my
goddamned life in your hands," he had said, getting up. "Now
I know how Marie Antoinette felt on her way up the steps
to the guillotine."

Rubens had clapped Marion on the back, embraced him.
"Is that how you think of us, my friend? As a revolutionary
council? And after the marvelous job you've just turned in?
My God, man, you're—we're *all* going to make this film into
the biggest grosser of all time!" He squeezed Marion's shoulders. "Trust me. We haven't let each other down yet, have
we? And we're not going to. You have my word on it."

Even with all that, perhaps it was safe to say that Marion
had not been totally convinced, Daina thought now, as she
watched the audience erupt into wild applause. Swayed, yes.
Definitely swayed enough to give Rubens his consent. But
until now, Daina knew, doubts had churned in Marion's
heart, gnawing at him. After all, this was America; his big
shot. If it turned out a bust...Tonight he was wreathed in
smiles.

Daina stood between them, Marion and Rubens. She felt
their presence only as if it were some ghostly contact, as if
she stood in a haunted house, shaking hands with wraiths.
All that truly existed for her was the wall of noise building
like a tidal wave in the theater, echoing on and on until she
walked the length of the place and, going down the long aisle,
turned to face them.

She heard her name being called and turned her head. But
it came not from one mouth, nor two or three. It was as if the
multitude was calling to her and in that massed sound her
name, so terribly familiar to her for all of her life, took on

a new meaning, new form and shape, gaining substance until it seemed to hang in the air.

She watched their eyes, seeing an expression that was unique. From face to face, in the light and in the shadows, she saw the same thing. On long faces, round faces, pimply faces, and perfect faces there was a common point that bound them together here, some banner that covered them all, fused them into one entity with one mind, one heart, one dream. And with a thrill greater than any she had ever before experienced, she knew she was that dream.

Daina turned up the high collar of the full-length Canadian lynx coat Rubens had bought her. She pursed her lips, blew a warm breath. Condensing in the frigid air, its mist hung in front of her face before dissipating in the night.

Here in New York, it really felt like Christmastime. Strings of lights lit up Sixth Avenue and, looking northward, the pale spare branches of the trees in Central Park looked like spectral brooms angrily trying to sweep away the darkness—or the cold.

No T-shirts and sneakers parading down Sunset in December here; no open sports cars; no surfboards carried down to Laguna.

Here December meant winter and, although there was no snow to speak of—just the dirty remnants turned to mottled gray and black ice by the traffic—still it was as chill as she remembered it. Taxis, their cheery for-hire lights ablaze, cruised up the avenue and, down the block at 53rd, a sidewalk Santa rang his bells for the Salvation Army or some other charity. Just a few short blocks away, on Fifth Avenue, Saks would still be open to accommodate the holiday rush and St. Patrick's would be festively floodlit.

Rubens stood next to her on the sidewalk, waiting patiently. Alex held the back door of the limo open for them. Marion had, moments before, climbed into the warm, plush backseat.

Rubens put his arm around her. "What are you thinking?"

She continued to stare up Sixth Avenue toward the park. "I don't think you'd believe me if I told you."

"I'd believe anything you told me." He shivered a little, drew on his pigskin gloves.

"What a foolish thing to say. That's not like you."

He shrugged. "However, it's perfectly true. You are the

only person in my life who has not lied to me at one time or another."

"But perhaps I have not always told you the entire truth."

"That's not," he said slowly, "at all the same thing. Now"—he drew her closer to him as if needing her warmth—"tell me what is on your mind."

"I was thinking of this city. . . ."

"The city?" He seemed puzzled. "I don't understand."

"It's been almost five years since I've been back, Rubens. A lifetime. But now I'm here, it's like I've never left. I'm a junkie. And here's where I get my fix."

"I don't understand," he said again.

"You should. You're from New York. You should understand what this city means."

"A city's a city, Daina. It's there to be used. I neither love New York nor hate it. I come back here when there is work for me here. I left it years ago because L.A. was where the film business was. I'm glad it's there. I like the sun and the climate. I never got used to playing tennis indoors or living twenty-five stories in the sky or, alternatively, taking the Long Island Railroad in from the Island. I come back here often enough."

"But what do you see here, Rubens? Is it just concrete and glass?"

"Yes," he said, the frown still on his face. "That's all. Just that and nothing more. I go where I have to and I don't miss any other place while I'm there."

Daina said something so softly he was not certain what it was. It sounded like "Pity." Then she had ducked her head and climbed into the limo. Rubens soon followed her.

Alex went around the front of the car, got in behind the wheel. He started up.

"I don't," Daina said, "want to go to the party just yet. Too early."

"Beryl's set up that TV thing with Eyewitness News," Rubens pointed out.

"I know. Fine. She told me four times before she left for the party."

"That's only because she went to a lot of trouble—"

"They'll wait." Daina shot him a glance. "Won't they?"

Rubens looked at Marion out of the corner of his eye. "I don't imagine they'll leave."

"Sure," Daina said. "Beryl'll handle it. That's what she's being paid for."

"Where d'you want Alex to take us?" Rubens said quietly.

"I don't know. Into the park, okay? You like the park, too."

Alex made a left onto Sixth, shooting out across Central Park South and into the stony hissing darkness. The nighttime glitter of the city seemed to recede by miles instead of blocks.

Out of the silence in the car, Daina said, "You think it's happening, don't you? That it's all catching up to me." Her head was back against the velvet seat, the light from the sodium lamps silvering her profile as, one by one, the limo came up on them, came abreast and quickly shot away. In those moments of illumination, like tiny intense spotlights, her eyes seemed to be glittering amethysts, deep and stark and wholly ethereal. "Slow down," she whispered, staring out the window. "Slow us down, Alex."

The bodyguard braked around a stone-lined turning and they came upon the Tavern on the Green, its surrounding trees hung with tiny lights like spun gold. "When I was a child," she said, "when I was sad, I'd go to the Planetarium and watch the stars come out. Day slid into night but not before, in the dusk, the silhouettes of the city were outlined all around the circumference of the dome. Then the night. And only the stars." But she was remembering some other time, was telling them this story now because she could not bear to talk about the other one.

"I don't think anything of the sort," Rubens said as if there had been no time in between.

"Like one of those old movies, it'll all disintegrate in the fire. Every scrap burned inward from the corners until all that's left is ashes that blow away in the slightest hint of a breeze." She turned her head to the side, smiled a ghostly smile at him. "That's what happens to all of us, Rubens, isn't it?" She smiled again, this time with great luminosity. "Well, you know what? That's all a crock, dreamed up by some Hollywood hack screenwriter, driven half drunk by turning out a dozen scripts a year." She pursed her lips. "All that matters is now." But her pounding heart told her otherwise.

"That's why we go from one project to the next without a second thought," Marion said.

She put her arms through his, kissed him on the cheek.

"See how he is, Rubens? He's really sweet under all that barking. And smart, too."

"Oh, yes. A bloody genius." Marion sighed. "But you missed my point. Somehow we all seem to miss the human factor...the one element that should make everything work. But we never seem to learn how to handle the excesses of fame. We become distanced from the majority of people, and this only makes us feel more superior. It feeds on itself, d'you see? We're all spiteful babies at heart—always rebelling, asserting an independence we never had as children." He eyed them both, a peculiar expression on his face. "Psychiatric blather, don't you think?" But clearly he did not. "That's why we're all such bastards in the end—as my ex-wife so artfully pointed out to me over and over. But then she was no different so she had to give it up in the end." He laughed. "It's so very amusing, in a way. I'm such a *bloody* lazy sod at home. But at work that's just not on.

"The theater is perfectly exhilarating—there is absolutely nothing like the live performance—but, in time, it becomes extremely self-serving in a way. It's so tightly knit, so monstrously *structural*, you see, by its very nature, so insulated. It was becoming far too *comfortable,* a kind of niche, and I began to see in myself a slothfulness which I came to despise. I began to see that I was no longer working full throttle, although for the longest time, it seemed, I had been hoodwinking myself into believing that all was well.

"For me, the film world has always been a kind of gigantic entity that, by its size alone, was scary." He grunted. "And coming to *Hollywood* as opposed to New York was another wrench. I grew up in the darkness of theaters, watching the fabled labors. To go there to work was like ascending Mount Olympus."

"And now I suppose," Rubens said, "you're going to tell us you long for a return to the bucolic days when you were a director in the theater, making, what, a hundred pounds a week. Good, honest work." Sarcasm hung heavy in his voice now. "Uhmm. Back to the land, old boy, isn't that it? To bathe your hands once more in those footlights."

"Christ no!" Marion laughed. "I wouldn't go back now for all the tea in China or, to be a bit more up to date, all the coal in Newcastle." He shook his head. "No, I think one only finds bucolics in children's books like *The Wizard of Oz.* And, you notice, that's written by an American. None of that 'Oh, Auntie Em, there's no place like home!' in our *Alice in Wonderland,* none of that stern Protestant morality there."

"No, of course." Rubens laughed. "The English are far too bent for that sort of straight and narrow."

"Too bloody right!"

Daina sat forward as they came out of the north side of the park. "Alex," she said a little breathlessly, "don't turn around yet."

"Where to, Miss Whitney?" He watched her in the rearview mirror, his eyes very dark and perfectly unreadable.

"Go north," she said, "past 116th and then come back down Fifth Avenue."

"What are you up to?" Rubens asked.

"Nothing," she said, not turning around. She gripped the metal edge of the pulled-back glass partition. "Just leave it alone."

There was silence in the car as they swung up then turned east for a short time; slid to a stop at a light and she watched the passing black faces. They seemed part of another world, as remote from her as Pluto was from the Earth—and with about as much to offer.

The light blinked green and they slid forward, turning right onto Fifth. She saw it from more than a block away. It stood on their right, high and far less blocky than many of the smaller buildings around it. It still had that odd quasi-European air, the detailed curlicues, the ornamental cornices, shadows of peering gargoyles, and she did not see what was wrong until they were almost abreast and she saw the boarded-up windows, the broken doorway, littered with shards of beer and pint wine bottles. Sheet metal, smeared with black aerosol graffiti: "MARK 2 GONE DOWN ZEE RAKHEEN ZOMBY S." was nailed across all the lobby window spaces. There was no glass at all save that which littered the sidewalk along its front. As they sped by, she caught a glimpse of a sign, black type on white, announcing—

But it was past too quickly, the building itself having held all of her attention. She put her forehead down against the backs of her hands, closed her eyes while Rubens and Marion talked softly on so as not to disturb her, Rubens' hand on her back, circling, circling like an unheeding gull.

"Go on now," she told Alex in an odd echoey voice. "Go on

downtown to the party." She picked her head up, slid to the
back of the seat.

"It's not enough," she said from between them.

Rubens looked at her. *"What's* not enough?"

"All this," she said. "Everything that's happened up till
now. Everything that's going to happen tonight."

Rubens seemed mildly amused. "Don't you even want to
give it a quick tryout before you condemn it?"

"No. I can already feel it. I'm a cannibal now, just like the
rest of them. All the money and the...fame just feeds on
itself...instead of being an end in itself. It isn't that at all.
And I really...truly thought it would be. I'm just a baby. I
want, I want, I want. That's all I can think of with no thought
as to whether it's good or it's bad. All differentiation has
become absolutely meaningless."

Rubens turned to Marion. "D'you understand her, by any
chance?"

"Just let her alone. She'll be—"

"You aren't, for Christ's sake, crying the blues," Rubens
said.

"No." She shook her head violently. "That's not it at all.
I'm just trying to...understand it, that's all."

He grunted. "Well, forget it then, 'cause there ain't no
way. You're trying to intellectualize an intangible...a feeling. It's come—it's hit. Let it wash over the side." He opened
the bar, poured himself a vodka on the rocks. "And just be
glad it's you."

Windows on the World was on the top floor of Tower One
of the World Trade Center. It was the northernmost building
and its range of windows looking out on the vast cityscape
was awesome. It seemed to stretch onward forever, away and
away, and not even the filthy Hudson, the sludge too thick
for it ever again to completely freeze over, seemed a barrier
tonight to the spread of the metropolis onto the cliffs of New
Jersey.

The brilliant lights of the city rose into the black sky as
if they were the illimitable stars creating a geometric universe where the rounded softness of the human structure
seemed an outsider.

All this was afterimage of course. What greeted them as

they stepped off the high-speed elevator onto the 107th floor was a mass of lights and people. It was already hot and smoky and Beryl, perfectly calm and in control though they were over an hour late, took Daina's hand immediately and led her off to an alcove where the Eyewitness News people had set up their lights. They already had plenty of shots of the party itself.

Because of Marion's involvement there were more than a scattering of theater people currently on Broadway. They could not have come to the screening, but the party began after the curtain had come down on their shows and they had all been anxious to come. In fact, Rubens had wangled a second print out of the studio in order to invite them to a special Sunday-evening screening he had set up for their convenience.

Spengler came and took her away from the bright lights and shining mikes. He seemed to know precisely when to do it. He wore a silver-gray shadowstripe silk suit over an oyster-colored shirt and a navy raw-silk tie. He stood with her under the enormous marquee logo that had been devised for the film: scarlet letters with white hairline trim against dark blue shadow type.

He was all smiles tonight. He had never said a word about Monty; had not come to the funeral. But his flowers had been there along with a brief note. Monty's widow had read the card, her thin lips moving silently. She had looked up, staring straight at Daina, and had torn the card into confetti.

"Rubens was right about how to handle this project," he was saying to her now as he led her away from the immense logo.

"He's almost always right," she said. "You'll find that out soon enough."

"Yah yah. I know. I've heard that before."

"But it's not often the truth."

"Everybody's gotta come crashing down sooner or later."

She swung away from him, stood face to face. "I really think you'd better explain that remark."

He raised his hands, palms outward, and that radiant smile bathed the immediate vicinity. "Hey, c'mon. I didn't know you were high strung. It was just a casual remark, is all." The grin went into high gear. "You know, now's a crucial time for you. You can't be too careful."

"Meaning?"

He shrugged, as if to say, Don't take this too seriously, but that smile, continuing to burn at 200 watts, was proof enough of his seriousness. "You make him out to be something more than human. That could be dangerous, that's all I mean. He's as fallible as the rest of us. You put all your faith in one place—" He shrugged again.

"You know," she said pointedly, "I think you've forgotten about that little incident."

Spengler put one hand over the other, rubbed at its back. "I haven't forgotten. But that doesn't make me afraid of him either. He's not so tough."

She smiled then, put her hand up to his cheek, just touched him there. "Neither are you," she said softly and went away from him.

The party was in full swing and she was immediately swept up, seized as if by a giant fist, squirted from person to person, cluster to cluster, and it was as if they all wore masks, all were on parade, about to be judged at any moment. There was nothing of consequence, not even the compliments.

"*Ay chica,* how you have grown!"

She whirled about, saw a golden-skinned face, dusted by freckles. The hair was still reddish and, oddly, the extreme shortness now in fashion. There was a mustache now, trim and narrow and somehow making that wide slash of a mouth all the more lethal-looking. And there were some lines now scored into that singular countenance, downward from the edges of the nose to the corners of the lips, skeins at the outer corners of the eyes. But those eyes themselves had not changed at all. Pale blue and flat as stones under water, they were the unblinking constant in a face of shifting emotions.

"*Qué linda muchacha!*" Aurelio Ocasio said, taking her hands in his. The grip was cool, firm. She felt the hardness of an expert; a professional.

Ocasio laughed to see her face. "My God, you don't remember me!" Those eyes peered at her and, as his face shifted position and the flat planes of his freckled face caught the overhead pinspots, the color drained out of them and she had the eerie impression that they were just two holes bored down into his skull, that she could see the brain pulsing wetly there.

"Can it be, *linda?* Can it really be?" He pulled back, held her at arm's length. He wore a fox-colored worsted suit that was obviously custom-made. His shirt was a pale yellow silk and his tie was thin, striped umber and burnt sienna. He wore a yellow carnation in his buttonhole. By his side had stood all this time a tall slim blonde in a peach satin affair that showed just a touch too much of her thrusting breasts to be altogether classy. She stood with her long-nailed hands in front of her, clutching a fox stole and a red-brown lizard-skin bag.

"Perhaps it's this," Ocasio said, running a stubby fingertip along the perfect line of his mustache. His face sagged in sadness. "Or perhaps merely time. It's been"—he snapped his fingers briskly—"let me see, twelve years. Is that right? Yes, yes I remember perfectly. Twelve years. We first met in a restaurant uptown. You don't recall, *chica?* You were so young then. You were with someone. Now let me see, what was his name? You know"—and now he seemed somewhat chagrined—"for the life of me, I cannot remember his name...."

"Baba."

"Yes!" Snapping his fingers again. "Yes, of course! I see you *do* remember me after all." He bowed slightly. "I am most flattered." Almost immediately his face fell again. "Unfortunately, we did not have a chance to become as close friends as I would have wished." He lifted his forefinger into the air. "But even then, *linda,* I could tell that great things were for you! Yes, truly. You had a certain quality. An... I don't know how to put it into words, especially English. Had we been able to become closer, spend more time together... I am so happy for you!" He covered her hands in his, brought them up to his mouth, kissed their backs. "A bravura performance, *linda!* Truly one of a kind!"

"What are you doing now?" She almost choked on the words.

"I run a specialized consulting firm." He seemed to smile, his long yellow teeth gleaming. "I have, you might say, only one client: the mayor of the city of New York." He threw his head back then and laughed as shrilly as a macaw. "You must stop by the office if you have time while you're here. No, no. I insist. See the operation. Ah hah! I'm certain you'd be fascinated, *chica,* ah yes! But now I see they are calling

for you. There's important business afoot, I imagine. There
you are. Go on now. I'll see you again before I leave." He blew
her a kiss. *"Adios, linda!"* And shook his head as she was
whirled away from him in the dense jungle of sweating bodies.

"'Daina Whitney creates the kind of on-screen magic
rarely seen in film these days. Hers is a performance of stunning complexity, combining mysteriousness, sexuality, vul-
nerability, and—not at all paradoxically—the kind of bravado previously the exclusive preserve of male performers....'
my God!...."

"Go on," Rubens urged. "What else does the *Times* say?"

"It goes on and on," Daina said, a bit breathlessly. "Christ!"

Rubens laughed. "Well, are you going to keep it all to
yourself? You've even got Alex on pins and needles."

She glanced up, over the sheets of newsprint, saw the
bodyguard's eyes, dark as olives, in the rearview mirror.
"Watch the road, Alex, would you? Now's certainly not the
time for a pileup." Then she began to read again from the
Times review:

"'On the outside, we have a fairly straightforward story
of a political hijacking. That, in itself, is a timely subject, but
be forewarned, this is no action-adventure film, per se.

"'Some comparisons come immediately to mind, most no-
tably Francis Coppola's *Apocalypse Now*. However, where Mr.
Coppola failed to peel away the heroic facade of war to show
its inner workings, Marion Clarke, who coscripted *Heather
Duell* with Morton Douglas, reveals to us, layer by layer, the
clockwork mountings of terrorism and a frightening vision
it is, too.

"'Yet without Miss Whitney's multidimensional rendering
of the title character, the film could not possibly have succeeded. For she is the hard center that must hold against the
whirlwind of forces. If she is not believable, there is, literally,
no film.

"'As it is, the film takes wing from her riveting performance to achieve true greatness....'"

Daina let the paper fall from her lap to the carpet of the
limo. She put her head back against the seat, watched the
lights of Manhattan flicker by in a slow dazzle, building itself
into a golden statuette with chaste, clasped hands. Behind

her eyelids it lived. Soon, she thought, it would live on the outside as well.

Monika was dying. She had a disease with a very long name. Daina heard the words strung together and, in typical medical style, they made no sense to her. The doctor could be speaking Martian for all she understood him—which was just the way they liked it, she thought. Doctors are far more secure when no one understands what they have said; there's less chance of being sued for malpractice.

But Daína did understand this: what her mother had was something like cancer, only worse. What could be worse than cancer? she thought. A disease without a cure. There was no cure for what Monika had, either. It was progressively degenerative.

"I understand you haven't seen your mother in some months," the young, clean-shaven doctor said. He had the artificial smile of an airline steward and the sunken eyes of a war veteran. He sighed a lot when he thought he was unobserved. "Now I don't want you to be shocked when you see her." They stopped before the closed door to Monika's hospital room. "She won't look the same, so be prepared and try not to be frightened." He patted her shoulder and left her at the door.

He had managed to scare her witless, an art some doctors seemed to be born with. She heard soft footfalls, whispered voices, the squeaky trundle of a passing gurney, a brief sob, stifled, the quiet chiming of the hospital page. But these were all behind her. In front of her was Monika, dying.

She reached out a hand until it touched the door. Slowly she pushed it inward. It seemed far too heavy for her to budge. She went into the room, holding her breath.

Monika lay on the high bed, tubes running into her nose, the inside of her elbow. There were black bruises on her arms where the needles had gone in and come out. She seemed to be sleeping and, in that slumber, appeared already dead. There were hollows in her face that had not been there before. It was as if something was stripping the flesh from her from the inside.

Daína felt compelled to approach the bed, and as she did,

Monika opened her eyes as if sensing the nearness of her daughter.

"So," she said softly, "the prodigal daughter returns." Her hand fluttered across the bedcovers, a wounded bird.

Daina was startled more by the eyes than by her mother's voice. For, despite the dire warnings of the doctor, those eyes were the same as they had always been, as dryly humorous, as mocking, as angry as when Monika had been ten years younger. That bastard doctor, Daina thought. He's only looking at the outside. Nothing can change what she is inside.

"You look different," Monika said. "Did Dr. Geist help you?" It was not a question. She glanced down at her own hand, empty atop the thin blanket. She shivered. "I'm cold," she whispered.

Daina reached down to the foot of the bed, unfurled the second blanket folded there. She tucked it in under her mother's chin. Monika's hand came up, closed around her wrist. "If you're better, you'll find it in your heart to forgive me." Her tone rose and fell with the beat of her pulse in the hollow of her throat. "I did what I thought was right."

"You deceived me, Mother."

Monika's eyes closed and tears began to edge out from beneath the lids. "You would never have listened to me. You would have turned your back on the truth."

"The truth is, you always tried to keep me from Daddy." Part of her cried out, How can you talk of this now? But another, larger part told her it must be said before it was too late.

Monika's grip on her wrist tightened. "You were always so beautiful, so pristine and innocent. And your father...had that way of looking at you. It was so...special. He never looked at anyone that way, not even me."

"But he loved you. How could you—"

"He loved *women,* Daina." Her eyes opened, larger, brighter than ever in that withered flesh. "I knew about it before we were married but I assumed it would stop when he was my husband. It didn't."

"Mother—!"

Daina attempted to pull away but Monika's grip had become fierce. Her head came up off the pillow. "You're old enough to hear this now. You wanted to know—you *must* know now." Her head fell back and for a moment her eyes closed again. She seemed to have difficulty breathing.

"Your father could not or would not stop. I suppose he must have loved me, in his fashion. He did not want to leave me. But I always suspected that was because of you. I knew he could never bear to part with you so he took the whole package...and in his spare time carried on." Her eyes squeezed shut. She was crying. "Oh, God help me." Daina thought she must be in pain and was about to ring for the nurse when Monika continued. "I grew to resent you, yes. You were my only link with him. I couldn't keep him but you could."

"But Mother—"

"Keep quiet until I've finished, Daina. I haven't the strength to fight with you." Her fingers moved upward until they entwined with her daughter's. "I know I drove you out of the house. I know what I did to you. I was drunk on the freedom your father's death gave me." She smiled a little. "I know you must think me callous but try to see it from my point of view. Try to see what he did to me; what I did to myself. Yes, I wanted you out of the house but"—tears spilled from her eyes again—"it was only after you had left that I began to understand what I had done and...how much I loved you. I had never...you see, I think the problem was I could never think of you as an individual. Before, you were always the object that kept our marriage together, the bridge between your father and me.

"Then when you came back I saw in your eyes it would be the last time I'd ever see you. I was afraid for you. God knew where you were, who you were with. You were in school only on and off and the people there talked me into going to see Dr. Geist. I thought they knew what they were talking about. They were authorities—" She stopped abruptly, biting her lip. She drew Daina closer to her. "Was it awful, darling? You must tell me. Please."

"No," Daina lied. "It wasn't so bad."

Monika's eyes seemed to clear and she smiled again. "That's good," she whispered. "That makes me feel much better. I was afraid—" She looked into her daughter's eyes. "But then I'm afraid all the time now."

Daina leaned over, kissed her mother on the lips. "Daddy told me, once, how much he loved you."

Monika's eyes opened wide. "He did? When?"

So Daina told her the story of their fishing trip on Long Pond, of the weather, the sights and sound and the smells, of the tension in the line, the feel of the rod jerking as the fish took the bait, the excitement of the tug of war.

"And what did he say?" Monika wanted to know.

Daina told her. "He said, 'You know I love your mother very much.'" Monika seemed to be sleeping. "Mother ...Mother?" She rang for the nurse.

It rang and rang and rang. Daina jerked upward in bed, her heart pounding. She wiped the sweat from her forehead. She turned her head. Rubens lay beside her, asleep.

The telephone continued to ring. She glanced at the bedside clock. The luminous digital numerals were just clicking over to 4:12. In the morning?

Automatically, she grabbed for the phone.

"Uh uh uh uh..."

"What?"

"Huh. Dain...?"

She rubbed at her eyes. "Chris?"

"Uh uh uh..."

"Chris is that you?"

"Dain, Dain, Daina..." The voice was thick, slurred.

"Chris where the hell are you?"

"Hum ummm..."

"Chris for Christ's sake!"

"...ew York...."

"What? I couldn't—Did you say New York? Are you here? Chris!"

"Yah yah yah."

"You should've come to the party...." An intuition. "Are you here...."

"Ak ak ak..." It almost sounded like laughter. Almost. "Alone Dain. All 'lone."

"What the hell are you doing here? Chris, are you okay?"

"Hidin' out Dain. I'm here incog..." He could not seem to get the rest out. She could hear his breathing now, shallow and ragged.

"Chris, just tell me where you are."

"Uh uh uh..."

"Chris!" Rubens rolled over, stirred toward waking, and she got up off the bed, walked as far away from him as the cord would allow. She turned away from the bed, cupped her hands over the mouthpiece. "Just tell me where you are. I'll come right over." A cold kind of dread had begun to infuse her, like ghostly fingers stroking her spine. She shivered involuntarily.

"...otel...."

"*Which* hotel?" Each moment now increased her fear. What was going on? "Chris, which one? The Carlyle? The Pierre?" She named his favorite haunts.

"Ak ak ak..." That sound again, so similar to laughter yet so utterly chilling. He gave her a name: The Rensselaer.

"What?" She almost yelled. "I don't know where—" But he was gone like a puff of smoke, exhaled and useless.

She did not bother to call his name, went instead back across the room, replaced the receiver in its cradle. She pulled on a pair of jeans, stuffed them into high leather boots, slipped a turtleneck sweater over her head. Then she knelt beside the night table, pulled out the Manhattan directory. Got "Hotels," ran her fingers down the columns, one by one, until she found it, said, "Oh, my God" under her breath. The hotel was on 44th Street, off Broadway. Any closer to a flophouse and he'd be on the Bowery. There was *no* reason for Chris to pass by a place like that, let alone be staying there. That was her thought as she picked up her shoulder bag and quietly slipped out the door.

At 4:20 in the morning, the avenues of New York seemed as wide as the boulevards of Madrid, the city so quiet she could almost hear the neon billboards blinking on and off. *Deep Throat* and *The Devil in Miss Jones* were still the double bill to beat at the Frisco Theatre on Broadway. Across the street a new twin movie house had sprung up, showing Spanish-language films exclusively. Tonight it was *El Brujo Maldito* and *¡Que Verguenza!*

The taxi swayed and dipped as it raced downtown over the pitted asphalt. Great plumes of gray-white steam hissed from manhole vents, luminous as they picked up and reflected back the street and theater lights. Each time they passed through a cloud it was like passing through a curtain and she, still half asleep, perhaps expected to see the structures of another world just beyond.

But it was not until she stepped out of the cab onto the sidewalk at 44th Street that she understood what it was she had been searching for. It was the gray glitter, the oh-so-kinetic grime, the jungle line of her outlaw youth. She wanted, desperately now, to know that it was still here, had not been plowed under, boarded- and graffitied-up like the gargoyled apartment building up in Harlem, whose beautiful shell would soon feel the humiliating crunch of the wrecker's ball. Yet it was not her youth for which she longed. That was a time, in fact, to which she was happy never to return.

She wanted to witness no victory over this outlaw world. Its inviolate existence was a reassurance to her; the ultimate proof that what she had learned here was valid. For here lay her power and it was stronger than that of the Red Brigades or the Black September or the Baader-Meinhof.

She took a look at the Hotel Rensselaer. It had a dark, dingy front of soot-blackened metal and wire-reinforced glass, giving it more the air of an ancient police precinct. It was bounded on the west by an iron-gated and padlocked stamp store with a display window full of sun-bleached cracked plastic folders sandwiching one stamp here and one there, and on the east by a porno theater that had but recently given up the ghost. Affixed to its slight marquee were two lines of black type. The first read: "XXX"; the second: "HOT CROSSED BUNS."

Over the revolving door of the Rensselaer hung an old and ponderous sign that every so often creaked on its iron limb as if about to make the final ignominious plunge onto the sidewalk below.

Just to the left was an iron grate in the pavement through which steam heaved, reeking with the sulphurous odor of New York's sewer network. A man lay atop this spot of sidewalk warmth, having first spread out an open leaf of crumpled newspaper. He wore a pair of pants far too short for him, held in place by a length of twine. He wore no socks and his shoes—or at least at one time they had been shoes—were full of holes. He was fast asleep in the vapors, his back against the grimy brickwork of the hotel's frontage, one hand tight around the neck of an empty pint bottle of Irish Rose.

The night wind rattled his newspaper bedding, making it seem as if he were riding a magic carpet. No princess for him, Daina thought, when he wakes up.

She leaned back into the open driver's window, handed him three bills. He had his radio on. On a talk show, someone was berating the mayor for underpaying the police. A spate of irate calls were coming in.

"You want I should wait, Miss Whitney?" the driver said. He was a sallow-skinned young man with a full beard and red eyes. "Business is lousy right now. I got a book. I don't mind."

She smiled thinly, walking away. "It's all right," she said. "I don't know how long I'll be."

He turned off the engine. "Don't make no difference. Better me than someone else, huh?" He rolled up his window almost all the way, began to pore over a dog-eared paperback copy of *Magister Ludi*.

What've I got to worry about? she thought as she went through the creaking revolving door to the hotel. Nothing ever changes.

Inside, the lobby looked like a heavyweight punk who had just gone the distance with the champ. Everything was broken down and seedy. Dust hung in the air as if it were being waved from place to place instead of disposed of.

She walked quickly across to the reception desk. No one was around. There was no book but a small plywood box within which sat a sheaf of three-by-five index cards.

She went through them without finding a "Kerr." Then she remembered the name he used on tour—all the band members had pseudonyms for security reasons. And there it was: Graham Greene. It used to amuse Chris no end. Room 454.

Replacing the card, Daina hurried across the lobby. It smelled like stale sweatsocks. A shuddering elevator eventually deposited her on the fourth floor. She took a hurried look around, almost ran down the hall.

Room 454 was at the end—one of two corner rooms. She did not even think to knock—or even that she might need a key—but reached down and turned the knob. The door swung open. She went in, closed the door behind her.

It was pitch dark in the room but even so she could sense that she was in the foyer of a two-room suite. She had not known that hotels such as this one had suites.

She moved cautiously forward, one hand outstretched, sliding along the papered wall. She could feel its scratched and shredded surface, as pocked as the skin of the moon. Somewhere along here, she reasoned, there must be a light switch.

She found it just at the end of the narrow foyer and flicked it up. Nothing. Silence. She stopped still, her heart thudding.

She was about to call out his name when she noticed that the air was heavy with scents. She sniffed like an animal on point, could define the sweet musk of weed, the sharp pungency of incense—patchouli—and the acrid odor of sweat. She caught her breath. It was not the smell one builds up after a hard day's work or the heady tang of aftersex relaxation—rather it had about it the stink of sickness and fear.

She moved into the first room, trying to pierce the blackness with her eyes. And she became aware of the guitar, strumming plangently—acoustic not electric—and she thought, He's all right.

Then she heard the bass, synthesizer, and drums come in, knew she was listening to a recording. She went quickly across the room and, at the threshold to the bedroom, heard his rich tenor begin to sing: *I'm tired of the lies/The thighs/That unwind at night/Like sails/Dark clouds billowing/Bewitching the endless blue skies*. Melody welling, the beat hypnotic.

"Chris?"

I'm tired of the sighs/The squeals of animal delight/Invading my mind/I find/I'm no longer willing/To fight/For what I want. Moved easily into the chorus: *I'm on a line/A bluebird on a line/Waiting for the sound/Of a gun to shoot me down/I'm on a line/Just paralyzed/Waiting for the sound of a gun to shoot me down....*

There was a short instrumental bridge, an electric guitar solo and then the chorus repeated itself until the music died away on dark, synthesized wings.

"Chris?" she said again. She went into the bedroom and almost immediately tripped over a pile of disheveled clothing.

Said "Damn!" and picked herself up. The tall shape by the near side of the bed turned out to be a lamp and she turned it on.

"Oh, Chris...."

It was a mean room that flared up at her, long and narrow; the kind that seemed old even when it was new. Now it was beyond redemption. The cassette machine was atop a scarred

wooden bureau, half hiding the flaking oval mirror behind
it. On the other side of the room one lone window fitted with
sooty glass gaped out on an alleyway too narrow for a man
to stand in sideways. The blank brick rear end of another
building abutted this so that it might have been midnight for
all the light that could seep downward even in midafternoon.

The bed, which dominated the room, was one of those
heavy iron affairs, bolted to the floor so that it could not be
budged. Bedspread and top sheet were thrown back in a tangle of slips and whorls, cascading down over the end onto the
throw rug that had, at some time long passed, grown thread-
bare. It was impossible to tell what color it had originally
been.

The rattling of ancient plumbing came from the half-open
door to the bathroom along the wall next to the window.
There seemed to be tiny movements in the corners where the
lamplight could not reach.

"Chris," she breathed.

He lay naked on the bed, soaked in sweat. His long hair
was matted and wet; he had a growth of beard and perhaps
this was what made his face seem so terribly thinned out.
That or the horrid harsh lamplight crawling across his face
like the advent of an eclipse. His eyes seemed enormous,
almost exophthalmic, with layers of blue-black around the
sockets as if he were made up for some macabre stage play.

The planes of his face were streaked with dirt and dried
sweat, and the skin of his body seemed so white he might
have been just unearthed.

"Chris, Chris...." Her heart breaking, she climbed onto
the bed, smelled before she saw the dried vomit that had
turned the undersheet on the left side of the bed to plaster.
She took his slippery head in her lap, stroked the hair out
of his eyes.

For one unbearably long, terrifying minute she thought
he was so far gone that he could not recognize her but it was
only that he was having difficulty focusing. His muscles were
corded, knotted as if from some long and titanic struggle;
there seemed to be not one ounce of fat on all his body, only
muscle and bone.

His lips tried to work but they were cracked, as rough as
leather. She got up and ran into the bathroom to get him a
glass of water.

Towels were strewn all over the place, damp and smelly, and along the narrow glass shelf over the worn sink, its white porcelain green and mottled brown from years of running water, were lines of men's and women's cosmetics, jumbled like a toy army in the confused aftermath of war.

There was one filthy glass resting precariously on the edge of the sink, which she washed out and filled with cold water. She turned around, heard a crunch under her boot sole. She kicked away a towel, saw the syringe and the torn corner of a glassine bag. No one had to tell her what the bag had contained, yet she bent down, put the bag into her pocket.

He had trouble drinking at first but there was no doubt that he was monstrously dehydrated. Holding his sweating head, watching the convulsive movements of his throat, she wondered how this could have happened to him in such a short time. What was he doing here? *Hiding out, Dain.* She could hear his words to her over the phone. *I'm here incog*...Incognito. But why?

"Dain..."

She opened her eyes, not having realized that she had closed them for any time.

"I'm here, Chris."

"You came." His voice was a reedy whisper and it was obviously difficult for him to speak even short sentences.

She felt his body tense, his eyes open wide and she let go of him just in time. He arched up abruptly, sitting, turning away from her, and vomited all the fluid out of him. For a moment his entire frame was wracked by convulsions, then the spasm seemed to subside and he was able to relax enough so that she could help him back down onto the bed.

She reached for the phone. "I'm going to call a doctor." But she never got as far as lifting the receiver from its cradle.

"No," he said furrily. His fingers were around her wrist, still with surprising strength. "None o' that."

"Someone in the band then. Didn't Silka come with you?"

"Don't," he said, "call *anyone.*"

"Chris, what's happened to you?"

His eyes looked at her dully. "Dunno."

She took his shoulders, fairly shook him. "Yes, goddamnit, you do!" She took out the glassine bag, held it in front of his face. "What kind of shit is this?"

He turned his head away from her. His bony chest heaved

and a film of sweat was breaking out all over him again. He mumbled something.

"What? What did you say?" She shouted so loudly that he jumped in spite of himself.

"Know what it is," he rasped. "Horse. Must be some bad shit." His muscles knotted and she thought he was going to retch again. "Real bad shit. Don't know. Never happened t'me before." His hands were fists, white and straining, the nails digging into the flesh of his palms. She thought she could see the fluttering of his heart beneath the pallid skin of his chest. "Gotta do somethin', man...." His eyes crossed with the pain. "Everythin's shuttin' down...."

"What are you—"

He arched off the bed, his lips pulled back from his clenched teeth in a terrifying rictus. It was like watching a skeleton come to hideous life. "Beat me. Beat me, Dain," he managed to get out. "You—you gotta."

He collapsed then and immediately she put her ear to his chest. Nothing. Not a beat.

"Christ!" she said and got up on the bed, straddling him. She lifted her right arm, closed her hand into a fist, brought it down as hard as she could on the spot directly over his failing heart. She counted five beats, did it again, grunting with the effort. Wait. A third time. It was like hitting dead meat.

She leaned on him, listening. Nothing. "Come on, damnit! Don't die on me now!" She reared up, hit him again and again over his heart, the beat like a great tympan in her ears. Sweat rolled off her, stinging her eyes, dripping dolefully into his pale flesh. The bed creaked rhythmically, violently, just as if they were making love.

"Come on, come on come on ... Chris ... don't do it ... come on, come on, come on!..." Her voice defined itself as a litany: a plea to him but also a goad to herself not to give up, not to stop until there was no hope left at all. But as the seconds stretched out into minutes and those minutes seemed to pile up, what hope she had been holding on to close against her heart, began to dissipate until she found herself weeping as hard as she was pounding on him, hating herself fully as much as she hated him for doing this to her, for having the temerity to drag her all the way over here at four in the morning only to flutter away from her like a dying bird.

"God *damn* you!" she shouted. "Wake up!"

And he did. Magically, miraculously his eyelids flickered as if he were dreaming and then, through her tears, she saw him staring at her, felt his great muscular chest taking enormous heaves as if he could not get enough oxygen.

She stopped what she was doing, began to cry all the more. "Oh, Chris...Oh, Chris, I thought you were dead, you bastard!"

He blinked once, opened his lips, shut them, said softly, "I think I was. I really think...Dain...don't stop now...."

"What?"

"You can't. You gotta keep it up...until you're sure I won't pass out ag—again." His eyes began to flutter closed as if he were too tired to remain awake. "You can't—can't let me go under...'nother time, Dain....I won't—won't wake up... ever...."

She rose up again with a groan from deep inside her, balled her hands into fists and struck him. He trembled under the double blows and she gasped in horror. But she did it again and this time his eyes flew open. He was unable to speak but she saw him staring at her as she continued to beat him, that soft loving look that seemed to go on forever. And she wanted to see that now, needed to see it more than anything else. She knew it was his only lifeline, that as long as he continued to stare at her, he was fighting, that he would not slip away without a battle.

She beat a strong tattoo against the flesh of his arms, his chest, his belly, thighs, sides, even his neck. And with each blow now he grunted like an animal. His straining body spasmed beneath her. His skin was as white as milk, as pale as the porcelain of the sink in the bathroom, seeming as translucent as tissue paper.

She could see the pulsing blue of his veins as they distended, rising to the surface and she closed her eyes. Hot bitter tears squeezed their way through her shut lids and she had trouble breathing. She sobbed as she struck him, finding that it gave her the strength to continue until it seemed to her that no real effort was required any longer. Her fists flying through the air were virtually weightless while striking him with the force of sledgehammers.

Now she thought of herself only as the bringer of life, as she rose and fell, rose and fell as inexorably as the tide.

The room around her faded like an old photograph subjected to blistering sunlight. There was only the two of them locked in a terrible embrace far more intimate than sex, connected by an odd umbilical. She was no longer aware that she swung in cadence, that she thought, that she even breathed.

Time seemed to stand still. Sweat ran like glue between their heaving bodies and her open mouth gasped in air.

Crying out, Chris tried to heave her off him, turning this way and that. But still she continued her violent tattoo upon him until, with a titanic effort, he twisted onto his side, vomited again and again over the side of the bed.

He moaned.

"Chris, Chris, Chris..." And never remembered where she got the strength to get up on all fours, back off the foul-smelling bed, dragging him with her, until he bumped heavily onto the floor and across it, over the low sill into the bathroom. Kick, kick, kick at those *goddamned* towels, heavy as concrete lumps, and roll him into the bathtub. Blindly she reached out, spun the cold water tap on full. Heard the great rush, the spume of the spray and gave a great startled cry as he snorted, sat up and, convulsively, pulled her into the shower with him.

"This bloody water is pissing cold!" He moved to get out and she pulled him back.

"Stay here," she said, "for a while." She had to raise her voice to be heard over the hissing heavy spray cascading over them.

They shivered together, their skin raised in gooseflesh.

She took his head in her hands, cradled it against her breasts. "Talk to me," she said. "I don't want you going to sleep now."

"I don't—" He coughed, choking on the water. He snorted again. "I can't think straight."

"Well try, damnit! What the hell are you doing in this flytrap anyway?"

"Hiding out."

"From whom?"

"Everyone."

"Come on!"

"Th' *bloody* band, all right?"

The water crashed down onto their heads, sucked and gurgled around their flanks.

"What did you do, Chris?" she said quietly.

"Just what you said I *should* do. I quit th' band."

"You didn't!"

"Thought Benno would go into cardiac arrest. Turned bloody blue in his face; sputtered'n'screamed...."

"What about Nigel?"

"Didn't say nothin'...." He paused as if remembering the scene all over again. "It was th' queerest thing. He didn't say a word. Jus' turned away an' looked at Tie." He snorted. "Ol' Rollie, he said, 'Aw, bollocks, Chris,' and Ian kicked in his amp, he was so bloody chuffed. I began t' walk outa there... can we go dry off now? I'm gettin' as wrinkled as a pensioner."

"In a minute," she said as if he were a schoolboy. "After you finish this." As if she were offering him a sweet as a reward for being a good boy.

"I began t' walk outa there, y'know, an' Nigel, he turns round an' says, 'You better remember, boyo. It'll change your mind right enough.'"

Daina stared at him. "What's that mean?"

Chris pulled a little away from her. "It's just between us— th' band members." He looked away from her. "There's a kind o' pact we made, see, years'n'years ago. In another age, it seems like."

"What kind of pact?" She began to feel a chill that had nothing to do with the water.

"A pact is all."

She laughed. "Oh come on. You can tell me." She poked at him playfully. "Something signed in blood I'll bet—"

It was meant as a joke so she was startled when he said, "Might as well've been."

"And it's still binding on all of you after all this time? What could—"

He whirled away from her, stood up and stepped out of the shower. Shivering, he bent down, began to towel himself off.

Daina twisted around, turned off the water. She climbed out, stood waiting while he bent again, handed her another towel.

"You'd better tell me what the fuck is going on, Chris."

He stood as still ~~as~~ a statue. Behind them both, the faucet dripped dolefully. A rattle came from over their heads as someone upstairs flushed the toilet.

He turned around slowly until he faced her. There was something in his eyes she had not seen before and she wondered what it was.

"All right," he said slowly, "you asked for it and...in a way you've earned it. You're one of us now"—he gave a gurgling laugh—"though Christ knows Tie would—" He stopped abruptly, eyed her appraisingly. "But no, perhaps now she wouldn't, eh?" He gave her a small smile. "It isn't once you've saved my life, but twice."

"I don't—"

"I know, Dain. Tie told me; thought she'd turn me against you an' it almost worked. For a couple o' weeks I was so bloody pissed at you I couldn't see straight. Until I thought about it, that is. Then, gradually, I began t' understand what you'd done—and knew that even Tie hadn't gotten it." He draped the towel over his shoulders. "She don't understand you at all, Dain, you know that? You dumbfound her—and scare th' shit out o' her."

He laughed shortly, weakly, stared down at his naked body. "Just look at this," he said. "An' us not ever havin' gone t' bed." He closed his eyes, swayed a bit and she reached out a hand to steady him. But the smile was still on his face. "It's such a relief, really." His eyes opened. The whites seemed a bit clearer though there was still a slight tinge of yellow to them. "I'm always thinkin' with my cock." He sat down on the edge of the tub, his uncircumcised penis hanging down between his thighs. He looked up at her. "I'm surrounded by a bunch of bloody vampires, ain't I? How in Christ did I ever let it happen?"

"Don't expect any sympathy from me."

He shook his head. "Sympathy's the last thing I need right now."

"Chris," she said slowly, "you've been wanting—I mean really wanting—to leave the band for a long time, haven't you?"

He put his head in his hands. "Yeh. I reckon I have."

"That music—"

"What music?"

"The song I heard when I came in—"

"I don't remember."

"I'm not surprised. What was it?"

He looked up again, smiled at her. "'On a Line.' Tune for th' solo album. Dain"—he stood up—"th' writin', it's all done. I've just got t' go into th' studio an' finish recordin'....I don't have everything I need at home. Just did some o' th' basics there."

"What's taken you so long?" she asked. "You've been so unhappy."

"'Cause I'm a bloody weak-minded bastard," he snapped savagely. "'What if,' I thought. 'What if I go out there an' I stiff? What a berk I'll look!'"

"But that isn't all, is it? Chris!" She moved to shake him.

His eyes were closing again. He slumped heavily against her as if all the strength had abruptly drained out of him. "Tired, Dain...so tired...."

She slapped his face. "For Christ's sake, Chris, wake up!" She shook him violently. "Oh, Jesus, don't go to sleep now! Talk to me. Chris! Talk to me!"

"Wha..."

"Anything! Chris!" She thought desperately. "Tell me how Jon died."

"Jon? Huh?" His eyes opened and he stared glassily, his head lolling as if he had just come back from a three-day drunk. "Jon?"

"Yes, you remember. Jon—your friend Jon. He died. Chris!" Slapped him again; stood him up, groaning with the effort.

"Ummm. Common knowledge." His voice was furred. "In all th' papers. Coppers wouldn't let us alone...three weeks..." All she could see were the whites beneath his partially opened lids. "Till Nigel came up with th' idea o' doin' a free gig in Jon's memory. 'Do it in Vondel Park, in Amsterdam,' he said. 'It'll get th' heat off an' us out o' here.'" His lids fluttered and she slapped his cheek again, hard enough for it to go white, then red as the blood rushed back in. "On'y...on'y wasn't Nigel's idea....Not really, no. Was Tie's. But then *all* th' great promo—promotion ideas were hers. When you come right down t' it." He giggled. "But she was using Nigel just like she used Jon. Like th' bloody Delphic Oracle. Knew bloody well we wouldn't go for pro—nouncements from her. But if we thought all those ideas were Jon's..." He laughed, his head rolling back and forth against her shoulder. "Christ but she was right. Th' bitch! She had th' right ideas, all right. They got us... a lot, a bloody helluva lot."

"And so you did the concert in Amsterdam."

He nodded. "Banners with Jon's face on 'em, bloody slogan-mongers chanting up'n'down th' streets for hours afterward, calling his name, calling his name." He sniffed. "After that, it all died down...just like he—ah, ah, *she*—said it would. Coppers buggered off t' hound th' Beatles or some such. Who th' hell knows!"

"And Jon was dead...."

"Oh, yeh, Jon. My good friend Jon. My mate." His voice dripped sarcasm. "Th' bloody band almost blew itself apart 'cause o' him. He was drivin' us all round th' bend, he was, with his orders an' his—Christ, we couldn't count on him for nothin'! Had t' hire some bruiser, finally, t' drag him along t' rehearsals'n'gigs. Didn't tell *him* that, though. Wouldn't dare. He'd slip away'n'hide from us all. No, no. Told him we'd hired him a bodyguard 'cause he'd gotten t' be such a big star. He liked that, our Jon did, oh, yes indeed. Got him right where he lived. If we hadn't—if he hadn't died, who knows where we'd all be now?

"Stupid bastard." His head shook from side to side like a wounded animal's. "Stupid *bloody* bastard. You know th' band was his idea in th' beginnin'. Yeh. Jon was a bloody genius in many ways. Not like Nile, mind you, makin' shit sound like a symphony. Not like that. But he could arrange th' music. An' then he'd scarper an' not even Tie would be able t' tell us where he went.

"Jon'd take all our songs, Nigel's'n'mine, an' he'd turn 'em into magic. Don't know how he did it....Christ knows I'm not even sure how Nigel'n'I managed to write what we did.

"But they hated each other, y'see...Nigel'n'Jon. Always like oil'n'water." He tried to stare into her eyes, failed. "Oh, well, not always, maybe. I was th' glue what held th' band t'gether in th' old days...med—mediatin' between th' two berks...but I was also th' reason they hated each other.

"Jon was jealous of my writin' with Nigel. Badgered me so much that I tried it with him once." He shook his head back and forth. "Was no go. He cried for three days...took a scarper an' we had t' cancel a weekend o' gigs. You c'n

imagine how that kind o' shit made Nigel feel...he's dead
if he ain't on th' bloody road.

"As for Nigel, I'd always assumed it was merely Jon's
weaknesses he hated. Jon wrote his own stuff an' often
enough he'd be in th' studio by th' time th' rest o' us arrived.
He'd look up at us as dewy-eyed as a kid an' say, 'Here's a
new one for ya.' But he wouldn't be able t' play a note...he'd
be fucked up one way or 'nother." His voice had softened
somewhat. "He'd break down'n'cry, holdin' on t' that deep red
Gibson o' his like it was a Teddy bear an' Nigel'd turn away
an' say, 'Christ Jesus, somebody come'n'clean him up.'

"It was Tie, of course, who got under Nigel's skin. I reckon
he just couldn't understand how she could be living with Jon.
We were on tour in Munich when she first showed up backstage. No one had any idea how she managed t' bypass th'
security people. But she had a lotta friends an' in Germany
at least you gotta have that t' get anywhere.

"She latched on to Jon right away. Well, it wasn't so sur-
prisin', really. Jon was a good-lookin' berk...always in some
trouble or other with a dolly's old man. Must be a lotta his
kids growin' up right now, ha ha! All he had t'do was bat
those long lashes o' his an' th' dollies'd melt dead away. Not
that *any* o' us had trouble. But with Jon...well, he was always a special case. But Tie was special too in her own way
an' she became th' first...an' only...t' move in with Jon.

"Then, one day, I came round t' Jon's flat. It was a day
just pissin' rain...cold'n'fouler'n'hell. I found him face down
in th' mud. 'Here, m'lad,' I said, 'what's happened t' you then.'
He'd been beaten an', I thought, robbed. But no. It'd been
Nigel. 'Christ,' I said, 'what th' fuck did you say t' him?' He
looked at me rather sheepishly. 'Don't think I c'n tell you.'
'You'd bloody well better, m'lad,' I told him. 'I don't want t'
have t' hear it from him.' He nodded then an' I took him outa
th' rain. Tie wasn't home an' I sat in front o' th' fire, starin'
at th' flames an' gettin' warm. 'Cept that ol' Jon, he couldn't
sit still for a bloody minute. He paced back'n'forth so fast, his
corgi got a crick in its neck from watchin' him. An' at every
sound from th' street he jumped three feet.

"'You bloody well better get it over with,' I said, 'before
you have a nervous breakdown.'

"He came an' stood over me then an' I could tell by his face
that it was no laughing matter.

"'I'm afraid t' tell you,' he said. 'I'm afraid you'll hate me, th' way Nigel does now.' He broke down. 'I couldn't take that, Chris. They're all against me as it is. But if you...' He put his head in his hands. 'I don't know what I'd do.'

"I took his hands in mine, said, 'Don't you worry none, mate. Nothin's gonna break good mates like us up. Just never you mind 'bout all that rubbish. What's this about then?'

"'I told him.' He sniffed. 'I told Nigel I wanted t' sleep with you.'

"I don't know why I'm starting to laugh now—it certainly wasn't funny. Not in th' least. I knew then that in at least one respect Nigel had been right 'bout Jon. What he wanted, he reached out an' took. No matter what it was. Proscribed or no—didn't make a bloody bit o' diff t' him. In that respect, he was a child of sorts.

"He was irresponsible but brilliant. He'd start th' day with amphetamines washed down with a tumbler o' gin. Then he'd snort some coke, do a bit o' morphine, drop a tab or two o' acid or, failing that, THC—whatever was in easy reach—an' maybe a codeine pill or two.

"Seems impossible, I know, that the human body can endure such abuse. Was it any wonder then we'd find him in th' studio, unable t' play, sobbing, 'But I did it just before, played it perfectly...they heard me. Ask them. Wasn't th' tape runnin'?' But there was no one there 'cept him.

"Then, on other days, miraculously, he'd be th' one that'd launch us in the studio...we'd all be lurchin' around without a direction an' he'd come in an' it'd all gel in just seconds. It used t' gall Nigel no end. His face'd go white, he'd turn away an' hit th' wall with his fist. Yah. He had th' knack, all right, did Jon.

"But even that couldn't stop the resentment from buildin' up into hate. An' Tie, she was always in there, bein' Jon's backbone, makin' him bolder than he ever coulda been on his own. An', I suspect now, she backed him even when she *knew* he was wrong—just t' twist th' needle that had got under our skins, again an' again until we all began t' jump at shadows."

He was shivering now, the sweat flying off him like rain and she held him close, squeezing and squeezing as if that act would bind all the life that was left in him inside. His eyelids flickered.

"Don't stop now," she said sharply. "Chris, I want to know how Jon died."

His eyes opened to slits. "Jon, yeh. Jon's death." He took a deep shuddering breath. "Still an' all, I reckon it was America what finally did it. We came over on our first tour in sixty-five...it was th' winter, I remember—bloody miserable weather. We were huge in England but here, only one radio station was playin' our stuff when we came t' New York. Sometimes we headlined but most often we were th' supportin' act, goin' on first while the kids were still comin' in. It was a tough adjustment for all o' us...we saw a lotta empty seats.

"Jon cried an' screamed all through th' tour an' we had t' hire someone t' make sure he wouldn't scarper. He made our lives even more miserable...wouldn't listen to Benno or any of us when we told him th' U.S. was where it was at if we were t' make it really big worldwide. 'I don't care 'bout bein' as big as th' Beatles or th' Stones!' he'd scream. But we all knew better. He *did* care...a great deal. He just found out he hated the States. Hated it worse'n anything. It was too big, too demanding...and far too cold an' uncarin' for him ever t' feel he had a chance to conquer it.

"Finally, thankfully, th' tour came to an end an' we flew back t' London. Not a word was passed between us on that long flight. But I know th' same thoughts were goin' round in all our heads. It'd all become too much t' bear.... An' then, in England, it began. Just when we thought it couldn't get worse...Jon began t' shoot his mouth off about how he never shoulda started th' band in th' first place...we'd warped his concept o' th' music, he said."

His teeth began to chatter and Daina turned him around to face her, hugged him to her, whispering in his ear for him to continue.

"I forget...."

"Jon's death."

"Jon's..." He nodded, his chin on her shoulder. "It was durin' th' summer. Ian'd just gotten a new house in th' country...Sussex. With a pool. He invited all o' us out. That included Tie an' she decided t' make a party o' it. Asked a bunch of her friends—really stunning birds an' a gaggle of theater nances...dancers...actors, I don't know what. Some

English and Scots but a lotta Germans'n'Swedes'n'that Aryan lot."

His head lolled against her and she had to remind him to keep going, not to sleep. "I remember...Nigel got pretty fed up with th' nances right away—he's never had any tolerance for that lot. Used t'...I remember, he used t' go after them down in Brighton summers when we were younger an' had nothin' much t' do. Idle minds..." He seemed to drift away for a moment but it must have been on a memory because he came back without any prodding.

"We'd all been drinkin' a lot, dropping—hell, we were pretty well out of it....Nigel got chuffed at a couple o' th' nances necking...tried t' throw 'em out. 'Course, Jon got in th' way....Jesus, he began t' defend 'em. 'Oh, that's lovely, that is,' Nigel said nastily. 'You bloody queen.' Jon said nothing, just stood there, weavin' back'n'forth while Tie screamed at Nigel: 'This isn't *your* bleedin' party—butt out!'"

He shook his head. "It all happened so fast. Nigel slapped Tie an' she fell over a lawn chair an' that made Jon take a run at Nigel.

"They went at it, y'know—th' way only streetfighters can. It was nasty...bloody nasty. 'What you standin' 'round for, gapin'!' I yelled. 'Get 'em apart!'

"But no one moved. No one did nothin'. Not until I went over an' pulled Nigel away. 'C'mon,' I said. 'Let's you'n'me'n'Tie get these queens outa here. They don't have t' see this.'" His head dropped. "An' on th' way back is when it happened...."

"What happened? Chris?" She lifted his head. "Chris!" Slapped him across the face.

"We were in th' kitchen...all o' us an' someone—I don't know who—said, 'What would happen if th' gas were turned on an' Jon came in here to light up?' We all laughed, higher'n'kites. But then, after a while, it wasn't so funny an' the smell got t' us an' we all went back outside." He sniffed. "By that time Jon was askin' for more shit an' someone said: 'Th' kitchen, Jon. It's in th' kitchen.'"

He stopped for a moment, listened to his own breathing. "I wonder," he said slowly, "if I'm gonna die."

"We're all going to die."

His eyes focused on her. "I mean here...now...'cause o' that shit."

"If you do," she said sharply, "it could only be suicide."

He thought about that for a moment. "I don't want to die!" His whispered voice was like the rustle of the wind through tall evergreens.

"Keep talking," she said, "and you won't."

He closed his eyes for a moment and when he opened them again, they were full of tears. "I remember...Oh, God help me, I remember it all." He began to cry, softly and silently, his tears sliding down his cheeks onto her flesh.

"We were such young punks then," he said after a time. "And we had only one thing on our minds: makin' it. But it's what kept us together, what made us strong. It was how we survived...all the filthy...shit they throw at you day after day an' expect you t' swallow without a pip o' protest. What's friendship compared t' that?"

There was a small silence for a time, until Daina said, "Then what did you do?"

"Nothin', darlin'. We all just stood there an' thought o' that godawful American tour, of how much money we'd lost but for all that how our album sales had picked up by th' time we'd left...how th' offers'd begun t' come into Benno for more dates...bigger halls...more money. But most o' all we thought o' how Jon'd refused t' fly again. How he despised America....How he was holdin' us down from what we all thought of as our...destiny. Yes, our destiny. That was th' word Tie used...."

"You mean she stood there and watched her lover walk inside?"

Chris shook his head slowly, sadly. "Oh, no, no. She went over t' th' side o' the pool an' sat down with her legs danglin' in th' water—"

"My God!"

"He'd never've left th' band on his own, no matter *what* he told everyone, no matter how much he complained in public. We all knew that. He was nothin' without th' Heartbeats—just like th' rest o' us. But it was worse for Jon. He wasn't no survivor. He had only one lifeline that kept him above th' waterline with th' drugs....Without th' band..." He shrugged.

"So you let him die."

"It was a sacrifice, Tie said. In all greatness, in all genius there must be pain, a givin' up o' the old in order for th' new t' take root an' grow. With Jon, we were going nowhere. It

was him or us an' there was no other way. He would've... It
would've happened fairly soon, anyway. His liver, his kid-
neys—his heart, even, how long d'you imagine they could've
taken th' abuse, huh? How long? *How long?*" He was screaming now, screaming and crying and beating against her with
what little strength he had left.

It was light when they emerged from the bowels of the
Rensselaer onto the tattered sidewalk. Steam no longer blew
from the iron vent in the pavement and the derelict had
moved on to better climes or worse, taking his newspaper
with him. The empty bottle was still there.

And so was the cab. From somewhere west on Broadway,
the smell of steaming coffee came to them.

Daina bundled Chris into the backseat with the sleepy
driver's help.

"You sure this bastard's all right?" he asked, chewing on
a toothpick. His breath smelled faintly from tuna. "He's as
pale as a corpse."

"Just take us back to the Sherry-Netherland," Daina said,
getting into the back and slamming the door shut.

"He sure must be a good friend of yours, Miss Whitney,"
the cabbie said, switching on the ignition. He stared at them
both in the rearview mirror. "Hey, don't I know him?"

Chris lay back in the seat. He was still trembling but the
crisis seemed to have passed. His eyes opened and for a long
time he watched the buildings passing by.

"This isn't London," he said thickly.

"No," she said quietly, trying to comfort him. "We're in
New York."

He nodded then. "Yeah. New fuckin' York." He closed his
eyes. "Get me t' th' airport," he said in a firmer voice that
she could almost recognize as his own. "I want t' go home.
Back t' L.A.... I got an album t' finish."

12

She did not, of course, think she ever wanted to see him again; not after what had happened between them. She was wrong.

She knew she was wrong the moment she returned from New York, put her hand in the pocket of the Canadian lynx and found the glassine envelope she had picked up off the floor at Chris' hotel room. She looked at it for a moment, put it together with the slip of paper Meyer had given her, which bore two lines of writing in a neat, controlled script:

> *Charlie Wu*
> *Cherries, Van Nuys B.*

and felt a kind of exultation at being able to lay in Bonesteel's hands two possible keys to Maggie's murder. It was more than he had done for her but she did not mind. She wanted to see the look on his face.

She did not want to call the precinct house and give him any advance warning. She passed up the silver Merc that seemed old and somehow shabby to her, climbed into the black Ferrari the studio had given her just after *Heather Duell* had wrapped. As befitting Southern California, it had an all-letter license plate: HEATHER. It was low and sleek and very fast. Never had she found driving such a sensual

and invigorating experience; it made her want to give up
using limos—almost.

It suits me, she thought as she paused at the verge of Bel
Air, turning left onto Sunset. It slid through the traffic like
a dream. She sat so low in the vehicle she felt she was part
of it: plugged in to the mighty engine, the electronicized circuits just as she did when a scene was going right and she
was making love to the camera. The Ferrari made her feel
as if she were making love to the city as it whipped by.

Part of her drifted away. It was as if a great multilayered
puzzle had been forming in her mind and now she was beginning to see a pattern emerging after seemingly months
of blindly fitting one piece to another without getting a
glimpse of the whole.

With the dream-memory of her mother's death flooding
back to her in New York, the skein of her past was complete
and she could at last understand it in the context of what she
was going through now. She realized, after waking up from
the dream, that all anger she had felt for Monika had leached
away from her at bedside. It was as if all the intervening
years had never taken place and she and her mother—
stripped of the accretion of jealousy, envy, fear and rage—
had come upon the basic core of their relationship: the love
between mother and child.

To Daina it no longer mattered what Monika had done or
hadn't been able to do. In the thin balance between life and
death, she knew that love was all that mattered. She did not
want Monika to die and, turning away, she had cried, silently
and bitterly, perhaps as much for herself and what she had
given up, as for her mother. She wished at that moment that
she had the power to turn back time, to erase all the years
she had wasted. But she had no power. She was helpless
before this unknown, unseen onslaught against which Monika fought bravely to no avail.

She knew, too, that in an odd way Monika had been right.
She had hit the streets to run away from everything she could
not bear to face. While she had scorned her friends who turned
to drugs to obliterate reality and, in doing so, had felt so
superior, she had merely taken another route.

Baba had known that and that night when they had finally
made love, she had sensed he was about to send her away for
the last time. "Fo' yo' own good, mama," he would've said.

Everyone knew better than me, Daina thought as she headed for downtown L.A. Christ, I was such an innocent in those days. But everyone is, once, and the first disillusionments are by far the worst.

The traffic cleared in a snaking lane in front of her and she shifted up to fourth, depressing the accelerator, and the leashed beast beneath her thundered, pressing her back against the wine-colored seat. Go, she thought. Go, go, go!

For the first time in her life she felt complete. There was an element inside her that had not been there before. She felt, for the first time, fully as competent as a man in everything. Yet it was most certainly not a masculine feeling, of that she was certain. What was happening to her? She thought of what she had done for Chris. Only now did she glimpse the truly terrifying nature of the episode. What if she hadn't.... But she already knew the answer to that one. Chris would be dead now.

And what had possessed her to take the glassine envelope? And why give it to Bonesteel now? Would he find traces of anything but heroin in there? She felt a premonitory shiver go through her. What have I become involved with? she asked herself. Maggie the granddaughter of a famous political figure, killed by a hot shot. But she had been tortured first, as if it had been politically motivated....

She downshifted, braking into a turn, moved up again to third. That hot shot, she thought, sticks in my mind. And there, in front of her eyes, was a vision of the glassine envelope lying on the floor of Chris' hotel room; a flicker of emotion, Chris calling out. What if Chris had been given the same kind of hot shot? What if there was no coincidence but the dovetailing of an M.O.? Or, she thought, it might all be an illusion of my fevered imagination. Somehow she could not convince herself of that, though she took the devil's advocate's part for several minutes. She did not believe in coincidences of that kind.

The precinct house looked just the same as it had before— as if it were a wagon train crouched in a circle awaiting attack. She was just getting out of the Ferrari when a voice said: "Miss Whitney!"

It was Andrews, the patrolman who had taken her to Bonesteel's office. He was just coming down the steps to the street.

His longish hair was streaked by the sun; his eyes a deep blue.

She gave him a big smile. "Well, how are you?"

"Fine, Miss Whitney. Just fine." He grinned and pointed. "Some set of wheels you got there." His hand stroked the flank of the car as if it were alive. "Leave us all in the dust."

"You know, Patrolman, I don't know your first name."

"Pete, Ma'am." He jerked a thumb over his shoulder. "And this is Harry Brafman." The other man, shorter and darker than Andrews but about the same age, nodded. "We're both on Lieutenant Bonesteel's staff."

"D'you know where he is? I've got something important for him."

"Sure. He's down by the pier at Santa Monica. We're just on our way over. You can follow us."

"I don't know about that, Pete," Brafman said, frowning. "You know what's going on there. We're not allowed to let civilians into a restricted area for any reason."

But Andrews waved aside his partner's words. "Miss Whitney and the lieutenant're old friends, Braf. If she says she's got something for him, he'll want to hear about it."

Brafman's dark eyes flowed up and down Daina's body. "I can't argue with that," he said with just the trace of a smirk.

There was indeed something up along the piers. Even before they arrived at Santa Monica, Daina could hear the piercing wails of the sirens and she was glad of Andrews' escort; she never would have gotten close without it.

She counted at least half a dozen patrol cars and, as they drove up, an armored SWAT unit vehicle rumbled away. Sawhorse barricades were up and everyone was being thoroughly screened.

Andrews and Brafman got out. They got another patrolman to guard the Ferrari while they took her behind the lines.

The pier was awash with cops, all of them in plainclothes. There was an ambulance with its red light flashing silently and its back doors gaping wide. It was empty inside. Around to the left and farther down the pier, a pair of white-jacketed paramedics were lifting something onto a wheeled stretcher. Daina recognized the tall assistant M.E. who had been at Chris and Maggie's house the day of the murder. He seemed to be cramming the back half of a cheeseburger into his mouth.

Beside him stood Bonesteel, resplendent in a silk-and-linen-weave suit of pale gray. He seemed the only cool one on the pier. He was looking down at the thing on the stretcher when Daina came up between Andrews and Brafman.

For a time he was oblivious to them. Then he looked up and, without taking his eyes from Daina's face, acknowledged their presence.

"You got here in record time," he told them. He did not move his head. "The shootout was at the far end. You know what to do."

"How's Forrager?" Andrews asked.

"Right shoulder. Not too bad."

"And Keyes?"

Bonesteel hesitated just a fraction. "He didn't make it." His eyes flickered. "I'm sorry, Andrews."

Beside her, Andrews stood stock-still, as if he were made of lead. His handsome, sharply chiseled features seemed to have aged in just that moment. A light breeze stirred his fine, cornsilk hair. It was, Daina thought, like baby's hair. But he's not a baby anymore.

Brafman walked by her, touched Andrews on the arm. "Come on, Pete. We've got work to do." He pulled Andrews away and, with their backs to her, they seemed just like two ordinary men strolling down to the end of the pier to see the ocean.

"Keyes was his brother-in-law." It was the first sentence Bonesteel had directed at her. "Andrews and his sister are very close." He said it as if the concept was inconceivable to him.

"Hello, Bobby."

"The boys bring you?"

"I asked them to. I have something for you." She waited a moment. "I don't want Andrews to get into trouble."

"Don't worry about it." His eyes dropped to the cloth covering the thing on the stretcher, an edge of which he was clutching in his right hand. "Have something here that might interest you." He began to draw away the cloth.

"Are you being funny?"

His hand paused in midair. "Funny? No. I'm quite serious."

With a flick of his wrist, he uncovered the corpse. "Meet Modred."

Daina had been determined not to look but curiosity got the better of her. She gazed down on a face that was in every way perfectly ordinary: eyes not too large, not too small, a nose that was just a nose, an unremarkable mouth. It was, in short, a face one would never look at twice or possibly remember. He was one of the crowd and had stepped out only because he was a psychopathic murderer.

His skin was white and he looked as if he were sleeping the peaceful slumber of the innocent. Then she saw that down below, where the cloth still covered him, it was turning red in three or four places. She put her hand out to steady herself and Bonesteel took it.

"What happened?"

"Let's get away from here," he said, "and I'll tell you."

He took her down the highway, to the beach. She took off her sandals but he kept his shoes on as they went across the sand. To one side perhaps a dozen bronzed kids were playing volleyball. Behind them, on the steaming asphalt, girls and boys in bathing suits and hot pants were roller-skating to disco music, as thick as the stalled traffic along Ocean Avenue. They were nearer Venice than they were to the Pacific Palisades.

"The shrinks were right about one thing when it came to Modred," Bonesteel said against the background of the music. "He wanted to be caught." He put his hands in his pockets. "He left us clues but either they were too warped or we were too stupid. Either way we never got close. So he called us and set up this meeting. We knew it was him because he told us some things over the phone...details we hadn't given out, that only the killer would know." He gave a grim laugh. "And he wasn't shy. Not at this stage. He told us everything."

Bonesteel sighed, looked away from her, into the haze. "Christ," he said disgustedly. "We knew he was dangerous and still I let him get two of my men."

"Bobby, how could you know?"

"How could I know? How could I know?" he echoed ironically. "My captain said the same thing. He's being very goddamned decent about it. 'Look here, Bonesteel,' he said to me. 'There's the other side of the coin. This maniac's gone for good. We're going to make hay of this. I've already been on the line with the publicity people. Your men went down in the line of duty. They're heroes.'"

Bonesteel ran a hand through his hair. "Heroes," he snorted. "They died because of stupidity."

"Not because they were brave?"

"They were too young to be brave. They just didn't know any better." But he looked at her finally and nodded. "Yes," he said. "They were brave."

"And they were your men." She looked at him. "So you blame yourself."

"They were under my command!"

"Did you do everything you could to protect them?"

"I should've known that psycho would carry a hidden gun. He had his hands up. I told Forrager and Keyes to go out and get him. He was grinning, crazy as a bedbug. One moment his hands were empty, the next he had a derringer. It must've been spring-loaded up his sleeve." His slate-gray eyes clouded with the memory. "Forrager and Keyes were very close. I don't think they even knew what happened. I heard the first shot and ordered the snipers to fire. They blew him back six feet but by that time my men were down." He brushed his hand across his face and she thought he had wiped away a stray tear.

"You protected them," Daina said. "What happened was unavoidable."

"Now you sound like my captain again."

"Perhaps it's because we're both a bit more objective than you are."

"You won't have to visit the widows, either."

"No, I won't," she said. "But that's part of the job, isn't it? There isn't one without the other."

"That's why I'm getting out after this last case. I can't take it. I'm a coward."

"Getting fed up isn't the same as being a coward."

The wind ruffled the bottom of his jacket, exposing the lining. "That's what I am, you know."

She shrugged. "Now you're just feeling sorry for yourself."

"It's what I think."

"Oh, come on, Bobby. I'm tired of True Confessions. Can we get on with—"

"Daina..."

"No," she said with a soft kind of finality. "We had our chance. Now that's over and I see it's better this way."

He turned abruptly away from her and she watched him

walk down the beach. Girls glanced clandestinely at him, lusting in their own way, for his bulk. He was a very desirable man. But he isn't for me, she thought. Once upon a time but no more.

She walked up the beach to the sandy concrete steps to the parking lot. She went to his dark green Ford, got in to wait for him.

In time he reappeared. He leaned on the side of the car, put his head through the open window. "I did some checking on your story. About Maggie."

"I thought you didn't believe me."

"Let's just say I was skeptical."

"What happened to change your mind?"

"I put in an order to get the body exhumed and got nowhere." He opened the door and got in behind the wheel. It was stifling inside and he rolled up the windows, put on the air conditioning. When it had cooled down, he said, "I also did some further checking on our friend Nigel Ash." He turned to look at her, his voice back to its old neutral self. "Did you know he was half Irish?"

"Irish what?" Daina tried to hide her astonishment.

"Irish Catholic. His mother was born in Andytown, a hotbed of IRA activity in Belfast."

"I know. How did she get to marry an Englishman, of all things."

"Not English," Bonesteel said. "Welsh. But, according to neighbors, it was the cause of their fights."

"I see you've been busy."

"There's more," he said. "Nigel's got a sister."

"I've never heard her mentioned."

"You wouldn't. I understand he never speaks of her."

"You mean they don't get along."

"I didn't say that, exactly," Bonesteel said. "Maybe it's because she lives in Belfast."

"Are you telling me she's a member of the IRA?"

"If I said that, I'd be lying. Our British cousins can be awfully close-mouthed when they want to. I haven't heard a yes or a no but they gave me her address. It's in the Falls." It was where Sean Toomey was from. "What you got for me?"

Daina pulled out the glassine envelope. "First," she said, "I'd like your lab to do a chemical analysis on the contents."

Gingerly he took it from her, held it up to the light. "Horse?"

"Yeah," she said. "Maybe that's all."

He slipped the envelope into an inside pocket after first sealing it. "Where'd this come from?"

She told him what had happened in New York and about what she thought the powder could contain.

Bonesteel shook his head. "It's a very outside chance. Junkies, you know, they get beat on street shit every hour of the day. Stuff's always cut. The question is with what. If it's a benign enough substance, well, then the potency's cut and that's it. But if it's something else, you can wind up dead on the bathroom floor. He was lucky you were around."

"Will you do it?" And when he didn't answer, she said, "Tell me one thing. Is street stuff ever cut with strychnine?"

"Not that I've ever heard of. Not unless it's on purpose." He looked at her, touched the outside of his jacket where the glassine envelope lay. "Consider it done." He got out his keys, fired the engine.

"Why don't we," Daina said nonchalantly, "take a ride out to Van Nuys Boulevard?"

Dusk was coming down and in the lowering light it was just possible to ignore the dust lying soft along the edges of the palms lining the highway.

"Van Nuys?" Bonesteel said. "What the hell d'we want to go out there for?"

Daina showed him the slip of paper Meyer had given her. "Who is Charlie Wu?"

"Someone," Daina said, "who might know who killed Maggie."

Bonesteel eyed her suspiciously but he turned onto the beginning of the Santa Monica Freeway. "Where'd you get this?"

"Can't you take anything at face value?" she said annoyedly.

"If I did," he said, "I'd be one helluva lousy cop." But he smiled then. "Okay, okay, we've all got our secrets. You keep this one."

At West Los Angeles, he made the long sweeping turn to the left, got onto the San Diego Freeway heading north toward the valley.

"You did some job keeping Chris alive," he said and she

could hear the note of genuine admiration in his voice. "How's he now?"

"Oh, fine. He's still in the studio. It's taken him a bit longer than he thought to finish up this first solo album of his. There was a fire a couple of weeks ago and one of the master tapes went up. He had to start three songs over from scratch. He's mixing the last of them now."

"Out by Oscar time, huh? You'll be an even bigger deal then."

The traffic was atrocious and Bonesteel swerved to the right, got off at Mulholland, going west until he hit Beverly Glen Boulevard into Sherman Oaks. The valley was coming up and as soon as they crested the rise, Daina knew, she would see the valley choked before the coming of night with the filthy brown smog that hovered for weeks on end. A heat inversion, the weather forecasters called it. And if it kept on long enough that industrial slime would begin to seep through the Santa Monica Mountains to inundate Beverly Hills and Hollywood. Already she could see the rosy glow of the valley reflected high overhead as if they were approaching a city in the heavens.

"What d'you care?" she said. "I'm already too big a deal for you."

He laughed bitterly. "We just weren't made for each other. Let's leave it at that."

But Daina knew neither of them would. They'd probe at each other until one or the other gave in. It was in their nature. It was a very fragile truce they had here, she realized.

"How are you ever going to be a successful writer?" she said. "You're still a cop at heart. You always will be."

"Every time you take a chance," he said slowly, "someone steps right on your face." The dying light showed her his eyes fierce and cold and just a little bit sad.

There were no oak now but plenty of cottonwood and scrub brush as they headed down off the mountains. Ahead of them, glowing like the neon heart of some monstrous robot of the future, lay Van Nuys. After a moment, they hit Ventura Boulevard, then through the underpass over which thudded and hissed the blurred traffic along the Ventura Freeway. Under them ran the culvert for the Los Angeles River. Immediately they hit the other side, they were on Van Nuys Boulevard.

As, at one time two decades ago, the Sunset Strip had been legendary at night, so now this boulevard had turned into a street of nighttime dreams. It was here that the youthful surfers from as far away as Laguna Beach came to strut their stuff; where the young dragsters, in the process of winning their speed spurs, rambled in nonchalant array; where kids from the high schools at Hollywood and Van Nuys hung out, getting high and getting laid while thinking shallow shadowy thoughts on the nature of evil.

Golden-haired girls in luminescent ciré hot pants and brief multihued halters as gaudy as Christmas trees, their faces more heavily made up than any three women on Rodeo Drive, roller-skated between the endless, six-laned caravans of Chevy vans, Camaros and Trans Ams. Amber fog lights from the thick lines of traffic threw odd articulated shadows across the boulevard and the buildings, in the doorways of which young boys leaned like brilliantined lounge lizards.

The air was thick with light beams and Rolling Stones backbeat throbbing from ten thousand radios, the ragged mainline melodies seeming peculiarly appropriate to this time, this place. The rock and roll was a spice in the air, heady with harsh defiance, and as she breathed the night air in, it seemed to tingle her nostrils as if it were ozone.

It was a brittle, brutal world, glossy and seamless, filled with a fearful kind of restlessness: like a nightmare or a horror film given life, there was the flicker of flight in those shining amber lights, the sickening stench of a fear ungovernable because it could not be faced. Daina understood such a fear just as she recognized this stark, brooding, hedonistic playground. The passing shadows of fantasy were not so very far from her own time of flight. And again she thought, There is nothing to fear. It all remains the same.

They joined the unhurried caravan heading north toward Panorama City, which would, long before that, turn around to head back south the way it had come. Clouds of exhaust rose as greasily thick as hoards of mosquitoes from the tarmac of the boulevard, enigmatic smoke signals from a primitive tribal society.

Just in front of them a plum-colored van came to a halt. Along one side, a Hawaiian beachfront was painted in a dizzying array of brilliant colors. Palms swayed to one side but the scene was of course dominated by the ubiquitous hero of southern California: the bronzed surfer, carrying his board, about to plunge into the high surf to challenge the Bonzai Pipeline.

A girl, as lithe as a wood nymph, her long streaked hair flying out behind her in a thick ponytail, detached herself from the darkness of a shallow doorway. She wore a pair of shorts so white they dazzled the eye and a fire-red tube top. She seemed to have no breasts at all, to be almost entirely composed of spectacular copper leg. The curbside door of the plum van opened and she climbed in. It jerked forward, began to accelerate to catch up to the car ahead of it and, as it did so, Daina could make out the sticker on its rear bumper: "Don't Laugh—Your Daughter's in Here."

Perhaps a half mile farther on, Bonesteel nosed the LTD into a parking space quite near the ornate front of a large, heavily trafficked bar. It seemed a schizoid place. The architecture could not make up its mind whether to be mock-Spanish or mock-Moroccan. There were a pair of half-moon arches, rising from white corkscrew pillars textured to look like sandstone but that were, in all probability, nothing more than concrete heavily dolloped with sand. Above the arches, bougainvillea twined, phosphorescent in the light, surmounted in turn by the establishment's name, spelled out in an arch of violent vermillion neon script: Cherries.

In the dense sea of sound and motion, a blue pickup cruised slowly by. In its flatbed back two boys sat cross-legged smoking out of a tall glass bhang.

"Bet there's plenty of grass around here," Daina said.

Bonesteel glanced at the back of the receding truck, grunted. "Sure there is. Kilos of it. But those two ain't smoking any. That's Quaaludes going up in smoke there."

"I didn't know you could smoke them."

He shrugged. "There's a new wrinkle coming up every day around here. They're so inventive." He took his hands off the steering wheel, kept a watch out on the entrance to Cherries.

Down the densely packed boulevard she could see a Bob's Big Boy and, just beyond, the red, white, and blue revolving shield of a Chevron station. Horns hooted in time to the music that collectively seemed to flow out of the night.

"You know anything about this place?" Bonesteel asked, flicking his thumb at the arching gateways of the bar.

"I've heard of it, certainly. Who hasn't? But I've never been in."

"And that's all you know?" His eyes were alive, darting back and forth among the clouds of kids moving easily in and out of the place. His face seemed livid in the wash of colored neon flashing.

"Uh huh."

She thought there might be something else forthcoming but he was silent. He shook out an unfiltered Camel, lit up. He aimed the smoke out his window and she thought, Even the cops have images to live up to here. Immediately she recognized this as being unfair and did not mind a bit.

The entrance to Cherries was choked with lank-haired boys in sleeveless sweatshirts and bleached jeans, their exposed biceps gleaming in the amber light as if they had been rubbed with oil; girls with deep tans, clouds of freckles across the perfect bridges of their perfect noses, painted with dark lip gloss, turning their mouths into pouting fruit, their eye sockets into iridescent slices of snakeskin. The girls' flowered print dresses seemed incongruous and anachronistic and the sleek sapphire and ruby arsenal of Spandex clothing of their peers, appearing much more like undergarments found on a bordello's floor than they did street clothes. These girls, in contrast, looked soft and vulnerable, much more like children who had inadvertently wandered away from the safety of their parents' sides.

Amid the ebb and flow, a still pond of four boys stood in the semi-shadows. The ends of long palm fronds brushed them and, every few seconds, the amber fog lights picked them out, slid by them in an unhurried wash. One boy was obviously the leader. His blond hair was so light it appeared to have been spun from platinum. He had light eyes, deep-set, widely spaced, a thin nose and a rather pouty mouth. He was talking to a long-waisted girl on a skateboard while his fellows looked on with hooded eyes. One of them bit his nails, another took a swig from a bottle of beer he held in a brown-paper bag. The platinum-haired boy nodded sharply and money changed hands. He patted the girl on her behind and she took off across the sidewalk, jumping the curb.

She picked up speed on the tarmac, weaving in and out of the traffic as she crossed the boulevard. On the far side, she swung to her right, went along the gutter for perhaps a block. Once more she jumped the curb with no break in her flowing line.

Daina watched her, smelling the stink of the accumulating exhaust, held in the air by the smog, the heat inversion, the perverse southern California spirit. She was dizzied for an instant. Then other scents came strongly to her on the draft created by the caravans of slowly moving cars and vans: chili, tacos, burning grease, grass.

In the fog-light-illuminated darkness, she picked out the girl heading toward the moving shadows along the side street, saw the Mexican youths come briefly into the brilliance of the boulevard, skimming furtively, outsiders to the cocaine and Quaalude set but still kings of marijuana and beer.

The girl had made her buy, was turning around, sidewalk surfing along the gutter, about to make her first sharp swerve into the six-lane flow when Daina was distracted by the harsh guttural roar of a powerful motorcycle's exhaust.

Out on the boulevard a cycle peeled off from the caravan, nosing into the curb beside the entrance to Cherries. Even without immediately recognizing the crimson and transparent plastic nacelle of the bike, Daina knew it was Chris. He wore an iridescent helmet without markings, a worn leather jacket from which the arms had been cut and straight-legged denims. He dismounted very quickly and, without taking off his helmet, went across the pavement.

Bonesteel stopped her with her fingers on the door handle. "Don't do that," he said softly. "Just stay where you are."

"Why?"

He would not answer, merely kept his eyes on the double gateway to Cherries.

Moments later, Chris emerged with a girl in tow. She seemed no different from the hundreds of others in the place: long blond hair, loose, flowing over her sunburned shoulders. You could tell she had breasts, though, even through the loose-fitting yellow camisole top she wore over tight emerald ciré pants. She rolled easily on a pair of luminescent custom-made skates. She did not look around.

The four boys at the entrance watched her departure with the same degree of indifference they seemed to view everything. None of them had short hair, as had become the fashion on the East Coast. It fell to their shoulders, an odd androgynous twist to their otherwise studiedly perfect macho image.

The girl had climbed on the cycle behind Chris. His right leg pumped up, down once and the machine started with a throaty roar and a brief burst of blue vapor. Chris twisted the handlebars and peeled out with a screech of burning tire rubber, weaving in and out of the traffic until he made a U-turn, headed south, back toward Hollywood.

"Christ," Daina said. "You knew about this all along."

"Dirty laundry, remember?"

"You're very big on surprises today," she said sharply, thinking of Modred's pale bloated face.

The girl on the skateboard had returned with her load, had deposited the transparent bag of grass into the cupped hands of the boy with the platinum hair. He leaned forward, kissed her hard on the mouth. One hand came around her back, searching lower. He cupped one finely molded buttock and her hips arched in lasciviously against his proud body. He gave her a pat as he broke away from her—as if his choice had been the girl or the drugs—and she skated into Cherries. By the time Daina looked again, the boy had dispersed.

"Three to one, Charlie Wu's pushing something," Bonesteel said as he opened the door.

They went across the jammed sidewalk that seemed to sizzle of the streaked lights plying back and forth from the boulevard.

The interior of Cherries was dark and smoky, filled with ponytail palms and ponytailed girls and boys. There was a long bar to the right, stained dark and gleaming, behind which was a series of beveled mirrors and glass shelves filled with bottles. The sides of the bar were black lacquer, as were the tables along the left-hand wall. About halfway back, the room took a dogleg to the right, opening up to twice the width. Behind a glass wall and double glass doors Daina could see people dancing in the disco. The light was subdued, the noise level remarkably low.

Daina turned to Bonesteel. "How the hell are we going to find Charlie Wu in all this?"

Someone was singing from the speakers hung from the tiled ceiling: *You wear those eyes that never blink/You always were the missing link....*

"Let's talk to the bartender," he said, leading her over to a leather-covered stool.

You paint your mouth you let me know/You really are the only show....

"What'll it be?" He was a beefy man with a cinnamon-colored mustache that drooped down around the sides of his mouth. He had long hair and intelligent eyes.

"A coupla beers," Bonesteel said. "Kirin, if you've got it."

Just take your time/'Cause it's not too late/Just take your time/'Cause it's not too late....

A Heartbeats song came on. Chris' voice low and menacing. Daina said, "D'you know a man by the name of Charlie Wu?"

The bartender tore up their check, jerked a thumb toward a table in the shadows near the glass wall of the disco. "Been here every night, waiting for you, Miss Whitney." Someone down the bar called to him and he moved away before she could ask him anything else. It could only be Meyer, she thought, who could set all this rolling. It humbled her. She still had a long way to go. She led Bonesteel through the packed room.

Charlie Wu was one of those Chinese men whose features were so delicate he could have passed for a woman. He accentuated the illusion by wearing his hair very long so that he evinced the aspect of a hermaphrodite.

There was nothing female about his voice. It was softly toned but quite deep and rich. He smiled when he saw her, stood up. But his smile soon turned into a frown when Daina introduced Bonesteel.

"I was told I'd be talking to one person," he said. "You. I got no beef with the cops but I don't have to talk to one either."

"I didn't say he was a cop," Daina told him.

"Huh!" Charlie Wu snorted. "You didn't have to. Cops all walk alike." He peered hard at Bonesteel. "You sure don't dress like any cop I've seen, though."

"This has nothing to do with you," Daina said. "If that's what you're worried about."

"I've got nothing to be ashamed of," Charlie Wu said, "especially when it comes to the cops. I'm just telling you what the deal was."

"I'm changing the deal," Daina said. "Bonesteel stays."

"Nothing doing."

"You wait here," Daina said to Bonesteel. "I'll just make a call."

For the first time a flicker of emotion showed in Charlie Wu's eyes. "Don't make any calls," he said unhappily. Daina turned back. "You vouch for this guy?"

Daina nodded.

"And it's all off the record?"

"You're clean as far as I'm concerned," Bonesteel said.

"I wanna hear it from the lady, too. She knows the source I'm interested in."

"You've got my word, Charlie."

"Okay." He nodded. "Let's sit down." He ordered another round of beer for all of them. He watched a young girl no more than thirteen pass by, her long sun-streaked hair bejeweled with beads and tiny feathers. "They're a little young for me here," he said as if in explanation, "but the management knows me and everyone leaves me alone." He shrugged. "I don't work regular hours."

"Just what *do* you do?" Daina said.

"I'm a mechanic."

"A mechanic?" Bonesteel echoed. "Who're you trying to kid, buddy. We know you're running drugs into—"

"You see what I object to?" Charlie Wu said with genuine sadness on his face. "You would never talk to me that way, Miss Whitney. I have assurances about you. But him..." He shrugged.

"He's right, Bobby," Daina said as quietly as she could over Chris' amplified voice. "Leave it alone." After a moment, she turned back to the other man. "Okay, Charlie. You fix cars."

He shook his head. "No, planes."

"You're an airplane mechanic?"

He nodded.

"What's this got to do with anything?"

"Quiet, Bobby," Daina hissed. "You work on small planes? Two-engine—"

"Well, I'm qualified," Charlie Wu said, "but I specialize in jets. 707s, widebodies, private stuff, that sort of thing."

"But you don't work for an airline."

"Nah, I'm strictly free-lance. Make more money that way."

"I'll bet," Bonesteel muttered.

"Listen," Charlie Wu said, "I'm usually a very patient man but could you put him on a leash or something? He's beginning to annoy me."

Daina restrained Bonesteel with one hand. "Let's get something straight," she said to both of them. "This is my show and I'd appreciate it if everyone backed off a bit." She lowered her voice. "Goddamnit, both of you stop sparring!" Now she had lost her train of thought, something Charlie Wu had said. What was it? "What kind of jobs've you had over the past six months?"

"Been kinda slow lately." He smiled slowly. "But even if it weren't, I'd know what it is you want. I been through this before, you know." He downed the rest of his beer, ordered another. "I get this call. Someone wants me to take a run out to LAX, one of the private hangars to take a look at a Longhorn Series 50." He looked at her. "Know what that is?"

Daina nodded. "It's a private widebody. Seats about ten." And, to answer his approving look, "I've flown in one. Possibly it's the same one."

"Got the Heartbeats' star-guitar logo on it?"

"Yes."

"Then it's the same one." Charlie Wu stirred his beer with a thin forefinger. "They were just blanking them out so it would look like any other Series 50."

"What did they want you to do?"

"When a plane—any plane—goes on a long trip, you want it checked out thoroughly, if you're smart."

"What about the plane's regular mechanic?" Daina said.

"Nobody around," Charlie Wu said, "but me and the guy doing the whiteout. Neither of us paid any attention to the other. Draw your own conclusions." He took a sip of his beer.

"Ever see the guy who called you?" Bonesteel said.

"Nah. I got a key to a post-office box in the mail. Got paid that way. Left the key in the box and that was it." He held up a finger. "Except for one thing. It wasn't people they were planning to carry, at least not on this particular run. I sneaked a quick peek inside. They'd taken all the seats out."

"What was in there?" Daina said.

"A lotta nothing. Just empty space. But there was tons of it."

"Not a drug run," Bonesteel said, half to himself.

"Why go to the bother of taking out the seats?" Charlie

Wu said. "No, it was something big—and heavy." He finished his beer, wiped his mouth. "Well, that's the lot."

"Wait a minute," Daina said. "When did all this take place?"

"Oh, 'bout six months ago. I'm a wiz at dates, too." He smiled. "Nice meeting you, Miss Whitney." He stood up, turned. "Oh, and Mr. Bonesteel, right? We never met."

Bonesteel got them off Van Nuys and out of the valley in record time. He turned onto Mulholland and they headed toward the top end of Topanga State Park. They drove in silence for a time. Bonesteel shook out a Camel, lit it with one hand. He took a long drag, blew the smoke out the open window. The glowing end of the cigarette seemed like the only light alive in the night.

Just inside the park, he turned off and they immediately hit a rough-paved narrow road, which quickly turned to packed earth. He rolled the LTD to a stop, turned off the engine. The quiet ticking came in counterpoint to the resumed chorus of crickets and tree frogs. There was a rustling in the branches above their heads, then the sound of wings beating against the sky, diminishing.

Bonesteel finished the cigarette, carefully crushed it to death in the ashtray. He stepped out of the car. Daina did not ask why he had brought her up here, only knew that they weren't finished with each other. She got out on the other side of the car. It was cool here, as damp as the sea. He looked up as he heard the soft crunch of leaves and grass disturbed at her moving.

"What I want to know," he said quietly, "is why you asked Charlie Wu about the time factor."

"It's odd," she said, looking at him. "At first I thought it was just an arbitrary date I pulled out of my head. You know...six months seemed like a natural time limit." His face was almost entirely in shadow and she found herself having to visualize each feature separately, setting it in place as if she were a plastic surgeon working on the most complex reconstruction of her career. "Then I realized what had triggered that particular period of time. It was something Silka said to me—I can't remember when—about Chris and Tie. He said they were alone together about six months ago."

"Where was Nigel?"

She could not see him at all now and she wondered if he

had moved or if it had somehow gotten abruptly darker. She kept her head pointed in the direction of his voice; it was all she had to go on. "Away was all that Silka said."

"Away." It was the same word but when Bonesteel said it, it took on hidden meanings.

In the ensuing silence, she felt herself suddenly afraid. "Bobby," she said softly, "what are you thinking?"

"I'm thinking," he said slowly, "that I've been wrong all along. This isn't any drug run Nigel's involved in. No, it's much more than that."

"What are you talking about?"

"Just think about it a minute," he said, and she could hear him moving now. "The pieces are all there in front of you. Nigel, half Irish Catholic with a mother who was almost assuredly a member of the IRA. A father who hated the Catholics, who abused his wife and who, finally, left her. A sister in Belfast, gone underground.

"Now switch back to the States for a moment. You're in an internationally known band with your own jet. Now how often d'you suppose that jet's in official use? Three, maybe four months a year tops, when the band is on the road. And what is it doing the rest of the time, huh? Sitting on its haunches in a hangar at LAX, idle. Now who's to know if you 'borrow' that plane for, oh, two or three quick trips a year? Say, two days apiece? No one."

"But use it for what?" She could see the gleam from Bonesteel's eyes like a predatory beast coming out of the darkness.

"Think, Daina. You're half Irish Catholic, your sister's a member of the IRA. What would *you* use the jet to transport?"

Daina did not know but, she found, Heather did. "Guns?"

Bonesteel smiled, cocked a thumb and forefinger. "Guns."

She took a deep breath. "And Maggie?"

"Maggie found out. Or"—he stopped very close beside her— "it was what it seems to be now: an IRA execution ordered in retribution for the raids planned by Sean Toomey."

"But why connect the fact? Why make it seem as if Modred had committed the murder?"

"That's obvious, too. To protect the killer. He's been very well placed—and hidden for years. Why expose him now?"

"Either way I don't like it."

He laughed harshly. "It wasn't made for you to like. This is something you have no control over."

"You'd know about that, wouldn't you?" she said nastily.

He walked a little away from her as if to get away from her words. "You can't see much of anything from here," he said. "The trees, the high hills block out everything, except that dim glow high up in the east." He turned away from it. "It's better that way."

He took some time to light another cigarette, careful of the night wind that swept over them, rustling the leaves all around them.

Daina was silent, thinking perhaps her own thoughts, feeling dim emotions, uncertain now of precisely where Daina left off and Heather began.

"Forget about Silka," Bonesteel said into the night. "He's an interesting enigma. But, after all, he's only a runner; small potatoes; just another fish incidentally caught in the net we're throwing. It's Nigel I'm after."

"But how can you be so certain?" She came around the front of the car, stood next to him. The air was clearer here over the hump of the mountains; the sulphurous, burnt-rubber stench of the smog lying low in the San Fernando Valley like a leper hiding out gradually fading from their nostrils. She took a deep breath. Somewhere, there must have been a conduit to the sea for she could smell the dampness, the heaviness, the phosphorus almost as if she were on the beach in Malibu.

Bonesteel's body was rigid, his silhouette like a black stake driven deep into the earth by her side. Just the livid red eye of his cigarette describing brief arcs in the darkness as he lifted it up to inhale, swung it back down again to his side. She heard the rhythmic hissing of his exhalations just as if it was the surf creeping sluggishly over the sand.

"Once upon a time," he said so abruptly she started, "I knew a girl." His laugh, when it came, was as harsh as a broom scraping over a cement sidewalk and just as unpleasant. "That was a long time ago."

Daina watched him carefully. He was looking at nothing. Not at her or at the trees or even at the low, hard, brittle sky.

"She was a dreamer, Marcia was. Full of ideals and hopes. She was a romantic." He dropped what was left of his Camel into the grass at his feet, ground it under the toe of his shoe. "She was beautiful, like my mother was only more so. Long auburn hair, eyes the color of Irish mist or ... well, that's how she always liked them described. And she was right."

He took a deep breath. "I met her just after I became a cop. I was very dedicated then. Very certain of what I wanted and, worse, of what was best for me." He shrugged. "It seemed much more complicated then. Marcia was a bit appalled at what I was, what she thought I believed in. But that didn't stop her from loving me, merely made it difficult and complex. All this goddamn approach-avoidance.

"We fell in love, we lived together for a while...a year and a half maybe. It was too long and not nearly long enough. We loved each other to distraction. So she left, finally. It was the only way we could both survive. 'I'm going away from you, Bobby,' she said that night. 'As far away as I possibly can.' She paused for a moment. 'I'll write you,' she said, 'only if you promise not to come after me.' So I promised.

"A month later, I got a card from her. It was from Florence. Six weeks after that, Granada and then, finally, in the middle of summer, I received a postcard from Ibiza. 'I've met someone special,' she wrote. 'I'm sending you this card not to hurt you but to tell you that finding this man has brought home just how much I love you. I'll always love you, Bobby. And never forget you. Love, M.'"

Bonesteel crossed his arms over his chest. Daina put an arm up, touched his shoulder. But he seemed not to be aware of it.

"By that time, I was into other things, made friends with other people, left her behind. But, you know, the really odd thing was that, in a way, I *hadn't* left her behind. Just as she wrote to me from Ibiza, I knew that she would always be a part of me. Some girls come and go. Like that. They fade in and then they fade out. Not Marcia. And I've never once regretted meeting her, even after all the pain...of parting. In a strange, direct way, we were good for each other in those wild, storm-filled days and nights. We built up each other's confidence to press on alone."

Daina forced her hand underneath his arm, pressed closer in against him. "Then this story has a happy ending after all?"

"Not quite." He began to walk and she went with him. It was late enough now so that a light ground mist was building through the long grass, curling around the low bushes, obscuring the boles of the trees farther away from them. They seemed totally cut off from the rest of the world, as if they were strolling through an imaginary land with time at a standstill.

"For a time, I lost track of her or, rather, I didn't hear from her. During that time, I had moved. That plus the fact that there was insufficient postage on the letter caused it to arrive six weeks after she had written it. She was in London; she had a baby. And no one else. She was alone, without friends...anyone to help her. I took an emergency leave and flew over. I thought the least I could do was bring her back.

"But I was too late...too much time had..." He moved forward again until they came to the verge of a sweeping dell. In the daytime, it would be a magnificent sight but now, shrouded in darkness and mist, it seemed only to be a hole ripped out of the ground, black and bottomless. He stared into it for a time. "She was gone, the baby was gone. She had turned on the gas, using her last sixpence, and left the light off. I read it all in black and white at New Scotland Yard. They had been brought in because she was an American. She had no family, no one and they had been at a loss as to who to contact. I was the only one and I didn't bring her back. I held the service there, found a place to...bury them." He hunched his shoulders. "It was a long flight home, but when I got there, I found one last nasty surprise. One last letter from Marcia. It had been written just a day after the other one. 'Don't blame Nigel,' she wrote. 'It took me a long time to understand him. It seemed forever that I hated him, thinking that he had betrayed me. I believed in him, in what he was, in his great life-force. It wasn't him that was the lie, only me. He's just a baby and therefore blameless. He has no moral code so he cannot be evil. It's me, me, me. Something's wrong with me. I don't belong here. I don't mean London. Good-bye, Bobby. You're all I remember now.'"

The night seeped in around them as if it had been holding its breath up until now. The tiny sounds of the crickets, the night birds calling plaintively, the intermittent swish of the underbrush as stalking nocturnal animals slid by, all combined with the thudding of her heart, to remind her that life after all continued here with a ceaseless kind of fury that could not be denied. A shiver ran up her spine and she held on to him more tightly, putting one arm around the small of his back.

"Come on," she whispered, as if afraid that her raised voice would disturb the life flowing on around them and plunge them again into the dark despair of his tale. "Let's get out of here."

But he refused to budge. "Don't you want to know," he said, his voice dripping acid, "who that Nigel was?"

"I already know," she said gently. "Come on now."

This time she managed to turn him around and, slowly, they made their way back to the car. Dew dampened the bottoms of their pants and Daina's feet were wet through the sandals.

When they were at the open door, she said to him, "You shouldn't be on this case at all."

For the first time in what seemed like a century, he looked at her directly. "I know that." Shadows crisscrossed his face, moving with the hissing of the branches of the surrounding trees.

"And naturally your captain knows nothing of this... previous involvement."

His gray eyes were dark with feeling. "He hasn't a clue."

"So I thought. Otherwise you'd be yanked off this case in less time than it'd take to tell him. That much I know."

He said nothing, continued to stare into her face. He smelled slightly from tobacco but also from cologne and, even more faintly, from sweat. It was not an unalluring combination.

She cocked her head to one side. "And I suppose it was pure coincidence that you got assigned to this case."

There was just the ghost of a smile on his lips now, fading. "There's no such thing as pure coincidence. I conned Fitzpatrick into giving it to me."

"How'd you do that?"

"Simple. Told him I wouldn't take it, nohow. The poor bastard's very predictable. He rammed it down my throat."

"That rule about personal involvement. It makes a lot of sense."

"I know that too." His face was grim. "It was Nigel's kid, Daina. *His* responsibility, no matter what Marcia thought. I'm not saying the sonovabitch had to marry her. But she didn't deserve...she didn't deserve that."

"You're going on."

"All the way," he said, leaning slightly forward, "to the end."

* * *

"It's almost time." Beryl Martin said it in her hard, clipped manner of speech. There was no doubt that it was a statement of fact and not an opinion although, to her way of thinking, the two were perfectly interchangeable if only they came out of her own mouth.

"There is a great ticking in this town," she continued. "Like a time-bomb set to go off. Everyone knows it, Daina. Even your enemies can feel it and it's making their palms sweat."

Rubens glanced at Dory Spengler, back to Beryl. "There's no time now," he said, "for anything to go wrong."

Beryl gave him a wide smile, the center of which was partially obscured by the end of her nose. "Nothing will."

The four of them were sitting at an impeccably laid table near the back of Le Troisième. Outside, on Melrose, it was dark and raining, the kind of still, windless rain that only comes to Los Angeles as if in retribution for some ancient transgression. But here, inside the restaurant that, for at least this period of time, was *the* place to eat, the lights were soft and low, giving a glow to the cream and dark green decor, the fine crystal. The waiters wore black tuxedos and starched white shirts with black bow ties and Antoine, the maître d', was so elegant it set your teeth on edge. In short, the interior of Le Troisième was as Old World as anything could possibly get in southern California.

Beryl, as resplendent as a cockatoo in an off-white dress that did absolutely nothing to conceal her bulk, picked up her glass and, after peering at a frosted-glass-shaded lamp through the white wine, sipped delicately at the liquid. The bottle lay at an angle in a silver bucket, set in ice, wrapped in a damp towel, at her left elbow below the level of the tabletop.

"To return to the sweating palms," she said, putting the glass down, "you'll never guess who called me up this morning." She did not wait for an answer and it was perfectly clear she had not expected one. "Don Blair."

"The agent?" Spengler fiddled with his fork. "What'd he want?"

"One of his clients has got a film up against us next week."

She looked now as if she had just swallowed a delectable morsel. "Mark Nassiter's the director."

Daina's head came up and Beryl's eyes shifted to meet hers.

"*Skyfire*," Rubens said. "I've seen it. About the war in Cambodia. It stinks. So what?"

Beryl ignored him for a moment, said to Daina, "Someone you know?"

"Used to know," Daina said. "Just another face from a long time ago."

"Of course." Beryl smiled benignly, broke the contact. She shrugged. "Anyway, it doesn't matter. Don rang through the first thing this morning, wanted to know what the hell we were up to.

"'Contrary to what any of you might think,' he said, '*any* film that's nominated has got a chance to win.' I could hear the sweat on his voice. I only wish I had taped the conversation. 'All you bastards,' he said, 'are acting as if you've got the Oscar all sewn up. There's a week to go. Anything can happen.'"

"What'd you say to him then?" Spengler wanted to know. His grin said he was relishing this story.

"I told him," Beryl said carefully, "to go out and see *Heather Duell*." They all laughed.

Spengler poured more wine for all of them and the waiter slid soundlessly up, bowing slightly and handing them great buff-colored cards, hand-lettered in green ink. He told them the day's specialties and they ordered the food and another bottle of Corton Charlemagne.

"Seriously now," Beryl said, "the New York launch—for which we all have to thank Rubens—was an unalloyed success. The national press that one week generated is still coming in, and we're hard at work on the L.A. opening. *Newsweek* was understandably miffed that *Time* beat them to the cover story but they couldn't squawk much at us because it was offered to them. They want to do one now." She smiled again but this time there was a sardonic hint to it. "Of course what I used for bait was the exclusive on Daina's new film. I know, I know"—she held up both hands to ward off Spengler's protests. Her myriad gold bands clinked together—"you and I have been over this before. I am well aware that the studio wants to hold on to it, play it close to the vest. That's because of Brando. Well, to hell with that, I say. Brando's going to do the film. The contract's already been signed, isn't that right, Dory?"

Spengler nodded morosely. "Sure but what is that? A piece of goddamned paper. I know Brando better than any of you. Anytime before the cameras begin to roll, he could back out. Even afterward. In my opinion, jumping the gun with this could—"

"Picture this," Beryl interrupted. "It's released as a cover story in *Newsweek,* breaks open nationwide the same week as Daina gets her Oscar. I don't have to tell you what it'll do for her."

"I'm thinking of—"

"Rubens," Beryl said, once more cutting Spengler off, "what d'you think?"

The appetizers came, set down one by one as gently as if they were priceless porcelain. Rubens stared down at the perfect row of asparagus. He waited until the waiter had spooned three generous tablespoonfuls of the rich creamy hollandaise sauce across the tips. When the waiter had left, Rubens took up the remaining sauce, ladled it over the rest of the spears.

He picked up his knife and fork, looked up directly into Beryl's face and said: "Do it."

He took three bites of his asparagus, turned to Spengler. "Don't for a moment," he said softly, silkily, "forget who you are and *what* you are. You're here only because I've allowed you to be. You may think you're as fallible as the rest of us"— he paused, watching carefully as the deep scarlet flush crept up Spengler's neck and into his face, as he recalled the words he had said to Daina at the party in New York—"but you're only kidding yourself. You're much more fallible. *And* more expendable. You were stupid once and that's enough. Don't get stupid again." He slid the tines of his fork into the soft flesh of an asparagus tip, lifted it up. It dripped hollandaise, once, twice back onto the plate. "You were right about one thing, Dory. I *am* only a man. But just think what that makes you."

Spengler was red-faced now. An erratic pulse beat a silent tattoo high up on his forehead. "I let you walk all over me once." He began to get up.

"Dory, sit down and behave yourself," Beryl said easily.

Sweat had broken out along Spengler's upper lip and his jaw seemed to be trembling. "You've no right to talk to me like that. I'll call Brando and—"

"Don't do it," Rubens said softly. "If you leave this table you're never coming back. You'd better think about the implications of that before you go off half cocked."

Spengler was as motionless as a statue and as stiff.

"Anyway," Rubens continued between bites, "I figure you had it coming. You stepped from the shit into a garden full of roses." His fork stopped halfway to his mouth. "And they weren't your roses either." He chewed on the asparagus tip. "What'd I ever do to you, that you should kick me like that, huh? I hand you this and still you're not satisfied. You've gotta have the whole enchilada. Did you really think you could cut me out?"

With an audible sigh, Spengler slid back into his seat. He took his crumpled linen napkin in one fist, rubbed it across his face a couple of times. "I was sore, is all. I'm treated like a busboy."

"Without you we wouldn't've gotten the Brando film deal so quickly," Beryl pointed out.

"I know that but—"

"You don't like the way I treat you," Rubens said. "That it?"

Spengler looked at him.

"Well, buddy, you better learn something fast. You've got to earn our respect around here. Don't expect to walk in and think you've been handed a cushy job. We've all got work to do around here. We don't do it, we sit around all day admiring our reflections, nothing gets done. You think you can get away with that, you know Brando better than his old lady, I don't care. You can just drift away with the wind. Happens to people around here every day. One minute they're useful, the next they're yesterday's news." He pushed the empty plate away from him. "Listen, you've got brains and you've got guts...at least I thought you had, otherwise I wouldn't've recommended you to Daina in the first place. Just get your head on straight and we'll all be cosy as mice again."

The waiter came to take away the plates. He left Spengler's where it was.

"It's okay," Rubens said, "we'll wait while Dory finishes his first course."

* * *

"Do you love me?" he said when they got home.

"Yes."

"I never thought I'd ask any woman that."

"Didn't you ever ask your wife?"

"I always assumed she did." He touched her, sliding the palm of his hand along her arm, upward to her shoulder. "I've never wanted to hear the truth so much in my life."

"Why?" she whispered. "It's you who'll leave me in the end."

He looked startled. "Why do you think that?"

"Because," she said, putting her fingertips over his heart, "I'm never sure of what's in there. Sometimes I think you have a heart of glass—no, plastic: you can see through it but you can't break it. You're like this city, Rubens. A city that's no city at all; there and not there at the same time." She put her head against his chest.

He gathered her into his arms, holding her tight. "And what would happen if I left you?" he said.

"Nothing," she lied. "Nothing at all."

Bonesteel called late in the morning after Rubens had left for the office.

"You up?"

"Give me a minute." She rolled over in bed, stretched. Had she been asleep or just daydreaming? She could not remember. She thought about guns and women in uniform; George and the PLO, Nigel and the IRA.

"All right," she said. "What's going on?"

"The lab found traces of strychnine in the horse you brought us," he said without preamble. "You missed your calling, like I said. You shoulda been a cop."

She sat up in bed, wide awake. "That means he's still in danger."

"Could be. Maybe he stumbled onto Nigel's gunrunning game." He paused for a moment. "Maybe I ought to come over."

"What for?"

"If Chris is in danger, chances are you are too. You two

have spent too much time together for the killer to think that whatever it is Chris knows, you don't."

"That's ridiculous," she said. "He'd have to be a mind-reader."

"Suit yourself," he said nonchalantly. "By the way, I put a tail on our friend Charlie Wu. Maybe he'll lead us somewhere interesting."

"Bobby, I gave my word—"

"Don't worry," he said, "I won't nail him. Neither of us said anything about using him, did we? Who knows, maybe I'll get lucky. I could use a little luck at this stage. I'm so close to breaking this, I can almost reach out and touch it. But all I've really got is a lotta speculation, a fistful of air and I can't move. I feel like a fly stuck in a web."

"You know what I think," Daina said. "I think you're pushing this. You can't be objective—we both know that. Turn it over to someone else. There must be plenty of detectives who can—"

"The hell with them!" he said harshly. "This case's the only reason I'm still a cop. Nothing's going to get me off it now."

"Bobby, you're a law officer."

"That's exactly what I am."

"But you can't twist the law to suit your own purposes."

"Let me tell you something about the law, Daina. It's perverted every minute of every day. I learned very early as a cop that some days the law is your friend and on others the best thing for you to do is just to step very carefully past it. If you let it lie there, asleep, it won't bite you." He snorted. "What d'you think your boyfriend Rubens thinks of the law, huh?"

And for one brief, blinding moment, Daina thought he must know about Ashley and who had ordered his death. She began to choke just as if she still had Dr. Geist's rubber T-bar in her mouth.

"All those guys with the multimillion-dollar pockets use the law, Daina," Bonesteel was saying. "It's how they got where they are. But this is all academic, anyway. I know what I know. Nigel's the one. It's in his blood. He's fucking callous. He doesn't care about another human being besides himself."

"Bobby, please—"

"I am the law, Daina. And I'm gonna make him pay for what he did to Marcia. Old friends deserve to be remembered. You know that, don't you?"

But what if Bonesteel was wrong? Daina was not sure what or who to believe. She only knew that Bobby was driven by an inner hunger that was self-devouring. She knew he was fully capable of convincing himself of Nigel's guilt irrespective of the evidence. But what if he was right?

She called Tie and invited herself over to Nigel's. She had not thought this all the way through but she knew she had to try it.

Tie met her at the door, embraced her.

"Are you happy back with Nigel?" Daina asked her.

"Now that Chris has left the band, it doesn't make much difference," Tie said unhappily.

"The band won't break up." But she did not really believe that. She was certain now it would and Tie confirmed this.

"Nigel says they'll go on just like before but I know him too well. He's weak. Whatever creative spark he once had has burned out. He's been riding Chris' talent for too long."

Nigel was out by the swimming pool. Like most displaced Britons, he seemed constantly amazed to be living in a place where the sun always shone. He was relaxing in a chaise. Silka, having apparently just mixed him a drink, was setting a tall glass down on a side table next to him.

"Silka," Tie called, "fix Daina a drink, will you?"

He stood waiting, cool and calm, the hint of a smile playing around his mouth. "Stolichnaya on the rocks with a twist." That was Rubens' drink.

"No," Daina said deliberately. "A piña colada would be perfect."

He nodded his head, went toward the bar. Apparently he already knew what Tie wanted.

Nigel turned his head at their approach. He was sunglassless and he squinted up at them. He did not say hello. She knew he must blame her for Chris' decision.

"Shit, you got your nerve coming 'round here."

"I came to see Tie," Daina said.

"You got some very odd ideas," he said to Tie, "an' I don't like any of 'em." He jerked his head. "Get her out o' here."

"Stop acting like a baby," Tie said coldly, looking down at him. "Daina will stay as long as she likes."

"Who's payin' your mealticket?"

"You don't really want me to leave...again."

"Silka!" Nigel bawled. "Do something!"

Silka came across with the drinks, handed them to the women. "What would you have me do?"

Nigel opened his mouth, looked at Tie, closed it again. He waved a hand. "Oh, go fix yourself a drink or somethin'." Silka looked at Daina before he turned away.

"Christ!"

They all turned at the exclamation.

Nigel was running toward the house.

"What is it?" Tie called after him. But he had already disappeared through the window-door, the off-white curtains billowing slightly in his wake. He emerged a moment later. There was a blunt-barreled Mauser in his left hand.

They were all looking at him. Daina put down her drink, untouched, ran to where Silka was standing. She felt Tie just behind her.

"Nigel—!"

"It's that bloody coyote, Tie!" He ran swiftly around to the back of the house and they followed him. For perhaps three hundred yards, an exotic garden stretched away from the house. Then, quite abruptly, a rolling hill, part of a series leading toward Topanga, rose rather steeply. It was lined with bramble and verdant underbrush that fought for space among a densely packed stand of reedy, rustling eucalyptus and broad-banded acacia.

Very quickly, Nigel was into the thickets. He did not wave the pistol around but held it quite steadily at his side as he moved upward. Perhaps there was some sort of half-overgrown path because he was scrambling up the hill at a surprising rate.

Thaïs led the way as they ran after him. It was difficult work after all and by the time they caught up with him, sweat and dirt streaked their faces and they were panting in the heat.

Sunlight streamed down through the trees, dappling Nigel as he stood at the near edge of a small clearing. His eyes were wide and his nostrils were dilated. The Mauser looked very large in his fist.

Tie began to speak but Nigel waved her to silence with his free hand. "Bastard's right 'round here, I know it. I saw him from down there at th' pool, just starin' at me, darin' me t' come up here." His head swiveled as if, without that movement, his eyes could not change their focus. "All week I've been seein' him, hearin' him nosin' around."

"Perhaps he's just hungry," Daina said, watching the foliage. A butterfly darted away with no particular rapidity and, above, dark brown finches darted and chirped contentedly. Everything was as it should be.

"No, no," Nigel whispered. "Ain't got a cat here. He's after somethin' else."

"Like what?" Daina asked.

But Nigel said nothing, waved them down into a crouch. He swiveled this way and that on the balls of his feet.

"I'm beginning to feel foolish," Daina said as she rose.

But Nigel hissed hard at her. "Now that you're here," he said, "you'll stay till I've found this bastard."

"I don't," she said softly, "take orders from you."

Nigel swiveled and she saw his eyes like flint. And she became aware of him: lean and brown and hard-muscled. "What'd you come up here for, anyway? This's huntin' territory."

"Only because you say it is. I'm not in the least interested in your coyote. Leave the damn thing alone."

"It's been tormenting me!" he screamed.

"You'd know about that, wouldn't you?"

He was in a patch of shade but either the sun was slipping or a breeze high aloft was moving the leaves because a sudden spear of sunlight caused his eyes to glitter as they stared hard at her.

"What are you talking about?" Tie asked her.

Daina shook off her arm. "I'm talking about murder," she said.

"What th' fuck you mean?" Nigel had not moved from his crouch. The Mauser lay on his thigh.

"Someone tried to kill Chris when he was in New York. His heroin was cut with strychnine—"

"You're out o' your—"

"In just the same way Maggie's was."

"Maggie," Silka said softly, "was killed by a maniac. We were all told—"

"I know what you were told," Daina said evenly. "The police caught that psychopath but he didn't kill Maggie."

"How d'you know that?"

Daina ignored Silka. She was staring into Nigel's face. Was Bonesteel right about him? It was very still around them and the heat seemed to ricochet back and forth, building. Whatever breeze there had been before had died. They were all dappled in patches of light and dark, inhaling the tang of the dark earth.

"None of us knew anything about what happened to Chris," Tie said, looking from one to the other. "Did we?"

"No one tried to kill Chris," Nigel said. "You're dreamin'."

"Then maybe I'm dreaming too that Maggie's real last name was Toomey and that she was the granddaughter of Sean Toomey."

Nigel barked a laugh. "Now I know th' heat's got t' you."

"Shut up, Nigel!" Tie snapped. She looked at Daina. "Is this the truth?"

"Yes. It was a political murder; retribution placed at Sean Toomey's doorstep."

"Christ, Nigel, d'you know—"

But Tie did not finish. Nigel's left hand moved and the snout of the Mauser came up, pointing in Daina's direction. It was a large-caliber pistol and the muzzle seemed as black as the night and just as huge.

Daina jumped and Nigel squeezed the trigger. The gun exploded, bucking in his hand. Daina heard the high cry from behind her and to one side, felt a bursting spray of hot stickiness.

She whirled. Her left shoulder was spattered with tiny droplets of blood, beading on her skin. Not her own blood. She smelled a stench.

Nigel was on his feet, racing past her. "You cocksucker!" he cried. "I've got you now!"

13

The alarm went off somewhere in the depths of the limo. It was soft and high and sounded like the chiming of a ship's clock.

The darkness through which they sped was shot through with bubbles of light, like champagne held up to lamplight.

The air conditioner hummed on the threshhold of audibility. Outside she could see the smog, the high dusty palms standing motionless as if time itself had frozen them in some long-unending Polaroid snapshot, and the illusion—caused by the deeply tinted glass—that they sailed through the reefs of night was gone. Outside, she knew, it was merely another hot late afternoon. Night, already, in New York.

"Thirty minutes to magic time," Rubens said. He sat relaxed and confident beside her in a midnight-blue custom-tailored tux over a white ruffle-front silk shirt and a velvet bow tie. He looked as if he owned the world.

"How can you sit there so calmly?" Daina wanted to know. She fidgeted around on the seat beside him, plucking a cigarette from his case, twirling it between her fingers like a baton before breaking it apart. Angrily, she brushed the strands of tobacco off her lap. The sinuous salmon-colored

521

Zandra Rhodes dress rustled like a living thing as it slithered across her stockinged thighs. It was faintly iridescent, hand-painted with deep blue oblique pinstripes that gave it a cascading look as if she were cloaked in water.

Rubens put a hand on her knee. "There's nothing to worry about."

"God's the only one who should be able to say that and mean it." She shook her hair out, opened her clutch purse, searching for her compact.

The Dorothy Chandler Pavilion was ablaze with klieg and TV camera lights in shining addition to its own. The crowds were enormous, straining against the purple velvet-covered chains that lined the steps.

The limo slid to a stop and the driver came around to hold the door. Mikes were thrust in their faces, questions were asked. Flashbulbs were going off at an awesome rate. Daina spoke to Army Archerd about the film but when he asked her about the rumors concerning her future plans she merely smiled her thousand-watt smile and, with Rubens on her arm, sailed past him, up the red-carpeted stairs.

"This is where it's all going to pay off," Rubens said. All that publicity work...including the six-week talk-show tour she had done with Marion two months back. It had been a breakneck cross-country tour that some bright spark at the studio had thought up. Whoever it had been, she had been right. The combination had been perfect. Marion, normally a rather reticent person in front of the camera, faced up to the blitz of the American media machine with Daina at his side. As a result, midway through the tour, they had discovered that an impromptu routine that they had somehow come up with during the "Mike Douglas Show" taping was an instant smash—as only something on television can be. So that by the time they climaxed the tour with an appearance on "The Tonight Show," during the premier week in L.A., they had no difficulty in stealing an extra ten minutes beyond the time allotted them.

Behind them the steps were filling up as the celebrities walked slower and slower for the TV cameras, clutches of twos and threes, widely spaced, coming on in such slow motion they seemed trapped in amber.

There were shouts and ripples of applause as stars made their appearance, began the long walk, longer than a wedding's, longer than a funeral's, seeming to go on forever, all the electricity draining from the projector into her limbs so that the film ran more and more slowly, grinding down to a golden haze, and she became excruciatingly aware of every movement, every shout, cry, scream, noise, push, shove, adoring look. But it took some time for her to understand that this hard accretion of sound and fury was vectoring in one direction, funneling inward from its widest point at the far edge of the throng to a pinpoint grappling.

Perhaps it was not until they broke through the velvet-covered chains and she found herself in the eye of a hurricane of uplifted arms, dangling strobe-equipped cameras, uplifted faces with pulled-apart lips, that she realized they were screaming for her. The New York Film Critics' award, the Golden Globes all seemed a prelude to just this moment.

Rubens ducked his head as someone swung, trying to get an autograph book in position, grabbed her around the waist. He began to pull her away.

There were brittle shouts and a great milling vortex that threatened to pull her under. Lights swung around and she heard the voice of Army Archerd, reporting still, coming up on the swirling commotion, leaving Charlton Heston or Sally Field or whoever it was.

Daina began to move, feeling pulled in two directions, knowing she must go, that crowds out of hand were no place to find oneself, recalling that poor girl almost trampled by the mob following the Heartbeats' limo in San Francisco, but wanting all the while to remain, feeling reluctant to let this demonstration of mass adoration pass too soon.

So she resisted Rubens' urgings just enough to keep her within the outer fringes of the mass while they strove to touch her, to talk to her, to kiss her and, it seemed, even that thousand-watt smile turned on them, was enough to keep them coming up. Someone tripped, went down, bobbed up again, kept coming.

There was more pushing and shoving now as they approached the first set of glass doors to the theater. The crowd knew, with the communal certainty that often sweeps through such masses, that their time was drawing to a close and they pressed forward at once, surging like a tidal wave.

Someone reached out a hand, caught her arm, pulled, and she almost went down. Rubens caught her, dragged her away. Whistles were blowing now and the harsh wail of a police siren could be heard cutting through the high babble.

The cops came in, wading through the throng, pushing people aside, moving forward with lowered shoulders and drawn nightsticks. They formed a wedge, dispersing people to the right and left. Someone cried out in pain or in longing and then the first of the cops was beside them and they were propelled through the first ring of the doors.

One other patrolman squeezed through the doors and the two of them stood to either side. The others, still outside, fanned out along the top steps. More police cars came screaming down the street, lights flashing and a riot van turned the corner.

"Are you all right, Miss Whitney?" one of the patrolmen inside asked her. He was young and blond with hard blue eyes and wide shoulders.

"Yes," she said. "I think so."

The back doors of the van opened.

"And you, Mr. Rubens? All okay?"

Cops came spilling out like salt from a container, but without Daina on the steps the crowd had pulled back, all the movement drained from them.

"Yeah, yeah," Rubens said disgustedly. He brushed his hands across the front of his tux, down the thighs of his trousers. "Where the hell *were* you guys?"

"Sorry, Mr. Rubens," the cop said without really meaning it. His tone said, If you weren't who you are, I'd tell you to mind your own damn business. "We came as quickly as we could. No one expected anything like this." He gestured vaguely with one hand. "I mean we're not in New York." He came away from the doors, took a pad from a holder at the small of his back. A ballpoint pen clicked in his hand. "I wonder, Miss Whitney...would you mind?" He offered the pad and pen and, smiling, Daina gave him the autograph.

"It's all right, Officer." She smiled at him. "You came just at the right time." At that moment he might have walked through a sheet of glass if she had asked him. "Perhaps you could wait around until the awards ceremony's over and give us an escort home."

"Hey, Mike," the other cop said, gesturing. "I don't know—"

"Phone it in," the blonde said without turning around. And in a softer tone of voice, said, "We'd be happy to, Miss Whitney." He took the pad and pen back from her. "You just look for us whenever you come out."

"Thank you, Michael. Mr. Rubens and I would appreciate that." She managed to stress the "I" and the rest of the sentence seemed to fade away. She turned, took Rubens' arm.

"Oh, Miss Whitney?"

"Yes?"

"Good luck, tonight. We're pulling for you."

"Why, thank you, Michael. That's very kind of you."

Color had come to his cheeks and he turned away.

Daina and Rubens went through the second set of doors into the lobby proper and she saw him the moment she stepped through.

He came quickly up, his dark hawklike face held high. He was in an ill-fitting tux that he must have rented at the last minute. His hair was a good deal longer than she remembered it, its pitch blackness relieved now by strands of silver, and his full beard was shot with white. It seemed ages since she had thrown him out of her house.

"I've been waiting for this moment," he said. His voice was the same, that peculiar metallic quality making his sentences seem clipped, foreign. It was just one of the elements that made him such a good public speaker. He seemed uncomfortable in the tux, his neck welted from twisting it back and forth against the chafing collar.

"Rubens, this is Mark Nassiter."

They ignored each other with the ferocity of sworn enemies.

"What d'you want?" Daina said.

"Just to see you again." There was a bit of tobacco on his lip. "To see what you've become." His dark eyes were hooded. "To see what they've made you into."

"Whatever I've become, Mark, is because of me. These are *my* dreams."

"You sure about that, honey?" He leered at her, leaning in on the balls of his feet, a habit he used to counteract his lack of height.

For the first time she was able to recognize the hardness

in his face; there was an adamantine quality to his eyes that she was certain now had been there all the time.

Mark pointed. "You so sure that this Svengali isn't at the heart of it all, pulling his strings." His mouth twisted with contempt. "How's it feel to be sleeping with a power junkie?" His hand snaked out, touched the line of her jaw, briefly cupped her chin. "That's all that's happened to you, baby."

Daina felt the forward surge even before she saw Rubens move.

"Now just a goddamn minute, you sleazy punk!" Rubens' hands were balled fists.

Mark beckoned with his finger. "C'mon, you fat cat. I ain't afraid of you. I ain't afraid of anything!"

Daina stepped between the two of them. She looked at Mark but she spoke to Rubens. "That's enough," she said tightly. "Leave this to me."

"The hell I will." Rubens took a lunge past her. "This bastard deserves everything he's gonna get from me!"

She spun around now, glared up into his face. "I said I'll handle this!"

Mark grinned sardonically. "Oh, that's the way, baby. Yeah, yeah. Assert your little self. Take it while you can. Who cares that it's only an illusion. This's the battle he'll let you win 'cause it costs him nothing to lose. But when it comes to the war, honey, he's already bought you, sold you, and packaged you like a side of ham. And the funny thing is—I mean the *really* screamingly funny thing is that you won't even know it until the army's gone on to a new, even bigger campaign and left you far behind."

"You're awfully sure of yourself, aren't you?"

He snorted derisively. "Sure enough so I don't have to kiss the asses of the power."

"Oh yeah," Daina said. "I can just see the scene now between you and the people at Columbia." She eyed him. "I'm certain they enjoyed scarfing down your polemics while shoveling over the extra eleven mil you needed to finish up *Skyfire* after you ran over budget."

Rubens laughed when he saw the expression on Mark's face.

"You disgust me." Mark turned to go.

"You through with us so soon?" Daina said sweetly. "I thought you were just warming up."

"I've seen enough," he said savagely. "*More* than enough. It's what I came here for."

She reached out quickly, took his arm in a strong grip, pulling him back to face her. "Oh, no, my lad, you won't get away with *that*." He started to pull away from her but she merely tightened her grip. "I'll tell you why you came here. You came to pick up your Oscar. You who won't kiss the asses of power. Well, here's the power tonight, Mark, and you know what? You're right here with the rest of us, aren't you?"

"When I win," he grated, "I'll be able to say my piece. That's what I want."

Daina shook her head so that her honey hair brushed her cheeks. She smiled. "If you had any guts at all you would've stayed away like Brando or Woody. But you couldn't. You're too weak. You lack even the conviction to face up to what you really are." She let go of him as if he were a three-month-old piece of meat. "You're all polemics; all steamy-voiced and angry-eyed in the dead of night. But when it comes right down to it, you won't strap on your guns and shoot. You're no outsider. You play at being an outlaw but that's all it is. Face it, Mark. You're a kid and that's all you'll ever be."

Mark's hands were clenched fists at the ends of stiff arms and the corners of his mouth were white with tension.

"Is everything all right, Miss Whitney?"

Daina turned her head slightly, saw the blond cop behind her. He had left his post, come in through the second set of doors.

"It's all right—"

But he was not even listening, pushing on past her. He stopped in front of Mark, tapped him on the chest with the tip of his forefinger as if testing for life. His other hand rested lightly on the top of his holstered pistol's stock. "You giving the lady any trouble, bud, I wouldn't advise going any further." He pushed once softly against Mark's chest. "Go on," he said lightly. "Beat it." And pushed again so hard that Mark stumbled back a pace before turning and disappearing into the crowd.

The blond cop turned around. "Anything else I can do, Miss Whitney...." He touched the peak of his cap.

"That's all right, Michael," she said softly. "Thank you very much."

"Not at all." He went out through the doors to join his partner.

"What's the matter," she said to Rubens as they went through into the theater, "cat got your tongue?"

"I don't know," he said. "I'm just a little dazzled."

She was perfectly prepared for the moment when they would call her name. Rubens was certain it would come even though she was not.

It was a time when the fear creeps in on silent dangerous feet, oozing through the mind, clamming the hands. It was like being a child all over again and knowing, just knowing, that there was nothing hiding over there in the corner where she'd piled her clothes and the closet door stood half open, in the night; in the dark with the rain spattering against the windowpane like lonely tears and the lurid neon radiance of the lightning forking down and the thunder rolling like waves against a rocky coast, rattling the windows at the moment it broke apart the sky.

"...all these jokes. The nominees for Best Actress in a Motion Picture are..."

But, somehow, at those times, knowing did no good at all because some *other* part of her mind was at work, creeping out when she wasn't looking, taking hold with steel talons and gaining an ascendancy, laughing hysterically at the rational world.

"...Daina Whitney for *Heather Duell....*"

So now she sat there on top of the bed covers, cross-legged and goosefleshed, her nightgown bunched up around her thighs, and she bit at her nails, stared at that black corner as if it were a pit and broke out into a cold sweat.

"...for *The Powers That Be....*"

And she thought she was perfectly prepared for whatever it was that was going to spring out at her from that dark place.

"...but then Jodie Foster's only nineteen." Laughter. "Now here's the all-important envelope. Sally, would you do the honors?"

It's only fear, she thought, that can cloud men's minds.

"...easier opening envelopes, wouldn't you? Oh here we

are. The winner is...Daina Whitney"—shouts and applause almost drowning out the rest—"for *Heather Duell!*"

So then she thought: What is it I am going to say now to all of them? Now that I've been chosen, now that my name has been called, now that the four others who were nominated have dutifully hidden their disappointment for the cameras but who, later on, for tomorrow and tomorrow, until it's nothing but old news, will whisper their resentment and envy to anyone who will listen. Is there anything to say to this community, to this city, to the world?

The film's theme swelled in the theater as she climbed the plexiglass steps to the stage with the rising applause ringing in her ears, the bright lights flaring in her eyes, and walked, breathless, to the thin podium where Sally and Bob waited, strangers to her now, smiling and waving.

On the podium's thin platform: the gold statuette.

Silence. And within the silence, a rustling as if she were alone in a field full of insects on an endless drowsy summer's afternoon.

She looked out over the audience, looking at no one at all. "I've thought of so many things to say...at a moment like this. Once I thought they were important things. But never having experienced a moment like this before, I find that everything I thought I would say is inadequate.

"It doesn't matter. Nothing I say here matters. This award"—she grasped the statuette around its ankles, holding it aloft—"isn't for words. It's for actions. It means more to me...I can't tell you. It's been a dream for so long, so long. Thank you Rubens and Yasmin and George and, especially, dear Marion. Thank you all for proving that this town hasn't lost its touch for making dreams come true."

Rubens' house seemed to be transformed as more and more people arrived to join the celebration. Six statuettes stood beside Daina's, including Best Supporting Actress for Yasmin, Best Director for Marion and Best Film for Rubens.

Daina felt as if she were standing atop the highest mountain peak in the world and below her, spread out on the most immense carpet in the world, were all the millions of people, their faces upturned in rapturous radiance, their arms outstretched toward her while she whirled and whirled and whirled.

From Rubens to Yasmin to Marion and back again as the four of them stood in the center of the room, standing on the plush pillows of the couch in the sunken conversation pit, holding their Oscars aloft while a battery of drunks shot off their SX–70 Sonars. Snick-snick-snick. The resulting flurry of photos filled the air like confetti. Daina winked at the fat sleek mermaid on the wall.

She downed champagne at a record clip. There was more Taittinger Blanc de Blanc there than anyone had seen in one place in a long time.

She had stayed in the Zandra Rhodes but had taken forty minutes in the bathroom with Mandy, the makeup artist from Reiko's in Beverly Hills.

She had emerged looking like a tigress. Mandy had used the entire top half of her face as her canvas, employing paints of opalescent oyster-white, glittering gold, a deep earthy umber and hints of a hard searing green. She had used all horizontal strokes, expanding Daina's eyes, giving the startling illusion that they went all the way around to the sides of her skull.

Above and below the white-painted sockets, the sweeps of the darker colors filled and highlighted, the glitter used sparingly only on the highest sections of her face: the points of her cheekbones, the ridges directly over her eyebrows, which now arced out and up into the thick tangle of her hair.

Mandy had removed the diamond band that had swept Daina's hair back and away from her face for the awards ceremony. She brushed it out and up until it resembled the mane of an enormous cat.

Daina had stood up in front of the mirror, shaking her head back and forth. She stared at herself in the warm rosy light, growled deep in her throat. Then she threw her head back and laughed.

"Go out there," she had told Mandy, patting her on the flank, "and have yourself a good time."

Now she threw her champagne glass into the empty fireplace. She felt as if she could open her arms and encompass the night. She wanted to go outside, to press all the stars against her breast, to feel their cold ethereal burning there and to know with quiet certainty that she and she alone had accomplished that.

People kept arriving at the most appalling rate; no one left. Men and women sat on the sofa, two and three at a time on the chairs; they lounged against the walls, reclined on the carpet, danced past the fireplace, kissed atop toilet seats, sprawled across the beds, antagonized Maria to the point where she threw up her hands in disgust and walked out; crawled across the tennis courts outside, draped themselves over the net and threw up, collapsed into the pool, snorting and spouting water to the confusion of the dolphin that bucked and rolled there, splashing those close to the edge.

And still they came. In dribs and drabs, in torrents they pushed their way inside, bearing presents of food and wine. She thought she knew them all but she could not be certain. Nothing mattered except her Oscar, which she alternately put on the mantelpiece so she could stare at it from across the pulsing room and held clutched tightly to her breast.

She spent a fascinating fifteen minutes speaking to an odd-looking man, tall and impossibly thin and gaunt. He had sallow skin, a black beard, a long hooked nose and eyes like bits of coal. She lurched away finally only to discover that she had been talking to the El Greco.

"...all the way."

"Huh?"

"Darling, come on," Yasmin said softly, taking her about the waist.

"It's my party." Her words were slightly slurred.

"I know. I only want to talk to you a minute." She smiled into Daina's face. "You can get back to that in a minute."

They went outside. It took them a year and a half. The forest of people kept shifting and there was no clear path to follow. The world was a liquid and they were finless.

Outside, amid the trees and the grass and the carefully sculptured foliage there seemed to be fewer people but that might have been only because there was more open space to move around in.

Their heels grated grittily against the concrete flagging around the pool. The underwater lights were on as well as the speakers and the water was a shifting rainbow of colors. No different from the land.

The dolphin rolled and snorted through its blowhole, diving and then spinning upward, breaching the surface and leaping high into the air to the accompaniment of raucous applause from the crowd of onlookers. The creature undoubtedly reveled in the attention, understood the nature of the guests, for it repeated this maneuver again and again, seeming to reach new heights with each successive leap.

Yasmin put her head to one side as she watched the creature's antics. "What d'you suppose he thinks of?" she wondered aloud. "They're supposed to be the most intelligent creatures on earth after us." They walked on. "Or perhaps there's nothing in its head but dreams." She turned to look at Daina. "That would be nice wouldn't it?" She took a deep breath of the night air. "Nothing but dreams."

"Then we all must be dolphins tonight," Daina said, looking up at the night sky, the burning stars, and remembered her wish. They did seem close enough to touch.

"I've got something to tell you," Yasmin said and Daina turned to look at her.

"Nothing bad, Yasmin," she said. "Not tonight."

Yasmin smiled, her teeth white and shining in that sensuous dusky face. Her eyes had never seemed so huge or so liquid. "I got word just before I left for the awards. I looked for you before but in the crush I couldn't find you and then afterward...there was just no time." She took Daina's hands in hers. "I've been offered the female lead in the new Scorcese film."

Daina stared at her. "Yasmin. Really?" She pulled Yasmin to her, hugged her. "That's wonderful! I'm so happy for you."

"The thing is, I'm off tomorrow for preproduction work in Lucerne. I'll be there a couple of weeks before shooting begins in Luxembourg, Madrid and Malta."

Daina sobered for an instant. "Tomorrow but—"

"I'll be at the Grand National in Lucerne. I'll call you as soon as I get settled."

"I'll never see you again, will I?"

Yasmin laughed. "After what we've been through together how can you say that?"

Daina felt near to tears, could not understand why. "It's just a feeling."

Yasmin stroked her neck. "Don't be sad," she said. "Not on a night like this. I'll be back. And, anyway, you'll be leaving soon for the Brando project. Didn't I hear Singapore?"

"Singapore, yes."

"Well that's what you should be thinking about. My God, it's the part of a lifetime!"

"Maybe I could get you written into the film," Daina said hopefully. She looked around. "Where's Rubens? I'm sure he could fix it."

"Daina—"

"No, no. There's no problem. Anything I want I can get now." She laughed, squeezed Yasmin. "Won't that be great? The two of us together in—"

"Daina, I'm leaving tomorrow morning." Yasmin took hold of her shoulders. "I want that part."

"But—"

"I've got to be on my own now. Don't you see that?"

Daina felt an unreasoning anger bubbling up inside her. She wanted desperately to control the situation. There was no good reason why Yasmin should not leave yet Daina wanted her to stay. Maggie was gone and now Yasmin was going too. "All I see is you leaving me."

"That's not true. All I'm doing is—"

"Oh, Yasmin, don't go!" The music beat louder and louder, popping in her veins like carbonation, a jungle line through the house, streaming outside into the spangled night. Flashes of color filmed her eyes and she felt spasms like jolts of current racing through her system. Her muscles jumped involuntarily under her glossy sweat-streaked skin as if they were threatening to take over.

"Daina, please. I don't want us to leave each other this way. We're friends—"

"Damn you!" Daina cried. "I could fix everything up for you! Everything! Christ, you don't know when you're well off!" Yasmin tried to reach out for her. "No, no. Don't touch me! Get away!"

She went lurching away to find Rubens but ran into Marion instead. His face was flushed from drinking but his eyes were clear and he grabbed her as she was about to stumble past him. "Hello there!" he said. "My God what a bash!"

"Oh, Marion!" She fell into his arms.

"Daina, what is it?"

His words somehow penetrated the fog in her brain and she pulled her face away from him. Hadn't she been told that water would not take off her extraordinary makeup? She shook her head, her tangled hair brushing her shoulders. "Nothing but good news tonight, Marion, right?" She smiled at him.

"Christ," he said, "you look like a bird of prey. That makeup's quite remarkable. Perhaps they could do the same for me."

She laughed, took his arm in hers. "Oh, Marion," she said. "What a place to be! Where else on earth could a night like this happen?"

"I cannot imagine." He looked at her soberly. "What's upset you so?"

"Oh, it's nothing. Just Yasmin acting like a fool. I offered her a part in my new film but she'd rather leave."

"Do you blame her? She's got a leading role in a very important film. How could you expect her to give that up?"

"But look what I'm offering her!"

"All you're offering her is an opportunity to hang around you, to be second best—"

"To be my friend!"

"Look here, my dear," he said sternly, "if she were your friend, you'd want her to do what's best for her."

"Oh, Marion, you don't understand at all!"

"On the contrary, I understand perfectly. Don't think I haven't seen what's been happening to you. This film...I tell you frankly, Daina, I'd never make another one like it again, even if I were assured of winning another Academy Award. I've thought about this a long time. I'm not so proud of that award. I'll take it back to England with me, put it on the mantel of my study and every week the cleaning lady will come and dust it off. What does it mean? Nothing.

"We all gave up too much for this film. It's taken an incalculable toll on all of us. You, me, Yasmin, George. None of us are the same people anymore. The film's changed us, marked us for life. I don't recognize you...I don't even recognize myself."

"No," Daina said, shaking her head. "You can't mean that. It's everyone around us. *They* see us differently so they react differently."

"Don't be a fool!" he hissed furiously. "Can't you see what's right in front of your eyes?" Yes, she thought. I see it. But, oh, I don't want to say it. "Look at George. He flew to Paris tonight. D'you know where he's headed? Southern Lebanon.

Christ only knows how he's arranged it, but he's being taken into one of the PLO base camps there. I'm quite certain he'll be screened but after that"—he shrugged—"he'll be one of them."

"George, a real live terrorist?" Daina stared at him. "He doesn't have the balls."

"On the contrary," Marion said easily. "George has become a very dangerous man."

"George is unstable."

"That's what makes him so dangerous."

"Does Yasmin know this?"

Marion shrugged. "I haven't told her. There's no reason for her to know."

"He loved her."

"All the more reason not to tell her."

Abruptly there were tears in her eyes. "I love her too, Marion."

He held her to him, kissed her forehead. "I know you do, darling. You're very good friends."

"I don't want her to leave." Her little-girl voice was muffled by his clothing.

"I'm quite certain she feels the same way. I'm leaving too, you know. I can't bear to be here another moment. I don't think I really remember why I came. All I know is I miss England terribly."

Daina kissed Marion on the cheek. "I want to see her. I want to talk to her before she leaves."

She spent more than an hour searching for Yasmin but, though she looked everywhere, she could not find her.

It seemed a very long time before the guests began to leave. In fact, it was near dawn before the majority of them staggered out. Some had to be shaken awake, force-fed strong black coffee so that they could make it to their cars, down the deserted streets to their diverse homes and still there would be more than one traffic accident, sirens breaking apart what was left of the night, red and white lights strobing. Blood seeping. Sleeping it off.

But for Daina, there was no thought of sleep. It seemed as far away as death. And the adrenalin flowed as if from some vast reservoir without end.

The house was unrecognizable. It did not matter. She and Rubens left the interior guarded by El Greco's dour intellectual and the exophthalmic mermaid perched smugly on her glistening rock, went back out into the dripping garden.

They made violent love beneath the palms whose slithering crowns chittered in the freshening breeze of dawn, with the sky beginning to pearl, just faintly, above the low rooftops; an indirect glow to the east as yet no threat to the brilliance of the stars. A crescent moon was near to setting, appearing and disappearing between the tufted palm leaves. The crickets sang and the sound of the dolphin leaping and twisting in the nearby pool made her dream they were lost on a desert island, surrounded by nothing but the sea. The sea.

The second time was quite different. He was still in her, wetly, rethickening. And he was never so gentle, so tender, so absolutely loving, and, at the very end, she was certain that he cried but it could just as easily have been his perspiration that dropped onto her shoulder, oiling her before rolling off the convex surface, absorbed by the earth beneath them.

Stillness. Just their breathing and the sound of the birds announcing the sun's arrival.

Daina fell asleep in the grass, the mingled sweat and juices from their lovemaking drying slowly on her skin, her long thick hair spread out like the tail of some demigod, her flesh tanned and glowing in the quicksilver of the reflected light: in the translucence of dawn, a painting by Rousseau.

While flies buzzed in the growing patches of sunlight, while a gold and green butterfly alighted on her one upraised knee, drifted away with the breeze, she dreamed she was back in New York, back in another time.

It was April and everywhere else it was already spring, but here in the gray steel canyons winter had not yet relinquished its icy chill. She wore high brown boots, the toes and heels spattered with snow the color and consistency of mud, faded jeans tucked into her boot tops and her old Navy peacoat with its dark plastic buttons engraved with an anchor.

Her honey hair was pulled severely back from her face, tied tightly in a ponytail. She wore no makeup. With her hands thrust deep into the pockets of her peacoat, she walked hunched forward against the harsh scrape of the wind barreling down the gutters. Her cheeks and the tip of her nose were red and her teeth chattered.

She kept on walking north, saw buildings sliding by her as if on a conveyor belt. Every once in a while she looked for street signs but she could not find them. She came to no corner.

Abruptly, she was in front of the restaurant and she went through the door into the warmth inside. She recognized the glazed Italian brick, the low pressed-tin ceiling. The thick odors of cooking food engulfed her.

Moonfaced and mute, people watched her as she hurried past their tables, piled high with food and liquor. She had begun to sweat and shiver but she did not think to unbutton her peacoat.

She went right to the table in the back, the most favored one in the restaurant, the one that overlooked the back window. Outside: the backs of buildings, their filthy brickwork overgrown by graffiti. A lean dog prowled amongst the rubble, lifting its mangy leg.

The face at the table was stuffing itself with cuchifritos. The great blunt hands, the pincerlike fingers shoveled the food into the wide-open mouth in such heapings that many of them fell back onto the plate with each delivery.

She stood very still, staring at the face: the pale, pale eyes, the red-gold hair. Grease stained the thin lips and flecks of breading stuck to the pink cheeks.

She called out a name, *his* name, and the face turned slowly toward her. In her pocket, her right hand curled around the warm pistol's butt. Her forefinger found the trigger and she drew the gun, fired point-blank again and again into the sweaty and grease-slicked face.

Nothing happened and, in horror, she stared at the gold statuette she held out, head first, toward the gaping mouth.

The face let out a roaring laugh. Tiny bits of grease and breading spewed from the pulled-back lips, from the honed edges of the white, white teeth, and she saw the dark hollow cavern of the mouth, as huge as the night sky. The braying laughter filled the restaurant, reverberating down off the low pressed-tin ceiling, echoing from the tiles, and she turned to run. But the hard blunt hand shot out, encircling her wrist.

"Here, my dear," the mouth pantomimed and she found a real gun pressed into the palm of her open hand. She gripped it, pulled the trigger without thinking and the pistol exploded, jerking again and again.

But the ruined face, dripping blood and gore, she found before her was not Aurelio Ocasio's. It was George's.

And the laughter came again, harder now, crueler and she fled out into the night, distance diminishing it not at all....

She was crying in the grass. High above her head a bright-plumaged bird, a cardinal perhaps, was squawking raucously, sounding suspiciously like the runoff from last night's party or the laughter in her dream.

She squeezed her eyes shut for a moment, still half asleep, not really knowing where she was. Somewhere between New York and L.A. Her dry lips opened and she sat up, called, "Rubens?" in a voice as low as a whisper.

She shivered, drew her legs under her, rested her spinning head in her hands. A fierce headache tore at her and she grunted like a wounded animal as she opened her eyes to the bright sunlight. I ought to get up and move into the shade, she thought. But she stayed where she was.

Ohhh! "Rubens?" She looked carefully around. There was the high green wire fence surrounding the tennis court and she looked quickly away. It was burning in direct sunlight. Her mouth was dry and sticky and she had trouble swallowing. Dehydration, she thought and then again, My God! as she held her throbbing head.

"Well," Rubens said, coming up to her through the foliage, "at last you're up."

"Shhh!" she cautioned. His voice sounded like a twenty-one-gun salute going off in her ear.

He squatted down beside her, dropped a silk dressing gown across her knees and held out a glass of orange juice. "Here," he said more softly, "drink this down. Maria just squeezed it. She came back, decided to give us another chance."

"Where did she go?" Daina said dazedly.

"It's a long story. Come on." He pressed the cold glass into her hand, wrapped her fingers around its side. "Drink up. I dropped a couple of Tylenol in."

Gingerly she put the rim of the glass to her mouth and began to drink. It tasted so good that she downed half before coming up for a breath. She squinted through the sunlight at him. "You certainly don't look the worse for wear."

He grinned at her. "Instant recovery." He was dressed in a lightweight linen three-piece.

"Don't tell me you're off to the office so early."

"It's two-thirty," he said. "In the afternoon."

"Oh shit! I wanted to call Yasmin."

"I didn't want to wake you."

"Goddamnit, Rubens!"

He stared down at her while she put her head in her hands. "You acted like a real shit last night. She was crying when she left."

"You saw her leave?" It was an idiotic question and he did not bother to answer her.

From somewhere behind them, past all the foliage and land, she heard a car door slam, coming quick and sharp in the air as it always did this time of the year. A dog barked several times and was still; she heard the rhythmic thump of a basketball against asphalt, the spang of a backboard's recoil, a young boy's shout of triumph.

Daina got up and went around to the pool. It was cool and clear. No animal rolled there, splashing. Back to Marineland, she thought, and took a dive into the deep end.

The cold shock revived her, made her head throb all at once. She broke the surface, swam to the far side, climbed out. To her left the sprinklers were on, hissing over the verdant lawn. She saw a glimpse of the Mexican gardener's assistant working on the hedges but she made no move to cover her nakedness. She turned back to Rubens, shading her eyes with the edge of one hand.

"Don't take a full day at the office. Let's have dinner on the boat."

He came toward her, grimacing. "Sorry. I thought I told you yesterday. I've got to fly up to San Francisco. If I don't close the Stinson Beach project deal today it's no go for this year's taxes."

"Oh, Christ, you don't have to. Not today."

He kissed her. "Schuyler says it's vital. I'll lose a half million in write-offs if I don't. Even *I'd* call that vital." He caressed her back. "But I'll be back in two days, three tops, and then I promise you a long weekend on the boat, okay?"

He left her standing by the side of the pool in bright sunlight, surrounded by the small careful sounds of afternoon.

She said nothing, seeming tall and browned and confident, as fit as an athlete.

She was quite still, listening to the sound of the limo as it started up, the crunching of the gravel as it began to roll down the driveway, taking him from her. She wanted to break into a run, to fly through the garden and the house, to stop him somehow. But there was no way and she did not make a move.

Tiny beads of water continued to roll off her shoulders and back, hips and buttocks, running in hot rivulets down the inside of her thighs. Soon the sun had dried her completely, turning her skin taut with heat. She put on lotion, facing the gardener's back, silently daring him to turn around.

When he did not and she had finished, she lay down on a chaise and closed her eyes. Only sounds came to her now but they seemed disjointed, separate, as if they had no connection to her or even to where she was. She seemed to float for an endless time. The whizz-whir of the sprinklers continued but the kid playing basketball must have gone inside. Soon all she could hear was the wind moving through the tops of the palms.

Her closed eyelids were red with bright sunlight and wind whipped her long hair back off her face so that it trailed behind her like a pennant.

Her arms were tight around him and she could smell the wonderful worn-leather odor of his jacket, the scent of his long hair, a touch perhaps of some cologne or, she thought with a start, just him after long hours of intense work.

For her it was not truly a sexual scent but a masculine one. Her breasts heaved with her breathing and she could feel the bending of his spine as he leaned further into it, the tension in his frame as the excitement and exhilaration of the speed raced through him. It was contagious; it spread through her and she lifted her face up until her lips were against his ear.

"Faster," she shouted. "Faster, Chris!"

He had come up to the house on the Harley while she had been stretched out by the side of the pool. He had been in the studio all night and had no desire to stay still. Neither, at that point, did she.

She opened her eyes when they came hurtling down off the Pacific Palisades and she saw the ocean, heavy and dark in the low troughs, shining like liquid gold where the sunlight struck it. Her heart turned over and she found herself longing again for the sharp blue violence of the Atlantic.

This ocean is such a poor substitute, she thought now. No raging tide this...only a sluggish swell, dulled by the long dusty years here, calm to the point of somnolence, lulling, hypnotic.

She closed her eyes again, dreaming.

Felt the centrifugal force dragging her as he took them around to the right and onto Old Malibu Road. He twisted the accelerator and they shot forward like a bolt from a crossbow.

The wind howled in her ears, whipping her hair. Her bare arms tingled with the scrubbing.

She felt him jump a lane and then pour on more speed. She opened her eyes. Pacific Coast Highway was a blur as she turned her head to look: the houses, trees no more than lines moving up and down like fingers of colored light, the tip of a paintbrush. It was a game she used to play in the back of the car when her parents took her up to the Cape during the summer.

Bubbling laughter burst from her throat and she squeezed her knees hard against Chris' hips as if she were riding a horse.

"Faster," she urged him. "Come on. Faster!"

There was a surge as if a giant's hand had reached out, sent them spinning. They whipped past two cars as if they were standing still, heeled slightly over as they went around a long lazy bend to the right, following the shape of the shoreline. Far up ahead a pair of great semis lumbered, spilling gray smoke from their vertical tailpipes as if they were cloudsowers.

"Hold on, babe!" His words, torn from his mouth by the screaming wind, boomed thin and harsh, something broadcast over a cheap P.A. They began to pull away from the traffic behind them, slowly at first as if they were riding a rocket straining to break free of the Earth's atmosphere as well as the awesome tonnage of its own inertia.

They were flat out.

Now the world was one long howling tunnel down which

they flew and it seemed to her as if they left the tarmac of
the highway, patches of light and dark racing by too swiftly
to focus on, becoming part of the wind itself.

Abruptly she felt a kind of fist at her left side pushing her
over. She began to turn her head. The cycle rocked on its
shocks as the vehicle's shadow shape drew abreast of them.
It was very close, blotting out a great deal of light, and this
was on her mind as Chris bellowed back at her, "That bloody
bastard, taking us t' th' cleaners like that."

It turned into a scream. The Harley's shattering windshield blew a rain of vicious black ice back into her face. She
felt a searing pain high up under her eye on the right side,
streaking around past her ear. Instinctively, she unwrapped
one arm from around Chris' waist, brought it up to her face.
And in the process, swung off dangerously to the right. Desperately, she tried to grip his thighs harder with her knees
but the howling wind was forcing her torso back away from
him.

She felt the painful reverse bending of her spine low down
at her coccyx and, like a junkie at the first moment of her
fix, she became aware of many things at once as the primitive
organism, in mortal fear for its life, began to break down the
environment into workable segments.

In front of them, the highway was clear all the way to the
high rear ends of the lumbering semis perhaps a quarter of
a mile ahead. Light oncoming traffic but the speed-blur made
it next to impossible to—Something was blocking the vision
on her off-side eye and she used her fingers to wipe at the
right side of her—wet and hot and sticky. Saw the crimson
color at the periphery of her vision.

Still she was aware of the solid-seeming shape to her immediate left, as black as night; Chris' helmeted head coming
up and another sound, so high up the register it set her teeth
on edge. Chris' head began to whip around like a bowling
ball hurled down an alley.

Then the wave of thunder hit them and they left the dark
shape, running right, over the verge of the highway. Airborne
for an instant, all vibration leaving the frame, floating free,
her buttocks leaving the seat, oddly carefree, then the jarring
crash back to earth, running bumpily over the dirt, the beginning of grass and she smelled the heavy scent of clover.
Terrified, a bird cawed, lifted.

It was the jutting rock formation that decided the spin. The front wheel of the Harley hit it at such an angle that they went right over it, the handlebars jerked right out of Chris' clawing hands. But the shock was too much for Daina's one-handed grip and she was flung head over heels backward, landing on the base of her spine. She was spun around, her face scraping along the ground, bounced up on one knee.

She lifted her head, saw the cycle riding crazily back across the crowded tarmac of the highway. It shot obliquely forward while oncoming traffic screeched and whirled away in a welter of colored angles.

Right across the highway it screamed, leaving black smoking rubber in its wake. There was a stink in her nostrils of burning oil and blood.

"Chris!" she called, trying to get up.

But the Harley, with Chris still riding it, had already made the far verge, slamming into the flank of a parked car, spinning away and, seeming to gain momentum still, slamming through the window of a seaside house. Bright sheets of flame erupted and a bang like the end of the world. Billowing smoke hurling skyward like raven's wings and someone screaming again and again. Traffic piling up, horns blaring and the screaming, going on and on, and the flames licking delightedly upward, traveling at the speed of light, and that stench, that awful stench invading her nostrils, a dog eating its own tail. Just the screaming and the darkness coming down.

Coulda sworn I saw you/On the streets yesterday/And I envied you/And that was my first mistake...

Squeak, rattle, bump.

Well it must have been a mirage/As I was caught up in the backdrops/Just waiting to surface and destroy...

"...in here. No, I don't want any of that. Not here." A banging over and over, reverberating in the cathedral of her mind.

Changes come like bullets/Shock but no pain/Dear me I see I'm alone again....

"...Christ's sake, have that black bastard turn the goddamned thing off!"

Silence, cool and crisp, and softly, softly, "All right, buster, you can do that at the other end of the hall...."

Gray spiderwebs arcing away from sunlight. Mist like granules of sand, lightening, whitening, peeling away layer after layer like gauze coming off the eyes.

"...aina, what happened?"

And the wind buffeting her, the rocking back and forth, *Oh, God, I'm falling!* and the lurch like a quake, the ground coming up, the jarring impact and then the film of the shooting star running away from her, hitting, being hit, sending crimson and black signals into the sky, steaming the afternoon, *Chris, Chris, oh Chris!*

"...right, all right. It's all right."

She was sitting up, shaking, sobbing into the hollow of his neck.

"Doc?"

"This is better than a shot right now. Later..." The sentence was left like that, hanging.

"Where am I?" she whispered. "Not by the sea. Dear God, not there."

"You're in a hospital, Daina." It was Bonesteel's voice. She recognized it now.

"Bobby?"

"Yes."

"Bobby." She clung to him. "The cycle. Something... it...it..." Her voice was as thin and reedy as rice paper.

"It's all right," he said close to her ear. "You're safe now. You're all right."

"Chris," she whispered. "What happened to Chris?"

She felt some movement as he looked at the doctor. "He's dead, Daina—"

"No! He's not!" But the raven's wings were still spreading out across the blue, blue sky and the flames licking hungrily just after the harsh push of the explosion's shock wave, oxygen sucked from her lungs, and the screaming echoing in her mind again. Horrible.

She was shaking again. "He can't be...." But the rage was gone and she said it softly almost as if it were a benediction. Oh, Chris, you had a whole new life now. I can't believe it. My heart is beating and yours is not. Can anyone explain that? She clung to Bonesteel's torso, but into the tendon of his shoulder.

"Daina"—his voice was gentle, comforting—"I need to know what happened. I had someone following you, but he lost the Harley."

The taste of the earth in her mouth, dust and sand, choking her, her shoulder jammed against the ground and the pain ripping through her, the blood streaming and half blinding her but the vision plain just the same, the shooting star losing the earth, gaining ascendancy over the air just before it bounced, crashed, *whoosh!* and the *flames,* the screaming going on and on. *Her* screaming.

She lay back on the pillow, tears streaming from her eyes. "First," she said, "tell me where I am." She looked at his face, into his eyes.

"You're in the emergency room of Santa Monica Hospital. You've got some superficial cuts—the worst of which is just under your right eye—plenty of abrasions, a couple of bruised ribs and a shoulder that the doc here tells me will give you some pain for the next month or so. No tumbling, he says." He smiled but she could see the strain coming through like bone popping flesh.

The phone rang somewhere close and someone moved to get it.

"Now, what happened?"

"Lieutenant, it's for you."

"Be right back," Bonesteel said.

The doctor, a young man with sallow skin and a bushy mustache that made him look like a sea lion, touched her cheek with his fingertips. "There are only two stitches," he said. "Can you feel this?" And when Daina shook her head, he went on probing. "In a little while, you'll begin to feel some pain. That's good so don't worry about it." He grabbed at his mustache, turning it back and forth between his fingers. "You were very lucky, Miss Whitney. An inch or so to the left and there'd have been some nasty nerve damage." He smiled. "All the X-rays were negative."

Bonesteel set the phone down, came and sat by her side. He waited until the doctor had left, then said, "Let me have all of it."

She told him everything she could recall, until the sting came again and the raven's wings flapping, expanding....

"... wait a moment," he cautioned her. "Give yourself some time." When she was breathing easier, he said, "You told me you felt a shape coming up on your left just before the crash. D'you know what it was? Did you see it clearly?"

"Some kind of truck ... or a car. But a high one."

"At this point you were flat out, right? Doing over a hundred. The windshield shattered. At that speed it coulda been anything—a stone thrown up by the traffic in front of you. Shit." He looked at her. "That it? Can you remember anything else, even the tiniest ... an impression maybe?"

"No. I—Wait, I do remember ... just after the windscreen went, Chris' head whipped back and ... away from the center of the highway."

"He turned his head?"

"No, no. It was more like ... I don't know, this is just an impression I had. It was like *something else* had twisted his head, pushing at him." She closed her eyes, nauseated again and thought, Oh, God, oh, God. I can't believe I'll never see him again.

"Daina, is there anything else?"

"No, I ..." How could she be so stupid? "Yes. Something Chris said while ... we were riding." She had to think hard for a minute to get through the rising stink in her nostrils, the sensation of tremendous forward motion abruptly stilled; silence in thunder. "He said, 'That bastard ... taking us to the cleaners like that.'"

Bonesteel's face was so close to hers she could feel his hot breath on the side of her face. "Which bastard, Daina? Who was it? Nigel?"

"I don't know."

"Daina!"

His voice like a steel-tipped arrow through her head and she squeezed her eyes shut, her stomach rolled up into a ball. She began to sob but no tears came. She held on to herself, thought, Rubens, Rubens, Rubens, where are you?

"That's enough," she heard a voice say softly, recognizing it as the young doctor's.

"Listen, you, if she has the key to this in her head—"

"Her head," the doctor said calmly, "is in no condition for this interrogation. She has to rest now. I must insist, Lieutenant."

"All right, Doctor. All right. Is it permissible to talk to her for one moment more? She won't have to answer another question."

"Go ahead."

Bonesteel's face came back into her view. She saw the worried look on his face. "I'm sorry about pushing you," he said softly, "but now the case has blown wide open. The tail I planted on Charlie Wu finally paid off late last night. He led us to a warehouse. Know what we found inside? Two hundred and fifty cases of guns. M-15s, semiautomatics, submachine guns." His eyes were fever-bright; he looked like a hunting dog at last released. "Don't you see? It's no more speculation. We've tied the shipment to the next run in the Heartbeats' jet."

"And Charlie?" She was worried about her promise to Meyer and to Charlie Wu.

Bonesteel's shoulders rose, fell and he grinned. "Dunno. It was the damnedest thing but with all those cops there he managed to slip away. Naturally, I've no idea where he is now."

She smiled a little. "Thanks, Bobby."

"Now listen, Daina"—his face had sobered—"I've got to get back to the site of the accident...if that's really what it was."

She clutched at his arm. "What d'you mean?"

"What I mean is that one attempt was made on Chris' life. Maybe this crash was given a little help by someone."

"Lieutenant, I do not want you frightening my patient."

"Listen, Doc, this lady has a right to know where she stands. We might be in the middle of a very serious situation."

"Maybe, could be. I'm going to have to ask you to leave, Lieutenant, and I mean right now. This is doing Miss Whitney no good at all."

"Daina, I'm leaving a man with you...one of mine. You remember Andrews?"

"Yes."

"He's a good man. He'll stay with you until I can get back, okay?"

She nodded wordlessly, turned her head away from him, overcome again by the howling, the shrill biting edge of hot metal scraping against the tarmac as the beautiful bike went slewing across and Oh, God. Oh, Chris, I'm sorry. And through it all, she heard her own voice booming as if from far away: Faster. Come on, Chris. Faster! A bolt seared behind her eyes. Something about going faster. What was it? Her head throbbed and she thought, I want to go home.

The doctor was dead set against it but he could not hold her there and, at last, Andrews took her home.

The afternoon was fading in maudlin splendor. Behind her she could hear the traffic from 16th Street and, turning her head, she could see the Pacific shining out past Lincoln Boulevard, white sails racing in for shore as the light came down, quickening, flattening the sea until it sparked with hard dazzling light, making her turn away.

She could hear the sound of the gulls fading in and out through the traffic's drone. Somewhere a baby was crying and she could hear Spanish being spoken in short angry bursts like quick combinations at a boxing match.

She remembered nothing of the ride home or how Andrews got the door open. He must have carried her inside like a husband with his newlywed bride for when she opened her eyes again, she was in her own bedroom. All that was missing was Rubens lying beside her. She rolled over, put out her arm, stroking the empty place where he should have been with the tips of her fingers. She began to cry.

"Miss Whitney, is there anything—"

"Just talk to me."

Andrews was silent for a moment, perhaps debating with himself over subject matter. "I thought you were very strong the other day," he said finally.

"What other day?"

"When Brafman and I took you out to Santa Monica to see the lieutenant."

"Oh, yes," she said softly. "Are you all right?"

"Ma'am?"

"Bobby said your...brother-in-law? Yes, brother-in-law had been killed."

"That's right."

"You're all right, Pete."

"Yes, Ma'am. I'm with my sister a lot." She could hear him moving closer. "Why don't you try to get some sleep now? The lieutenant will be here as soon as he's through."

"You're very kind," she whispered, falling away into sleep.

She saw nothing, smelled nothing, heard nothing. But she felt violent motion. She was hurtling through a canyon, the sheer size of the walls seeming to accentuate her speed. She tried to slow down but she could not. Every time she did, she seemed to go all the faster. She was following a shape and, once, when it turned around she could make out the glistening snout with its blunt black nose and its nostril slits. The eyes were lupine, round and almost pure gold save for their centers which were black vertical slits.

When she caught sight of this face she no longer wanted to slow down but rather felt such a strong desire to go faster that she shot forward as if blown from the mouth of a gun.

And woke up. It was pitch black. The dead of night. For a moment she lay where she was, listening to her heart race. She closed her eyes but behind the lids she saw again that terrible lupine face. Her eyes snapped open. I was going so fast, she thought, recalling the dream. And then, in a blaze of lightning, Bobby's words came back to her: *At that speed it coulda been a stone thrown up by the traffic in front of you.* But that wasn't true, she knew now. *Oh, God!* Her knuckles were white with tension. Why hadn't she remembered this before?

There had been no traffic in front of them. Only the great ponderous semis a quarter of a mile up ahead and she urging Chris on: *Faster! Come on, Faster!*

Bonesteel was right. It *hadn't* been an accident. And that high shape. That car. An old Rolls-Royce Silver Cloud. Nigel's car, glimpsed in the rearview mirror of the bike just before . . .

She sat up in bed. "Pete?" she called. "Pete!"

She swung her legs over the side, got up. She had to tell Bobby what she had remembered. She reached forward, turned on a light. And stood stock still. Her closet doors gaped open, the drawers of her dresser lay tumbled and smashed on the carpet. And her clothes. Her dresses had been ribboned with shears or a long knife, her blouses ripped through at the bodice, her jeans and pants had been dismembered.

She put her hand to her mouth, moving backward, away from the terrifying display. She felt the side of the bed against the backs of her knees and whirled.

The lamp sent a pool of light onto the bed. She saw the slight depression on the left side where she had slept and just to the right of it a pale balled object. Without thinking, she leaned over to get a better look and caught a whiff of male scent so strong that she almost gagged. But still she had to make sure and she touched the pale object.

"My God!" she breathed. She was staring at a pair of her own silk panties, heavy and musky with a pool of cooling semen.

She lunged for the phone and moaned. The receiver was dead in her hand.

She threw the phone from her, whirled away. The black hallway yawned at her as if it were alive. She rummaged through her clothes, her hands wet and shaking until she found a pair of jeans that had been left whole. She drew these on, discovered a whole T-shirt, pulled it swiftly over her head. Then she went down the hallway. Halfway to the living room she paused. She was barely breathing as her senses quested outward for a tangible sign of Nigel's—it must be Nigel!—presence.

The stillness was overwhelming. Her senses seemed to have become sensitized by her fear so that now she was becoming aware of the multitude of minute noises she had never before known were there: the brief rasp of wood settling, the dry scrape of a branch against the side of the house, the hum of the refrigerator in the wet bar across the expanse of the living room.

In that moment as she crouched in the hall, her palms leaving streaks of sweat along the walls, all these tiny humdrum sounds were chillingly transformed. In her mind's eye she could visualize the dark face in the shadows, the drawn weapon in the taut-fingered hand, the coiled musculature of the figure stalking her. She thought of the piece of pale silk lying obscenely so close to where she had lain asleep and a shudder went through her. The air seemed to flutter in dread.

She peered ahead into the gloom of the living room as if willing her stalker to appear. So much space in this house, she thought. So many rooms to hide out in. And where was Pete? She knew that she could not stay in this position much longer. Her muscles would begin to cramp and then she would be no good at all. She must rise and methodically go through each room—or leave. Now. Get up and run. These were her only choices.

She needed a weapon and for that she would have to get to the kitchen. Rubens kept no guns but there was a set of large carving knives in the kitchen, on the wall next to the eye-level microwave oven. But first she had to see if all the phones were out. The nearest extension was in the living room, inside the deep drawer of the cocktail table in the conversation pit.

Again she strained to see into the darkness. Nothing. She ceased to breathe long enough to listen. Nothing but the booming of her heartbeat in her inner ear. Her flesh began to crawl.

She took a deep breath, steeling herself, then went swiftly down the hallway, turning on the lights in the living room, out back in the pool, the tennis courts, the enormous garden. She needed light now in the same basic way she needed food and water. There was about it the element of survival: the primitive organism clamoring against the bars of its cage in terror; darkness was equated with death.

The obese mermaid watched her tenderly from her froth-rimmed rock as she made her way toward the sofa in the center of the room. The back of it was toward her and she could not see down into the pit until she was very close. Then she jumped, screaming a little until she had the presence of mind to bite back on it.

The drawer to the cocktail table was open, the base of the phone upended. The long red cord to its receiver was stretched taut, wrapped again and again around the neck of Patrolman Pete Andrews. Daina stared at his face, unable for the moment to turn away. The cheeks and eyes were fully as bloated as those of the mermaid in the painting. His tongue, so swollen it was round, protruded part way between his lips and there was a foul stench as if he were a baby who had not yet been toilet-trained.

There was a burning behind her eyes and her head began to throb on the side where she had been hurt. Tears came to her eyes but she berated herself, balling her fingers into a fist. Don't! she screamed at herself. It won't do you any good to weep for him now. She turned her mind toward Nigel instead, remembering what he had done to Maggie and perhaps to Chris.

She skirted the conversation pit, running for the kitchen now. The knives stood out in her mind like shining swords. That room was empty, too, but when she turned on the light, she moaned. The empty wooden box had been ripped from its place on the wall. Methodically, now, she went through the drawers and cabinets looking for anything she could use against him. There was nothing more lethal than a spatula.

Back in the living room the mermaid mocked her smugly, safe on her perch and, on the mantelpiece, the two Oscars—hers and Rubens'—stood together like a pair of tin soldiers.

She crossed quickly to the fireplace, took down her statuette. She hefted its weight in her right hand. It was heavy enough to inflict a good deal of damage provided it was swung with enough force and aimed correctly.

She went up the three shallow steps to the window-doors at the rear of the room. The linen curtains were closed. Transferring the golden statuette to her left hand, she reached out, took hold of one edge of the curtain. It fluttered as if from a breeze and she froze. A breeze was impossible. All the windows were closed. She looked carefully around until she realized that her trembling hand had set off a ripple effect in the light fabric.

Cautiously she pulled aside a tiny section of the curtain, bending slightly to peer outside. In the floodlit night, she saw part of the tennis courts, the extreme left-hand side of the pool, sprayed by the multicolored underwater lights, staining the facade of the white wooden lattice-work cabana, and beyond—the cabana!

There was a phone in there on a separate line. Few people knew about it because Rubens used it exclusively for business. If I can just make it across to the cabana, she thought, feeling the weight of the statuette, I'll have a chance.

She shifted a bit until she was near the seam of the double window-doors. She reached down slowly and, behind the barrier of the curtains, pushed the small metal V lever that unlocked the doors.

Her hand moved downward, gripping the knob to the left-hand door. She turned it, careful to make no noise and, when it was hard over, pushed the door open inch by inch.

When there was enough of a gap for her to slip through, she went out.

The night chittered on around her. She heard the soft slap-lapping of the water against the pool's side. The crickets sawed away and once, far off, she heard the dull booming of a car's exhaust diminishing.

She put the statuette in her right hand, swung it back and forth slightly like a pendulum, getting her muscles used to its weight and mass distribution. No use lugging it around if she wasn't going to be prepared to use it.

All right, she told herself. This is it. Take a deep breath and you're off.

She sprinted off to the right from the side of the house and was rounding the shallow edge of the pool when a voice said sharply: "Daina!"

She ignored it, went on running.

"Daina!"

It came again and now she saw movement, heading out from the trees toward her.

"Daina, don't!"

The great booming of a pistol shot brought her up short. She stood there panting not more than twenty feet from the safety of the cabana. But she knew if she made a move of any kind now, he would fire again and this time hit her.

She lifted her head as she heard rustling off to her right in the garden. She saw the black bulky silhouette.

"Silka!"

He came toward her in long confident strides. He was dressed in black jeans and a matching turtleneck. He wore crepe-soled shoes that made no sound when he walked. In his right hand she saw the long snout of a Magnum .357.

He smiled as he came across the grass and she sighed in relief. "Am I glad to see you," she said. "This makes twice you've saved my life."

His smile turned into a grin, the grin into a leer. He lifted the muzzle of the gun, pushed it into the spot between her breasts. His voice was like liquid silver. "I saved you that time in San Francisco so I could have you at this moment. Ever since I held you in my arms that night I've thought about you; what I wanted to do to you." He moved his face in toward hers and she pulled back, a frightened mouse from the hypnotic swaying of the adder's head.

"I don't—"

"That's what I thought about while I watched you sleeping; while I used your panties to—"

"You!" she gasped and tried to bolt.

His free hand came out, gripped her painfully, pulling her around to face him again.

Daina could not bear to look into those eyes any longer. They were as vast as a universe, blotting out everything. She closed her eyes, moaned slightly.

She heard the tiny clatter of sounds near her and her eyes flew open.

"Now," Silka said, "we'll just give you a little shot of something to, uhm, soften you up." The thing looked like a miniature coffin. He opened it up and Daina saw the shining syringe, the tiny vial of clear liquid. "Something"—the leer came again—"to put you in the mood."

He extracted the syringe from its box, began to fill it. Daina did not have to be told what was going in there: horse cut with strychnine.

"Christ," she said, her heart pounding and the fear flooding through her, "you don't have to do this."

"Oh, yes," Silka said. "I do."

And all she could think of now was how wrong Bobby had been about everything; how his obsession with Nigel had caused him to miscalculate and would now cause her death. Once she had been injected, she knew, that would be it. There would be no guardian angel for her as there had been for Chris in New York. And, in any case, Silka would have recalibrated the dosage.

He pushed the plunger slightly on the inverted syringe and several drops of the liquid spurted out, silvery in the light.

Silka nodded. "All right." His filled hand was moving, the tip of the syringe looking sharp and lethal. The point was leveling off as he prepared to plunge it home into the soft flesh on the inside of her elbow.

In that moment, she lifted her right arm, which she had allowed to hang lax and perfectly still at her side, smashing the gold statuette against the side of Silka's head.

He stumbled to the right, off balance, and Daina began to run to her right, heading for the thick tangle of the garden.

With each step the small of her back ached, tingling just as if that fat steel-jacketed shard of death were about to strike her.

Heard a booming and she flung herself forward and to the side, crawling the last three yards past the first line of hedges.

Panting, she sat up, moving on hands and knees farther into the foliage. A booming came again just like the last one. Instinctively she ducked, moments afterward realizing that the shots were coming *from* the foliage, not into it.

Crouching, she half ran in a zig-zag course toward the

sounds of the gunfire. Past the great privet hedge she saw him crouching there, aiming carefully. He must have heard her approach but he could not break his concentration. He squeezed off another shot and then she was beside him.

"Bobby! My God, he's a madman!"

"A fanatic," Bonesteel said, sighting through a gap in the leaves. He fired, said, "Damn! This bastard's good. Very good." He glanced at her. "He's a fanatic and that's not the same thing at all. He's mad all right but in a very canny way." Quickly, he reloaded, fired off another shot.

"I came as fast as I could," he said softly. His head was darting back and forth as he searched for a sign of Silka. "I buggered those poor lab guys until they gave me what I wanted. Chris was shot in the left temple. We pulled fragments of a .357 slug from what was left of his skull. You were—"

"Silka's carrying a Magnum .357," she said.

"I'm not surprised...now."

"You were wrong all along about Nigel."

"Come on," he said, taking her hand. "Let's move. We'll be sitting ducks, otherwise."

He took her through the bushes on an acute tangent from the vector of his last shots. They crouched down. Daina could smell the harsh stink of cordite and the heavy scent of fear. Scenes from *Heather Duell* flashed through her mind like lightning. There seemed to be no difference to her between what she felt then and what she felt now; the two had merged, seamlessly.

"I want this bastard," she whispered, "for what he did to Maggie and to Chris. For the misery he's brought."

He reached out, put his hand on her arm. "I want you out of here. It's too volatile now...the whole place is a red sector."

"If you think I'm leaving now you're—"

"You'll do as I say!" he hissed savagely, pushing at her. "Get the hell away. I'll eat this bastard for dinner by the time you're—"

The explosion and his grimace seemed to her to occur at precisely the same instant. Thinking back on it, of course, that could not have been the case.

Bonesteel's body leaped toward her, against her, bowling her over. She felt his heart hammering against her, colliding with her own.

"Christ," he whispered. "Jesus Christ."

She could see the pain written across his face. His brows were knitted with it, his eyes filled up with it, dark and haunted. His face was filmed in sweat and she felt a widening pool of wetness between them.

"Bobby," she called. "Oh, Bobby!"

She heard the sounds of the foliage hissing, saw the long stalks bending in toward her and, without thinking, tore the .38 revolver from his grasp, wriggled out from under his inert bulk and scrambled away.

A booming and a shot whined away just to her left. She gasped, changed direction and kept on going, past tree boles and high swaying ferns.

She turned once and, seeing some movement, pulled the trigger. The gun bucked in her hand, the force catching her unprepared, and she had to use her other hand to stop it from flying away. She moved onward, shivering. The fear was driving everything Jean-Carlos had taught her right out of her mind.

She caught herself crying, berated herself. *Come on!* Pull yourself together. If you don't, you'll surely die. There's no one now between you and him.

Behind the bole of a tall palm, she crouched, listening. It was very still. The gunfire had sent the birds upward, screaming, and even the crickets had ceased their chatter. But, on the other hand, the reports could easily be mistaken for a car backfiring. She could hold no hope for the neighbors' response.

She could feel her heart laboring, the stink of fear hard on her. And she thought, At last you've gotten what you wanted; achieved what you first went to Baba to find so many years ago.

She inched her face around the bole of the tree, looking to right and left, shrank back as a bullet thunked into the wood, whined away into the night like a bee. She put up the gun, squeezed off a two-handed shot. This time she was ready and the bullet went where she had aimed it. She shot again.

Stillness.

Where was he?

Just the tops of the high dusty palms moving somnolently.

Time to move. She got up, took one step to her left and a bullet whined away, taking a tuft of grass with it. It had struck not four inches from the toe of her shoe. She pulled back, thought, Christ, he's got me pinned down.

She felt utterly helpless and with that feeling all energy seemed to drain from her. She could not move from this spot and to wait for him to approach would be suicide. Even if she had had years of training with Jean-Carlos instead of weeks, she could not hope to defeat a man of Silka's expertise and massive strength hand to hand. Some things were just beyond the range of reality.

Despondently she opened the cylinder of the .38. Her teeth ground together. Well, that cut it. Two rounds left. She snapped the cylinder shut, closed her eyes. Her head throbbed and she began to cry again. Is this how Heather would act? she asked herself. Oh Jesus, stop kidding yourself. This is no film. The cavalry's already come and been shot down.

Bobby. She thought of him. What of Bobby? And Chris and Maggie. What of them all now? No one will know what happened. Even she, as close as she was to the puzzle, could not fit all the pieces together. How would anyone else be able to?

A wind sprang up, drying the sweat on her skin and she shivered. Above her head the palm fronds fluted, dipped, and wavered as if they were trying to warn her.

And what of Heather now? How false an image was she really? Up until tonight, Daina would have wagered all her money that that character had not been false at all.

She had not waited for the cavalry to come. She was the last stop on the train and without her . . . Was that just some fantasy they had all conjured up between them? Had she been a man, she could've, she would've . . . But I wasn't born a man, Daina thought savagely. I am what I am and it should make no difference. But it does, God help me. I see now that it does.

She stared hopelessly at the pistol held in her hands between her upraised knees. There had been no sound for a while and now she heard clearly the rustling of the foliage as if some nocturnal predator were alive there, stalking her. The sound was coming toward her, she could hear that. There was very little time left.

She turned around on her knees, peered beyond the scaly trunk of the palm. But there was nothing to see. It was as if Silka had turned invisible. Jean-Carlos had not covered any of this.

And then her mind seemed to clear, as if the imminence of death had turned the inside of her head to crystal. The days fell away like leaves, all the weeks, the months, and she was back in that oddly lit loft on West 3rd Street, hearing Jean-Carlos say, *Never trust your life to an automatic. They have a tendency to jam when hot.* She stared down at the .38 Police Positive. It was a revolver. Something about revolvers. But what?

The jacarandas whispered her name and she lifted her head. A thin trickle of sweat broke out, rolling agonizingly down the indentation of her spine.

Christ, she thought. He's here. And I still can't see him. He's only playing with me.

Playing!

She gasped, whirled back around to the other side of the palm. Her mind was racing now, her pulse hammering. She had it now. Jean-Carlos had said, *From a woman's point of view, situations are often difficult...many times seemingly untenable. The thing is never to give up.* His eyes had bored into her and she could imagine him breaking out of Morro Castle, the pain of leaving behind everyone who meant anything to him. *Where your opponent expects a lack of strength, you give him guile. Here, let me show you a trick and you will understand why I myself only use revolvers.*

With trembling fingers, with her breath whistling through her half-open mouth, Daina opened the cylinder again. There they were: her last two rounds. She had to be very careful now, turn it just so. There! The tip of her tongue came out, licked at her parched lips. Now she knew what she had to do.

She turned around, waited for him to appear.

The night was very still, the breeze that had sprung up dying in midflight. It must have come from the Pacific for now she could feel the humidity as if it was a layer of wax on her arms and torso.

Saw a movement between the hedges very close to her— closer than she had imagined—and she aimed the .38, slowly pulled the trigger. A loud snap as the hammer cracked down and nothing else. Just an echo as if a mocking laugh from the empty chamber. Silka could not have known that Bobby had reloaded the gun just before he was shot. Had he been counting the shots? Daina would be surprised if he hadn't been.

And now he emerged, like a Satanic Adam from the midst of the tall flowers and hedges of the garden. He came straight at her, his Magnum swinging loosely at his side.

She aimed the .38, fired again, heard only the loudest click in the world, echoing on into the night. "Damn."

Silka threw his head back and laughed. "Nothing left for you now, honey," he said heavily, "but this." Tilted the muzzle of the pistol up, not even bothering to aim it at her. There was no need now. He could afford to take his time. And, she reflected, he was the type of man who would. Because he enjoyed what he did. Not just a professional but something more. Much more than that.

Now was the time, while he was coming on. She had won an Oscar for her performance in *Heather Duell,* but that would be nothing compared to this one. If she failed to sell it now she surely would be dead inside of five minutes.

She put the fear of God into her voice and on her face. It did not take much. "You don't have to do this, Silka," she said. "I could be very good to you. Where's the sense in killing me? Don't you want me still?"

"Yeah," he said, coming on. "And I'll have you yet. Just before I press the Magnum to your head and blow your brains out." He grinned savagely. "It sure will be pleasure, doing that. You caused me a lotta trouble." He shook his head. "Broads will do that, insinuate themselves into the picture until they're embedded there...like lice.

"Now I gotta abandon it all, the sweet racket I spent so long setting up, using the band's own money to buy the guns, using their jet to transport them to Northern Ireland." He looked down at her with burning eyes. "If Chris hadn't gotten too smart for his own good, he never would've checked the books and found that even the Heartbeats' habits couldn't account for all the missing money. He never would've even suspected me, and I wouldn't've had to kill him. Now it's all led, inevitably, to this bloodbath."

He shrugged. "But I'm used to death; freedom's built on bloody corpses." His footsteps seemed to shake the ground as he came toward her. "My two brothers were so idealistic, disappearing into Northern Ireland after our father, hooking up with the Provos. Then, one day, I got a letter from Dan. 'Ned's been killed,' he wrote. 'The bloody Proddys did him in in a raid.' Ned was only seventeen, the youngest of us. He and Dan were putting together an operation. 'We need you now,' Dan wrote.

"I was just out of the Marines. I wanted to fight. But for something I could really believe in. I went to Belfast, saw how we're treated in our own homeland. Six months later, Dan and I came back to Boston, engineered that raid on the National Guard armory. Took those cases of M-60 machine guns down to Mexico and then had 'em shipped over.

"Dan went back with 'em but I stayed here. In Belfast I'd met a dark-haired girl with eyes as green as emeralds. She too had been working on a plan but she had required just the right operative if it was to work. Many in the IRA hierarchy said it would not; she knew they were all wrong."

"That was Nigel's sister," Daina said.

Silka's colorless eyes opened wide. "Yes," he said, "it was. So now you know it all. The embezzlement scheme, the gun-running...all her idea. How she hates her hedonistic brother who made so much money but turned his back on the cause of a free Ireland. I had a lotta contacts over here and I made sure I was at the ASRM dinner, sitting next to Benno Cutler. He was the easy one to sell—it was the band who was difficult."

He towered over her, his legs slightly spread. "They were dangerous, all of them in their own way. But, on the other hand, they were like babies: they responded well to instant gratification. With my connections, I was always well-supplied with dope. They liked that. And they liked the fact that I was tough; physically tough. They had hired me and they could order me around. It gave them a good feeling inside."

His face was as hard as granite, his eyes unblinking. "Ten years I've been ripping them off and they never knew it. 'Course she had a very elaborate plan to get the money out of them but the funny thing is none of it was necessary. There was so much money already going for drugs and it was painstakingly kept off the books, I had no trouble as long as I was careful.

"'Course Jon gave me a bad turn that once when he stumbled in on me. His eyes were glazed and I thought he was too far gone to notice what was happening. But Jon wasn't stupid and when he brought it up to me later, he wanted money and...other things to keep his mouth shut. Poor sadistic Jon."

Silka shrugged his massive shoulders as he stepped over a low, perfectly manicured hedge. "Well, there wasn't much of a choice after that. He had to be gotten rid of. But discreetly, you understand. Discreetly. I couldn't afford even a ripple."

He smiled. "It was so simple, really. Jon was an addict so his death by overdose wouldn't cause much of a ripple. It's expected, really, something amiss if it *doesn't* happen.

"But then I saw what was happening within the band and I thought, my God, this is better than I ever coulda hoped. I'll let them kill him *for* me." He shrugged again. "'Course, a little strychnine in his horse sorta helped ol' Jon to that great gig in the sky." He laughed, a harsh barking sound. "Fucking amateurs. He'd've smelled the gas, otherwise."

He stopped just before her. "Now," he said thickly, "I'm going to get my reward for all these years of faithful service to the band and to a free Ireland. Assassinating Maggie was my last assignment from the IRA. I'm going home for a long rest with a lotta money in my pockets." He took a step toward her and Daina lifted the .38.

He was so close that she did not have to aim, merely pull the trigger. An instant before it happened, she saw the understanding come into his face—his own death mirrored in those cruel frozen eyes.

She felt the enormous tension come into her arm, traveling down her arm into the thin bones of her hand. A tiny muscle twitched in her forefinger as she began to squeeze and not, for God's sake, jerk the trigger.

Images flooded through her mind, blotting out Silka's bulk so close in front of her. The busted-up interior of Chris' house, the violent anarchy leading to the emptied speaker box filled with blood and flesh and broken bones that had once been a thinking, feeling human being.

The pad of her finger felt the blood-heat of the metal, the singing tension of the trigger mechanism awaiting enough force to release the cocking hammer.

Saw in a blur the other weapon—that enormous horrifying hole at the end of the Magnum's long barrel—moving upward with appalling swiftness, and she knew that with each passing fraction of a second, she was losing the advantage that one moment of shock had given her.

Pain lanced through her face, half closing one eye, and her body felt as if she had just leaped out of a six-story window. But the adrenalin was pumping, keeping the mass of the pain at bay for the moment.

Her forefinger was on the move and she heard the screaming again: tires black and smoking, streaking the crowded tarmac, and the cycle beginning its determined slide toward oblivion. Only the back of Chris' helmet visible, the sunlight lancing like a laser burst off its convex surface and *that smell,* the gull lifting away, screaming, screaming while the window caved in and the fireball ballooned, the raven's wings spreading....

The report of the .38 was deafening in the confined space between them. Silka shot backward even as she pulled the trigger a second time.

He was lifted off his feet by the enormous impact at close range, spun around. Blood spurted, splattering across the grass like rain. She had aimed for the heart and Jean-Carlos would have been proud of her.

She stood up, went over to where Silka lay, the gargantuan Magnum just past his outstretched right hand. There was no expression on his face now; no sign that he had ever once been a thinking organism, filled with hate and lust and rage. His glazing eyes were now truly as blank as lenses.

Daina let the empty .38 slide from her fingers as she turned away, running back to where she had left Bobby. He was still alive and she left him again, went across to the cabana, her heels sounding very loud against the flagstone and then the brick near the pool.

When she had used the phone, she came out again, went to where Bobby was lying, to be with him. She propped his head in her lap and after a time his eyes opened.

"Where is he?" It was just a whisper.

She put her face close to his so he could hear. "He's dead, Bobby. I shot him."

His eyes seemed to flicker. Far off she could hear the high-low ululations of the oncoming ambulance and police cars.

"I was only doing my job," he said. "I think I should've stuck to writing." The wailing was stronger now, coming in through the trees in increasing waves.

The blood seemed to be coming out of him in torrents and she used her palms to press against the ripped flesh. She thought of Baba. "Keep quiet now, Bobby." She touched his shoulder. "Rest a bit. The ambulance is almost here."

* * *

She rode all the way to Cedars-Sinai in the ambulance with Bonesteel, gripping his hand as if that force of will expressed through human contact, flesh to flesh, could keep him alive. His face was pale, barely recognizable beneath the translucent plastic cup of the oxygen unit. And all she could hear, above the wailing of the siren, was the harsh stertorous rasp of his ragged breathing.

When she became terrified that he would not make it, she thought of technicolor sunsets where everyone lived happily ever after and of her power as an icon to evoke those sunsets.

Bobby was on the operating table for more than six hours and she told herself in a kind of litany to keep out the panic that that was good, that if he was going to die, it would have been right away.

In that time, she did not leave the waiting room, except to urinate. She did not eat. When someone brought her coffee, she drank it. Otherwise she sat on a plastic-covered couch the color of a crudely painted sunset and stared at her whitely clasped hands.

The first hour and a half was a snap. The cops were crawling all over her, taking down her statement. She gave it all to them, everything she knew—holding back only Bobby's confession concerning Nigel: it could only do harm to them both now—and, after a while, it seemed to mollify them somewhat, considering how put out they had been about finding three bodies in one place and one of them a detective lieutenant of the LAPD. A plainclothes detective who she thought might be Bobby's partner eventually intervened, clearing the lot out before bringing her a cup of ersatz tomato soup, tasting of metal and time.

After that, it became increasingly difficult because there was only herself to be with. Without interest, she watched the detective, halfway down the hall on the phone. She was desperate for Bobby to live, conjuring up so many scenarios that she became dizzy. Until she thought of the film, convincing herself for the rest of those long agonizing hours that if she only *believed* he would be all right, then he would.

She got up from the uncomfortable couch, walked across to the windows. They faced west, toward the Pacific. Traffic was snarled on West 3rd Street. Someone got out of his BMW, shook a fist in the air like a defiant salute.

Half a block away a pair of girls so young their chests were still as flat as a man's, roller-skated across the street. They were lithe; as tawny as lions, their long silken hair fanning out behind them like fairies' wings. They held hands, as childhood friends will do, and threw their heads back, laughing at the confusion they were causing while continuing to weave back and forth in patterns so complex Daina was reminded of Astaire and Rogers. Faster and faster the golden pair swung, like pendulums under their own momentum, executing breathtaking maneuvers one after the other, cut loose and free at last, absorbed in the dance.

She knew she loved Bobby, not as a lover but as a friend. But he was, she realized now, almost as dangerous as Silka had been; his obsession had turned him away from being a good cop. Given the opportunity, he might even have shot Nigel.

She did not know how she felt about anything else, except that there was a great fissure inside her now, black and as fathomless as space itself, growing wider with each passing moment.

She heard a brief clatter from the other end of the hall. The place was alive with reporters and TV cameramen. Three uniformed cops were all that stood between her and that mob. The detective had his hands in his jacket pockets as he talked earnestly into a bristling bouquet of mikes thrust before his face. But he and the men under his command would not give way.

Outside, the girls had gone and the liquid line of cars was again on the move, from East Los Angeles to Encino, earfood blatting at them from their turned-on radios. Like cream from a jug, she thought. It was as if the girls had never existed.

She heard the sound of running feet and the doors to the operating theater banged open. When the sweat-soaked surgeon appeared, she knew before he opened his mouth.

"He didn't make it. I'm sorry, Miss Whitney. We did everything we could." His words passed through her like the wind. "There were three of us." Like a matador fresh from the *corrida,* he had been too tired to remove his wet red-veined gloves, the regalia of his work. He began to peel them off.

They made a terrible high squeaking sound. "If it's any consolation, he fought hard. Very hard."

"No," she said, turning and walking away down the green-tiled corridor, past the white-faced detective. "It doesn't mean a goddam thing."

14

When Rubens returned home, he found her waiting for him in the hallway. The morning was very bright and he had forgotten his sunglasses on the plane. When he opened the door, the interior of the house seemed very dark to him and he paused for a moment to allow his eyes to adjust.

He saw only her silhouette at first, tall and slim and quite superb—almost, he thought, like a perfect piece of sculpture.

Then she stirred and he smelled her soft scent; he felt a peculiar tightness at the back of his neck and was at a loss to explain it.

Then he saw her. She wore a pale grape-colored cotton dress, high-necked and low-backed. Over her right shoulder, the sad, wise El Greco face stared at him.

"I heard about it on the way in from the airport," he said. "The same time I heard about Chris. I guess I'm a little late." He stood stock still, staring at her from across a small amount of space. His eyes seemed frightened as if because of his absence she might have been damaged. "Are you all right?"

"Perfectly."

"Your face?"

"Will be fine. In time." She looked at him quizzically. "Don't you want to touch me?"

As if that were a command freeing him from bondage he dropped his briefcase and overnight bag. Took her into his arms.

At his touch all her cold resolve, all the fright and passion she had been desperately trying to keep in abeyance, spilled out and she melted into him.

"It's over now," he whispered, gently stroking her hair. "All over." But it was he who was trembling.

"What's the matter, Rubens?" She held on to him, feeling his strength flowing into her.

"I was afraid you were dead." His voice had taken on an odd echoey quality that made the short hairs at the nape of her neck stir. "Or had changed somehow."

"I'm the same," she said, not believing it at all. "I'm the same as I always was."

He looked down the hallway into the living room. "It doesn't look like anything happened here at all. Like it was a dream or something." He looked at her. "Let's call it that. A bad dream." And kissed her hard on the lips as if by this gesture he could banish all the evil that had been played out here so short a time ago. "Where's Maria?"

"In the kitchen."

"You stay here," he said brightly. "I'll go tell her to fix us a huge lunch and we'll take it out to the boat." He smiled at her. "I haven't forgotten my promise."

They set sail in clear weather but were soon wrapped in a low sea fog so that, though they were fairly close to shore, Daina could make out no land. They moved leisurely south-westward, heading in the general direction of San Diego. Rubens had not mentioned a destination and Daina did not think to ask him about one. There seemed no need. The sea was their only destination; their only purpose to be together.

Maria had outdone herself, fixing a sweet-and-sour cold chicken that, to Daina at least, always seemed more Chinese than Mexican, tortillas and enchiladas, a salad of tomato wedges and slivered onions in oil and basil. She had also included a fresh-baked loaf of French bread with plenty of sesame seeds, the way Daina liked it, and a bottle of robust but dry Italian gattinara.

Afterward, they held hands on the bridge, taking turns steering the boat, talking in short bursts about nothing of any consequence. Rubens went below to take a short nap, leaving the wheel in Daina's capable hands. When he emerged at twilight, he had on his midnight-blue cotton sailing pants, a knit short-sleeve shirt and his battered espadrilles. "We'll eat in an hour," he said.

He anchored with the running lights on and they went below. Over dinner, he said, "I've a surprise for you."

She looked at him, studying each feature in turn—his dark, depthless eyes, his strong, hawklike nose, his expressive mouth—and wondered how she ever could have been afraid of this man. "What is it?"

His eyes were sparkling. "A present," he said with the flourish of a prestidigitator. "Anything you want."

Of course she knew he was joking. "Oh, anything at all? Let's see. How about the Taj Mahal?"

"Give me a week," he said, perfectly seriously. "If you're really serious about it, that is."

"The Taj is a little grand," she said. It occurred to her then that she was missing something. "You're not joking, are you?"

"No." He took her hand. "I want to give you the one thing you want most in the world. Something no one else can give you. What'll it be?"

What, indeed, she thought giddily. Furs, clothing, jewels. A trip around the world. She thought of a Rolls Grand Corniche, a Formula I Lotus, a Lear jet. She thought of paintings: the old masters and the moderns; a Rembrandt might be nice, or a Picasso. She had always loved Monet. What she wouldn't give to own a Monet! But she could say nothing. It was too dazzling. My choice will have to wait, she thought. At least until tomorrow. He seemed disappointed when she told him that but he understood.

That night, they made long languorous love that seemed in perfect concert with the gentle rocking of the boat. But as Daina was drifting off to sleep, as she hung on that thin, ephemeral ledge between both worlds, she felt her heart touched by the fibrous tentacles of anxiety. She tried to search inside herself for the source but by that time sleep had claimed her and she dreamt.

She awoke from a dream into a dream, it seemed to her.
She had been walking the streets of a European city. A city
by the sea, though she could not say which one. The sun was
warm on her shoulders, the tiles beneath her feet echoing the
spectacular sienna color of the hills on her left. She felt thirsty
and had paused under the striped umbrella—slightly frayed
and faded—of an outdoor café for an Americano. It came but
when she brought it up to her lips it was so salty she could
not drink it. She called to the waiter over and over again,
trying in vain to get his attention. Calling, calling....

A calling had awakened her. Or a sound very much like
it. She lay in the double berth while Rubens slept beside her,
waiting for that sound to come again. She knew it would. In
the meantime, she thought about her dream. That city. Surely
she had been there before, it had seemed so familiar. She
thought hard. By the sea. It had to be the Mediterranean. All
right, then, which...Naples! Of course! It was Naples. But
she hadn't been there, in oh, ten years at least. What was it
about Naples...?

Then for some reason she thought about Bullfinch's My-
thology. There was a summer when she had read it avidly
from cover to cover and when she was through, she had
started all over again. Naples.

Then she had it. The legend of the one Siren: Parthenope,
who was so distraught at having failed to lure Ulysses to his
doom, she threw herself into the sea. But instead of drowning,
she had been cast up at Naples. Daina remembered the
Americano she had ordered in the sun-drenched café and how
salty it had tasted; sea-salty. She shuddered.

And at that precise moment she heard the sound that had
awakened her, a soft calling that seemed to come from everywhere at once. It was even a vibration racing through the
hull of the boat. She sat up in the berth, looked around. The
sound went on and on for a very long time. A song plaintive
and almost hypnotic.

She got out of bed, pulled on jeans and a turtleneck
sweater, went on deck. Day was breaking. The fog had lifted
and the sea lay before her for as far as she could see in any
direction. There was no wind at all and the surface of the
water lay as still and smooth as glass. Not a wrinkle disturbed
its timeless skin.

She went to the taffrail, leaned her elbows on it, breathing deeply of the richness of the air. It made her think of breathily chill weather, of slush in the gutters, glutinous and black with soot, of long dark streets peopled by shining brittle faces, filled with blaring radios set to WWRL, James Brown blasting the night, weeded yards, the forecourts of bombed-out buildings, sinking into a swamp of garbage, the belching steam from underground.

It was the underworld she had conjured up, across the river Styx, hard by the Zanzi Bar. The black shining faces, yellow-eyed and white-teethed, staring at her foreign self as she was shepherded into the ghetto.... Memories of another time.

Her heart hammered in her chest as she heard the soft wailing come again across the vast bosom of the Pacific as if it were the calling of the sea itself. The pale down along her arms lifted. And abruptly all her thoughts were as insubstantial as the wind. All but one of them, hanging in her mind like a brilliant golden sword, twisting, twisting in the center of her mind. I tried once, she thought, her pulse racing, but I was only a kid then, thinking voodoo might do it for me. Well, I'm a woman now. And I've got the power.

Then Rubens was beside her, mugs of steaming coffee in his hands. She took one from him, drank greedily, her fingers and palms pressed hard against the hot ceramic.

She knew what she wanted to say to him but her throat blocked so that she had to wait a moment, rest before she opened her mouth again and in an odd thick voice said, "There's a man. A man in New York. I knew him... a long time ago.

"He killed a... friend of mine, someone I loved. Slammed into his apartment and shot him down like he was an animal." She was dizzy now, her stomach in a knot. No one ever knew this but her. "He didn't know I was there, that I saw him do it." What was it Bobby had said? You can't forget old friends. Never to forget; oh no.

She stared up into Rubens' face, aware that the sounds of the sea were coming again like invisible waves, the Sirens' hypnotic call. "What happened to Ashley...." Rubens was staring at her in a very peculiar way, his eyes hard and dark and filled with a quicksilver anger. "You asked me what I wanted more than anything else," she said, starting over. "I want the same thing to happen to this man."

Rubens put his arm around her and together they walked to the bridge. He pressed a stud and the anchor was weighed. As he prepared to get under way, he said, "Listen. You can hear the whales calling to each other, a long lonely song." Then he spun the wheel, heading for home.

When they got back to the house, Daina told Rubens the man's name: Aurelio Ocasio. How odd it sounded on her tongue. She had not spoken his full name in so many years. It was the name of an alien.

While Rubens went to the phone, she crossed the living room, pulling open the window-doors out to the garden. The pool shimmered in the heat, sunlight turning its surface to diamonds. If I dive in there, she thought, I'll surely break my neck.

She stepped outside and the sunlight hit her like a hammer blow so that she staggered. Her stomach knotted and she thought she might vomit. She stumbled, reaching quickly out for the metal top of the nearest chaise. Her legs were trembling and sweat had broken out along her hairline, under her arms. My God, she thought. This is the moment I've longed for since I saw Ocasio standing over Baba's body. I wanted him dead. I was so full of hate for him, for my father for dying and leaving me alone with my mother.

That hate had been a closed fist encysted within her heart, a part of her for so long she had lost its true meaning somewhere inside herself. Instead, it had grown as she allowed it a life of its own. She saw very clearly now in a flash so sudden and so powerful it dizzied her, how she had become lost within that hate and with this last act would be drowned by it.

For an instant she felt as helpless, as utterly alone, as terrified as she had during her long incarceration with Dr. Geist, and she began to weep.

Idiot! she berated herself. Why are you crying? You still have the power. Use it!

"Rubens!" she cried, tearing her hands from in front of her face. "Rubens!"

She leaped up, ran through the garden, thinking, He was just picking up the phone when I went out. "Rubens!" she called him again. How much time had passed? "Rubens!"

He was hanging up the phone when she hurtled into the

living room. "My god, no!" Her eyes were open wide, staring. She seemed to be having trouble breathing.

"Daina, what—"

"Rubens, is it done?"

"I was just talking to Schuyler. He—"

"The call to New York!" she screamed. "Did you make it?"

"I was just about to. What's this—?"

"Oh, thank God!" Her eyes closed and she took a deep shuddering breath.

He came across to where she stood, trembling. He put his arms around her. "Darling, what's the matter?"

"I don't want you to make that call." She looked up into his eyes.

"It's your present. Of course I—"

"Just don't do it!" Consciously she softened her voice, put a hand up against his chest. "That's all."

"I thought this was something you wanted very badly. Did I get the wrong impression?"

Daina closed her eyes again and he felt a shudder run through her. "No, you didn't. Ocasio's death was something I had prayed for for eleven years."

"Then let me make the call. Let me make you happy. You have the power now, don't you see?"

"That's just it. I *do* have the power, just as you do. Marion was right. It's not getting the power that's so difficult. It's knowing what to do with it after you've got it. I think Meyer feels the same way—"

"Meyer?" His eyes got hard. "What d'you know about Meyer?"

She looked up at him. "Rubens, when I was in San Francisco he came to see me."

"Why didn't you tell me before?"

"I didn't think you'd understand. He's worried about you. He thinks you've become too much like him. He's right."

"What makes you think I'll understand now?"

"Because now I'm sure you love me. I can't live like this anymore, Rubens. I've lived with violence all my life but I've never really understood it. I see now that I—you and I—have been sinking deeper and deeper into a kind of quicksand without even knowing it. I was your most willing pupil but now I understand what I've become.

"Once I saw what you'd done to Ashley I promised myself

I'd never let that happen again. It was the same promise I made to Meyer. He's smarter than you or I gave him credit for. He made a deal with me: he'd help me find out who murdered Maggie if I kept you safe from harm. But he was giving me a lesson to learn. He was offering me violence and I took it; took it willingly.

"Now I understand that we'll be outlaws for the rest of our lives if we don't stop now; there'll be no turning back. Once, long ago, in the days I knew Aurelio Ocasio, that's what I wanted to be: an outlaw. And every decision I've made from then until this moment has been to further that end. Now I know I don't want it; that I mustn't have it.

"Ashley's dead. There's nothing either of us can do about that. But the future's another story."

Their eyes locked for an interminable time. "I'm leaving," she said finally.

"To go where?"

"I don't know. Anywhere. Naples is as good a place as any to start." There was a long silence. "I want you to come with me, Rubens."

Daina watched his eyes for any telltale signs. She had not known until she had said it just how much it meant to her. Her heart was pounding. What would she do if he chose to stay here? She was going anyway, she understood that. The decision had come from the very core of her being and there was no turning away from it; she did not want to. But the thought of leaving him was so painful that she was certain her heart would crack open.

"The use of fear's all I've known for so long."

"You have me now," she said.

"I don't want to lose you," he said thickly.

"Then come." She took his hand, squeezed it. "It'll be as scary for me as it is for you. But at least we'll know it's what we both want; learning things all over again."

"I'm not too old to do that." He smiled. "Let me get packed—"

"No," she said. "Let's just leave. Now."

"Well, at least let's take the Oscars."

"What for? They belong here, don't they? They'll be waiting for us if we ever come back."

"And the house?"

"Let the Mexicans take care of it; they always have."

They went out of there then, through the wide-open door into the hot sunlight and the dappled shade. They came down off the steps and walked across the lush grass. The soles of their shoes crunched against the gravel as they reached the silver Merc. Daina got in behind the wheel. For a moment Rubens stood looking back at the house, the grounds, one hand on the car door.

Then he got in beside her and she started up the engine. The Merc gave a throaty roar as she wheeled it around in a U-turn, going quickly down the long snaking drive, between the dusty soughing palms.